Niccolò Rising

DOROTHY DUNNETT

A DELL BOOK

Published by
Dell Publishing
a division of
The Bantam Doubleday Dell Publishing Group, Inc.
1 Dag Hammarskjold Plaza
New York, New York 10017

Originally published in Great Britain by Michael Joseph, London.

Dell ® TM 681510, Dell Publishing

ISBN: 0-440-20072-5

Reprinted by arrangement with Alfred A. Knopf, Inc.

Printed in the United States of America

July 1988

10 9 8 7 6 5 4 3 2 1

KRI

Characters

(Those marked * are recorded in history)

Charetty company, Bruges and Louvain
Marian de Charetty, the owner
Felix, her son by her late husband Cornelis
Mathilde (Tilde), her daughter
Catherine, her younger daughter
Julius, her notary
Claes, an apprentice
Gregorio of Asti, a lawyer
Henninc, Bruges manager
Astorre (Syrus de Astariis), mercenary leader
Thomas, Astorre's deputy
Olivier, Louvain manager
Cristoffels, Louvain manager

Medici company, Bruges, Geneva and Milan
***Angelo Tani,** manager, Bruges
***Tommaso Portinari,** under-manager, Bruges
***Francesco Nori,** manager, Geneva
***Francesco Sassetti,** Geneva
***Pigello Portinari,** manager, Milan, and brother of Tommaso
***Accerito Portinari,** factor, Milan, and brother of Pigello and
  Tommaso
***Cosimo di Giovanni de' Medici of Florence,** head of the Medici
  Bank
***Pierfrancesco de' Medici of Florence,** nephew of Cosimo

The company of Thibault & Fleury
Jaak de Fleury, Geneva
Esota, wife of Jaak de Fleury
Thibault, vicomte de Fleury of Dijon, elder brother of Jaak
Maffino, Milanese agent of Thibault & Fleury

The company of Strozzi, Bruges and Naples
***Jacopo di Leonardo Strozzi,** manager, Bruges
***Lorenzo di Matteo Strozzi,** son of Jacopo's cousin, and under-
  manager, Bruges
***Niccolò di Leonardo Strozzi,** Naples, elder brother of Jacopo
***Filippo di Matteo Strozzi,** Naples, elder brother of Lorenzo

*Caterina di Matteo, sister of Filippo and Lorenzo, and wife of Marco Parenti
*Marco di Giovanni da Parenti, silk merchant of Florence, husband of Caterina

Merchants and noblemen, Flanders
*Anselm Adorne of the Hôtel Jerusalem
*Margriet van der Banck, wife of Anselm Adorne
*Jan Adorne, eldest son of Anselm
*Anselm Sersanders, son of Anselm's sister and Daniel Sersanders
*Louis de Bruges, seigneur de Gruuthuse
*Marguerite van Borselen, wife of Louis de Bruges
Guildolf de Gruuthuse, grandson of the seigneur's bastard cousin Louis
*Jehan Metteneye, host to the Scots merchants
Griete, wife of Metteneye
Mabelie, Metteneye's servant
*Pierre Bladelin, household controller in Bruges to Philip, Duke of Burgundy
*João Vasquez, secretary to Isabelle, Duchess of Burgundy
Tristão Vasquez, kinsman of João, and married to Lucia of Kilmirren
*Charles, comte de Charolais, son of Philip, Duke of Burgundy
*Henry van Borselen, seigneur de Veere
*Wolfaert van Borselen, son of Henry and Count of Buchan, Scotland
*Mary, sister of King James II of Scotland and wife of Wolfaert van Borselen
*Charles van Borselen, son of Wolfaert and Mary
Florence van Borselen, half-brother of Henry
Katelina van Borselen, elder daughter of Florence
Gelis van Borselen, younger daughter of Florence
*Michiel Losschaert, knight of Bruges, formerly in Constantinople
*Giovanni di Arrigo Arnolfini, merchant of Lucca in Bruges
*Marco Corner, merchant of Venice in Bruges
*Jacques Doria, merchant of Genoa in Bruges
*William, Governor of the English merchants in Bruges
*Colard (Collinet) Mansion, writer, translator and artist in Bruges
Oudenin, pawnbroker of Damme

Scots of Scotland and Bruges
Alan de St Pol, lord of Kilmirren, Scotland
Simon de St Pol, son of Alan's younger brother Jordan
*James Kennedy, Bishop of St Andrews, cousin of King James II of Scotland

*George Martin, factor of the Bishop of St Andrews
*Alexander, Duke of Albany, son of King James II and Queen Mary of Guelders
*John Bonkle, illegitimate son of Edward Bonkle of Edinburgh
*Stephen Angus, kinsman of the Bonkles and agent of the Scots in Bruges
*Sir Alexander Napier of Merchiston, controller of King James II's household
*Richard Wylie, archdeacon of Brechin and procurator at the Curia
*John de Kinloch, chaplain of the Scots in Bruges
*John Reid of Boston, Scots merchant trading in England and Calais
Muriella, sister of John Reid

French and Franco-Scots
*Louis, Dauphin and heir to King Charles VII of France
*Charlotte, daughter of Louis, Duke of Savoy, and 2nd wife of the Dauphin
*Gaston du Lyon, chamberlain and equerry to the Dauphin Louis
*Raymond du Lyon, brother of Gaston and man at arms in the Dauphin's guard
*Isabelle, sister of King James II and widow of the Duke of Brittany
*Antoinette de Maignélais, mistress of the rulers of France and Brittany
*Sir William Monypenny, seigneur de Concressault, adviser to King Charles
Jordan de St Pol, vicomte de Ribérac, financial adviser to King Charles
*Patrick Flockhart, captain of King Charles' men at arms
*Andro Wodman, archer serving under Flockhart in France
Lionetto, a French mercenary captain serving in Italy

Flanders galleys: Venetians
*Alvise Duodo of Venice, commander 1459
*Piero Zorzi of Venice, commander 1460
Quilico, ship's surgeon to Alvise Duodo
Loppe (Lopez), Guinea slave from Alvise Duodo's galley
*Piero Bembo, agent of Venice

Milan and Genoa
*Cicco Simonetta of Calabria, secretary to Francesco Sforza, Duke of Milan
*Alessandro Sforza, lord of Pesaro, brother of the Duke of Milan
*Prosper Schiaffino de Camulio de' Medici, envoy of the Duke of Milan

*Francesco Coppini, Bishop of Terni, papal legate and secret envoy of Milan
*Federigo da Montefeltro, Count of Urbino, captain of the Duke of Milan
*Giammatteo Ferrari da Grado, professor and physician to the Duke of Milan
Tobias Beventini of Grado, his nephew, physician to captain Lionetto's band
*Count Jacopo Piccinino, mercenary captain, son of Milan army leader Nicholas
*Prosper Adorno, future Doge of Genoa and kin to Anselm Adorne
*Tomà Adorno of Chios, kinsman of Prosper Adorno

Naples
*Ferrante, King of Naples, bastard son of Alfonso V of Aragon
*John Duke of Calabria, son of King René of Sicily and claimant to Naples
*Margaret of Anjou, sister of Duke John and wife of Henry VI, King of England
*René, King of Sicily and Duke of Anjou, father of above and uncle of the Dauphin Louis

Greeks and Levantines
*Nicholai Giorgio de' Acciajuoli ("the Greek with the wooden leg")
*Bartolomeo Giorgio/Zorzi, alum farmer and silk merchant of Constantinople
*Agnolo Acciajuoli, banker, grandson of Donato, Prince of Athens
*Laudomia Acciajuoli, sister of Agnolo and wife of Pierfrancesco Medici
*Giovanni da Castro, godson of Pope Pius and ex-dyer at Constantinople
*Caterino Zeno, merchant of Venice with Levantine connections
*Violante, wife of Zeno and granddaughter of Emperor John of Trebizond

BURGUNDY
and the
ITALIAN STATES
1460

Peter McClure

0 20 40 60 80 100
Miles

ITALIAN STATES

(To smaller scale)

0   100
Miles

SWISS CONFEDERATION

Tyrol

VENETIAN REPUBLIC

Venice

DUCHY OF SAVOY

Milan

Turin

DUCHY OF MILAN

Mantua

Genoa

Bologna

Ligurian Sea

Pisa

Florence

Adriatic Sea

CORSICA

Siena

Urbino

PAPAL STATES

Tolfa

Abruzzi

Ragusa
(Dubrovnik)

Civitavecchia

Rome

Tyrrhenian Sea

KINGDOM OF NAPLES

Naples

Sarno

SARDINIA

Rhine

Basel

Middle

SICILY

Sea

Alps

L. Maggiore

L. Como

Bernard's Pass

DUCHY OF SAVOY

DUCHY OF MILAN

Milan

Pavia

L. Garda

VENETIAN REPUBLIC

Turin

Po

Mantua

Adige

Venice

Istria

Croatia

Genoa

Modena

Po

D. of FERRARA

Po

D. of MODENA

Bologna

REP. of FLORENCE

Adriatic Sea

Chapter 1

From Venice to Cathay, from Seville to the Gold Coast of Africa, men anchored their ships and opened their ledgers and weighed one thing against another as if nothing would ever change. Or as if there existed no sort of fool, of either sex, who might one day treat trade (trade!) as an amusement.

It began mildly enough, the awkward chain of events that was to upset the bankers so much. It began with sea, and September sunlight, and three young men lying stripped to their doublets in the Duke of Burgundy's bath.

Of the three, Claes and Felix were watching the canal bank for girls. Julius, his instincts blunted by an extra decade, was content to sink back, agreeably fortified, and forget he was anyone's tutor. A good astrologer would have told him to get out at once.

The sun warmed the bath, and the water bore it along on the last stage of its meandering journey. From the leadfounder's in England it had crossed the narrow sea to the Low Countries in a serviceable wind-battered caravel. It had been unloaded with some trouble in the crowded harbour at Sluys, and strapped with some trouble athwart a canal boat with a scratch crew of oarsmen.

And now, here it was. Lumped with cherubs: a bath for the noble Philip, Duke of Burgundy, Count of Flanders, Margrave of the Holy Roman Empire and all the rest of his high-yielding honours. A communal bathing-basin now on its way to the Duke's occasional residence in the merchant city of Bruges. And working their passage inside it, Julius, Felix and Claes.

For the moment, there was nothing to do. In the peace, a wave of philosophy overcame Julius. "What," he said, "is happiness?" He opened his eyes.

"A new hound," said Felix, who was seventeen. His crossbow lay on the points of his pelvis and his ratlike nose was red with the sun. "The kind with big ears."

Julius curled a lip, without malice. So much for Felix. He turned his gaze towards Claes, who was eighteen and built like an oak tree with dimples.

"A new girl," offered Claes. He jerked open the wine flask, gripping the neck like the hock of a stallion. "The kind with . . ."

"That's enough," Julius said. Philosophy was wasted on both of them. Everything was wasted on Claes. Julius was sometimes glad that civilisation had reached the advanced stage it had, so that it could stand up to Claes. The Greeks would have gone back to tents.

Claes looked at him, pained. He said, "I've only had—" Beside him, young Felix was grinning.

Julius said, "Drink! Drink! I said that's enough about girls. Forget I said anything."

"All right," said Claes, surprised. He drank. He inhaled. His nostrils were indigo blue. He said, "This is nice."

Julius refrained from agreeing. A dyeshop apprentice would find any change nice. Felix (his charge, his employer's son, his daily burden) had enjoyed the day's rabbiting, but didn't deserve to. Only he, Julius, had left his cares in the dyeshop and had a right, for one day, to indulge himself.

The canal banks glided past. The lightermen bickered companionably and dropped into snatches of song as they paddled. The sun-warmed cherubim lodged three indolent heads, cheek by jowl round the bath-rim. Julius found the wine flask in his hand, and eclipsed the whole sun with its bottom. *A conscientious youth, yet with a troublesome lightness of character.* So they had assessed him, while he was earning his scroll at Bologna.

God take all law schools and dispose of them. This is Flanders, not Italy. You volunteer to unload a bath from a ship. You accept a lift in the bath back to your place of residence and employment. You close your eyes the better to ponder. Where is the lightness in that? Julius, notary to the Charetty family, closed his eyes. Almost at once, so it seemed, he endured a nasty blow to his ribs. Half-awake, he flung out a fist in return. He hit something.

"Hey!" said Felix and, his face flushed, made to kick him again. Julius rolled over, escaping the foot. The sound of rushing water told him why Felix had wakened him. They were approaching the lock.

Felix's voice was continuing, monumentally resonant because of the bath. "You've knocked my hat off," boomed Felix. "You've broken the feather."

The lightermen, steering up to the lock, glanced round appreciatively, and so did Claes, who had got up to help them. The truth was, it was hard to hit Felix and avoid hitting his headgear. This one had a peak and a long pointed brim like a paper boat. Its osprey feather curled, broken-backed, on the rabbit-bag. Where the hat had been, Felix's brown hair was sweaty and flat, and his curls had sagged into corkscrews. He looked furious.

Claes said, "You said you were tired of the feather. It's time for the beer, Meester Julius."

Claes had been with the Charetty since he was ten, and being a family by-blow, he got to speak that way to Felix. Through the years Claes had become not only an apprentice but a kind of servant-companion to the Charetty heir. Felix tried to batter Claes regularly but mostly put up with him. Felix's mother, thankful for peace, let Claes off his dyeshop duties whenever Felix demanded it. Julius, equally thankful, hoped that Claes' spasmodic apprenticeship would last long enough to see Felix into maturity, if not old age and burial.

Julius, an easy-going sort of man, had nothing much against jonkheere Felix. He could control him. Claes, of course, had no writ to control anyone, which was why he got beaten so freely. It made him very helpful. Julius watched Claes give a last shove with his oar, put it down, and then walk round the end of the boat and hand Felix his hat. All anyone remembered of Claes were his size and the dents in his cheeks and his helpfulness. And that nothing female under twenty was safe from his endeavours.

Julius could see his mouth opening and shutting outside the bath, and hear Felix booming back from within. Julius didn't join the discussion, which was on the usual subject. Of course, he liked watching a good-looking woman. He had his share of vanity. He knew his sort of looks drew attention. He had had to extract himself more than once from some developing situation with a client's young wife. It was not, either, that he contemplated taking Holy Orders; or not up to the present. But if a good chance came along, a man ought to be ready. He was moderate. He didn't raven, like Claes; or yearn like poor Felix when brought to sail the canalised river between Sluys and Damme, passing three miles of ankles and a handful of knees, if you were lucky.

Accessible ankles, what's more. You didn't find grand ladies with steeple headdresses and shaved brows and pearls on their slippers among the quays and sheds and warehouses and pens and tie-posts of the two ports of Bruges. You got pertly laundered white caps and slyly hitched work-gowns: enough of them to please even

Claes, Julius thought. The liveliest girls called down to one youth
or the other. Men sang out too, and boys ran alongside, keeping up
with the rowers. One tossed a pebble into the bath, and it chimed
like the tongue of a church bell. The tongue of the thrower soon
drowned it, as his father hurriedly thrashed him. Even from Brussels, or Dijon, or Lille, Duke Philip could hear things.

Claes stayed on his feet beside Felix. Felix was signalling master-
fully with his hat, from which Claes had adopted the feather.
Three feet long, it waved from his thatch like a fishing line. On the
other side of the boat, Julius helped throw up the ropes at the
sealock, and heaved up the statutory can of Bruges beer to the
lock-keeper.

The man looked at him twice before naming him. Without the
gown he wasn't Meester Julius the notary; he was just another
young pest in his twenties. In his more sober moments, Julius was
aware that exploits such as these were unseemly. In his less sober
moments, he refused to be bothered. The lock-keeper had no trouble recognising Felix or Claes. Everyone in Bruges and Louvain
knew the Charetty heir and his slavish attendant.

There were no other craft in the lock: another mark of the power
of the Duke. The lighter entered, and behind it the tidal gates
waded creaking together. The lock-keeper, stowing his beer,
walked off to open the sluices. Perched high on the water, Julius
looked ahead, beyond the shut wooden gates, to where the canal
ran straight over the marshlands which led to the far spires of
Bruges. Immediately outside the sluice another barge, seaward
bound, lay double-moored to the bank, waiting for them to emerge.

It, too, lay low in the water. It, too, bore only one item of cargo:
a single thickly wrapped object some fifteen feet long which did
not, like the Princenhof bath, project beyond either gunwale, but
lay snugly within the barge well, hardly moved by the swell of the
water.

Above it, in a cleared and cordoned space on the bank, stood a
group of undoubtedly very grand persons with an authentic steeple
headdress drifting among them. From the superior height of the
lock, Julius gazed upon them. So did Felix and Claes and the lightermen.

There were banners. There were soldiers. There was a group of
well-turned-out local churchmen escorting the figure of a medium-
sized, broad-shouldered bishop with precious stones winking all
over him. Julius knew who he was. He owned the Scots ship *St*

Salvator, the largest vessel they had seen back at Sluys. It had already unloaded and had been taking on cargo for Scotland.

Felix said, "That's Bishop Kennedy, the King's cousin, come to winter in Bruges. That's the party he brought with him from Scotland: they must have been staying in Damme since they landed. What are they waiting for?"

"Us," said Claes happily. His feather waved slowly.

"The lighter," said Felix. Occasionally, the future burgess surfaced in Felix. "What's that thing in the lighter? Cargo for the *St Salvator* maybe?"

Occasionally, Felix was right. "Important cargo," said Julius. "Look. It's got Duke Philip's own seals all over it."

Hence, of course, the escorting soldiers and the other overdressed dignitaries. There was the ducal flag, with the Duke's deputy controller in its shadow. There was the banner of Bruges, with the Communal Burgomaster and a couple of échevins under it. Also the cleverest agent in Bruges and one of the wealthiest: Anselm Adorne in a furred robe, his long poet's face wreathed by the scarves of his hat. His wife was with him, her wired headdress sensibly hooded, apparently brought in to shepherd the only female in the Bishop's small party. The female, turning, proved to be a fine-looking girl in a temper.

Felix said, "That's Katelina van Borselen. You know. She's nineteen. They sent her to Scotland to marry. She must have come back with the Bishop. And I may be blind, but I don't see a husband."

Married or unmarried, the girl called Katelina was wearing the steeple headdress. The hennin had caught the wind and was furling and unfurling its veil like a flagpole so that she had to hold it with both tight-cuffed hands. She wore no ring, but there were two possible suitors beside her, presumably off the same ship. One was an elegant older man with a beard, wearing a draped hat and gown Julius would swear came from Florence. The other was some silly gallant.

A good astrologer would, at that moment, have taken Julius by the arm. A good astrologer would have said, Do not look at the Bishop. Do not speak to the lady. Keep away from Anselm Adorne and the Florentine with the beard. And above all, my friend, leave the boat now, before you make the acquaintance of the man you call *some silly gallant.*

No one took Julius by the arm. Fate, which had a better idea, let

him conquer his pang of jealousy and recognise that before him on
the quay was a fair-skinned man of quite striking good looks, wearing a silken tunic as brief as a shirt-tail. Between cap and ear, the
fellow's hair was bright as church gold. Between high brow and
cleft chin, his expression was one of impatience, mixed with ineffable scorn.

From the badge of his henchman he was of consequence. The
henchman held, with some care, the leash of a muscular hound
with an identical crest on its back-cloth. Hand on sword-hilt, his
master was posed like a painting, one shapely limb flexed in its blue
hose, the other stalwartly straight in its white. His gaze, idly scanning the onlookers, discovered the stare of a serving-girl. The nobleman lifted his brows and the girl, hugging her pail, coloured
brightly.

Claes, transfixed beside Julius, allowed his feather to wander.
Julius sneezed without ceasing to gaze at the paragon who, in turn,
had caught sight of the bathing basin. It seemed to amuse him.
Snapping his fingers, he acquired the leash of his hound and began
to stroll up to the lock, throwing a remark, as he went, to the lady.
He looked as if he might snap his fingers for her as well, Julius
thought, but he didn't. And although she looked after him, she
didn't follow.

The well-dressed magnifico came closer. He was not as young as
you might think; at a distance. Thirty-three, thirty-four. His blue
taffeta was French cut, and so was the one-shouldered cloak and
the tilted plate of a hat with its ruby. In his two years at Bruges,
Julius had never seen him before. Felix had. Felix, his fingers
plucking his own atrocious pinked velvet, spoke in a voice of unwilling awe. "That's Simon," said Felix. "Heir to an uncle in
Kilmirren, Scotland. They say he's never had a refusal. The rich
ones think he'll marry them, and the poor ones don't care."

"What?" said Julius. Claes said nothing. His feather had come
to a halt.

Felix said, "The rich . . ."

"Never mind," Julius said. Simon of Kilmirren came to rest on
the bank just beside them. The underwater sluice gates had opened.
The water they were floating on began to crease a little and swirl,
and a line of wet appeared on the lock wall. The lock-keeper came
up.

The man called Simon said, "My poor man, you take your time,
you Flemish clods, don't you? I saw some beer."

His Flemish was very good. The lock-keeper had no trouble accepting insults from gentlemen, especially if he saw a profit in it. He said, "It's a custom, my lord. Beer during the passage to Bruges, and the dues paid on the way back. My lord is going to Bruges?"

Julius wondered how anyone, even a lock-keeper, could imagine he saw a promise of beer in that smiling face. The Scots noble called Simon continued to smile. "My lord has a thirst," he said. "Waiting for this rubbish to pass down the lock. If you have beer, I'll take it."

"Excuse me," said Julius.

It could have been that his voice was not loud enough. Certainly the water, by now, was swirling outside the lock as it emptied, causing the waiting vessel to joggle. The lighter on which Julius stood was now sinking steadily, so that his eyes were level with Simon's trim waist. Simon did not turn his head. Only his dog, attracted by something below, straightened its forelegs, steadied, and leaped lightly down beside Julius, dragging its lead from Simon's grasp. Felix said, "Oh no, you don't!" and grabbed its collar, separating it from the rabbit-bag. The Scotsman turned then, with surprise, and looked down at them.

Julius said, "I'm sorry, my lord, but the beer represented part of our dues. To be fair to the man, you would have to pay him for it."

The charming face stared at him. It inspected, in turn, the faces of Felix, Claes and the lightermen. Its gaze returned and settled on Julius. Simon said, "Stealing a gentleman's hound. The penalties are, as I remember, quite serious."

"And what about stealing beer?" Felix said. "And eating other men's rabbits? If you want your dog, come down and get him."

Felix had a great deal to learn. Julius let him go on complaining. Above, the Scotsman turned, ignoring them, and stared at the lock-keeper who went off in a hurry and came back with the beer. He put it down in front of Simon. The girl in the steeple headdress, Katelina, had walked up beside him. She said, "I thought only workmen drank beer."

There was a glint in the handsome eyes, quickly concealed. She had surprised him by coming. Simon said, "When stuck in a sty, do what the pigs do. I offer you beer, or another half hour of the Bishop."

"Beer," she said calmly. She was speaking in Scots, which was not easy to follow. "Pay the man. Or the children."

The lock-keeper had revised his opinion of Simon. He also understood Scots. He said, "Thank you, demoiselle. Meester Julius will tell you its worth. Meester Julius is a Bologna-trained lawyer."

The Scotsman failed to blench. The Scotsman let his considering gaze drift again over the crew of the lighter, and fixed on the most miserable member, a lighterman with three days' growth of beard and a rash. "Meester Julius?" he said.

"Meester Julius?" said Claes in the same moment.

"Never mind," Julius said. He knew he was being baited. He also knew he was going to get his money, if he had to ransom the dog for it.

"Give him a coin," the girl said. "Look." She tilted her head, so that the hennin wagged like the mast of a ship, and began to unclasp the purse at her waist. She had dark, well-marked brows and a fine skin, its colour a little heightened by amusement or annoyance. Julius gazed at her.

"Meester Julius," said Claes.

The Scotsman, smiling, laid a finger over her hand and instead delved into his own handsome wallet, drawing from it a handful of small foreign coins. He cast them with deliberate abandon into the barge, and watched smiling as they spun and hopped in the bath and sank among the bottom-planks and the ropes of the barge. Then he stopped smiling and said, "Take your hands off my dog!"

He was speaking to Claes. Julius looked round. Now they were sinking more rapidly. The mooring-rope slid through the lightermen's hands. The group of dignitaries on the lower bank vanished from view, every head turned in their direction. The wall of the lock towered above them, green with weed.

As always, there were leaks in the wall. Gorged with water, it spewed carefully into the barge, splattering Felix's smartly stuffed lap. It found and spiralled down the favourite toque Julius was wearing. It hit the Scotsman's hound, which skipped aside, growling. The hound had been standing, Julius saw, astride the Kilmirren crest of its own unstrapped back-cloth, now spread like a bathmat beneath it. It was glaring at Claes. The crest was not what it had been. Claes said, "I'm sorry, Meester Julius, but I had to do something. The Duke of Burgundy wouldn't like it."

Julius began to laugh, just as a jet of real virulence suddenly sprang from the wall and cascaded over the barge. It increased in power. It began to fill, with dynamic effect, a corner of the Duke of Burgundy's bath, which proceeded to urge its barge sideways. The lightermen, already mesmerised, allowed the slack in the rope to run upwards. A further discharge, more violent than any so far, hit the opposite side of the bath. It started to spin just as the lock gates on the inland side proceeded to open, and the mooring ropes fell.

Far above them the Scotsman was saying something, his face pink and white with annoyance. Beside him, the girl Katelina bit her lip, the beer standing forgotten between them. In the lighter, equally, no one was thinking of picking up money. It was Felix who said, "We're going backwards."

"Sideways," said Claes. He said it thoughtfully.

"Forward," said Julius.

The lock gates continued to open and the Duke of Burgundy's bath prepared, giddily, to emerge into the canal. The lightermen jabbed with their paddles. The leaden rim of the bath rose, sank and rose. The slop in the bath flowed backwards and forwards, soaking their sandy boots and their hose and the rabbit-bag and cleansing the Kilmirren crest as it rippled. The bath-rim struck the wall with a clank and drove itself and its barge swirling out of the lock where it bounced off one gate and bucked off to visit the other. The dog, staggering, barked.

From the corner of his eye, Julius saw the Scotsman make his way quickly down to the group on the bank. There, every startled face was turned to the lighter. The dog redoubled its barking, and on the shore men began to shout very loudly.

Julius could see what they were shouting about. He could see— everyone could—what was going to happen. He had time to wonder what was in the ducal parcel so handsomely stowed in the long barge at the side of the waterway. He had time, even, to examine it as the Duke of Burgundy's bath leaped towards the shuddering outward-bound lighter containing the Duke of Burgundy's personal cargo. The two boats collided. The lighter, held by its ropes, had no way to escape as the boat containing Julius, Felix and Claes pitched into its planks and sheared its side off.

The bath tilted, ejecting Claes and Julius briskly into the waterway. It sluiced Felix down to its deep end where he wallowed, his submerged hand firmly clutching its coping. Then it righted itself.

The crippled outward-bound lighter tugged its mooring ropes, burst them, and shed its cargo with languor into the watery gloom, capping it with its own weedy bottom.

As it went, Julius rose to the surface. His eyes opened on horrified faces, Burgundian and Flemish. His ears, streaming water, caught the first ejaculation of moment which did not come from the Flemings at all, but from the Scottish Bishop. *"Martha!"* exclaimed that figure in a voice of bronchial protest. "What have you done? What have you done? You have sent Martha, you fools, to the bottom!"

No one laughed. Especially Julius didn't laugh. For now he knew what had been in the barge, and what they had ruined.

There was no one to warn. Claes, his feather lost, was floundering over there and Felix, swimming briskly, had nearly got to the bank, neck and neck with the dog, which scrambled up past him. The boat with the bath was tied up, and the lightermen already stood, a sheepish group, on the towpath. Dripping, Felix got out and, commendably, went off and joined them, shadowed by Claes. Feeling old, Julius climbed up and squelched after them. The dog shook itself, and its master's man, scowling, got it warily by the collar.

From the circle of eminent persons, severe voices had continued to rise. The Bishop's demands could be heard: "Will you take some action, my lords! Get your engineers, your dredgers, your seamen!" And later: "Unless, of course, the insult is deliberate. My cousin of Scotland is promised a gift, and the gift is lost by the Duke's own officers in the Duke's own waterway. What am I to think?"

The commandant hurriedly spoke, and the Burgomaster. Then at last came the calm voice of Anselm Adorne, who had held, in his time, the highest office in Bruges and whom Julius would trust to smooth anyone's feathers. "My lord, you have lost only a wind and a tide. The Burgomaster will escort you to Bruges. The commandant will take these men into custody. The canal will be dredged and the object retrieved or replaced. It was, I believe, purely an accident, but the city will pursue its enquiries and make you their report. Meanwhile, we can only offer our humble apologies."

The Burgomaster said, "That is so. That is so. The lightermen will answer to the dean of their guild, and if negligent, they shall be punished."

"They were not all lightermen," someone said. "Those three. Those three wear no badges." The voice of Simon of Kilmirren, newly arrived from the lock, negligent in blue taffeta, his fair face perfectly bland. Someone gripped Julius hard, from behind, by the arms. "And," continued the same amused voice, "they owe the lock-keeper money."

Anselm Adorne turned his head, glanced at Felix and Claes and remained studying Julius. His hollow-boned face, deceptively monkish, was noncommittal. He said, "I am acquainted with Meester Julius. Any mistake over money was, I am certain, an oversight. But I must ask. How did you three come to be on this boat?"

"We were asked," Julius said. "With so many ships in the basin, crews were pushed to serve everyone."

"The Duke cannot command a lighter crew when he wishes?" said the Bishop. He had pushed back his hood. He was not very big, but he had the chin of a fighter.

The man in the Florentine gown had lost interest. Turning his back on the Bishop he had strolled to the quay, to watch the water lap at the lock. Adorne's wife was still present, and the girl Katelina, picking her way down from the lock, chose to stand between her and Simon, looking pensive. Then she turned towards Julius, who was pouring water from doublet and jacket and hair, and she smiled. It was not a smile of sympathy; and when the fair Simon murmured something in her ear, she broke into a low laugh that was even less sympathetic. Returned without a husband, they said. With Simon, who had never had a refusal. The rich ones think he'll marry them, and the poor ones don't care.

"My lord, there were enough lightermen," Julius said. "But none who could care for the bath. An officer asked us . . ." He heard himself, a well-schooled, responsible notary, stumbling through his explanation. Rolling back from the rabbit-hunt, full of good wine from the grateful dune-herder, ripe for novelty, heading in any case seven weary miles back to Bruges—who would not have taken the chance to travel in the Duke's bathing basin?

He ended as best he could. "And indeed, minen heere, neither we nor the lightermen are to blame for the accident. The walls leaked, and the basin became uncontrollable."

The man called Simon drifted to the Bishop's shoulder and stood there smiling. "Uncontrollable! To Bruges lightermen, conveying such property! Who was steering?"

No one had been steering. Everyone had been steering. One of the lightermen, pressed, admitted suddenly that that apprentice called Claes had been steering.

All eyes on Claes. My God: goodnatured, randy, innocent Claes, who knew nothing but how to make jokes and mimic his betters. Claes, with the biggest mouth in Flanders. Claes who, standing in a pool of light mud, opened his eyes, large as moons, and said, Of course, minen heere, he had been steering, but not inside the lock. The osprey feather would have been an improvement. His hair, darkened to the colour of gravy, hung in screws over his eyes and coiled over his cheeks and dripped into the frayed neck of his doublet. He shook himself, and they all heard his boots give a loud, sucking sound.

A liberal smile crossed Claes' face, and faded a little when no one responded. He said, "Minen heere, we did our best, and got a ducking for it, and lost our day's sport and our crossbows. And at least the Duke still has his bath."

"I think you are insolent," said the Burgomaster. "And I think you are lying. Do you deny, Meester Julius, that the youth Claes was steering?"

"He was steering," said Julius. "But—"

"We have heard. But he ceased when you entered the lock. That is, you saw him stop. But he may have started again."

"He didn't," cried Felix.

"I know he didn't," affirmed Julius stoutly. And uselessly. He saw the lightermen exchange glances. And knew, as if he'd been told, that the lightermen would not give the same assurance. They couldn't afford to. His legal training told him it was all entirely unfair. His experience of courts ducal, regal and churchly told him that fairness had nothing to do with it. He hoped his employer, Felix's mother, would keep her head. He hoped the Bishop was less vindictive than he looked, and that some god would stain, tear or even drench the taffetas of the exquisite Simon, who was still murmuring to Katelina van Borselen, watched, as they all were, by the devouring gaze of the onlookers.

The serving-girl with the pail was also still there. She had stopped courting the glance of the taffeta, and there was concern on her round face, not blushes. Perhaps Claes felt her eyes on him. He looked up, and found her, and gave her one of his happiest smiles. Mary Mother, thought Julius. He doesn't even know what is happening. Should I tell him? That the Duke's cargo that sank was a gift—a gift from Duke Philip of Burgundy to his dear nephew James, King of Scotland. A fifteen-foot gift of some import. To be plain, a five-ton war cannon, grimly christened Mad Martha.

Someone cried out. It was, perhaps, thought Julius, himself. Then he saw, to his surprise, a mass of dishevelled brown hair dart

past the Bishop, and recognised the athletic figure of the girl Katelina. And behind her, also running, was Claes, followed by an
increasing number of soldiers.

At the lock edge, the bearded man in the long robes had turned.
He saw the girl coming. He tried, stepping hastily, to move out of
her way. Then he saw what she was after and stretched out a hand.
Her hennin, blown off by the wind, rolled and skipped at his feet.
He stooped, just as Claes, sprinting, passed the girl and started to
pounce in his turn. The two men collided.

The bearded man fell, with a sickening crack that could be heard
all round the basin. Claes, his feet trapped, dived over the body and
plummeted, with a fountain of unpleasant water, back into the
canal. The girl stopped, threw an annoyed glance at the water, and
then stooped with a frown beside the prone, convulsed form of the
Florentine.

The grip on Julius had gone. Felix, also free, said, "Oh my
God," and rushed to the water's edge. Julius followed him. Between heads, he could see Claes splashing about in the water.
When the apprentice glanced up, it was at Katelina van Borselen,
now come to the edge, and not at the soldiers lined above him at
all.

"It's buckled," said Claes, with regret. He referred, you could
see, to a soaked steeple headdress captured firmly in one powerful,
blue-fingered hand. He coughed, examining it, and water ran out of
his nostrils. He paddled carefully back to the steps and gazed up,
with apology, at the hennin's dishevelled owner.

Katelina stepped back abruptly. Claes climbed the steps. The
soldiers seized him. Claes' circular eyes opened wide, winking as
water ran into them. He gave his attention to the soldiers, and to
Katelina, and to the hennin, which was no longer a snowy cone,
but a battered scroll mottled with indigo. She accepted it in a
dazed manner.

The generous lips widened in that marvellous smile which had
bewitched every servant in Flanders. "I took the weeds out of it,"
said Claes to Katelina von Borselen. "And the mud will wash off in
no time, and Felix's mother's manager will get rid of the indigo.
Bring it to the shop. No, send a servant. A dyeshop is no place for
a lady."

"Thank you," said Katelina van Borselen, "for troubling yourself. But perhaps you should save your concern for the gentleman
whose leg you have smashed? There he is, over there."

The way his face changed made it clear that Claes had been
unaware of the other's misfortune. He was a good-hearted boy. He
made to move to his victim, but the men at arms stopped him
instantly. They buffeted him as they did it, and went on striking
him every time he opened his mouth. The biggest mouth in the
country, and the best-beaten back. Julius looked at his young master Felix. Felix said, "It's all Claes' fault. He never seems to grow
up."

Echoes of Felix's mother. If they crucified Claes, would she
blame her notary? There was no one else to worry about him. Claes
was the sort of unfortunate bastard (Julius sympathised in a way)
whose relatives were either dead or indifferent. Julius said, "The
man whose leg he broke. Who was that?"

No one knew. A Florentine. A guest of the Bishop's, come from
Scotland with the Bishop himself, and the beautiful Simon, and
Katelina van Borselen who, if God had been kind, would have
found a husband in Scotland and stayed there. Whoever he was,
they would find out soon enough, when he or his executors demanded Claes' hide for his injuries.

They watched as Claes was dragged off. He went unregarded by
Anselm Adorne, which was a bad sign. But Adorne was occupied,
like the rest, in anxious ministration to the man with the beard.

Like most of the rest. The exquisite Simon, taking off his blue
taffeta doublet, had offered it rolled like a bandeau to the lady; and
was now binding it round her loose hair. It looked very pretty. He
fastened it with the ruby, still talking. After a moment she smiled,
in a cursory fashion. If you were interested, you might have wondered what the girl Katelina had against the young lord. Perhaps,
on the journey from Scotland, he had ignored her, and had now
changed his mind? Or had he once gone too far? Or had she se-
lected a rival, and he was trying to lure her back to his company?

Julius considered these things, watching Simon. Then he turned
his back on him with decision. But for that sportive nobleman, he
and Felix and Claes might have escaped without notice. It did not
occur to Julius then that the fair Simon's interventions could have
been other than idle. And yet he knew the practices of the city.

And he knew, as the fair Simon knew, which of the three would
suffer for it most, in the end.

Chapter 2

Whatever profound legal argument Julius had with the commandant on the way back to Bruges, it was ineffectual. It didn't save himself and Felix from prison. Before noon, they were locked up.

By divine intervention his employer, Felix's mother, was away at Louvain. Julius sent a soothing message, wrapped in money, to Henninc, her dyeshop factor in Bruges, and three others to people who owed him a favour. Then he hoped for the best. It seemed to him that no one was really interested in himself or in Felix. If one person was going to be blamed for everything, it was going to be Claes.

It was late afternoon when they got the first news of him. The turnkey, bristling through the bars, mentioned that their young friend had been put to the question. The lad, who wanted a tile or two, had talked for a turn of the hourglass about nothing else but the rabbit hunt. Of course, he had done himself no good, although he was a great comic, everyone said: as good as one of Duke Philip's dwarves. Maybe Duke Philip would take him on as a jester, if he got over the beating. They'd made a better job of it than they usually did, hoping for a confession. Julius was sorry for Claes. Fortunately, Claes took this sort of setback philosophically; and in any case, he had nothing to confess.

Then the news came that he had been brought into prison. Naturally, he was lodged in the famous Dark Chamber. Julius (also philosophical) paid for warm water and cloths and wrote a promissory note for the bailiff, stolidly counter-signed by the town notary, to buy Claes the right to the upper floor, where his masters had bedding and sustenance.

The idiot was dragging irons when he arrived, and Julius had to pay to have these taken off also. He added this to the careful running note of his expenses, which in due course would reappear, neatly itemised, as student equipment for Felix.

Naturally. Methodically honest himself, Meester Julius had learned which of her son Felix's experiences Marian de Charetty was prepared to pay for, and which she wasn't. In the past two years, she had taken the occasion once or twice to refresh her notary's memory on the subject of his contractual duties, which did not include boisterous exploits with Felix. In point of fact, before the notary came, Felix's exploits had been more than boisterous. Felix got excited. Felix never knew when to stop. Even Claes, who got into worse trouble than any of them, never went into passions like Felix.

Up to now, horses and dogs had claimed all Felix's deepest emotions. But at any moment, there would be girls. So far, girls either tantalised Felix or neglected him, for he treated them roughly, the way he treated his own little sisters. But that would change. Julius hoped that it would be Claes, and not himself, who had to handle that bit of coaching. And that it would take place back in Louvain, where people understood students. But that said, there was no harm in Felix, kneeling there like any good horse owner helping to doctor Claes' muscular back, and doing more harm than good, especially as he kept stopping to argue with everything Claes was saying.

Claes, the colour returning a little to his good-natured face, was engaged in describing in five different accents what it was like on the lowest floor of the Steen, where there was no food and no light, and you had to beg as best you could with a bag on a pole through the window bars. Someone had given him a turn of the begging-pole because he was bleeding, and when he drew it back in, it had a poke of butter inside.

Felix stopped. "Butter?"

"From the wool vats. For my back. Someone took it before I could use it. I wish I had it now. Have you got your jousting-gloves on? You've got hands on you like thorn bushes. It came, the butter, from Mabelie."

"Mabelie." It stopped Felix again.

"Standing outside the prison window. Didn't you see her at Damme? The girl with the big plait of hair and a bucket. I didn't know her name either. It's Mabelie, and she works at Jehan Metteneye's."

"And she brought you butter." Julius found he had stopped attending to Claes' back as well.

"Well, she was sorry for us. Everyone's sorry for us. There was quite a crowd out there in the Burgh. The hatters' men, I meant to tell you, Meester Julius. I told them where to go for their rabbits, but they weren't too pleased. I reckon if Meester Cambier is raising the cannon, he would lift the rabbit-bag too for a favour, and maybe even my lord Simon's money. Two of your clients were there, Meester Julius, wanting to know if the contracts were still legal if they hanged you. And Henninc from the shop, saying he was sending to Louvain, and anything you had promised to pay would come out of your wages. And all the boys from the yard, with beer. You should have left me in the Dark Chamber," said Claes nostalgically. "I would have had the butter and beer and all before they hang us."

"They won't hang us," said Felix confidently. "We did nothing wrong. It wasn't our barge. We weren't in charge of it: the lighter-men were. The lock-keeper got his beer back. And we've got you, Julius. You know more law than any of them."

Julius said, "Felix, the Bishop was angry. He's the Scottish king's cousin. The Scottish queen is Duke Philip's niece. The Scottish king's sister is married to Wolfaert van Borselen. Something has to be done to convince all these people that the offence was an accident."

Claes smiled at Felix over his shoulder. "So someone's got to be punished. You see? If it wasn't an accident, they wouldn't dare punish anybody."

Claes, for whom no tangled issues ever existed, often depressed Julius, particularly when he knew what he meant. Felix was merely incensed. "That's crazy," said Felix. "They'll punish *us*? For doing nothing?"

"They punished me," said Claes the apprentice. He turned round cautiously to let them fasten the cloths over his front, and settled crosslegged with his shirt over his shoulders. His hose had dried in folds and wrinkles all over his thighs, and his hair had dried too until it was thick and flat and frizzed a little just at the edges, as if someone had singed it.

"Of course they punished you. You broke that gentleman's leg," said Felix with justice. "And you weren't respectful. And you certainly made a fool of the girl this lord Simon was making up to, and he's a Scotsman as well. That Katelina. She didn't want her stupid hat returned once it got into the water, you fool. She could buy twenty others."

"Your hair's come out of curl," said Claes sympathetically. It was not surprising, Julius thought, that Claes got beaten so often. He remembered something important. A girl called Mabelie worked for Jehan Metteneye, and the Metteneyes of Bruges had been innkeepers and brokers for incoming Scottish merchants for five generations.

"The girl Mabelie," Julius began.

"A great thick plait of hair down to here, brown as a fox. A full mouth of teeth as good as your horse, and cheeks pink as paint and a nose like a plum and a great white neck with muscles in it going down to—down to—"

At the wrong moment comprehension came to Claes, and he stopped before the terminus. "She says the Scots are out for our blood. They needed the gun to make war on England. She says the Duke will blame Bruges, and the Burgomaster will have to protect himself. She wants to meet me under the Crane at eleven tomorrow."

Julius closed his eyes. You would say it was fantasy, if you didn't know Claes. You would say that even Claes couldn't receive an invitation through prison bars from a girl he'd never spoken to in his life. On the other hand, when you knew Claes, you knew what his smile did. All the same—

"In two pieces?" said Julius. "With your face blue and your tongue hanging out? Or are they going to arrest all the lightermen and let you and me and Felix walk home to the dyeshop tomorrow?"

"That's what I meant to tell you," said Claes. "If you hadn't jabbed at my back. I couldn't think while you jabbed at my back. All the boys from the shop were there outside the prison."

"You told us that," said Felix.

"Yes. Well, all the Dyers' Guild members came there as well, and the dean and the chaplain. They said they'd sent to the écoutète and the échevins and the counsellors and the deputy controller and of course Meester Anselm with a very big complaint and talk of outrage and even talk of ceasing to do trade with Scotland, and all the officials had put together their heads and agreed that, provided we satisfied Meester Anselm of our innocence, there would be no further action apart from a significant fine from the Charetty family—"

"Oh," said Felix.

"—which the Dyers' Guild and the Lightermen's Guild would each assist them to pay. They're letting us out in the morning. Under the Crane at eleven, she said."

Meester Julius stared at the family apprentice. "You knew that when you came in."

Claes gave his generous smile.

"And," said Julius, "the bailiff knew that, and probably the gaoler and both the turnkeys who took all my money." He could feel himself sickening for a cold, so he contented himself with delivering a cutting, well-phrased and annihilating diatribe, which Claes received with proper humility, even if Felix giggled all the way through. Then he rolled over and submitted himself and his cold to an uncomfortable, but not a doom-laden night.

The three children were brought before Anselm Adorne in his handsome house next to the church of Jerusalem the following morning. His remit was to make an enquiry, and to give them a fright.

Children? Two were youths, and one was a highly trained notary only seven years younger than Anselm himself. But they were still children in terms of diplomacy. The family Adorne had had nearly two hundred years of regional power in Flanders since they came from Italy to settle in Flanders with the Count of the day, who had married a daughter to the King of Scotland. A long, long sequence of Adornes, with their well-bred faces and quizzical eyebrows and fair, curling hair, had served the town of Bruges and the Dukes of Flanders, in that order. They never forgot, either, the other branch of their wandering family, which had served the republic of Genoa in Italy for even longer, as men of business and men of money and, very often in the highest post of all, as Genoa's rulers, her Doges.

To a man of family and of property like Anselm Adorne, trained in knightly skills and in letters, Latinist, fluent in Flemish and French, German and English and in the dialects of the country of Scotland, the three foolish young men who had overturned the Bishop's new cannon were simply children. He did not rise when they were brought into the great room of his house, nor did his wife of sixteen years move from the far end of the hall, where she had placed herself with her visitors, her serving-woman and the older of their many children.

The gothic chair in which Anselm sat, like the beams over his head, bore the entwined crests of his mother and father, Bradericx and Adorne, and the blazon appeared again, in coloured glass, in the tall gothic windows. The notary had been here before. On the quayside at Damme, Adorne had recognised the slanting eyes and

taking, blunt features at once. Meester Julius was a good deal more
subdued now, in his proper collared black gown, with his hat-scarf
over his shoulder, and the tools of his profession slung at his belt.
But his soft-shod feet had a firm enough grip of the ground, and
the inkhorn and pencase hung steady and still. The young man had
the pride of the convent-bred clerk and the scholar. But escapades
were for students.

The others were common material. The boy Felix had bid fair to
run wild after Cornelis de Charetty died, but he had a sensible
mother. Whether he had the shrewdness of his father was another
matter. It had been Cornelis who had kept his head in the panic
two years ago when the Lombard pawnshops all failed, and had
rescued his wife Marian's father by taking over his trade.

It was recognised as being good business, mixing pawning with
dyestuffs. The Louvain shop had flourished, and de Charetty had
several houses there, it was said, as well as his Blauw verweij, his
woad-dyeing workshop and house here in Bruges, and his excellent
bodyguard. He must have had small enough time for his children.
But a man like Cornelis should have been wiser: should have
looked to the future; should have considered who was to follow if
he died before his time. Now there was only his wife Marian, and
the managers who were as reliable as managers usually were, and
that maniac of a mercenary and the boy. This boy Felix, who
enjoyed pranking with his apprentice friend Claes, and had no
thought of the business at all.

Anselm Adorne looked at the apprentice then, last of all, and
made an observation. He said, turning, "I will not ask you to sit
down, Meester Julius, for you are here to be sentenced. But tell me
first. Has this fellow been chastised?" He spoke in Flemish.

The youth Felix opened his mouth and, receiving a look from
the notary, shut it again. The notary said in the same language,
"Minen heere, Claes was beaten for the injury to the Bishop's
friend. He was also beaten for what was taken to be an imperti-
nence. Both were unintentional."

"He was impertinent," said Anselm calmly. "And he did cause
harm to Messer de' Acciajuoli. He was beaten for no reason concerned with the cannon? No proof or confession of guilt has attached to him?"

"No, minen heere," said the notary. He spoke with firmness.
"Claes had no designs on the cannon. It was an accident. Nor was

he steering when the mishap occurred. If minen heere will allow, there are many who could confirm."

"There are, by now, many who might think it in their interest to confirm," Adorne said. "I see no purpose in widening this enquiry, which to my mind has become too public already. Whether or not I accept that the affair was an accident, it is a fact that an ally of the Duke and the Duke himself have been much offended against. Meester Julius, as notary to the family de Charetty, you were responsible for these two youths yesterday afternoon?"

"I am answerable to the demoiselle de Charetty," Julius said.

"I shall then leave it to the demoiselle de Charetty to deal with you as she thinks such an employee deserves. You, my good youth, are heir to your father's business?"

The boy Felix said, "Minen heere, Meester Julius wasn't at fault. We made him take us shooting. We all decided to climb on the—in the—"

"You had all drunk rather much, and decided you would enjoy a ride in the Duke of Burgundy's bath. It is understandable, in very young children. You are no longer very young children. You are servants, as I am, of my lord Duke, and must respect his property and the dignity of his rank and that of all his friends. Would your father have disregarded such things? Does your mother? What have you done to her name and her pocket, you her son, you her notary, and you her apprentice?"

The boy Felix had gone red. The notary said, "We will have care in the future. We did nothing with malice, nor ever will."

A barb? No, he thought not. Meester Julius had sense, and was making the best of it. The boy Felix saw only the injustice: there were tears in his eyes. It was time he learned about injustice. The apprentice Claes stood with perfect stoicism; the stuff of which good workmen and good soldiers were made.

Adorne spoke to the notary. "You have been told of the fine, and of its conditions. My judgment is that the payment laid upon your employer and your guild is punishment enough for what you have done. You are excused further detention. To mark it, I offer you wine in my house. Meester Julius, there is a stool for you, and one for your scholar. Margriet!" He had left the boy Claes where he was, standing before him.

There had been no real need to call. His wife knew his ways, and had caught his eye long before, and sent for his steward. Now she rose smiling. Adorne rose too, as she came forward, though she pressed the boy and the notary back to their stools. "My lady," said Anselm Adorne. "We have a young fellow here who performed a service yesterday for our friend Florence's daughter, and who has not yet been rewarded. Have her come over." He watched the three men as he spoke. None of them, he was well aware, had noticed Katelina van Borselen at the end of the room. Two of them turned, reddening. The apprentice just stood where he was, waiting patiently.

Anselm Adorne was amused by people, but never acted from mischief alone. He was not satisfied that he had plumbed the apprentice. He also wanted to find out the mood of the girl, first cousin to Wolfaert van Borselen, at the end of these three (unmarried) years abroad as maid of honour to the Scots Queen.

It didn't take long. Today, instead of a hennin, she had bundled her hair into one of those nets, with a screw of curled hair at each ear. It made the best of her neck, which was long, and she wore her gowns narrow and plain, in the Scottish court fashion. She had the Borselen eyebrows, at present drawn closely together. The apprentice turned, and the eyebrows separated.

"Ah," said Katelina van Borselen. "The bath attendants. I don't know when I was last so amused. And this is the retriever. He looks different, dry."

"Yes, my lady," said Claes. He smiled, with perfect and transparent good will. "So do you, my lady. I think Meester Adorne means you to apologise to me."

Adorne saw his wife's face twitch and straighten. He was sorry, but not very sorry that he had failed to take the boy's entire measure. He said, "Claes—that is your name?"

The boy had the open smile of the child, of the idiot, of the aged, of the cloister. He said, "Claes vander Poele, minen heere."

The surname had been given him. He had none of his own. Anselm's steward, who could nose out anything, had known all about Claes. The youth had come as a boy of ten to serve in the Charetty dyehouse. Before that, he had lived at Geneva, in the merchant household of Thibault and Jaak de Fleury, being Jaak's niece's bastard. He had never gone back to the de Fleury family, who seemed to have discharged their duty towards him when they paid his apprenticeship fees to the dyers. It was a common story. A servant of one household or the daughter of another made a mistake, and the mistake was reared thriftily, and appeared with blue nails in Flanders.

Minor gossip didn't interest Adorne, but Bruges and its business life did. One day Felix de Charetty would belong to that community, and it was the duty of the community to see that he came to it without prejudice or unworthy companions. Anselm's steward said this apprentice was sweet-natured and simple. Such things were easy to test. Anselm said, "You should understand then, Claes vander Poele, that a lady does not apologise to an apprentice."

"Why, minen heere?" said the apprentice. "If I offended her, I should apologise to the lady."

"Then apologise. You have offended me," said the Borselen girl.

"Because my lady's hair came down in the wind in front of my lord Simon. I know it. I am sorry, my lady," said the apprentice.

Anselm Adorne was conscious of his wife's twinkling face in the background, and of the sharp stare of the girl he was talking to. "And you brought me under your roof to suffer an encounter with *him*?" said Katelina van Borselen. "Scotland was more civilised."

"Perhaps it will be better in Zeeland, my lady," said the apprentice. "The winds may moderate. Or if my lady would like, I could bend her a framework that wouldn't blow off. I make them for Felix's mother."

"Claes," said Julius the notary. "With the permission of Meester Anselm, I am sure you could retire."

The sunny smile turned on Adorne. "May I retire? May I first, minen heere, speak to your children? We know each other."

Adorne knew that, from his wife. He had not finished yet with this particular rascal, but to allow matters to take this course might be interesting. He inclined his head.

It was not his eldest son Jan and his cousin the youth made for, he saw, but the little ones: Katelijne and Antoon and Lewijse. The lady Katelina watched him pass her with well-bred amazement, and then turned to talk politely to her host and hostess, waiting patiently from time to time if Meester Julius were invited to speak. Little bursts of laughter came from the children at the end of the room. They seemed to be playing a board game. Later, he saw the boy Claes displaying his hands, with some sort of pattern of thread held between them. Later still, he heard voices he could have sworn belonged to people he knew, such as Tommaso Portinari, and the Scottish Bishop and Meester Bladelin the Controller and the guild-dean of the fruiterers, who had two upper lips, may God give him comfort.

Then all the voices stopped, and he knew that Nicholai Giorgio de' Acciajuoli had, as if on cue, entered the hall. He was dressed as he had been yesterday on the quayside at Damme, with the draped hat and the silk brocade robe, created in Florence. He dominated the room. His combed black beard was Italianate, but the quality of his skin and the close-set dark eyes were Levantine. His lips, edged with red, revealed fine teeth. A Greek of Florentine origins: the guest from the Scots ship whom the apprentice Claes yesterday had sent flying. Whose leg Claes had audibly broken.

Beside him, Adorne saw the notary stiffen. The boy Felix, nostrils wide and mouth open, lost some colour. At the end of the hall Claes rose to his feet with painful slowness. Then he smiled. He said, "I wondered, monsignore, why I could get no news of your injuries. I have to make my apologies. I had no thought of harming you."

He spoke in Geneva Italian, and was answered in Florentine.

"A bruised elbow," said the bearded man dryly. "You were intent on other things. I hope you thought it worth it."

What blood he could spare rose for a moment into the boy's face and hesitated there, with his dimples. He said, "So long as monsignore forgives me."

"Oh, I forgive you," said the lord Nicholai Giorgio de' Acciajuoli. "So long as you do not repeat it. I had one replacement. My other limbs are in Boudonitza. Your friends look amazed. You had better explain to them."

But the notary had it by now. He also had Italian, Adorne remembered, and possibly even some Greek. He had trained in Bologna. The notary said, "You have—it was wooden, monsignore?" Relief and embarrassment mottled his face.

"I have a wooden leg," agreed the other. "Which makes it difficult to rise up when deprived of it. Which makes it agreeable also to sit, if my host will permit? Beside, perhaps, the lady Katelina whose presence alone made our late voyage supportable." He sat. "And now, introduce me to your three youths."

Anselm Adorne made the introductions. Then with equal solemnity, he introduced his one-legged guest, using Flemish.

He did not expect them to know the name of the princes of Athens. He introduced this descendant merely as Nicholai de' Acciajuoli, now touring Christendom to raise gold to ransom his brother, captured when Constantinople fell to the Turks. He did not complicate matters by explaining further. Monsignore had done well in Scotland. The King had been touched and the Bishop had collected a good sum for monsignore's brother. The other part of the Greek's mission to Christendom had been less successful. Like everyone else in the East, he wanted a new Crusade to free Constantinople.

Just so. But the rulers of Christendom had troubles enough without going into all that.

A conversation began in Italian. At his side, Adorne was aware of Katelina van Borselen's displeasure, and disregarded it. The boy Felix, excluded also, began to pick at his nails. The word "Greek" entered the talk.

The noble lord from Boudonitza was gazing at Felix. He said, in extremely slow Greek, "I am told by your friend that horses interest you."

It had a surprising effect. The youth Felix turned crimson and he clasped his hands quickly together. Then he started to speak. Whoever taught Greek at Louvain was not a supreme master, and the youth, it was certain, was not the world's brightest linguist. But he was crazy, it seemed, about horses, and the stud of the Acciajuoli was famous. He stuttered and ganted and listened.

Katelina van Borselen said, "What are they talking about now?"

Anselm Adorne told her. From the corner of his eye he identified his wife in a state of mild discomfort. He was not behaving, today, like a host.

"I am afraid," said Katelina van Borselen, "that I can't spare the time for a Greek lesson on horses. Margriet, may I trouble you? I promised to help my father receive some Scottish friends. The Bishop. My lord Simon."

"You'd be better getting a Greek lesson on horses," said the boy Claes.

Anselm looked at him. After a moment he said, "The Scots are allies of our Duke, boy. You have been brought into civil company. Don't abuse it."

The tone of their voices, perhaps, had caused the Greek to break off his laboured discussion with Felix. He had also recognised a name, and an expression. He spoke in Italian, unexpectedly, straight to Claes. "You do not like the handsome Simon, young varlet? You are jealous, perhaps? He is well dressed, and talks to beautiful demoiselles such as this lady? But he cannot speak Italian, or make children laugh, or be concerned for his friend as you are. Why dislike him?"

The youth Claes considered, his overbright gaze on the Greek. Then he said, "I don't dislike anyone."

Adorne said, "But you hurt them. You mock. You mimic. You offended the lady Katelina yesterday and today."

The gaze turned on him. "But they offend me, and I don't complain. People are what they are. Some are harder to pity than others. Felix would like to dress like my lord Simon, but he is seventeen, he will change. My lord Simon is not seventeen, but he acts like an oaf, and has the talents, you would say, of a girl; which must be a mortification to his father. But I think, Meester Adorne, that he does speak Italian, because he made a joke about you in that language. The lady Katelina will remember."

It was Messer de' Acciajuoli who took control before Adorne himself got his breath back.

"I think," said the Greek, placing a manicured hand with care on the apprentice's arm, "that the time has come for Claes to make for his home, if his beating is not to overcome him. Perhaps his friends would see he gets there. Honesty, Messer Adorne, is not a commodity that recommends itself everywhere. I am glad to have made its acquaintance, however, and I would not have it penalised."

"It has been penalised already," said Adorne. "And you are right. We have been talking, these last five minutes, about the inclement weather. Meester Julius, you have leave."

He could not stop the children from running after Claes into the yard, or from touching him. He hoped the notary would have the sense to take this apprentice straight to the Charetty dyeshop and keep him there until things had settled. Or better still, send him back to Louvain, and the boy Felix with him. He wondered, since Margriet was bound to ask, if it were true that the lad made Marian de Charetty's headgear; and scooping up and studying the tangle of cotton the children had dropped at his feet, decided it probably was.

He saw to the departure of Katelina, and returned to find the Greek talking to Arnolfini, the Lucca silk merchant, whom he could not remember having invited. Messer de' Acciajuoli had in his hands the children's board game, and was idly settling the pieces. They both looked up as Anselm came in, and Arnolfini and he exchanged greetings.

The Lucchese had called, it seemed, for no particular reason. "Except," he said, "out of regard for your selfless service. You gave of your leisure, I am told, to spare the échevins this dangerous case of the sunken gun. We are all impressed."

The Greek spoke gently, his gaze on the board. "Heavy fines were imposed. But the Guilds are rich."

"Indeed," said Arnolfini. "Rich and solvent. I hear that payment has been made already. Before even the sentence was delivered. Who invented this very odd game?"

"I cannot remember," said Anselm Adorne; and was not surprised to see the Greek look up, smiling.

Chapter 3

The sky was blue when Katelina van Borselen left Adorne's house with her maid, and the wind barely stirred her cut-velvet cloak. She had been home in Flanders for two days.

The town house her father had taken in Silver Straete lay on the other side of the town. The painted canal boat of Anselm Adorne waited for her at the foot of the gardens, with three servants to care for her. She had them row her home the long way, past the convent of the Carmelites, and St Giles' church, and the great pile of the Augustines, and the handsome church of St James, from which could be seen the towers of the Princenhof, to which the Duke of Burgundy's bath had just been dragged with such trouble. She would not think of that, or the considering gaze of the notary Julius. She made them row her almost as far as the Friday market.

They said Venice had bridges too, but Bruges must have a hundred: in stone with almond-eyed saints and dulled gilding; in wood, with treacled timbers and bosses of greenery. The roads were thronged but the river, split and skeined and channelled everywhere, was the highway where boats passed gunwale to gunwale, hooded, laden, crammed with bags and boxes and beasts and baskets and people: with nuns and officials, merchant-burghers and aliens, churchmen, consuls and innkeepers, and masters of ships laid up at Sluys, who skimmed past in their skiffs on the stretches, sloping their masts to slide under the glittering arches.

And on either side passed the crooked banks of tiled houses, drunkenly cobbled with crazy windows and flower-pot balconies and roofs fluted like pastry-crust. Their feet, their watergates, their warehouse doors were set in the canal. Their boat-steps led up to small secret gardens whose roses still tumbled over the wall, and swayed to the draught of a passing boat, and posted their mingled scents after it.

The van Borselens were Zeelanders, but Katelina understood how it felt to be a Bruges townsman.

Edinburgh was grey stone and grey, silvered wood and every roadway was vertical. Bruges was flat. Bruges was speckled warm brick, its roads cloistered with towered mansions and palaces and tall houses, laddered with windows, where the businessmen lived. Bruges was the multiple voice of working water; and the quality of brick-thrown echoes, and the hiss of trees and the flap of drying cloths in the flat-country wind, and the grunting, like frogs in a marsh, of quires of crucified clothes, left to vibrate in the fields of the tenters. Bruges was the cawing scream of the gulls, and the bell-calls.

Bells rang from all the towers in Edinburgh, but a Bruges man was born to the beat of the womb and the belfry-hours. The work bell four times a day, when mothers rescued their young from the feet of the weavers. The watch bell. The great bell for war, or for princes, that you could hear from the poop-decks in Damme. The marriage bell. She would not think of that either. She had come back from Scotland in disgrace, having refused the lord whom her father had picked out for her. No one did that. A daughter's duty was to marry as her family's fortune directed, and her father had no sons. So now she had only two choices. The cloister, or a marriage to someone else of her father's choosing. And she knew who the likeliest suitor would be.

Simon, heir to Kilmirren had not so far declared himself. Back in Scotland, she had attended the Queen wherever the court might find itself, and that was not always in Edinburgh, where Simon's uncle kept a town house, and where he did all his business. She knew all about Simon for several reasons. His sister Lucia had been maid of honour in her time to two Scots princesses, one married to France and the other to Katelina's cousin Wolfaert.

A child then herself, Katelina did not remember her. In any case, Lucia had very soon left, betrothed to her Portuguese nobleman. But gossip about Lucia's brother, the handsome blond Simon, had entertained the Borselens for a long time after that. So Katelina knew that he had had a wild youth in France, and had been sent home in disgrace to his uncle, the head of the family. She had met Alan, lord of Kilmirren. A mean and slow-witted man, comfortable with the gun-masters who were his gossips and ambitious for nothing more than an easy life, he was not the man, clearly, to handle someone like Simon.

It had been left to the family steward, she heard, to take Simon in hand. For five years, they said, he had resisted every effort to tame him, and had made what splash he could with his French dress and manners, on the small income his uncle allowed him.

What had changed his mind one could only guess. The need for money, Katelina suspected. The steward died, and Simon took over. By the time Katelina came to Scotland, Simon was steward of his uncle's lands in Kilmirren and Dunbar: a reasonably rich man with a flair, intermittently exercised, for ideas and management, who earned enough for his needs, and employed a factor for business that bored him.

He enjoyed, she knew, a roving courtier's role in Scotland and Flanders, but had been careful to shackle himself with no public offices. He had no wife, and they said he was a libertine. This appeared to be true. On the other hand, the uncle was childless, and Simon himself was an only son. One day, Kilmirren would be his, and he must therefore marry. She had known as much during her Scottish stay, but then she had been intended for someone else and had neither looked at Simon, nor he at her. During the ship journey south she had been too wretched, too apprehensive to want anyone's company. Pride had come into it, too. To reject her father's choice and to appear to hanker instead after the exquisite Simon would be less than dignified. Especially as the exquisite Simon might fail to offer her marriage.

When, in the latter days of the sail she had allowed him to come near her, it was plain that he wished to attract her and, perhaps intrigued by her withdrawal, was to some degree attracted himself. By the time they landed at Sluys, she knew he had made up his mind to try for a conquest.

She did not show that she was flattered. If he offered for her, her father would approve. So, presumably, would Simon's uncle, and Simon's estranged father, if he were ever asked. There was money and land and a minor seigneurial title. Of the several young men whose parents had shown an interest in her, he was the most eligible. Outside, that is, the lord she had refused. The lord she had refused had been forty years older, and vicious. Simon the nephew of Kilmirren was physically qualified to endear himself to any girl living. She was not widely travelled, but she at least had never met any man with his looks. Why then did women of all classes (they said) make him free of their beds, but never marry him? Why did he never marry them? Of one thing she was sure. Without marriage, he would never have her. Whether she wanted him with marriage was something she did not yet know.

Katelina van Borselen entered her father's house thoughtfully, and prepared to receive her father's guests with composure.

* * *

Felix de Charetty and Claes his shadow spent the afternoon lying on the grass by the Waterhuus, with those of their friends who had an excuse to escape work.

Felix had no excuse, having been told quite distinctly by a tight-lipped Julius to get back to the dyeshop and stay there. But Julius had been waylaid by a group of men wishing to talk about rabbits, and Felix had made his escape, dragging Claes with him. Retribution would come when his mother arrived from Louvain, as she undoubtedly would. He was unconcerned. Felix had little interest in people who worked for a living, although sometimes his friends swore they saw old Cornelis over his shoulder, when he drove a sudden, sharp bargain over a trifle. One of the reasons he liked Claes was that he had no possessions.

The group on the grass were talking a mixture of languages, because they were mostly the young of the trading community. Among them was Anselm Sersanders, Adorne's nephew, and John Bonkle, the source of the worst of their English vocabulary, and one of the Cants. Also, Lorenzo Strozzi was there, feeling miserable. They did what they could to relieve his misery and, indeed, it became quite a strenuous afternoon. It was almost over when Strozzi happened to mention the gathering taking place in Florence van Borselen's house, and the fact that he and Tommaso had been invited.

Felix's hair was uncurled again under the high blocked and brimmed hat he had been made to put on by Julius, and the bagsleeves of his sober doublet were wet to the elbows, but his energy had not diminished. "Go!" he said. "Lorenzo, you must fetch Tommaso and go!"

"Felix wants to know what Simon is wearing," said Claes.

"Tommaso won't go for you and Claes," said Lorenzo nastily. "You know how he hates the way Claes copies him flashing his rings."

"It may stop him from flashing his rings," said Sersanders. "Anyway, Tommaso will go, if van Borselen invites him."

"Of course," said Lorenzo. "Tommaso has only been invited because the manager of the Bruges branch of the Medici bank is away on business, and they have to make do with the assistant manager. I have only been invited because the head of the Bruges branch of the Strozzi company is also away, but at least the manager is my father's cousin, so they may be sure I will know how to

drink wine without spilling it. I am not going. I don't need to go.
They are Flemish pudding-makers."

"Say that again," said Felix. He took his hat off.

John and Anselm, on either side, changed position discreetly so
that either could get hold of his dagger arm. Claes said, "Felix
doesn't like the young Borselen lady. He kicked her headdress into
the water."

The glare in Felix's eyes was replaced by a look of normal exasperation. His shoulders slackened. He said, "I told you. You
shouldn't have jumped in after it. But Lorenzo shouldn't—"

"Lorenzo's brother is sick in Naples, and he is worried," said
Sersanders.

"Lorenzo misses Spain," said John Bonkle. "Imagine being sent
to Spain at thirteen. All those black serving-girls and the climate.
Felix, why not a branch of the Charetty in Spain? You would be
agent, and we'd all come and help you. You could leave Julius
behind with your mother."

Felix flushed. To compare the Charetty to a great house with
branches all over Europe was a compliment. He said, "Oh, I would
take Julius. He's a good man."

"And me?" said Claes. His hair had got damp and had risen up,
as it always did, into a dun-coloured floss. He was, with reason,
lying on his face, as yet unaware that Felix had untied the waist-
bows attaching his hose to his pourpoint.

"You?" said Lorenzo. "You would have half Christian Spain and
half Muslim Spain breeding before a month had gone by."

"I'll stay in Bruges, then," said Claes. "Lorenzo, why did Felix
want you to go to the van Borselens'?"

They all looked at Felix.

"He doesn't dislike the girl after all: he fancies her," John Bonkle said. "Go on. That's why, isn't it?"

Felix grinned blandly. In fact, he wanted to know what Simon
was wearing. And he found out, too, because Lorenzo, aware of
having tried his friends' patience, did walk round to the Strozzi
residence in Ridder Straete and, having put on dry clothes, presented himself with Tommaso Portinari at the house of van Borselen and his daughter Katelina.

In Silver Straete, men and their wives had called all afternoon to
pay their respects to the lady Katelina, newly returned (unmarried)
from Scotland. Her child sister Gelis watched them, counted them,

and informed Katelina, sometimes hardly out of earshot, which of the ladies was pregnant, and by whom.

The reception was held in the garden, a modest paved plot set about with handsome tubs and small trees and a fountain. There was also a cushioned stone bench, upon which Bishop Kennedy of Scotland had been placed, with his agent attending behind him.

It was, of course, a gathering of those who held Scotland in favour, since Wolfaert van Borselen was married to the Scottish king's sister. The prime topic, indeed, was the overturning of the Mons cannon Mad Martha, which was universally deplored, and not least by the French wine importers. No one hinted that, if the Scots bombarded England, England would find it hard to spare troops to invade France, which would please Bishop Kennedy and benefit the English king, Henry the Sixth. No one mentioned that a number of fugitive English who did not approve of King Henry were at that moment conspiring to cross into England and take the monarch into courteous custody, with the white rose as one of their emblems. No one mentioned the heir to France, the Dauphin, at all.

They talked about Madeira sugar and pepper prices. They discussed salted salmon and answered Bishop Kennedy's questions about exports of good slate and quarry-stone. They touched, politely and warily, on the sensitive subject of ship insurance. The conversation, studded with pitfalls, ambiguities and unexpected fragments of news, was of a rare fascination, so long as you were a merchant.

Katelina saw her possible future husband Simon on the other side of the room, toying with his smart dog, and taking no part in these useful exchanges at all.

She wondered if he lacked an instinct for business. She wondered, since he glanced at her from time to time, whether he was impatient for other reasons. She noticed that Tommaso Portinari, the young Florentine from the bank of the Medici, was talking more than suited his elders. She noticed that his companion, the sulky young Strozzi boy, appeared more interested in Simon's garments than in the good Scottish Bishop's opinions.

Simon, of course, was as always worth looking at, with his brief, cinch-belted tunic, his broad padded shoulders and the tall, roll-brimmed hat on the neat, razored bulk of his hair. His chin was smooth as blond wood, and looked unyielding. Once committed to

something (look at the way he had spotted these stupid young men
at Damme) he could be obstinate.

But there were muscles, too, under the padding. In Scotland, he
had jousted frequently, and successfully. It was how he made his
superior conquests among the high-born widows and neglected
wives watching. If he had bastards, she had never heard of them.

She talked to everyone: Jacques Doria, Richard Wylie, Sandy
Napier. Mick Losschaert had just got out himself from Constantinople, and knew the Greek Acciajuoli family. Bitter and yellow-
skinned still with privation, he was not slow to disparage them.
Jumped-up Florentines who had reached Greece through Naples,
and founded a line of Athenian princes. There were still Acciajuoli
in Florence. Medici men.

He begged leave to doubt, said Mick Losschaert, whether Nicholai Giorgio de' Acciajuoli really expected the combined fleets of
Christendom to sweep through the Middle Sea and destroy the
Sultan Mehmet of Turkey. He rather thought, said Losschaert,
that all Messer Nicholai Giorgio had in mind was to pay the ransom of his brother Bartolomeo, so that Bartolomeo could continue
trading in silks with the Sultan. He wondered aloud where the
money was that had been collected for Acciajuoli in Scotland; and
who was to have the pleasure of transferring it.

A certain constraint fell on the company, and the Bishop's
breath whistled. Five feet eight inches in his sandals, he had the
lean, folded face and balding head of a man much over his true age
of fifty. On shipboard, Katelina had learned not to underestimate
him. When he spoke, you saw the thrusting eyebrows and jaw of a
lively, muscular man who was at least agile still in mind and de-
bate.

Now he shot a glance up at Losschaert from where he sat on his
bench and said, "I miss my guess if my cousin James, King of
Scotland asked his people for gold so that a silk merchant in Constantinople could resume his trade. Or those worthy men—you
must have heard the names, they are famous—who came to Mantua from the East to beseech the Pope weeping for help?"

"My lord Bishop, you misunderstand," Losschaert said quickly.
"I meant merely that there are many interests at stake in time of
war as well as time of peace between the eastern world and the
west. With single supplicants it is wise to be careful. Where the
whole Christian church of the East asks for the friendship and
succour of Rome, it is a different matter."

Tommaso Portinari, Katelina saw, had accepted a goblet of wine and joined the fringe of the discussion. The Bishop's eyes moved to him. The Bishop said, "Well, if you have doubts about the money collected for Nicholai de' Acciajuoli, I fancy you had better express them. The sum was entrusted to me to bring to Bruges, and I have placed it in the good hands of Messer Tommaso here. From Bruges, I understand, it will be transmitted to the Medici branch at Milan, who in turn will transfer it to Venice. From Venice, after due negotiation with the Turk, it will be taken in appropriate form to Constantinople, and there exchanged for Messer Nicholai's brother. Am I right, mynheere Tommaso?"

"It is so, my lord," said Portinari. He wore melon sleeves and a low-crowned beaver hat and had rings on most of his fingers, which were white and fine. The rings were not very expensive: he was only under-manager. Tommaso Portinari had come to the bank as a twelve-year-old. Katelina had known him all her life, as had everyone else. Hence his need to impress.

He said, "The bank is much engaged in arranging Christian ransoms, as Monseigneur knows. Our Rome branch does little else." He spoke Italian's Flemish tinged with other accents, of which English was one. Only that morning, Katelina realised, she had heard someone imitate him. She frowned, remembering.

Tommaso, seizing his chance, was continuing. "Mynheere Losschaert is not, perhaps, aware of the trust the Curia place in my company. Naturally, for the remittance of money. My lord Bishop brings us fees accruing from new Church appointments, and we transmit these to Rome. But we are agents for other things also. I am at this moment sending three suits of tapestry overland to one of the Cardinals."

"You trust the Alpine passes in winter?" said Doria. "With money?"

"Nowadays we send bills of credit," said Portinari. His manner combined firmness and deference. "But yes, under proper guard, we would send silver if need be. You dispatch goods that way yourself, when the Flanders galleys come in with something that won't wait till spring. They are late this year, my lord Bishop."

"They are near," said the Duchess of Burgundy's secretary. He removed from his nose the flower he had been smelling and, bending, tucked it behind the collar of Simon's seated dog, which thumped its tail and galvanised the folded half of its body a couple of times by way of encouragement.

Messer Vasquez straightened. "We shan't have to wait long, I think. They say the auction was held up this year, and the galleys were late leaving Venice. I am told the silk will be good, and they carry exceptional spices. The Duke has been informed."

Tommaso turned quickly, so that Katelina could see his high cheekbones and long nose and the brightness of his eye under the fringe. He said, "Has Monseigneur heard who is the commander?"

Messer Vasquez did not mind sharing his news. "One of the Duodo, I hear. I understand it may be Messer Alvise, who used to sail from Venice to Trebizond. If so, Bruges may look for good entertainment. When the Turks attacked Constantinople, Alvise Duodo broke the boom and led most of the trapped fleet to freedom. A wealthy tribe the Duodo, and not wanting in style."

He smiled at Katelina. "Now is the city's busiest time, demoiselle Katelina: when all the cellars are empty and waiting for the two precious cargoes. But as a child, you have seen the Flanders galleys arrive?"

She was silent. Come Lent, the ecstasy of the Carnival. Come late summer, the wonder of the great galleys sailing in with their treasures from Venice. The two marvels of a child's year which she had most missed in Scotland. For which she had yearned even more than the wide skies and the water and the warm, speckled brick.

"Occasionally," said Katelina. "Monseigneur, will you take a little more wine?"

Simon remained to take supper with them, and was amusing. It would have suited her father more, Katelina thought, if he had fallen into discussion of what had been said that afternoon, or asked questions, or given his opinion of those who had spoken, and hinted at a little gossip from Scotland.

But of course, Simon knew that. He was sure, then, of receiving her father's blessing if he sought it (or perhaps he had it already?). And he had elected instead to impress her. She spent some time not being impressed. But he was remarkably easy in manner. He made her father's chaplain smile, and bandied anecdotes with his secretary and drew out both her father and herself on the subject of the court at Veere, where Simon's own sister Lucia had once served the Scots princess. Her father asked after this sister, who had married a Portuguese in the Duchess's train and was now at home in the warmth of south Portugal. They had a son, it appeared, and Lucia was more than contented.

"Content to be so far from home? Are you sure of that?" Katelina spoke from mischief, but Simon answered her with composure.

"You missed home during your three years in Scotland. But marriage is a commitment. The six sisters of my king were flung all over Europe. You know that the princess at Veere is still happy. So are the others, all except two who were sent home to Scotland. Ask them if they enjoy being back in Scotland or not."

"Are they still alive?" said Katelina.

"Come Katelina," said her father. "That is hardly courteous. These ladies cleave to their lords, as they should, and willingly follow the mode of life which duty lays on them. Whether it is warm or cold, or hilly or flat does not signify."

"Or whether their husbands are warm or cold, or hilly or flat?" said Katelina. "It must signify, or the convents would all be empty."

The chaplain pursed his lips, looking at no one. Her father said, "Demoiselle, you have not learned delicacy, it would seem, in your travels abroad. This is not talk for the board. My lord Simon will excuse you."

She rose slowly. So did my lord Simon, and took her knuckled hand to lead her out from her chair. He said, "If, Monseigneur, you would excuse your guest Simon also. There is a fine sunset in the garden which would cool us both, if one of your servants would attend us."

There was a pause, then her father nodded, and signalled with his eyes to one of the younger serving-men, whose eyes were glistening with interest above the badge on his pourpoint. She thought of refusing to go, for she was in a rebellious mood. She had been a long time away from paternal authority, and her last suitor was still overclear in her mind. She walked out of the room and across the tiled passages still in two minds, and annoyed because he still held her hand, and because a pleasant scent of some sort came from his clothes, and his hair was a shade she had once prayed to the Virgin Mary to bestow upon her.

When the servant opened the door to the garden she moved her trapped hand half out of his, and was alarmed to find it detained. But he kept it only long enough to raise it to his lips, and then gave it back to her keeping again, and followed her docilely into the garden. The servant dropped out of sight but not, she supposed, beyond hearing. She said, "Why are you in Flanders?"

He had stopped walking. Back at the house, the shutters were rimmed with yellow lamplight except for the open, aromatic window of the kitchen, where a cat sat on the sill. In front of her the little trees, moving, masked the lamps in other houses being lit, one after the other as the evening light waned. The sky was full of pale marzipan colours, and so was the water in the fountain basin, and the glimmer that came from the well. Something pricked her through the gathered voile over her collarbones, and again at her temple. She said, "Gnats. We shall have to go back indoors."

The bench was beside them. He said, "I was going to answer your question. Am I not worth a gnat?"

"No," she said. "Tell me another time. Or drive them away. There are some leaves. Smoke would do it. Ederic?"

By God, not out of earshot. Her father's servant appeared. "Fetch a brand from the kitchen," said Katelina. "And throw it on those leaves. You were saying?"

Simon watched the servant disappear tranquilly enough, and led her to the bench, where he took off his jacket and spread it for her. "I was saying that, like everyone on the good Bishop's fine ship *St Salvator*, I was in Bruges to sell part of the cargo, to invest the proceeds, to buy and to lay orders and, most of all, to enjoy the arrival of the Flanders galleys. You could have asked me all that on board."

The trees were darker. A strengthening light, advancing, told that Ederic was coming back. "I wonder why I didn't?" she said. She sat down.

He said, "Because you were afraid I might give you another answer. There is a time for everything."

"And this is the time?" she said. Ederic, stooping, was introducing the brand to the pile of damp leaves. The leaves hissed, and a little smoke showed, and a trace of movement from the first moths. Simon made to sit down. "If you stand," said Katelina, "you could tend the flame while Ederic takes the brand back to the kitchen. It is not the time to burn down my father's house anyway."

Blue smoke rose from the fire. Ederic looked at his mistress and left. Or at least, withdrew from sight. Simon surprisingly knelt by the fire, staining his hose, and, bending, blew into its darker regions. The darker regions retorted. "If you wish to see me blackened," he said, "I have no objection. As to your question, the art of timekeeping is one that is peculiarly Flemish. When the hour arrives, I expect a Fleming to tell me."

"You seem to have waited a very long time to be told. Perhaps you may find yourself waiting as long again. Oh."

Simon said, "I am afraid, if you sit over there, that you will continue to be stung. Let me recommend this side of the fire, where the smoke will blow past you. Why did you refuse his lordship? He had a fortune, and he would have died very quickly."

"Would he?" said Katelina. She considered, and then rose with his jacket and, spreading it, dropped by the fire. He was right. The smoke was just enough to ward off the gnats, but it flowed in his direction, not hers. Already his fair skin was flecked with soot, changing its classical contours, and his eyes shone.

"Of course he would, with you as his wife, demoiselle. Although I am told he prided himself on his embraces. You didn't experience them?"

He must know perfectly well that Ederic was within earshot. She said, "I cannot really remember. I find courting tedious."

He had removed his hat. His hair and eyes gleamed in the fire-light. The sky was lurid; the garden was dark. Her gallant Scotsman bowed his head, examining the erratic course of his fire. "Look," he said. "So damp and so miserable. But at a touch"—he bent and blew—"the right touch, of course . . . Warmth. Light. Comfort."

Katelina van Borselen, black from her brow to her bosom, looked back at him. And then round at him, because swiftly, he had slipped round beside her.

He said, "And sometimes, the right touch is not comfortable at all. But how can I find out whether my courting is tedious unless we are both black as well? My black hands here and here, and my black lips where you would like them. Katelina?"

His breath was scented. The silk on his arms and his body was warm. His lips, arrived at her mouth, tasted of wood ash.

His black lips were on hers, and his pink tongue was inside her pink mouth, disturbing her. Her chin, when she jerked it away, was wet and sticky. She wiped it with trembling fingers.

"Mother Mary," she said. "They said you had the conduct of an oaf and the talents of a girl, to the shame of your father. Now I believe them."

One hand remained caught at her breast. The other lay slack at her neck. He became perfectly still. He said, *"They?* Your father?"

She could not lie about her father. She twisted her shoulders, and his hands fell away. There was a space between them. His soiled face, intent on hers, glimmered in the firelight. Gnats, moths, flared, died, and dropped on their laps. She said, "Has no one told you that before?"

"Who?" he said. "Who said that?"

"No one you need be afraid of," she said. "Except that I heard it. Except that it's true." Without him, her skin wavered between cold and hot, and she was still shivering.

Very slowly, Simon of Kilmirren stood up, and the smears on his face were not comical. He said, "Your father does not think so. Do I begin to see why you refused his lordship, and are unmarried at nineteen? You are malformed?"

She stood also. "Yes," she said. "If it means I have a dislike of fumbling attentions."

"You invited me here. I see. So all you want is a convent?" The anger in his voice was so well controlled that it hardly carried. His voice itself was low enough to escape any listener.

"All I want is a gentleman," said Katelina loudly.

And found herself, somewhat naturally, alone in the garden.

Chapter 4

Drawn from the comforts of the van Borselen kitchen, the servants of the noble Simon had to scramble to put on their jackets, collect the hound and attend, torch in hand, as their master, without taking leave of his host, set off at a smart pace for the market place and the Bridge of the Crane, beyond which lay his lodging. The dog, which he ignored, skipped and barked, excited by his streaked face, his blackened shirt and his air of displeasure. His servants walked carefully.

Curfew fell at nine o'clock, and all those in the streets were home-going. After that, the only lights would hang at the gates of the wealthy, or flash from passing boats, or glimmer from pious niches, illuminating little.

The night-life of Bruges after nine o'clock was pursued with minimal light or none at all. Despite the patrols of the Burgomeester van de Courpse and his officers, there were taverns and bath houses and certain other establishments which did not shut their doors at nine, but these were careful to show no outward lights.

No lights were carried by the officers of the peace who stood, turn about through the night, at the foot of the belfry, nor by the men who watched with bell and horn from the top. The nine closed gates and the five miles of ramparts were not lit, since Bruges was at peace. Only, from the country outside, you might see a tint in the clouds here and there, where they hung over a palace or courtyard or friary. And from within, observe from the cracks between shutters and the broad underfoot traps of the cellars, which householders were still up, and busy.

Later, animals would prowl rustling among the refuse that would be swept up so excellently by the scavengers in the morning. The dredging boats would move slowly from canal to river, scouring the silt and netting the day's quota of bloated pets and rotting vegetation. Near the bridge (here, where my lord Simon walked on without sparing a greeting) the kranekinders were checking and

greasing the Grue, the town crane, a task which could only be done
at night, when business was over.

Their lanterns flickered on the ground, illuminating the huge
wooden framework raising its snout to the sky, with its pair of vast
treadmill wheels roofed like farmhouses, and its mighty double
hooks dangling. At its peak, from whatever whimsy, had been
erected an effigy of the bird which gave it its name, and smaller
cranes perched single-legged on the long sloping spine of its neck,
freed by night from the jostling abuse of the seagulls. Familiar as
the belfry to those who lived in and frequented Bruges, it drew no
glance from the Scots servants of the fair Simon, steward of
Kilmirren. Only one of the felt-capped men lying inside its wheels
whistled between his teeth to the other and jerked his head, so that
a drop of grease splashed on his cheek and made him curse amia-
bly. Neither left his job, and indeed they had no need, for every
man with night-business in Bruges came by the Crane sooner or
later.

At the lodging owned by Jehan Metteneye, one of the Kilmirren
men had to pull the bell to have the courtyard door opened, and
the lantern over the gate gave the porter an interesting view of my
lord Simon's appearance. The room he shared with Napier and
Wylie and another couple of Scottish merchants was upstairs and
usually empty at this hour, but naturally he met Bishop Kennedy's
factor George Martin outside the eating-room and Metteneye's
wife on the stairs, and fell over John of Kinloch, the Scots chaplain, coming out of the dormitory, having used the last of the
washing-water. It was a good half hour before he was able to come
downstairs decently groomed and eat his supper while he entertained the others with the more amusing parts of his adventures.
John, the St Ninian's chaplain, irritated him, and he forced himself
to be especially charming to him.

At the same time, he had no doubt at all how he was going to
pass the rest of the night. He had already brought down, in a roll,
the papers he required to study before his first purchasing mission.
He asked and received from the demoiselle Metteneye permission
to use the innkeeper's office, with its lamp and its worktable, where
Jehan kept his chests and his ledgers.

She was fifty and her smile made him flinch, but he smiled back
when she trimmed the lamp, and brought him a better stool, and
asked if there was anything of which he had need. He said no, and
then changed his mind. He asked whether Mabelie could bring him

a flask of the wine she had put specially aside for him. It was a risk, but a small one. Jehan was unlikely to let his wife come running here twice.

He unrolled his papers and opened the inkstand, but after the door closed, made no attempt to read or to write. As always, coming back to a town, he had run through his mind the tale of his past conquests and part conquests, and had arranged them, half in idle anticipation, half in amusement at himself, in descending order of attack.

Mabelie this time stood at the head. He had found her in his last days at the Metteneyes', a virgin of splendid charms and piquant simplicity, from which status he had led her with quite unwonted enjoyment. She was a servant, of course: one of the myriads of poor cousins and children of cousins which provided the staff for every good burgher's household. There would be no hurry therefore to find her a husband. He had hoped, when he came back this time, to find her still in the house. When he saw her with her pail on the quay, still bright-eyed, still blushing, he had been quite touched.

Last time, she had come to him here, and later he had bribed the two other maids to sleep elsewhere, while he came to her attic. Sometimes, such were the pleasures of Bruges that the dormitory stayed empty all night, and they could take their ease there. It was the only way he could pass such a night, without leaving the house. Women were not permitted in the inns and halls of the merchants.

When a quarter of an hour had passed and Mabelie had not come, he became impatient, and opened the door. One of the menservants was passing, and he shut it again. Five minutes he tried again, and nearly knocked over the demoiselle Metteneye, advancing to knock with his wine. He produced a brilliant smile, and detaining her chatting, asked after Mabelie. The girl, she said, was a trial to her at times, as all girls were, but a hard worker for the most part, and earned her keep in times like these, when everyone wanted service and didn't care whom they ran off their feet. She would be off perhaps making up beds for the new gentlemen who had come in that day. She couldn't say. But my lord Simon would no doubt see her about, tonight or tomorrow.

He tried again ten minutes later, and this time found a maid that he knew, whom he avoided as a rule because of the leer with which she accepted his bribes. She giggled and said that, of course, she would tell Mabelie that the gentleman was working late. But indeed, monseigneur, Mabelie was working late herself. Leer.

She was a fool. There had been no mistaking the look he had given the wench on the quay, or that she had come there on purpose to see him. He let the girl go and, wine in hand, wandered idly all through the house, from the servants' quarters to the kitchen, being charming to everyone, and growing angrier. A game of cards was in progress in the commonroom. He stood and watched, chatting and drinking. Other servants came and went, but not Mabelie. He would have to go out. He had almost decided when the courtyard bell jangled and jangled, so that the cardplaying stopped and heads turned.

Voices. Barking. Someone had disturbed his hound. Metteneye's voice, and then Metteneye's face round the doorpost. "No need, gentlemen, to be alarmed. Someone has reported open bales to the mercers' men, and they have come to search. It will not take long to prove their mistake. Everything is in order."

They groaned. It happened every now and then. Foreign merchants had to abide by strict rules. Goods might be sold in their lodgings on certain days and at certain times only, and must be corded up when that time was over. Uncorded goods meant fines and confiscation. The native traders of Bruges were well protected. One was polite—as now—to the officials who came in with their strapped caps and heavy jackets and broad shouldered servants standing behind. And agreed, of course, to descend to the cellars where the great bales were kept, and from which light, said a passerby, was showing at every trapdoor.

The tramp of feet was sending his dog hysterical, so Simon let it out and took it down the cellar steps with the rest, his fingers tucked under its collar. It snuffled and tugged, even when the cellars proved, of course, to be totally empty but for merchandise, and all the merchandise neatly corded and baled as it should be. Metteneye crossed to snuff the rogue lantern, which some fool had left burning untended.

The dog nearly knocked him over. Wrenching itself from Simon's hand, it leaped past Metteneye, round a pillar, through an archway and, scrabbling, vanished behind a great stack of kegs. They followed it. It had stopped before five bales of forest and brown and middling wool and a sack of skins which had just been inspected. It was barking in front of the bales as if they either threatened its peace of mind or contained its dinner.

Simon walked forward. Between the bales and the wall was a space. Upon the space, a makeshift bed appeared to be laid, composed so far as he could see of an assortment of fox, cat and hare skins, imperfectly cured. The portions of fur obscured a single undulating shape which separated, as he watched, into two distinct forms. A white article, evincing itself at one end, resolved itself astonishingly into the cap on the winsome head of the servant called Mabelie, followed jerkily by her shoulders.

She would have stopped there, but crowding round her, the mercers' men and the Scots merchants had already begun to break into laughter. They dragged her out, guffawing, while she kept her eyes shut and her scarlet face hidden as best she could. She had her stockings on. Otherwise the only part of her clothed was her waist. Metteneye, smiling angrily, took off his jacket and flung it over her.

Simon took three steps off. He stood at the other end of the warm heap of furs where his dog was still barking, and he had in his hand the little dagger which foreign merchants were permitted to carry, to protect themselves against robbers. He bent, perhaps to probe with the blade, or perhaps to defend himself. He had no need to do either. Under his eyes, there emerged slowly a dishevelled head of dust-coloured hair, a pair of brawny shoulders and a sweating chest half encased in a madeover shirt of limp canvas and, over this, an even cheaper pourpoint whose laces did not seem to be entirely attached to their stockings.

Simon knew the face. He knew the broad brow, the moon-like eyes, the nose, precise as an owl's between the dimpled cheeks, and the deprecating, disarming smile.

Claes, the Charetty apprentice. Claes, whose expression at this moment was neither apprehensive nor rueful nor mischievous, but something of all three. Who said, shutting his eyes with a sigh, "I won't deny it. I admit it. I've the conduct of an oaf and the talents of a girl, and there's nothing surer than this, that I'm a mortification to my father, wherever he is."

It was the biggest joke of the evening, thought the mercers. Instead of a nasty scene with the Scots, a court case, a lot of ill feeling, there was a serving-wench being given her business by Marian de Charetty's great smiling lout Claes, lying there in his undone laces, talking his way into his next beating.

It made you wonder, too, when you saw how the fellow Simon was taking it, whether the noble Scots lord might not have had an eye on the lassie as well. He had certainly gone a queer colour. Indeed, for a moment, the knife he had in his hand flashed once or twice, as if he wouldn't mind using it.

And perhaps the fellow Claes thought so too, for all of a sudden, with a heave and a jerk, he was out of the furs and thrusting past the dog and between two of the lads standing laughing at him, and through the arch and round the pillar and up the steps and off through the house in the direction that led to the courtyard. The merchants and the mercers' men looked after him guffawing, and someone slapped Metteneye on the back. Then the noble Simon seemed to come to himself, and he burst out laughing as well, and sheathed his knife, and called to his dog and said, "Well, what are we waiting for? That's a rogue needs a beating, and all we have to do is catch him!"

Immediately, his companions saw what he was after. The joke was good, and it needn't be over yet. Apprentice Claes, the great lover, was a long way from his attic at the Charetty house. The least they could do for poor Metteneye, with his trust abused and a good servant maybe in the family way, was to catch the fellow and make him regret it. Crowing and hallooing, they streamed out of the cellar, leaving Metteneye to grip the little piece by the arm and drag her up the steps to his lady.

The trouble was, of course, the odour of fox, and cat, and hare, and even a faint residual tincture of rabbit. And yet the lad was inventive, by God. He nipped round into St John's Place and past the English merchants' house before you could blink, and then dived straight across and into the Englishmen's tavern, where they were not at all welcoming as he dashed through, spilling the beer and the dice and the card tables, and still less so when a quantity of pursuers burst through the door, including those well able to see what the dicing stakes had been. By that time, Simon's dog had been joined by another.

By the time they fought their way through to the back door, Claes had gone, but there was a wicket door swinging loose in Winesack Street with both dogs barking before it, so they flung it open and poured through, and across a courtyard, and up to a door which opened courteously when they hammered on it, revealing a stout, shiny gentleman in towelling robes, loosely—too loosely— swaying at dog-height.

No one consoled him. Ignoring advice from the better-informed, merchants and mercers pressed past him, following Simon. They bounded from passage to parlour and into a medley of chambers furnished, like Paradise, with nothing but white clouds and se- raphic pink bodies. Among them were several more mercers, a midwife, two counsellors, the chief clerk of the tonlieu, a Grand Dean, two guild-sisters and a bell-founder with muscles like anchor-chains.

No fleeing apprentice was visible through the steam or, indeed, rigorously sought. Two of the pursuers had the misfortune to miss their footing on the slippery tiles and fall into the baths, overcome with the heat, the noise and the inadvertent movements of bathers. Those who emerged, streaming, into the September night might have gone home at that point but for the sight of Simon, running fiend-faced and light-footed before them, with three or four dogs at his heels.

They followed, and were rewarded with the sight of the boy, the randy big bastard who had caused all the trouble, dashing through the darkness to the quay and down the steps to the water. A moment later, one of the long barges moored there swung out and began punting out into midstream, pointing towards Damme. On the steps, Simon paused and then, turning, sprang up to the quay and began running hard with the dogs for the next bridge, followed at an increasing distance by the breathless merchants and mercers, to whom had added themselves a curious householder or two and the porter of the bath house, exuding general goodwill and a willingness to be bribed by almost anybody.

Powerfully though the apprentice might drive his oar, he was only one man in a barge too broad for punting. The boat came sluggishly up to the bridge just as the Scots lord, perfectly trained, flung himself onto its incline and, balancing, jumped.

The reek must have met him in mid-air. Before he hit the laden barge, he would know what it was he'd jumped into. As it was, he first crashed into the boy, who dropped his oar in the water. Then the lord Simon's feet hit the cargo, and he stumbled and sank into something which responded with squeals and forced grunts and queer pipings, each of them borne on a belch of unpleasant vapour. Air from the bellies and bladders of Bruges' deceased dogs and cats and the little dead pigs of St Anthony, retrieved from the water each night by this, the regular scavenging barge.

Sadly, the Scots lord was lying among them. The only oar was overboard. And so, in an ungainly plunge, was the youth Claes, forging, for the second time in two days, through the doubtful water of the canal to the far bank. Choking audibly, Simon of Kilmirren rose to his feet also, stepped up and, diving, began with ease and style to overtake the flapping apprentice.

On both banks the merchants followed him, and the dogs. By their lanterns they saw him master the interfering cross-sway of the water, and follow the darkened head jerking through the water ahead of him, beyond which was the bridge of the Poorterslogie, and the tall latticed bulk of the building itself, the clubhouse of the great White Bear Society.

The lad was no swimmer. He must know how swiftly the lord Simon was gaining on him. The youth would have to land at the Poorterslogie, and if he got there—and he might—before Simon, he wouldn't get there ahead of the dog-pack. A pity. A pity to let it go so far, poor silly boy. For the water might rinse off the worst of the odour, but plenty would stick. Every brute in the place would be there on the bank with a welcome. And swimming coolly, effortlessly, at his back, the Scots lord Simon wasn't going to rescue the apprentice. Not after all that had happened.

Simon got to the bridge a little after the dogs. Above the racket of barking, opening shutters rapped one after the other. Squares of light fell from their windows and showed the dogs grouped, growling and yapping at the head of the steps and the apprentice half out of the water, hesitating at the foot.

There were men there as well. They weren't householders, because the light shone on badges. Drawn by the barking, they were a passing party of hondeslagers, the patrolmen paid by the city to clear the streets of stray dogs. Obligingly, they were cuffing the beasts from the steps; holding them back from young Claes. It annoyed the Scots lord, you could see. Thinking the youth might escape, he drove himself swiftly forward and lunging, seized the boy by the ankle and wrenched. The youth toppled off-balance and hit the steps with his shoulders. He exclaimed. The dogs, driven to frenzy by the redoubled odour, broke loose and pounced on the two men, one fallen, one upright. Claws ripped down the lord's doublet and he took out his knife. The men, swinging leaden clubs, set about them, and dogs hurtled squealing, and dropped as the apprentice got to his feet, three quarters naked. The Scots lord straightened behind him.

The merchants, running up with their lanterns, didn't know what Simon was thinking, although they might guess some of it, and Claes might have worked out the rest. The echoes of forgotten, festering hurts. The memories that included Mabelie's shy, inviting smile and fresh body. The insolence on the quay. The caustic voice (but neither the merchants nor Claes knew about that) of that shameless Borselen woman: *"No one you need be afraid of."* And the other, swinish words she had repeated that had come, as Simon now knew, from the spiteful adolescent before him. Who, amusing himself, had used them again just now, to Simon's face, sure that Simon would be none the wiser.

He had the knife still in his hand, and he intended quite simply to use it.

Claes turned round just as Simon lifted his arm. It was too late to duck, with his legs encumbered with men and dogs. He snatched the only weapon at hand, the leaden club in the hand of the man next to him, and parried the blow as it came, and the next. He went on wildly swinging.

Enclosed in the general fighting, the duel attracted no attention. The hondeslagers, profiting from the mix-up, beat about them with a will, and if a dog got away, it was lucky. The quayside and half the bridge were covered with what, in skin and fat money, would keep them in beer for a fortnight. Lanterns jostling, the merchants stumbled here and there, laughing and calling until the fray started to slacken, the last dogs were being disposed of, and even the fight in the middle was changing. When it stopped altogether the merchants, even then, hardly noticed. When they remembered at last to look for the cause of the trouble, all they found was the handsome Simon, alone, in a great state of fury.

Alone, because the lad Claes had got away somehow. That is, he'd totally vanished.

A pity, you'd say. But Christ, he'd given them all sport enough. So had Simon, standing dripping and reeking, so that you had to go upwind to talk to him. Of course he was angry. He even accused the dog-killers of shielding the youngster.

He had a point, if it mattered. There had been a circle of men—it was hard to see how the youth slipped between them. But where else could he have gone? Not over the bridge. Not back into the river. Not down the quayside along which they themselves had been advancing. Unless he had risen into the air?

It was John of Kinloch, recipient of too many slights, who expressed the kind hope that friend Simon's own hound was uninjured. Baying after another, Simon had forgotten his dog. He looked round for it. It was easy to find by its collar: a magnificent beast, lying dead at the feet of the hound-chief.

The hondeslager blanched. To touch the dog of a knight meant a flogging. A collared dog, a branded dog must be distinguished at

night from all others. Therein lay the skill of their office. And here,
in the half-light, he had killed the hound of a noble Scots merchant. He said the only thing he could say. He said, "My lord, you
saw your dog, jumping about. It could have hurled itself into the
path of anyone's club. None of my men killed it directly. I swear to
you. As for myself, how could I? There is no club in my hand."

"A hondeslager without a club?" said a cynic.

"The boy took it. The apprentice. You saw him," said the dog-
man to Simon.

Simon said, "And he killed my dog? It must have been him or
you."

The dog-killer was silent. A decent man, he kept his gaze strictly
level. Simon started to speak, his face darkened. From the wall of
the lodge high above them, a cheerful, resigned voice forestalled
him.

"Oh, the shame; the shame of it!" said the Charetty apprentice.
"Friends, I have to admit to it all. For the lawyers will never
believe you."

The crowd of men lifted their eyes. From its tall, hooded niche
on the corner, the oldest burgess of Bruges, the White Bear, the *het
beertje van der logie,* does not look down at his peers but up, to the
clouds and the rooftops. He wears a high golden collar, and golden
straps cross the white painted fur of his chest, and between his two
paws he clutches the red and gold shield of the city.

He stood there that night, his gaze lofty, and ignored the two
battered arms which encircled him; the thicket of dun-coloured
floss at his cheek-bone; the amiable chin which pressed on his
shoulder. From one of the embracing fists, hopelessly damning,
dangled the stained leaden club of the hondeslager.

"Take me. I'm yours," said Claes peacefully. "I don't deserve to
have a nice girl like Mabelie and then go off killing dogs; and I'm
giving a terrible smell to your beertje."

"Come down," said Simon softly.

The youth embracing the bear nodded agreeably. "But when the
sergeant arrives, if you don't mind. And if there's a Christian
among you, would you tell Meester Julius I'm in the Steen again,
and he'll need to have a word with a bargeman?"

Chapter 5

The group of apprentices outside the Steen the following morning was even bigger than it had been the day before. Weavers running to work, wellwishers on their way home paused to grin through the window bars. The two crane-repairers were among them.

This time, there was no Mabelie to put butter for Claes in the begging-bags, but her name hung in the air, as if written on bunting. Even when the work bell rang and the space outside the prison reluctantly cleared, there remained one or two curious burghers who stood on their toes to spot the stolid face of the apprentice and who, before passing on, threw him fruity reprimands in voices less than severe.

Left standing also was a tall, black-bearded man of mild aspect who was not a Fleming. "Well, Claes vander Poele?" he said to the prison. The inmates, who owed Claes the worth of a night's entertainment, pushed him heartily up to the window and pressed round him, grinning.

Claes' battered face showed, also, his customary cheerful smile. "And give you good day, Messer de' Acciajuoli," he said. "If you're collecting for me, don't try the King of Scots this time."

Nicholai Giorgio de' Acciajuoli pursed his bearded lips, but his eyes were amused. "Nor the Duke of Burgundy, I must assume," he said. "After the episode of the bath and the cannon. Nor, I suppose, those innkeeper-brokers with pretty serving-girls. Do you cause so many upsets in Louvain?"

Claes tilted his head and brought it cautiously upright again. "Perhaps," he said. "But the university is more used to them."

"Where, of course, you attend your young master. And his mother, the widow of Charetty, oversees you. Is she strict?"

"Yes," said Claes, and shivered.

"I am glad to hear it," said the Greek blandly. "I hear from Messer Adorne that she is on her way to Bruges to deal with these matters. Master Julius has already called to discuss your case, and you may well be freed before nightfall, if a price can be agreed. Do you think your employer will retain your services, which are costing her so dear?"

"Monsignore," said Claes. Two lines had appeared on the untroubled brow.

"Yes?" said the Greek.

"I thought I would be out by mid-morning. They let you out after a beating."

"Are you complaining?" said Acciajuoli. "By offering money, your master the notary has spared you a second beating so soon after the first." He paused. "Or did you have another assignation?"

Behind the bars, the brow cleared. "That's it," said Claes. "And my friends have left. And if I know him, Meester Julius won't let Felix come and see me. And—I don't suppose, monsignore, I could trouble you to convey a message to Felix de Charetty?"

Nicholai de' Acciajuoli, of a race of Athenian princes, who had merely paused from curiosity on his way from Messer Adorne's house to a pleasant rendezvous in a tavern, was moved to laugh. He said, "In Greek? I very much doubt if it would be possible. In any case, why should I?" He might have agreed, so clear was the boy's smile.

"Because you stopped," said Claes.

Messer de' Acciajuoli paused. His feelings at that moment were of a sort that Julius would have recognised. He said eventually, "And what would be the message?"

"Tell him not to do it," said the apprentice simply.

"Tell him not to do it," repeated the Greek. "And what is he not to do?"

"What he is doing," said Claes. "He'll know."

"Presumably he will," said Messer de' Acciajuoli. "But I am going to the market place to join my good friend Anselm Adorne after his magistrates' meeting. I have no idea where to find the shop of the Charetty."

"Monsignore, there is no difficulty," said Claes. "Felix will be with Meester Julius in the Two Tablets—in the same tavern after the fine is paid. The magistrates meet upstairs to consider these cases. I hear that Turks are damned souls and drink nothing."

It was time to go. "Some of them drink," the Greek said. "But I don't know if you could consider them saved as a consequence. I can make you no promise, young fellow. If I see your young friend, I shall tell him."

The great smile returned. "Monsignore," said Claes. "Tell me, if any day I may do you a favour."

The Greek laughed. Afterwards, he remembered laughing.

If the angriest man in Bruges that day was the Scots nobleman Simon, the next was Julius, the Charetty notary.

By noon, of course, the news of Claes' folly was all round the town. Of the repercussions in Silver Straete, where Florence van Borselen heard an uncensored account with some disappointment, and his daughter a censored one with contemptuous laughter, Julius knew nothing.

He learned, as everyone did, that the town had taken advice, quietly, of the officials involved, and was not proceeding against anybody. It was assumed that the injured Metteneye family would complain to the long-suffering Charetty family about the conduct of its apprentices, and restitution would be made. The owner of the scavengers' boat had been content with the price of an alepot.

The man Simon had lodged a formal complaint about the death of his dog, and Julius had just finished another unpleasant interview with Meester Adorne and two magistrates in which Claes' liability had been defined in terms of large sums of money.

If the final amount to be paid by the Charetty company to the Scots merchant was less than it might have been, they had the Scots bishop to thank. From his residence with the Carmelites, Bishop Kennedy had disclosed his disapproval of unseemly night brawling. My lord Simon had lost a fine dog, but he had himself at least partly to blame. Compensation was due, but not prodigal compensation. He trusted his good friends of Bruges to see to it.

Breathing hard, Meester Julius crashed downstairs to the public room of the Two Tablets of Moses after that interview and threw himself onto the tavern bench occupied by Felix, who had collected round him a number of unreliable friends such as the Bonkle boy and Adorne's nephew Anselm Sersanders and the Strozzi undermanager Lorenzo, who seemed to spend such a lot of time, looking discontented, away from his employer's business.

Someone said, "Aha! The party of dog-lovers. Julius, my little friend, your mistress is on her way to chastise you. Stick to ink and parchment and numbers, my dear. It takes men to control men."

It was the voice of one of the most tiresome Frenchmen in Bruges. Lionetto the condottiere was sitting at the next table with the baldheaded doctor Tobias and all his other friends round him.

Tobias was drunk, and so was Lionetto. In Italy and in Geneva, Julius had seen enough of drunk mercenary captains to know at least how not to handle them. He said, "Do you want Claes? Take him."

Lionetto gave a long laugh, which emerged in two phases with a central intermission. He was one of the few mercenaries Julius knew who looked not only low-born but proud of it. But that might have been the red hair, too coarse to curl, which brushed his shoulders, and the pock-mottled skin and ripe nose. He had a chain over his doublet with rubies in it. Or glass maybe. But the gold of the thick links was genuine.

Recovering, Lionetto said, "Pay me and I'll take him, if you're afraid of the widow. Hey, Felix! Your mother's coming, you know? Get your backside stripped off for the horsewhip! You too, Julius! Hey?"

Beside him the doctor, grinning, let his elbow slip off the table and knocked over Lionetto's full tankard. Lionetto, cursing, smacked the doctor over the head and then, leaning forward, ripped off one of the man's stained black sleeves and mopped up his splattered hose with it. The doctor looked annoyed. Lionetto shouted.

"Julius, my little man! Give me your naughty dog-killer and I'll give you a sot of a physician in exchange for him! One pint of Gascon wine, and he'll abort you quintuplets. That is, if you could ever get quintuplets between you. You've only got one man at the Charetty, and he's your fornicating apprentice!" Lionetto frothed. "Claes'd have your mother under him if she wasn't too old."

Felix missed it, thank God. There was only one sort of man who could handle Lionetto, and that was another condottiere. Wait, Julius thought, fuming. Just wait till Astorre gets to Bruges with the demoiselle. Then we'll see about horsewhips. He saw Lionetto open his mouth and steeled himself to do something about it, and then didn't have to. Everyone quietened. Everyone looked at the stairs. From above, solemn in their long gowns, the magistrates were descending to take their customary refreshment in the common room. Anselm Adorne was among them.

And as they seated themselves, and talk began to resume, a second interruption caused it to wane again. The tavern door opened, and in walked the Greek with the wooden leg. The one who was begging gold to ransom his brother. Acciajuoli, that was the name.

Nicholai de' Acciajuoli looked around, smiled at Meester Adorne who was signalling to him, and crossed steadily to where Julius and his assorted juniors were sitting. He was looking at Felix.

Lionetto's attack, surprisingly, had not upset Felix. Felix was subdued today. Or rather, that flattered him. Felix was quietly sullen. Sullen to Julius, that is. To his friends he turned a different face. Coming downstairs, Julius knew he had heard the wheeze of suppressed laughter. Julius had just spent an hour making feeble excuses to magistrates. If you weren't the company notary, last night's escapade no doubt appeared side-splitting.

The face Felix turned to the Greek was therefore half hostile and half expectant. This was a house guest of Anselm Adorne. He was going to be censorious, and Felix was going to be impertinent. Julius could see it coming.

The Greek said, "Messer Felix, I have a message from your friend Claes, who is in the Steen."

He spoke in very clear Greek. Julius, disciple of Bessarion, understood him. On his feet before Felix could speak, Julius said, "Monsignore . . . I thought he was released."

The Greek sighed. "Perhaps so," he said. "It was early this morning. I should have delivered it then, but I was overtaken with affairs. Is it too late?"

Belatedly, Felix stood up beside Julius. "Too late for what?" he said.

"Felix," said Julius. He turned to Messer de' Acciajuoli. "Forgive us. Please tell us what Claes has said. It was generous of you to trouble."

"It was no trouble," said the Greek kindly. "And a very short message. He requires you, Messer Felix, not to do something."

"What?" said Julius.

"What?" said Felix rather differently.

The Greek smiled. "That is all. He said you would know what he meant. Forgive me." And smiling again, he turned with care, and made towards the table of Anselm Adorne and the magistrates. Felix remained on his feet.

"Felix?" said Julius.

The Bonkle boy tugged Felix's tunic and he sat down.

"Felix?" said Julius again, really sharply.

Under his breath, the Sersanders boy said, "I told you."

"Well," said Felix angrily.

The Sersanders boy said, "I told you Claes was in trouble enough."

Julius stared at him, and then at Felix, and then at John Bonkle, who wouldn't meet his eye. He said, "Oh my God, what has he done now?"

By then, other people could have told him.

In the pleasant little garden of the van Borselens the fountain, playing gently while the family took the air, chatting, suddenly became possessed of Satan and thrust its jets hissing into the air, to fall drenching across my lord's head and into my lady Katelina's satin skirts.

In the yard of the Jerusalem Church the well overflowed into the piles of newly-mixed mortar, spreading its white sticky porridge over and into the timber stacks, and the feet of the masons and carpenters who were adding the latest improvement to Anselm Adorne's splendid church.

In the egg market, the casing shot off a waterpump and frightened a goat, which broke its tether and demolished three stalls of eggs until someone caught it.

The waterpipe running under Winesack Street sprang a leak under uncommon pressure and the water, rising, found its way into two cellars and the bath house, where it put out the boilers, injected the bathwater with a stream of noisome brown liquid and nearly choked the proprietor, the porter and the clients with a surfeit of steam.

The barbers' bloodpit, sharply diluted, overflowed. Joining the rivulet from a parting pump joint, the stream moved into the Grand Market and towards the wheels of the Great Crane. This, powered by two running men, each treading the curve of his wheel, was currently raising a net bearing two tuns of Spanish White, two chests of soap and a small cask of saffron.

By bad luck the water reached the Crane from behind, striking the wheels at a time when they were spinning hard in the opposite direction. The effect was to halt the spin suddenly, pitching each running man severely forward to the hurt of his features. The twin hooks, almost wound to the height of the Crane, then unwound even more quickly, dropping the Spanish White, the soap and the saffron and breaking every container.

Rivers of gold, rivers of white, rivers of scarlet and a scum of expensive bubbles made their way over the square and began to spread, pervasively, under the double doors of the Inn of the Two

Tablets of Moses, while far across the town, at the Waterhuus, an exhausted horse drooped, a wheel of cockeyed buckets jerked and creaked to a crawl and the level of the town cistern began, bless-edly, to lower at last.

They stemmed the flood under the inn door with brooms, and then swept a path outside so that the magistrates could emerge and survey the novel carnival aspect of the market place. The magis-trates were about to emerge when Claes slid hastily in, followed closely by a trail of yellow footprints.

Halfway to Felix he slowed, becoming conscious perhaps of an area of peculiar silence.

Half the inn's clients, it appeared, were vastly amused, among them Lionetto and his companions. By contrast Julius, Felix and all Felix's friends stood in a huddle, looking at Claes. Adorne and the magistrates were looking at him as well, and the Greek, stand-ing quietly beside them.

The owner of the Two Tablets, unsure what was happening, rushed to reassure. "As you asked, my lords, a constable has been sent to the Waterhuus. And a sergeant. And the town surgeon, to see to the cranemen."

The doctor Tobias, lifting his head with some trouble, said with drunken solemnity, "No need for that. I'm a surgeon."

He rose, arms outstretched, single sleeve dangling, and began to weave his way to the door, slapping his feet into fresh floods of colour. Rainbow bubbles rose from his heels. Arrested, he stamped, making more of them. He watched them rise. He turned and blew them, with a large and deliberate bounty towards the swaying Lionetto, upon whom they burst like fried eggs.

Julius, swiftly calculating the cost of the silk doublet under the gold and (glass?) rubies, was not surprised to see dawning rage on the captain's roughened face. The Greek said, "Ah, there is our friend Claes, come to chastise me. But indeed, I did deliver your message to Felix. He will tell you."

"Forgive me." It was Anselm Adorne, intervening, in Italian. "Forgive me, Messer de' Acciajuoli. You saw the boy this morn-ing?"

No unspoken message from Felix, no fierce counter-appeal from Julius, no beseeching gaze from the rest of the youths prevented Nicholai de' Acciajuoli from saying what he wanted to say.

"Through the prison window, of course. Unfortunate lad. He

gave me a message for this young gentleman. What was it? *Not to do it."*

"Not to do what, Monsignore?" said Adorne gently.

The Greek smiled. "That is his secret. Something, no doubt, they had planned together. Do you imagine it is safe to go out?"

Anselm Adorne turned his fair head and divided his gaze between the pale face of Felix de Charetty and the artless one of Claes the apprentice. "Yes. Tell us," he said. "Is it safe to go out?"

Claes and Felix looked at one another, and Julius shut his eyes.

The expression on the apprentice's face was not without cloud. It was, perhaps, more that of one who meant to please, and hoped to be liked for it. "It should be," said Claes. "If everything went according to plan, it should be, monsignore. Meester Julius, is it true that—"

"My doublet is ruined," said Lionetto. The doctor had gone.

"Meester Julius—"

"Do I understand," said Lionetto, "that this lout is responsible for the mess that has ruined my doublet?" His admiration of Claes, it was clear, had undergone a transformation.

No one answered. Anselm Adorne, eyebrows raised, looked at Julius. Felix looked at Claes, his lips parted. Claes, persevering, said, "Meester Julius. Is it true that the lady is coming from Louvain, and captain Astorre with her?"

"Yes," said Julius shortly.

"Oh," said Claes. His saucer eyes rested on Julius.

"Astorre!" hissed Lionetto. "Astorre!" he repeated, voice rising. "That block of criminal stupidity is coming here, to Bruges, while I am in town? Is he tired of life, Astorre? Or is he wooing the widow, Astorre? Retiring from the lost battles to take his ease in a dyeshop? Is that why he is here?"

Anselm Adorne turned. "The widow of Charetty employs him, captain Lionetto. I fear your doublet is stained. Would it not be wise to have it attended to? The way is clear outside, I believe."

Julius said, "Minen heere, it is not known yet what caused this."

Adorne's smile had faded. He said, "But it will be known fairly soon. I think, Meester Julius, you should take your pupil and your apprentice back to their residence, and stay there until your mistress arrives. She, I make no doubt, will have something to say to you. By that time so, perhaps, will we."

Felix said, "Meester Julius had nothing to do with it. Nothing. And Claes was in prison." He had flushed.

"It has been noted," said Adorne. "It will be our endeavour, as always, to see justice done. It is a pity the need should arise quite so often."

But he was not looking at Julius at all, but at the Greek.

Chapter 6

Within a week, the widow of Charetty arrived at the Ghent Gate of Bruges and passed over its bridge and through its prudent defences, thick as two castles, to settle the question of her erring son Felix. Her unmarried daughters, aged eleven and twelve, rode beside her. Behind her came five horse-drawn wagons, one smith, one carpenter, two clerks, three servants, a cook, and her bodyguard led by a professional soldier called Astorre, an abbreviation which had long since replaced his original name of Syrus de Astariis.

With the Flanders galleys almost due, she would have to have come anyway. It was an annual journey, but not one she enjoyed. Louvain to Brussels; Brussels to Ghent; Ghent to Bruges the roads had been as crowded as the canals and worse to navigate, what with other people's draw-oxen and broken-down carts and inn-keepers' rumours of brigands lying in wait round the next hedge.

Which was usually rubbish. Which needn't, anyway, concern the Charetty company, which had its own bodyguard. More than that, its own band of mercenaries. So no one molested them and, at last, they had come to Bruges. For her entrance she wore a good cloak of rich mulberry and had an extravagance on her head, a voile contraption fronted with seed pearls. Astorre and all her servants behind her wore the Charetty blue, the special dye Cornelis had concocted which she preserved in his memory. Her horsecloth and those of her daughters were of gold wire and velvet, and their harness was silver. Bruges should know, when one of her burgess-widows rode into town. To erase the impression made by her son Felix.

She had forgotten how noisy it was. First the creak, the groan, the thud of the windmills. Then the long portal-arches into the city which trapped the jingle and clatter of stamping horses and the squeak and thunder of cartwheels and the din of country voices.

In the streets, the leaning houses smacked the same noises between them. In September, every workshop and every shutter was open. She heard the rasp of a saw, and the slap of the baker and the clang of his ovens. She heard the buzz of the grinding stone and the chime and clash of the smith and voices raised in anger and voices raised in mirth, and dogs, and pigs, and the crow of a cockerel. She heard the gulls disputing above and the uniform creak of the house signs and she heard, most of all, the clacking of looms, resounding in street after street like a clog-dance.

In the three months she had been at Louvain, there were changes as well. She noted them, and made, courteously, the correct responses to her fellows who called to her, but she made her way to her own home without stopping. Her home and her business. It was the same thing.

And here was the entrance to the dyeworks Cornelis had been so proud of: well-swept, with no grass between the cobbles: good. The reek of warm dyes and the stench of urine. Smells which disturbed other people, but not her. And there in the yard (of course: why forego the chance of an hour off their labours?) stood her loyal employees to greet her.

The dyers in their aprons, with their hands hanging like indigo pumpkins. The male house servants in neat coifs and caps and their summer cloth doublets, black at the cuffs with nose-wiping but with no unmended holes about them. And the women with decent gowns, and head-napkins carefully ironed and folded round under their chins. The grooms, without waiting, skipped to help with the horses.

In the middle was her manager Henninc, in cuffed hat and sideless coat that reached to his calves at the back and his knees at the front because of his belly, which had not got any smaller. Because of her food or her wine, she was not sure which. But an honest man, Cornelis had always maintained. Plodding, with no head for figures, but honest.

The need for a man with clerk's training was what had led to the appointment of Julius. There he was. A sturdy stance, but one that avoided defiance. Or deference, if it came to that. *Too handsome by half,* Cornelis had grumbled at the hiring. Not from any distrust of herself: he knew better than that. But that blunt, heavy-boned face with its slanting eyes and nose so straight it might have been broken—that could cause trouble among burghers' wives as well as the girls in the house and the market place.

But in fact, Meester Julius had given no trouble. Either his discretion was absolute, or the opposite sex had no part in his calcula-

tions. Nor, even more mercifully (it appeared), had the same sex.
At the same time, he had been a fool with Felix.

And there her son was, dashing out of the house with a stupid
hat in his hand and his crimped curls bouncing. No less gaunt—
was he wasting: what kept him so puny? No less boisterous. No
less . . .

Dismounted, she stopped him with her voice before he could
reach her. "Felix de Charetty, return to the house. When I wish to
speak to you, I will send for you."

Hurt eyes: the mutinous lip beginning to bulge. Then he lowered
his gaze and said, "Yes, my lady mother," and turning, walked
with dignity back to the house. Good.

Now her own daughters had dismounted and were standing behind her. Tilde and little Catherine, demure, obedient; shooting
glances from under their hoods. *Look at us. Grown women with
husbands to find.*

"And Henninc," said the widow. "You are well? Come to my
office in five minutes." She took her time. She ran her eye over all
her workers, all her servants, and acknowledged their bobs and
their curtseys before she brought her gaze round to her notary.
"And the good master Julius. Can you spare me some time, a little
later?"

"Whenever you wish, lady," he said. He inclined his head.

"And your troublesome apprentice?" she said.

Henninc said, "Claes is indoors, demoiselle. The magistrates
wished him kept indoors until you arrived."

"No doubt," said the widow de Charetty. "But there was no
need to agree with them, surely? Unless of course the town intends
to recompense me for the loss of his labours? Or was this your
arrangement, Meester Julius?"

He looked her straight in the eye. "I fear," said the notary, "that
the magistrates would accept no appeal. If I may, I shall explain
when we speak."

"So you shall," said Marian de Charetty. "And so shall the
apprentice Claes." And nodding, disengaged the clasp of her cloak
and walked across to her door, her daughters following.

Her steward, panting, reached it in time to set it open for her.

Felix went up to the attic where Claes sat on his pallet, fiddling
with a knife and a lot of wood shavings. Felix said, "Mother's
home. Henninc and Julius first."

"Warm or cold?" Claes said, tilting the box he was working on. Claes was always making toys, and other people broke them.

"Freezing," said Felix heartily. He was a little pale.

"That's a parade for the yard," Claes said comfortably. He squinted along an angle and, taking his knife, niggled at something. "Tell the truth and don't rely on Julius. He can't cover up all the time, and Henninc will have to come out with it all anyway, to save his own skin." He put his contraption on the floor and poked about till he found a small wooden ball.

Felix said, "It's all very well for you. You're not her son and heir. The honour due to your father's fair memory. Future of his beloved business. Goodwill of the clients and the respect of those who will one day work for you. (That's you. Don't laugh, damn it.) Lack of consideration for good notary Julius, doing his best in unhappy circumstances. Wasting Henninc's time. Wasting the time of my tutors at Louvain. Besmirching the very reputation of Flanders in the eyes of the foreigner . . ."

"Costing a lot of money," said Claes. He dropped the ball gently into a socket, and inside the rough little box a number of trifling things started to happen, apparently of their own volition.

Felix cast it a fraught glance. "It doesn't play a tune," he said disparagingly. "The last one had bells there, and a drumstick. She'd save money if she took me out of university."

"Well, you can't have bells all the time. You'd have to work," Claes observed.

"I worked at university!" said Felix indignantly. When Claes didn't look up or answer, Felix picked up the newly-made box and dropped it on the floor, glaring at him. Bits of wire and slivers of wood fell about everywhere.

Claes looked up. Not with a hurt expression, or an angry one. Just obediently, thought Felix, furious. *Claes was always making toys, and other people broke them.*

For the same reason that people beat him. He didn't mind.

Julius, downstairs, was having a worse time with his employer than he had anticipated. He had put himself into an untenable position, which made him resentful and angry. On the other hand, although young, he was intelligent, and he had had a lot of experience. One would not stay all one's life with a pawnbroker and a dyeshop. But a dismissal would hardly advance him.

He adopted therefore an attitude in which courtesy, firmness and regret were equally mingled. Standing (she had not asked him to sit) before the tall chair in which was seated Felix's mother, Meester Julius explained the business of the Duke's bath, and the injustice of the judgment. He went on to represent, a little vaguely, the commonplace nature of Claes' peccadillo which, a little unfairly, had caused some rather merry gentlemen to chase him and take the joke too far. He thought it most unlikely that Claes had touched the gentleman's dog, but of course it could not be proved. And as for the manipulation of the waterhuus supply and its piping—"

"He planned it with the rest, but my son was responsible for carrying it out. I had gathered as much," said Marian de Charetty.

He disliked working under women. When Cornelis suddenly died, he nearly left forthwith, and then thought better of it. She might well stay a widow. She was ten years at least older than he was. If he could put up with her, he would have more scope for his skills than ever Cornelis would have allowed him. And so, in a way, it had turned out. Except that it was only his notarial skills that she needed him for. In most other ways, her brain was quite as sharp as that of her late husband, and because she hadn't had the same time to establish authority, she was both harder and tougher. This year she had pushed them all, at the Louvain end and the Bruges end, and she had gone too far with Felix.

What was happening with Felix was a rebellion, caused by that, and the loss of his father, and fear of the approaching weight of the business. And come to that, it was probably true of himself. He was sorry for Felix and the other youngsters. He got tired himself, sometimes, of the long, solid hours of negotiation and ledger work and trying to drive Felix through alleyways of learning when all Felix was worried about was that he hadn't yet managed a girl. Well, at least that was one problem that Claes didn't have.

Meester Julius gazed at his employer as, in the yard, she had gazed at him, and with thoughts that were, in the long run, not so different. Tall commanding women he could dislike in comfort. He disliked the widow of Charetty quite a lot too, but he could see that others might not. Marian de Charetty was small and round and active, with a stare that was none the less of the brightest blue, and vermilion dye in her veins, which made her lips naturally scarlet and her cheeks naturally rosy under short chestnut brows. He had never seen her hair, which was always rigidly covered, but he could imagine it.

He thought it might not be good for her business, to be comely like that. No one in the workshop, naturally, would step out of place, but dealers and brokers might come to expect favours. His own manner he kept carefully formal. At the moment, his hands were clasped behind him, indeed, to help him subdue his fury and remain formal. He wished to God she were a man and they could simply bark at one another. Women either burst into tears or dismissed you.

He answered her questions about the magistrates' decision, the fines and the damages, and watched her write the sums down. At the end she looked up.

"Well?" she said. "And how do you see your part in all this?"

He looked at his feet, and then upwards frankly. "Insofar as Felix was in my care, I suppose mine is the ultimate blame," said her notary. "You may think me unfit to guide him in future. You may also think that part of the responsibility for your losses should fall on me."

"All of them, surely?" said Marian de Charetty. "Or do you think my son should pay in some way as well? I leave out friend Claes, who has no money, and who must assuredly therefore find some other means to pay."

"He has paid," said Julius quickly.

"On the contrary," said Marian de Charetty, "As I understand it, I paid to save him a second beating. I may even have to pay a second time, to satisfy this bloodthirsty Scotsman. Perhaps I should simply offer him Claes instead?"

Claes was a boy apprentice. Claes had been with the Charetty family since he was ten, sleeping in the straw with the rest, and sitting round the apprentices' table. Claes was her son's shadow.

Julius said, "I think the Scotsman would kill him."

The blue eyes opened. "Why?" said his employer.

God in heaven. Carefully, Julius answered. "He is rumoured to be jealous, demoiselle."

"Of *Claes*?" she said.

He thought she understood perfectly well. God damn it, she must: old Henninc would have told her all that, at least. Not the bits about Felix, but all the titbits about Claes, so that she would get rid of him. Julius supposed that she would. He said, "He's a good worker, and trained. Other yards would pay to have him."

"I'm not concerned about Claes," said the widow. "Nor am I greatly concerned about you. You have investments. If you wish to remain with me you will, I am afraid, have to liquidate some of them. If Felix goes back to Louvain, you will return with him, leaving in Felix's hands and in mine an exact accounting of your personal finances. For any misdemeanour of Felix's, your funds will suffer and I shall then force him—in time—to repay you. In other words, if you find yourself unable to build his character, then clearly I must. The only redeeming feature in this entire crass chronicle has been the regard you have shown to some degree for one another. Your regard for other people has, of course, been non-existent." She viewed him critically. "And you find all this unfair? You wish to leave?"

"It depends how much money you want," he said bluntly. How did she know what he had?

"Enough to teach you a lesson."

"I might teach Felix something you don't want him to learn," he said.

She went on looking at him, brushing the side of her mouth slowly, back and forth, with the ruffled edge of her quill. Then she laid it down. She said, "You negotiate very patiently, on the whole. You can sustain an argument or an attitude. Then you lapse, like that. Why?"

Because I don't like working under a woman. He didn't say it. He said, "I'm sorry, but it has all been rather a worry. I am not a rich man. As you know."

"And therefore," she said, "if I am going to use you as a means of training my child, I am not likely to be so unreasonable that you can do nothing but leave. You must have thought of that."

He said, "I was surprised. I thought my private affairs private."

"In Flanders?" she said.

He did not answer.

She said, "We do not all finish our training at twenty, Meester Julius. None of us. What drives you to a childish escapade in a bath is what drives you to make an unwise remark in negotiation. That is the lesson you are paying for. You will thank me one day. I shall send you a note of my precise decisions by tomorrow. Meanwhile, you may send my son to me."

He hesitated, and bowed, and left, and after he had called Felix, he locked himself in his own room, and thought. He had still reached no conclusions when, some time later, he heard a door bang and realised he was listening to Felix emerging in turn from his interview.

Julius unlocked his door and, dashing downstairs, was in time to catch his pupil, sullen, raging, red-eyed, and bear him off to a quiet spot to deal with. It came to him, in the middle of this, that he appeared to have reached a conclusion after all.

One of the servants was sent for Claes, and they all watched as he thumped downstairs and knocked on his mistress's door, and was admitted. They all lingered, but the door was thick and the mistress never raised her voice anyway. And old Henninc came along in any case and chased them away. One of the boys said the Widow had a whip with three thongs and wire on it, but they didn't hear any whip sounds either.

When Claes went in, Marian de Charetty was writing. She went on writing until he closed the door gently, and then looked up as he crossed the floor to her table. She said, "Turn round."

His open face smiled at her. He said, "There is no need, demoiselle. It's healing well. Meester Julius cared for me. And the second time—"

"He paid. I know. You'll die, Claes. You'll die before you are twenty unless you quieten down. The cannon, surely, was nothing to you?"

"The cannon?" he said, astonished.

"Or did someone pay you . . . No of course they didn't." She answered herself, staring at him, frowning. "You would arrange it to fall overboard simply for the pleasure of tricking somebody. Don't you want to know how I guessed?"

He stood, his hands hanging at his sides, perfectly composed. "I expect the Duke's officers paid the fine for the demoiselle," he said. "But of course, Meester Julius could not be told."

"Julius has already told me what a hard and valuable worker you are," said his mistress. "Do you suppose the direction of your talents has escaped his attention?"

He took her up wrongly. "Jonkheere Felix would still get into trouble, even if I weren't with him. Young gentlemen do."

"Thank you for the news," said his mistress. "I know, and Meester Julius knows, that when you are there, the mischief is usually harmless. What Felix does on his own is not so considerate. The waterhuus warden will be beaten and dismissed at the least. That I know you didn't plan."

He was silent. Then he said, "Of course, the demoiselle is correct. Jonkheere Felix requires work, and away from the well-meaning elders who remember his father. The demoiselle is considering, then, that he might leave university?"

She tented her fingers against her mouth. "I thought of that. But I felt Louvain was important."

There was a pause. Then he said, "The demoiselle would find, I think, that it has served its purpose."

Another pause. She said, "And if I were to send you to work with him?"

She had learned, through the years, not to listen to what Claes said, but to watch his eyes. He said, "Jonkheere Felix is getting older. He might be better with the company of his own kind."

She went on studying him. "But he would not resent Meester Julius?" Then, reading his smile, "Or, I see, the reverse. Meester Julius might become restive under Felix. So I send my son away, and you and Julius stay and help me operate my business? Beginning with an achievement like yesterday's?"

"The brush with the Scotsman?" he said.

"The Scotsman," she said sharply. "An act of deliberate malice. Of folly. Of madness. What have you to say?"

"It was an accident," he said. He was looking at his feet.

"Like the cannon?" said Marian de Charetty. "Except that this time, it was personal. You saw this man at Damme. You took a dislike to him before you even knew who he was. You decided to hold him up to ridicule."

"Demoiselle," said Claes. He had looked up. "I didn't expect to be discovered. I was the one to be made ridiculous." She said nothing, but simply stared at him until he spoke. He said, "People act according to their nature. I wondered then what he was made of."

"And now you know, of course, after one angry encounter. And as a result, there is damage to be redressed. My client is offended. Felix's patrimony will suffer. All because of this *accident.*"

Claes said, "My lord Simon is going home after the galleys. I'll keep out of his way. I suppose he will now keep out of mine. Demoiselle, I have some news about alum."

She said, "You certainly will keep out of his way. I won't have a feud while you're under my roof. You don't have the means to survive one. God knows you have the means to start one. Your trouble is the same as Felix's. You need work."

He smiled. His palms, as he lifted them to her, were thickened with calluses.

"What sort of a fool do you take me for?" she said. "I know that. In the eight years you have lived with this family your arms and legs at least have earned your keep. The pity is that none of the rest of you, it seems, is even born yet. What is to become of you?"

He shook his head, smiling the brimming, affectionate smile he turned on all the world. "The Duke will hang me, perhaps?"

"No," said Marian de Charetty coldly. "The King of Scotland perhaps. The King of France almost certainly. If Meester Julius leaves, you might do worse than go with him."

"Will he leave?" said Claes. He looked surprised.

"He might," said Marian de Charetty. "When he finds I will not take him into partnership. But with what he now owes, it will take him a little time to save what will make him independent. By that time, Felix will be grown."

"And I, perhaps, will be hanged by the King of Scots," said Claes. "So where will you go for an honest notary to help you guide jonkheere Felix?"

He spoke as if thinking aloud. She allowed Claes to speak freely quite often. Now, before she could think of an answer, he had suggested one. "There is Meester Oudenin. His daughter is the right age."

She felt her colour rise, and she inhaled abruptly. It left in her throat the faint smells of ink and parchment and leather, and sweat, and sawdust. Sawdust?

She said, "I think that will do. The beating you certainly deserve would do nothing but lose me even more of your labour. I shall tell you in time what other punishment I have devised. Meanwhile you will return to work, no matter what the town says. I shall take care of the Scots gentleman."

The footsteps she had heard became clearer, and Astorre's familiar fist banged on the door.

Claes smiled, and she fought not to smile in return. Another bang came to the door, and Astorre's voice saying, "Demoiselle!"

Claes said, "I wrote it down. About the alum. It's Phocoean, and the Venetians were hoping to keep it all quiet. The Guild would be interested." He withdrew a creased scrap of paper from his pouch and laid it on her table; then glancing up with another smile, slid one of her other papers across it. Then, receiving word-less permission, he crossed and opened the door for Astorre, before himself bowing out.

The door shut. She did not look down at the paper. The soldier, as she expected, was carrying a heavy box under either arm. He crossed the room with his bow-legged tramp and set them heavily down beside her money chest. It was why she had to bring a strong bodyguard every year, carrying extra groats to pay for what she bought from the Flanders galleys.

Astorre straightened, his breathing hardly disturbed. Twenty years of hard fighting showed in the puckered scar over one eye and the scarlet frill which was all the surgeons had left of an ear, but he was as fit as a twenty-year-old, with not a thread of grey yet in his beard. He said, "So you've told him?"

"No, I haven't," said Marian de Charetty.

"He'd make off? I wouldn't have thought it," said the captain.

"No. He's grown a lot in a year," said the Widow his employer.

"Too much?" said Astorre, and laughed, hawking. He spat in the rushes. There were captains with courtly ambitions and those who aimed lower. It was his small size, she always thought, which kept Astorre's manner brutish as well as belligerent. He was an astute and experienced man. But even before Cornelis died, she could manage him.

She said, "He's grown in some ways. I don't want trouble with Claes until the galleys are in. Then I'll tell him."

"As you like." Astorre was unworried. He went out to get the rest of the boxes and she watched him. She thought it very likely that Claes had already guessed what she was going to do with him. And if he hadn't, he would soon sniff it out, among all those other yards and kitchens and offices where he ran his messages, and was always made welcome.

He would sniff it out, but he would do nothing until she told him publicly. She could rely on that as she could rely on nothing else in her life. She thought of Claes defending Julius, and Julius defending Claes, and was aware of a shadow of jealousy.

Chapter 7

"I'll keep out of my lord Simon's way," Claes had promised.

Marian de Charetty saw that he did. She placed him under house arrest, and did the same for her breezy son Felix. She did not think, unfortunately, of restraining her mercenary captain Astorre, whom she considered an adult. When, a few days later, the merchant galleys sailed in from Venice, it seemed to the head of the Charetty company that her household was under control, and she had nothing now to distract her from her business. At first, she was right.

Without Claes or Felix, the fifty thousand people of Bruges, more or less, covered by foot or by rowboat the few miles to the harbour at Sluys, there to see the two slender ships from Venice move in and drop anchor.

It was never less than marvellous, every year. To see the sunglow slide through the silk of the banners, and the blaze as the oars unscrolled every one from the water and stood erect on each side like two combs. To hear the flagship begin to make music: first the drums and pipes with a rattle and chirrup, and then the burping of trumps from the poop. Above the flash of the brass, the fringe would blow and wink on the canopy where you would see, each year different, the thick sprawling embroidery of the commander's device.

And across the water, you would swear you could sniff it all; the cinnamon and the cloves, the frankincense and the honey and the liquorice, the nutmeg and citrons, the myrrh and the rosewater from Persia in keg upon keg. You would think you could glimpse, heaped and glimmering, the sapphires and the emeralds and the gauzes woven with gold, the ostrich feathers and the elephant tusks, the gums and the ginger and the coral buttons mynheer Goswin the clerk of the Hanse might be wearing on his jacket next week.

It was a trick, that was for sure, like the Duke's performers at Carnival time. It was no accident that the galleys always downed sails and entered harbour in daylight, with the decks sluiced and

the rowers and sailing-masters in livery and the noblemen commanding each ship in a stiffened gown in the crazy Venetian mode,
their beards newly trimmed, with perhaps a chained marmoset on
one shoulder.

It wasn't a difficult trick. The Flanders galleys never spent
nights at sea like the round ships, getting dirty with no time to put
things to rights before landing. The Flanders galleys put into harbour every night in their highly-paid voyage from Venice, fanned
down the Adriatic by the thick summer airs, drifting into Corfu
and Otranto, nosing into and out of Sicily and round the heel of
Italy as far as Naples; blowing handsomely across the western gulf
to Majorca, and then to the north African coast, and up and round
Spain and Portugal, dropping off the small, lucrative loads which
were not needed for Bruges; taking on board a little olive oil, some
candied orange peel, some scented leather, a trifle of plate and a
parrot, some sugar loaves.

But never anything crude, or bulky, or coarse. The Republic's
Flanders galleys were the princes of Venice's fleet, expensively
manned and expensively built to outrun any thief in the seaways,
and designed for luxuries only.

They came every year, and every year reached the Narrow Seas
and separated: two for Bruges and one for London—or Southampton, if Londoners happened to be campaigning against foreign merchants that year. The total freight of three Flanders galleys, they
said, was worth a quarter of a million golden ducats. Yes, there was
that much money in the world. So they said. And look, to prove it:
the Doge and that lot in Venice voted twenty pounds a year to
bribe the customs clerks at Bruges to undervalue the cargo. That's
true. I tell you. I had it from one of their widows. And ten times
that much to spend on a sweetener for Duke Philip himself.

So the crowd would say, watching the customs men being rowed
aboard, two to a galley, and the Sluys reception committee, and
later the fellows done up in their gold chains from Damme, and
much later—for some folk would sire their sons after the christening, if they thought it would add to their dignity—the big bell on
the Bruges tower would start tolling and someone—Jan Blaviet,
that's who—would come riding a mule with a hat on him like five
ells of bandaging caught on a thorn bush, followed by Anselm
Adorne and Jan van den Walle and a clutch of grooms and servants and soldiers with the Bruges blazon and flag. And with them,

the Venetian agents—big Bembo and thin Contarini and that great bloated miser, Marco Corner.

And later than that—for the Venetians got first whack at the scriveners' lists and the unloading, just as they got the first chance to get their goods on before sailing—the rest of the partnerships who were expecting consignments.

Such as Tommaso Portinari, with all his rings on, if he could persuade Tani to let him handle it, which he probably couldn't. And Jacopo Strozzi, who might bring young Lorenzo with him, if his gout was bad. And Jacques Doria and Lommelin and the rest of the Genoese. And Pierre Bladelin, the Duke's household controller, to check on the goods the Duke had especially asked for, and João Vasquez, to do the same for the Duchess, with Figuieres and the other Portuguese with him. Someone from the Corps of Hosteliers, to see who needed putting up. The Germans from the Hanse, anxious to hear about rates. And the Lucchese, with Giovanni Arnolfini and his long, pallid face, who knew the Duke's taste in silks and had a few private commissions worth a groat or two.

Oh, a lot went on behind the scenes when the Flanders galleys came in. The big men never came out in the early days to the harbour, just waited until it all arrived by barge at the Staple in Bruges and the Waterhalle. The real haggling went on, they said, at the meetings afterwards. After all, there was all winter for wheeling and dealing. Six months while the galleys sat in the harbour and every tavern and brothel in Bruges and the waterside entertained four hundred seamen.

The Flanders galleys had come, and the bells and the trumpets were merely the prelude to the deafening jingle of money.

Unwisely, on the third day after the galleys' arrival, Marian de Charetty released her son Felix from his duties, on condition that he did not set foot outside Bruges. That put Sluys out of bounds.

She assumed, with some reason, that he would go straight to a tavern, from which Julius would later be sent to extract him. Julius himself was at Sluys, with Henninc her manager, taking a close interest in some bales of weld and woad and kermes and some sacks of brazil blocks, and a wistful interest in a valuable item called alum. The demoiselle de Charetty herself was due at a meeting of the dyers' guild, to which she hoped that Julius would come with his bulletin. She sent for Henninc's deputy, placed him in charge, and went off on foot, with a maid, to her meeting.

Henninc's deputy, a hardworking fuller called Lippin, remembered that there were shears to be brought from the grinder's and, finding Claes handy, dispatched him forthwith on that errand. That Claes had not been allowed to leave the premises for a week had not entered his mind, and Claes left in a trice, in his clogs and piss-spattered apron, in case it should. He found Felix in a deserted office of the Medici, in the tall consular house near the market. Felix was not pleased to see him. "Who told you I was here?"

"Winrik the moneychanger," said Claes appeasingly. Winrik, patrolling the streets with his money booth, was the best source of gossip in Flanders.

Felix sneered. "And in return you gave Winrik a long, helpful check, and found a mistake in his daybook and three miscalculations at least in his ledger. This stinking artisan," said Felix to his sole audience, an infant trainee newly sent out from Florence, "—this Flemish moron tells numbers for pleasure, as you and I drink, or fart, or plan how to spend money."

"Well, if you're going to spend it, someone's got to save it," said Claes with reason. His large gaze drifted over the packets and letter-books of the Medici. "Save you money too," he volunteered to the office boy, who looked him up and down, so far as he was able, and stepped back beside Felix, and then farther back still, as the smells from Claes' apron pursued him.

"There," said Claes, running a set of large indigo fingers over an order book. "What's that and that?"

The boy hesitated.

"Oh, never mind," said Felix wearily. "Don't humour him. It's a disease." He looked at Claes again. "What have you got Mother's shears for?"

"They've been sharpened," said Claes.

"Then isn't she expecting you back?" said Felix, a touch of his father creeping into his manner.

"No," said Claes without blinking. "What are you waiting for?"

"Tommaso's boat. He's going to Sluys. It's the day of the private deck sale on the Flanders galleys. I want a monkey."

"You want to be sent back to Louvain," said Claes. "She'll find out you've been outside the city."

"I'll tell her that you bought it for me," said Felix.

Claes considered. "You mean I have to come to Sluys with you?"

"Well, yes," said Felix, reviewing for the first time the practical problems of the immediate future. "That is, if Tommaso can get rid of his priests and his monks. He's choosing a tenor for the Medici chapel in Italy." His face brightened. "Terrible, isn't it?"

Through several doors, sounds emerged which might have been singing. It was indeed terrible. Claes grinned at the boy. "How many has he heard?"

The boy turned his back on the apron and replied, pointedly, to the youth with the good clothes and the hat. "This is the third. Brother Gilles is from the choir of the Augustines. He is a friend of the soldier Astorre of your company. The man Astorre waits, too, to travel to Sluys."

"Oh," said Felix. A ringlet, out of habit, fitted round his finger, and he twisted it.

"He is severe, Astorre?" said the boy. "You do not wish to see him?"

Felix said, "He's only my mother's captain. I'm going to Sluys."

"He'd do your shopping for you," said Claes. "Monkeys. Leopardskin mantles. A new sort of feather?"

"I'm going to Sluys," repeated Felix. The singing had stopped.

The door opened. "I heard that," said captain Astorre. "Jonkheere Felix—"

"I'm going to Sluys," said Jonkheere Felix for the third time.

Claes never sighed. He just said, "And so am I," and grinned cheekily up at the soldier, who cuffed him absently across the face and said, "Well, what are we waiting for?"

That was Astorre in a good mood, because his friend Brother Gilles had been picked for the Medici chapel. The clouds cleared from Felix's face. He grinned at Astorre, at Tommaso Portinari, entering briskly to lead them all to the company barge, and even at Claes, following obediently in his stocking soles with his clogs round his neck to save the boat-planks, and his shears under his arm, wrapped in his apron.

They embarked without a qualm, and even Tommaso looked cheerful. They were all off to Sluys, and the Venetian galleys.

Afterwards (but he was lying) the notary Julius used to say that it was the worst moment of his life, that sunny day in September when he squinted down from the deck of the Venetian flagship and saw the Medici skiff being punch-rowed along the canal towards him.

In it were his employer's son Felix, who had promised not to leave Bruges, and his employer's apprentice Claes, who had been under house-imprisonment in her dyeshop, and Tommaso Portinari, to whom his employer did not wish to owe favours and who, by the cramped look of his nose, was going to exact from someone the price of suffering the smell from Claes' apron all the way from Bruges to Sluys.

And last and worst, there in the prow was the pullet body and cockerel face of his employer's captain Astorre, his beard pecking the air as he vaulted out. Then he stood on the quayside, the button eyes attacking the palaces of crates, the terraces of bulging bales, the landscapes of sacks and baskets and barrels through which chains and clusters and units of men were moving about, transferring their environment piecemeal to cart and barge and warehouse under the swinging stalks of the cranes.

Then the beard pointed shipwards and Julius drew carefully back. There were, after all, two galleys lining the wharf, and you could only pray that Felix and Claes and Astorre would choose not to come on board the flagship.

Two galleys with a hundred and seventy oarsmen on each, and thirty bowmen, and the navigating officer, and the scrivener and his assistant, and the caulkers and the carpenter and the cook and two doctors and the notary, all with their boxes open on deck displaying their little items for sale, and their price lists.

It was one of the perquisites of the Flanders voyage, the right of the crew to take small goods for private sale at the ports they touched at. He shouldn't wonder if the priest hadn't a bag below deck there, with a morsel of incense and some quite expensive church vestments inside it. And the commander's cabin, you could be sure, was stacked to the arras with sweet wine and some items smaller and heavier, like gold dust from Guinea, where that woolheaded slave came from.

But all that, of course, was a matter for the friends of Ser Alvise Duodo, and not for vulgar public huckstering. The Greek with the wooden leg, Monsignore Nicholai de' Acciajuoli, was in there with Duodo now, no doubt seeking news of his captive brother in Constantinople.

It was a pity that the Greek had not come alone. It was a pity that he had brought with him the noble merchant who had sailed with him from Scotland, the ungentle Simon. For the present, the curtain of the poop cabin was drawn, but at any moment, one of them might emerge before Julius finished his business. It was a pity, as well, that Julius was not entirely sober.

Julius did not, after the incident of the cannon, the girl and the dog, wish to draw the attention of Simon to himself or any member of the Charetty household. Already he had successfully dodged his gaze once: something not hard to do on a deck one hundred and eighteen Venetian feet long, and packed with people and boxes. As well as disliking Simon, he was inclined to be deeply envious of him. He wished he could watch Simon, but without being seen. He was aware that he had delivered an extremely capable seven days of work to the demoiselle de Charetty after his berating, and that he had celebrated the fact just a little too early this morning. He particularly, therefore, did not wish Felix and Claes to come aboard. As for Astorre, it would be a disaster. Julius cautiously raised his head, shaking it slightly, and looked over the rail.

It was a disaster. The boat with Tommaso in it appeared to have gone. But Felix's head, wearing a hat like a bagpipe, was already visible as he climbed from the quay to the flagship. Behind him was Astorre, in a flat cap and a smart leather jerkin, with brocade sleeves stuffed like a goose pie. Behind trailed Claes in his felt working cap and sweaty shirt, its drooping neckline exposing his muscular chest and the upper selvedge of that silky dun-coloured thatch with which Nature, as Julius had envious cause to know, had endowed his virility.

Felix saw his tutor, smiled in an alarmed fashion and trained his bagpipe vaguely towards the vendors who were shouting most loudly while his eyes hunted for the object of his desire. Astorre, his gaze on some distant and glorious prey, ignored Julius altogether. Claes, his albuminous eyes glowing with the simple joys of communication, said, "Felix wants a monkey. The demoiselle has gone to her meeting."

"I've sent Henninc to join her," said Julius, frowning to keep his eyes in alignment. "You were right. The ballast was alum from Phocoea. Who told you? The Greek, Nicholai?"

"Oh no, Meester Julius," said Claes. "The scrivener's list says the alum is from the Straits, at Castile prices, and I'm sure Monsignore de' Acciajuoli would agree. That's what the Venetians were buying. Phocoean alum would be much more expensive."

"So it would," said Julius, frowning more deeply. Alum, that white, innocent powder that got dug out of the ground like rock-salt was about the most important ingredient in the world to a dyer, for it bound the colour to the cloth. Claes would know that. All the same, Julius wondered from time to time if Claes understood what he was really saying, as he carried these tales from place to place. It had been unlikely, after all, that the Greek would tell him anything. Claes simply heard things, by virtue of passing from office to office, in a city where artisans were invisible.

Julius said, "Well, you'd better watch out. Our dog-owning Scottish friend Simon is in there with Messer Nicholai and the commander, and it would be just as well if he didn't lay eyes on you. Also—"

"God save us," said Claes, with no more than a simple expression of interest. "There's the captain Lionetto and his friends. They've bought a black man."

Anyone could see they hadn't bought the black boy, but were merely scrubbing him to see if his colour would come off. Julius, on occasion a man of discernment, said, "Wants a monkey? She wouldn't stand for it."

"I expect the price would be too high anyway," said Claes with optimism. He had continued to gaze at the Guinea slave, who had stopped tugging his chain and was rolling about as the powerful arms of captain Lionetto jabbed at him with a deck swabber. "They'll have to buy him if they damage him. Unless Felix would like a black boy instead of a monkey. The demoiselle might like that."

"Felix's mother?" said Julius. His eyes watered with laughter. He said, "Tell Oudenin the pawnbroker over there. It'll help his courtship." Everyone knew that Oudenin had been throwing his daughter at Felix's head, but really fancied an armful of the widow.

To his surprise, Claes assumed a willing expression, laid down his apron and left him. With disbelief, Julius watched the apprentice squeeze and squirm his way over the deck until he reached the pawnbroker's side, and there, sitting down, engage him in some sort of artless conversation, in the course of which they both rose.

Whether or not Claes had been talking about Marian de Charetty hardly mattered. As he got to his feet, the soldier Lionetto said, "Hah!" and, gripping a friend on each side, began to force his massive way through the crowd to the apprentice. His ginger velvet and his hair were the same colour.

"Hah!" said Lionetto. "And whose doublet are you staining today, my silly lout? And what fool gave you leave to foul the air of this ship with your stinking rags? You need a wash. Give him one."

Undoubtedly slowed by the cups of wine he and Henninc had shared, Julius steadied his gaze upon Lionetto's two cronies who had gripped the apprentice and were beginning, to a general rumble of appreciation, to lift him at the proper angle for a quick dispatch over the side. No one showed any special anxiety on Claes' behalf, nor indeed did he himself show any positive resentment as he hung, looking mildly astonished, from the soldiers' muscular grasp. A bald man remarked, in merest commentary, "Maybe he can't swim."

Claes could swim, and he needed a bath. Julius pondered the situation, and concluded, hazily, that it was not an emergency. They got Claes under the armpits and swung him back, as the crowd scattered.

They didn't swing him overboard, because the sinewy person of captain Astorre took three steps forward and kicked one of Claes' captors in the kneecap, causing the man to kneel inadvertently, screaming. For a moment, Claes and his other captor stood hand in hand, and then the second man threw Claes' fist away and advanced on Astorre.

He was forestalled by Lionetto.

Disregarding both his own soldiers and Claes, who continued to stand looking puzzled, Lionetto neither punched the other captain nor shouted at him. Instead, breathing heavily, he dropped one shoulder and, closing his fingers about the other man's wrist, lifted Astorre's unresisting right hand and held it, enclosed with his own, at waist level.

Encircled by their joint grasp was a standing-cup of enamelled pink glass, thick with gilding.

"That is mine," said Lionetto gently. "I ordered it last year from the sailing master."

His beard six inches away, Astorre exposed yellow teeth in a grin. "Indeed. He forgot to say so. I have paid for it."

"How childish you are," said Lionetto. "It is hardly worth my while taking it from you. Give it up, and I will give you what you paid for it."

"Take it from me?" said Astorre. "My poor baboon. This silly boy and I between us could strip you to your small clothes. To your inadequate organs if we felt like it. But the commander is a guest in our country and gentlemen do not brawl on his deck. I will take my property."

"My property," said Lionetto.

"Paid for by me," said Astorre.

"Signori!" said a voice of some weight.

They turned.

The curtain of the commander's cabin had been drawn back and in the entrance stood Messer Alvise Duodo, the hero of Constantinople himself. The Greek Nicholai de' Acciajuoli was beside him, today wearing a velvet hat over his handsome cowled cloak. And behind them both, Julius saw with misgiving the arrogant clean-shaven features of the nobleman Simon, whose dog had nearly beggared the Charetty family.

"Signori!" said the commander again, causing, as he had intended, one or two of his bowmen to look up alertly. You could see, when the *capitano* turned his head, that his puffed hair was razored up to the ears, and his overjacket and his buttons and the style of his flat cap and marbled silk doublet were marvellous. Only members of rich families like the Contarini or the Zeno or the Duodo were picked by the Senate and Republic of Venice to lead the Flanders fleet, and some of them were good sailors into the bargain, although that was not what they were there for. They were there because of the skill which allowed the seigneur commander to recognise, from a few murmured words of the Athenian's, that the makers of the disturbance were mercenary captains of some value as well as some potential danger. The lord commander, walking forward, said, "Ah. Il signore di Astariis and il signore Lionetto. I was seeking you. Pray to settle your difference and come and take wine with me."

Bulky and diminutive, the figures of the two captains stilled. Their faces turned, relaxing, towards the source of this flattering statement. Between the two formidable bodies the goblet remained for a moment, firmly held by one hand of each, while they sought a way out of the dilemma.

It was solved for them. Not by Messer Nicholai; not by the seigneur commander; not by either of the contenders.

Simon, the blue-blooded Scottish guest of the commander, made his elegant way towards the two captains, paused, and with a sudden, nicely-judged blow, propelled the glass spurting upwards from the half-relaxed grasp of the captains. The trajectory was oblique, and exact. To a wail of delight and of horror, the thing rose in the air, spanned the gunwale of the galley and, in a glittering, rose-coloured arc, descended to drown itself, finally and expensively, in the depths of the harbour.

Everyone looked at Lionetto, whose white-hot glare, muting, resolved itself into a flashing smile, directed at the Scotsman. Then, turning, everyone looked, with greater hopes at Astorre, who had purchased the goblet.

Astorre put his hand on his dagger, and took it off again. Then he put his hand on his purse, opened it, and withdrew and held up a coin. For thirty feet and more, trading, already slackening, came to a halt. Ignoring Lionetto; ignoring the Scotsman; ignoring, with magnificent aplomb, every factor against him: "A florin," said Astorre, "for the man who will dive for my property."

"Wait!" said the commander. The deck, which had begun to tilt, righted itself swaying under his feet as swimmers and non-swimmers paused on their way to jump over the side. The Greek smiled.

"Let me suggest," said the commander easily, "that more success might attend the efforts of just one man. Let the slave perform. It is his trade, diving."

He was the commander, so those who grumbled, grumbled quietly. Instead of jumping, they struggled for viewpoints. Nearest the companionway were the captains Astorre and Lionetto.

The African brute was unshackled. He was instructed by dumb show what he was to do, and then instructed again by an oarsman in broken Spanish. Then, as the devil still hesitated, they flung him over the side and pointed a few arrows at him, in case he thought of swimming all the way back to the Guinea coast.

When he came up to the surface from time to time after that, they flung whatever came to hand at his head and shoulders until he went down again. Nobody wanted to be there all day.

The commander watched with patience, having already chosen the moment when he would declare, with regret, that the search was void. It was therefore with astonishment not unmixed with annoyance that he saw the dull wool-head and broad shining features shoot up yet again from the water, accompanied this time by an upflung arm bearing the captain's vulgar pink goblet, unbroken.

He could hear, from the two ridiculous men, the hiss of indrawn breath as they caught sight of the goblet: see the smile on the face of the owner and the rage of the man Lionetto.

The negro had reached the steps and was dragging himself upwards. At the top, stabbing the air, were the long arms of Lionetto and the short arms of Astorre, awaiting him. The African hesitated.

The Greek said something to the commander, and the commander spoke to the Spanish linguist.

"Tell the slave to keep the goblet from the two captains. Tell him to throw it to the other men of the—what?—the Charetty household. Where messer Nicholai indicates. The three men you see over there."

The first Julius knew of this inspiration was the tilting backwards of all the heads in front of him, as if to watch the flight of some firework. In a perfunctory way, he looked up as well. Arching high in the air, there rushed towards him something gleaming and pink that looked very like the stupid standing-cup Astorre was carrying on about. Julius staggered, jabbed by Felix's elbow as Felix started to jump, trying to catch the thing.

He was annoyed with Felix. It pleased him to see Felix teeter in turn as Claes calmly took his place, raised his large, secure hands and caught the goblet.

Julius could have sworn, afterwards, that he caught it.

It was hard to tell, therefore, how a second later it was not in Claes' hands at all, but smashed into a shower of rose-coloured particles which glittered everywhere you looked: in bits of fur and folds of silk and majolica bowls and screws of sugar and people's boot-tops and purse-bags and scabbards.

Or empty scabbards, in the case of Astorre and Lionetto, who were thrusting together towards the unfortunate Claes, a blade in the fist of each. Behind them on the rail, the nobleman Simon was smiling.

It was Lionetto, who had not paid for the goblet, who suddenly stopped, looked at his dagger, and then dropping it back in its sheath, threw back his head and started to laugh. "That silly boy and you between you could strip me to my small clothes! That's what you said! Astorre, my poor fool! You couldn't even hold your own goblet, and he couldn't even catch it! Strip me to my small clothes!"

"Ah," said the Greek softly. "What a pity."

"Is it?" said the commander. "I should not have given much for the boy's chances. Now they are at one another's throats again. Really, this is now a discourtesy. Master, you will be good enough to tell the captains that your commander regrets that time no longer permits him to offer them wine, and that he would be glad if they would settle their differences upon shore. Tell me when they have gone. Messer Nicholai?"

Holding the curtain back for the Greek to re-enter his cabin, he saw that Monsignore de' Acciajuolo's gaze was resting on the pleasantly-endowed young man from Scotland who had just shared their collation: the yellow-haired person called Simon. It occurred to Messer Duodo to wonder, idly, what the Athenian's tastes might run to. He said, "I doubt if our Scottish friend intends to come back. It would seem that he regards himself as a friend of Lionetto."

And as the Athenian, without replying, hesitated on deck, as if about to recall the Scot to the cabin—"Indeed, Messer Nicholai," said the commander. "I think you and I have wasted time enough on this nonsense. We have that to discuss which, after all, requires no audience." And the Greek turned, the curtain falling behind him.

For whatever was about to take place, he could do nothing about it.

Chapter 8

With dismay, Julius watched authority leave, and Astorre and Lionetto freed to stride down to the wharf, and lock horns at last without hindrance. The loss of the commander's invitation was barely remarked, so intent were both captains on battle. They took their stance face to face on the quay, pursued by three or four dozen spectators and surrounded each by their friends. Behind Astorre, somewhat bemused, gathered Julius, Felix and their henchman Claes, with his recovered apron rolled under his arm. Behind Astorre stood the group of men who had supported him, Julius remembered, in the tavern of the Two Tablets of Moses. They included the bald man, whom he placed, blearily, as the drunken doctor Tobias, who had looked after the cranemen when Claes had damaged their faces.

Claes. Oh, God: idiot Claes. What were they to do with him?

Then Julius saw that the group about Lionetto included the Scotsman Simon, and realised, chilled, what someone wanted to do with him. Julius pulled himself together, and grasped the arm of the Charetty mercenary Astorre. He said, "Captain. It's over. We should get back to the Widow."

Jeering, Lionetto caught the words. "Oh, yes. Run back to the Widow. Why fight, if you can earn your living between the Widow's cordial legs? Was that what you wanted the goblet for? A bedding gift? I'd not blame you. No more nights in the mud under canvas; no university throw-outs to give you orders, no . . ."

Scarlet-faced, Felix leaped at him. Julius lunged, but Claes was before him, as Simon was before Lionetto. The collision of the apprentice and the Scotsman was of the briefest. It was the third time they had met in a matter of weeks. It was the first time they had touched one another. It was an encounter of greater moment than any other. For as the Scotsman fell back, it could be seen that the side of his fine lemon doublet was spotted with blood.

Simon caught his breath. Then, one hand over the wound, he stretched forward the other and drew from under the apprentice's arm a rolled apron with a gleaming point, blotched with red, stick-

ing from it. In silence, the Scotsman grasped the point and, unfurling the apron, held out for all to see a pair of finishing shears.
Lionetto took and examined them.

Simon said, "This man has attacked me. I claim the right to
punish him."

Felix said, "You have no right. He is a servant. He was protecting me." His face was scarlet.

Julius said, "My lord, it was an accident. The shears had come
from the grinder's, and Claes was carrying them rolled in his apron
for safety. And, if you will forgive me, this is not your quarrel."

"Indeed," said Simon. His clear blue eyes, catching the sun,
reminded Julius of his reputation with women. They said that
shrew Katelina van Borselen had turned him down, and he had
lain with every high-born woman in Bruges between then and now.
He looked sinewy enough to have done it and, eyeing him, you
could be sure that those chosen enjoyed it. Mesmerised, Julius
stared at him.

Simon said, "It may not be my quarrel, but this is, I must assure
you, my blood. Captain Lionetto, you and captain Astorre are
great leaders, whose lives are precious to kings and republics. What
excuse could Bruges give, if the world should lose such men over
an idle quarrel? It was I who flung the goblet overboard. It was the
lout here who broke it. Why not let me fight on your behalf, and
the youth for the Charetty captain? As it is, honour demands that I
should chastise him."

He paused, looking around with a half-smile pulling his lips.

"And unless you think it unfitting, because of the difference in
our degrees, I would assure you that I will not take a gentleman's
weapon against an apprentice. He may choose what he is used to.
A stick, a baton, a pole—I will engage to match him with anything."

There was a rumble of approval. Beside Julius, Astorre said,
"That's fair enough, considering the Scotsman has to fight with a
hole in him."

Julius said, "It was nothing. Look. It isn't even bleeding now.
Astorre, Claes doesn't fight."

"Everyone fights," said the captain irritably. "He's twice the
width of this pretty fellow, and younger. Anyway, he dropped my
goblet."

So Astorre wasn't going to help. And there was no one else to
stop it. The noblemen and chief officers of the galleys had long

since prudently absented themselves; the bowmen had no orders
and therefore only the avid interest of any layman in a forthcoming
fight. There were no officials remaining from Sluys or Damme or
Bruges to see justice done, and only Julius to keep badgering Astorre, and Felix to harangue Lionetto in an unavailing effort to
dissuade them.

For Lionetto and Astorre, being professional soldiers, had every
wish to kill, injure or otherwise dispose of a rival, but not in single
combat, like schoolboys. For that, one became a laughing-stock.
There were other, more adult ways of attaining that object.

So it suited each to perfection to seat himself, Astorre on the
landward side and Lionetto by the wharf edge with their coteries,
while a space between them was cleared of sacks and boxes, and
two broken oars found, and made equal in length, to serve as quar-
terstaffs in the Picardy fashion.

It was not the sort of match worth a wager, but good enough to
pass an afternoon, such as men in camp were well used to. Lionetto
had no particular interest in the Scotsman, whom he thought too
stuck up about his own looks, especially when, as now, he was
stripped to hose and under-doublet and thin, fancy shirt, and made
a finer figure, Lionetto was aware, than Lionetto himself.

However, there was no doubt he, Lionetto, had a better champion than that pig Astorre, whose man was this paint-spreading
artisan with his toes sticking out of his leg-covers. The fellow was
nothing but eyes. He reminded you of an owl in a tree, with five
men with longbows beneath it.

Someone yelled, "Go to!" and they started, with no special ceremony. Their weapons were six feet long, and heavy. The Scotsman
wore an amused smile.

He had cause. With no advantage of reach or of height, and with
a build infinitely more slender, he had all the trained skills of the
fightingman which the labourer lacked. It was as it had been in the
canal water. One performed like a thoroughbred, and one like a
boor. Claes would open his powerful shoulders, but before the pole
had swung through its arc, the other man would have slipped
through his guard to buffet his thigh or crack the hard wood
against shoulder or elbow.

These, indeed, were Simon's first targets: the means by which
Claes gripped and guided the pole. Those and the callused blue
hands, grasping it.

Perfectly fed, perfectly exercised, the nobleman Simon was fit as a lion. The muscles of his shoulders and back rose and sank beneath the fine cloth. His sleeves, loosely rolled, showed the developed forearms of a swordsman, and beneath the whipping cords of his hose, the contours of thigh and calf were firm and swelling and classical. His hose, soled in leather, gave him a footing on the uneven cobbles as he swayed and side-stepped and swung, double-handed: cracking the vibrating pole with precision against his opponent's; but not quite hard enough to knock it out of the other's broad fists.

He took his time. To Julius, who had held a sword, it was painfully apparent that every blow of the apprentice's was being anticipated. At leisure, smiling, even talking cuttingly as he circled, the man Simon was watching the youth with practised eyes: noting the smallest change in Claes' breathing, his footwork, his shoulders, the flickering glance of his eyes.

Then Claes would thrust, or swing, and Simon's club, cracking, would deflect the other and then, driving on, would hit where Simon designed. On the joints. Across the knuckles. Once, full in the chest so that the breath momentarily left the other man. Once, glancing off the side of the head so that Claes staggered back, frowning, and only, by some bemused instinct, managed to dodge the swift return blow which ought to have felled him.

He had a hard head. You had to give him that. When he straightened, he had his senses again, and this time, you saw that he had learned something. Instead of relying on schoolboy whacking, turn about like a game of palm-tennis, he too was trying to watch, to guess his opponent's next move.

Sometimes he was successful. Twice Simon was careless, and Claes' heavy pole struck him; once on the shoulder and once on the wrist, in a blow which made the nobleman draw in his breath and swing fast out of range, until the strength came back to his grip.

An experienced man would have given him no time for recovery, but Claes had neither the skill nor the energy. Instead, he stood and shook himself, reviewing his muscles, thought Julius, like a general reviewing his troops and recalling them to the standard. But all the time, his eyes were scanning Simon, and when Simon lunged, for the first time Claes was there before him, and their poles crashed together, and dropped, and disengaged.

But after that, Simon was careful, and whatever Claes might have learned, it was not enough to protect him from the buffets which reached him, over and over, out of the scuffling dust of their engagement. And Simon was still fresh. His face, when you saw it, was smiling, and between clenched teeth he was still, now and then, throwing out some tempting jibe.

Claes, on the other hand said nothing. The ebullient, talkative henchman, the clown who could imitate anybody, was shuffling now instead of dancing, and stumbling when he swerved. Where he had been struck on the knuckles, one hand had begun to swell and blacken, and there was scarcely a patch of unmarked skin on the blue-stained fluff of his arms, or above the torn hose at his thighs, or on the half-bare feet stubbed by the cobbles. As they watched, Simon contemptuously leaned forward, feinted, and driving the broken end of his pole down the wall of Claes' chest, tore the youth's sodden shirt to the waist, leaving behind a track of red gashes.

The conduct of an oaf and the talents of a girl. And a mortification to your father.

Felix said, "Stop it. Astorre, I order you. Stop the fight, or I will."

The crowd didn't want it stopped. They liked Claes well enough, and they had no particular love for the Scotsman, but one man baiting another was always good value, and this was better than Carnival time, when the Duke set a batch of blind men to round up wild pigs in the market place. *"Kill him!"* some woman was yelling to Simon.

Julius said, "Astorre, you heard him. Stand up and admit defeat, for God's sake. Do you want that fellow Simon to kill Claes?"

Astorre's beard had an obstinate set. He said, "If someone else wasn't giving him a drubbing, I would. Anyway, he's a powerful lad. And it's for the Charetty honour, isn't it? Would you want the Widow to have the name of employing nothing but cowards? After what that animal Lionetto said about her back there?"

Felix lifted his fist. Envisaging, for a frightful moment, a parallel brawl developing between his employer's son and his employer's mercenary, Julius thrust forward and grabbed Felix, who struggled. Then they both became still, watching what was happening before them, on the quayside.

His face and limbs swollen, his lungs labouring, his legs without strength, Claes could not even pretend, now, to study his enemy, or predict where the next blow might come from. He merely fought defensively, his pole held between his two hands, protecting his face and his body.

And this, of course, allowed Simon to do what he wished. He made no attempt to hook the other man's pole or otherwise disarm him, which would have finished the fight. Instead, sometimes swinging his pole, sometimes using it as a battering ram, he proceeded methodically, but without haste, to reduce his opponent.

You would say Claes was beyond thought. Indeed, from the beginning he had used his brains, Julius thought, little more than one of Astorre's pensioned soldiers, stupefied by too many blows on his helmet.

But one spark of an idea must have entered Claes' head. He waited until, after a succession of glancing blows, Simon swung his pole to the horizontal like his and prepared, spanning it with his hands, to attack in a different way. Claes hardly signalled what he meant to do next. Only his eyes flickered, once, and Simon, smiling, lunged in that direction.

Even then, he clearly could not believe that the flicker had been a deception. But there was Claes, on the wrong side, not only still gripping his pole horizontally but rushing at him, with a desperation that told he had gambled on this one movement all the strength he had left.

There was no time to sidestep. Claes was on him, and his pole was against Simon's pole, and the impetus of the rush was carrying Simon back, at first for a quick pace or two and then, as he dug in, more slowly. But still back, because the only advantage Claes had was in weight. And for once, Simon had no advantage at all.

Breathless, the spectators watched. On one side Astorre grunted, with Felix and Julius, still gripping each other beside him. And at the wharf-edge itself stood Lionetto, in a clear space with his cursing friends crowded about him.

Behind the resisting figure of Simon, men moved out of the way. Behind Simon was a stretch of a dozen paces and the edge of the quay, and the water. Astorre grunted again, with displeasure. "God blast them. Who wins if both dolts fall over?"

"At least it will stop it," said Julius. His teeth were sunk in his lip. Surely the Scotsman, with all the fight in him yet, was going to break the deadlock and duck long before he was shoved to the edge? Or would he let himself be run there and twist, sending Claes under his own impetus over the edge, and thus end the battle?

If that was it, thought Julius, someone had better act quickly. Someone would have to fish out the poor beaten idiot before he drowned from exhaustion.

Perhaps the touchy Scotsman had intended to throw Claes over. Perhaps he intended to play with him, recovering at the last moment and driving him back to a worse beating than before. Certainly a scuffle of sorts developed as if Simon had changed his position, but was finding it less easy than he had expected. Later, although no one knew for certain, those nearest the quayside swore that Claes threw away his pole and, gripping his opponent by the arms, hurled himself and the other man into the water together.

Certainly, before they left the quayside, both poles had dropped, cracking and bouncing to the cobbles. Lionetto himself, who was standing quite near, agreed, when pressed, that the Scotsman had been carrying no pole when he passed him.

What was visible to all was that moment. The moment when, locked together, Claes and his tormentor hurtled off the quayside and into the depths of the harbour.

The shouting rose to a roar, and died away. On the quay, instead of the duellers was dust, and a scuffed and empty arena. In the water of the harbour was a widening ring, its edges slapping the quay wall.

Then people, exclaiming, began to mill about at the edge of the wharf. Only Julius, throwing off his notary's robe and ripping off his purse-belt, thrust both at Felix and, in an extremely good doublet, jumped straight out into the water.

He saw the yellow head of the Scotsman quite quickly, progressing sedately towards the wharf steps, and in no evident need of retrieval. Claes he could not see at all nor, when he shouted an enquiry, did the other swimmer even turn his face towards him.

The water still pooled and danced, where the two men had plunged. Julius swam towards it. He was quite near, in fact, when he saw the blood, spiralling up like whelk-red in a dye vat.

He took a strong breath, and dived, and found the cold, drifting bulk of Claes' body.

Because the boy appeared to be dead, which might have been a nuisance, the seigneur commander Duodo made his stately way along his deck to the wharf, followed by the Athenian de' Acciajuoli and the ship's surgeon. When they got there everyone else drew back, with the exception of a bald-headed man who continued to kneel, busying himself in a bad-tempered way with the inert, half-naked body of the apprentice. It was grotesquely discoloured.

Messer Duodo said gently, "This is an unfortunate business."

Lionetto and Astorre looked at one another, and Lionetto moved forward a little. "Oh, they've got the water out of him," he said. "They mend quickly, that class. I dare say he'll be none the worse in a week or two."

"Ah, the lad is alive," said the commander. One would have been deceived. The youth's eyes were shut, and distressingly sunken. Also, there appeared to be blood. He said, "What are you stanching? Perhaps my surgeon can help?"

Without looking up, the bald-headed man said, "I am a surgeon. I could do with proper bandages, and some ointment. It's a stab wound."

It was the Greek who said sharply, "A stab wound?"

There was a pause. The ship's surgeon laid down his box and, kneeling, opened it. The second mercenary, the one they called Astorre, said, "The Scotsman snatched the shears as they went over, and stabbed him."

The first mercenary, Lionetto, had flushed. "It was the boy who took the shears. You heard the Scots lord declare it. The boy had stabbed him once already."

"There seems to be some confusion," said the commander mildly. "Did no one see precisely what happened?"

The answer, as he expected and, indeed, counted on, was in the negative.

The Scots lord, wet and tired after the combat, had left with his servants. The notary here, who had saved the youth's life, had seen no more than anyone else. There was no need for the lord commander to trouble himself further over an idle dispute. The good pawnbroker Oudenin had offered to carry the lad to his house until he could be moved back to Bruges. The ship's surgeon, if the lord commander permitted, could supply immediate medicaments. The bald-headed man, whose name was Tobias Beventini, was also willing to help. Master Tobias was a fully qualified medical officer, already attached for a year to the mercenary army of this Lionetto.

The commander was mildly surprised that one of the company of Lionetto should care for an employee of his antagonist's household. Indeed, the man Lionetto objected, but the doctor Tobias continued to work, and paid his captain no heed whatever.

The commander, it seemed, was expecting a buyer almost immediately to discuss the price of his Candian wine. He murmured a few appropriate comments, gave carte blanche to his surgeon, a languorous person burned by the Levantine sun who called himself

Quilico, and paced back on deck, leaving the Greek to watch, since he was interested.

The Greek said, "The wound. Is it serious?"

The bald-headed man said, "Yes. He needs warmth and attention quickly. Once we see how matters go, he can be taken back to Bruges by canal." He looked up, his drinker's eyes narrowed. He had a small flexible mouth like a fish, and a pallid face with a fuzz of pale hair round his cranium. He said, "And if you are going to ask, I didn't see what happened."

"I am more concerned," said the Greek, "with the young man's recovery. He may need constant medical attention."

"He will have it," said the bald-headed man shortly. "I have nothing to do. Messer Quilico will be about. The pawnbroker is helpful, and I will stay with the boy through the night. It may be possible to move him tomorrow."

Around them, the crowds had thinned. Lionetto, after lingering, had turned abruptly and walked off with his friends but without this man he called Tobie. One or two crewmen from the galleys stood about, and nearest of all, of course, the Charetty boy and the factor Julius, his black gown flung round his shoulders over his soaking doublet.

The mercenary Astorre, who had caused all the trouble, said, "Well, my lord, if you mean that, I can tell you that the Widow— that the demoiselle de Charetty, who employs him, won't see you out of pocket at the end of it. Send the accounting to her. Or to Meester Julius here. Meanwhile, we ought to be going. Jonkheere Felix? Meester Julius?"

"You go," said the notary briefly. "We're staying."

Nicholai de' Acciajuoli looked at him. He said, "I think perhaps, if you will forgive me, that the demoiselle de Charetty might be more reassured to hear the tale from your lips or her son's than from—anyone else. No doubt the surgeon here would appreciate your help in taking the boy to the pawnbroker's you speak of. But I am sure Messer Quilico and Messer Tobias will engage to give you any news of a change in his condition. Indeed, I am myself staying here in the castle, and will see to it."

An autocratic bastard, concluded the surgeon Tobie, when he had time to think of anything but the task of transferring the bleeding carcass of his patient from the quay to the house of the pawn-broker.

The man Oudenin, who seemed eager to help, settled him comfortably enough on a pallet in a room full, so far as Tobie could see, of kitchen utensils and seamen's clothing. Then, after a fairly useless consultation with Quilico, they left him alone with the boy, and the medical provisions the galley doctor had supplied him with.

The apprentice was still unconscious. A hell-raiser in his own little way, so they said, but a long way from being able to deal with the nobility when bent on raising their particular hell. All right. To work, before the youth woke, so that the worst of it was out of the way. His hands this morning were steady.

Devil take Lionetto. Tobias Beventini of Grado knew very well, looking at the passive, marked face below him, that he was only doing this to score off the captain. If he didn't watch, he'd be reduced like a child to taking umbrage. Since the day of the flooded tavern, Lionetto had never insulted him in public again and wouldn't, when he was sober. Nor would he let him, when he was sober. Lionetto needed a good medical officer, and he had been the best of his year in Pavia. And it was his choice to work with mercenaries. It was still his choice. The Dauphin's piles and the Pope's feet were for sycophantic men like his uncle.

He preferred to sharpen his skills on common men, like this one. Yellow bubbles. He remembered laughing over it at the Crane, while he was tending the cranemen's burst noses. By God, he had been drunk. But there was no doubt, this lad caused his elders a lot of trouble, and it was not surprising if they levelled the score now and then.

But not like this. Not the way that Scotsman had done.

Much later, during the night, the youth—Claes, was it?—stirred and opened his eyes, and the surgeon lifted over the soup he had ready, and prepared to give it him. For quite a while, as was natural, the apprentice didn't seem to understand where he was, or what had happened, and said nothing when Tobie put the necessary questions about his condition. Then suddenly he seemed to gather his thoughts together, and answered quite sensibly, in a low voice. In return, without being asked, the surgeon described where he was, and what had happened to his companions. He didn't mention the man Simon, or ask questions about the source of the wound.

Curiously, when Tobie referred to the pawnbroker, he thought the bruised face responded with a glimmer. But when he looked again there were, as before, only the effects of shock, and pain and a primitive kind of endurance. Finally, after taking some food, his patient slept. Tobie wondered if the youth would ever know how lucky he was, how nearly those blades had pierced his heart. There was, of course, no guarantee of recovery yet. There would be fever to come. The journey to Bruges would be troublesome. Lionetto, as well, was quite capable of finding some task for his surgeon that would give him little time to fuss over the sick of an antagonist. Yes. He would have to decide what to do about Lionetto.

Now, his patient at rest, Tobie slipped out quietly to rejoin the pawnbroker and his daughter at their table, since they had invited him. The daughter kept talking about the boy called Felix, and he wondered if there was an affair going on there, but was too bored to pursue it.

He had left a light by the youth's pallet, and the door a little ajar so that he could enter the room without sound. So it was that on returning he saw, without being seen, that his patient was awake, and had somehow moved on the pillow, so that the light came from behind him. But it was a wax candle, especially clear and brilliant, that Tobie had left. It shone into Oudenin's brass pots and copper kettles and they returned the light, mellowed, to the helpless man's face.

Tobie studied it. The broad low brow and discoloured cheekbones and swollen, extravagant lips. The darkened eye-sockets, big as candlecups, and the repressive loop of the nostrils. The hair which had dried like dragged wool. The face of a buffoon, pressed to the pillow, where something glistened, ceased, and then glistened again.

Till he was sure, Tobie stood watching. Then he retreated with care. The voice the boy needed was not that of a doctor. The voice he needed didn't exist. There was nothing Tobie could do. And in any case, the poor, silly fool wanted no help. Or this would not be happening, as it was, in painful and absolute silence.

Chapter 9

The dangerous business of the Charetty apprentice and the Scotsman was reported to the city that night, and was briefly debated. It was decided to wait and see if Nature might dispose of the difficulty. It was recognised, on the other hand, that Master Tobias Beventini of Grado was an excellent surgeon.

Considering that he was wrestling most of the time with his own problems, the surgeon Tobie lived up to their fears, or expectations. He gave his patient the required amount of expert attention. And when the time came to dispatch him to Bruges, he found something to render the boy insensible, both to the rigours of the trip and to any attempts to interrogate him. It had already struck the shrewd surgeon Tobie that there might be trouble ahead, depending on who was supposed to have tried to kill whom. Tobie had, before now, patched up a man and seen him go to the gallows. That was, however, no business of his.

In Bruges he deposited the boy in the house of his employer, saw him settled, and went off with the announced intention of (at last) getting drunk. He had earned, Tobie saw, the contempt of the Charetty heir Felix. That for Felix. If anyone needed help, there was Quilico. Tobie wondered, from his experience of the inside of Quilico's box, what Quilico had actually been treating, all those years in the colonies. He promised himself a long talk with the Levantine physician.

His interpretation of Felix's glare had been correct. Surprisingly, it was Felix whom the whole affair had cast into a frenzy. His passionate intervention on the quayside had come of course from wounded dignity: a compulsion to defend his mother, her business, and Claes, the property of that business. In themselves, these emotions were new to him. Whether any of these protective feelings applied to Claes as a person Felix did not consider, and would have been offended if asked.

Felix overslept on the essential morning. Otherwise at first light he would have set out with Julius and his mother to collect Claes at Sluys. When they came back he hovered about getting in everyone's way as the unusually inert figure wrapped in blankets was hauled from the barge at the foot of the yard and wheeled in a barrow to the demoiselle's household quarters, and not to the common sleeping room, which was certainly noisy. When Tilde his sister burst into tears, Felix was rude to her.

It annoyed Felix that Claes was not prepared, or able, to speak to him, and that, when he apparently went off his head and started a fever, it was to Julius that one doctor or the other gave his instructions, and Julius and his mother who sat by Claes and dosed him when they had time.

For three days, Felix had the door shut in his face. It was unfair. He needed some facts from Claes. When, on the fourth, he began to repeat his complaint, his mother cut in with unusual acidity. If he wanted to pick Claes' brains through the hole in his chest, he was welcome to try, she informed him.

Felix was thrilled. Quite unchastened, he bounded to the sickroom, displaced a blushing girl on her lingering way out with a dinner tray and sat down on a stool by Claes' mattress.

"Well. Who did it?" he said. He bent forward. "You should see your face!" said Felix. "I'll get a mirror. Remember that vat that went wrong, and came out sort of grey streaked with yellow?"

Claes was quite normal after all, because the dimples appeared and disappeared. Claes said, in nearly his usual voice, "You should have seen me yesterday. What happened to Astorre?"

"He proposed marriage to Mother," said Felix. "All right. I can't help it if it hurts you to laugh. He said Lionetto had impugned her honour and it was up to him to set it right."

"Did she accept?" said Claes.

"She said she'd give him his answer at the same time as Oudenin," said Felix. "And you've no idea how keen Oudenin is to marry her. You know what? He bought that black boy. You know. The one that dived for the glass you broke, you silly idiot. He bought the black boy, and he's handed him as a present to Mother. To Mother! . . . Listen, I can't help it. You asked," said Felix impatiently. "Will I get somebody?"

He watched, intrigued, as Claes' face turned yellow, and then white again. He then helped Claes to be sick, which everyone who ever went to a tavern was used to doing, and said morosely, as he dumped his head back on the pillow, "I can't hold much of a conversation if all you do is splutter."

His eyes shut, Claes grinned. "Tell me something sad," he said.

"Anselm Adorne came this morning," said Felix, which was the most boring item of news he could think of. "Oh, and Mabelie's been twice, so now everybody knows you're still seeing her. And Lorenzo. And John. And Colard, saying something about pigments. If you've been promising shearing-lakes to those painters, Mother will have your ears."

"She can have them," said Claes drowsily. "It'd spare me your recital."

"Well, I came specially to see you," said Felix, getting up crossly. He realised, suddenly, that he had been led away from the vital purpose of his visit. He said, "You didn't say, anyway. That bastard Simon. Did he do this?"

Claes' lips, reduced to normal, produced a reposeful snuffle. Felix, used to this also, opened his follower's eyes by the simple expedient of grasping a handful of hair and pulling it tightly. "Simon?" said Felix.

"Pontius Pilate," said Claes rather sourly, and would not be wakened again.

Normally, Felix would have persevered but, as he found to his astonishment, Julius put the entire blame upon him, Felix, for some imagined relapse in Claes' condition, and barred the door to him for a day. In the end, even Tilde and Catherine got in before their older brother.

As someone had remarked, Claes was of a class that generally mended well, and he was strong. He also had, freakishly, the attentions of two doctors. When Quilico wasn't there, Tobie frequently strolled in, mostly sober. Once they both came at the same time and went out together and got drunk. The day after that, Tobie sat on the sill in Claes' room and said, "Why the interest in plants?"

Claes, swathed and propped up with cushions, looked like a plaster cast of a Roman with eyes round as coin-dies. He was getting back his lung power and had just finished giving a very good imitation of what Quilico had said on his last visit, with a lot of Greek swear words. Claes was, Tobie was aware, also memorising every habit of speech and action that he, Tobie, possessed. It was sometimes quite difficult, talking to Claes, to keep your speech normal.

Now Claes said, "I was trying to get his attention. I didn't want him to give me an enema. Doctors and dyers are always able to talk about plants. For instance, I might want a hair dye and you might want a love potion. Or the other way round."

Talking to Claes was like walking in sinking sands. Tobie said, "I hear you were discussing alum. Naturally, of course. Surgeons use it for blood-stopping and dyers for fixing their colour. Do you know, I made a little enquiry. Before the Turks took it over, alum was coming into Florence alone at the rate of three hundred thousand pounds weight a year. For the Arte della Lana. The weavers."

"Fancy, Master Tobias!" said Claes. He shook his head in an amazed way. He looked happy.

"So?" said Tobias. "Holly, for one. I've got a note of the rest. So have you, I am sure. All the plants that grow on the Phocoean alum mines."

Claes still looked happy. He said, "But that's a long way away, Master Tobias. On the east of the Middle Sea. Beyond Chios. Beside Smyrna. And the Turks have taken it over. You couldn't get hair dye from there. Or a love potion."

Tobias Beneventi was an impatient man, but he could disregard provocation if he had to. He said, "Did he tell you where else these plants grew?"

He waited. He tried to look calm. A few times, Quilico had come to the point. And then had had another drink. And then had slid under the banquette.

"Yes," said the Charetty apprentice. His eyes had grown a little too bright, but he was smiling still. He said, "But you don't need a hair dye. And in any case, I've already forgotten the name of the place and Master Quilico's no longer in Bruges. I don't know whether they told you? He got very drunk, and the commandant was vexed and shipped him out in a carrack for Djerba."

Tobie said, "Do you know what you're doing?"

He knew he should stop. He was a doctor. The boy knew enough, too, not to risk losing his grip on himself. He said, "Well, you should know how people rave on their sick beds. You could try me again when I'm well and see if I say the same things."

"Don't worry," said Tobias. "You haven't said anything. All right. Lie down. I don't know why I talk to you."

"Don't you?" said Claes. His eyes were shut, but he looked quite serene. Even mischievous.

Tobias didn't go back: there was no need. And in any case, he couldn't make up his mind what to do about it.

In a week Claes was up, and in another he was able to sit downstairs clothed, his lap littered with books and documents, while Julius completed the laborious paperwork resulting from the Widow's purchases. It was during one of those sessions that Felix, scarlet with anger, burst into the room, shouting, *"What is this?"*

Julius laid down his pen. Claes looked up.

Julius said, "Not now, Felix."

"You didn't tell me," said Felix. "I've just heard. You didn't tell me." His naked, shallow-set eyes switched from Claes to his mother's notary and back again. "If you're going, I'm going," said Felix in what, if you didn't know Felix, sounded like a blind affirmation of staunchness and loyalty, but in fact, as Julius well knew, was mostly pique.

Julius said, "Your mother wished to speak to Claes first. Felix, go upstairs. Your mother will talk to you about all this later."

Claes, who was not of the class to know anything about tact, was looking enquiringly from Julius to his employer's son instead of continuing quietly with his task. Julius opened his mouth.

"They're sending you off," said Felix flatly. "To—"

"Felix!" said his tutor with the finality that Felix did, sometimes, obey. Then Julius got up and, with a restraining gesture to the apprentice, led his employer's son forcefully out of the room and closed the door. When he opened it again, ten minutes later, it was to usher his employer into his own tall-backed chair behind the table.

Claes rose from his stool and waited, his lustrous eyes resting on Marian de Charetty as she seated herself. Julius left. Claes, obeying a gesture, sat down. There was a short silence, during which his mistress studied him. Then: "Well, Claikine," she said.

It was a name he was used to: the name he had had as a child when, hard-used and filthy, he had come to the Charetty. She had taken him in for her sister's sake. Her sister who had no connection with the unwanted child, but had married into the family that had produced it. The de Fleury family, of Dijon and Geneva.

Sitting by his bedside during the past weeks she had employed the boyish name now and then: to recall his attention when it was wandering, or to turn his thoughts when, in his confusion, they strayed in directions which offered small healing. But for the last two weeks, she had left his nursing to others.

He smiled. He said, "There's no news to break to me, demoiselle. Of course not. I am only grateful you kept me and were so kind in these last weeks when I couldn't serve you."

She wondered what he remembered of the early days of his fever: of the late-night alarums when a frightened maid would come for her, and when she was not dressed in her daily uniform: this thick, moulded dress with the narrow sleeves and smothering neck; the velvet cap cuffed by stiff lappets with its wired widow's peak which covered all of her hair. It was a blessing, really. When she grew grey, no one would know of it. When she became thick in the trunk, the folds of her train could be tucked up to disguise it.

Or did that matter, in any case? Neither Astorre nor Oudenin nor any of the several others who had offered for her knew what she was actually like, any more than Cornelis had, those last years of his illness. She was the widow de Charetty, a bit sharp of tongue, a bit hard of manner, who owned a thoroughgoing medium business capable of expansion.

To this young man whom she had known since he was ten, in the days when she was serenely married to a vigorous, cheerful Cornelis, she said irritably, "You guess you are to be sent off, and you make no complaint, you have no anxious questions to ask. Don't you even want to know where?"

"You remember my great fault," said Claes. "I'm easily contented." And then, his smile widening, he said, "I don't mean to annoy you. But I feel sure it must be somewhere of exceptional amenity if Felix wants to go with me."

"You stood between him and Lionetto," said the Widow. "Or so I heard."

He said nothing, but rested on her unaltered the same kindly gaze. He would not delude her about Felix, and she must not delude herself. She heard herself saying, "It is not Felix's attitude which concerns me, but yours. You protected Felix, and from that stemmed the trouble that followed. To be turned off now must seem the height of ingratitude."

Again, he cut through all she intended to say. He said, "Of course not. I had meddled long before that. I put myself in the market place."

He had been reared on French, and his Flemish still held an undercurrent of it. His own voice, when he was not play-acting, or mimicking, was soft and even and practical, even when uttering such a remark, which silenced her for a moment with the very complexity of its implications. Round a guild table; in the midst of some subtle, three-sided negotiation in a Hanse office, she sometimes thought of Claes, and of the dawning, in increasing numbers, of moments such as these.

She said, "Then you may be able to guess who has already approached me to ask for your services."

The smile she received now was like none she had ever received round a guild table. "So I may," he said. "But I don't think you would expect me to tell you."

She rearranged the papers before her. "I have had a request from Ser Alvise Duodo the Venetian," said the Widow. "If I wish to release you, he will give you work on board the Flanders galleys till spring, and then give you some training on the homeward voyage which will obtain you a paid post in Venice. He would interview you."

"And the other?" said Claes gravely.

"The other comes from the Dauphin. The Dauphin Louis of France, who is staying at present with Meester Bladelin. He remembers clearly, it seems, meeting yourself and Felix on one of his visits to Louvain. Felix engaged him in conversation about hunting. He proposes for you a post with his huntsman, combined with that of—he said—a resourceful errand lad. The post, he said, was too menial for a son of mine."

"But Felix wants it," said Claes.

This time she chose not to answer, watching him; waiting for him to return the stroke in this delicate game . . . the fourth, the fifth, the sixth such conversation she had held with him, perhaps, since she had found him grown, suddenly, out of childhood. Six such conversations, sensibly spaced.

Mabelie had called twice, not being able to dispense with . . . conversations.

Claes said, "Or no, I see. Felix longs to be the Dauphin's huntsman, but he doesn't know yet that there is a third offer. Then I give you best. I don't know what it is."

"It is mine," said Marian de Charetty steadily. "That you join captain Astorre and his mercenaries on their trip to Italy, and if he finds you suitable, stay with him to fulfil any contract he may make on my behalf. When the contract ends you may choose to stay, or return here."

He changed colour. An involuntary response was the last thing she had expected: in her turn, she was shaken. Even then, she could not tell whether he felt pleasure or fear.

To give him time, she said, "You and Julius have always maintained that the mercenary troop ought to be the most lucrative side of the business. Astorre has given me good reason to think that is so. The Duke of Milan and the Pope are recruiting mercenaries for the Naples war: we have well-trained lances on reserve pay who have only to be called. Captain Astorre with the best of these will go overland to Milan before Christmas. If Astorre obtains a contract, he will send for more men by the spring."

He said, "But the Flanders galleys would take me out of reach of my lord Simon just as effectively."

That was to test her. But her thoughts on this matter had occupied many nights. She said, "Do you suppose you are being chased out of the city by Simon? There is no question of that. You maintain that the shears fell into the water and became entangled between you. My lord Simon, it seems, will say nothing, except that he regrets the disgrace to his rank in being led by his temper into chastising a servant. For him to seek you out now or attack you would make him a laughing-stock."

"And you don't think *I* would attack *him*?" said Claes.

"I think I know you," she said. "That is why I have asked Astorre if he will take you. There are things you need to learn."

"Such as how to fight," he said. His tone was neither joking nor bitter but idle, as if his thoughts were quite elsewhere. He said, "Demoiselle, I am content, as I told you. If you know me, you know that."

She said, "But you have put yourself in the market place," with a little sadness. And then, as he did not answer, she said, "And, you must know, the city is concerned. They won't press charges for what has happened and they won't order me to send you away. But it would be wise to leave Bruges for a while."

She broke off again. Claes said, "Geneva lies on the way to Milan. Will captain Astorre call there? Is that what you mean by having something to learn?"

When Claes wanted to know something, there was no avoiding the vastness of his gaze. He did not look distressed, although his face was more hollow than it usually was, with the faint rainbow colours here and there that reminded Felix, he said, of St Salvator's windows.

Claes had come to her from the kitchens of Jaak de Fleury of Geneva, whose late niece's bastard he was. Michelle her sister had been Thibault de Fleury's second wife. Her sister was dead, and Thibault old and out of his senses, but Jaak de Fleury continued to flourish. And his horse and his ass and his wife and his fine trade and banking company with its headquarters in Geneva.

Life was not fair. She had not seen Jaak for many years, not since Cornelis died or long before it. All she and the de Fleury company had in common now was their trading connections, stiffly maintained because both houses depended on them, but involving no warmth, no personal interest, no friendly contact. She did not like Jaak de Fleury, and he did not like her.

And if she did not like him, she could imagine how Claikine must feel. Although he had never spoken of his time in Geneva. Not consciously, anyway.

Now she was sending him there, however briefly. She looked directly at him and said, "Yes, Astorre will call at Geneva. What are you afraid of?"

He was looking at his darned hose, and smoothing one knee with a finger from which the blue dye had almost worn off. In the small cabinet meant only for Julius, he seemed to occupy all the air and all the floorspace, even though he was folded double on the low stool. He laughed suddenly and said, "You'd be surprised, demoiselle. I suppose, of ridicule I haven't invited."

"Then you should learn how to deal with it," the Widow said. "As I said, you have a lot to find out. Captain Astorre has no objection to teaching you. You will learn also from Julius. Indeed, I hope there are some things Julius might find himself learning from you. When you are not here, his totals for Felix's scholastic equipment frequently depart from the credible."

The finger on his knee stopped, and he looked at her.

She answered the query with a calmness she did not need to pretend. "Yes. Julius wants to go to Italy also. I hope, by the way, that you thanked him for what happened at Sluys."

Claes said, "Yes, of course. Why does he want to go with Astorre? What will you do? Who would help you here with the business?"

Her anxiety dissolved, for a moment, in amusement. She said, "Why shouldn't he go? Julius is ambitious. A well-led band needs a notary, a paymaster, a treasurer. He would do well, and it would give him the authority he longs for. And as for the business, I don't believe Julius really thinks that pawnbroker Oudenin will supplant him before the end of the contract. But Julius does know that I will not make him a partner, now or in the future. I need someone cleverer."

Silence.

Everything she said, she knew, had been understood. Everything

she thought . . . almost. She said, "I think I can manage. I may
make a temporary appointment. That is my concern. Your concern
is your immediate future. You have three offers. Which will you
take?"

She could see him physically take the decision: straightening his
arms so that his big hands hardened on his knees; firming, with a
long inhalation, the muscles which had held him politely at attention on the low, backless stool.

He said, "You have considered that, by law, you would receive a
fee from the galley commandant or the Dauphin for releasing me
from my apprenticeship?"

She was answered. She kept her voice, in spite of it, steady.
"Every time I look at my debit column, I consider it," Marian de
Charetty said. "If you go to Milan for me instead, I shall demand
large profits in compensation. Do I take it you have decided for
Astorre and Italy?"

His resignation was marked. "I have no alternative," he said. "I
was brought up obeying your every word. You send me to Milan. I
go there."

"Such martyrdom!" said the Widow. "We shall try to survive
your departure."

"I'm sure you will," Claes said abstractedly. His mind, it appeared, was on the business. He said, "As to the dyeshop, I think
I've heard you and Meester Julius suggest that if the fulling and
the finishing were to be farmed out, Henninc would enjoy giving all
his attention to the dyeing, with Lippin to help him. And a cheerful sort of clerk—we all know they are about—could work with
jonkheere Felix, now he's ready to be interested in what goes on in
the business. The investment side at Louvain can run itself for a
bit, but it really needs to attract more money. Julius says. I wonder
if Astorre and Julius and I could help?"

She said, "You can certainly help. If you get a contract to garrison Naples, it will give the business here some real capital."

"Yes," he said. "Of course. But I was thinking of something else.
If you like, you could send us south with a trading caravan. You
know. Merchants and men of business going to Italy and needing
protection. Merchandise to be escorted over the mountains. And
what would pay best—the job of taking boxes of letters and bills
and bulls from the Flanders banks to their Italian headquarters. A
winter courier service. The banks would give you a fee, and I could
carry them all on this trip. They could send silver even, with an

armed escort this size. And if they were impressed by us, they might approach you to hire men another time. You'd have to train your own couriers."

"I should," said Marian de Charetty slowly. Slowly, in tribute to the implications of all he was saying and the scale, she began to suspect, of the decision he had actually reached. He was eighteen.

She had known she was sending him from Bruges, and security. She had known she was forcing him to go to Geneva, where all his early misery must have been. And despite Astorre's prediction that the Naples war was defensive, that there would be no fighting next year if ever, she had known that she was sending Claes to learn the business of war, and take part in it, and that when or if he returned, he would be altered.

Yet he had to learn to defend himself. And he *had* meddled, as he had said.

She looked at him, and he said, "It is for the best, demoiselle," and gave a quick, comical grin of reassurance.

She smiled in return, with composure. She was good at that.

Among the merchant-princes of Bruges, the most useful social event of that autumn was the banquet given for the commander of the Flanders galleys by the Duke's wealthy Controller Pierre Bladelin. It was held in the Controller's russet brick palace with its octagonal tower and steeple in Naalden-Straate.

If the Duke had been present, it would have been held in the Princenhof, which would have been more interesting because, as everyone knew, there was a new bathing basin and several sumptuous retiring rooms (they said) filled with fruit and flowers and sweetmeats and perfumes and other unusual luxuries, for the use of the bathers before, during and after immersion.

While in residence in the past the Duke had been known at least twice to pick a new mistress from the society invited to meet him at the Princenhof. If such a lady proved fertile, the fortune of that particular family would be made. The Duke was quite prodigal towards all his bastards, and none of his mistresses or their previous or subsequent husbands had ever been known to censure him.

Katelina van Borselen had heard it all discussed often enough in her own family, and in that of her cousins. The subject came up again now, with their handsome invitations from Bladelin. The de Veeres had accepted, and so had her father. Her mother being in Zeeland, Katelina, regally trained, proposed to attend in her place.

The de Veeres agreed that, as it was, Controller Bladelin's house was grand enough, as it had cause to be, considering the appointments he held and the years he had enjoyed the Duke's favour, in spite of being born to a dyer of buckram.

Katelina, who had forgotten this detail, added it to the others already occupying her as she swept through the Controller's doorway, and under the wrought tabernacle and the shield and the handsome sculptured effigies of the Madonna and her host in adoration.

At this function she did not expect to meet dyers, or their sons or their notaries. But did dyers stick to dyers, and hence might ostracise the enemies of their own kind?

She had learned from Margriet Adorne (but not from her father) that the Scotsmen had closed ranks round Simon of Kilmirren after his excess of high spirits at Sluys, when he had given a beating to that impertinent lad. It had been a fair fight, they said, although marred at the end by some accident. Since then the victor, however mutinous, had been constrained to stay decorously at Jehan Metteneye's, or Stephen Angus's, or in the company of the Bishop or his factor. Once he had called on her cousin, because the Scottish king's brother was staying there. She knew, because apparently my lord Simon had asked Wolfaert about her.

That was something her father had not forgotten to mention. She understood that she was still in his town house at Bruges and not yet dispatched to Zeeland or Brussels because he was displeased with her, and hoped, while Simon was still in Flanders, that she would repent and repair matters between them. Oddly, she was in two minds about that. For a man gently reared, Simon's behaviour in the garden had been crass (she told herself). He was spoiled with easy conquests—but who wouldn't be, with such looks? She had been . . . She had been aware of his power herself.

If, as was rumoured, the girl found in Metteneye's cellar had been his property, then at least he had handled the matter with style. And as for the business at Sluys—the Charettys' rollicking labourer had by all accounts been the first to draw blood, and deserved whatever had happened thereafter.

She had noted the faint reserve with which men spoke of Simon. He was well over thirty. He had a long record of dalliance and only a short one of practical stewardship. She recalled, certainly, that she had met his unwelcome attentions on their last meeting with an insult which had sent him off in a temper. Afterwards, she wished she had managed it better. But it was marriage . . . marriage she had to engineer, not what threatened to swamp her that night.

Now, if she wished it, she had a second chance. Now, for example, he could not so well afford to reduce his circle of well-wishers. If she met him tonight, she would be amiable.

She had nothing to lose. She had no desire to enter a convent. She had served the Queen of Scotland without gaining a husband. The Duchess of Burgundy lived at Nieppe apart from her husband and surrounded by handsome Portuguese. Simon's sister had married one of them. But there was no guarantee that the Duchess's entourage would bring her a husband: it was just as likely to bring her the Duke.

She wondered if in that event her father would be shocked, and realised that he was probably hoping against hope that such a thing would happen. He had no heirs apart from Gelis and herself. He had borrowed heavily, she knew, to raise even the small dowry which would have gone with her hand to the objectionable—the abominable Scottish lord she had rejected. She had costly gowns. She had family jewels of some value, and some even rarer, presented by the princesses she had served. She had been allowed to keep these. They enhanced her value.

She wished she were a widow; independent; in control of her life and her intelligence.

She looked about. Soon, according to custom, the Controller's trumpeters would announce the principal guests, and a procession would form which would lead them to the banqueting room. The commander of the Flanders galleys would, one assumed, accompany the Controller. The Dauphin Louis, they said, had also consented to be present.

She had met him once in Brussels, a sharp-featured man in his thirties. She had been about to leave on her three-year exile to Scotland. He had just fled to Burgundy to escape the court of his father in France. One day he would be king of that country. He was welcome to it. Meanwhile . . .

Ah. Dyers did not, then, ostracise the antagonists of other dyers. There, on the other side of the hall, was Simon of Kilmirren.

Steering her father discreetly from group to group, Katelina van Borselen made her way across Controller Bladelin's crowded hall to where gleamed the remarkable hair of Simon of Kilmirren under a leafy concoction of taffeta. Trailing leaves feathered his over-

sleeves, and his jacket was buttoned with acorns. He had his back
to her.

His stance was unwontedly stiff, as if in the presence of royalty.
Yet he was one of a casual circle. It included Giovanni Arnolfini,
the silk merchant. The short dark man was her father's friend João
Vasquez, the Duchess's secretary and a kinsman by marriage to
Simon's sister. The two wearing damask with hat-jewels of vegeta-
ble proportions were without doubt Venetians. Conversing in halting French, they would now and then turn to Arnolfini for help, or
to the seventh of the group, whom she could not see, but whose
Italian sounded like Tommaso Portinari's efforts at French. Her
lips twitched.

Then her father entered the circle and Simon turned and saw
her. He frowned. *Frowned!*

"My lord Simon! How delightful," said Katelina, "to see they
have released you. Were you in prison for long?"

She spoke in French. Even the Venetians, she hoped, would manage to translate most of that. To her gratification, the volatile face
of her suitor went white with anger. Her father, gripping her arm,
said, "Katelina, what are you thinking of? Monsieur of Kilmirren
has not been imprisoned!"

She looked puzzled. "For killing that youth? Oh, forgive me! As
a foreigner, of course you would be exempt from our laws. What
am I thinking of?"

A sonorous voice at her ear said, "Madame, whatever your
thoughts, they cannot fail to enchant by virtue of their delectable
instrument, your noble person. Perhaps I might beg to be presented?"

The speaker could only be the seventh man, he of the Italian-
French. She turned, amused, and felt her confidence dwindle.

The florid words had not come from a smiling gallant, but from
a man in his early to middle fifties, whose substantial height was
only matched by his stoutness. The fur-trimmed velvet which fell
to the ground would have made the sails for a good-sized cargo
vessel, except that few fleet-owners could have afforded its price.
The jewelled chain round his shoulders was worth a castle and the
fur on his plain hat was sable. Below it, his clean-shaven face was
many-chinned like some fat friar's, but unlike the traditional fat
friar, held no geniality. The lips which had paid her the compliment were politely smiling, but the eyes were wintry.

"Ah, your pardon." The Duchess's secretary. "Madama Katelina, may I present le sire Jordan, vicomte de Ribérac? Monseigneur lives in France, and is here on business to do with the galleys. Monseigneur, Der Florence van Borselen and his elder daughter Katelina. And Madama, may I make known Messer Orlando and Messer Piero of the Flanders galleys?"

A slight movement of the fat man's broad shoulders appeared to constitute a bow. "Then continue, Madame Katelina, with your lively history," said the vicomte. "A Scottish war has broken out, here in Bruges?"

Someone laughed—the Lucchese Arnolfini. "Not quite, monseigneur. An episode involving an apprentice with no harm done on either side. Madame Katelina has clearly heard some false rumour."

"I am afraid she has," said Simon clearly. His face was still rather pale, with its frown firmly imprinted. He said, "Indeed, I see friends I must rejoin. Will you excuse me?"

He turned without waiting for leave. "Friends?" said Katelina as he passed her. And in a voice pitched to carry no farther, "Female friends, perhaps? The other kind seem to be lacking."

He paused. His back to the company, he kept his voice low, as hers was. He said, "Your apprentice friend has them too, you know. Indeed, you might well blame yourself for what happened to him. It was you, after all, who passed on his good opinion of me in the first place." Then she was left, frowning in her turn, gazing after him.

"Madame can tell us," said the mellow voice of the vicomte de Ribérac, again in her ear. She turned round resentfully. She understood, she thought, why Simon had looked so ruffled when she arrived. His anger had not been directed at her. And yet—he did have a temper. How had he discovered that it was the apprentice who had spoken those disparaging words in her hearing? It worried her. Because it made her responsible, too, for what had happened.

The fat man said, "Madame Katelina, you cannot leave us in suspense. Messer Orlando relates a wonderful tale of an apprentice attacked at shear-point by none other than our absent friend Simon. Can it be true?"

The tone was jocular. The eyes were not. Katelina said, "Messer Arnolfini is right. I know only by hearsay. My lord Simon conceived a dislike for an apprentice, and their paths crossed. There was a fight, which the apprentice lost. The stabbing was an accident, I am sure."

The vicomte de Ribérac's lips moved in a smile. "A feud between a nobleman and an apprentice! It would hardly happen in France. A youth is impertinent: he is beaten, not fought."

"Oh, Claes was beaten," said Katelina. "He replaced my lord Simon in the bed of a serving-girl and was responsible for the death of his dog. For both these things he was thoroughly beaten. And imprisoned."

"As is, surely, natural?" said the fat man. "Then the apprentice in turn, I deduce, tried to kill monsieur Simon? Messer Orlando?"

The Venetian in black damask put a finger to his beard, striving to understand. He said, "The fight? But it was the labourer, I am told, who wounded Messer the Scotsman with his shears. Messer the Scotsman, instead of having him killed, chose to fight him with staves, a weapon of the people. I consider this a mistake. A nobleman does not meddle with peasants. In the event, the youth received what he deserved."

"He was killed?" said the fat man.

"Nearly," said Katelina. "Because your noble Scotsman stabbed him with the same shears after beating him nearly to death."

The fat man smiled, and then turned to Vasquez, Arnolfini and Florence van Borselen. "The customs of Burgundy! Well," he said. "Is this rumour or fact? Monsieur Simon, who could have told us, has unfortunately left. But perhaps he is merely being modest. To best a brutish child of the people with his own chosen weapon is something, surely?"

"And to stab him is something else," said Katelina coldly.

Her father said, "Katelina. You know that isn't true. The shears became entangled between them. And the apprentice stabbed Simon in the first place."

"Did he?" said Katelina. "The *rumour* I heard said that it was an accident."

The cold eyes remained on her face. "You sound, madame," said the vicomte de Ribérac, "as if you were no friend to our noble young Scotsman."

She stared him back. "Then you are right," said Katelina. "I happen to think him—to know him—to be a self-indulgent, vindictive rake."

"So I thought. What a pity it all is," said the fat French nobleman, and heaved a deep sigh. "When you, my dear madame, comprise in all your magnificent parts my perfect ideal of a daughter-in-law."

Somewhere, trumpets sounded. The conversation in the great hall began to lessen. People moved, to make way for the Controller, for the Dauphin, for the brother of the King of Scots. People began to take their places to walk, two by two to the banquet. Only around one small group did complete silence fall; did no one move.

As if alone, Katelina van Borselen and the gross man called Jordan de Ribérac gazed at one another.

"What a pity," repeated the fat man, with no emphasis. "For—perhaps I should have told you? Forgive me if I did not think to tell you—your self-indulgent, vindictive rake . . . really? How very sad!—is my son."

It was Katelina's father, she realised afterwards, who, apologising with chilly courtesy, extracted her and led her to take her place in the movement to table. It was her father who, after conversing as duty demanded with his dinner partners, turned to her during the elaborate meal and said, "You were at fault, as you well know, in expressing immoderate opinions of absent persons in such company. But the greater fault lay with the Frenchman, in allowing such a discussion to take place without revealing his interest."

Then Katelina, who had thought of nothing else, said, "How could he be his father?"

Florence van Borselen said, "I have enquired. I, too, feel I have been misled. I was informed quite clearly that Simon of Kilmirren was nephew and heir of Alan, lord of that property, and that his own father, Alan's younger brother long living in France, was either dead or incompetent."

Katelina shivered. "Incompetent," she said, "is not the word I would have chosen."

Her father moved angrily. "I can certainly think of a better," he said. "There is a man over there, Andro Wodman, a Scot living in France who is here in Jordan de Ribérac's retinue. The vicomte, he tells me, was landless and of small fortune as a young man. He made his way then to France, fought for the King, gained a favoured place in the Scots Guard and, with advancing years, was given the estate of Ribérac by his grateful monarch. There he has invested his newly made fortune in trade and shipping and other such interests.

"He is a wealthy man now. King Charles leans on him as his

adviser. When the Flanders galleys come in from Venice, or the Florentine, or the carracks from Cyprus, M. le vicomte sends his factor to Flanders, but rarely comes himself. He and his son, Wodman says, have not met for many years, but de Ribérac keeps himself informed of all Simon does. His good name, as you see, is of importance to him."

"And Simon resents him," said Katelina.

"He would do well to hide it," said her father dryly. "From what I can see, he has in his father a powerful and unquestioning ally whom he may one day come to need. For instance, you had the vicomte's favour, it seems."

"And have forfeited it, it seems," said Katelina. "Are you as grateful as I am? Or would you have enjoyed including Jordan de Ribérac in the family circle?"

As it sometimes did, honesty overcame expediency in Florence van Borselen. "No," he said at length. "No. I cannot see myself or your mother, in truth, entertaining that man under my roof now or at any time in the future. There is something unnatural there."

"Then—" said Katelina; and did not need to finish, for her father put his hand over hers.

"Then," he said, "if you dislike Simon so much, I shall not force you. There is time. We shall find you a better husband, and one suitable yet."

The exodus to Sluys came later, by decorated barges and skiffs, making their way by glittering torchlight along the river, through the Damme gate of Bruges and out by the canal to where the two Flanders ships lay outlined in light.

Moving along the canopied deck of the flagship, winecup in hand, the chosen guests would watch from the rail as sailors performed high on the rigging of the sister-ship, and tumblers somersaulted, and tightrope walkers moved dancing from mast to mast, and from mast to quay. And the walls and wharves of Sluys itself would be packed with all those who had not been invited, but who flocked every year to the extravagant theatre brought them every year by the generous, the hospitable, the inestimable Republic of Venice.

Only Katelina did not go. Pleading indisposition, she received no reproaches from her father, who understood perfectly, and who was content to have her taken back to his house by two stout men at arms and her own sensible maidservant. He did not know, therefore, when she changed her mind, and instead of making directly home, had them take her to the dyeing establishment of Marian de Charetty.

The iron lantern over the courtyard doorway was lit, but knocking at first brought no response. She had turned to leave when light footsteps approached on the other side of the door, and a woman's voice made itself heard in civil apology, overlaid by the sound of withdrawing bolts.

The door, when it opened, revealed the short, neat person of Marian de Charetty herself, lamp in hand and, after the first flash of surprise, pleasantly collected. The Widow said, "Madame Katelina! Forgive me—all my household are off to gape at the galleys at Sluys. Please come in. What can I do to serve you?"

Katelina paused in the courtyard, her maid standing beside her. "It's late. I'm sorry. I wonder if your apprentice is here?" she said directly.

"This way. Please," said the widow Charetty. Holding open the door of her house, she ushered her visitor through a passage and up a few steps to a low-ceiling room where a fire burned and a single, high-backed chair littered with papers showed where she had been sitting. Clearing these with one hand, she gestured to Katelina to sit, and directed her maid to a stool in the background. Then, still standing herself, she said, "I have several apprentices, madame, and all but Claes are at Sluys. Which did you wish to see?"

Things done on impulse are not always easy to carry through. Her head in its elaborate veiling held high, Katelina said, "I have just heard in a little more detail what befell your apprentice Claes at Sluys. I feel some responsibility . . . The disagreement which led to his injury began with another incident in which I was involved. I wished to ask how he was."

The round high-coloured face opposite her broke into an open smile. "Don't blame yourself," said the widow Charetty. "There are few people as exasperating as Claes in the midst of some prank. He brings most of it on himself. And he is much better. Well enough indeed to have gone to Sluys, but the physician thought it best to harbour his strength for the journey. Wait. I shall call him. You will see for yourself."

"Journey?" said Katelina. But the Widow had gone, and when she came back, it was to usher the large figure of Claes himself to stand before Katelina.

Because, she supposed, he was not working in the yard, he was better-smelling than usual, in worn doublet and hose which were clean, and showed no change that she could see in the physique beneath them, which was broadly powerful. Lifting her eyes to his face she thought at first, on her little acquaintance with it, that nothing had altered. Then, as a log shifted, she saw by the flame that his eyes were set deeper than she remembered. Then the dimples appeared, like two thumbprints, and he said, "But how kind of the lady to trouble! Or was it by wish of my lord Simon? I heard Controller Bladelin had invited him."

Beside Katelina, Marian de Charetty's lips tightened. It was enough to set the thing in proportion. Amused, Katelina said, "That's the second time this evening I have been put in my place. The first time it was my lord Simon, as you call him."

"One must call him something," said the apprentice.

Marian de Charetty, sitting, said, "We hoped the matter was over. It created more gossip than it was worth."

"It will die when Simon has gone," Katelina said. "And Claes is leaving also?"

"Very shortly," said the widow de Charetty. "He is forsaking the dye vats for Italy." She glanced, smiling at her apprentice. "He is joining my captain, Astorre, on a journey to Milan. If it falls out as we hope, he may make his career in the field for a season. He is, you will agree, built for it?"

That, at least, was true. Gazing at the pleasant, firelit face of the apprentice, Katelina wondered what therefore seemed odd about the arrangement. Claes had never fought, rumour said. He had hardly known what to do against Simon. An apprentice such as this had no training. She said, "You will have a lot to learn. Do you ride?"

The dimples deepened. He shook his head. He said, "They're planning to put the horse on my back."

Katelina removed her eyes. She said to the Widow, "You think it better for him to leave Bruges. I think you are probably right. He has an enemy, I'm afraid, in my lord Simon, and another in the vicomte his father."

Chafed by her own recent ignorance she was soothed to note that here, too, there had fallen the silence of bafflement. The widow of Charetty said, "My lord Simon's father?"

"Jordan de Ribérac. He was at the banquet tonight. I'm told he lives in France."

"And he shares his son's . . . attitude towards Claes?" said the Widow.

"Yes. As I have cause to know," said Katelina abruptly. She turned to the apprentice, who appeared to have left the discussion. "There is something I have to apologise for. I quoted an expression of yours—an uncomplimentary expression—to my lord Simon. I did not tell him its source, but he seems to have discovered. Part of his anger against you is because of that. I am sorry."

He stirred, and then smiled fleetingly at her. "But there's no need. If it's the expression I think, I called him that myself on another occasion. An occasion which by itself angered him a good deal more, I think, than the names he was hearing. Don't concern yourself. And especially, don't fall out with my lord Simon or his father on my account."

Katelina stared back at him. Forgetting her training she said, "I don't need your account to bear the brunt of any falling-out between me and that precious pair. If I were an official of Bruges, I'd expel them."

He did not answer or smile. The Widow said gently, "I think, Claes, you should thank the lady and return to your room, unless she has more to say to you. Madame Katelina? You would allow him?"

He had been standing. She should have remembered his sickness. But one does not ask an artisan to sit, except among children. She said, "I'm sorry. I hope your health is restored in full, quickly. And that you prosper in your new occupation."

He thanked her briefly, and left. After he had gone, Katelina sat gazing at the wine the Widow had poured for her and said, "You will miss him, I imagine. Despite all the trouble, he is an amusing fellow."

There was a little silence. Then the Widow said, "Yes. He is an unusual being. The trouble is . . . The trouble really is that he cannot protect himself."

Katelina smiled. "Well, he will be able to do that very soon," she said. "He will make a good soldier."

"No," said the Widow, and her chestnut brows drew together, as she tried to make her meaning plain. "It is not that he can't protect himself, but that he won't. He is like a dog. He thinks every man is his friend."

But one did not devote thought, like that, to an apprentice. Or if one did, one did not discuss it with an acquaintance. "And every woman too, by all accounts!" said Katelina, smiling. "Indeed, it is time that boy left Bruges and learned common sense. Now tell me your plans for this son of yours. What about Felix?"

She did not know, after she left, how long Marian de Charetty stood in her doorway, looking across the deserted courtyard, before she came in at length and, shutting the door, made her way back to her room.

On the way, she passed the foot of the stairs to the apprentices' quarters and stopped for a moment, as if divining the quality of the silence which, upstairs and downstairs, invested all the rooms of her house.

Then she went, alone, back to her room, and sat down in the chair, and picked up and spread open her papers.

Chapter 10

A bold little businesswoman, that Marian de Charetty, the burghers of Bruges said to one another. Sending her captain and the pick of her company off over the Alps before Christmas. And her notary, who probably knew more of her business than she did. And persuading the Medici and the Doria and the Strozzi to confide their goods and their letters to the same Astorre, together with anyone else who had to travel south and wanted a safe journey. A gamble her man would never have taken, the Widow's friends said, compressing their shaven chins inside their furry collars. But a gamble, mind you, that might make her a fair fortune if they came back.

As the notary in question, Julius felt less alarm than they did. It was unpleasant, but nothing amazing to cross the mountains in winter, and in the short, bow-legged and violent Astorre they had the most experienced of caravan leaders. Whatever it looked like, assembling in the yard in a mess of carts and mules and sumpter horses and crates and barrels and packages, the cavalcade would be licked into shape long before it had completed the jolting three-week journey south through the lands of Burgundy to the freezing, windy and lucrative city of Geneva, where all the merchants and half the goods in the carts were to be deposited.

After that, sure enough, they had the long lake to skirt, and then the plunge up through the snow to the pass that would take them to Italy. But by then it would be a Charetty party. Astorre and his twelve cavalry and his six mounted bowmen and his eighteen varlets with their horses and mules. And with them (because Astorre was a man with a passion for food) an energetic Swiss cook called Lukin. And Astorre's smith, a German called Manfred. And Astorre's deputy, a grim-faced English professional who answered to Thomas, to whom poor Claes had been presented as helper and pupil. Felix had grudged that. Felix's face, watching Julius and Claes riding out of the yard, had been a study of anger and wistfulness.

All the men were familiar to Julius. Between contracts they

came about Bruges or Louvain, and he interviewed them and paid them. He had assumed that was to be the total of the party, before he heard the Widow's new plans. But not a bit of it. They now had a black servant. The one who had dived for the goblet. The one the pawnbroker Oudenin had given the Widow. And whom the Widow, not wishing to offend minen heere Oudenin or be indebted to him too greatly either, had sent on the expedition. A touch of luxury.

Nor was that all. They had the offices of a monk. A musical monk called Brother Gilles who, inconveniently, was part of the Medici consignment for Florence. In addition to three suits of tapestry, a quantity of Paris goldsmithwork embedded in fleeces, a satchel of letters and four expensive hackneys with breakable legs, a gift for Cosimo's nephew, Pierfrancesco.

And finally, and almost as disturbing, the bald-headed physician Tobias. Who had fallen out, it seemed, with the captain Lionetto and had applied, with success, to serve his rival Astorre instead. It was Master Tobie, indeed, who was busiest on the trip to Geneva, cutting lay corns and administering purges, or powders which, it was hoped, would produce the opposite effect. Julius, observing the daily training of Claes, was reassured when the surgeon showed no alarm, even in the earliest days when the embittered Thomas showed him small mercy.

Kill or cure it undoubtedly was, considering the sickbed Claes had left behind him; but it was amazing how weapon-play hardened him. The more punishment he got, the quicker he became to avoid it. And soon he could hang on to his horse at a gallop, even when they made his saddle fall off. You would see him jolting along, the iron brim of his round basin-hat clapping up and down on his nose like a pot-lid. It made everyone cheerful.

Later, Thomas found the boy an old two-handed sword and showed him a few tricks with his own blade before he knocked him out with the flat of it. And the horse-soldiers, discovering Claes didn't bear them a grudge and was a born teller of jokes into the bargain, accepted him round the fire in whatever barn they got into for the night (while Astorre and Thomas and the rest, naturally, slept five to the bed in the comfort of the inn) and were easier on him next day. Even the African seemed to take to him, and had to be beaten once or twice for sneaking off to the barn instead of staying on the floor beside Julius' bed.

He and Claes appeared to converse mainly in sign language and

Catalan, which they all knew bits of from Lorenzo. He was a very large negro, with shoulders like mattresses, and Brother Gilles was afraid of him and prayed when he came too near, which the negro seemed to enjoy. So they rode on sedately south, glittering with helmet, cuirass and leg-armour under the banner of Astorre, nobly horsed, with the nose-piece of his helmet supplying a profile of astonishing dignity, considering the convulsed and furious face that worked beneath it.

On the way to Geneva, Claes was thrown to the bowmen, and it was discovered that he had an accurate eye, which allowed a respite to some of his bruises. This lasted for a day, at the end of which an outburst of maniac inventiveness got him thrashed by Astorre himself. It had very little effect. His superabundant energy, it was apparent, had returned. He was cured. That was the night before they entered Geneva. Once settled in their chosen inn, the doctor tossed a phial-end of salve to Julius' African and told him to smear some on Claes' lacerations. The black man, who answered to Loppe rather than Lopez, appeared to understand well enough, and went off with it. The doctor said, "You know Geneva well and so do I, but what must these two, Loppe and Claes, make of it all? Or do we keep them too busy to think?"

Julius had been wary of Tobie at first. Astorre still thought he was a spy, and fingered his half-ear when Tobie contradicted him. Tobie had a tongue in his head like a whiplash but had shown no interest, till now, in the Charetty family. And even now, his box on a bench, the doctor was only chatting while working.

Julius was working too, a ledger laid on his knees and his tender backside sunk in a cushion. "Oh, Claes knows Geneva," said Julius. "Poor bastard. He was dragged up in the kitchens of the Fleury family till they kicked him out and Corneille de Charetty took him in as an apprentice. The Widow's sister married into the Fleury."

"Why did they kick him out?" said the doctor absently. He had cleared a space on the commonroom stool for his bowl and pestle, and was blending powders, crushing and grinding with circular movements, the candlelight glowing on his toughened, bald scalp.

"Why did he get a thrashing today? Too much energy and no sense of direction," said Julius. "Also, a peculiar household. Wait till you meet Esota."

"Esota?" He went on grinding.

"Wife of Jaak de Fleury. Jaak, the head of the business. Old

Thibault's sick; stays outside Dijon; does nothing now. Jaak runs it all. Was running it when I was there as his notary. Claes had gone by that time. I stuck it a year, until I heard there was work at the Charetty."

The blending was finished. Tobie released his spatula and exercised his fingers, looking up. He had the most unremarkable face Julius had ever seen. Sheathed in fine, spindrift hair, the bald head descended through a flat, faintly-lined brow to colourless eyebrows, round pale eyes and a small spare mouth, tinted pink. Its single decorative note was formed by the pads of his nostrils, which were round and fleshy and curled, like two notes of music. Tobie said, "We have to go there, don't we? How do you feel about meeting them?"

"Oh, we didn't quarrel," said Julius. "I left to be tutor to Felix. Jaak was angry because he was losing me, and he doesn't like the Charetty family—the demoiselle's sister was only a second wife, and the Fleury don't really recognise the relationship. But Corneille de Charetty was useful as a Bruges agent: buying stuff like pewter from England for de Fleury's clients, or herring or pictures or painted canvas. And in return, Jaak sells Charetty cloth at the Geneva fairs on commission. So he complained—didn't he!—when I left, but he didn't want to fall out with Corneille."

"So of course you don't mind going back," said the doctor. "Well-found, with authority, the notary of a promising war-band with excellent prospects. He'll regret even more that he lost you." He leaned forward and, lifting his bowl, began to fill a jar methodically with its scourings.

Julius gave a wry smile. "It will be amusing," he said. "I suppose it's Claes one should be sorry for. Poor bastard. Eight years later, and look at him. They'll be glad they got rid of him when they did."

Tobias said, "Well, you saved the boy's life there at Sluys. He seems quite attached to you. Is he frightened now? What will he do when he comes face to face with this family?"

"Smile," said Julius.

The doctor raised his brows. He said, resting his hands on his knees, "You make him sound simple. From all I hear of him, he can be highly ingenious when he wants to be."

"Well, of course he is," said Julius, irritated. "He's picked up reading and writing, and scraps from the classes at Louvain as Felix's servant. The Widow's harsh, but she's never stopped him improving himself. I've taught him myself. He's good at numbers. In fact, that's what he's best at."

"And still a dyer's apprentice?" said the doctor.

Julius' annoyance changed to amusement. "Well, can you see Claes in clerical company?" he said. "He'd empty anyone's office in a trice. He likes his life. He's happy. I sometimes wish that he wasn't. He lets other people do what they like with him. If he settled down and applied himself, he could get the better of them sometimes at least."

The doctor was mildly interested. "So," he said. "This sudden plunge into soldiering. Is it his idea? Or the only way the demoiselle could get rid of him?"

"Oh, the demoiselle," Julius said. "Bruges complained. Someone had to knock him into shape. And at least, now he's learning to defend himself."

"So I see. I hope my salve lasts out," said the doctor. "And what if he turns to the attack one of these days?"

"I wish he would," Julius said. "We all wish he would. I'd support him. In fact, if he really put his mind to it, I can tell you, I shouldn't care to be one of his targets."

"Yes," said Tobie thoughtfully. "I agree. He's a big fellow, Claes. I wonder if the demoiselle has really been wise? To put a sword in his hand instead of a dyestick?"

Julius didn't trouble to answer. Claes was Claes. Julius knew him, and Tobie didn't. All you could do was keep pushing him, and hope that one day he would take the initiative.

They passed through the gates of Geneva next day, with the dazzle of Alpine snows on the skyline, and the wind blowing straight off them. Not a big town, clinging to its steep hill at the end of the lake, but built where it mattered: where roads and rivers led north to France and southeast to Italy and south to Marseilles and the Middle Sea, and merchants from all these places could meet, and exchange goods, and spend money. The big stone fortified houses with their tower-staircases and their vast cellars belonged to the merchants, and there were well-kept quays down on the lake, and inns and warehouses and well-built market booths at the Molard, near the Madeleine, and rows of notary-benches up in the square by St Peter. But the burgess houses were narrow, and only of wood. Not all the town shared the wealth of the merchants.

Surrounded by traders, Geneva was also surrounded by predators. The Dukes of Savoy might currently control the city, appoint the Bishops of Geneva; name their sons as its Counts. But France's unstable monarch had a greedy eye on these Fairs which milked off the trade of French Lyons. And the Duke of Savoy was not always very wise. He had given help to the Dauphin, the King of France's estranged son, now sheltered by Burgundy. He had let the Dauphin marry Charlotte, the Duke of Savoy's plain young daughter. Periodically, the King of France leaned on the Duke of Savoy, and Savoy and Geneva periodically stopped plotting and cowered. They were too vulnerable to be brave about it.

Which was why, to be sure, the traders who dabbled in banking and the bankers who dabbled in trading tended to have, always, stout branches elsewhere. At the first breath of a threat, the assets of the Medici mysteriously would transport themselves in the form of ledger books and anonymous paper over the Alps to the safety of Florence and Venice and Rome. The house of Thibault and Jaak de Fleury hedged its bets through its connection with Bruges and Burgundy through the Charetty company. But it was very careful to keep the esteem of Charles of France.

So reflected Julius as the cavalcade wound its way, mules, wagons, soldiers and all, up the steep streets towards the Hôtel de Fleury where it was to unload and disperse. Claes, he saw, was quite near, labouring seriously on his horse, tin hat on his nose. On impulse, Julius said, "This is no pleasure for you, meeting Monsieur and Madame de Fleury again. I'm not looking forward to it either. They were severe with you."

Claes' caterpillar lips, expanding, paralleled the rim of his helmet. He said, "Oh, I forget. I got used to the hobble. And they always brought my head back in the morning until the string broke."

"They treated you like a serf," Julius said. "Even after you left, people talked about it. Don't you bear them a grudge?"

"I'll try," said Claes, "if you want me to."

"Don't be silly," said Julius shortly.

He spurred on. He reminded himself. Talking to Claes was a mistake.

Since, teasingly, the Charetty notary had not described the Fleury family in any detail, the surgeon Tobie was curious. He was curious, primarily, about Julius himself, who seemed an extraordinary mixture of innocence and ambition. The widow de Charetty, Tobie guessed, had disappointed Julius in some way. Now he appeared to

hope his fortune was going to be made in the train of a great
mercenary company. He was a good accountant, and he was possibly right. Tobie, with a year's experience of Lionetto's unlovely
ways, recognised in captain Astorre a man of equal ambition and
perhaps equal lack of principle, but with a rough regard for the
rights of his men which Lionetto had never troubled with. Before
age overtook him, Astorre wanted, Tobie guessed, the big prizes
that had so far eluded him—the great reputation, the statue in the
market place with laurels on it. Half a day in Astorre's company,
and he was sure of it.

Tobie knew Astorre was watching him, and moderated his own
abrasive style not at all. If Astorre didn't want him, he could say
so. But he would want him. Tobie knew about Lionetto, who was
after the big prizes also, and who had sworn to get in Astorre's way
if he hindered him. Some time, when he trusted him, Astorre
would ask Tobie about Lionetto. Meanwhile, at the thought of
Lionetto, Tobie's back occasionally twitched.

But Astorre would keep him, of course, for even better reasons.
Tobie was the finest surgeon this side of the Alps, and maybe beyond them. Maybe. That, in a way, was what he was trying to
prove. There was no medical crisis known to man that you didn't
come across treating an army, except maybe childbirth. He had
worked in a kind of furious ecstasy all the past year, and had found
out things and done things he hadn't believed possible. Including
curing the boy, which had led to his being here. The boy Claes,
who must come to no harm in the house of the Fleury. Or at least,
not until he and Tobie had had a talk about hair dye, and love
potions, and holly.

The Hôtel de Fleury was massive. The yard swallowed their cavalcade: the cellars accepted, in their various quarters, the furs from
the Doria and the barrels of salmon from the Strozzi; the goods
from the Charetty which Jaak was to market; the consignments
from the five merchants who had travelled with them and who
would pay, heavily, for the privilege of warehousing until the next
Fair.

The goods for Italy were stored in yet another area, ready for
transfer to packmules for the Alpine crossing, and the Lorrainer
carters paid off with their wagons and beasts. The horses for Pierfrancesco, with care, were led to the stables and housed with Jaak
de Fleury's own.

The consignment they called Brother Gilles, with less care, was required to wait in the biting wind in the emptying courtyard, listening to the raucous voice of the Fleury steward and his henchmen and the dwindling noise of the men at arms as they were led off to their quarters. At last, none was left in the yard but the captain Astorre, his deputy Thomas with Claes, Julius with his African servant, the silent, shivering singer, and Tobie. Then, and only then, the massive double doors of the Hôtel de Fleury creaked and opened: a servitor, bowing, stood back, and there emerged on the threshold the magnificent person of Jaak de Fleury.

Magnificent, thought Tobie Beventini, was the word. Not in the way of Popes or Doges, a tribute to status, to trappings, although this man had both. Magnificent in physique and in presence: a being to command. Jaak de Fleury was taller than most, and built like an athlete at the peak of his powers. His shoulders were of a breadth to wear like thistledown a gown of double cut-velvet lined with the finest of sables. His face below its wide jewelled hat was smooth and tanned and heavily handsome: the nose solid and straight in the French manner; the eyes dark and intelligent; the well-shaped lips smiling; the smile itself serviced by gleaming whorls: round the lip-corners, under the high, solid cheekbones, extending the full, well-lashed eyes.

Jaak de Charetty said, "Well, Astorre my poor man, how late you are. To be expected, of course. I expect you tried to tear yourself away from your employer as best you could. The ladies, God bless them, and fools that they are. You had better come to my bureau and—ah, I see my little notary with you. Both of you. My wife is somewhere, and will look after the rest of you. Is that a heathen I see? Not in the house, surely. Or the knave."

"They both come indoors," said Julius. The hardness of his voice surprised Tobie. Julius added, "The servant is mine, and is Christian. The young man is Claes."

"Claes?" said Jaak de Fleury without interest. His steward waited for orders, a bone-cracking grip on Loppe's arm and another on Claes' nearest shoulder.

"He lived with you," Julius said.

The luminous eyes studied Claes, from the dented bowl on his head to the stained and battered links of his shirt-mail, the uneven hem of his doublet, the darned stuff of his hose and the scuffed, borrowed boots on his feet.

"So many did," said Jaak de Fleury. "Which was this? The one who stole? They all did. The one who claimed my wife raped him? No, that was you, Master Julius, was it not? The one with the unusual rapport with the farmyard? Yes, that was Claes. I sent him, as I remember, where pissing might serve a purpose. To the Charetty dyeshop. How well I see he has turned out."

The notary had said Claes would smile, and Tobias saw that he was right. The smile was perfectly open, with neither guilt nor confusion behind it. Claes said, "All your training, grand-uncle. I told them."

"Grand-uncle?" said the merchant. He drew back and then yielded smoothly to laughter. "An intended insult, I suppose. An instruction from the Widow to embarrass me. Well it might, if you were my bastard and not my late niece's. But as it is, I forgive you. A light beating, Agostino; and lock the boy in the barn. Come. I am cold."

"Monseigneur, so are we all," said the voice of Astorre, hoarsely bland. He raised his short arms. With no apparent effort, the slave Loppe was disengaged from the steward's grasp with one hand, and the shoulder of Claes claimed with the other. "Don't concern yourself with this rubbish. It belongs to us, and will serve us indoors. There is a singer for Cosimo de' Medici dying of cold. Do we stand here all day?"

The fine eyes of Jaak de Fleury stared at the captain. He said, "You would loose these brutes in my house? For what harm they do, I expect compensation."

"You will have it," said Astorre. "Now, can we enter? There is business."

"Ah yes, there is business," said Jaak de Fleury. "Women's business at that. How charming they are in their innocence. God asks us to protect them, and we will. But who will repay us the cost of it? Not the heir. Not the delightful young gentleman Felix, with his beardless pranks. And so, dear Julius, they can no longer pay you your wages? You have to fight for a living like the brutes you professed to despise. How sad. And who is that man?"

Tobie said, "A physician. Tobias Beventini, Monsieur de Fleury."

The eyes trained themselves directly upon him. "A relative?" said Jaak de Fleury. "A relative of Jean-Mathieu Ferrari?"

No one else had asked him that. "A nephew," said Tobie. He could feel Julius looking at him.

"Trained in Pavia?"

"Yes, monsieur," said the doctor. "I am under contract to captain Astorre. I wish battle experience."

"Your uncle would not agree," said the merchant.

"Fortunately," said Tobie, "it is my affair and not his. My present concern is the monk here. The cold air could damage his throat. Messer Cosimo would be disappointed."

"It is of no matter to me," said Jaak de Fleury. "The Medici are my debtors. Signor Nori is responsible for the Geneva branch of the Medici. Signor Sassetti, once the manager, sometimes visits him. One or other of them will call soon, for their documents. Nori, plenty of money and always ailing. There's a gold mine for you. Sell him a cure. He'll pay. Sell him a cure for anything: he's convinced he has every disease there's a name for. Go that way. My wife will take care of you."

He walked off, with Astorre and the notary following. No Madame de Fleury appeared. After a moment, catching the eye of the Englishman Thomas, Tobie entered the house, his hand on Brother Gilles' elbow. Thomas followed, with the big African and Claes walking slowly behind, looking about them. A staircase offered, and Tobie was making towards it when a quick movement arrested him. From behind a door, drawn by the youth Claes, came the frightened figure of a middle-aged woman, one reddened hand clutching her apron.

"She doesn't recognise me," said Claes, grinning down at her. "Claikine, Tasse. Remember Claikine, aged ten? The boiled eggs under the broody hen?"

"Claikine!" The formless face, rough as pastry, divided into planes of amazement, and then recognition, and then pleasure. "Claikine, grown!"

"Like a hedge. The whole tale of my successes. And how is Tasse?" She dropped her apron and Claes put both big hands under her armpits and swung her up in the air. She gasped, and beamed, and gasped, and her hair fell out of its coif in grey ribbons.

From the doorway came another gasp. Hard on the gasp came a scream. "Murder! Rapine! Robbery!" screamed Madame de Fleury.

Chapter II

It could, thought Tobie, be no one else, even before Esota de Fleury moved from the doorway and into the light. The brush of a heavy gown, the glimmer of a jewelled collar, the scent of imported essences—that was Madame, or a mistress. And nobody had talked of a mistress. And then the not unmusical voice, trembling with fright: "Husband! Men in the house! Oh Tasse, Tasse, you are ruined!"

Her voice rose, in a way with which Tobie was familiar. He said, "Put that woman down!" to the youth Claes. He was aware of a tinge of professional pride that, so soon after his recovery, Claes could lift a full-grown woman and hold her. Then he started towards the agitated Madame de Fleury, who immediately fainted. Tobie caught her, staggering a trifle, and lowered her to the tiled floor. Claes, his smile gone, ceased hugging the servant Tasse and set her upright. The negro Loppe, without being told, took a lamp from its bracket and brought it over. Tobie leaned over Jaak de Fleury's helpmeet.

He expected to see, without doubt, a large woman. What else he saw was unaccountable. If her husband was, as he seemed, about fifty years old, Madame de Fleury was thirty or less, her skin unlined, her hair, uncovered and dressed as for a party with ribbons, a rich glossy brown. In a mask, apart from a certain lack of proportion, she might have raised a man's hopes. Without one, there was no denying that she was ugly. Gazing down at the bladdered nose and the great jaw, the low sloping brow and the thumbnail eyes, tightly shut, Tobie wondered, mildly, what the size of her dowry had been to persuade Jaak de Fleury to marry her. Below the face, the solid body was encumbered in velvet. Childless, the notary had said. And decked in emeralds. One of her hands, blindly raised, was groping towards him. He put his own over it. "Don't be afraid. We are guests, Madame de Fleury. From Bruges. From your kinswoman Marian de Charetty."

Her eyes opened, and then her mouth, on a large framework of teeth. She said, "Tasse. He was assaulting her."

Tobie slid his arm round her shoulders and helped her, with some trouble, to sit up. "He was greeting her," he said. "Don't you see who it is?" He was aware that, behind him, the Englishman Thomas stood impatiently scowling, while the negro Loppe had retired with care to the shadows.

Claes and the serving-woman stood side by side. The servant, who looked frightened, glanced at the youth. Claes had rested his gaze on the reclining woman. His expression was blank and without dimples, and his mouth occupied less of its line than was normal. Then of a sudden, in its familiar way it expanded. Claes said, "You won't catch me ravishing anyone with Julius around. He's the expert on that. Shall I fetch him for you?"

And the woman frowned, and moved weakly within Tobie's grasp, and then said, "Little Claikine?"

"No. Big Claes," said the apprentice calmly. He did not approach.

The woman gasped. "I feel . . ."

"Let me take you to your chamber," said Tobie. "I'm a physician. Your husband should have warned you of our arrival."

The mountainous face turned up to him, eyes timid. "I forget," she said. "He is busy. Wine for his guests. My servants . . ."

"They will look after us. There's plenty of time for that. Now. You should be in your bedchamber. I'll help you. Thomas, Claes, Loppe—stay till I come back."

He observed, as he helped her out, the glance she cast over her shoulder at Claes. But Claes, he saw, had already backed himself discreetly to share a wall space with Loppe, and was murmuring to him, and grinning. He thought he caught the reflection of his own voice. Tobie, labouring to lead the invalid lady of Fleury to her room, was conscious that this time, perhaps, he had uncovered a pattern of relationships which would have been better left alone. He could deal with it. He knew his own competence. But this—this did not promise to be pleasant.

It fulfilled its promise. The mistress of the house, excusing herself, was absent from supper. The master, when he eventually emerged with Astorre and the notary Julius, looked strongly displeased, and confined himself at table to biting courtesies. The inferiors Loppe and Claes, if they ate at all, were not visible, and Thomas, who was, soon learned to keep his mouth shut. The master of Fleury had no time to waste on the emissaries of his non-relative Marian de Charetty, and now their business was done, wished to be rid of them. A thing denied him until tomorrow, when Francesco Nori of the Medici would call on them.

They shared two bedchambers, as was natural, Astorre and the Englishman in one, with Claes on the floor; and Tobie and Julius in the other, attended by Loppe. Tobie, uneasily served by his digestion, made his way through the night to the appointed place in the yard and found himself accosted, returning, by a shrouded figure he recognised, alarmed, as his hostess. She, no less alarmed, muttered apologies and hurried off, her robes trailing. He took the trouble, before lying down, to check the whereabouts of all his party. In his own room, Julius snored, and so did Loppe. In the next chamber, sleep had claimed both Astorre and his deputy, but had apparently escaped the former apprentice Claes, who was nowhere to be seen.

He slept, and woke to an empty room and the sounds of pandemonium. He lay, waiting. It was Julius, finally, who opened the door and sat by his mattress, irony on his handsome face. "You hear?"

"I dare not imagine," said the doctor, "what has happened. But I might guess. Madame has been ravished?"

The straight-nosed, classical face relaxed its grimness. "I suppose you've met this before."

"It is common," said Tobie. "By the negro this time, perhaps?"

The face opposite him was bitter. "Where would be the pleasure in that?" said the notary.

Tobie sat up.

"Not—"

"Of course," said Julius. "Claes."

"What will happen?"

Julius said, "That depends on M. Jaak. If he insists, it will be a long imprisonment. Or they'll mutilate." He paused. "Astorre will try to prevent it. I'll do more. I shall see that they don't."

Tobie had met this kind of calm before, too. He said, "You won't help him by laying yourself open to punishment. Astorre has only to swear that the boy never left the bedchamber. Can't he do that?"

"Astorre and Thomas went to bed drunk," Julius said. "Everyone saw it. They wouldn't have noticed if Claes had brought Esota into the same bed and forced her between them."

The doctor studied him. "When he met us, M. Jaak referred to another incident. He accused you, I take it falsely. This, therefore, is something Madame de Fleury is accustomed to doing. Something of which her husband is well aware, and probably others. Would an accusation against the boy stand?"

"Oh yes," said Julius. "The lady has a reputation. That will spare Claes the ultimate penalty. But not the rest. He's rich, M. Jaak, and has the favour of the French king. And Claes was out of his room. So were you."

"Following Claes," said the doctor. "How can one explain such a coincidence? Unable to sleep, I visited the yard and finding him there, engaged him in conversation. It was dawn, I believe, before we returned, and fearing to waken his fellows, I invited him to return to my chamber. You must have seen him there yourself when you wakened."

A becoming colour had risen under the tanned skin of Julius. "And so," he said, "who visited Madame de Fleury?"

"A dream," said the doctor. "Unhappy creature, she is plainly subject to such things. I shall prescribe a soothing liquor. When I've informed our friend Claes of his own nocturnal movements. Where do you think I could find him?"

Perseverance being one of his attributes, Tobie discovered the locked cellar which contained the apprentice, and found his way, discreetly, to a useful barred window. It was close to the ground. When he sat down beside it and called, he was answered equally quietly. He was in time at least to prime Claes in his story, if not, he saw, to forestall his first beating from the de Fleury grooms. It was no more, said Claes a trifle shakily, than he had grown accustomed to from Thomas. And so where, asked Tobie mildly, had he actually been on the previous night? He gazed down into the cellar and Claes gazed up, Tobie's shadow on his disarming face.

A doctor is never surprised. Tobie Beventini was quite prepared to learn that something had taken place between his former patient and the woman de Fleury. She was quite capable of accosting the boy. The boy, for reasons of his own was quite capable, Tobie thought, of taking advantage of it. Revenge sometimes took curious forms. His reading of Claes was not the same as that of Julius.

Claes said, "She is abnormally made. He married her for her property."

"So?" said Tobie.

"So it helps her to believe she's desirable. Meester Julius knows. It's why he left. It's sad. But her husband exploits it."

"Then why should he accuse you?" Tobie said. "And where were you last night?"

"With their servants," said Claes. "But I wouldn't say so. I got away eight years ago, but many didn't. There's another niece . . . It doesn't matter. As for accusing me—it was just because I did get away. I have nothing to lose, so I might tell about Madame Esota's sickness."

"Sickness!" said Tobie.

Claes looked up at him sideways. "You're not ugly," he said. "Or married to Jaak de Fleury."

Tobie studied the boy. He said, "But for me, de Fleury would have destroyed you. Your notary friend too, very likely. You are very forgiving, my dear Claes. But if you don't take up your own battles, you leave a heavy task for your betters. Or perhaps that's what you want?"

Below him Claes moved, and straw rustled. Claes said, "Do you believe that? I hope not. I can't thank you enough for your trouble. But indeed, there was no need to do anything."

"Losing your nose or your hands wouldn't matter?"

Claes said, with diffidence, "It happens or it doesn't happen. It's for me to arrange, well or badly. Indeed. I appreciate what you did. A second rescue. But I don't mean to involve others this time."

"You haven't the choice," said Tobie. "No one has."

The other was silent. It was a deliberate silence. Tobie pressed him. "You'd never thought of that?" said Tobie.

"I think of people dependent on me," said Claes. The cellar was cold, but he sat quite still, his crossed arms tight round his body. "But no one needs to shoulder my burdens."

"Not even the people who are dependent on you?" said Tobie.

That disturbed the boy a little. He said, "You and Meester Julius are not."

"Perhaps not. But you are our conscience," said Tobie. "If we let injustice touch you, then we demean ourselves. Whether you want it or not, we have to interfere. As those who owe you something will do. You are not a free agent. Hasn't your employer told you as much, after one of those escapades of yours? But perhaps it's unfair to recall them. This time, there is no fault on your part. Therefore accept help willingly given."

"Help asked for, yes," said the boy. "Master Tobie . . ."

He could not fathom what the youth wanted. He waited.

"Master Tobie," said Claes. "These are unpleasant people, but to punish them isn't necessary. Especially to punish them mortally."

Tobie gazed down at M. Jaak's grand-nephew and prisoner. He said, "Who could punish them mortally?"

The face below him lightened a little. "The good Lord," said Claes. "Although you couldn't protect them from that. But someone, maybe, with potions."

"I see," said Tobie, and thought. Eventually, he said, "I don't see any danger of that. Don't trouble about it."

"Then I won't," said Claes, his upturned face smiling.

Tobie, leaving him, felt his own smile stiff on his face as he returned to his room, and his medicine chest. Nothing was missing, as yet. He locked the box . . . against whom? Astorre and his henchmen, objects of Jaak de Fleury's contempt? Master Julius, protective of Claes and vengeful on his own account? A plot of one of de Fleury's own abused servants, overheard in the kitchen? Or even Claes himself, afraid of being driven to the very kind of self-protection that he and Julius had been, in their exasperation, urging upon him?

But no. He didn't believe that. He didn't believe Claes was ever driven to do anything against his own judgment. He had only once seen him truly helpless, and that was on the quayside at Damme. His motive now was probably simpler than anything Tobie imagined. And sadder. For whoever harmed Jaak de Fleury or his wife, Claes would be blamed.

Thoughtfully, the doctor put the key in his pouch and went off to find his host, Jaak de Fleury, and make him party to the happy news of Claes' vindication. At first, M. Jaak would hardly believe that his wife had not been ravished. Indeed, unless you knew differently, you might almost think him disappointed. But when Tobie took him aside and explained the exact nature (in Latin) of Madame's unhappy illness, he began to recover his colour, and breathe more naturally, and even went the length (eventually) of thanking Tobie for his welcome diagnosis.

After a while, he recalled that the boy Claes was shut in a cellar, and sent to have him released. Asked about compensation to Claes for his beating, M. de Fleury promised to give the matter some thought. There was no sign that he did so. The only compensation Claes appeared to receive was the negative one of retaining his hands and his features. He emerged from the cellar some time later, with a little less than his usual ebullience but otherwise remarkably calm, and Tobie gave Loppe some more ointment. Then

Claes disappeared to the stables and the business of the morning began, almost as if nothing had happened.

No one suggested that the surgeon might visit his hostess in her chamber. In a way Tobie was sorry. He had been looking forward to asking her questions, with Julius on one side and her husband on the other to protect his character. Tobie found his way to the kitchens instead, and was given ale and a pie and had a long talk with the woman called Tasse, while Julius dealt with the representatives of the Medici, for whom Jaak de Fleury professed to care so little.

Many people might claim to despise the Medici, but few could afford to ignore them. In London, Bruges, Venice, Rome, Milan, Geneva, Avignon, their banks, carefully managed, controlled the business of nations. And the banks in their turn were controlled by the head of the family, that brilliant, gouty old man, Cosimo de' Medici, from his palace in Florence.

He had sons to succeed him. But better than that, generations of trained businessmen who followed each other from centre to centre. Julius knew some of them. The Portinari family, of whom Tommaso of the rings was the junior member, while his brothers looked after Milan. The Nori family, including old Simone of London and young Francesco here, many years in Geneva. And coming in with Francesco Nori at this moment, his senior Sassetti, just under forty, with his Roman nose and cropped curly hair, who bestowed on M. de Fleury the most sonorous and formal of greetings before turning to renew acquaintance, cordially, with Julius and clap the shoulder of Astorre, the Charetty captain.

Astorre had guarded consignments before. Astorre was used to these sessions. Astorre had, Julius noticed, a certain intensity of expression which reminded him that the captain, too, had money tied up here in Geneva according to a boast he had once made. M. de Fleury, it would seem, had offered him family rates, and an assurance that his money would be safe if anything happened to the Charetty company.

It interested Julius that, despising Astorre, Jaak de Fleury still wanted his business. Not the man, clearly, to let personal feelings interfere with profit. Good mercenaries could make a lot of money —a string of successes, a single brilliant capture, a season of looting could reward with uncounted gold any bank which was lucky enough to attract their investments. If Astorre got a first-rate contract in Italy and did well thereafter, de Fleury would make a big profit. His, Julius', own money was with the Strozzi. As Marian de Charetty knew, damn her. There were no such things as secrets these days.

So Astorre stayed through the dealings that morning. It was, in the main, a matter of checking and issuing receipts for the goods consigned from Bruges to Geneva. And there followed a formal inspection of the goods in transit from Bruges to the Medici in Italy. The tapestries were unroped and viewed, and the gold plate. Brother Gilles was summoned and introduced, but excused from an example of his vocal agility. Then there were led from stables to courtyard the four hackneys which were to delight Messer Pier-francesco.

Jaak de Fleury retained throughout his air of ineffable superiority, and was no more affable to the Medici managers than he had been to the servants of his distant kinsmen, the Charetty.

Julius, papers in hand, walked out with Astorre and the rest to see the horses brought out for inspection, and saw that Claes had emerged from the stables and was helping the grooms. Julius was relieved to see him free, and also tickled. Unlike Felix, a walking bible of blood lines and litters, Claes had no close acquaintance with animals. Despite his grand-uncle's recent jibe, the grand total of his experience extended to draught-oxen, the dog he might or might not have clubbed and the hard-mouthed horses from which he had fallen with regularity most of the way to Geneva. It was remarkable therefore that he had taken to the Medici thorough-breds, and they to him. The nights spent sharing their straw had led to some sort of companionship. He fed them illicit mouthfuls. When he went near them they nuzzled him so that his ears dripped.

So the animals and their handlers now came to rest before the two Medici managers, and Claes was turning away when Sassetti said, "Well, now. Am I mistaken, or is that a young man I used to know? Claikine?"

Claes turned and looked. The frizzled hair, flat from three weeks under his helmet, was the same colour as the rust on his mail shirt, his face was blotched as it usually was, and he had something very close to a black eye. He grinned. "Messer Sassetti."

"And Messer Nori. Well," said Sassetti. Waves of chilly affront emanated from the lord of the Fleury. The Medici manager ignored them. "And here you are, a soldier now, do I see? With capitano Astorre? About to make your fortune?" Sassetti turned to Julius and the doctor. "The liveliest child I ever saw in this household. A terror, were you not? But a good courier, a runner of fast errands, *volando.* I wish my office boys had your speed. Well—" dismissing him with a smile—"and these are the horses."

He approved the horses. There remained only, before they all froze, to return to the house and effect the formal handing-over of the Medici dispatches. Julius sent Loppe for the satchel, and opened it, and unwrapping the heavy oiled paper, spread the contents on Monsieur Jaak's board so that the waxen seals, firm and brilliant, lay in profusion like flowers.

First, he picked out the Medici packets: the seal of Simone Nori from London; the package from Angelo Tani in Bruges, and another from Abel Kalthoff, their Cologne agent, all with *il segno,* the pear-shaped outline topped by a crucifix and bearing those three imperial spots which signified the Medici. All intact with their seals and white thread. And all impenetrable, even had it been otherwise. For no banker in Europe would communicate sensitive information to another in open writing. And the Medici codes were the best in the world.

Nonetheless Sassetti and his companion turned them over, good humouredly, before enclosing them in turn in their pouches, and took the chance, as bankers will, to glance idly at the other packets waiting to be dispersed to their owners. A communication from Marco Corner, the Venetian merchant, to his relative Giorgio here in Geneva. One from Jacques de Strozzi to Marco Parenti the silk merchant, the husband of Lorenzo's sister Caterina who lived in Florence. One from Jacopo and Aaron Doria to Paul Doria in Genoa, care of the Milan representative of the Bank of St George. And a dozen at least addressed to the Medici bank at Milan whose assorted seals bore haloed figures in the most expensive of wax.

Sassetti stretched out a thick finger and exposed one of them. "The Bishop of St Andrews, Scotland," he said. "Annates, of course. Or perhaps a Papal collection? I see why our little consignment is so powerfully defended. What might happen to the Pope's attack on the Turk if the gold does not reach him?"

"My dear Sassetti," said Jaak de Fleury. The archaic cheekbones gleamed with irony in the handsome face. "Who could imagine this former ladies' man at the Vatican ever collecting enough money to send off a rowboat? Will Burgundy help him? No. Will Milan lift a finger? And all those odorous hermits he has conjured out of the East to join churchly hands in a Crusade—what do they want but a house and a pension and sufficient literate pupils to praise them in Greek for posterity?"

The merchant raised his splendid shoulders and gave a civilised groan. "The King of Scotland must be mad, sending money. His sister, at least, is a fool. She stayed here for years, betrothed to the Count of Geneva until the King of France pointed out how unsuitable such a marriage might be, and they sent her back to Scotland."

"She was Bishop Kennedy's cousin," said Julius. "Perhaps there is a dowry to retrieve."

The Medici men, who would know, maintained an appearance of tranquil attentiveness. Julius, taking the hint, dropped the subject. The money from the Bishop of St Andrews, he knew very well, was ransom gold for Nicholai de' Acciajuoli's brother. If the Greek planned to beg here as well, it would do him no service to underline the size of his takings.

The conversation dwindled to a close. M. Jaak de Fleury did nothing to protract it. M. Jaak de Fleury, Julius knew very well, could hardly wait to get rid of the Medici, and then see them all on their way off by nightfall. M. Jaak de Fleury did not enjoy their company.

A difficulty emerged. Collecting now in the bank of the Medici was a fresh batch of reports for Milan. Messer Nori would bring them tomorrow. And the Charetty captain, he hoped, would undertake the task of conveying them. The price offered was excellent. M. de Fleury refused point-blank to entertain the Charetty company any longer. Julius, negotiating swiftly and decisively, obtained an agreement from Nori. If he returned now and assembled the letters, Julius would send a man to the bank to collect them. He was happy to have thought of it. When, later, it came to choosing the man, he thought Claes, familiar with Sassetti and Geneva, deserved the small excursion.

That M. de Fleury might not approve did not cross the notary's mind. He packed his papers, and went off to help Astorre get the cavalcade loaded once more and assembled. The peremptory summons came then, to appear before M. Jaak in his cabinet. The interview was disgusting. Julius emerged from it white with suppressed anger and marched towards his room. The first person he encountered was Claes, carrying Thomas's luggage. "So you came back!" said Julius.

Claes looked surprised. "I had to wait. The letters weren't all ready."

Julius flung himself down on a mattress. "The old monster was convinced you'd run off, or were giving away all his secrets."

Claes looked sympathetic. "Did he threaten to cut your hands off? No, they gave me some beer and asked about Meester Tobie. I told them about Lionetto and his glass rubies."

"And about de' Acciajuoli?" Julius said.

Claes' brow wrinkled. "No. They have their own silk factory, the Medici. You know that? I told them about Messer Arnolfini: does that matter?"

"No. That's only trade between Arnolfini and the de Fleury company; it doesn't matter," said Julius. "The Charetty don't handle silk."

"It's just as well," said Claes. "What they said about the Widow!"

Julius sat up. "About the demoiselle?" he said sharply.

Claes looked defensive. "Well, about women in business. You heard M. de Fleury already. They don't like the cloth she's been sending. And they say she puts too high a price on it."

Julius stared at him. "That's nonsense. We price it below the market, if anything."

"Well, it doesn't sell at that price," said Claes cheerfully. "And it's mouldy."

"What!"

"Maybe M. Jaak is storing it in a bad cellar," said Claes. "The one I was in was rotten damp. Maybe someone should tell him."

"Maybe," said Julius slowly.

"You talked to him," Claes said. "Did he mention it?"

"No," said Julius. "Maybe I should have taken his offer. Someone seems to be making a profit out of the Charetty company."

"Offer?"

"He wanted me to come back to the company," said Julius shortly. "After enquiring whether the Widow meant to marry again, and if Astorre or myself were proposing to be her next husband."

"The captain!" said Claes.

"Yes. Although to do him justice," Julius said, "M. Jaak didn't seem to favour Astorre as head of the Charetty business. He was kind enough to say that I would make a very good master for that sort of woman. Then, when he was sure that wasn't what I was after, he offered to take me back in my old post, now I saw what a poor thing it was to hang on to some woman's skirts."

Julius paused. Normally, it was not the sort of thing he would mention to a youngster like Claes, but he had to tell someone, and Claes was handy. More and more, Claes was handy. Julius wished, not for the first time, that Claes would come to his senses, and make a responsible contribution and attain some sort of standing so that a man could discuss matters with him.

Claes said, "Well, it depends, like everything else. But I expect you refused."

"Then he tried to buy Loppe. Loppe!" said Julius.

"That's because his voice is so good," said Claes, nodding.

"*Loppe,*" repeated Julius wearily. "Not the monk. How did Astorre become friends with a monk?"

"You're thinking of Brother Gilles," said Claes in a friendly way. "That's the one whose voice isn't very fine, but he was the best Tommaso could find when the Medici wanted a tenor. The person singing Gregorian chants with the good tenor voice is the Guinea slave Loppe. He learns anything. He was with a Jew, and then a Portuguese, and then a Catalan, and then Oudenin and the demoiselle de Charetty and you. Five languages, and the Gregorian chant."

Julius looked at him. At length, "Brother Gilles has been teaching him?" he said.

"No, he picked it up. Brother Gilles was impressed. They sing in counterpoint."

"And Monsieur Jaak heard him," said Julius.

"And wants to buy him, of course. He's worth a fortune. Did you sell him?" said Claes.

"No," said Julius. "I wouldn't sell that man a dog. But if Loppe is valuable, what do we do with him? He was Oudenin's gift to the Widow."

"I told Messer Sassetti about him," said Claes. "He thought the Duke of Milan would be interested. Oudenin wouldn't mind if Loppe went to the Duke of Milan. Loppe thinks he would like it: I asked him. And Astorre and Brother Gilles would be pleased. We might get better terms for the contract."

Sometimes Claes could surprise you. Julius gazed at him.

"If we get him over the Alps, that is," Claes added thoughtfully.

Chapter 12

Crossing the Alps in November made a good story, of course, when you got back home again, and why not. It was no pleasure for Africans (or elephants) who had never seen snow before. Well-educated young men had written of how, bravely, they had been towed over the mountains blindfold on a sledge. Someone spoke of making the traverse on a wheeled litter pulled by an ox on a prudently long lead, with the reins of his horse in his hand.

Astorre's only concession was to reload all the merchandise onto packhorses and mules, and muffle the four gift horses in blankets. As an afterthought, Loppe got a blanket too, above which his broad black face rose like a smoothly-buffed moulding. He was unhappy.

The roping and packing was assigned to Claes, who had proved in the journey from Bruges to be an instinctive expert in the distribution of weight, and who could design knots like a sailor. Although the snow glistened on the Jura mountains on their left and the Alps on their right, the lakeside was still green and without the carts they moved briskly, the harsh bitter wind bending and whipping their standards and the new-dyed plumes on Astorre's shining helmet.

Four days, they reckoned to take, from Geneva to the St Bernard's hospice on the top of Mount Jove, and, with luck, no snow until they had left the lake and climbed as far as St Pierre. In fact, they achieved it in three, because traffic to and from the Pope's Crusading Congress had squashed down the snow and given the inns and monasteries a reason for being warm and well-plenished and lucratively efficient.

There were, of course, other ways of crossing into Italy. Armies went by the Brenner Pass, which was gentler and good for supplies. Germans such as Sigismund of the Tyrol went by the St Gotthard. French and Flemings and English who didn't want to travel by Lake Geneva could ship their goods south on the river Rhône to Marseilles, and in the sailing season, make for Genoa.

But it wasn't the sailing season, and in any case, Genoa was controlled by the French. So, his frilled ear blue and his beard spiked with frost, the captain led his little company through Savoy, which was controlled by the French as well, in the sense that King Charles told the Duke of Savoy what to do. But then, as everyone knew, the Duke's wife and all her relations from Cyprus also told the Duke what to do.

Facing all ways, that was the Duke of Savoy. His father the Pope, who had died eight years before, had at least known what he wanted, and how to get it, if not how to look it in the eye. *A cross-eyed monkey,* the present Pontiff had been heard to call the late Pope Felix, in Latin naturally. Gossip about Pius the present Pope lingered, discreet and titillating, in all the inns and monasteries Astorre's company called at.

It might seem a delicate topic, but there were others more dangerous. There was an English party at St Maurice, stiff with armorial bearings, and you wouldn't choose to talk to them about their idiot Lancastrian king and his Yorkist rebels. Or about their French queen, whose brother you were actually going to Naples to fight. It was safer to chat about the Pope's fearful visit to Scotland nearly twenty-five years since, and its well-known consequences. A half-Scottish bastard, soon perished, for one. And a barefoot pilgrimage for another, which had afflicted the feet of Pius Aeneas ever afterwards. You would have thought that Papal feet would have interested this great doctor Tobias. But he just sat and drank, and watched Claes a lot. Astorre noticed him.

At the next meal, a Milanese on his way north deafened them on the same topic till Meester Julius felt roused to put in a word for the Pontiff. "All right. He's had a couple of bastards," said the notary. "Then why should this poetic homewrecker take Holy Orders, become Pope, and then devote all that energy to a campaign to retake Constantinople?"

"Met him, have you?" said the Milanese. "Well, some say it was a change of heart. Myself, I might do the same, with his conscience. At any rate, my Duke's not complaining. His crusade is going to leave while there's a war going on in south Italy. If the Pope wants Milan to fight Turks, then he's got to do something first. He's got to help Milan beat those greedy French dogs who want Naples."

"That's what we heard," said Meester Julius.

"They told me. Oh, they'll take you on in Milan," the other man said. "The Papal army'll take you, or the Milanese army; or they'll send you straight down to Naples to help King Ferrante hold out, if that's what you fancy. Mind you, you have to watch how you go. A lot of French-lovers about, making for the Mantua congress. Don't overtake *them,* if you can help it."

It was good advice, if hard to keep in the heights where snow fell in thick felting layers, like wool in the napping and shearing sheds, and began to choke the trodden ways. The horses' heads hung, and men's cheeks turned raw and blotched between their beards and their eyebrows, and when they blew their noses, their face-guards stuck to the skin of their fingers. Then, whatever company loomed through the whiteness, you caught and thankfully kept with, for there was safety in numbers.

By the time the final, multilingual cavalcade reached the monastery built by St Bernard, even its English component had unbent, and ate and drank with the rest in the steaming warmth of the refectory, and told their servants to answer when Claes tried out John Bonkle's English on them. But next morning, it was Astorre who was first on the floor, arranging his convoy for the second and harder part of their journey. He left the roping to Claes, who had to be retrieved from some congenial courtyard where he had been effecting a repair to a pump.

The blessing Claes received from the Prior was, Astorre considered, excessive, but might possibly serve to keep the youth on his horse until they were over the mountains. Although the fool was improving. Listening to the sound of the talk, Astorre could tell that Claes was less of a butt to the soldiers, although some of rougher kind still took the chance, now and then, to play tricks with him.

A captain less experienced than Astorre might have stopped them, before an arm or a leg could get broken. But that never did any good. Men simply resented what they saw as protection and beat their victim up worse on the sly. It was up to Claes to learn fast enough to protect himself. Which he was doing. And the journey was designed by the devil to exhaust experienced men, never mind youths with a turn for trouble-making.

Astorre even said as much to Tobias who, as a former companion of Lionetto, had so far lived under the cloud of Astorre's darkest suspicions. Time, however, had revealed the doctor surprisingly as a hard man much after Astorre's own heart, with a tongue on him that could make a lazy trooper jump as sharply as Thomas's. Astorre had spent some time, in fact, reconciling

Thomas to the fact that the company now had four officers to it instead of two, and that no company with ambitions could manage with less.

Contracts, letter-writing, book-keeping were all part of the business, and time was too short to spend half the day scouring a town for a notary, or taking the services of your employer's man, who would cheat you as soon as look at you. And good fighting men stayed where there was a good surgeon. Good food, good pay and good doctoring was what kept men together. And a leader who knew his business, took no foolish chances but knew how to save the best efforts for the best promise of plunder, and would divide booty fairly.

Up to now, he was willing to admit, the company had lacked organisation. It was never twice the same, for one thing. Men under contract mostly turned up when called, but not all of them. Some of them had got themselves killed. Some had formed winter bands and turned to plunder and wayside robbery to keep them in food and drink and girls through the winter as well as the arms they were supposed to be supplied with. He'd been half waylaid more than once by faces he had recognised, who had withdrawn when they saw who it was, and the number of his lances. And a lot of these were caught and hanged or cut down before spring arrived. Then others would find a captain who paid more, or had a better reputation for prizes; or some might even be paid by the other side not to come.

The companies who did well—the really great companies who gave themselves a grand label, and could name their own price in a big war—these were companies with their own chancery, like a lord would have, and a council, and a treasurer and pension funds and everything, just like a city state. And these companies were good because they stayed together, and their men knew each other, and often never went home at all, but stayed in winter quarters (paid for) when the fighting died down, and were all there and ready to begin again the following year.

That was what Astorre was aiming at. He wasn't born a soldier-prince. He hadn't had the chances that made a Hawkwood or a Carmagnola. He didn't expect to be courted by monarchs. But with Marian de Charetty's backing, he could get himself noticed. The ducal leaders would ask his advice. He would become known, not just as he was, as a good man with a small company who could be relied on. He would be the man they thought of when they wanted a spearhead for a special siege, a special battle. Men would come to his banner, and there would be money to pay them. And finally, some prince might buy the company from the Widow and give them a permanent home. These sorts of men could be gener-ous. He knew captains who had been given towns in lieu of pay, and then got to keep them. That was what Astorre wanted. That was what Lionetto wanted too. But Astorre was going to be first to get the men and the money and the backing and the conquests. For the first time, this year, it seemed possible. And Lionetto had better not get in his way, or he'd smash him.

Of course, it wasn't an easy life, on the big campaigns. No wives and no homes—or else several, like a sailor. But camp followers—yes, you had to have those. He would have to have those even with the smaller numbers he expected to join him from Flanders and Switzerland and Burgundy. Women to cook and wash and make homes of the tents and the huts and keep the men happy. There were times when he wished, himself, he were back in the days when he was just part of a lance, with his cronies about him, and not a care in the world but to think up a worse name for the old bastard up there who was leading them.

Then he remembered how good it was, being first with no one to stop him. Good, at any rate when you weren't crossing the Alps in a snowstorm with your slitted eyes streaming. They were on a single-track now, between towering snow-cliffs which were only the foothills to higher and steeper snow-mountains behind them. His horse didn't like it. Astorre was pressing it on when he realised that Tobias the doctor was trying to attract his attention. Astorre slowed and looked back to where the doctor was pointing.

Behind the bobbing snow-capped helms of his company, and the nodding shapes of the packhorses, was a long interval of unten-anted white. Beyond that was a horse, standing riderless. And be-yond that was a trough in the snow, partly filled by a low che-quered form which stirred feebly.

"Who?" said Astorre angrily. He would have to stop. Anyone left in this snow would perish. He halted, and the caravan crowded up and then came to a halt at his back. He scanned the faces behind him, noting all his officers, and the boy Claes and the negro Loppe. One of the soldiers, then, curse him.

The doctor said, "He must be hurt. I'll go back, if you can pass me. No. Look. There's another party of horsemen behind him. They'll pick him up for us."

The notary Julius had edged forward. "If they don't slit his throat and take his armour."

"He hasn't got any. It's Brother Gilles. It's captain Astorre's monk that's fallen off," said Claes the apprentice. His face was raw but quite cheerful, and his hat was plumed with white snow like a Janissary's. He added, "I think it's the Lancastrians. The English party. They wouldn't harm him. But I'll make sure it's them, shall I?" And kicking the horse, he turned its head to the nearest small ridge.

Astorre did nothing to stop him. He was getting tired of Brother Gilles, who had performed some unspecified favour for one of Astorre's many sisters and was now collecting his reward. Decency required, however, that the monk should be rescued—unless, of course, the odds were impossible. Astorre scanned the heavy grey sky, and swore quietly. The two college men exchanged clever glances. Claes, arrived up on a ledge, boldly stood in his stirrups and focused his watering eyes on the flags of the oncoming riders. Then his face cleared. "It's all right. Worcester's banner. It's the Englishmen."

Everyone looked relieved. Tobie settled his reins and prepared to ride back to the monk. Astorre grunted. Only the fallen man, seeing no move to assist him, and himself at the mercy of strangers, raised an arm from the snow in distress. Then he opened his mouth. You could see it, a dot in his white face.

Tobie and Julius saw it. Astorre stiffened. Later, Tobie realised that Claes, high above, had also paused for a moment. By then the blazons must have been perfectly clear, and the plumes, and the horsecloths.

Claes paid no heed to the English. Instead, he trained his eyes on the monk and, with a sweep of his arms, cupped his hands to both ears in the universal gesture of one willing to listen. And so invited, Brother Gilles called to him.

His voice could not be compared to Loppe's, but he was frightened. For the first time perhaps in his life he hit a true note at the top of his compass. Brother Gilles shrieked, "Help me!" And panicking, repeated it over and over.

Astorre's head was down like a bull, and his eyes, turned up to Claes, had red veins in them. Astorre said, "Make him stop. Quickly."

Claes, his hands removed from his ears, glanced down enquiringly. Astorre spoke again, his voice rumbling. "Make him stop. Sign to him to stop shouting. Or he'll start a God-blasted—"

"He has," said Julius shakily.

Tobie looked.

The monk had stopped shouting. He was looking upwards. The English party, which had nearly reached him, was looking up also. On either side of the recumbent man, puffs of snow like thistle-down wreathed the sides of the steep snowy walls, through which could be seen grey patches and fissures as chains and blocks of snow began sliding towards the track on which the monk lay. A blizzard of snow, rising upwards, told where the first lumps had fallen.

The slope was short, and the momentum enough to knock a few men off their horses and give the rest an unpleasant moment or two, but no more than that. The haze cleared for a moment. Tobie saw that some of the English party, thrown off or dismounted, were pulling a smothered Brother Gilles out of his hollow. The rest had backed out of the line of fall and were waiting until the cascade had settled. It got quiet again. It got so quiet you could hear a sort of low drumming, very like a cavalry charge.

It wasn't a cavalry charge.

Julius was still laughing when he saw the expression on Astorre's face, and followed his gaze to the high peaks. There, too, the snow was steaming, and fissuring, and sending gently down to their miniature creek a rumbling sound which had nothing to do with a few hundred-weights of snow shocked from a cliff-face, but everything to do with an Alpine avalanche that uprooted forests and overrode valleys and wiped men and horses clean from the mountains. Astorre said, *"Ride!"* and dug his spurs into a trembling horse which set off, lurching and staggering, along the path they had been taking when stopped. Julius, his horse pushed from behind, struggled, looking at Tobie.

Tobie said, "Go on. I'll follow."

Julius hesitated, and obeyed. Tobie dug in his spurs and forced his horse to the side of the track, against the oncoming, buffeting stream of his own frightened company. Above him, Claes was leaving his ledge. As his horse came stumbling down, Tobie confronted him. He had the words on his lips: *"You and I are going back."* He had no need to say them. Claes had wrenched his horse round already and was urging it back to the smother of snow where the initial fall had filled up the pathway. Above, the noise of the high fall was louder. The puff of snow had become a cloud, travelling fast down the face of the mountain towards them. Through the haze ahead of them a group of riders became clear, plunging over the snow. Some were bare-headed, their pennants snapped, their shields missing. Their shadowless faces were haggard. The leader was dragging the monk's horse. Brother Gilles, caked with snow, groaned and shook in the saddle. A broken leg dangled.

Tobie said, "Who else needs help? I'm a doctor." Claes was already dismounted.

The English party were all there, and fit to ride, although a horse had been killed. The monk was thrust with rough care into Tobie's wide grasp, while the horseless man took his place in Gilles' saddle. The monk groaned, and Tobie gripped him one-handed. Speed. Speed was all that mattered. They had to outrun an avalanche, riding tired horses—his with two men to carry. Claes, remounted, was by him. They set off, slipping and struggling, and the rolling drumbeat of the snowfall attacked them, repeating from every towering face. They weren't going to escape. They couldn't. He saw Claes take a deep breath, and wasn't sorry for him.

Claes said, "We have to reach the turn of the track over there. It's past the line of the fall. And there's an overhang." He spoke in English. A flash of angry impatience told what the English leader thought of the theory. Tobie said, "He may be right. If so, we can ease up. Or the horses will founder."

He caught the end of Claes' glance and was not sure, himself, why he had displayed faith in him. Snow slapped him in the face: falling snow and thrown snow and impacted snow flung from the hooves all about him. Through the whiteness he saw the turn of the track, and a looming shadow behind, which was the overhang. Claes, straining beside him, suddenly tipped his head back and inhaled through his nose, the unaccustomed lines lifting. "Which isn't to say," said Tobie between his teeth, "that you don't deserve the thrashing of your young life. And will get it."

"I know," said Claes. "There. We're safe." They struggled round the sweep of the widening bend. Under the cliff was a hollow, big enough to contain them all as they stumbled in. By then, the thunder above and behind was like deafness. Tobie thought about the weight of snow making that noise, and the speed it was running at. The overhang wouldn't save them. If the avalanche hit the overhang, it would split it clean from the face of the rock. But they had to risk it.

It missed the overhang. They all heard, seconds later, the wall of snow strike the track where they had been, and the roar of stone and wood breaking as the shelf fragmented and slipped, taking splintered trees with it.

From their place of safety, they sat their horses in silence, watching the spectacle of the fall. The edge of its path was just short of the overhang, where Claes had predicted. Either a piece of astrology, or a simple matter of calculation—or of local knowledge. Claes had been reared, after all, in Geneva. Tobie could hear him saying so at this moment to one of the English party, a swarthy young man who had crossed, perhaps to thank him. Tobie, his attention half on the monk, wondered what else they were saying. Then he lost interest, for a moment later there was a flurry of movement beyond them and Astorre appeared, with Julius and all the others, come back to make sure of their safety. They didn't wait long. Now the shock was over, no one wanted to linger. They helped Tobie secure and settle his patient, and then they and the English party set off together.

Tobie could see Astorre looking for Claes, but Claes was wisely invisible. The English leader explained to captain Astorre what he thought of imbeciles who screamed in the mountains and, to Tobie's admiration, captain Astorre answered mildly. He could do little else. Publicly, the matter was over. And Brother Gilles was the only real sufferer.

"He ought to ask," Julius said, "what he thinks of imbeciles who encourage imbeciles to scream in the mountains. Did you see Claes?"

"Of course I saw Claes," said Tobie. "He was right in front of my nose. If you also want my interpretation, he was hoping for a nice little avalanche, and he got a big one. And a fright to go with it. He was as white as the snow for a bit, was our little friend Claes."

Julius was looking at him. Julius said, "I've seen him get more than he bargained for. I've seen him frightened. But I tell you something. Underneath all the fright, the bastard enjoys it. Or he'd stop. Wouldn't he?"

The tone was impatient, but under it there ran a thread of something almost like wistfulness. Tobie rode on, and left the question unanswered.

Chapter 13

Led by their captain Syrus de Astariis, known to the trade as Astorre, the spearhead of the Charetty company rode into the city of Milan eleven days after leaving Geneva. From far across the green Lombardy plain, travellers had a view of the red massive walls of the capital, and its spires and its towers. The duchy of Milan was one of the Five States of Italy, rival to Venice, secret ally to Naples, open friend of the Pope. The duchy of Milan stretched from Tuscany to the Alps and was at this moment beloved of Florence, which could not reach its northern markets without it. And Florence, at this moment, meant the Medici.

Milan was not latticed with water like Bruges, or built on it like Venice. Milan was protected by two concentric circles of canalised river and ramparts of handsome red brick, pierced by six portals. Astorre proposed to enter through the Porta Vercellina. It was a provocative entrance, planned all the way through Aosta, Ivrea, Vercelli and Novara, where they had spent a whole night, Julius remarked, polishing gear like a wife on the eve of a bankruptcy sale.

Julius himself did his share, however: presenting himself with his papers at dawn at the drawbridge, and employing the pure, persuasive Italian which belonged to his notarial years in Bologna. By midday he was back with a permit and a paper from the Duke's secretary allowing them wood, wine and lodging in the Inn of the Hat and its annexes. An hour later they were riding through the Visconti portals, and past the hunting-grounds of the Castello Visconteo now being transformed, in a maze of cranes and shovelling men and red fork-tailed battlements, into the Castello Sforzesco.

For the heiress of the Visconti had married Francesco Sforza, son of one of the greatest condottieri, God save us, that Italy had ever known. And Francesco Sforza, these nine years Duke of Milan, was the man to recognise a professional turn-out when he saw one. So the Company Charetty paced through the crowded Milanese streets, helms and shields and knee-armour glittering, and lances erect as the masts of a war-fleet. And other captains, equally lured from their hearths by the aroma of war, looked appraisingly through tavern windows as Astorre's charger picked its way over the paving, the horsecloth heavy with expensive embroidery; the harness glistening over its chest and netting its hips in intricate leathers.

Captain Astorre had ostrich-plumes today in his helmet, and a fur collar which covered his quarter-ear, and rings on top of his gloves. Today, he had no wish to be part of a lance, rollicking round a barn fire and complaining about women and usurers. Perhaps he was less sure the following day when the head of the ducal Chancery summoned him to the Court of Arengo, the old Visconti palace beside the cathedral, to make known what services he and his company offered.

A fighting man, after all, was at his best in the field and not stumbling over his sword in the presence of noblemen. Astorre supposed he could rely on the wits of the notary, whom he was taking with him. And he had a fine gift for the Duke in the African Loppe, who had been dressed up in red cloth quilted over his chest so that given only a pillow (said that chatterer Claes) you could go to bed in him. They'd got him two-coloured hose into the bargain, and a Sforza badge for his hat with the viper and eagle in gold thread, bought ready-made from a booth in Vercelli.

On behalf of the Widow, Astorre expected to get his money back, in some form or another, as was customary. Loppe, who had already picked up some Italian, had expressed no views on his destination in Astorre's hearing. Naturally. Nonetheless the captain was edgy as they set out for the palace, and snapped at Thomas when he tried to delay him with the news that some great signor wanted to see him.

Thomas, left over from the English war in France, possessed peasant English, peasant French, hideous Flemish and almost no Italian. The "great signor" proved to be Pigello Portinari of the Medici Bank, arrived to collect his letters, his horses and his tenor. Julius, already mounted, said, "Tell him the captain and I have gone to the palace. We'll call on him tomorrow. If he wants the letters, he can take them now if he signs for them. Claes knows where they are."

"I'll get Master Tobie," said Thomas.

"No, you won't," said Astorre. Master Tobie was presently in a back room with a knife, a needle and a box of ointments, trying to put together Cosimo de' Medici's damaged tenor.

"Claes gets the letters, Claes shows him the paper to sign, and Claes carries them to the bank for Messer Pigello, if he wants."

Claes, captain Astorre refrained from saying, was a Flemish dye-shop apprentice and therefore prevented by status and language from the sort of indiscretion which Thomas without doubt would have perpetrated.

Astorre got on his horse and joined Julius and the neat escort he had arranged for the short journey to the palace. There was mud on his armour, splashed up from the street dirt. It got worse as they crossed the square with the half-done cathedral in it. Astorre thought they should have left the old church alone. All that was left of it was the front. The cathedral wallowed behind it like a hog with a truffle. They were going to start knocking down bits of the Arengo soon, so that the cathedral could grow. Then the Duke would have to move to the Castello. It was a piece of nonsense, spending money like water instead of where it was needed. States went bankrupt, building cathedrals.

There was the archway to the palace. He remembered it, and the size of the courtyard. Galleries, and a loggia, and a lot of people asking brusque questions. Astorre began to run over numbers again in his head. The worst that could happen was that the Duke wouldn't take him, or would offer a sum that would make them no profit.

No, the worst that could happen was that the Duke would take Lionetto, and not Astorre. And if that happened, it could be remedied. By God it could. He would see to it.

In the tavern behind him, nothing fell out as he had planned. Pigello Portinari, to whom Thomas took instant exception, did not wish to be served by a youth, or an Englishman who spoke like a yokel. Medici dispatches were not letters from country cousins. What his manager had written from Geneva, what his brother Tommaso had to tell him from Bruges, were matters on which much might depend. Were there no Italian-speaking gentlemen in the Charetty company? Claes, mutely pink, was dispatched for Tobie, who rose loweringly from Brother Gilles' bedside and stalked into the chamber set aside for Astorre and his henchmen, Claes following willingly.

Tobie, who had no deep acquaintance with the staff of the Medici, saw before him a man with very little resemblance to Tommaso Portinari of Bruges, and markedly older. Not being an under-manager and possessing, moreover, the favour (they said) of the ducal family, this Portinari was lavishly gowned, and the trimmings on his swathed turban hat caught even the doctor's attention. Tobie, whose aureoled bald head was hatless, wiped his bloody hands on his stained apron and said, "Well?"

The visitor remained calm. "I," he said, "am Pigello Portinari, manager in Milan for Piero and Giovanni de' Medici. You have some papers for me. If you will come to my offices, they may be properly examined and paid for."

"Good," said Tobie. He stuck out a thumb. "The name of that fellow is Claes. He will come with you now. If you want anyone else, you wait until later."

The Portinari eyebrows went up. "You are butchering something?"

Thomas, trying to follow the correct Italian, was scowling. Claes' face got pinker.

Tobie said, "If I had any sense, I'd be trying to. You an expert in music?"

Pigello Portinari looked at him thoughtfully. "It is customary—" he began.

"Your brother isn't," said Tobie. "I'm trying to save the leg of a croaking fool of a monk your Tommaso is sending for the chapel of your chief in Florence. We brought him alive over the Alps. He has been delivered alive here in Milan. You let him die because you want me running attendance on you, and you have to explain to Messer Cosimo de' Medici. And the Duke."

"The Duke?" enquired Messer Pigello with composure.

"The Duke of Milan. Your Duke. My uncle is his physician."

"Your uncle? Giammatteo Ferrari da Grado?"

"My uncle. My father was the ducal notary who officially transferred the dukedom from the Visconti to the Sforza nine years ago. My name is Tobias Beventini of Grado. The name of that fellow, as I told you, is Claes. He speaks Italian. Take him."

"With pleasure. How fortunate," said Pigello Portinari, "that we met, and have resolved a confusion. Instruct your excellent youth to box the papers and come with me. And perhaps, later, we may tempt you to visit the Palazzo Medici?"

"Well, someone will come," said Tobie briskly. "You've got four horses to collect and pass on to Florence. And Brother Gilles, of course. But that won't be for a while yet. Excuse me."

He departed. So in due course did Messer Pigello, followed by

Claes and his satchel. Lacking a good astrologer, no one saw any harm in it.

Claes was still away when Julius and the captain made their triumphant return from the Arengo. Tobie heard them come back. Deservedly well-supped and lavishly irrigated, the doctor lay on his pallet with his hands under his head. The jaunty clack of their hooves, and the pitch of Astorre's voice bawling at Julius, conveyed everything. They had succeeded. The contract, the condotta, was captured.

And so it turned out. A cheer from some nearby quarter below told that good news had been announced to the fighting-arm. Then Astorre's padded glove punched back Tobie's door and the captain strode in, wrenching off his monstrous helmet and handing it back, without looking, to Julius, who passed it to Thomas, arriving behind. Tobie sat up. Astorre shot him a self-satisfied glance and began to walk up and down, his bow legs hinged like a lobster's, while he reeled off dates and numbers and figures relating to the hiring of the Charetty company by the Duke of Milan.

His voice, at battle-pitch, made the ears sing. One hundred lances and one hundred foot, to be got down to Naples by spring. That was what he'd engaged to supply. And they'd take more if he got them. He'd signed a six-monthly contract at nine hundred florins the month, not counting their plunder entitlement. And pro rata terms from now until April, what's more, depending on how many soldiers he took south this winter.

Within the next twenty-four hours, Cicco Simonetta, head of the Chancery, would pay out the money. And in six days' time, when the horses and lances were rested, he, Astorre, would lead them all down to Naples. How? Was he the expert? They would be told. On foot, probably. Or on foot to Pisa, perhaps, and then south by sea. It would depend, wouldn't it, on the weather, and where the enemy was, and how active? And he, Astorre, would send runners to all those towns and villages in the Low Countries and other places where men were paid by the Charetty to stand by for fighting. *Come!* the orders would say. *Come to Naples and help yourselves to a fortune!*

Julius was flushed too, as if he had spent all day drinking, which he certainly hadn't. There were things Tobie wanted to know. So they were to join King Ferrante. So the terms were more than generous. So what else had Astorre and Julius learned? What about the Pope's troops, and the Duke's own army and the whereabouts of the other free companies? The rival companies, after all, were important. They might have to join one of them. There was the army led by Count Jacopo Piccinino which at present (said Julius) wasn't down near Naples at all, but on the opposite coast. And the Count of Urbino led another. The Count of Urbino, thirty-seven, one-eyed and brilliant, was about to marry the Duke of Milan's niece. Years ago, the Duke of Milan had promised an offspring to Count Piccinino himself. Mercenaries were popular sons-in-law.

Tobie knew all that already. To put it mildly, Julius' answers were airy. It annoyed Tobie to be less intoxicated with wine than Julius was with relief and complacency. He continued, undeterred, with his questioning. "And the palace? What did you think of it?"

Astorre, still pacing up and down, tried to snap his fingers and then began to fight his gloves off. "Offices, that's all it is. Officials, ambassadors, apartments for the family of course, but the Duchess has only four women and the Duke has no style. None. God knows what use he'll find for the African, though we'll hear. The secretary hinted there would be something appropriate. I should hope so. They spend money on some things. Tutors for the children. There's a foolishness. They'll turn out badly, you'll see. Latin orations at eight. All that nonsense. We met their physician . . ." He turned.

"Ah," thought Tobie.

Astorre bent and brought his stitched eye, as he sometimes did, close to Tobie. Angled downwards, like a bird's foot, it glittered. "You didn't say," said Astorre, "that you were nephew to Giammatteo Whatever. Him. The Duke's physician."

"Or the son of Beventinus Whatever. The Duke's famous notary," Julius said, his face glistening.

Tobie sat up on his pallet and, stretching out, poured himself a fifth cup of wine. He said, "I didn't ask you for your breeding chart. Anyway, I hadn't decided whether to stay with you or not."

"Careful," said Julius. He whipped the cup from Tobie's fingers and before he could stop him, had drained it. Julius said, "I think you are implying that it was only your connections that got us the condotta?"

Astorre's face, which had receded, came closer again.

"No," said Tobie. "I fell out with all of them years ago. That was why I nearly stayed with Lionetto. I knew if he tried to get an engagement in Milan they'd refuse him. So, see, it's a compliment. They took you in spite of me. Do have some of my wine."

"I'll send for some more. Where's Claes?" said Julius vaguely.

"Took the papers to the Palazzo Medici. Then they sent him back for the four horses."

"You let him take the horses?" barked Astorre.

"Three expert grooms to lead them, and Claes. He was the only one who could recognise a receipt. It's all right. They got there all right. The grooms came back and reported. Claes is coming back too, once the paperwork is all done."

"I think," said Julius, "I ought to go and fetch him. The Palazzo Medici?"

"One of those slums," said Tobie hazily. "No, that's where he went with the papers. The horses were for Cosimo's nephew. Christ, Tommaso made enough fuss about it. The horses went to Pierfrancesco de' Medici."

Satisfactorily, Julius was now more sober than he was. He even sat down. He said, "Tobie. Pierfrancesco de' Medici is in Florence."

"I know," said Tobie. "But his wife is here. Staying with her brother. Her Florentine brother who has a great big house in Milan where he sometimes stays for months at a time. Such as now. With great big stables. Because the family go in for horse-breeding."

"Who do?" said Julius.

"Pierfrancesco's wife's family. The Acciajuoli," said Tobie patiently. "Pierfrancesco de' Medici is married to Laudomia Acciajuoli. Cousin of the Greek with the wooden leg. Remember? The bearded mosaic who was collecting money in Scotland and Bruges to get his brother ransomed from the Sultan?"

Tobie paused. "And talking of wooden legs, my captain, you may be glad to hear that your friend Brother Gilles will survive. In about a month's time he will not only walk, he will be able to leave us. If we only had some wine, we could celebrate something."

The next morning, shutting his eyes against the glare of the rainfall, Julius accompanied his captain and four well-armed men to the Chancery to obtain the first down-payment of the contract. He expected a box of florins. Instead, he was given one thick sheet of paper addressed to Pigello Portinari, manager of the Medici Bank of Milan.

"Money?" said the secretary's secretary. "We don't handle

money. Make your wishes known to Messer Pigello. At the old bureau beside St Ambrogio. Or the new palace beside the Castello. Turn right before you get to the walls, and look for St Thomas's."

With a jerk, Astorre nocked his tough beard and aimed it. "Last time—"

"It's all right. Take the paper," said Julius. "The Medici will pay you. It's their way of loaning money. Then the Duke sees they get it back with a profit."

"That's usury," said Astorre, glaring at the secretary's secretary.

"No, it isn't. It's God's way of rewarding an honest, hard-working banker with a vigilant eye on the money market. Let's go. Never mind the old Medici office. I want to see the new Palazzo."

Proceeding there in the rain with an argumentative Astorre, Julius felt a quiet satisfaction. The youth Claes was hardly representative of the Charetty company. It was time he and Astorre redressed the balance.

There had been some intermittent concern last night when it was remarked that the receipt for the horses had not yet returned in Claes' keeping. But when they woke in the morning the papers were there by Julius' hand, and someone said that Claes was asleep with a smirk on his face, having come in later than anybody with the toes out of his stockings again and a list of addresses. Something would have to be done about Claes.

There was a lot of wet sand and mortar round about the Palazzo Medici as well when they got there. Taking shape was a long block of an edifice built of squared stones. There were a dozen arched windows on the upper storey, all pillared and garlanded, and the middle portal had been done by Monsignore Cosimo's own architect, Michelozzi. The dizzy top of the arch bore the Sforza shield and medallions. On either side were paired life-sized sculptures, two of youthfully virile Roman warriors and two of exquisite ladies in Florentine dress.

Neither of the men looked like a relative of Tommaso Portinari. About the provenance of the ladies Julius had no knowledge either, but entered the court with high hopes. *Semper droit* had been carved all down the archway. He supposed it could be held to sum up the beliefs of the Sforza, the Medici and the Portinari, if it came to that. He was not so sure of himself.

There was building going on in the courtyard as well. It was huge. When it was complete, its reception rooms and domestic quarters would be big enough to contain the owner and his whole household, should he ever visit. The rest would presumably hold the permanent staff of the bank, its storehouses and its offices.

Inside, in a warm room on the first floor dark with tapestry, Pigello Portinari and his brother Accerito came forward to greet them with a stately cordiality. The Roman army would not have had either of them. Especially the old one, Pigello. Gaunt, balding and chinless, he had nothing of young brother Tommaso about him except perhaps the long pointed nose. And a liking for rings: he had two on some fingers. Except that Pigello's rings were large, genuine rubies and diamonds and emeralds, and his sleeves weren't turned out with sheepskin. Pigello was rich.

Astorre and Julius were given carved chairs. They were brought refreshments. The name of Tommaso entered the conversation and left it almost at once. When the time came (and they were not detained long), Pigello moved over the shining tiles to a table big as a sarcophagus, chubbily carved, from which he drew papers, and read from some of them, and caused others to be signed. Then he took out a number of keys and opened seven locks on a great chest in a corner. Its lid, which required two men to lift it, was lined with extravagant clockwork, reminding Julius of one of Claes' elaborate game boxes. Pigello brought out a bag. "Gold, I think," he said. "I should suggest gold. I know Messer Cicco talked in terms of florins, but it is not a good time for currency. Not today. It will correct itself, of course. Now, Master Julius, you will keep note of this. And then you may use my bodyguard—I shall arrange it—to escort you back to the inn."

Relating this later to Tobie, he was disbelieved. "Gold?" said Tobias. "He *suggested* you took gold, when ordinary currency would have been cheaper for him?"

"There it is," said Julius, who had just finished a long, noisy stint paying wages and was tired of arguments. "Don't complain to me if he was generous. It got him Astorre's investments anyway."

"What?" said the doctor.

"Pigello offered Astorre double the interest Fleury were giving him, and Astorre's transferred his business to the Medici. There's a vote of confidence for you. The Medici think Ferrante is going to stay King of Naples. Unless you think they are humouring us because of your uncle."

"My uncle the Duke's physician? No," said Tobie. "He came to visit me while you were away, and has made it very plain that he considers I'm on the losing side. So you have to think of it another way. Ferrante fails, Astorre is killed, and the Medici don't have to pay anything. I'm not really interested, but has Lionetto come to Italy yet, and if so, which side is he joining?"

"Why?" said Julius. "If it's Anjou and the French and not Ferrante, will you cross back to him?"

"With my gold? It's tempting," said Tobie. He had pushed his hat to the back of his scalp, and his face with its neat, curled nostrils was passive. He said, "You should have taken our numerical genius with you to count it. Where was Claes last night?"

"Second column from the left, third name down," Julius said. "I haven't got a copy of the list yet, but they're selling it in the yard for beer money."

"Well, let's get it," said Tobie. "I'll find Claes. Does he always do this?"

"I don't know. I've never been in a new town with him before," said Julius. "I suppose he's looking for something."

"Safety in numbers," said Tobie laconically.

He did not trouble, when Julius had gone, to send for Claes, as he knew from his uncle what Claes was doing, and where. He simply rammed down his hat, brushed off the short black gown of his profession and, wrapping himself in his cloak, set off for the delightful mansion of the Acciajuoli.

Chapter 14

The Milanese house of the Acciajuoli lay between the dust and mud of the cathedral and the dust and mud of the Castello, not far from the merchants' piazza. There were unbroken lines of arcaded houses in squared stone and red brick and worked marble. There were impressive blocks with projecting eaves and arched windows and coats of arms over the doorways. There were churches, some inside enclosures. There were towers and staircases and balconies and upper-storey projections in timber that sheltered the streets and sometimes arched across them.

The big bell of the Broletto clanged out as Tobie left the crowded market streets for ones where there were fewer women, and the men, meeting briefly or hurrying to get in from the cold, wore wide or tall or draped hats, or the black caps of the professions, and kept warm in heavy gowns over padded damasks. Tobie looked in peoples' faces as was his habit, and drew conclusions about the health of the city. Now that the Duke had it in hand, it was well run. The undernourished, the crippled, the surgically punished were not to be seen in this quarter anyway. You would find them where the common houses were, and the workshops. And other afflictions known to the medical man, such as the burns and dull ears of the armourers.

But misery was not what Tobie mostly remembered, from his days calling there as a student. He remembered the heat, and the din, and the cheerfulness. In winter, you could get hot roasted chestnuts in Milan anywhere. He used to eat them with his friends, swinging his legs on a bench by the anvil, and shouting to them and the smiths. It was talking to the smiths, he sometimes thought, that made him the kind of doctor he was.

The house of the Acciajuoli was the sort that banking families liked to build. It was wide rather than tall, with a good big double-door that led not to a room, but to a short vaulted passage which ended in a square courtyard, pleasant even in rain, with evergreens placed on the cobbles, and a rank of solid buildings on its far side which presumably held the stables, and the horses brought with such pains for Pierfrancesco Medici of Florence, who had married an Acciajuoli. Somewhere, he could hear the mewing of goshawks. To one side, a balustraded flight of steps gave access to the principal floor. The porter, who had displayed no surprise at his arrival, showed Messer Tobias Beventini up the steps, from which a narrow balcony ran along the face of the building. Part of the way along this was another door which opened on his approach. Immediately inside was his uncle.

"Well, turd," said Giammatteo Ferrari da Grado. "You were in no hurry to come. Here is where you put your cloak. You are prepared for what is going to happen?"

"I don't know what is going to happen," said Tobie coldly. "I can only repeat. There is no connection whatever between this boy and myself. Whatever he has done is his own responsibility."

When little more than his own age, his uncle Giammatteo had been professor of medical logic at Pavia University, founded by a Duke of Milan. In a long career spanning thirty years Giammatteo had never moved from the faculty except to minister to the current Duke, its protector. Or, of course, to give his services, at a price, to those of the well-born and the famous whose appeals or whose politics touched the Duke's heart.

When Tobie, resoundingly qualified, had rejected the sedate satisfaction of university life in favour of rampaging about with merchants and mercenaries, Maestro Giammatteo had publicly washed his hands of him, thus neatly preventing his nephew from exploiting his name. That, and the other things he had said at the time had not endeared him to Tobie. Neither had the fact that, although well over sixty, the professor was florid and hale, with all the positive features in his merry face which Tobie himself lacked, in addition to a beard and a full head of speckled brown hair.

Tobie said, "Is he here?"

"Oh, yes," said his uncle. "As you know, he brought the horses for Pierfrancesco. Messer Agnolo and his sister made a point of inviting him back, even before they sent for me. A most amenable youth. We have all made it our business to speak to him. He shows a charming gratitude for all you have done for him. Your skilful nursing at Damme; your act of mercy at Geneva. We know how close you have been. You must see how, when you left captain Lionetto so suddenly, it might appear that the boy's affairs had attracted you?"

"No. As I told you. It was captain Lionetto's affairs which repelled me," said Tobie curtly. *Affairs,* his uncle had said, with a certain slyness. Deviation had always amused Giammatteo. Tobie found it reassuring. That, then, was why he was here. It meant, at least, that his uncle knew nothing of hair dye, and love potions, and holly. Or of a possible fortune, in the hands of an enigma whom he might, or might not, bring to confide in him.

"As you now repel Lionetto, I am told," his uncle was going on cheerfully. "Your former captain is in Milan, on his way to Piccinino. You would do well to be careful. Well, your young man is in the family chamber with Messer Agnolo and his sister and friends. You had better come with me to collect him."

"In the family chamber?" Tobie repeated.

The professor smiled. "Playing cards, I believe," he said with benevolence.

The leisure room of the Acciajuoli was little more than a painted cabinet, although the fireplace was handsome, and bright with a flickering brazier. All the other light in the room was placed round the card table at which four people sat, while three others stood bending behind them. As Tobie entered with the professor, one of the players turned with an abstracted smile and raised a finger. "One moment! We crave your indulgence. Marco, Giovanni—perhaps our guests would take wine while we finish."

The ushering servant had gone. The men thus summoned to help were two of the three standing guests, the third being a young and pretty girl. Tobie knew none of them. Smiling his social, doctor's smile, he took a precise inventory.

Of those playing cards, the speaker was no doubt his host. This man, thickset, sallow and commanding, must be the banker—Agnolo Acciajuoli, grandson of Donato, Prince of Athens and kinsman of Messer Nicholai, the one-legged Greek who had travelled from Scotland to Bruges. And the woman next to him must be Laudomia, his sister, wife of the absent Pierfrancesco. Or halfsister, perhaps: a handsome woman, many years younger than Agnolo and dressed in Florentine fashion, her hair and sleeves crossed with jewels and her unveiled bosom and neckline in elegant partnership.

Next to her, there sat someone familiar who was not a Greek or a Florentine. A lean, dark-skinned man, young but soberly dressed, whom Tobie had last seen somewhere quite different. In the party of Lancastrian Englishmen. In the English party which had stopped to rescue Brother Gilles and had been caught in the first of Claes' avalanches.

An Englishman, here?

Then the supposed Englishman, smiling, said something to Claes in an idiomatic French which was quite patently his native tongue, and Claes, replying politely in the same language, addressed him as "Monsieur Gaston." The woman, laughing a little, put down a card and herself spoke to the apprentice, this time in Italian. He answered at once: not entirely correctly, but with the clear Bologna inflections he must have picked up from Julius, instead of his early Savoyard. He had an exact understanding of the question.

They were, of course, toying with him. Tobie's uncle, cup in hand, murmured in Latin, "Why not try him in this language? Or Greek?"

Claes gave a smile, his eyes on his cards. "Maestro, spare me," he said. "I cannot both walk on my hands and contest a game with such players." He laid down a card and shot a glance at Tobie. It was full of conspiratorial delight. If he could, Tobie would have cancelled on the spot both the misguided, cavalier deeds at Damme and Geneva which had linked him with this dangerous lunatic. He glared at Claes, full of suspicion.

The boy's manner, damn him, was perfect. Deferential, with glimpses of spirit and simple humour which made his elders laugh. He was clean. Beside the others, his clothes were those of a servant; but the Charetty livery was the best that the Widow could afford, and despite all the travelling, the blue cloth of Claes' doublet had enough stiffness in it to set off his straight dyer's shoulders. The soldier's belt cinched his waist where the stained apron had always hung, and the high collar defined a well-placed throat and neck. His monstrous gaze and wide grin nothing could be done about, but there was equally nothing vacuous about them. It was a discovery Tobie had made at Bruges.

It was the youth's turn to play again. The hands holding the cards were no less callused than they had ever been, but at least the fingertips were not blue. As Tobie watched, they strayed over the sheaf of oblong cards and, picking one, laid it on the table.

There was a short silence which Tobie, ignorant of the game, could not interpret. Then the woman Laudomia, her grey eyes cold and clear, looked at him smiling and said, "Again!"

"Arabic," said Claes. "You should have asked me to talk in Arabic. Then you would have won it all back." The cards were

hand-painted, in red and blue and gold. The pack was worth everything Claes was wearing, Tobie calculated, from his head to his
toes.

"Wait," said the Frenchman called Gaston. "Before we all lay
down our hands. Niccolò my friend: what cards are we holding?"
Niccolò?

He was looking at Claes, whose colour had risen. Claes said,
"You don't know? Monsieur, you must lose a great deal."

Messer Agnolo moved. He smiled, catching the eye of the man
called Giovanni, who came and stood by him. "Tell me mine, my
young friend," he said. "What do I hold in my hand?"

"A bearing-rein," said Claes without rancour. "Well, monsieur,
you began with a nine, and never let it go. Then you picked up and
kept a three and a Queen. Those were all *bastoni*. Later . . ."

He named one by one all the cards in the other man's hand; and
then, when he was asked, those held by the others. As he did so,
Giovanni leaned over and checked them. They were correct.

Claes looked both relieved and embarrassed. "It comes from the
dyehouse," he said. "Long lists of recipes, very good for the memory. And verses. We make them up to sing when we're stirring. By
the time we've added in all the people we like, they can get to be
very long."

He looked round, in an accommodating way, as if ready to sing,
too, if invited. Messer Agnolo said, "Do you hear that, Giovanni?
You were a dyer. We shall expect no less of you, next time you play
cards with us."

Beside him, Tobie was aware that his uncle was smiling. His
uncle said, "May I introduce my nephew Tobie, or do you wish us
to go away while you start another game with this budding arith-
metician?"

Play, it seemed, was over. Their host rose, with his sister, and
came forward. Guests were seated and reseated. Introductions
were made. The pretty girl was called Caterina, and Marco Parenti
her husband was a merchant in Florence who used to export silk to
Athens and Constantinople. More than that, he was a writer. More
than that, he visibly did not care for the fact that Caterina had
picked Claes to sit beside.

Giovanni da Castro was the Pope's godson, and held a post in
the Apostolic Chamber. The Holy Father made use of his business
experience. Before that, Messer da Castro had been a dyer. There
was a coincidence. A dyer of imported cloth in Constantinople,

before the attack by the Sultan six years ago. He had escaped with his life. He was lucky.

Tobie's expression, he hoped, remained calm. It was an Acciajuoli household. Why be surprised if all the guests once did business in Constantinople or Athens or the Morea? He remembered one member of the family who had not been mentioned. He said to da Castro, "You were luckier than Messer Bartolomeo, the brother of the Greek with the . . . of the kinsman of Messer Angelo's who toured Europe raising funds to ransom him. Is there any news of him? Will he expect to be freed when the gold is collected?"

Ever since Bruges, the subject of the Greek and his captive brother had acutely interested Tobie. He was surprised when da Castro did not immediately answer him. It was Laudomia, the captured man's relative, who said, "My dear Messer Tobias! The man was freed months ago. It was the firm of Medici who paid the ransom and who generously agreed to stand out their money until they can be recompensed."

"By which time, of course, the rates would have changed," said Tobie.

Monna Laudomia smiled. The Pope's godson, entering the conversation, quickly said laughing, "It is the one thing which never stands still. But of course, the matter had to be settled to allow Messer Bartolomeo to continue trading. At a price, of course. The taxes on Christians are unbelievable. But with one thing and another, Bartolomeo Giorgio will never go short."

"You mean," said Tobie, "he is still trading in Constantinople under the Turks? While you had to leave?"

There was again a second's pause, and then da Castro shrugged. "There is religion, and there is business. Sometimes, one has to choose. No. I don't grudge his fortune to Bartolomeo. I shall do well enough here."

"And what," said Tobie, "if your godfather launches his Crusade, and it takes Constantinople back from the Turks?"

Messer da Castro looked surprised. "Then I may return to my trading there if it suits me. And Messer Bartolomeo will be able to continue without Turkish taxes. A happy outcome."

"If he survives," Tobie said. "What does he trade in? Is he a dyer as well?"

Again, the pause. Again, Laudomia Acciajuoli supplied the answer. She said, "Bartolomeo is from Venice. You may think it hard to justify a kinsman who cleaves to the heathen. But the Sultan favours Venetian traders. The Sultan permits them their own customs and worship, and in return they pay highly. Bartolomeo buys raw silk from the East, and sells or exchanges it in Constantinople for woven silk from dealers like Messer Marco here. He is also much concerned with alum."

"*Alum?*" said Tobie. He cleared his throat.

Laudomia Acciajuoli looked at him. She said, "I thought his brother possibly told you. Bartolomeo controls the alum mines of Phocoea for the Sultan."

Claes, you bastard, thought Tobie. And dear uncle Giammatteo over there, studying the roof-beams. What am I in? What do they think I'm in? What do I do? Continue as if nothing had happened. Tobie said, "I can see why you must be hoping for a crusade."

"Or another source of alum," said Monna Laudomia. "That is your great dream, is it not, Messer Giovanni? That the Pontiff your godfather will allow you the means to prospect for minerals in his territory? Think what it would mean if alum were found!"

The Pope's godson rose. He said, "It is, I am afraid, a remote chance at the moment. Monna Laudomia, Messer Agnolo, I must take my leave."

Tobie was not surprised. He played his part in the leave-taking and stood absently watching his host escort the Pope's godson from the room. His uncle, smiling in a way he did not like, made a business of seating himself again, and after a moment, Tobie did so as well. Claes, when he shot a killing glance at him, was seated between Marco Parenti and his wife, and they were all talking Italian.

The cardplaying Frenchman had taken a stool next to Tobie's uncle. Tobie's uncle leaned over and said, "Tobias. You haven't met M. Gaston du Lyon."

"On the contrary," said M. Gaston du Lyon. "M. Tobias and I had a snowy encounter some days ago, and he is asking himself why I was travelling with Englishmen."

At the moment, Tobie didn't want to think what the answer might be. He said, "I hope you were none the worse for the soaking."

"I was not harmed in the slightest. No, I was merely riding with my lord of Worcester for safety. He was under the impression, I think, that I was a loyal citizen of King Charles of France making my devout way to Rome."

"But Claes knew who you were?" said Tobie.

"I should be annoyed if he did. No, he did not. He has been, if not penitential, at least polite on learning my identity."

"Which is?" Tobie said.

"Oh, I am French," said M. Gaston. "But I serve not the French king but his exiled son the Dauphin. I am chamberlain to the Dauphin Louis, and am come on leave to Milan for the jousting in February. I live for jousting. It is my great joy."

"It isn't mine. I spend too much time repairing the victims," said Tobie. He thought of the avalanche. He thought of Claes, so obligingly patching up pumps, and picking up all the Savoy gossip. Whatever the naive M. Gaston might think, Tobie for one was sure that Claes had known exactly whom M. Gaston represented. Before the avalanche, too.

Tobie felt agitated: even trapped. The conversation between Claes and the pretty girl and her husband had broken up. Suddenly Claes was standing between each and calling him over. "Master Tobias! You met Messer Marco and his wife. Do you know who she is? She is Lorenzo's sister!"

"Lorenzo?" said Tobie.

"Lorenzo Strozzi! From the House of Strozzi in Bruges? They've just had a bereavement—a brother—and there are letters from Lorenzo for Monna Caterina and her mother this very moment in my satchel at the inn. She'll have them tomorrow." In deference to the bereavement, Claes' face registered a sort of happy sympathy. He turned to the girl. "Lorenzo misses you so much. We cheer him up, but he needs to come back to Italy."

"It is what I have always said," said the girl. "My brother pines, Marco. He longs to have his own business."

Claes looked interested. Messer Marco Parenti looked annoyed. Tobie, bent on extricating himself, heard the girl speak again, and Messer Marco muttering, "Not here. Not now," in a husbandly way.

A hand gripped Tobie's arm, and drew him aside. "Now," said Tobie's eminent uncle cordially in his ear, "do you not perceive the value of well-placed acquaintances? They have taken measure, in their own way, of the youth. I find him of interest. I congratulate you on your sponsorship. I have been able to tell Monna Laudomia that you, as my nephew, are the most reliable man they could find."

"Could find for what?" said Tobie. *"Sponsorship?* I've nothing to do with Claes. What do they want him for?"

His uncle looked surprised. "His gifts," he said. "You must know how much he was in demand when he left Bruges?" He paused. "And he really does know much more than he should do."

Tobie thought of Quilico, and then decided that his uncle couldn't possibly know about Quilico, who was so familiar with what grew by the Phocoea alum mines. And who was apt, in his cups, to talk about other, undiscovered alum mines to sick, cunning youths and their doctors. Then he realised that the professor might know all about Quilico if Claes had told him. But why would Claes tell him? "You will have to explain," said Tobie carefully.

"Is this a physician who speaks?" said his uncle. "Diagnosis, my boy! You saw the cardplay. The youth absorbs languages, can manipulate numbers. What will such a man make of a private courier service?"

From pure relief, Tobie found himself smiling. So that was it. The courier service. He should have guessed as much. Tobie thought of the satchel Loppe carried everywhere on the journey, and the handsome letters with their threads and their seals. A person who carved intricate puzzles had a touch fine enough for a thief or a forger. And the cunning to disentangle other men's writings. The men who created the ciphers in the ducal Chancery, in the Medici offices, were of this sort exactly.

Tobie said, smiling still, "They're buying him off, or employing him? Or pretending to do both, while slipping something fatal into his winecup?"

"I expect they thought of that," said his uncle mildly. "But not when they found he was a friend of my nephew. That was when they brought me in to advise them. I was, I am, happy to help."

"A friend of mine?" Tobie said. "Thank you, but that lump is a dyer's apprentice."

"Well, you saved his life. Or so I'm told," said his uncle. "And followed him to Milan. And showed an intelligent interest in a piece of information you picked up in Bruges. Or haven't you even got the sense, turd, to realise what this is all about?"

The smile left Tobie's face. He would never make assumptions again. They were not, after all, talking of nothing but a courier service. They were talking of alum, and they knew—even his uncle knew—a lot more than he did. And they were trying to implicate him. A profitable bargain with Claes was one thing. Being manipulated by the entire Acciajuoli clan (including possibly Claes) was another. Tobie said, "I see. Well, if they ask me, I'm having nothing to do with it."

"Afraid?" said his uncle. "He's not afraid, your young Niccolò."

"He's nothing to lose," Tobie said.

"You have a point," said his uncle. "But it hardly matters. You're involved. You can't get out anyway."

"Allow me to differ," said Tobie.

Tobie tried to leave twice after that, and was restrained twice by his uncle. Nobody asked him anything or offered him anything except food and drink and innocuous conversation, which maddened him further. Denied a chance to explain, rebut or refuse, he contented himself with ignoring Claes wherever possible. It was an outrage that, when he finally managed to get away, his uncle should foist Claes upon him. They were returning to the same inn, Giammatteo pointed out. It was safer, after dark, for his nephew and the young man to walk there together. Messer Agnolo would lend them both a lantern.

Claes carried the lantern. Fuming, Tobie walked down the stairs ahead of him and crossed the courtyard. Claes jiggled the lantern. Tobie's shadow leapfrogged from pillar to pillar and stalked grotesquely over walls, its chin in the air. When they got out into the street, Tobie swore aloud and, turning, stopped the youth by gripping his wrist. Then he pulled the lantern towards him and extinguished it.

The dim light of the Acciajuoli porch showed the reproach on Claes' features. Claes said, "Now I can't read the list."

The doctor snapped. "What list?" Then of course, he remembered.

Claes was already undoing his purse. Silver glinted inside. Tobie said, still snapping, "You were playing for *money*?"

"It makes it more interesting," Claes said. "They would have let me win, anyway." He had a list in his hand. "Second column . . ."

"Second column from the left, third name down," said Tobie. "Or that was last night, wasn't it? In any case, don't let me keep you. I'm going back to the inn."

"Well, so am I," said Claes. "But not yet. You can't talk there.

Third name down. It's an apothecary's shop near St Maria della
Scala. Round the corner."

"I don't need to talk," said Tobie. "I can tell you without moving a step that I'm having nothing to do with it."

Relief spread over Claes' face. "That's what I hoped," he said.
"I've nothing against your uncle, but I've explained that I don't
need a partner. All we have to do now is think how to get you
out."

"I'm not in," said Tobie, for the second time.

"Of course you're not," said Claes. "We just have to decide how
to convince people. It won't take five minutes, and then you
needn't think about the alum again."

The alum. Well, it was worth five minutes to get this nonsense
out of the way.

The apothecary's was, of course, shuttered and dark. Tobie
stood stiffly back while Claes delivered a few gentle tappings and
finally, after a great rattling and scraping of bolts, the door opened
a trifle. The man who let them in carried a candle. He seemed to be
alone. At the back of the room was a truckle bed with a sag in it
where he had been sitting, and a trestle table with a hunk of bread
and some olives. At night, a lot of shops used an apprentice as
guard-dog.

This was a bigger place than it seemed. Near the door was the
apothecary's selling-table, with the scales on it and a counting
board and bags of counters and bowls. The drugs and spices most
often used were on the shelves behind that, in jars of glass and
pewter and earthenware. A dirty mortar stood on a stool.

The smell was a choking mixture of medicated syrups and brim-
stone and salammoniac and ointment and turpentine mixed with
pepper and ginger, cinnamon, anise and nutmegs, cloves and
cumin and saffron. Tobie could smell comfits and paint, wax and
perfume, vinegar and raisins. There was mustard somewhere, and
oil of wormwood, and soap. Tobie sneezed.

"May God bless you," said Claes. The man with the candle was
leading them towards the back of the shop. They passed more
shelves, and a cabinet, and some bales. Tobie sneezed again.

"May God bless you," said Claes. "Is it asthma? Your uncle was
treating the Duchess for asthma, he was telling me. And the Pope
for his gout. He says the Pope is sitting this minute with a pipe of
warm water trained on top of his head. Maybe that's what you
should have. He says the Pope has never been the same since he

had that bad time in Scotland, and his feet froze and his teeth began to fall out. May God bless you. But not his hair. Long, golden curly hair. The Pope kept his hair a long time. May God bless you. You haven't paid a visit to Scotland, Meester Tobie?"

They were entering a low door at the back of the shop. The strong scent got stronger. The ceiling was hanging with objects. Tobie brushed a bundle of herbs with his scalp, dodged, and was fetched a light blow by a pestle. Through the door he caught sight of a bed, a hanging curtain, and another bed. He turned on his heel.

Claes' hand slipped inside his arm and wheeled him round again. Claes said, "There's no one here. We have half an hour before anyone comes. They don't understand Flemish."

He drew Tobie into the room and shut the door behind the apothecary's man. The bed and a low cushioned chest with a candle beside it were the only articles on this side of the curtain. Claes sat on the chest with his knees together. Tobie remained on his feet.

Tobie said, "Before we talk about how I get out, I want to talk about how I got in. Who brought my uncle into it?"

The youth's large gaze was pacific. He said, "I expect it was the Greek with the wooden leg. When I didn't take the post with the Venetian commander. He would write to his cousins the Acciajuoli and tell them all about you."

"Why?" said Tobie. He sneezed, with passion.

"Because you were questioning Quilico. You remember. The galley doctor who'd worked in the Levant. He thought Quilico would make me interested in the colonies. He didn't realise that he'd brought together a dyer and a doctor and an alum company man, and that we might make deductions. I expect he was quite worried," said Claes. "I expect I should have had a little accident if he hadn't found out who you were. Your uncle is a great man, isn't he?"

"Never mind my uncle," said Tobie. Without thinking, he sat on the bed. He said, "The Greek with the wooden leg. Did you know his brother had the Phocoea alum concession?"

"Not then," said Claes. "I think Anselm Adorne did."

"Adorne?" said Tobie. He retrieved Adorne from his memory. The fine-looking burgher in Bruges with the Jerusalem church and the kinsmen who were Doges of Genoa.

"Well, yes," said Claes. "The Genoese have been running their Levantine trading posts for two hundred years. The Zaccharia, the

Doria, the da Castro, the Camulio. Adorno has been one of the great names on Chios for nearly as long. If you'd been interested, you should have got to meet Prosper de Camulio, here in Milan. He knows as much about alum as anybody."

Tobie said, "Da Castro. Now there's a point. Why was Giovanni da Castro there tonight? There's a world shortage of alum. The deposit at Phocoea is best, and Venice and the Greek's brother Bartolomeo have the Turkish franchise of it. It can't be in their interests to have a rival mine opened. So why entertain the Pope's godson, who's hoping to raise money to find one? Why entertain you and me, knowing that you knew from Quilico of another mine and thinking that I did?"

The large eyes shone. Claes waited expectantly, as if for the end of a nursery story.

Tobie opened his mouth and produced a sneeze. He pulled out a kerchief. He said through it, as bitingly as he could, "My guess is that the Acciajuoli are backing both you and Giovanni da Castro. In exchange for the profits of the new mine, they're going to pay you to help da Castro exploit it."

He blew his nose. Claes said, "May God bless you," and went on looking at him intelligently. Tobie said, "Isn't that right?"

Claes said, "Oh, no. I'm sorry. No. Giovanni da Castro hasn't begun to look for alum yet. He isn't in any special hurry. I think he was there because the Acciajuoli would be glad if I killed him. Of course, the Phocoea alum interests don't want another alum mine found."

Tobie said, "They're buying your *silence*?" He felt a spasm of awe, and wiped it off with his kerchief.

Claes said, "And yours, of course. They think you know what I know."

Tobie gazed at the former apprentice. "I should be hard put to it," he said, "to sustain that impression."

"About the information they're buying as well," said Claes cheerfully. "It's a new contract. I've sold them a courier service. That's why M. Gaston was there, and Marco Parenti and the Strozzi sister. That's nothing to do with alum. That's ordinary business. The Charetty company provide the couriers and I provide the special information. They hoped, they said, that you would stay in Milan maybe and supervise it. You don't provide anything. You just collect money and look as if you did. And keep quiet about alum."

He paused, and his brow wrinkled earnestly. Claes said, "The trouble is, if you don't collect the money, they'll think you aren't going to be silent."

Tobie said, "Thank you very much. You've embroiled me in a plot to safeguard an alum monopoly. Now you've linked me with spying."

"Spying?" said Claes. "I wouldn't know about that, Master Tobie. Ambassadors spy, and envoys and special agents. I don't move in those circles. I just overhear things brokers' clerks talk about, and dealers' stewards, and smiths and carters who know where horses are going, and food is being collected, and money paid. Gossip. Nobody notices someone like me."

"Claes," said Tobie. "Tell me about the cannon that had an accident on its way to the King of Scotland. And the avalanche that fell on the Lancastrian English. And this famous knack you have with puzzles and numbers. And then try to make me believe that you're sitting with straws in your ears, picking up stable gossip."

Sitting cross-legged, Claes gazed back at him. He looked exactly like someone with straws in his ears. He looked like a large, clean-shaven hermit about to make out a case for a new hut. Bitterness filled Tobie. He saw no reason not to tell Claes exactly what he thought of him.

Tobie said, "You want to be rich, of course. You want to force the people of Bruges to bow to you instead of beating you. You want clothes and jewels and a mistress who isn't a servant, and you want to parade them in front of Jaak de Fleury and his wife, and Katelina van Borselen, and captain Lionetto and the Scotsman Simon. You've picked Julius' brains, and got him and Astorre safely off to battle, and you've got an excuse to go straight back to Bruges with secrets to trade, and no one to answer to but a vapid youth and a widow who needs an intelligent, lively young person to help her. Will you marry her, Claes?" said Tobie. "I'm sure she'd have you. You have such a way with the girls."

Claes said, "I told you I don't want a partner. You became involved by mistake. You'll hear nothing more about any of it."

He spoke in a different voice. Nor did he look like someone with straws in his ears.

Tobie said jibingly, "In spite of someone knowing that I know all that you know?"

Claes said, "All they're concerned about is preventing the appearance of a new alum mine. If you withdraw, they have nothing to worry about. You're the only person who could have found it."

Tobie's eyes opened, watering. He sneezed, and was not blessed. He thought, quickly and intensively into his kerchief. He took his nose out. He said, "I see. So much for hair dye and love potions and all the talk about plant patterns? Quilico *didn't* tell you where he thought the alum might be?"

Claes said, "Only that it was in Lazio, which is a very large area around Rome, and inside the Papal States. That's why there's no point in backing da Castro. As soon as it's found, the Pope and no one else will exploit it."

Tobie said, "How wise of you not to have told me. I might have embarked on the whole scheme myself, with my uncle's protection. I still could, couldn't I? Find the mine, if it exists, and produce proof of it. Because the Phocoea company won't otherwise pay to suppress it, will they?"

The friendly look had returned to Claes' face. He said, "I don't see why you shouldn't do just that, Master Tobie. Someone might as well have the use of the information."

Tobie said, "Why not you? You said you didn't need a partner."

"Oh," said Claes. "That was for the courier service. No. People would talk, wouldn't they, if I spent weeks tramping hillsides and interviewing Levantine merchants and alum miners. Sooner or later, other people will find the deposit anyway. It offered a quick profit, that's all, for someone who could give time to it now."

"I see," said Tobie. "And what have you told the Phocoea operators?"

Claes unfolded his legs to the floor and put his hands between them. "That they'll have proof by the spring that an alternative mine does exist. If you want, I'll tell them the proof will come from you. If you don't want that, I'll tell them that there's no mine."

Tobie said, "They won't believe you."

Claes smiled. He said, "You'll be safe."

And, of course, he would. Because of Giammatteo.

The candle wavered. Half an hour. It must almost have gone. Tobie said, "You know you deserve what's happened. You set it all in motion. If they don't believe you, they'll do to you what they hoped you'd do to Giovanni da Castro."

"Then I'll have to hurry, won't I, and dig up some secrets to defend myself with?" said Claes. His gaze was profoundly amiable. He said, "If you don't want to make the decision at once, I needn't say whether you are withdrawing or not. The friends of Phocoea don't expect my report till the spring."

Which was shrewd. It was an offer Tobie liked. And there was no need, either, to make a specific reply. Ignoring the alum question as if it had never existed, Tobie said, "I want them told *now* that I have nothing to do with your courier service."

Claes said, "I understand. That's easily done."

"So now you can keep all the profits," said Tobie. "What will you do with the money?"

"Force the people of Bruges to bow to me instead of beating me," said Claes. "Invest some of it."

"Oh?" said Tobie. He rose from the bed and smoothed his crumpled gown. "A little property somewhere? A share in a wine tavern?"

"Both those things. What do you think of handguns?" said Claes.

Tobie stopped picking feathers from his skirts. He said, "You're going into business?"

"Well, I'm in it already," said Claes. "The money belongs to the Charetty company. Captain Astorre ought to have handguns. And there are a few other things a credit would be useful for, apart from buying property. Louvain needs more capital."

"The Widow?" said Tobie. "You're doing all this for . . . She's willing to take money from this sort of source?"

"There's nothing wrong with a contract for a courier service," Claes said blandly.

"And she doesn't know about the alum scheme either? Only the Greek and Anselm Adorne," Tobie said. "You know, I'm surprised about Adorne. A man with a family church protecting a Turkish monopoly. You won't deny that's what it is, even if the Venetians are working it?"

A further thought struck him. "Christ. And if what you're saying is true, protecting it at the expense of the *Pope*?"

He hoped he looked horrified. He was afraid he looked the way Claes was looking. Claes said, "I didn't say Adorne knew any details. Anyway, trade and high thinking usually manage to put up with each other somehow. That was a knock on the door."

Tobie had heard it. He said, "You didn't arrange . . ."

Claes got up. Large, smooth-skinned, sunny, he looked capable of every athletic feat Tobie had ever heard of. He could imagine Claes exerting himself happily for hours and hours, with one girl or several. There were two beds. Vistas of endless embarrassment opened before him.

Claes said, "Don't be worried. No one will ever mention alum to you again, unless you open the subject first. And as far as you know, I am running a perfectly respectable courier service. I'm going back to the inn. Stay if you want to."

Status had to be maintained in some fashion. "That depends," said Tobie unhurriedly. He strolled to the door, and opened it on a small, charming person with a coral necklace and one exposed breast. He said, *"Cateruzza!"*

"Second column from the left, third down," said Claes. "They said you used to come from Pavia to see her. I thought you'd like to know she was still mixing trade and high thinking. I'll leave you the lantern."

Tobie stood at the door to the shop, and watched Claes find his way past the herbs and the pestle, and leave.

Tobie sneezed.

"May God bless you," said Cateruzza musically from beside him. The sneeze, he saw, seemed to have unveiled her other breast.

He shut the door. He felt surprised. He felt tricked. He felt like investing all his recent blessings at once—quicker than at once—in the revealed and trim lap of Cateruzza.

That was when Tobie began to enjoy Milan. He saw Claes a few times after that, discussing practical things. Girls, alum and spying were never mentioned.

Julius was annoyed about the courier service. Even when it was explained to him how much money it would put into the company's coffers, he was resentful. He had expected Claes to go with them to Naples. He didn't see how Claes, having been appointed to Astorre's army, could suddenly elect to do something quite different. It annoyed him even more that Astorre didn't seem to mind.

The only one who seemed to mind was Thomas, who would have Claes' society when he set out north to collect the rest of the company. And, perhaps, some of the men at arms, who had got used to Claes' serial representation of Astorre fighting his way through the duchies of Europe, collecting screaming cooks who had to make veal jelly, and smoked ham and pounded pork fried in the way that he liked it, until there was no tent big enough for his cooks, his latrines or his belly. Claes also did a superb imitation of Lionetto, which Tobie did not wholly appreciate.

Captain Lionetto had arrived in Milan, and he and his former medical officer had had one clash in public already. Lionetto had a new cloak lined with dormice, and was covered in coloured stones which this time were quite clearly not glass. Someone was being very good to Lionetto, and Tobie suspected that it was not Piccinino, who had hired him. Nor was it the Medici, about whom Lionetto had told two shocking stories and professed an attitude of deepest contempt. Especially when he heard where Astorre had placed his money.

Tobie had told Astorre about the encounter, less to shake Astorre's trust in the Medici than to invoke Astorre's vigilance in case Lionetto sent three men after him, Tobie, with hatchets. It spoiled his pleasure at the thought of remaining in Milan over Christmas, which he had been at such pains to arrange. Julius had complained about that as well.

It had fallen to Tobie to point out that Brother Gilles was in no shape at present to travel. Despite captain Astorre's fading interest, someone had to attend to the poor fellow's leg. He undertook to do that. Then to deliver the monk to the Medici in Florence. Then to join Astorre and Julius and the others in Naples, where they would have spent the winter getting fat and surrounded by leeches of one sort or another. By that time, the spring fighting should be about to begin. Astorre would fight. Julius would count the wounded. He, Tobie, would heal them. Wherein lay the objection to that?

"It's that girl," Julius had said. "Isn't it? By God, you're as bad as Claes. I never see him either."

"The trouble about you," Tobie had said, "is that you think nobody is busy except yourself. Girls? Claes is at the Castello, learning to be a little soldier called Niccolò. The Duke's Chancellor insisted, if he was going to protect the ducal packages. Me? I'm going to Piacenza tomorrow with Thomas and Manfred. We've the guns to order for Fleury, and I'm buying handguns for Astorre."

"He didn't tell me," said Julius. "Out of the condotta fund?"

"I suppose so," said Tobie. "Either that, or Claes is playing cards for money again." He slapped the notary's shoulder, which was solid and made his hand sting. He rotated it abstractedly all the way to the door, looking satisfied, while Julius sat and stared after him.

Chapter 15

Gossip, hurrying over the Alps with departing Papal delegates, got to Bruges before Thomas or Claes. It included a tale that captain Astorre had won a useful contract for the Charetty company, and was sending to call south his fightingmen. Gossip, less believably, tried to make out that the Charetty had won some other contract to supply an accredited courier service between Flanders and Italy, run by—but no. The greatest lords, the greatest men of business in northern Italy entrusting their dispatches to Claes, that scatterbrained lump of an apprentice, who had marched out of Bruges with the company just three months before? Was it likely?

Felix de Charetty, stuck in Bruges with his sisters while his mother was storming about managing the business in Louvain, was one of the first to hear that piece of news, and he believed it all right. Trust Claes. All the best riots, all the best jokes they'd ever shared had begun with some idea of Claes'. He envied the couriers the fun they would have before it all collapsed about their ears, like the Waterhuus prank. He tried to imagine the beating Claes would have to put up with this time.

When the first of the country people, coming in through the St Catherine's Gate, reported a grand papal nuncio's cavalcade on its way into Bruges (that little bishop Coppini) and, guess what, a group with the Charetty flag keeping them company, Felix yelled to his sisters and found and rammed on his beaver hat with the tall crown.

Tilde, who fussed the way his mother once did when his father was living, rushed up to him with his cloak, and stood looking wistfully after him. At Catherine's age she would have screamed to go with him, but thirteen had its dignity. Catherine, on the other hand, jumped up and down, pumping her sister's sleeved arm and chanting. Since Claes left, Catherine had become a woman. She thought she might like to marry Claes, especially if he was away a lot, and brought her presents from Italy.

Naturally, the arrival of the papal nuncio had been heralded, and by the time Felix and a number of his friends had arrived at the St Catherine's Gate, the ducal representatives and the sires of Ghistelle and Gruuthuse and the burgomasters and the Chancellor of Flanders and the dean of St Donatien and the Provost and Receiver of Nôtre Dame and the clerics of St Sauveur and the monks from the Minorite Friars and the Augustines and the Jacobins and the Carmelites were all standing in the February cold, with the town trumpets and drums, greeting the Bishop as he rode up with his escort.

Behind, waiting to make a less elaborate entrance, was Astorre's deputy Thomas. With him were half a dozen men at arms and a figure with a pointed helmet and huge elbow-guards and glittering leg-armour and a stout horse as good as Thomas's. The figure was Claes. His new armour was striped with bird-shit from the pigeons disturbed by the trumpeters. Terracotta within its circular frame, his face beamed at his fellows with its remembered, undisturbed, dazzling smile. What was more, Thomas was grinning as well. Thomas!

Elbowing his way through the respectful ranks of the crowd, the heir to the Charetty won to the rear, his fellows following, and pulled off and waved his beaver hat at his mother's servants. "What do you think you're doing! Back to the dyevats!" shouted Felix, snorting with laughter. John Bonkle stood grinning behind him, and Anselm Sersanders, and Lorenzo Strozzi, and two of the Cant boys.

His apprentice Claes raised a gauntleted hand and made, also grinning, a vast and explicit gesture. He said in the burgomaster's voice, "Boys! Boys! Remember the great city you represent!"

Among the men at arms and the spare horses, it could now be seen, a group of baggage mules stood also waiting, their canvas bales bulging. It was Lorenzo Strozzi who looked it over and said, "I thought couriers didn't stop to trade?"

"That's what I told him," said Thomas.

"Trade?" said Claes. "It wasn't trade, it was a free gift, as you'll be the first to agree. There was this band of freebooters——"

"Robbers."

"Highwaymen."

"And you destroyed them?" said Felix.

"No! No," said Claes. "Someone had done that already, and all their old armour and weapons were being sold off cheap at Dijon. Half price or less. It was a bargain."

Felix said, "How did you pay for them?" His narrow face had somehow got narrower.

"Out of my wages," said Claes. "And Thomas's wages. If your mother doesn't want them, we're planning to sell them off at a profit. But of course—"

"What do you mean? You're her employee. They belong to her. You'd better come along to the yard," Felix said. The smile began to spread again. "And wipe the dirt off all that tin. No boiled leather leggings now, eh? And princesses in your bed, speaking Italian."

"Speak?" said Claes. "Let them do one thing but gasp, and you're done for. Thomas will tell you. If you stop for a rest, they scream for their fathers and there you are, made a Duke."

Thomas was still grinning. "That's a lie," he said. "But they're good enough wenches. Claes is right."

"And we've brought something for you," said Claes to Felix.

"A girl?" said Felix. The note in his voice said it all. He saw, by the deliberate pause, that Claes heard, and was impressed.

"No," said Claes. "I see it isn't wanted. I'll take it back. It was a porcupine in a cage."

"That's a girl," said Lorenzo Strozzi, returned to gloom. "And how was Meester Julius? And the rest of them?" The ecclesiastical cortège had moved on, allowing them to enter the town in their turn and make their way, noisily, through narrow streets where every other man called a greeting, and quite a few girls as well.

Claes said, "Meester Julius is fine, so far as a humble person like myself could tell—all his days spent in one palace or another, drawing up contracts and arguing about fees and clothes and provisions, and dancing on his toes with fine ladies."

"Astorre too?" said Anselm.

"The finest court dancer in Italy," said Claes. "If you caught sight of Astorre hand in hand with the Duchess, with his hat full of flowers and his frills and ribbons so long they need a page-boy on each side to carry them, you would weep for admiration. As for the doctor, your brother-in-law had better look out, Messer Lorenzo. That sister of yours is the prettiest girl in Milan, and Meester Tobias wasn't the last person to notice it."

"You saw Caterina?" said Lorenzo, his eyes brightening. "And my mother? Was there news of Filippo?"

"And Loppe? And Brother Gilles . . . ?"

"The horses? Did you see Lionetto?"

"And girls? Come on, what were the girls really like?"

It was a merry homecoming.

Even when, late that night, the others had gone, and the two entranced sisters, flushed and wide-eyed, had at last been coaxed to their chamber, Felix sat before the fire in his mother's little cabinet, talking and talking while Claes listened. A shrewder eye, looking at Claes and recalling how far he had travelled, might have wondered why he remained.

Some of his business was done. With the Widow away, there was no one to report to. After the unloading, the men at arms had been sent off to take their ease, Thomas with them. Then Claes had made the required trip to the dyesheds to have his shoulders slapped by his friends, and answer all manager Henninc's less searching questions. After that, Claes had quartered the town, as a courier should, to deliver his letters. Some doors were shut, and some merchants absent. Undelivered documents had come back with him: he would have to arrange for them. He had some oral reports still to make. Some clients, curious, wanted him back for a refreshment. He had to see Angelo Tani tomorrow. Today. It was very late.

". . . That was after the explosion," Felix was saying.

"The explosion?" said Claes. He had heard, first of course, about the girl. The girl who—at last—had coaxed Felix out of his virginity. It was not, as he had wondered, the girl Mabelie, but someone new, from Varsenare, come in to do kitchen work, and the sailors hadn't even got to her yet. (Oh yes, the Flanders galleys were still here. Half the seamen, of course, were kept busy in the boatyards on caulking and repairs and refitting and the town took good care to think up work for the rest, but all the same, every night was carnival night to those foreign pigs. Which reminded Felix . . .)

"It's not long till Carnival night. Yes, I know. I'll be here for it." "What else?" had said Claes. And had been told, in detail.

He gathered that the city fathers, once Claes had gone, had lost all sense of humour and had made a ridiculous fuss over the smallest thing, which in turn had put Felix's mother into a rage, just like a woman. All those things Julius had talked about? Well, he had done some of them. He'd found someone to make buckles, and they'd bought some sheets of copper from England, from a boat that didn't want to put into Calais. A woman had agreed to sew helmets. But then there had been that trouble over the hawking, and by the time it was over he didn't know what his mother had done.

Detailed account of the trouble over the hawking. Specifically detailed account of this splendid girl, whose name was Grielkine. Mabelie, he ought to tell Claes, was now the friend of John Bonkle. Now Felix thought of it, he'd forgotten that the Bonkles were a half-Scottish family, but it didn't matter. That bastard Simon had gone back to Scotland anyway, and so had Bishop Kennedy and so had the cannon. Katelina van Borselen was still about, and still unmarried. The Greek with the wooden leg had left, with his begging bowl. Felix couldn't remember his name. Claes didn't enlighten him.

Louvain? Oh. Well. What did Claes want to know? Oh yes: his mother was there just now. Well, she spent half her time there. My God, the new manager there was a handful. It was like listening to Goliath and David, his mother and that fellow standing up to one another. Bark, bark. Yap, yap. No. He was wrong. Goliath and God-damned Goliath. Felix couldn't imitate them as well as Claes could. It would make John and Anselm and the rest spew up into their beer. They went to a new tavern now: they'd fallen out with the old fool at the other one. That was after the explosion.

"What explosion?" said Claes tenderly.

But Felix had veered off the subject again. Felix always resisted direction. He had, however, drunk quite a lot and, before too long, was steered back, mildly aggravated. The explosion. What about it? Numbskull incompetence, as was usual. One of the dyevats went up like a cannonball, shattering the suction pump and cracking the sewage pipe and losing a whole list of cloth and a boiling of crimson. It had taken a week to replace everything, and his mother had foamed at the mouth for a fortnight. Useless idlers! They deserved all they'd got.

"What did they get?" Claes asked.

"Red faces," said Felix adroitly. He made a space for the laugh. "Ernout was worst—remember that idiot? The others lost a few yards of skin here and there, but that's nothing."

Claes said, "I thought I saw a few new faces."

"Personally," said Felix, "I think they're all Henninc's nephews, but when I say so, he just gets angry. I've found a man who can cut taffeta in the French way. You know. It's expensive, though. What did you pay for those arms you bought at half-price?"

But Claes, unaccountably, had fallen asleep and did not hear him. When Felix kicked him a couple of times he merely grunted, and turned over on the settle he had appropriated, which was high-handed enough, for an employee. With some trouble, Felix tipped the settle over, depositing Claes on the floor, where he continued to sleep. From experience, Felix knew that there would now be no awakening him. He lifted the waterjug and emptied it, concentrating, on the fire. Then he made his way, with slight difficulty, to the door, the staircase and his bed.

He was still in bed early the following morning, when Claes left sedately to pay a social call, as invited, on the Medici bank. It was, on the face of it, a minor event. Tobias Beventini might have warned them otherwise.

Angelo Tani, the manager, had shown, in arranging the interview, the qualities his Medici masters had honoured when they made him managing partner of the Bruges company, with five hundred shares of its capital, and a right to one fifth of its profits. His deputy was Tommaso Portinari, whose two elder brothers controlled the Medici bank in Milan. It was Pigello Portinari who, in some distant convulsion of madness, had entrusted this youth with a courier service. Hence Tommaso was to receive Claes as well.

Angelo was well aware that Tommaso Portinari was a jealous young man; jealous even of his own brothers. Angelo did not enjoy the sensation that every now and then mysterious reports on his own shortcomings found their way to Florence, but he put up with it. Ambition was a hone to performance, and his own record for a youngish man was unshakable.

Tommaso had some ability. Left in charge, he could wriggle out of a law suit; placate a customer. But he also liked flattering patronage. When Tani came back, he would find a few deals, a few loans on the books that he and his masters had doubts about. And, criticised, Tommaso would go off and commune in a corner with his opposite number, that fool Lorenzo Strozzi. At such times, Angelo would rub his round head of frizzled curls and draw his pen towards him and arrange for Tommaso, with his fine, ascetic face and diligent culture, to take trips to Brussels and Nieppe, and make himself agreeable to Duke Philip and his independent Duchess and his better-dressed courtiers.

It was good for business, and social success kept Tommaso contented. He wished sometimes that Tommaso would marry, instead of embroiling himself in long-standing contracts with large, stupid women. He supposed that, like all good Florentine mothers, Caterina di Tommaso Piaciti had forbidden her son to marry anyone but a Florentine. Pigello was married already, with two promising sons. One never knew. Perhaps when one of his plain mistresses gave him a plain son, Tommaso would be encouraged to have a bride sent out from Italy. Or perhaps what he wanted was not, in any case, to found another branch of the Portinari dynasty, which stretched back already more than two hundred years. Angelo often wondered how the Portinari felt, serving the Medici. But then, the Portinari had never won fortunes, or cities, whereas Cosimo had done both.

So Angelo Tani drew his under-manager into his room before the new courier came and said, "I think it would be wise, Tommaso, to forget that this boy Claes has been an apprentice. There are those in Milan, it seems, who think him useful. We should make him welcome."

Tommaso had acquired another ring. The stone was Oriental. It represented, no doubt, some sort of discount on the goods he had bought from the Flanders galleys. Tommaso said, his eyebrows disappearing under his stylish arrangement of fringe, "He will be duly astonished. The last time I saw him downstairs he had a pair of shears under his arm, and an apron you could smell from the belltower."

Tani said, "I don't propose, naturally, that you carry him up the staircase and then wash his feet. But a courteous recognition of the fact that he has received a deserved elevation—that should not seem out of place. Unless you would prefer not to see him?"

Vain hope. Beringed and fastidiously dressed, Tommaso was there beside Angelo Tani when the parlour door opened on Claes. Today the Charetty servant wasn't wearing an apron and there were short boots on his feet instead of clogs. The rest of his clothes certainly hadn't tied up a fortune. The Widow had outfitted them all in blue cloth before they went to Milan, and that, clearly, was what Claes was wearing: a stiff-collared doublet with a short, plain jacket over, and a double-brimmed cap. He was professionally shaved, and his old frayed purse had been replaced by a newer one with a good latch, but otherwise there was no difference that leaped to the eye. His cheeks shone, dimple-buttoned. He said to Tommaso, "You've got a new ring. Duke Francesco has one like that. And a brooch to match. Made by one of his goldsmiths. What did you pay?"

Tommaso pondered, and then named a figure.

Claes, emitting an unfocused whistle, sat down on the bench offered him. "No, I couldn't find you anything better than that. That was a bargain. You stick to your supplier. Messer Angelo, thank you. So you read the letters? Were they in order?"

"My friend, in excellent condition," said Angelo heartily. He poured wine into three of the good cups, handed it, and sat himself beside Claes. "Considering the road, and the weather. And, no doubt, you had several others to carry."

"You would think all the world was writing to its master," said his courier cheerfully. "The letters for Messer Nori at Geneva alone! More, I dare say, than even Messer Pierfrancesco has written to you. And, of course, the letters to be forwarded to Lyons. Everyone seems to be buying their helmets at Lyons these days. Not so fine as the Milanese, they say, but much cheaper."

"Cheaper than Bruges?" said Tommaso.

Claes lifted his face from his cup. "You'd have to ask the Justiniani. The Venetians. They bought some, I'm told. Or Messer Corner might be able to tell you: I brought a letter for him. They say the Venetians pay cash. Of course they can afford to. You can pay cash and allow credit, can't you, if you're as rich as they are, and the Lucchese."

"The Lucchese?" said Angelo Tani. "We know our Lucca merchants in Bruges are capable men, but their town is hardly as rich as Venice."

Claes looked mildly surprised. He said, "I'm sure you're right. But they're allowing such credit on their silks—you'd hardly believe. It'll suit our Duke and his Duchess, at any rate. I shouldn't be surprised if all the court turn out in matching cut velvet for the Holy Blood Procession this year. I gave a fat letter to Messer Arnolfini (from his backers, I suppose), and he looked very pleased when he opened it."

"Have some more wine," said Angelo Tani with generosity, and without catching the eye of his deputy. The Medici silk-making business in Florence was managed by Angelo Tani's father-in-law. Only two years ago he had written to Florence begging for permission to sell silk on credit to Burgundy. Begging. For permission to make a huge profit. But the agreement, when it came, was so circumscribed that it was hardly worth getting. In general, of course, he was in accord with the company's credit policy. His contract made his duties quite clear. He was to lend money only to merchants or master-artificers. Sales of foreign exchange on credit to nobles and churchmen were expressly forbidden except by written consent of Cosimo's two sons, or Pierfrancesco his nephew. Angelo observed the rules. He saw that Tommaso observed them. But in every business, there were exceptions.

He was glad he had thought to have the boy visit. He acknowledged Pigello's acumen. He welcomed the new courier service and would tell Pigello that he hoped it would continue. Angelo Tani, sitting back, led the talk genially into a discussion of the current market in silk and then, smoothly, in the direction of the other missives which the youth had carried. The Spinola were mentioned, and the Doria. Savoy and Cyprus and sugar. The traffic in hides and the effect of the English-Scots truce.

The boy had asked about that. Before Angelo could reply, his deputy gave a winsome smile and, forgetting, flashed his rings. "Don't rely on it to keep your noble friend Simon away from us for long. Scotland can't make up its mind whether to favour the English King Henry or the Yorkist rebels. There seem to be heralds at Veere every other day conferring with the van Borselen. The rest of the time they're at Calais. Has anyone asked you to carry messages to London yet? That could make you a few enemies."

Angelo moved his feet. He did not want the boy ruffled or scared out of Bruges. The dashing Simon might have returned to his own country but the peculiar father, the fat French merchant de Ribérac, moved in and out—buying gunpowder, the rumour went, and small arms. From whom, Tani wasn't sure, nor under what sort of licence. The noble Simon's Scottish uncle, they said, had a taste for gunnery.

Angelo watched the boy's face, but it was innocent, he saw, of anxiety. The boy said, "And the van Borselen want King Henry to stay king of England, do they? Like Bishop Kennedy did?"

"It is as well," said Angelo Tani, "to consider them neutral. As is your illustrious Duke."

"Duke Philip?" said the newly elevated courier with, unfortunately, the familiar candour of Claes. "But he prefers the Yorkists, they say. Otherwise he wouldn't be sheltering the Dauphin. Which reminds me. They have a fine menagerie in Milan. I brought back a porcupine for Meester Felix, but he doesn't want it, and it's to be a prize in the lottery. Unless you want it, Messer Angelo?"

"My God," said Angelo Tani.

Tommaso smiled, and then grew serious as he understood this as an expression less of disgust than of consternation. Tani repeated. "My God. The ostrich."

"The ostrich?" said Claes helpfully.

The governor flicked a hand. "It's no matter. A request in the Milanese dispatches. We were a little unwise, sending four fine horses to Messer Pierfrancesco and failing to consider a gift for the Duke."

Tommaso said, "But Messer Pierfrancesco was buying the horses. And the Duke breeds his own."

"Of course. But Messer Pigello your brother has pointed out, rightly, that it is not seemly for the Medici family to be seen in Milan making better display than the Duke. We should have sent him an offering at the same time. A spectacular offering. Messer Pigello has suggested an ostrich from the Duke of Burgundy's menagerie. An unsolicited gift between the two duchies which Milan would appreciate, and which would cost Burgundy little. The animal—"

"Bird," said Tommaso.

"—creature," said Angelo Tani, "would be sent at our cost. Tommaso is to interview Messer Pietro Bladelin on the subject tomorrow."

Tommaso, he was glad to see, sat up abruptly.

The courier stood. "I can see," he said, "you've a lot to talk about, and I mustn't waste all your time. I'll thank you for the wine, Messer Angelo, and get on my way. I've enjoyed listening to everything. That's how you learn, isn't it? Listening to great men and the business of nations."

He bowed himself respectfully out and controlled his inclination to laugh until he was in the street, and round the first corner. From there, he sped to keep quite a different appointment at the unsavoury tavern newly patronised, he understood, by the junior riffraff of Bruges.

They pelted him for being late, and pelted him again for being clean, and hammered him good-humouredly until his chair broke for talking about Dukes with every breath. When he could get a word in edgeways he told, spluttering, the tale of the ostrich.

Anselm Sersanders, who knew everything, said, "The Duke hasn't got an ostrich at Bruges."

The Bonkle boy, cross because of his burden of guilt, said, "How would you know? He must have, if Sforza's got his eye on it."

"No, he used to have, but it died last year," said Sersanders. "Poor Angelo. He'll have to send something else."

"Mabelie?" said Claes.

John Bonkle went crimson.

Claes grinned at him. "She wouldn't leave, would she? It's all right. I took the owner's label off before I went away. All right, what? Felix's porcupine? No, the Duke has one."

"Wait!" said Lorenzo Strozzi.

Since the topic had nothing to do with money, they all looked surprised. Strozzi said, "Wait! Don't you remember I told you? We've an ostrich in Spain. Unless it's died. In Barcelona."

"That was Loppe," said Claes.

"No! An ostrich. Messer Angelo can tell Pierre Bladelin, and the Duke can buy it, and ship it to Milan as a gift. It won't have come from his menagerie, but that won't matter."

They looked at one another. It was Claes who punched Lorenzo's shoulder and said, "What ideas you have! Of course! Why didn't I think of it! I'll tell Messer Angelo as soon as I've had my drink."

"Oh," said Felix suddenly. "No. You'll tell him tomorrow. I forgot. Mother's back from Louvain. I was to tell you to report to her instantly."

The serving-girl, her hand on Claes' shoulder, had already asked Claes what he wanted, and he had probably told her. She and Claes were smiling at one another. Claes said, without looking round, "You forgot to tell me."

"I didn't," said Felix. "I've just told you. And you'd better hurry as well. She's in a fair temper."

"When I've had my first beer?" said Claes cajolingly. "Or half of my first beer?"

"Now," said Felix sharply. "She employs you."

A chorus of appeal, not unduly strong, was raised on Claes' behalf. Felix remained adamant. He looked round, frowning. "He's my servant," he said. There was no gainsaying that. Claes rose, pulled a face, and trudged off with a dejection so precisely that of Henninc after a bad night at the dice that they all sent catcalls after him.

Outside, he straightened. The smile lingered, and lessened, and faded. Then he set off at an even pace through the streets that led back to the yard, and the Widow.

Chapter 16

Leaving the inn, Claes regretted the heavy wool cloak he had left behind that morning. It was cold. Colder than the Alps, because of the dampness. Now, on the way to the dyeshop, there was time to notice it, as there hadn't been yesterday, in the scramble to deliver his dispatches.

He had been away often before. Every few months, the Charetty cavalcade had left Bruges for Louvain. Then had followed the weeks of trying to persuade Felix in from the hunting-field, away from the kennels, out of the taverns and brothels to attend his lectures. Julius, of course, had helped too. Some of the time they had both been successful. Some of the time they had all grown impatient of the responsible world at the same moment, and had embarked on some escapade which got them all into trouble. Well, now Julius was with Astorre, and that was possibly where he ought to have been all along. And he himself was back in Bruges after three months. After an absence no different from any other, as far as time went. It should all look the same.

There had been heavy snow not so long ago. It lingered in darkened wedges on cellar-steps, and it edged towpaths like tarnished drawn-thread work. Where river-water still flowed, ice followed the frozen mud of its banks, faithful as a lace collar. Where the water was still, the middle was crazed with welded floes, broken and broken again to let barges through. The thudding of ice-breakers' hatchets went on all day. There, the water's edge was dark and liquid from the warmth of the houses, and cats prowled, watching for comatose fish to rise gasping. And there too, you saw, as you saw every winter, a child's dress on a pole stuck by a canal bank, hanging stiff and frozen. Clothes were not easy to come by for some folk, but no one would take it: not until the parent of the drowned child had been found, and the child named. Sometimes, of course, it was an infant, and there were no clothes to hang on the pole.

He passed the Crane, idle this morning, but although the men recognised him in spite of the blue jacket, he walked on with a cheerful wave of apology. It wouldn't do to keep the demoiselle waiting. The gates of the Charetty business were open, but whatever train the Widow had brought back from Louvain was already disbanded and invisible. Claes saw men in the yard he had spoken to yesterday, but today they didn't look round. It was odd, in fact, how little attention they paid.

In the house it was the same. He saw the Widow's cook pass in the distance. He caught the flash of her face, then she hurried off. A bad sign. Not even Henninc, to tell him where he was expected to present himself.

Common sense told him that she wouldn't receive him in her parlour, although her son had. The storm, whatever it was, waited for him no doubt in her office. He reached it, and hearing nothing, tapped with caution. "Demoiselle!" he said. Here, one word was enough to identify him.

"Enter," said the voice of Felix's mother. There, too, one word was enough.

He gazed at the latch in his hand. Then he rapped it down like the spring of a stone-thrower, and made his way in. She sat behind the desk. Her face, matching her voice, was chilled and rigid. There was a man seated beside her. The man smiled. "Perhaps," he said, "you are going to claim that you don't know who I am?"

The thought had entered his mind but he had dismissed it. There was no doubt who this was, even although he had never met him face to face. A man of perhaps not more than fifty, but of so large a framework and so heavily fleshed that he topped his reed chair like a marrow. But an opulent marrow. His robe fell to the floor, lined with marten. His jowls sank into the layers of muslin, quilting and fur which lay on his solid shoulders. His hat, a double cartwheel infilled with drapery, had an enamelled crest set with gems on its underbrim. The same crest hung from the jewelled chain over his shoulders. The face under the hat was fresh-coloured and vast; the mouth small; the eyes sparkling.

Jordan, vicomte de Ribérac, wealthy and powerful merchant of France who had attended (so he had heard) the autumn banquet for the commander of the Flanders galleys. Yes, there could be little doubt. Monseigneur de Ribérac: the French father of the Scots nobleman Simon.

No one spoke. The fat man's eyes, fixed on him, continued to sparkle. Claes said, "You are well known, monseigneur."

The fat man turned to the Widow. "Without a change of expression! You see? I commend your teaching, demoiselle. The youth is a model of composure. He answers, they tell me, to the good farm-yard name of Claes."

The bright eyes quizzed Marian de Charetty, and she returned the look with hostility. She was wearing, Claes saw, a gown stiff-ened like leather, and her hair was locked into some sort of con-tainer. Her colour, too high to have left her entirely, had confined itself to a bloom on either cheek, above which her blue eyes glit-tered like lapis. She said, "Farmyard? Claes is merely a short form of Nicholas."

"To allot him three syllables would, I think, be going too far," said M. de Ribérac. "The Flemish form, after all, is proper for artisans."

"It is true," said the Widow, "that our artisans are worth more than another land's aristocracy, but Claes is no longer one of them."

She sat without moving, holding down but not hiding her anger. Claes stared at her, and then switched his gaze to the man. The older, dangerous man.

The fat man said, "Has he been made a burgess, then, since his last exploit? He has been chosen by some very strange people to run errands for them. So, boy. You run fast, do you?"

"If I have to," said Claes.

"And carry letters for the Medici. And others. You open them, do you?" said the fat man.

Claes said, "I can't, if they're sewn with thread and then sealed."

The chilly eyes stared at him and then, measuringly, at the hands that hung at his sides. "I think I believe you. And of course, even if you opened them, you couldn't read, could you?"

The demoiselle's eyes flashed, but he didn't need the warning. He said, "I can read." He added, his voice helpful, "I read the ones I can open, unless they use cipher."

The fat man smiled. He said, "Now I am pleased with you. We are having an interesting conversation, are we not? You read the ones you can open, and the news that is not in code. And you pass that news on. Who to?"

"The people who pay me," said Claes, showing surprise. "I earn money."

"So I realise. And are you earning it for yourself, Claes, or for your employer here? For you still belong to her company, don't you?"

Claes smiled at his employer. "Yes, of course. The demoiselle de Charetty employs me."

"And so you take your wages, and bring her back all the profits. How kind of you. Do you imagine she and I are imbeciles?"

Pause. "No, monseigneur," said Claes carefully.

The fat man moved. "Then why are you smiling?"

"Because," said Claes, "I have had this conversation before. With Master Tobias the doctor. He wondered if I wanted to be rich, or powerful, or just get my own back on other people."

"And what did you tell him?" said the fat man.

"What he wanted to hear," Claes said. "But we fell out, just the same."

Silence again. Then the fat man said, softly, "You spy. Don't you?"

"I told you," said Claes.

The fat man said, "Ah yes. But for yourself, not for the demoiselle here. You spend a great deal of time with Agnolo Acciajuoli. Have you told anyone? What use can these meetings be to the Charetty company? You fall in—was it accidental?—with Monsieur Gaston du Lyon, the Dauphin's chamberlain, on his way to Milan for—what was it? The jousting? And when he suddenly breaks off his jousting and makes his way to Savoy, you know that plan too? Don't you? And sell it to whoever pays highest?"

"Well, I'd be an imbecile if I did that," Claes pointed out earnestly. "Because if I offended the Duke of Milan, or the Medici, or the Dauphin, they wouldn't pay me any longer, would they? You have to think of things like that, you know, in this business."

A smile came and went, on the demoiselle's face. Good.

The fat man said, "I see you are someone who thinks deeply. So, when you earn money, after such deep thought, for your employer —why do you then invest it in your own name? And not in Milan, but in Venice?"

Claes looked at his employer. Then he hung his head.

She said, carefully, "I think you had better answer."

Claes said, "The Medici made the transfer."

"From Milan to Venice. So my informant tells me. They clearly thought it worth their while to pay a certain price for your services?"

Claes studied his boots. "They thought it worthwhile because I had given them the wrong rates for Venice. In one of the letters I opened. It wasn't in cipher."

"You falsified a dispatch?" said the fat man.

Marian de Charetty's face had lost colour again. She said, "You idiot, Claes. That's the end of you."

"But you won't tell." Claes reassured her, reviving. "And it'll make a fine profit."

"I won't tell," said Marian de Charetty. "But have you forgotten who he is?"

"No, I haven't," said Claes.

"I'm glad you haven't," said the fat man. He lifted a hand. "Come here, clod."

Claes stirred. Then obediently he moved along the side of the desk and presented himself.

Jordan de Ribérac looked at him. He said, "You made a childish attempt on the life of my son. You failed to kill him. But you will try again, won't you? Once you have money and a little authority, and people no longer laugh at you and fling you in the Steen. That is why you are suddenly ambitious?"

"Your son?" said Claes. "How would I kill him better with money?"

The fat man's eyes never ceased watching. "You fought him," he said.

"He fought me," said Claes. "You've paid no attention to him before, that I've heard of. Why suddenly champion him now? You won't change what's wrong with him; it's too late. You won't change what's wrong with me: you don't even know what it is."

"You underrate me," said Jordan de Ribérac. "I could begin with your name."

Marian de Charetty said, "He hasn't harmed the Medici by anything that he's done."

The fat man looked at her. "Misreporting market rates to his advantage? Demoiselle, that is theft, and we all know how theft is punished. Does he know whose bastard he is?"

She flushed.

Claes said, "I know."

"Yes," said the fat man. "Whatever I think of my son, when someone lays a finger on a member of my family, I like to find out all I can about them. As I think I have shown you. So let us talk about bastardy. You know, you say. So you know about your poor, silly mother, who fornicated with servants?"

The crash from the table was the demoiselle's fist. Claes looked at it, and her face. She was scarlet. She said, "M. le vicomte, you may leave."

The fat man's bright eyes surveyed her. "Why? The story is old news. None dispute it. *You* have no need to be disturbed, demoiselle. The boy is no blood of yours. His grandfather took your sister in second marriage. You are his great-aunt only by marriage, as the Geneva merchant Jaak de Fleury is his great-uncle. Did you enjoy visiting him, Claes?" said M. de Ribérac. "You did pass through Geneva?"

"I didn't kill him either," said Claes. "I disappointed his wife, but that's another matter. I think you are disturbing the demoiselle."

She didn't look as if she thanked him for that. She was breathing quickly. She said, "The demoiselle is quite capable of having a gentleman escorted from her premises, if his language warrants it. Is that all your business, M. de Ribérac? To warn Claes not to injure your son? I have told you before, mónseigneur, your son is a vindictive man."

"You don't like him," said the fat man. He examined her.

She said, "He is handsome, and has many friends, I am sure. No, I don't like him."

"Neither does the lady Katelina van Borselen," said the fat man. "You are right. He has been wrongly reared. And who is to put matters right but his father?" His mouth smiled and then, compressing its chins, became vertical. He gave a parody of a pout. "But I live in France, and whom can I trust to help me over here? Who will watch over Simon's movements, report to me what he does, warn me if he becomes engaged in unseemly designs, or makes inappropriate attachments, or seems about to forget the family honour?"

He paused. He made a large gesture. "Who but a young informer already under threat of exposure? You, my dear Claes, will become, unknown to him, my son's shadow. For the best of reasons, my personal spy. That is why I have come. To offer you an appointment."

Claes took his time over answering. No one was going to interrupt him. He analysed the suggestion, like a puzzle. Half the pieces were missing. He said, "Because, monseigneur, you want me to kill him?"

The fat man smiled, but said nothing. Claes said, more slowly,

"Or because, after this talk, it ensures that I shan't kill him in case it would please you?"

The fat man's smile broadened. He said, "So subtle! You will have me thinking of you as Nicholas. You will do it then?"

Behind the table, the demoiselle made a slight movement, and stopped herself. Claes ignored it. Claes stood in front of the fat man, and heard his heart beat through the soles of his boots. He said deliberately, "You forget your own manhood. Even an artisan is excused from dealing with animals."

Palms on his chair, the man slowly rose. As tall as Claes and twice as broad, he levered upright his bulk, steady as the town crane, until he stood face to face with the youth. He went on, with a relic of grace, to lift one thick arm until it stretched, like a dancer's, high over his head. The hand, heavily ringed, lay curled in the air, as if about to curvet in a greeting. Then M. de Ribérac swept it downwards. His palm remained cupped towards him. His outer hand, with its heavy quartz ring, burst its way carefully down Claes' cheek, from his eye to his chin, holding its blood-infilled course till the end. Then he drew his wrist back and let it dangle. Below the ring, blood appeared on the floor.

Marian de Charetty, on her feet, had seized her handbell to ring it. Claes moved, his hand on her arm, and prevented her. The fat man, smiling at Claes, spoke to him as if nothing had happened.

"If we are trading insults," said the fat man, "try that for another. I made you an offer. To refuse it with crudity was an error. You will observe, in the weeks ahead, other tokens of my interest in your affairs, and the affairs of your employer. You will notice, too, when I have groomed my son to my taste."

"If he survives it," said Claes. He let the demoiselle's arm go. Blood, dripping from his jaw, was reddening his shirt and he lifted his fingers in a vague gesture to stem it.

The fat man looked at him, and then at the Widow. He sighed. "Who knows what lies ahead of him, or of you?" he said. "You will remember today. Especially, of course, when you look in the mirror. It is not, my dear knave, the face of a Nicholas, is it?"

Marian de Charetty was standing, her hand still on the bell.

Jordan de Ribérac smiled. He said gently, "Demoiselle, you have not been wise. God give you good day."

The door closed behind him. There followed the sound of his ponderous tread, moving away. Without asking leave, Claes sat down suddenly and bowed his head. Between his knees, his hands gripped each other, and blood splashed on them.

He was not often out of control. His body and brain had a good partnership and the difficult moments, if any, were always in private. This one was not. His skin pricked and crawled and the frame of his bones held a wasps' nest. He became aware that Marian de Charetty was beside him, and saying things in an abrupt voice.

"That was assault. Why did you stop me? I'll call in the magistrates."

When he paid no attention, her voice died away, but she was still there. Something touched his torn cheek. He put a warding hand up and found a cloth there. She relinquished it into his fingers and took a light grip of his shoulder. Then her other hand moved to the nape of his neck and spreading, blanketed it.

She held her palm there, warm and firm, as he had seen her do for her children. When he stirred, she moved it away. He saw her face bent over him. She looked half-smiling, half-agonised. She said, "My dear. What a homecoming." Below the wired headdress, her brow had puckered, like roughened water.

My dear. He tried to think about that, but it escaped him. The cloth was sodden but he kept it to his face. His other hand, palmed on his knee, wanted to massage and work like a fuller. He fell into speech. "Why should he do a thing like that?"

There was another stool in front of him. The grip left his shoulders and the demoiselle de Charetty went and sat on that, and looked at him. "Because he is an evil man," she said. "We couldn't warn you. He threatened us with what he could do to you." She paused, and then said again, "If we could only have warned you."

"I think I guessed," he said. "He wanted to lie in wait. He hoped to learn something." His brain began, sluggishly, to work again. He said, "The threats were nothing. But you shouldn't have heard them, or the insults. I'm sorry. And you defended me."

Before he finished, his mind had begun to stray back. She must have realised then that her first reply answered the wrong question. She said, "It was a trial. He expected you to refuse. Claes?"

She had begun to start from her chair. She stopped and, changing direction, took time to find a fresh napkin. She held it out. "In a moment, I'll get you some water."

There was blood all over his clothes. The fresh cloth to his face, he blotted idly here and there with the old one. He said, "If it was a trial, there doesn't seem much doubt of the verdict." The lightest touch of the dressing was painful. It wasn't the same as the back lash he was used to. Scarred for life by a ring. By a man's ring, at that. No one would believe it. Not Julius, anyway. Tobie, maybe.

He began, at last, to be able to handle the matter. He turned fully towards the demoiselle. He said, "Oh, no magistrates. There's nothing very much that would help matters. Nothing even worth talking about. He forced his way in. You couldn't stop him. It would have been silly to call in half the yard over that. I'm only sorry you had to put up with it."

"There is the matter of your face," said Marian de Charetty.

"No," said Claes. "What action could I take that would do any good? And it isn't for you to take any. I wouldn't let you. He won't come back. He has a feud with his son, and he tried to involve us. He knows now where we all stand." He paused. He made to smile, and stopped very quickly. He said, "Put it behind you. I shall. He's just an unpleasant man with an unpleasant son and too much power. I know what went wrong. You didn't ask him if he was thirsty."

But she was not prepared to be hurried. She said, "And the threats? They didn't sound like nothing to me. What have you been doing?"

Claes said, "You can judge for yourself. Let me get clean and come back, and I'll tell you."

"Everything?" she said. She had risen and gone to her cabinet. She turned, flask in hand. She said, "You need some of this, first. What was it in Felix's tavern? Beer?"

"It would have been," he said. "Except that my employer summoned me just as the rim touched my lips." He began to say, "Your son has very bad timing," and then did not say it.

She said, "This is the strongest wine I have. Don't tell Henninc I have begun to drink it. It has been that kind of winter." She paused and added, "For everybody, I think. And Felix has done very well."

He emptied the full cup she gave him in a single long swallow, and let her refill it. He took it with him to the sleeping room that he shared, which was empty, and stood in silence for a moment before the piece of mirror, before he went to find water. The demoiselle had offered to help, but he was used to all this. More or less.

He was quick. He cleaned the deep ragged cut and changed his shirt and scrubbed the marks on his doublet and hose, holding fresh cloths to his face as the bleeding stopped and started. He had put ointment on the wound, and alum. It was the correct styptic, of course. It was also a small, personal gesture of defiance.

After all that, he went back to the demoiselle's office, and found that there was a tray of assorted meats on the table, and more wine. She was dressed from chin to floor in one of her usual gowns, but not the same one, and of a softer material. She was rather pale, and extremely efficient. He was not very hungry, but was glad to drink again. She said, "You deserve to be speechless, but perhaps after your report, rather than before it. Is it painful to talk?"

"Not about this," said Claes with confidence.

It wasn't true. His face ached and bled and he kept dabbing at it. But the need to talk kept his mind occupied. He had already laid on her desk the reports from Astorre; the details of the Milanese contract and the Naples posting, the lists of men and horses, supplies and equipment copied neatly for her by Julius. Now he sat in the high settle and spoke to it.

The demoiselle took her platter to her own table. While she ate, she held her pen in the other hand and used it, noting and checking his figures.

He still drank intermittently, but not enough to make him careless. The items went by one by one. The negro Loppe had been safely delivered to the Duke, and there was a letter about him. The Medici goods, including the horses, had arrived in good order. Julius was with Astorre. The doctor had remained in Milan to deal with an accident to Brother Gilles. A very slight accident.

She queried that, and received a brief account which said nothing of avalanches or Gaston du Lyon. She did not query the equally brief account of the business transactions, such as they were, which had taken place at the house of Jaak de Fleury. He mentioned having bought some cheap armour on the way north in case Astorre needed to refit or add men to the company. She asked questions, and he gave her answers, but went no further than that. Not just yet.

Then he turned to his own work, and spoke carefully. He had delivered the bills and the letters, and had found a sure market for a good courier service. They would require relays of men, and extra horses, but he had orders already to cover the outlay. He named clients in Milan. They included Pigello Portinari and the Florentine friends of Pierfrancesco Medici. He had promises from the Strozzi and the Genoese and the Venetians and even the Curia. And the Duke's secretary had been impressed, and said that he might well place dispatches with him from time to time. It would require someone in Bruges to train the couriers and to supervise the relays. Perhaps someone in Milan also. It was for the demoiselle to say who. These were the receipts so far, and these the draft contracts.

She laid her pen down and began to look at the receipts, slowing down as she proceeded. She laid the last one on the table and looked up at Claes. She said, "These are very large sums."

"Yes, demoiselle," said Claes. He sustained her blue stare.

She said, "You know very well these are extraordinary payments for a courier service. In fact, they are not for a courier service, are they? This is what Jordan de Ribérac was talking about. These are fees for information already received, or bought in advance. Is that so?"

He had known, uneasily, that he was going to have to explain that. He said, "Every state pays for information, and every courier opens papers. We might as well get the profit as another."

She said, "I would have believed you if M. de Ribérac hadn't made a point of it. He mentioned the Acciajuoli and Gaston du Lyon. Neither name is here."

Claes said, "Because they're indirect clients. I met Gaston du Lyon, and he may recommend us to the Dauphin. The Acciajuoli are the Florentine friends of Pierfrancesco Medici. The Medici are clients, and I hope they'll direct the Bruges branch to use us. I saw Angelo Tani this morning."

The diversion didn't work. She said, "I'm waiting for you to tell me why de Ribérac made a point of mentioning them. I take it the Acciajuoli are relatives of the man you hurt at Damme?"

His cheek was beginning to thicken. He said, "The ones I saw come from Florence. The other branch of the family stayed in Greece and became dukes of Athens and princes of Corinth, until the Turks came. Since then, of course, they've all been captured or exiled." He glanced at her. She raised her eyebrows, and kept them raised. "—Or trading under licence with the Turks," he said reluctantly. "That's what the vicomte was hinting."

She said, "Trading in what?"

He said, "Anything. Silk, of course. They're importing already from Lucca, and the Medici are within a sneeze of negotiating as well. Of course, as Christians they're not supposed to."

He saw her trying to read his face, and then look away from it. She said, "Well? Why are you interested in the Greeks, and the

Greeks in you? We don't sell silk. They dye their own cloths in Constantinople."

Claes said, "It would be useful if the Pope launches his crusade. To have a connection, I mean."

She stared at him. She said, "You don't want me to know. But if something goes wrong, I shall be ruined as well as you. You heard de Ribérac."

"There's nothing to know," he said.

She said, "And the other things he was talking about? The letters you carry? I never knew a man more able than you to unsew a letter or copy a seal or decipher a code. Thank God, at least the Medici are safe. They change their code every month and use Hebrew into the bargain."

There was a silence, during which he turned over meat with his knife-point. He failed to think of something to say, and paid the price for the failure.

"Loppe!" exclaimed Marian de Charetty. "Loppe was owned by a Jew? And you are spying, of course. Probably for and against everyone. And the Medici are going to find out. And you are going to hang a rich man. Or would, if I let this go on. It is not to go on. You are to go back, cancel this contract, and join Astorre in Naples. Do you hear me?"

He said, "How can you stop me?"

"I can disown you," she said.

"Then you'll receive your profits from me as a present. Disown me, of course, if you're truly afraid. But you needn't do it yet. And demoiselle," said Claes. "You can't really believe I could put you in danger?"

She was sitting bolt upright, staring at him. She said, "Claes, double-dealing is mortally dangerous. Double-dealing where there is an enemy about like de Ribérac is stupid. These people your clients are jealous and powerful. He mentioned the Dauphin. If the Dauphin enrols you and has reason to doubt your loyalty, then we may as well shut the business and go into exile."

Claes said, "I know all that. Those kinds of risks can be avoided. As far as the Dauphin is concerned, I'd never expect to deceive him. For a prince, he's far too astute."

There was a pause he didn't understand. The demoiselle picked a piece of meat herself and toyed with it. "Felix would agree with you," she said. "The house has rung with the Dauphin's praises for a month. Or with praise of his hounds. It's the same thing."

He waited. When she added nothing, he said, "You've been in Louvain a lot, then. It must have passed the time for Felix."

"Well, of course, he and the Dauphin met in Louvain," said the Widow judicially. "But nothing, I can tell you, surpassed the splendour of that first summons to the court at Genappe. I thought Felix would swoon. You probably swooned, listening. I dare say he talked about it all night."

"He talked all night," said Claes. "But I am sorry to tell you that I slept through half of it. Perhaps Felix will take me there some time. It depends what you want done about the courier service. If you let me run it for you, I couldn't go back with Thomas and rejoin Astorre."

Marian de Charetty said, "I understood that you had already declined your post with captain Astorre and were presenting me with an ultimatum. Either you run the courier service for me, or without me. I should be interested to know how you propose to raise the money for it on your own."

Life consisted of starting to smile and stopping again. He said, "From the Medici. But of course you would have a permanent call on the profits. The scheme and the first expenses are yours."

She was thinking. She said, "You would do some of the riding yourself?"

"Perhaps," he said. "I'd need to stay a few weeks in Bruges to arrange it. I'd need to go back to Milan to confirm contracts. After that, I'd spend my time between the two places, very likely. If Bruges will receive me back from time to time. They probably would. It would be in their interests."

He knew how stubborn she was. She was brushing the quill of her pen back and forth over her lips. She put the pen down. She said, "The business needs money. Astorre and Julius have laboured to arrange a fine condotta. From all you say, I can imagine how much work this list of yours must represent. You did it for the company, and it would be a poor company that didn't thank and reward you. Yes, I shall back you. Yes, you may run the service for the Charetty company, provided you keep me informed, from day to day and minute to minute, precisely what you are doing, my friend Claes."

She broke off. She said, "You're not afraid? Even after today?"

He didn't try to hide his relief. It wasn't only relief, it was happiness. He cracked his cheek open, beaming at her, and shoved a cloth at it and went on beaming at her through it. He said, "You won't regret it. You really won't. Never mind today. Today won't come back. I've something funny to tell you."

Instead of smiling back, she was angry. "Something funny," she said. "That I should like to hear. What about? The Turks? The war in Italy? Felix? Simon? Monseigneur de Ribérac? The explosion?— No, we must keep the explosion for another day, and a few other problems. What is your amusing story about?"

Her voice grated. He suddenly saw how tired she was, and that she was angry with herself now, instead of with him. He clutched the cloth and bestowed on her the warmest, largest, most enveloping smile in his power.

"Well, really," he said. "Well, really, it has to do with an ostrich."

Chapter 17

That afternoon, the biggest entertainment in Bruges was the split face of the Charetty apprentice who had gone to be made a soldier. The household saw it first, as the big lad began clattering about and hopping up and down stairs, collecting papers and other things he needed for all the errands he had to run, he said, before the Festival. Those who had seen him arrive the day before, or had talked to him in the yard, swore that his face was all right then. It wasn't the work of some narrow-minded husband, because he'd slept in the house all last night. One or two merchants had come for their letters, and there had been a call from this fat French lord, but the Widow would have screamed to the magistrates if the fat lord had done it, or would be screaming to Claes, which she wasn't, if Claes himself had upset her.

Asked how it happened, Claes told a different story every time. Some of them were truly marvellous. None of them could be believed for a minute. He was a real joker, was Claes.

He himself had thought of staying in, but there was too much to do, and Felix hadn't come back, which meant he was still in the tavern. By the time another hour had gone by, his face had swollen, half closing one eye. He closed his satchel and took up his cloak and went off to make his calls. Everyone he met had a different witty provenance to suggest for his spectacular stripe, a whipping from the Widow being by far the most popular.

He seemed to meet all his acquaintances at once that day in Bruges, but that was because he had no working routine to follow. It was uncanny, in this familiar place, to hear the command of the bells and not to obey them. Not to hoist the cloths out of the vat and stagger off at a run with his team, to get them pegged out before the noonday peal drove them to dinner. Not to herd with the others for meals and for prayers; to report to his yard master or to his employer; not to be safely one of a group. The group he was now in was not a safe one.

As he suspected, Felix was still where he had left him. He joined him there, because it had to be done. It was not a good place: an inn serving no wine, but just beer for artisans, and the artisans resented rich young fellows like Felix occupying the benches all day, and taking the owner's attention. By the time he got there, Felix and his circle had eaten and then had settled down to some defiant drinking. When Claes came in, the more alert of his friends noticed his slit face at once and, convulsed with laughter, vied with one another, naturally, in accounting for it. Felix, rousing himself, heard his mother's name associated with some impolite fantasy and, jumping up, charged the speaker head down.

Three of them in the end got him quietened, and ready to transfer his aggression to the bowling alley they currently favoured. On the way, Felix changed his mind and, skidding on frosted cobbles and frozen dirt-paths, led them unrelenting through a light blizzard of snow to the Burgh, where the lottery queue wound, cold and grumbling, along the wall of the Treasurer's office and half round the church of St Donatien. A number of well-built men in town livery, patrolling in pairs, made sure that, however cold and however impatient the crowd, the queue remained orderly.

Standing stock-still, the heir to the Charetty company studied it fiercely and then suddenly grinned. Felix, it transpired, had been set upon during the last heavy snows and pelted outside his inn by a group of journeyman drinkers. There they were. Waiting for lottery tickets in their employers' time. And caught helpless at that, unless they wanted to give up their places.

"Felix," said Anselm Sersanders.

"Felix," said Bonkle.

Felix, stooping, paid no attention, although he did, hazily, wait until the nearest patrolman had turned before he started to throw. His aim was not very good and Claes, with relief, saw a distraction. He said, "There isn't enough snow, yet. Come on. There's Colard waving."

The makers and sellers of books were usually in the yard of St Donatien, but in bad weather they packed up their booths and went indoors. Colard's little room was above the cloisters and imposed its own toll on visiting stomachs, being kept retching-hot by the fumes from his candles and brazier, not to mention the chemical reek of his inks.

Today being a work-day, fumes and flames were streaming inward, thrust by air and snow from the unshuttered window from which he had waved to them. In the few minutes they had taken to climb the stairs he had reseated himself at his desk, his knee-stockings twined round its frame like old pennants. He had pushed his shirtsleeves up to his elbows, and his tousled hair was plush on one side where he had been writing too close to the candle.

His tongue out, his face ruddy with health, he was completing a line of careful French script, his hairy wrist moving over the vellum while his eyes flickered up to the Latin work propped on his lectern.

"The Penitence of Adam," read Felix. "Here! Any pictures?"

The translator's lips opened at either end, leaving his tongue where it was, for some moments. Then he said, "Two words to finish. Wait. No. No pictures," he added.

"Aha! Liar! I've found one!" said Felix.

"Put that down!"

Ignoring this, Felix had laid hands on a miniature and was examining it with authority.

He turned it this way and that. "Well, you've drawn a proper Adam," said Felix. "But Eve! You'll have to show that hand of hers in another place. Might not be Eve at all. Might be another Adam."

"He needs a model," said Claes. "You remember. He has a short memory, Colard."

Colard swung round, his writing posture intact and his eyes lit with fury, one on either side of the beak of his quill. "Put that down. It isn't my painting."

"I could get him a model," suggested John Bonkle.

"But it isn't his painting," Claes pointed out.

"Then who did it?" said Anselm Sersanders.

"No one you know. Anyway, he has a model," said Colard, giving up. "She goes about with her hand there all the time. If he ever wants an Adam to match it, I'll recommend one of you animals. I've got some beer, but if you don't want it, just don't do what I tell you."

It was a well-rehearsed routine. They helped him find the beer and the drinking-pots, climbing over boxes and crates and bundles of papers and poking between rocking piles of manuscripts on his shelves. Anselm, who had just had a birthday, sent out to a roast shop for two brace of pigeons with mustard, again a matter of custom; and they sat baiting Colard while he devoured a good deal more than fell due to him.

"Make the most of it!" said Felix gloomily. "Eels from Wednesday onwards."

"But the Carnival first!" said John Bonkle cheerfully. He was a cheerful lad. He said, "Come on then, Collinet. Who are you taking?" He then, belatedly, turned a deep crimson.

"No, then, Jannekin," said Felix maliciously. "Much more interesting. Who's going with you? If it's Mabelie, you'd better watch out. Claes here gave her a good time. High marks. You might lose her again."

"Shut up," said John heatedly. Claes, glanced at hurriedly, proved to be grinning with no visible rancour, although it made beads of blood come out all over his cheek and he had to fish, swearing, for a kerchief. John said, "It's up to Mabelie what she does. She won't be with me. You know that's not what the Carnival's for."

"Father got you in the marriage market, has he?" said Felix. That, as everyone knew, was what the Carnival was really for. One of the few times the rich as well as the poor mingled on the streets of Bruges, and danced, and met, informally, with no commitment on either side, young women to whom they had not been introduced.

Oh, there was no mingling of ranks. However well the masks fitted, the nobles were marked out—by their clothes, by their servants in livery. Gentlemen could expect the hospitality of the great houses, which offered music, refreshment and dancing. And any nobleman, dallying in the streets and meeting a lady of quality, could (so the custom ran) show her his name on a scroll and, if she agreed, make her his partner all evening for whatever sport she might choose, except that he was sworn not to speak.

Those were the rules, and they worked well. Couples met in relative freedom and relative decorum, and good contracts often followed. The very young, however, were well-guarded. At thirteen or fourteen, a girl or a boy followed the impulse, and of such stuff were unfortunate marriages made.

Colard Mansion said, "Well, John's old enough. He ought to be married. So ought you. What's your mother got planned?"

Felix stared at him. "Do you do what your mother says? I don't want to be stuck with another woman. Not till I've had some freedom. I'm taking Grielkine, what did you think?"

Claes opened his mouth.

"And you're taking Tilde and Catherine," said Felix crossly.

"I am?" said Claes. "Who says so?"

"I say so," said Felix. "I don't need to do everything my mother says. I wish she'd get married herself."

"Do you?" said John in surprise. "Who's she going to the Carnival with?"

"Oudenin, if he has his way," Felix said. "But of course that's no good. No. She wants to marry someone rich. Someone with a seigneurie, a bit of property, a title."

"Someone like Jordan de Ribérac?" said Claes.

"Well yes, he's rich, isn't he?" Felix said. "And could keep his rotten son Simon from taking us to law every five minutes."

Anselm Sersanders said, "That's nonsense, Felix. If you don't like your mother running your life, you're not likely to enjoy handing over all the company to a stepfather. After all, you're the heir."

The curls had all come down again round the high cheekbones, and Felix's eyes were heavy with beer. He said, "Keep me in hounds, keep me in drink, keep me in armour and anyone can have the God-blasted business."

"Armour?" said Claes.

Felix laughed frothily. "Thought you'd learn to be a soldier under Astorre, didn't you? Astorre!"

John Bonkle looked from the one to the other. Sersanders, catching Claes' look of polite puzzlement, undertook to explain. "Since you left, Felix has become an expert in jousting. Haven't you, Felix? Except that the demoiselle won't pay for all your equipment—not yet."

"That's a detail," said Felix. "Don't need equipment to show what a man can do. Not quarter-staffs, eh, Claes? Swords maybe? Or blunt lances, if you can ride. Can you ride?"

"You'll have to ask Thomas," said Claes. "He usually carries me part of the way, and then jumps off the horse as soon as it's running properly on all four legs. Who's been teaching you jousting?"

Sersanders smiled and said, "If you can coax Felix to tell you that, then you'll know more than we do. He's found a master at Louvain. The only trouble is, it's all a bit expensive, so that we all see his point. If the Carnival brings him a rich stepfather, he won't much care who it is. Will you, Felix?"

Claes said, "Oudenin. I always said it. And Felix can marry his daughter. Colard, why did you wave to us?"

"What?" said Colard, who had picked up a sheet of vellum and become lost in it. He laid it down.

"You waved at us," said Sersanders patiently.

"I waved at you," said Colard. "Message. Your uncle wants you. And Claes too, if he has any letters. He's at Giovanni Arnolfini's."

Claes said, "Colard. We've been here an hour. Two hours, maybe."

"I don't mind," said Colard. "But there isn't all that much light left, it's quite true. Perhaps you'd better go."

Sersanders said gravely, "Perhaps we'd better. Claes?"

Claes said, "Yes. I'll come. Felix?"

"What?" said Felix, opening his eyes.

"What was that about your two sisters tomorrow? Your mother asked you to take them to the Carnival, didn't she?"

"And I'm telling you to take them instead," Felix said. He opened his eyes a little bit further. "You're not going to pretend you can say no?"

"Felix!" said Sersanders. "That isn't fair. And your mother wouldn't like it anyway. That is—"

Felix said, "Then she'll have to put up with it. There isn't anyone else. Oudenin of course would be delighted, but he's the last person, thank God, she'd apply to. There's always Henninc; but even Claes, you will agree, is better than that. Despite the face. What brawl did you get into, anyway?"

"I was attacked by the porcupine," said Claes with brevity. "All right, I'll take the girls on one condition. That you tell your mother you've asked me, and get her agreement. Otherwise I'm going down with the plague."

"You are the plague," said Colard Mansion mildly. "Would you all mind getting out of my light?"

They parted outside, Felix with Bonkle in tow making belatedly for the unfortunate bowling alley of his choice. Claes, with Anselm Sersanders, set off west to the market, and then north to the consular house of the Lucchese in which dwelt the rich merchant Arnolfini who was entertaining Sersanders' uncle, the elegant Anselm Adorne.

It was not easy to hurry. The snow had stopped, and had turned to sepia mud under the swarming feet of the workmen delegated by the town and the Guilds to decorate the square, the hall, the belfry, the inner dock and all the houses around for which they had obligations, in preparation for the Shrove Tuesday Carnival on the morrow.

Ladders, sparsely escorted, trudged from road to road and

flailed round corners. Carts full of paper lanterns jostled for place
with wheelbarrows full of candles. Collapsible booths, meant to
nourish by daylight the crowds gathered to witness the drawing of
the lottery tickets, and by night the thronging crowds attending the
Carnival, arrived, were erected, and collapsed. Officials with news
attempted to traverse the town, as was their duty, and proclaim it.
Who was bankrupt. Who was dead and who was to marry and who
needed a wet-nurse. Interesting news, if you could hear it.

Men with flags hammered in nails for flags. Painters painted.
Drays trawling kegs of wine and kegs of beer rumbled from tavern
to tavern, drawn by horses like pumpkins, some already bearing a
cocky plume over one eye. A file of bawling urchins followed a
two-legged barrel which had once contained beer, but which now
contained Poppe, a seller of unwashed Lenten ginger, parading the
streets for his error.

Anselm threw him a kindly snowball in passing, which washed
off some of the egg on his forehead, and he and Claes stopped to
bestow one or two more on Witken the weaver, standing tied to a
pole and decked in his own deficient wool, to remind him that
weaving in frost was unlawful.

Both victims swore in response, without rancour. You dodged
the law. You got caught. You put up with it. Next time it happened
to Claikine, Poppe and Witken would take their cheerful revenge.
With dung, maybe.

The Lucca house was in the same street as the house of Pierre
Bladelin; past the Bourse, with all the lottery placards, and near to
the house of the Genoese merchants. At the door Sersanders, to his
surprise, was turned away with an errand. His illustrious uncle
asked him, of his goodness, to find and comfort his cousins Katelijne and Marie, who were skating with their brother nearby on the
Minnewater, and to tell them that their father would be with them
shortly.

A kind young man, Sersanders had no fault to find with small
cousins, although there were times when he felt he had heard
enough of their brother Jan's exploits in Paris. But being percipient
as well as kind, he made no demur and went, leaving Claes.

Claes, led by the steward, walked through the Lucchese consulate to a small yard, up a stair and into the presence of three men
seated at a long table draped in rich cloth. One of the men was his
host, Giovanni Arnolfini. One was Anselm Adorne. The third he
knew by sight as William, the Governor of the English merchants

in Bruges. He stood still, controlling with ease an automatic impulse to smile.

Messer Arnolfini said, "My dear Claes! What have you done to your face?"

It was becoming, there was no doubt, a tiresome question. One might ask the same, if one were unkind, of Messer Arnolfini. It was twenty-five years since Jan van Eyck had painted that pale, cleft-chinned face with its hairless lids and drainpipe nose ribbed at the tip like a gooseberry. Giovanni Arnolfini hand-in-hand with his future bride.

Well, Monna Giovanna, to be sure, still sported horns of red hair of a sort, but Meester van Eyck was dead, and Messer Arnolfini half dead by the look of him. All that was the same was the convex mirror, though one of the enamels was recent, and the silver-gilt chandelier overhead with its six candles burning politely.

Everything tended to be well-mannered about Messer Arnolfini and his kinsmen in Bruges and London and Lucca. From silk-merchant, he had become Duke Philip's money agent. He had the franchise, for 15,000 francs every year, of the Duke's wily tax on all goods (such as English wool) passing to and from Calais through Gravelines. He bought cloth for the wardrobe of the Dauphin of France. And he lent the Dauphin money.

Claes said, "Monseigneur, it was an accident. You wanted news of Milan?"

The pallid, clever face smiled. "I have that already, from the letters you left for me. No. I wished Messer Edward, the English Governor here, to meet you. And I have instructions for you. The letters you carry from Italy for Monseigneur the Dauphin are to be delivered to me."

Contained in that were four pieces of information, which one might as well follow. The first move was obvious. Claes said, "Willingly, monseigneur. Monseigneur has the instructions in writing?"

He had.

"And the armour, monseigneur?" said Claes.

"The armour?" The merchant leaned over and flicked a finger at the stool on the other side of the table. Claes sat.

Claes said, "The armour of my lord prince the Dauphin. Last year's gift from my noble lord the Duke of Milan. My lord Dauphin's envoy began to bring it north, I understand in the autumn, but had to lodge it at Geneva. At a pawnbroker's. To pay for his own transport home?"

"Well?" said Messer Arnolfini. His two guests were studying the handsome roof-timbers.

"Having gold with me," said Claes, "I redeemed it. I have it safe in the Hôtel de Charetty with my lord Duke's letters for my lord prince the Dauphin. I shall deliver them to you forthwith."

"You redeemed it with your own money?" said Arnolfini.

"Of course," said Claes. "On the advice of M. Gaston du Lyon. Who is in Milan for the jousting."

There was a pause. Messer Arnolfini said, "And, my good Niccolò, you have the pawn ticket? In writing?"

He had, in his purse.

"Then," said Messer Arnolfini, "allow me, when you bring the armour, to reimburse you on behalf of *el mio Monsignore el Delphino.* Now tell us, if you will, what news you have of those whom you met on your journey. For example, the Bishop of Terni, my lord Francesco Coppini?"

"An illustrious churchman," said Claes. "Entrusted with collecting pounds groat for the crusade of His Holiness. From Flanders, that is. His Holiness has already said that he despairs of aid from England, racked by civil war, or from Scotland, remote as it is at ocean's farthest bounds. Nevertheless he has sent Bishop Coppini to go there if he can, although he is very small."

"To go where?" said the English Governor in excellent Flemish, which was to be expected of a son of Flemish-occupied Norfolk who had worked for fifteen years now in Bruges. Claes knew, as everyone did, of the friendship between the Governor and Adorne that went back to their teens. And of the friendship between the Governor and the bookseller Colard.

Claes gazed at the Governor and said, "I suppose Bishop Coppini is to go to England, Meester Willem. To reconcile King Henry with his kinsmen of York. Or perhaps to go to Calais, to reconcile the Duke of York's son with King Henry. I wouldn't know, not being on terms with my lord Bishop. Although, of course, we all saw a lot of his chaplain in Vigévano."

"Ah," said Messer Arnolfini. "And did the Bishop's chaplain despair, too, of seeing the English war settled, and a brave English army set forth against the heathen hordes?"

It still hurt to smile, so he didn't. "I took it, monseigneur," said Claes, "that the Bishop's chaplain had great confidence in the

Bishop's powers to resolve the English dispute. And resolve it in time, perhaps, to allow an English army to set forth to battle with confidence. But against whom . . ."

"Yes?" said the English Governor.

"Against whom," said Claes with sorrow, "I was unable, monseigneur, quite to make out."

It told them, for he meant it to tell them, all they wanted to know; for these were three men who were not on the side of the Lancastrian English King Henry, but on the side of the pretender of York, and therefore of the Dauphin of France and of the Duke of Milan and of King Ferrante of Naples. For whom Astorre and his new-gathered company were about to sally forth and do battle.

It was a matter of some ingenuity to lead the conversation from that point to his own interest in arms, but in time Claes succeeded. He received, humbly, what advice the company had to give. Then the conversation moved to the city lottery, in which not so long ago Meester van Eyck's widow and a friend of the Governor had both been winners. "So I hope, my friend, that you have not delayed buying your ticket," said Adorne. "Who knows what you might win?"

He had not bought a ticket, but now he would do so. "Come. Walk with me to collect my energetic children first," said Sersanders' uncle. "You will not forget, however, to bring the letters and armour to Messer Arnolfini?"

He would not forget. The three seated men rose. Farewells were taken. Not altogether to his surprise, he found himself walking through the afternoon streets to the inner harbour with the great man Adorne at his side, his ascetic face sunk in furs. Adorne said, "You brought me letters from my kinsmen of Genoa. Is there any more news?"

A pile of sacks made them separate. When conjoined: "Monseigneur, what can I tell you?" said Claes. "Your kinsman Prosper Adorno will be Doge when the French king loses control of Genoa. But who can tell when that will be? Messer Prosper has many friends, but they don't wish to be named."

"So long as they are friends," said Adorne. "You know, my family supplied many Doges to Genoa. Because of the Levantine trading posts, they never wanted for wealth. But the Turks' arrival changed that."

"The loss of Phocoea," said Claes. "I heard about it in Milan. A lot of people in Milan are talking about it. It seems a shame,

Meester Anselm, that Venice has the franchise now. Of course, the Acciajuoli don't think so. But there's a fine man like Messer Prosper de Camulio, only waiting to be given some chance. And of course, Bruges suffers as well. The Charetty business as much as anyone."

"Yes," said Adorne. "I hear you are taking some care for your mistress's business. I commend you for it."

Claes dispensed, without smiling, as forceful an impression of pleasure as he could contrive. He said, "The demoiselle is the best of employers, but I have no experience. Monseigneur, I should like, some time, to have your advice? The demoiselle of Charetty is anxious to extend her business, and I think I may see a way."

"You wish to invest?" said Adorne. "I am no longer, as you may know, an officer of the city. But I have some knowledge of what property there is, and what may come on the market. Perhaps we should have a meeting about it."

"Monseigneur, how can I thank you?" said Claes. "A meeting would bring us both profit. I'm sure of it. And look. There are your children and Anselm your nephew."

They had arrived at the inner basin, which was a pity. There on the white sheet of the frozen Minnewater were the screaming figures of two of Adorne's older daughters, and the morose face of his eldest son Jan. With them were not only his nephew but a party from Zeeland. His lordship's secretary and chaplain had brought the de Veere princeling Charles, and with them were his father's cousins Katelina and Gelis van Borselen.

The young people caught sight of Adorne. With varying success, they skated towards him. First to arrive was Katelina van Borselen, whom Claes had seen three times before. Tittering with the lord Simon at Damme. Resenting the Greek's Greek in Adorne's home. Apologising . . . however badly, apologising . . . at the demoiselle's house for occasioning Simon's bad temper.

It was she, of course, who had warned him first of Jordan de Ribérac.

She looked today in better temper, and also in looks: her vigorous face with the well-marked brows and rounded chin was blooming with colour, and strands of dark brown hair had escaped from her hood and hung, like Katelijne's, in front of her ears. She wound them back, halting expertly before Anselm Adorne, and smiling, gave him a greeting. Then she transferred her gaze to Claes, and frowned, and then lifted her brows. "And our newest envoy. They tell me you have been rechristened Niccolò. With a knife, it seems."

Her voice was not abrasive, but Adorne, who set store by good manners, frowned in his turn and moved away to speak to his children, leaving Claes standing on the bank of the pond. Claes said with caution, "My face, demoiselle? I lay down and let someone skate over me."

Her expression was the one Julius wore, when he regretted unbending. Since he felt not at all unfriendly, Claes added, "It was a small accident only. The name was accidental as well. The Milanese prefer it to the Flemish version. It hasn't stopped anyone from calling me Claes."

"Or anything else," said Anselm Sersanders, arriving with a hiss of ill-fitting skates. "Look, I borrowed these. Want to try?"

He staggered. A small, stout girl of thirteen or fourteen withdrew her fist and said, "You were skating with me."

"Well, skate with Claes instead," said Sersanders. "He's very good."

"He's a servant!" said the fat girl.

Claes smiled at her. He said, "But that's what servants are for. I skate beside you, and you tell me how I may serve you. Look. I am going to skate like Controller Bladelin. He is very grand, but he's just the Duke's servant, after all. He skates like this."

He finished binding on the borrowed skates, and stepped onto the ice, facing the child and drawing his face into the shape of Controller Bladelin, when about to address a grand lady. It hurt, but was worth it. He made an elaborate bow, achieved a dangerous wobble, and offered his arm to the child, uttering a genteel invitation in a laboured French accent. It was one of the easier voices to imitate. The child's face, mesmerised, looked up at him and then back at Katelina van Borselen. He realised, a little too late, that this must be the younger sister. Ah, well. He repeated, "Distinguished lady: grant me the privilege?" and taking the child's unresisting hand in his own, skated off with her.

She said, "Do more of that."

He did more of Pierre Bladelin. He did both the burgomasters. He skated, daringly, like the Duke's libertine nephew, flamboyant and self-assured until the devastating fall at the end. He skated, with serious concentration, like the Duke's far from libertine son the Count of Charolais, which convulsed small Charles van Borselen, whose godchild he was. He skated like Jehan Metteneye trying out a bale of cloth and making an offer for it; and like the Provost of St Donatien trying to keep up with the rest in the Holy Blood Procession and like the men working the wheels of the crane after too many ale-jars.

His friends kept calling for one of his specialities, which was Olympe, the lady who ran the town brothel, but he resisted. This was for the children, who were in a circle by now, holding on to one another and shrieking. He imitated anyone they wanted, excluding present company and their mothers and fathers. He had been beaten up before. He kept Gelis, too, in the circle with him, and made her his partner. Her poor, doughy face blazed with excitement.

It was Adorne who brought it to a close, calling his family and waiting, too, to catch the entertainer's eye. He said, "You won't forget, my friend Claes, that you have letters to take to Messer Arnolfini."

He waited while the youth skated over, his arm round the child, and a crowd of disappointed youngsters trailing after. The young van Borselen woman, who had stood beside him in silence awaiting her sister, said nothing. The youth arrived. The child Gelis, her brows drawn together, said, "I want to go on."

Katelina van Borselen said, "I'm sure you do, but you mustn't exhaust your escort. He has to keep his energy for the Carnival tomorrow, when he has older ladies to entertain."

The wound, made pliant by the heat in his skin, had opened again, and Claes stopped it with his kerchief while, sitting, he began to take off his skates with one hand. Sersanders came to help him, talking over his shoulder.

"Ah, the Carnival. You'll never guess which fine ladies Claes is going to spend the Carnival with. Shall I tell them?"

"Come, Gelis," said the van Borselen girl.

"Who?" said Gelis.

Anselm Sersanders looked up. "Why, Mathilde and Catherine, Felix de Charetty's young sisters. Felix has just decreed it. Won't they all enjoy themselves?"

Gelis said, "I want to go, too."

Her sister Katelina said, "You are going. You're going with Charles."

"I'm going with this man," said Gelis.

Claes, who was having extreme trouble with one skate, covered his face with his kerchief.

Katelina said, "But he's—" and stopped. She said, "But what will happen to Charles, if he has no friends to go with? That would be unkind."

"He'll have Father Dieric and Meester Lievin," said her sister. "And, you know very well, many other children. I wish to go with someone older."

It was impossible to spend any longer over his skate. Claes looked up and, fatally, met the frowning gaze of Katelina van Borselen. He turned to the fat child and said, "Well, demoiselle: why not go with your charming sister?"

The charming sister flushed, and he rather regretted it. Of course, she would already have an assignment. Or, if not, her parents would have made sure that a number of suitable gentlemen would cross her path tomorrow evening. She was nineteen, and unmarried.

An older, wiser head resolved the situation. Anselm Adorne said, "Perhaps it would meet the case if the demoiselle de Charetty were to allow her two daughters to join my family party tomorrow evening. Our friend Claes would be welcome as additional escort."

"—But—" said the fat child.

"—And of course, so would the young demoiselle, if she cared to leave her cousin's son Charles for a spell."

Gelis said, "I'm going with him."

Claes rocked obligingly to the prodding figure and came upright on his haunches, and then to his feet. He said to Anselm Adorne, "It is kind of you. The demoiselle de Charetty will be most grateful, and indeed so shall I. What time . . . ?"

"Come this way," said the lord of the Hôtel Jerusalem. "Jan will take the children home. Demoiselle, you will forgive me . . . ?"

Katelina van Borselen forgave him, staring in a vexed way at Claes.

"I wished," said Anselm Adorne, walking away, "to mention, since you were speaking of arms, the store kept by the Knights in the Hospital of St John. Here. My father was Guardian. He used to say the Hospital would be as well to reduce their collection and replace it with sickbeds."

"Perhaps," said Claes. He knew the tower the armour was kept in. He looked up at it, consideringly, as they passed. "Unless, of course, the arms are old, or in bad repair."

"On the contrary," Adorne said. "I have no key, or I would show you. Brigantines, helms, leg armour. Coats of mail from

Hannequin's time, in good condition. Pikes and lances. Even some swords."

"Well, I can tell you, monseigneur," said Claes, "there are many who would be glad of them. There's little money for armour, once new guns have been bought. Captain Astorre is purchasing from Piacenza at this moment. From Messer Agostino, who is casting cannon for the Holy Father himself. One to be called Silvia after his own name, one Vittoria after the Pope's mother, and the third Enea after the Pope's name in the days of his . . . Before he had need of cannon. It can throw a stone ball through a twenty-foot wall, can Enea."

"Better than the cannon from Mons? You would hear," said Adorne, "that it found its way safely to Scotland, as it was bound to do in the end. Here we part. Or at least, here we must part, if you are to make sure of your lottery ticket. And tomorrow, you will bring your mistress's children to the Hôtel Jerusalem, prepared for the Carnival. Say at sundown?"

"At sundown," repeated Claes; and ducked his head, and watched Adorne walk away. He was happy.

He had the Dauphin's letters to fetch for Messer Arnolfini, and the bale containing the Dauphin's redeemed armour. He had to walk back to the Burgh and acquire (another) lottery ticket. He had to get hold of Felix, and sober him, and start finding out what was wrong with Meester Olivier, the disturbing manager at Louvain. He had to begin, cautiously, to sound out various tradesmen whose names had been mentioned as having property they might wish to part with.

Skating had made him hungry, but in other ways had restored him. The morning was far away, and the threats of the morning. He stopped for twenty minutes at one of his own favourite taverns and had a dish of tripe and a pot of beer with a lot of people he knew, including Thomas, who seemed pleased to see him. Then, full of energy, he set off on the programme he had made for himself.

Chapter 18

The coming of the Venetian galleys, and Carnival time. The two marvels of a child's year which Katelina van Borselen had missed, exiled with an exiled queen in Scotland. She remembered thinking as much, in her father's house here in Bruges, just before Simon of Kilmirren had taken her into the garden and had tried to embrace her. And she, independent fool that she was, had resisted him.

That had been in September, and galley-time. Now it was February, and time for the Carnival, which would decide whether or not she was to be packed straight off to Brittany to be maid of honour to the widowed Duchess, who was yet another sister of the Scots king. Another fortunate widow, now some thirty years old. At her betrothal, they said, her future husband wasn't upset when they warned him his fiancée was more than a trifle dim-witted and didn't know much of the language. It suited him, said that nobleman. All she needed to know was how to tell his shirt from his pourpoint. He made her a mother twice before he made her a widow, so she must have sorted it out.

Well, if she, Katelina, wanted to be a widow, she would have to be a wife first and tonight, of course, was her chance. So said her mother: a forceful woman whom Katelina disliked, and who had now taken in hand the matter of her daughter's future. From a list of suitable cavaliers, three had been chosen in face of Katelina's determined indifference, and friendly visits had been paid by her mother to the mother of each. Even now, as she sat with her parents looking down on the market square, young men of good family were probably eyeing her from below, and agreeing which would stand masked in her path after nightfall this evening, a scroll in his hand. Or agreeing, all of them, to plead a previous engagement.

The square was lined with houses of passive service like this one, whose owner vacated it in times of public festival so that eminent persons might, seated, enjoy the view from the windows and refresh themselves from the buffet provided. A comfort one ought to appreciate when, as today, it had been snowing. The tapestries hung over the sills were all powdered with white, and snow sat on the crow-steps of all the red gables, five or six storeys up, and flecked the brown brick and lodged in all the fancy stonework round the windows and doors.

The roof of the covered dock opposite was a long, smooth slope of white, and white capped the statues on the public well in front of it, and prinked the four-square bastion of the old trading hall filling the end of the square, with the bulk of the belfry tower straddling it.

It was the speaking-trumpet from the belfry roof they were using now, to relay all through the day the results of the lottery. The Bailli and the écoutète and both the burgomasters were there, on the wooden tribune erected in front of the hall, with the treasury officials of course, and some échevins and the constables of the sections. They all wore their fanciest hats and their heaviest robes in blue and green and expensive red and extremely expensive black, crowded together under the canopy with its swagged greenery and painted flags. The braziers crackled on either side and small tables stood at hand upon which pewter jugs appeared from time to time, and dishes from which steam was rising.

It was not, for the City Fathers, the most comfortable way of spending Shrove Tuesday. On the other hand, the lottery, properly run, could raise an excellent sum for the city. There were always generous donors, especially now, on the eve of the weights-test.

A porcupine in a cage had just been held up, with some care, by two officers. The crowds were so thick in the square and the roads leading out of it that the spectators were nearly immobile. They released their excitement by shouting, and by a jostling of coiffed and capped heads, like a field of clover whipped by a down-draught. Hoisted children flapped their arms, the only beings with freedom to do so.

A porcupine, of course, was no use to a laundress or a brick-maker or a lad from the fishing-boats, any more than would be a pair of gloves, or a wineglass or a drum or a falcon. In such cases the handsome prizes were turned into money in a matter of min-utes. Katelina saw her own father's steward standing patiently in the crowd, among the well-dressed, waiting to see who won the right to the good Spanish horse. Others, she knew, would have their eyes on the gospel the Duke had offered, or the hound, or the holy picture. Sometimes a wealthy guildsman—a shoemaker, a butcher, a tailor, a carpenter—would win and keep such a prize, or a nobleman from inside Bruges or outside its boundaries, for the lottery was advertised far and wide. But mostly the prizes were money, and each announcement was greeted with screams of be-mused joy.

The porcupine caused two commotions, she saw: one within a group of turnkeys from the Steen who appeared to have won it, and another in an assortment of people dressed in the identical blue of the Charetty company. The women of the Charetty household, she saw, were wearing new shawls, and the working men had fresh caps, with knots of ribbon lacing their jackets. The demoiselle their employer, small and round and polite as she had found her on their single encounter, had the reputation of being a sharp business-woman, harsh with her staff and not afraid to stand toe to toe with a man and speak her mind if she felt like it. But she knew, too, it seemed, the mark of good management: to relent on occasion, and be generous.

The Widow herself was not, naturally, in the market place al-though, peering, Katelina observed the son, Felix, dressed in an astonishing pleated garment trimmed all over with black and white fur, and with a lopsided fur hat apparently hanging with ermine-tails. He was howling with laughter and clutching the arms of two friends, one of whom, in dutiful blue, was the large apprentice called Claes. The one who had gone to fight in Italy and then had inexplicably returned. The one whose skating had so entertained Gelis yesterday.

You could see from here the thick red cut on his face, although today the swelling was less. He had been rude when she had en-quired about it. She had not phrased the enquiry, naturally, as she would have done to one of her own kind, but he had no right to resent it. She had, after all, made a special journey to the Widow's house that night last autumn, because she had thought him ill-used by Simon. Well, at least Simon was not responsible for fighting him this time. Simon was in Scotland.

The boy Felix howled again, drawing her eye. She perceived that the youth Claes had won something. A piece of armour. No, a token; a single mailed glove, being presented to him by one of the yellow-caps, a convalescent from the Hospital of St John, which must have donated it. Standing on the rostrum, answering ques-tions and smiling with his flock cap pulled off, Claes looked like the soldier he wasn't. Some of the squealing from the spectators undoubtedly came from feminine throats. He looked as if he was very aware of it, but didn't turn round and wave.

The truth was, thought Katelina van Borselen, accepting a sweetmeat and passing it to her small, omnivorous sister—the truth was that this young womaniser was rather clever, the last thing one wanted in a servant. Wit was for your lover, if any. For a husband, it was too much to hope.

She thought again of the three names on her mother's list of possible suitors. Two were the middle-aged heirs to modest seigneuries, one near Ghent, and the other near Courtrai. The third, and the best catch, was a member of the Gruuthuse family, one of the oldest and greatest in Bruges, into which her cousin Marguerite had married four years before. Guildolf de Gruuthuse, a charming boy of fifteen, was already well experienced. If she married him, she would have twenty years of child-bearing ahead of her, to a husband four years younger than herself. She was unlikely to become a rich widow.

It crossed her mind that she had been short-sighted in rejecting so passionately the mature spouse produced for her in Scotland. She even saw, with a pang, that her father had not been as unfeeling in the matter as she had believed. She realised that, at last, she had grown out of the rosy world of childish romance. Real life was different. One adjusted to it, while working to gain what advantages from it one could.

She turned her eyes from the fevered stew in the market place, and began to scan the more favoured windows and balconies for the devices of seasoned lords from Ghent and from Courtrai, and for the warlike cannon, the vigorous symbol of Gruuthuse.

Marian de Charetty spent the day with Tilde and Catherine, her two little daughters. With other members of the Dyers' Guild and their wives and children, she had watched part of the lottery prizegiving and, as it drew to an end and the crowd loosened, she allowed the girls to take her from stall to stall, and buy and eat what they wished. They watched the dwarves and the tumblers, and threw coins in the cap of the man with the performing dog, and guessed the weight of a pig, and saw a man with two heads in a cage, and a girl with a beard and an animal that was half a horse and half a cow, with a mane at one end and udders at the other that could be milked. They were selling cheeses from it and Catherine wanted to buy one, but her mother wouldn't let her.

It was there that she came across Lorenzo Strozzi and, re-minded, asked civilly how he was getting along with his plans for importing the ostrich for Tommaso. Listening to his answer (he had learned from a sea captain that the bird was still in Barcelona, and had sent off messages by land and sea to have it shipped to Sluys instantly) she studied the tension in the narrow shoulders and sallow, earnest face, and thought, as ever, of Felix. Juvenile, irresponsible, maddening—at least Felix did not look haunted, as the young Italians did, operating in the full glare of cousinly rivalry from the other trading branches of their huge families in London, in Florence, in Naples, in Rome.

As a mother, she tried to rule and educate her only son Felix, and when he defied or resisted her, it drove her wild with annoyance. But was this the alternative? Lorenzo's mother Alessandra, stranded in genteel poverty in her native Florence after the exile and death of her husband, had never stopped pushing her three sons and two daughters.

Her youngest son was now dead. Filippo, the eldest and ablest, had received the best training and was now honourably settled in Naples in the family business of his father's cousin, Niccolò di Leonardo Strozzi. Lorenzo had left Spain to come here to work for Niccolò's brother, head of the Strozzi business in Bruges. But, taught by Alessandra and their own pride and ambition, her sons saw this as servitude. In Florence, Alessandra sold off property; sent them money and advice while, writing between Naples and Bruges, Lorenzo and his brother plotted and planned and struggled and were unhappy.

None of them could go back to Florence, which had exiled them as well as their father. None of them, she noticed, attempted to marry, any more than Tommaso Portinari had done. Unless you could get a good Florentine wife, you made no binding arrangements. And if old Jacopo Strozzi died here in Bruges, would Lorenzo, son of a cousin, inherit? No, the business would go to the brother in Naples. And the brother in Naples, looking at Lorenzo, twenty-seven years old and hungry for money, might think it safer to appoint his own manager, and leave Lorenzo to run errands for the Medici on matters like ostriches.

She said, smiling, as Lorenzo finished his recital, "And I'm sure you have a partner for this evening? Felix tells me he is accommodated, although I haven't been told the girl's name."

Catherine, her mouth full of gingerbread, said, "We're going out with Claes."

To Lorenzo, children were a closed book. Remembering, no doubt, a number of heated arguments, he flushed and said, "Yes, I heard."

Marian was amused. Without thinking she said, "Arranged by Felix, I gather," and caught the flash of Tilde's upturned eyes. She went on, smoothly, "In fact, they've been invited to join the Adorne party, which they will all enjoy. Oh, to be thirteen again."

"You should be able to stay thirteen forever," Lorenzo said.

She did not know what to say, and let him go when he bowed and rejoined his companions.

In the afternoon, when it grew colder, she took the girls home for a rest, and something to eat, and so that she could set their robes to rights and comb their long hair and place upon each smooth hairline the rim of each expensive bag-cap, Tilde's in crimson, Catherine's in blue. The velvet wings, touching each shoulder, lent to the face of each child an engaging purity; and the back-fall, fringed with gold thread, showed off the straight childish shoulders under the cloak. Below that, the tight, square-necked dresses were of velvet with ermine on the tight cuffs. The Adorne would not be ashamed of her daughters.

Twelve and thirteen they were now; and no longer children. That angry glance from gentle Tilde had reminded her of that. What was to be done? She understood all too well how Felix had bestowed the task of escort on Claes. But he had done such things before and Claes was well able to outmanoeuvre him. She did not believe, either, that Claes was ignorant of Tilde's feelings. More than most, he was able to put himself inside the minds of other people. It was Tilde who had told her of the chest she had seen open in Claes' room, and the silver-gilt warming apple that had lain in it. A gift from Milan. But for whom?

But the silver-gilt apple had never been presented, at least not in this household; and she was afraid she knew why. And by the same token, he had found it convenient to engage himself for this long-awaited Carnival evening, neutrally, with her daughters. When he came to collect them, however, he was at his most cheerful: his face cloudless around the angry scar, his blue hose and doublet and jacket in order, and one of Felix's ermine-tails stuck in his cap.

Apart from this serviceable livery he had bought no new clothes that she had seen, except for a good purse and low boots, which he was wearing. To his friends, this was merely old Claes, the walking dish-rag. To the eye of Marian de Charetty, it was the fruit of a conscious decision: a signal of nonaggression to smooth his passing return to the herd. She could imagine Felix's reaction, if Claes had returned in the latest Milanese fashion.

She wondered if Claes ever longed for these things, and decided that he didn't. Or hadn't, so far. If he did, it would be some woman, no doubt, who would teach him. The little serving-girl Mabelie had taken up with John Bonkle—so Felix had let slip. And Felix himself, she was fairly sure, had found a girl of the same sort. She could not deal with that. Julius, so good in many ways, had failed her too in this respect. And it was one of the few areas where pride would not let Felix learn from Claes.

Did youths grow out of these wayward passions? Would the pretty face in the hedgerow always tempt them, up to and after the time when good sense said that they must found a family, or old age would find them with nothing? At what age did a man come to himself, and see that he must have security? Perhaps, for some men, it never happened.

Her home was empty. As Cornelis' wife, she would have kept open house for his friends, while the young went out in their carnival clothes and passed the night in undisclosed pleasures. A widow, she had already accepted the hospitality of the other dyers: she did not want, a widow, to join them in their houses this evening as one of the older generation, Cornelis' generation, which was not hers. She did not want, either, to join the throng in the market place, the throng of couples, of lovers, as a mother, a widow, a chaperone. But to stay in, alone, was not pleasant.

So she was surprised and delighted when, an hour or two after nightfall, a servant came to her door from the Adorne family, requesting her company at the Hôtel Jerusalem for the evening. The young people, said the servant, had all left, and the demoiselle Margriet had thought she might be alone, and free to join them until her daughters returned. Or, indeed, to stay overnight should it please her.

She asked the servant to wait while she prepared herself quickly and, locking and double-locking her doors, left the house to her porter. Then she stepped into the familiar street, and took time to pause for a moment. Beside her, the Adorne servant stopped too, obediently, his torch in his hand. But tonight, there was no need of light. The snow had vanished, except as a sparkling design upon buildings, tinted peach and rose and lilac and leaf-colour by the paper lanterns that clustered like birds by windows, doorways, walls and corbels in every street.

Tonight every gate-lamp was lit, and the corner niches with their holy statues shone bright and tended. And so, in answer, did all the towers and spires of the churches, outlined tonight in twinkling candle-lamps against the black, icy sky. The street, even here away from the centre, was crowded with thickly-cloaked, rosy people, and, somewhere, she could hear music.

Marian de Charetty stepped out. The night, which had promised nothing, now promised companionship. At the very least.

Under the same magical sky the former apprentice called Claes was entertaining, with artistry, a number of disparate young whose attendants knew less about children than he did. He had the sheer delight of the lanterns to help him. They walked about, their faces upturned. From the hump of each bridge, with its painted statues, its branched lights, its evergreen, they looked down on a fairyland reflected in water. The canals were tinselled like ribbons, and so were the children's faces, catching the light from them.

But then, after the lights, there was the rapture of the market place, far more exciting than it had been during the lottery-draw, with the booths all taper-lit, and selling everything that was wonderful—fruit and sugar almonds and nuts and figs and raisins. The stalls had flags on them, and there were flags all round the square and on the roof of the Waterhalle and the Old Hall, all lit by lanterns.

There were so many lights and so many people that you didn't really feel cold, but in any case there were braziers at the street corners and hot drinks and soup to be got at some of the booths, and even three men with an oven on wheels, pushing in dough at one end and raking out hot pies at the other with the speed of devils in hell, while their customers hedged them in shoulder to shoulder, eating and spluttering, red-faced in the glow from the embers.

There were braziers up at the other end too, on the rostrum cleared now for the town players—the trumpets and pipes and drums and timbals and fiddles—and the town singers, with the scarves of their hats spiralled round their valuable throats. The songs they sang were not the kind you would hear in a tavern, but when the drums and fiddles got going, the children would begin to dance up and down and then the older people, and a circle would start up somewhere for a country dance, and then break off, because it was early and everything was orderly yet.

The scaffolding, of course, had been taken down, Witken the weaver having completed his two days of penance and Poppe having reached, officially, the end of his mortification by barrel, although he was still wearing it, drunk, in the boisterous care of his friends. Then the seamen began to bring the ropes into the square for the tightrope walk they always did, with hoops, up in the belfry; and some of them were drunk as well, although not, you had to hope, the ones who were going to fasten the rope or the ones who were going to dance on it. By that time, Claes' young ladies were becoming extremely excited.

By that time, also, a number of things had happened.

Jan Adorne had left, for one thing. He was not, as a student, wife-hunting; but at fifteen he was undoubtedly on the track of something other than a group of small girls. The small girls, who did not regard themselves as such, resented this.

The two Adorne daughters, as it happened, were well-behaved and at home with Claes. He talked to them and made them laugh, and invented things, and introduced them to funny people (if Father Bertouche didn't stop him) and let them do interesting things that Mother would never allow, when Father Bertouche wasn't looking. They liked his jokes and the feel of his broad, capable hands on their backs as he shepherded them through the crowd. They were, of course, too old to sit on his shoulder, but now and then he would put his two hands round Katelijne's stripling waist and hoist her to get a clearer view.

When that happened, Father Bertouche coughed, or tapped Claes on the shoulder. He coughed partly from disapproval but partly because he had a raging cold. He also had aching feet, and was pining, explicitly, for his comfortable quarters in the Hôtel Jerusalem. The chaplain, therefore was little help, particularly as the Charetty girls paid no attention to him: Catherine because she had gone insane with excitement, and Tilde because she was Claes' chosen lady and insulated from the rest of mankind for the evening.

This was Claes' mistake. It arose, as his employer had suspected, from a very clear understanding of her elder daughter's mind. To wound Tilde tonight by treating her as another child was unthinkable. He accordingly announced that, as the elder of Felix's sisters,

Tilde was to take the place of her mother this evening, and would be his official consort. At the time, it had seemed a reasonably good idea. Tilde had flushed with pleasure, and he had been careful to keep the other children amused while giving her, when he could, a mock-courtly attention that she could enjoy without taking it seriously. Then Catherine, spurred by the noise and the lights and the strangeness, began to run wild.

When Felix exploded, Claes got him out of public view and then found a way for him to get rid of his energy. It was different with a young girl, who kept dragging her hand from the miserable chaplain's and hurling herself into the thick of the crowd—a crowd which by this time was not quite so orderly, or so sober, and which was beginning to be pushed this way and that by another element —the young nobility, in their silks and their furs and their grotesque and marvellous masks, walking in groups to and from their chosen mansions with their servants and their musicians and in the mood to slap aside a careless child who cannoned into them—or to take her by the arm and lead her with them.

Claes caught her twice and fetched her bodily back in a whirlwind of squealing and laughter. The second time, Tilde brought up her arm and slapped her sister open-handed on the side of the head so that Catherine screamed in earnest and glared at her, hand to cheek and tears in her eyes. The Adorne daughters stared at them both and the chaplain made a noise like a horse trotting in mud.

"Hey!" said Claes, closing his warm hand round Tilde's wrist and taking Catherine round the shoulders with his other arm. He shook Tilde's wrist a little, and tilted up her clenched hand. "Look at that fist! You frighten me! How can I escort a lady who might beat me at any moment?"

Catherine giggled. He turned to her. "And oh dear, look at Father Bertouche. He can't look after everybody, can he, while I'm running after you? He'll have to take everyone home, and we'll miss the tightrope walkers, and the bonfire and the fireworks. And you haven't even had your fortunes told yet."

"I want my fortune told," said Catherine.

"But I can't trust you, can I?" said Claes. "So I'll just have to see that you don't run away again." And holding her arm tightly in his, he unbuckled his belt, and adding it to her girdle, shackled her loosely to him.

It was what she wanted. Tears gone, she took his arm and

dragged him across to the astrologer's. Beside him, Tilde walked stiffly. She said, "Mother would have slapped her."

She was no longer his undisputed partner. Catherine skipped on his other side. Claes said, "Of course you must slap, if everything else fails, and there is some danger. But it's quite good to try other things first."

"Felix hits you," said Tilde. She paused, and then went on before he could answer. "But of course, my mother doesn't."

A roar went up. The tightrope walkers had appeared at the top of the belfry. The heads of Marie, Katelijne, Catherine, Father Bertouche and even of Mathilde turned involuntarily upwards. Claes blew, invisibly, a sign of relief and amusement that made his cheek crack. A commanding voice, shrill as a whistle said, "Ah, there you are! Where have you been? You were told to look out for me! You haven't been trying!"

Herod, where are you? Packhorses crossed the Alps with less trouble. Dragging her expensive furs to his side was a short, stout party he had seen before . . . Ah, Gelis. The young van Borselen girl with whom he had skated, and who had tried to command his services for this evening. Pushing through to stand behind her, thank God, came a liveried manservant and a cloaked maid in a white coif. Beside him, Tilde's head turned, and a moment later, the chaplain's.

The van Borselen sprig looked up at him sternly. You put a bag over their faces, that was all. A bag with a few oats at the bottom and they were perfectly happy. The van Borselen girl said, "I brought a cloak and a mask, in case you couldn't afford them. Here." The manservant, catching no one's eye, transferred to his mistress a long roll of extremely good cloth, with a vast concoction of feathers settled on it. She held the armful to Claes.

Claes said, "Demoiselle, you are welcome to join us. We were hoping you would. But there are too many of us for a masquerade. You know the demoiselles de Charetty? And of course, the demoiselles of Adorne. Father Bertouche . . ."

Father Bertouche, his inflamed nose in his kerchief, gazed with animosity at the threatened increase in his flock. He said, "Certainly, we are not joining in any masquerade. Indeed, we were considering whether, at the end of this performance, we should not make our way home."

"I should like to go home," said Tilde flatly. On Claes' other side, Catherine's face appeared, frowning. Beside the priest, the two Adorne girls were whispering. The older, Marie, flushing, murmured something.

"What?" said Father Bertouche.

The van Borselen girl looked at him with impatience. "She says her sister needs to go home," she said. "Don't you have a maidservant with you?"

The chaplain removed the kerchief from his nose, and his upper lip glistened ochre in the lamplight. He looked stricken. Claes smiled. "It's a common problem," he said. "I don't mind taking her, if she wants to be comfortable. I know a lot of girls here."

The Adorne child, poor thing, looked as stricken as the chaplain. She said, "I want to go home," in a strangled voice.

"All right," said Gelis van Borselen. "Take my maid. Matten, go with them. Help the demoiselle if she needs it. You needn't bother to come back."

Christ. Claes said, "Then we'll all go back to the Hôtel Jerusalem."

The fat girl stared at him. "I'm not leaving," she said. "And I've sent my manservant home. I'll stay by myself if you don't want to keep your promises. You did promise."

With undesirable but understandable speed, the group about him was dissolving. Untying Catherine, finding some sort of words to say to Tilde and the retreating chaplain, Claes caught the essential phrase and was in time to plunge after the vanishing manservant and drag him back by the arm. He looked frightened.

With reason. "I told him to go," said the child. "Or he would hear about it from my father."

"And I," said Claes firmly, "am telling him to stay, or your father will hear about this from me. Where did this cloak and mask come from?"

"I borrowed them." Her chin came up, improving the view slightly.

"I'm sure. And if you take them back in time, perhaps no one will say anything about it. So I shall make you an offer. Ten minutes here at the tightrope. Ten minutes dancing with some of my friends. Ten minutes for the fireworks and the bonfire. And then our friend here and I take you home to your sister."

Gelis said, "I'm not staying with Katelina. I'm staying at my lord of Veere's house where Charles is. Do you want to know why?"

She wasn't a bad child. Ahead of him, unexpectedly, glimmered the promise, at the end of it all, of an hour or two to spend as he pleased. With whom he pleased.

He listened, peaceably, to the item of information she was pressing upon him, and found it, indeed, nearly as interesting as she thought it was.

Chapter 19

A s children were taken home, masqueraders began to fill the streets. Gradually, among the fustian, there appeared thick cloaks of furred velvet with glimpses of pearled sleeve and gold fringe and silk brocade underneath. And next to the felt caps and decent hoods and white bonnets there would brush past a griffon, a jester, an eagle. A unicorn would turn to look at a pretty ankle, or a ship in full sail pass by laughing, or a goat or a Charlemagne pause to toss a coin and pick up a sweetmeat.

Katelina van Borselen was not yet among them. The cloak she was going to wear lay on the table by the great window in her parents' house. Every now and then, she paused by the window to see if her mother's three suitors were waiting yet. The house was empty but for its gatekeepers. They were there to protect it, for the other servants had leave to stay out, or were with her parents at the lord of Veere's house. They were there to protect her as well, in case her escort failed to come, or proved undesirable. Or in case (as was not entirely unheard of) one cavalier disputed with another, and she was left waiting with none.

Usually, however, there was no unpleasantness. The candidate proffered his scroll and was chosen or excused with courtesy. Unknown in his mask, he lost no face before a waiting rival. Unless, of course, he was confident enough to bring his liveried torch-bearers, his pages, his servants. As, glancing out, she saw presently that Guildolf de Gruuthuse had done.

She had missed his arrival. He was already waiting under the eaves of the opposite houses. He was cloakless. From the neck up, there was nothing of him to be seen but the pelt, eyeholes and fangs of a magnificent leopard-head. From the neck down, the lamplight displayed a brief, fur-hemmed tunic and the negligent line of his hose, exposed from mid-thigh to the soles of his feet. One gloved hand rested at his hip. In the other, exposed to the light, was a masquerade scroll. And behind him, with the Gruuthuse cannon on every shoulder, were six liveried servants. One of them held a ribboned lute like a cat by the tail.

He had just, she thought, taken up his stance, because the group he had come with were still in sight, calling and laughing. As she watched, others passed, and there were exchanges of some hilarity. This was normal. The moment she appeared, he would revert to the usage of chivalry. She ought to go down. She ought to make quite sure, first, that there were no other contenders (was it likely?). Katelina, with the greatest discretion, peered from the window.

There *was* another contender. A man both taller and broader than Guildolf, waiting serenely, scroll in hand, beside her own gatepost. He was alone, with no servants or device to distinguish him. Of his shape she could see nothing either, for he was cloaked from his mask to his boots. And of the mask itself she could make little in the uncertain light. It seemed to be made up of feathers.

She hesitated. Then she took up her cloak and descended the stairs of her father's house slowly. She crossed the yard, and spoke to one of the porters, who opened the gates. She stepped through them.

The big man with the cloak was, of course, nearest, but she must acknowledge them both. Katelina faced the distant leopard and dropped him a solicitous curtsey, but turned to deal first, as was natural, with the nameless suitor beside her. She dipped her skirts again, with marked refinement, and held out her hand for his paper.

He knelt, presenting it. The headdress, catching the light, proved to be the mask of an owl. The name on the scroll was that of the suitor from Courtrai, which was odd, as she'd believed him a short man. On the other side of the road Guildolf de Gruuthuse had set out to join her, and was crossing the cobbles with elegance.

So. There were no other claimants. She had to choose between the beast and the bird. Beside her the bird, who had risen, chuckled under his breath. Suitors were not supposed to speak. In mellow Flemish with an undertone somewhere of French, this one made a short statement. "Pick him if you like, but he plays the lute like a butcher, and squeezes his boils every morning at table. That's the idea of the leopard. By the time he takes the mask off, you've got used to them. He's keeping the rest of the skin for his bridal night."

She choked. Controlling herself made her eyes water. The handsome legs and the leopard-head arrived before her. The wealth of the Gruuthuses. Twenty years of child-bearing. Boils.

Katelina van Borselen curtseyed again to Guildolf de

Gruuthuse, but laid his scroll gently back in the hands which had offered it. "My lord, I am honoured, but you have been forestalled by another. God give you a happy evening and night, and may we drink together one day in friendship."

He was disconcerted in the extreme. It was, she saw, rather unlikely that he would drink with her or any member of her family again. She hoped that her mother, who had created this fiasco, could repair it with equal facility, and rather thought that she could. After all, it was her mother who had issued, as it were, three invitations. Someone was bound to be disappointed. The idea that three people might be disappointed was not, of course, something that her mother had contemplated.

Katelina was not greatly concerned. In her view, what mattered was whether or not the evening was likely to proceed in such a manner that she, Katelina, would not be disappointed. She curtseyed deeply, and the Gruuthuse boy bowed and marched off, his entourage following raggedly, with all their mouths at different angles. The man carrying the lute made, behind his master's back, a light-hearted manoeuvre with it that Katelina hoped she didn't understand. A low booming sound from under her companion's mask told her that he had noticed it too. She realised that she had chosen a vulgar man and was visited by a strong qualm.

Perhaps he observed it. At any rate, he made her a bow of elaborate and expert dimensions, presented his arm, and laying his hand on top of hers, proceeded to lead her up the street in the wake of the richly dressed courtiers ahead of them.

The first open courtyard they came to was the Controller's. On Carnival night, their clothes, their masks, their jewels were the only passkey gentlefolk needed. They swept under the archway and into the lantern-lit garden where fire-baskets glowed through the wine they took in their glasses. High in a tower, flutes and fiddles and viols penetrated the chatter, and a small diligent drum paraphrased it.

People moved, and circled, and went. Once, there came winding under the trees an arcade of dancers, linked hands high, sleeves swaying below finials of monstrous and beautiful headgear. In the icy February night, the women's headdresses bloomed like camellias or lily-spikes; or seemed fit for eating, like gourds and pastry-puffs and heaps of sugared sweet things, bound with angelica.

Tonight, she had left behind the famous hennin, and her maid-servant had pleated strands of her hair through a thin goldsmith's caul, and made the rest into a thick ribboned braid, long enough to be pressed by her cut-velvet skirts when she seated herself. To-night, her four-stranded gold necklace from Lyons lay upon bare skin instead of the eternal infill of gauze, and she had rings on most of her fingers.

Her companion, she saw, had none; not even a signet. It con-firmed what she guessed, although, observing the rules, he did not speak again. He knew what manners required. To begin with, she made few demands on him, but later, as they moved from Blade-lin's to the new-built courtyard of the Ghistelhof and from there to the house of Vasquez; from the palace of Jean de Gros to the Seven Towers or the hall of the Archers' Guild; when they ventured into the great mansion of Gruuthuse without meeting a leopard, and finished in the gardens of the Princenhof itself, guests of the absent Count of Charolais—then, tentatively, she ventured to take part in the dances and found that she had no need for concern, because he was skilled in their figures and deft in their execution. When she wished refreshment, he served her punctiliously, and also such of her friends as they met.

Sometimes, at a less formal encounter, he served them in other ways, making them gasp and laugh by the way he tossed and jug-gled their plates and made knives calmly appear or disappear. He was not vulgar, she found to her relief, but he was amusing. And he neither took off his cloak, nor did he touch her, except by the hand or the elbow. Only she noticed, while she was able to notice, that he so managed that she was offered a great deal to drink.

She was not disturbed. She let the evening go where it would lead her, knowing the pattern. At some point he would take her home—to the house empty but for the porters who, recognising her accredited escort, would allow them both in. She would lead him to her mother's parlour and, to thank him for his escort, would offer him wine and ask him for the privilege of seeing his face. And he would unmask.

Girls who had told her this much were rarely explicit about what followed. If a conquest had been made, the family of the suitor would pay a call on the family of the prospective bride and an arrangement would be come to.

That was next day. What happened on the evening in question was, evidently, a matter of discretion. But it couldn't, after all, be very much. The house might be empty, but it wasn't going to stay empty all night. And under normal circumstances, it didn't matter much anyway. You asked your approved cavalier to your home, and he came. That meant marriage. Simple, if you brought home the right man. Not so simple, if you didn't.

It made her tired, thinking about it. Her escort caught her when she stumbled the second time and said, "You must be weary. Shall I take you back to your house?" They were the first words he had spoken after the greeting, and she could not detect in them any accents at all of Courtrai. She said, "I think you'd better." Then she said, "After you've taken the mask off."

They had stopped facing each other. She waited for him to obey. Instead, the mask with its unblinking owl's eyes turned from one side to the other in explicit refusal. She stood for a while to see if he would give up, and when he didn't, she turned and walked off frowning. After a moment he caught up and took her elbow again, for which she was grateful.

At her gate, the duty porter recognised the mask, and being well-trained, merely wished them both a good evening and opened the gates without smiling. He went ahead to unlock the door which led into her hallway, and make sure that the lamps were all burning.

She led the way to her mother's parlour. She had drunk a great deal, but thinking of this moment, she had made sure that she was not in any discomfort, and he too, she was aware, had calmly absented himself from time to time. Another, if minor, sign of the adept. So now she could discover from whence all this expertise came.

The fire had burned low. She went to repair it and he said, "Watch your cloak," in the same level Flemish. She waited, allowing him to unclasp the garment from behind before she knelt: she felt his fingers brush the ruffled rope of her hair. Then, as she mended the fire, he crossed and laid her cloak on a stool.

She expected, when she turned and rose, to find that he had done the same, but he had discarded nothing. She said, "Now you reap your reward for all your gallant service this evening. It is only, I'm afraid, another cup of good wine but at least you may sit, and let me give it to you." She had reached the cupboard, smiling, but still he had not moved. She lifted two cups and a flask and began to bring them back to the settle before the fireside. She said, "I understand. There is an owl's face under the owl's face?"

The cloak was blue in colour, and thick, and fell straight to the ground. He made no effort to remove it. She bent, a little impatient, and set the cups and the flask on a stool and was aware, as she did so, of a lock of released hair swinging close to her shoulder. She tilted her head to collect it, even as she realised what had happened. In removing her cloak, he had released all her hair from its pleat.

She turned, lifting her eyes to question him. She found he was immediately behind her, and the owl mask inches away. He said, "And now the rest of the pretty laces."

She jerked away from his hands. She moved so sharply indeed, that she left her necklace still in his grip. "Oh no," said Katelina. "That isn't part of the bargain."

The owl stood where he was. You couldn't tell if he were dismayed, or angry or merely patient. He said, "I haven't made any bargains." He began, without haste, to walk towards her.

She was between a chair and the wall. She said, "You have. My mother's arrangement. The scroll gives you leave for an evening, as my escort. Now you must be content. If you want more, you can call on her tomorrow." She ran out of breath.

He had stopped at the chair. He said, "If *I* want more? But it's you, demoiselle, who wanted this, surely? You knew when you saw the scroll that I was not from the seigneurie of Courtrai. You knew when you brought me home that I was not one of the three suitors your mother had chosen. No one has made a bargain. No one has given me leave to be here, except you. And why, if not for this?"

"It was not for this," said Katelina.

"For the wit of my conversation? But I have passed the whole evening in silence. For the rapport between us? But we have never yet been alone with each other. Why then have you brought me here, if not to sharpen my hunger and satisfy yours? Sweet demoiselle, all the world knows you for a virgin and suspects you for an unwilling virgin. Why remain one any longer?"

It was not only going wrong, it was going wholly wrong. Even his voice was different. Katelina said, "It may be hard to believe, but rape was not what I had in mind." She paused. "Marriage, perhaps." Had he locked the door?

The mask produced a low laugh. "You were ready to entertain a proposal of marriage with the man you thought I was! Rubbish, my dear demoiselle. I expect to marry you, but only after I have introduced you to the very particular delights of the condition. Then I think, without too much persuasion, you will be quite content to be my wife. I am," said the owl, "a man, I am told, of exceptional powers. I am willing, since my son cannot please you, to put them all at your disposal."

"Your *son*?" said Katelina.

The great cloak, as she spoke, was being thrown back. The courtier's hands which had served her so skilfully rose to the amusing owl mask. The fingers, which had led her from dance to dance, which had taken that strong, considering grip of her clothing, gripped instead each side of the mask and lifted it carefully off. Underneath were the benign, mammoth features of Jordan de Ribérac.

He said, "Or do you dislike Simon so much? I sometimes wonder. But he, of course, is far too offended to make you an offer and, in any case, has a little feud of his own to settle first. Or thinks he has. He will find, I think, when he comes back that it has been settled for him. The churl still has two eyes, but he will remember me every time he looks in the mirror. I detest peasants and people who consort with peasants," said the vicomte de Ribérac. "You will notice this, when you come to France. I could not breed on you otherwise."

Claes. It was this man who had marked Claes. And what else was he saying? She put both hands on the chair before her. She said, "You want children to oust—"

He interrupted, smiling gently. "A single son: what a hostage to fortune! A wealthy man needs more than one heir."

She said, "You have a wife."

Jordan de Ribérac smiled. "There are many ways," he said, "of getting rid of a wife. Whereas a child-bearing woman is beloved of man and of God, as we will prove, you and I, if God wills it. The door is locked and the porters are bribed, demoiselle Katelina. I shall undress, and you, if you will be so kind, will place a little more wood on the fire. There is a draught on this floor. I can feel it already."

The door to the main house was locked. But the door in the opposite corner was not, and led to steps, and a yard, and a postern she knew how to get through.

She moved to the fire as if to mend it. He *was* undressing. He unclasped his overgown and began to drag his thick arms from the quilting. She waited no longer. She leaped for the small doorway, and took the stairs two at a time, hoisting gown, sleeves and underskirt out of her way as she went.

She heard him swear, and then start to follow. His footsteps drummed on the uppermost stairs as she plunged down the last steps and into the garden. Trees, tubs, the ill-fated fountain stood in her way. Beds of snow closed over her feet. She lost the postern door; found it; found the bolts had stuck in the cold. She hammered at them, hearing de Ribérac's footsteps behind her.

The first bolt gave way; and then the second. She wrenched the door open and rushed into Steen Straete, brilliant with light, thronged with merrymakers. Those nearest turned and smiled, and she dropped her skirts suddenly. She was safe. There was no need to call for help. She had only to cross the square to reach the Hôtel de Veere where her parents were, and Gelis. She thought de Ribérac had been lying when he had claimed to have paid off her porters, but that could wait until tomorrow. There was no need to go back to the Silver Straete house tonight.

She moved into the crown of the street, among the singing, laughing crowd of gentle and commonfolk, and turned and looked back. Jordan de Ribérac had emerged from the postern and was standing, hatless and cloakless, looking after her. He made no effort at pursuit but stood staring at her over the intervening heads. Then his great bulk moved, and followed by its shadow made its way, with deliberation, in the opposite direction.

He had offered her marriage and rape both, in her own house. After she had passed an evening with him. After she had invited him, warmly.

Of course, he had deceived her. The name he had shown her was not his own. He had not sought the approval of her parents. She must tell her parents, for she required their protection. But there was no need that anyone else should know. As it was, she saw in her mind's eye her mother's expression. The son of the seigneur of Courtrai, her mother knew also, was six inches shorter than Simon's father.

She found she was trembling, and walked more quickly, helped by the pull of the crowd. It must be time for the fireworks, and the bonfire. Somewhere here, very likely, would be the lord of Veere's party with Charles and Gelis and a reassuring circle of servants. And there, sure enough, was Gelis herself in the distance. But Gelis alone, with only a white-faced manservant behind her. Gelis with her shrill voice upraised and her plump face wild with distress, pleading vehemently in a swirl of indifferent, frolicking carnivallers.

Katelina picked up her skirts once again, and began to run towards her small sister. She called her name, and then opened her arms as the child fought with her elbows toward her. Without tears, without shrieks, Gelis said, "They won't believe me. We saw it from the tower. Two men came up and took Claes away. And I think they killed him."

With the child Gelis and her servant on his hands, it had seemed to Claes that he was already involved in the strenuous conclusion of a particularly strenuous day. Life being what it was, he would not have been greatly amazed to be faced with still more complications. Danger he did not think of at all.

Indeed, the time with the girl had been no hardship. He had found friends to circle-dance with them both and got her a place from which to watch the jugglers and found an acquaintance who would take them all up the tower of St Christopher's chapel, ready to witness the fireworks. Once she had got what she wanted, she was easy to handle. They all were.

After that, he was no longer in control of matters.

He settled Gelis and her man in the tower. He ran down to find and thank his acquaintance. He turned to come back, and a surge of sightseers all but swept him off his feet. When it slackened, he found he had travelled halfway to the Waterhalle and moreover was propping up a couple of drunkards who would not let him go. And finally, one of the drunkards raised a groggy arm which must have had something other than a hand at the end of it, for when it descended on his head, Claes experienced only the first flash of pain, so sudden was the oblivion.

He woke to the sound of harsh gasping, and realised it was his own, and that his chest was shuddering and groaning because there was almost no air. His other senses, slowly returning, advised him of a crashing pain in his split face and head, and then of the likelihood that he was not only blind but fully paralysed.

Intelligence, as he struggled for air, dealt with this nonsense. He was not paralysed. His limbs were cramped because he was huddled in a very small space, and he could not see because it was dark. He unfolded numb fingers and found the walls of his prison, which were wooden.

A coffin, presumably. Or intended to be. His mouth was open, wide as a fish. He could feel his lips stretched, his nostrils scoured and distended. There were pains in his neck and his chest. A wash

of faintness bedevilled him, and receded. Wood. He could break
out of wood, if it were thin enough. If it was not in fact a coffin. If
it was not in fact a grave, with earth above and around it.

Try.

His knees were already up to his chest. He pulled them higher,
and then hit out with both feet against the walls of his prison.
Total, obdurate, absolute resistance. A thud that might as well
have come from metal. Nothing. And another wave of faintness
that told him he had no reserves left to try that again.

If it was as thick as that everywhere. The lid, what about that?
Wriggle. Breathe slowly. Lift one hand, then the other. Explore.

Not just wood, but a familiar smell. Not a rectangle. Not the
smell of corruption. A smell as frail as the spoonful of air that
brought it to him, with a crazy, commonplace association. With
girls. With taverns. With good times in the past. The smell of
malmsey wine. He wasn't in a coffin. He was in a keg.

He wanted to laugh, but kept lapsing out of awareness. His brain
said, "If . . ."

He forgot what he was thinking about.

He remembered. His brain said, "If it's a keg . . ."

It was important, so he hung on to it. He clenched his hands. He
took long, shallow breaths full of alcohol fumes, and wanted to
laugh again, and stopped himself. If it was a keg, there ought to be
a bung.

Feel. His stiff hands brushed over the wine-roughened curves.
No bung. Move. That was harder. That meant shift, and half-sleep,
and wake up, and shift again. When he slept, his head and his chest
stopped hurting him. Why had he moved?

The reason eluded him. Trouble receded. He lay, gasping occasionally and pressing his hand on his chest. The back of his hand
brushed against something. Against nothing. Against a hole.

The bung. That was what he was looking for.

He lifted his hand with enormous lethargy and pushed his fingers into the hole. Through the hole. Out through the other side of
the barrel and into another body of wood. Not a bung. The side of
another—another two barrels.

He was in a keg with an open hole in the side. But the keg was
upside down among others and the open hole covered. He couldn't
break out. If he wanted air, he had to roll the cask over. Even if he
rolled it over, other barrels above him might block the hole just the

same. The effort of rolling it over might use up all the air he had. If he fainted for good, he would suffocate.

All right. If he was going to use air, why not shout with it? But how far would a shout carry from a pile of barrels? Were the barrels even in Bruges? Near passers-by? Near anyone? If he used the same energy to try to alter the way the keg was lying, the noise, perhaps, would be just as great?

It wasn't thinking; it was more in the nature of a long, disconnected dream. He reached that point. Then, carefully, he drew into his lungs all that was left of air in his prison. And lifting himself, flung himself bodily against the curved walls of the barrel, sideways, downwards, with all the strength he could gather.

Wood boomed against wood. Inside his prison the noise echoed like Cambier's cannon, exploding inside his ringing head. His teeth rattled with the jar of barrel meeting barrel and then rattled again as there was another echoing thud. His keg had struck its neighbour and had been hit by another.

A third collision followed, shaking him from side to side like a bird in its shell. His knees and shoulders hammered against the oaken staves and his split cheek suddenly took the brunt: even as he gasped, he realised what it meant. The keg had turned partly over.

Then he had no idea what was happening, because the keg was kicking and jolting in a succession of unbearable thuds like a tree being punished by axe-blows. His brain, deadened by pain and by airlessness, ceased to tell him anything. The movement, like a tree falling, became increasingly languid. The thuds, spaced out, became slower and heavier. The last, just above one of his shoulders, actually made itself felt through the demoiselle de Charetty's blue cloth. The corner of another barrel had burst through his own, and come to rest on his shoulder.

His new blue jacket. She would have it mended. It would do for someone else. Or Felix's dogbasket. He went to sleep. Poor Tilde. He woke.

He wasn't gasping. His head ached, and his shoulder. And, come to think of it, every inch of his body. But he wasn't gasping, because the keg that had splintered his own was letting in a strand of air. And light. And more air and light were playing on his midriff where (by dint, he assured himself, of ineffable pilotage) the open bunghole of the keg was now exposed.

It had worked. He could breathe. Whatever stackyard he was in, his cask was exposed to the air. He could shout from it; recover strength to burst from it; roll it stupidly to freedom if he had to. All he had to do was get his breath, twist to apply his eye to the hole, identify his whereabouts, and proceed to rescue himself.

His head throbbed with pain but he hardly noticed it. He had only one question for his guardian angel. St Nicholas. St Claikine. Don't laugh. It's the wine fumes. Don't laugh, but tell me. Why is the light from the bunghole bright red?

Feet up, shoulder down, head down. Eye to the hole. Answer: it is bright red because out there, something is burning.

A fire in a cooper's, a brewer's yard? Dangerous, my friend Nicholas. But there are watchmen, and horns and crowds and buckets of water . . . Crowds? But they're all in the market place, enjoying the Carnival.

I was in the market place. I was knocked on the head in the market place. There is no way that two men could have carried me through that crowd and got me as far as a brewer's yard. They didn't need to. There was a dray in the market place full of barrels. They had only to fling a keg over my head in the dark, like a butterfly net. And hammer on the lid as they carried it to the dray. And toss it aboard.

A dray, in Carnival time? A dray full of barrels of tar, making for the bonfire. The bonfire which this year, like every year, was not your landsman's pile of faggots. Not for Bruges. Bruges tied up an old barge to the bridge of St John, filled it with barrels of tar, and set fire to it.

He was on the barge, and in the bonfire, and against the roar of these flames, and the screams of the crowd, the voice of a burning man would reach no one.

You have air. You have wits, you like to think. Use them.

The bunghole, at his eye, was trained on the new-lit inferno of the front of the barge. The splintered gaps at his shoulder, on the other side, let in light that was dim. That way therefore, and quickly. What had been merely light through the hole was now blistering heat as barrel upon barrel of tar caught, and flared and rose into sheets of flame.

He kicked, this time with full force; but the bottom boards and the staves were immovable. So the lid, perhaps, was tacked down in a hurry. He forced one hand over his head and punched upwards. The nails gave. One side opened. There was no time for more. With the hand that was free he thrust out and found a purchase and pushed his barrel away, disconnecting from the intruder; starting, again, a dislodgement that turned him over and all but broke the arm protruding over his head.

He drew it in as the slide gained momentum. His barrel was rolling and so were others. Through the half-open lid he heard waves of shouting. All Bruges lined the canal, watching the fire and the fireworks . . .

Christ . . .

If the slide went the right way, he and the kegs with him might tumble off the burning barge.

If another cask hit his half-opened lid, it could kill him. When the half-open lid took the water, it could drown him. To stay and burn to death might really be preferable.

This struck him as very amusing. He realised that he was rather drunk. Under the circumstances, that was even funnier. Between laughter and hiccoughs, he thudded from side to side of his barrel as it rolled and bounced with the others. When it hurtled into the canal he had a swinging view of the crowds on the bank, their faces brilliant with light and euphoria; their voices raised in good-natured catcalls as the city's inept officials lost a dozen badly-packed kegs from the ship-fire. Among them, diamond-bright, were the faces of the drunkards he had met at St Christopher's. This time, they were sober and he was inebriated.

The canal was half-congealed. Some barrels bobbed in water; some crashed onto floes. His was one of the latter. The base of the barrel was stoved through and it fell on its side. Two staves cracked, but the bands held it together. Vaguely, he was aware that he was still within his container, and that it was sliding, self-propelled, over the ice. If they saw him they would, of course, lift his barrel between them and cast it back on the fire. So he must shout.

He had just reached this conclusion when the icefloe stopped, and the barrel tilted, dropped, and smacked into freezing water. It entered his barrel at one end and left at the other, drenching and nearly choking him and leaving him in a rocking pool. The barrel floated, bumping into the bank. No one lifted it up. No one had noticed it.

Claes considered, dizzily. Then he straightened his legs and pushed them through the broken base of the barrel. The cold of the water was numbing. He braced his elbows inside the barrel and, using his legs, propelled himself silently along the lee of the bank. Somewhere near was a watering-slope, an incline from bank to water used by horses. There he could slip from the barrel and merge with the crowd. Half-drunk and soaking wet, with two of his enemies a few yards away. And perhaps the person or persons who had paid them.

He was so cold by now he could hardly breathe. Another irony, but he had nothing left to laugh with. The barrel bumped on the incline he was seeking, and he felt for the ground with his feet, and found it, and tried, stupid with cold, to push the barrel from him and emerge from it. He was attempting to do this, at the bottom of the ramp, when the light from the top of his keg was cut off by moving figures and someone took hold of his barrel quite firmly in a two-handed grip and rammed it down on him again, wrenching off the lid a moment after.

Before he could see who it was, his entire head had been obliterated by an object crammed down on top of it. A familiar voice said, crossly, "Are we to meet this drunkard everywhere? You! Call yourself a friend of Poppe?" The voice of Katelina van Borselen.

Poppe. The gingerbread seller in the barrel.

She said, "Three of you. Look. He can't even stand."

She didn't know if he could walk. Slowly, he got to his feet, his body enclosed in the barrel, his head emerging, wearing whatever she had put on top of it. A carnival mask. A lot of feathers. A man's voice said, "I took Poppe home hours ago. I thought he was home."

"Well, he's got out again. Can't you see?"

Christ. A child's voice this time. The sister. The two van Borselen girls must be there.

Gelis. Of course. Gelis must have seen from the tower. And recognised the two pseudo-drunkards. And warned her elder sister not to give him away. But how were they going to explain Poppe soaking wet in a soaking-wet barrel? They didn't need to explain it. Just to get him surrounded by a helpful crowd who thought he was Poppe. That way, no one could harm him. Until they got to Poppe's house.

The barrel was incredibly heavy. Perhaps the punishment barrel had handles inside. Or a special lid, or rests for the shoulders. He had to half-carry this one, with people bumping into him on either side and behind. There seemed to be a small crowd willing to escort him. A popular fellow, Poppe. He wondered where he lived. He realised he was stumbling regularly and, but for the crowd, would be lurching all over the road. Occasionally, through the slits in his mask, he would glimpse the child's unlovely face, pasty with worry. And sometimes the demoiselle's, with a line between the black brows, but no worry. Rather a look of the fiercest concentration.

People were slowing. People were stopping. The house of Poppe. With Poppe asleep in bed no doubt inside, with his wife and family. Why was the demoiselle unworried? She had come to one side of him, he saw. And the child Gelis had come to the other. Someone said "Up!"

The barrel rose in the air and the demoiselle said, *"Get out and run!"*

It was more a case, he wished to submit, of ducking vaguely and falling flat on his face. But he had hardly got free of the barrel before someone—the demoiselle—had caught him by the arm and was dragging him sideways. The barrel remained behind, apparently tenanted.

"Gelis," said the demoiselle. "She'll set it down in a moment and disappear. She'll be all right. Gelis always manages. I told her to go to the Veeres'."

His teeth drummed together. The vibration made his head want to split open. The freezing cold in his face made yesterday's cut feel like an axe-blow. His brain had frozen too. She said, "I'm taking you the back way to Silver Straete. The house is empty."

He remembered being surprised that the van Borselen kept their postern unbolted. He remembered being led into a kitchen lit by the embers of a huge fire, and stopping dead on the threshold, and then realising why he had stopped and walking steadily forward. Steadily was a misnomer. He could not stop shivering. He remembered very clearly the demoiselle saying, "Strip!"

He said, "No."

She wasted no time, he granted her that. She dragged out the wooden tub, and poured cold water into it by the jugful, and then padded her hands and lifted the great cauldron from the fire and filled the tub with the steaming hot water. Then she said, "I'm going to get into dry clothes as well. Strip and get in."

The good blue cloth tore as he tried to get it off. He stepped out of everything all tied together. He had to do even that leaning against the kitchen wall. He held the edge of the bath, but in spite of that, slopped the water, thudding into it suddenly. He laid his arms on his updrawn knees and his head on his arms and his senses swam and returned and then left for good. The fire, built up by the demoiselle before she went out, became a healthy blaze and kept the tub and its contents warm as a copper.

He slept.

Chapter 20

A long time later Claes, born Nicholas, woke, and turned his head lazily on his arm.

A kitchen. The well-run, well-equipped kitchen of a household of means, smelling warmly of chicken.

He turned his head further.

A wooden tub. A scrubbed table with two truckle beds under it and a clutch of tallow candles on top. A wall covered with pans and pots of iron and copper and long-handled implements in iron and wood. A carved press, half-open, showing bowls of wood and earthenware and pewter and brass, and some pewter plates. A copper water-jug on the floor, and a meat-safe and a pail. A sugar barrel. A salt box. A bench with a young brown-haired woman in a loose robe sitting on it.

And he appeared to be naked, hugging his knees in a bathtub of water.

His wits would not immediately provide him with a reason. The girl displayed a well-bred and absolute calm, with a touch of amusement. Having no idea what response she expected, he returned the look with equal tranquillity. The effort made his head spin. It was already aching. All his body was aching. He removed his gaze from the girl and allowed it to wander to the fireplace. His clothes were spread before the hearth, drying.

He remembered everything. This was Katelina van Borselen, changed into dry clothes. Changed into a fine linen chemise with a loose mantle thrown over her shoulders, and her hair unbound.

All right. First things first. He confirmed, for his own peace of mind, that his present position was one of reasonable decorum. He remembered that she had said the house was empty when they arrived. He returned his gaze to her and found she was still looking at him. Not watching him. Looking at him, the way Colard studied a painting brought in by a foreigner. He said, "I seem to have been asleep."

"An hour," she said. "The house is still empty."

He said, "Thank you for drying my clothes."

"They'll be ready to wear in an hour or two," she said. "Get out. I have some broth heating."

He had dealt with variants of this often enough, in bath houses and out of them, and the result was a romp. In those cases, the girl was not Katelina van Borselen, and he had not just been in danger of losing his life. So this was not what it seemed. He set a course as straightforward as possible. He said, "You have me at a disadvantage."

She looked at him with contempt. She said, "Do you think I've never seen a whole man before? My parents sleep in a naked bed, and my servants, and my cousins."

There was no towel within reach. Matter-of-factly he palmed the tub-rim and hoisted himself up and over it. He treated her to whatever view she wished of his back as he walked without haste to the fireplace and, picking up his damp shirt, wrapped it round his hips and tied the points neatly to hold it. His fingers were withered with soaking and someone had unbuckled his muscles. He put a steadying hand on the chimney-piece and turned, smiling. "Now," he said. "There was something about chicken broth."

She hadn't moved from her bench. She said coldly, "Get it yourself if you want some. It's there at the fire."

He left trails of water wherever he moved. He saw that she observed it, but in her turn of mood was disregarding it. In any case, the room was heavily warm. He found the pot on its chain, and stirred it, and went to the wall press for two bowls, nursing his energy as it began to come back. He needed the broth, and hoped that he might have time to take some before hostility, for whatever reason, became open war. He filled the first bowl from the pot and placed it deftly on the table before her with a spoon. He said, "The demoiselle will also eat?"

He had presented her, somehow, with a problem. She said rather shortly, "We shall both eat at the table."

There was a second bench, on the opposite side of the table. He took his bowl there and sat. "God save the hostess," said Claes. She didn't look as if she wanted the broth. He picked his up and drank it off immediately, thick and warm and nourishing, dispatching the lingering taste of canal water and malmsey. He said, putting down the bowl, "You've saved my life twice. First the canal, and now the soup. I haven't thanked you yet."

He had no doubt she had questions to ask. There were quite a few he wanted to ask himself. Such as who else had seen what had

happened apart from herself and Gelis. Such as how she had come
to be there, unaccompanied. Such as why, having rescued him, she
hadn't raised an outcry and called in her parents, or the magistrates. And why he was here, like this. Had it been anyone else, he
would have known. It was a puzzle, like the Medici ciphers, to be
approached indirectly. All he could do was offer a comment, and
hope a conversation would follow.

Nothing followed. The lady Katelina dipped her spoon in and
out without answering. He waited politely.

She was a handsome girl, and nicely made, like a good piece of
wood-turning. Her breasts, under the chemise, were round as small
Spanish oranges. His gaze, on its way somewhere else, drifted over
the rest of her. The linen was so fine that you could see the colour
change, where the white of her skin ceased below it. His gaze
continued until it rested on his own bowl, which gave him time for
a little necessary self-discipline.

He knew his reputation, and it was mostly deserved. He liked
girls. He liked them, of course, for providing him with life's greatest and most inexpensive delight; but also he liked their company;
their opinions. He liked to make them talk. This girl was a virgin.
He was sure of it. Of these, he had little experience. Girls of that
sort who offered themselves were usually too young to be responsible: one did not take advantage. Sometimes, with an older woman,
it was a kindness.

This girl didn't look as if she wanted to talk. She was already
half-regretting what she'd done. It would be easy to make the situation quite impossible, so that she'd ask him to leave. A little
loutish behaviour would do it. But then what would she do? Better
to help her. He said, "Do you know, demoiselle, if Meester Simon
is in Bruges?"

Her hand with the spoon stopped immediately. She said, "He
was not responsible." Then she flushed. She added curtly, "He is
not in Bruges."

She was not a serving-girl, and she'd caught the other thought in
his mind. Now she would ask him to leave. He pushed the bowl
aside and made firmly to rise. She said with sudden fierceness,
"They meant to burn you to death."

He restored his weight to the seat. He said carefully, "They
failed, thanks to you, demoiselle. I know who they are, I think.
They won't do it again. You needn't worry. Tell your sister it's all
right."

He watched her. She couldn't have been alone on the streets. He had to know if anyone else knew. He said, "Did your sister come for you?"

The question alarmed her. She pushed her bowl away distractedly and, getting up, walked round behind him to the fire. There, where it had escaped his notice, was a striped towel, warming. She leaned over and picked it up as he turned on the bench, watching her. The firelight glowed through the fall of her linen, and he realised that she had left her outer robe on the trestle. She turned, the towel in her hands unfolded. She didn't answer his question at all. She said, "Did he cut open your cheek?"

He remained still. "Simon? No."

"Not Simon. Simon's father, Jordan de Ribérac."

It was like being in the barrel again, such was the buffet. Yesterday, she hadn't known how he came by his scar. Today, she was able to connect it with Jordan de Ribérac. And to imply—as surely she had implied?—that they both knew that Jordan de Ribérac was responsible for what had happened tonight. Yet she hadn't clamoured for help.

She was holding the towel bundled together before her, as if for comfort. He said, "You met him this evening? Monseigneur de Ribérac?"

"He offered me marriage," she said.

Marriage! He looked at her now with sheerest bafflement. The light from the fire flickered and gleamed over the expanse of his skin like the Northern Dancers.

She had spoken with bitterness. As if Jordan de Ribérac had offered her something else besides marriage. If he had, it would hardly have been in the street. So it was here, in the empty house. But how could Jordan de Ribérac get himself admitted to the house of an unchaperoned girl? In one way. Claes loosened his hands. He said gently, "He was masked? And he told you he wanted to harm me?"

"Something like that," she said wearily. "He said he had settled Simon's feud with you. Of course he had. He thought he had got these men to kill you. Gelis and I can testify to it. I shall tell my mother and father. He'll be punished." She was twisting the towel in her hands. She wanted de Ribérac punished.

Claes said, "Perhaps he did pay men to get rid of me, but I wonder what proof there is? Did anyone else hear him threaten me?"

There was a stool by the fire, and she sat on it. Her hair was brown tinted red in the firelight, and crimped where it had been plaited. She said, "He was here. I was the only person he spoke to. He was my partner for the evening. I thought he was . . . some-one else."

He had guessed as much. He said, "And the two men who at-tacked me? We'd need witnesses, or someone who knew them, or someone who could connect them with Monseigneur. Without that, accusing him would only link your name with his in a way you wouldn't like. He could twist what happened quite nastily."

"I don't know," she said. "I don't know who the men were. Don't you have any evidence against him?"

"Nothing that would be any good. Look," said Claes. "There's no need for you to do anything more about this. It's my battle anyway, although I'm glad you made it yours for a bit. Otherwise I shouldn't be alive. But now, forget about what happened to me. Tell your parents only that M. le vicomte deceived you and made an unwelcome proposal. He shouldn't trouble you again."

He watched her. There was relief in her face, as well as disap-pointment. He had said what she wanted him to say. There was also resolve. She said, "It hardly matters if M. le vicomte or any-one else makes advances to me now. They'll marry me off to some-body soon. In case I haven't told the whole story. It's a pity really that nothing happened. It might as well have done."

And so he knew exactly why he was there. She was nineteen and clever and capable; but in this matter, she was thinking like Gelis. As he might have said to Gelis, he said mildly, "Is the towel for me?"

She had forgotten it. Then she remembered and brought it for-ward and then, hesitating, placed it round his shoulders as she had probably once planned to do. Her hands lingered. They were trem-bling. He put up one of his own and drew her round and, still holding her fingers, seated her beside him, a space away on the trestle. The firelight struck through the stuff of her robe and told him something else. So, Claes, you need discipline for two. Let's see how you master all this.

He said, "Demoiselle, the world is full of bridegrooms. Don't be cruel to them because some of your suitors displease you."

She said, "You don't marry."

That line of reasoning he didn't propose to follow. He took an-other, speaking simply, to convince her. "Some day I shall. No one should expect too much, of course. But whoever my future wife is, she might regret having followed a whim."

"I expect too much," she said. "What I want doesn't exist. So—"

So formality wouldn't serve any longer, and what they were talking about would have to be made explicit. Which he regretted. Because she would end by loathing him. He gave her back her hand and, rising, stood, in his turn, bathed in firelight. "So you appoint me as surrogate. Thank you, but I'm not flattered," said Claes. "And you're wrong. There are many men who would make you happy."

She, too, had dropped all pretence. "Show me how," said Katelina van Borselen. "It's my whim. It's not your responsibility."

He stood, looking down at her. "Of course it's my responsibility. We're of different stations. There might be consequences."

"There will be no consequences," she said. "Or I shouldn't have brought you here in the first place. Are you afraid of something else? Or am I less than you're used to? In which case, can you recommend me to a friend?"

She spoke, as she had at Damme, with extreme harshness. There were tears on her lashes. He said, "Oh dear God," and kneeling, took both her hands again. He said, "Look. What you would lose, you would lose forever."

"Would you boast about it?" she said. And then, "No. I'm sorry. I'm sure I know you better than that."

"You don't know me at all," he said in despair. She smelt of some sort of fine scent. He tried to keep his hands steady and force his brain to work. Suddenly she pulled one hand out of his and laid it on his bare shoulder and then drew it down, sliding over the muscles of his bruised back, down and down.

Can you recommend me to a friend?

He said, "I shall show you what it is like. As gradually as I can, so that you can stop me before it goes further. After that, I'll try to stop if you tell me to. If I don't, you must use force. I don't know how much you know about men."

Her cheek was against his, and he could feel her smile briefly. He could feel her heart thudding. She spoke as if her throat hurt. "Gelis says that you're the most passionate lover in Bruges, according to all the girls she's been able to ask. And that you always tell them you can stop, but they never want you to."

She was a child. And because two men had been cruel and her mother heartless, he was going to have to seduce her.

Or the other way about.

Or neither. He was going to lift her and take her up to her chamber and lay her, as her future lovers would do, on her bed. Then, as carefully as his abundant energy would let him, he meant to unclothe her, and caress her, and lead her as sweetly as might be through all the intricate overture of mutual love-making. Then—if she did not stop him—he meant to arrive with force where he was needed, so that all her life she would remember the new pleasure, and not the new pain.

Like most of his better plans it fell out as he wanted, except that he went to sleep afterwards, which he had not intended to do. But which, under the circumstances, was understandable.

He woke in bed, with a slumbering girl in his arms, and her long hair coiled over his body. Even in sleep, her face looked different; warm with colour, and peaceful and contented. There was a smile still somewhere on her mouth, and he smiled in return for, no doubt, the same reason. Then, brought to reality, he looked to the window. Still dark, thank God. The household, to be sure, would hardly return before dawn, and the parents well afterwards. All the same, he should have left long ago.

He knew, normally, exactly how long to make love. When to tease it up to its climax. How long to allow for the courtesies afterwards. But this, of course, was hardly routine. For one thing, he had the kitchen to clear up and his clothes, for example, to remove.

With care, he eased himself free of the girl and left the room silently for the kitchen. There the sand-glass told him he had four hours perhaps before daylight. All the same, he did not take time to dress, but went quickly about the business of tidying. In the end it looked, he thought, as it had when Katelina had led him in from the garden. The broth would hardly be missed. Or the towel, which was upstairs for a very good reason. He looked round, lifted his clothes, and hesitated. He could dress here and depart, as he would have done had he not slept. But then, he would have taken proper leave of her.

As it was, he didn't quite know what to do. She seemed happy. She had been happy; of that at least he was sure. She had clung to him at the climax as if the gates of heaven were shutting. Afterwards, she had said very little, but had lain stroking him, over and over as if he were a new possession. And he had fallen asleep.

But he was glad about that. He was not ignorant of the ways of well-born women in bed. Some made no secret of what they wanted, and were frank and comradely both in your arms and out of them. Some wanted servant-lovers to whip them in bed and crawl under their feet the rest of the time. This girl was neither of these. He wondered what he had done to her. Perhaps, having taken the first step, she would never marry, but take a succession of lovers. Until in time she ceased to take heed of the calendar, or of the courtesies, and trouble and ruin would come.

Perhaps it would turn out well. Perhaps, like an overanxious child she would now be content to wait for a proper marriage. Or even look forward to it. He smiled a little, thinking of the kind of men, young and old, her family would propose for her. Perhaps he ought to have restricted the performance a little. But she was a delicious girl, well made and courageous. What else she might be he didn't know, any more than she could know him, whatever she claimed. They had hardly exchanged more than a few sentences in all their acquaintance. It was not his mind she or anyone else wanted him for. That he fully accepted.

He decided to go back and open her chamber door. She had only to pretend sleep if she wished him gone. If she were still asleep, he wouldn't waken her. In any case, she knew she could rely on him to greet her, when next they met, as a servant should greet a lady.

The line of light under her door told him that she had risen and renewed the candle. And, perhaps, dressed. His clothes, held one-handed before him, would have to represent the decencies: he wanted to end the matter, one way or the other. He opened the door.

She had risen, and replaced the candle, and lifted the sheet from the floor, but she had not dressed. She looked up, half in bed and half out of it. He looked at the long line of shin and knee and thigh and all the places where his fingers and his lips had rested. And then the white skin of the arms, and the frail ribs and the small breasts, round as oranges. And her lips, which were open. She was smiling. She stood, and he could trace the small incoherence of her breathing. Then she walked towards him, her eyes on his hand, and the sheltering twist of his clothes. "These need to be folded," she said. "And in any case, they are in the way." And striking them from his hand to the floor, she took their place.

That time, there was no courting at all. The next time, a great deal. The third time, when the sky outside the window was lightening, a desperate onslaught which he tried in vain to calm and contain.

In the middle of it, a door slammed below. She fought him, forcing him to continue. The resulting explosion paralysed them both for long moments. Then they lay, their heartbeats shaking the bed. They couldn't have moved, had the door opened.

It didn't open. One pair of footsteps shuffling about, far below, servant, intent on drawing water and setting fires for the returning mistress. Katelina, her nails skin-deep said, "Don't go. There's a way into the garden. Mother won't come for hours."

He lay still, his face buried. So much for self-control. He lifted his head from his arms and said, "Demoiselle."

"Demoiselle!" said Katelina van Borselen.

He turned on his side and looked at her. Now she was white, unlike the blooming girl of the first seduction, and her skin was damp, her hair tangled, the hollows blue under her eyes.

He said, "What other name can I give you? I've taken something precious from you. I've given you, perhaps, what you wanted. If it's wrong, it's wrong. But for more than one night—that would be greed on both sides."

She had not thought before of the question of pride. He saw her think about it now. She said, "If you were . . . a lawyer . . . would you marry me?"

So disarming, so cruel. He took her hand, full of affection, and said, "Even if I were a lawyer, you would be too far above me."

She closed her eyes, and opened them. She said, "They said you were clever. I think you are more clever than even they think. Surely you should have trained as a clerk? Why an artisan?"

"Because I like it," said Claes. "I did learn letters. But my mother died. Now I have all I need."

"I think," she said, "that you were lying when you said you wanted to marry one day."

He said, "Yes, I was lying. But that doesn't mean that I can come between you and your future husband again."

She said, childishly, "You don't want to?"

He sat up. He said directly, "Would you ask it of me? A servant?"

She had struggled up, too. "You're not a servant," she said. "In my eyes you are Nicholas."

He said, "Because I've done what I've done, you daren't think of me as Claes. But I am a servant. And a bad one. I've wakened you too far, Katelina. But what overcame me will overcome someone else, one day. You don't need a paragon of a husband. You carry delight in your own body. You know it."

She didn't speak. She watched him dress, the first time she had seen a man cover his body, he supposed. She must be wondering if it would be the last. There was nothing he could add, or do about it. When he was ready he stood by the bed, looking down, and she spoke then. She said, "If he knew about this, I suppose Jordan de Ribérac would kill you."

It had occurred to him. He said, "He won't know. Don't worry."

Her face was pallid white. She said, "Why did he mark your face?"

He said, "He wanted me to spy for him on Simon. I refused."

"Why?"

"Why did I refuse? Because if Simon gets killed, I don't want to be charged with the blame. A charming family. They hate one another." He thought about it for a moment.

She said, "Claes?" in an odd voice, but when he looked at her, she said only, "Be careful."

He said, "Of course. I must go."

She sat very still, the sheet folded about her like a habit, and he didn't try to embrace her. Instead he bent, and lifting her fingers, kissed her hand like a gentleman.

She shivered, and he left quickly.

He didn't realise that, once, he had called her Katelina. He didn't understand, in the slightest degree, what he had done.

Chapter 21

Headache-grey, the first day of Lent dawned over the city of Bruges and smoke began to rise, with reluctance, from its chimneys. In the bright and well-ordered house of Adorne the children rose, and were groomed, dressed and marshalled for Mass in the Jerusalemkerk with their parents, household and guests. Afterwards their guests broke their fast and left, including the widow of Charetty and her two daughters, who curtseyed daintily and were kissed by the demoiselle Margriete.

The two daughters, unusually silent, were taken off to their home by a manservant while their mother made her way to the town hall, where the city was wont to mark the day with a feast of freshwater fish and good wine. She did not know, or care, where the male members of her household were, or how they had passed the night.

Tilde had spent it crying. No one could blame Father Bertouche for bringing home the four little girls (he was in his bed today). It was a pity that the van Borselen child had broken into the party so forcefully, but no doubt Claes had been rescued eventually from her attentions. Someone—a servant; the sister Katelina perhaps?—would have to find the child Gelis and take her off home. It was not Marian de Charetty's concern.

She supposed Felix had spent the whole night with his new girl. Now he had got the knack he supposed, also, that she would have to speak to him, or half the servants in Bruges would claim to be bearing to him. Failing his father, the best regulator of that situation was a wife.

She needed help with Felix. But wives had fathers. As it was, she kept falling over the pawnbroker Oudenin at every step. She returned home after the dinner in time for the annual inspection of weights and measures, and found Claes had forestalled her and was already busy in the yard, stripped to shirt and a very old doublet. She left him alone and went to the kitchens, where she found Felix cajoling one of her women. He had won a sack of bells in the lottery and wanted them sewn on Claes' clothes.

Claes' clothes were already in the kitchen being pressed, and a great tear repaired. He had been pushed into the canal, said her woman, clearly believing it. Felix, his eyes brilliant with sleeplessness, clearly didn't. Neither did she. Claes had the same look as Felix, and his red scar crossed a cheek healthy as tallow.

Ash Wednesday. A day she had always hated.

Later there was a brief scene when Claes came in for his clothes and found bells all over the doublet and jacket. Forced by Felix and his friends to get into them, he went straight out of the door and came back in due course with a flock of goats, which he led jingling into the house and up to and through Felix's room, where they stood bleating and defecating anxiously. Felix was angry, but his friends, screaming with laughter, made him see the joke. A man, debited, no doubt, to Felix's educational equipment, came later to clean up the room, while someone snipped off the bells and Claes, in his old clothes again, got the keys of one of the cellars, and had a cart harnessed. A moment later, the Widow saw it rumbling out of the yard with Claes driving and one of the yard lads beside him.

Felix had gone off, without seeing her or asking her permission. Henninc, queried sharply over the cart, reckoned that no good had come of trying to make an apprentice into a soldier. Six months ago that was a good boy, who would never have thought of driving out of the yard in his mistress's cart, in his mistress's time, without asking.

"So why did he want it?" she said.

"Why, he's gone to get his lottery winnings," said Henninc. "A mail glove was all he got, but that's but the token. It could be a shield he has to collect, or a helm maybe."

"Or just the other glove," said Marian de Charetty. "In which case he'll look a fool with a cart, won't he? All right. We've got other things to bother about. Show me the scales that were altered."

The cart did not come back for some time. Catherine was fetched by friends, and returned later to say that there were dried-fruit stalls in the market place, and the van Borselen girl had been there in a worse temper than ever. Gelis, the fat one. Gelis had nothing to say about having Claes as a squire at the Carnival, except that she had had the dullest time she had ever had in her life, and had gone off home by herself. She didn't say who Claes had gone off with, but guess what. Gelis had a new hand-warmer. And guess what it was?

Naturally, a silver-gilt apple. Marian de Charetty wondered, wearily, if Claes had handed it over before or after his clothes were covered in bells. Or perhaps last night he had carried it with him. You never knew whom you might need to bribe—or reward—at a carnival.

At dusk, after everyone was indoors, the cart arrived back in the yard and she could hear the cellar door being unlocked. There was a tramping of feet which went on for a long time. Then the yard boy, looking cheerful, tapped on her door and said that there was some good new stock just come in, and would the demoiselle like to see it for the inventory? She folded a shawl round her shoulders, took a lamp and went out, her key bunch rattling. The wind blew under the fluted voile on her head with all its matronly gofferings, and tugged where the folds bound her chin. Claes was in the cellar alone, kneeling among sacks with the candles lit. She shut the door.

He turned his head and said, "I took the yard boy because he's a bit simple. He thinks half of this is wool. Look."

She walked to him and bent. Some of the sacks were already unpacked. Behind them were boxes, whose lids he was lifting. She saw, firstly, a packing of straw, and then metal, glinting dully. A steel cuirass, with another beneath it. Shoulder guards, nesting one into another, and thigh-pieces, and coudières. A sack of something which might have been cabbages, but in fact were iron helmets, in the German style. Another box of massive body-armour. Marian de Charetty let drop the lid of that box, and sat on it, saying nothing.

Claes, working quickly, pulled open the last of the sacks and checked their contents. Then, picking up his candle, he whirled it in an extravagant gesture, and bringing it over, set it beside her. "Well?"

She said, "I heard you won a mail gauntlet."

His skin was suffused, oppressed after all the bending. But no one had a smile as wide as Claes. He tapped a barrel, and then hitched himself on top of it. "Two dozen others in there, from the Hospital of St John. If anyone wants to know, that's all I won. You bought them from me, and Thomas will take them south to Astorre. Of course, he'll take the rest too, mixed up with the stuff I bought on the way north. That lets us outfit fifty more men than we contracted for. They supply the horses, and we supply the armour."

He was speaking to her man to man, as he often did now. She took her eyes from his rolled-up sleeves and the purple bruises all over his arms, and said, "And what am I paying you for the barrel of gloves? I had better know, I suppose."

"Not too much. They're old ones. I'll write it into the ledger. Of course, you don't pay me anything. All this came from the arsenal at the Hospital by arrangement with the Adorne family. There is no record of it, and none of us has ever heard of any of it, except for the barrel of gloves."

It was cold in the cellar, and the three or four candles he had lit did little to warm it. But she was far too stubborn to let him away with all this. She crossed her hands on her knees and said, "So how did you pay for it?"

"With promises," he said. "I'll tell you when Messer Adorne and I have had our meeting. I came across something interesting in Milan. A way to profit the Adorne family and the Charetty company. Messer Adorne doesn't yet know the details, but he was willing to make this much of an investment. And as I've said, we can put fifty more into the field, whether the scheme works or not."

She said, "Yes. I gathered you wanted me to buy Astorre an army. I don't see any weapons here."

"No. Well," said Claes. "I told you Messer Tobie was going to Piacenza. He had a commission to buy guns and powder for Thibault and Jaak de Fleury. I asked him to get fifty *schioppetti* for captain Astorre as well. Handguns."

"And pay for them?" she said.

"You know," said Claes, "it's a wonderful system. The Medici bank are backing Milan and King Ferrante of Naples, so their Milan manager—that's Tommaso's brother Pigello—is quite willing to advance us the money for the handguns, as well as recruiting money for Thomas to pick up fifty more men than Astorre is expecting.

"Then we go to the Duke of Milan and offer him fifty fully-armed splendid gunners provided he draws up another condotta. Then with the money from that, we pay back Pigello and the gunsmiths with a great deal left over."

She said, "Captain Astorre had not been made party, then, to this delightful scheme?"

"He doesn't like handguns," said Claes. "But Messer Tobie does. And so does Thomas."

"But Meester Julius doesn't?" said the Widow. "Or have you forgotten that I have a highly paid notary with the company whose job, I should have thought, was precisely to do with matters of commissions and contracts and purchasing?"

From a smile, his lips reformed in a small, bloated shape denoting conjecture. He lifted both hands and laced them on top of his head, narrowing his eyes against an invisible rainfall.

She said, "It's not such a difficult question, if you haven't got a headache."

He removed his hands. His smile, leaping back, acknowledged the hit. "It *is* difficult as far as Julius is concerned. He's a clever man. He'd rather listen to you or to Tobie than me."

"Meaning," she said brusquely, "that Tobie has your measure, and Julius hasn't. So why not say so?"

He said, "Has Felix been drinking?"

He never let a misunderstanding exist between them without cutting clean through. She should have remembered. She said, "Yes. He missed you. The bells . . . The goats . . ."

"Yes. I'm sorry," he said. "But I haven't much time to find a place where I can start. You're giving him money?"

She said, "Not for jousting armour." And as he still looked at her, "Not for ermine-tails either," said Felix's mother.

"Then—" he began to say, and interrupted himself. Then she heard it too. Felix's voice, calling outside.

She said, "Should we—?"

"No. Let him see it all," said Claes. "No details. Just a little underhand deal he's to keep quiet about. He will. It's his company."

"But—" she began.

The door opened on Felix and his ermine-tails. His shallow eyes were full of suspicion. He said, "They told me you were both here."

"Well, I hope so," said Marian de Charetty. "Since I left orders you were to be sent here as soon as you condescended to come in. Where have you been?"

"Out," he said. "What's all that?"

He took the candle from Claes and poked about, all the time she was telling him. He came back with a pointed helmet and stuck it on Claes' head unexpectedly, making him wince. Felix stood back and giggled. "Only one thing worse than that," he said, "and that's the stuff you had on when you arrived. Why don't you pick out a set and buy it from us?"

Marian de Charetty, rigid, opened her mouth. Before she could speak, Claes said, "I've got all I need. Besides, you'll want to pick the best of it for yourself."

Felix grinned. "The best of what? That's battle armour for soldiers stamping about in the mud."

"My mistake," said Claes.

"I should think so," said Felix. "You don't seriously think I'd appear—"

"Of course not," said Claes. "You see, I had all that teaching by captain Astorre. I forgot you hadn't."

Marian de Charetty said, "I'm cold. Felix, take that lamp and light me back to the door. Claes, that's enough. Blow out the candles and lock up."

Claes, rising obediently, began to walk over to blow out the candles. Her son, his back to his mother, stood red-faced in his way. Felix said, "What do you mean, Astorre taught you and didn't teach me? What do you think Mother got him for?"

"Your father got him," said Claes. "For a bodyguard."

"And so what kind of training do you get from a bodyguard?" Felix never had any trouble changing his ground, especially when furious. He said, "My God, a week in the company of a second-rate common soldier and you lecture me about fighting. A gently born man doesn't exercise by backyard wrestling. He jousts. Do you think I learned what I know about that from Astorre?"

Claes, waiting patiently, bent and blew out a candle round Felix. "Who did you learn it from then?" he said.

Felix drew breath and stopped. He said, "You're not paid to be inquisitive. You're paid to do as you're told. Blow out those candles."

He moved to one side. Claes blew them out, while Felix stalked with the lamp to the door. His mother followed. From the dark, Claes' voice followed them. "Captain Astorre teaches jousting as well."

Felix turned his head and gave a short bark of laughter. "And you think you can joust better than I can?"

"I haven't got a horse. Or a lance." Claes' voice was rather sad.

Felix turned fully round. He said, "Well now, that's no difficulty. I'll lend you one. You make yourself up a nice set of armour. We'll make it a loan. And I'll get the others to rig up a barrier outside the walls, say tomorrow, and we'll see what you can do. With a proper wager, of course. If you have the spunk."

"Felix! Claes!" said Marian de Charetty.

Her son, still carrying the lamp, brushed past her, crossed the yard and banged the door into the house, leaving yard and cellar in darkness. Behind her, she could hear Claes laughing under his breath. There was a scrape, and then new candle-light appeared behind her, sheltered from the wind by his hand. He had taken the helmet off, and looked a trifle more serious.

He said, "He wanted jousting armour. He must have it already. I wondered about the Brotherhood of the White Bear. Their big tournament after Easter."

She stared at him. "He wouldn't try for that!"

"He might. He'd be eligible, with the right backing. Anselm Adorne took the lance when he was very little older."

"But he was trained. All the Adorne family were taught by tournament masters."

"Maybe Felix is being taught by a tournament master. I shouldn't be surprised. He's very confident. But it might be as well to find out how good he is."

He had begun walking, but she stayed where she was. "How good are you?" she said.

"Not very," said Claes. "I'm hoping that we'll be evenly matched. Whatever happens, he'll have to win. So there's no need to worry. Nothing can possibly happen to Felix. And it'll be the first time on record that I've had a beating dressed in a full suit of armour. I could have done with it a few times in the Steen, I can tell you."

It took two days in fact to set up the unfortunate confrontation between Felix and his mother's servant. Most of the arrangements were made by Felix. Recruiting his friends, he began, grinding his teeth, to prepare on a scale close to that for total war. Then as time and the same friends did their work on him, he began, as usual, to forget his anger and enjoy himself. He resolved to show his paces, display his armour and score a decisive victory without undue punishment to his good if somewhat loudmouthed friend Claes. Thus, of course, winning the wager; which had reduced itself, at his mother's insistence, to a pair of mailed gloves.

It came to him, nearer the time, that he was not supposed to have any armour outside the usual household store. He helped himself from that, but could not resist retrieving from its hiding

place his own splendid helm, with the eagle's head and the plume
of red feathers. He told Guildolf de Gruuthuse to say he had lent it
to him. He began to look forward to the contest. A number of his
friends, stirred by the preparations, got hold of their fathers' horses
and asked to join in as well. A couple of serious town officers came
round and warned him that encounters of this kind were forbidden
unless properly ordered, even if only in play. He lost his temper at
the word "play", and John Bonkle had to pacify them and slip
them some money.

The day dawned, cold and wet. The whole house, it seemed,
emptied.

No: what nonsense. The dyesheds were full as they should be,
and the fuller's shop, and the house vibrated with the steps of its
servants. But Felix left, and Claes, and the rabble of young men
accompanying them, and a group of indolent horses, and a wheelbarrow full of armour, and a lot of pennants with the new paint
running down them.

Long before now, Marian de Charetty had ceased to feel any
apprehension over this nonsense. There was no venom in the affair
now. They were all old enough to be able to manage matters, and
she trusted Claes to keep both her son and himself from any real
damage. Standing now at her glass window, she saw, divided into
uneven diamonds, her son's face brilliant with excitement and
Claes beside him, marching about, booming in ecstatic embodi-
ment of the absent, impassioned person of captain Astorre. The
rest, Bonkle, Sersanders, Cant, the young Adorne were doubled
up, helpless with laughter. Claes himself she saw, she knew, was
cloudlessly happy.

They came back four hours later with nothing wrong but a
sprained wrist (Sersanders') and a bill for three pigs which Felix
had chased and stuck with the wrong end of his pennant after they
wandered by mistake into the lists and upset his charger. They had
also stopped off on the way home to show off their armour and
drink to the success of the tournament. This Marian de Charetty
deduced from the erratic clanking which preceded her servant
Claes' scaling of the stairs to her office. He knocked thunderously
on the door and came in apologising because he still had his gauntlets on, there having been a bet that he couldn't drink from a glass
without removing them. His face was scarlet, the scar crimson.

"If you must sit down," said the Widow, "I think that chair is
strongest. So it went well?"

He sat down. It sounded like a meal being dished up item by item. He was beaming. "I should say so. I don't know when I've laughed . . . Yes, it went very well. No trouble at all. That is, the pigs. We—I have to tell you about the pigs." He told her about the pigs, while she refused to smile. His face, blotched with sweat, grazes and tears of laughter, was a mess and he couldn't wipe it, either, because he couldn't get his gauntlets off and she wasn't going to help him.

It didn't seem to trouble him. She said, "I'm glad you've had such an enjoyable time. It must have been more interesting than earning your pay in the dyeshop."

Through the drink, she had his attention. He said, "Demoiselle? I'm sorry."

If she were as honest as he was, she would say what was in her mind. She would say, accusingly, "Why are you so happy, so often?"

Instead, she said, "What about Felix? That was the purpose of it all, surely?"

He said, "He has great promise, and courage. All the courage in the world."

"But not yet the skill for the White Bear tournament?" said Felix's mother.

"Nothing like enough skill. No. Not yet. And because he's brave, he won't recognise his shortcomings. He'll take risks, and run into danger. He should be prevented from jousting at Easter. Prevented at all costs," said Claes.

She was silent, trying to imagine herself forbidding Felix this thing he had set his heart on. She said, "How much danger would there be? Blunt swords, buttoned lances . . ."

"Men still get killed," said Claes. "And things happen that aren't accidents. Suppose someone wanted to ruin your business?"

She stared at him. She rose, and coming round her desk, held out her hand and said irritably, "For goodness' sake, get these gloves off. Felix is hardly the backbone of the business." She dragged, clanking, at one glove. "In any case, who would go to such lengths?"

"Felix is the heir," Claes said, offering the second glove, and then looking at the kerchief she was holding out to him. "That's the second time you've had to give me a cloth. You must be surprised to find I'm even house-trained." He paused and said, "As to that, if you remember the first time, you'll remember some quite distinct threats."

She stood, a glove in either hand. "Jordan de Ribérac?"

Claes dropped his eyes to the kerchief. "I had an encounter with two of his men the other day. Not a pleasant one. And don't start thinking of formal complaints: nothing can be proved. Indeed, he's gone back to France now anyway. But it made me think. For example, the vat explosion while I was away?"

She sat down, the gloves in her lap, looking at him.

He said, "I felt it wasn't an accident. I made them show me the new vat, and the new pump. They'd been connected up wrongly. You'd have had another accident in less than a week."

"Who—?" she said.

He shook his head. "Someone Henninc didn't know, with all the right credentials. I've told him to have no repairs done except by the men he knows well. But of course, anyone can be bribed. And if there's trouble here, there might be trouble at the Louvain end of your business."

She said, "We've had it already."

"I thought you might," said Claes. "I haven't much time. But I wondered if I ought to go and see the new man. Olivier, isn't it? Felix might like to go with me. And I thought I should also like to call at Genappe."

Sixteen miles south of Brussels, the compact moated castle of Genappe had been a favourite hunting lodge of the Duke of Burgundy's until recently. Until the Dauphin Louis, heir to the kingdom of France, had fled to his dear uncle for sanctuary and his dear uncle the Duke had presented him with Genappe, to be his home for as long as he wished to defy his own father.

Claes proposed to call on the Dauphin of France. Her servant Claes. Her remarkable, half-inebriated, wholly self-possessed Nicholas. Who was so happy, so often.

He clearly saw nothing odd about it. She said, "Well, you'd better make sure your blue doublet is properly mended."

The large gaze admired her; the caterpillar mouth expanded in a beam of complete and serene understanding. He said, "And put back all the bells while I'm at it?"

Chapter 22

Easter, that year, fell in the middle of April. The expedition to Genappe, Claes decided, should ideally take place just before it. In case circumstances changed, he became very busy.

By the middle of March, Marian de Charetty was a substantial property-owner, possessing three warehouses next to her own, a wine tavern close to the fish market and—at a cost that frightened her—a house and storerooms in Spangnaerts Street. Spangnaerts, or Spanish Street, was in the heart of the prime trading quarter of Bruges, near the Bridge of St John, across the canal from the English and Scots trading houses, and within three minutes of the customs house, the Bourse, the consulates of Florence, Venice and Genoa, and the Lodge of the Brethren of the White Bear. It was also next door to a house owned by Anselm Adorne.

Felix was given the task of supervising the refurbishing of the wine tavern. Astoundingly, he set about it with vigour, making a number of excellent innovations and causing concern only in the undue sternness of his dealings with both his staff and his customers. One of the Metteneye boys, who had been accidentally sick over one of Felix's new trestles, was more than surprised to find himself bundled into the street and told not to return until he could hold his drink properly. Felix's mother, called upon by the Metteneye mother, found herself having to apologise.

The money to do all this, it seemed, was being found partly by loan, and partly from the profit of some investment Claes had made with the Milan Medici.

Thomas, arriving with two hundred foot and horse towards the end of February, found accommodation, beer, food and fodder waiting for him, and a string of mules and hired carts bearing armour. Thomas, offspring of three generations of landless soldiers stranded in France by a succession of forgivable English defeats compounded by a succession of unforgivable English truces, began to soften still further towards foreigners, who weren't at all bad so long as you kicked the bastards from time to time where it hurt most.

After a week of pandemonium Thomas and his small army left, to join Master Tobias at Milan and proceed south to Astorre and Naples. With him went an extremely burly chaplain called God-scalc from northern Germany, and a Hungarian crossbowman called Abrami, both discovered by Claes. The function of the chaplain, he explained, was to help Julius with his clerking and keep Tobie from interfering, while reminding the troops that disobedience to Astorre's orders meant death and hellfire immediately. The job of Abrami was to help Thomas imagine he could handle everything, while handling all the things Thomas couldn't.

Marian de Charetty listened, questioned, objected, argued and occasionally won a point.

The pump in the yard had been set right, and a man brought in from Alost to do nothing but look after the equipment, keep friendly with Lippin, and obey Henninc's orders. Henninc was pleased and the man, who reported direct to the Widow and often got quite different orders, was discreet and able. What portion of Claes' network of contacts had produced him was not yet evident. Godscalc, Marian knew, had been a brother of the chaplain to the painters' guild: she suspected Colard Mansion had supplied him. The Hungarian, amazingly, was related to the wife of one of the seamen at Sluys. Henninc's new deputy, who spoke native Flemish, went by the name of Bellobras, which still caused Felix extreme amusement.

When she wasn't worrying about loans, the Widow felt like smiling as well. She had never before experienced so buoyant an upheaval: not in her girlhood; not in Cornelis' lifetime. She had envied Claes his disposition. All through the worst of his 'prentice excesses, he had always been lively to deal with. Employing him now, it would seem, as an equerry, she woke every morning alert and expectant, wondering what amazing battles she would have to fight, what new acquisitions, new experiences, new adventures would be packed into this day before it ended. She was never disappointed. She had never seen anyone work so prodigally in so many diverse arenas. The excesses of the past she now interpreted as mere spillage of all this vitality, and could only be thankful there had been no more of them. Speed, of course, was important because he had to get back to Milan, because of the courier service. That had been organised, too. She had asked to be kept informed about it, and was, to a fault. It seemed to be a matter of hiring riders and analysing information about horses and lodgings and tolls and other couriers. The Bruges branch of a number of banks, including the Medici, then made known their willingness to confide certain kinds of dispatches under contract to the Charetty. One of the new couriers had already gone south with a heavy guard and a satchel.

But managers like Angelo Tani wanted personal service, and Claes was ready to oblige. He would carry the letters. He had to report to Milan in any case, and set that side of the business in order. Tani would expect Claes to go as soon as the latest word came in from London. And as soon as Tommaso received firm news of the ostrich. Had it, or had it not been shipped by the Strozzi company aboard a Catalan ship in Mallorca?

The Flanders galleys, after lingering an inordinate length of time, had taken courage and set sail for London, to load English goods and begin the long journey home to Venice. The question was whether the English King Henry, with civil war on his hands, would commandeer the galleys for his own uses. The merchants in Bruges and London and Southampton waited anxiously.

Bishop Coppini, on his saintly mission for peace, departed along the coast to visit English-held Calais and converse with the English rebels, the Earl of Warwick and Edward, the son of the King's Yorkist challenger. They said a number of Scotsmen had been seen in Calais as well. They said the King of Scots, changing his mind, was now holding secret talks with both sides of the English dispute instead of just the reigning Lancastrian, and had sent to ask the Duke of Burgundy if he could spare any more guns.

They said the Scots king was sending some envoys to Brussels in the guise of merchants, one of whom was likely to be Simon of Kilmirren. Remember Simon, who made that fuss over his dog after finding young Claes with a girl in the cellar? Who took sides with Lionetto at Sluys against Astorre and the Charetty crowd? Who nearly did for young Claes with a pair of cloth shears? Or maybe it was the other way round . . .

The Widow heard that piece of gossip. She was in the mercers' hall at the time, pursuing a contract to do with yarn dyeing—one of the few parts of the business she still kept in her own hands. There followed three different meetings, held in various quarters, to which she was escorted by Claes, and during which she had no chance to talk privately. Riding back from the third, in St Lievens, he listened to her and was not apparently troubled.

"My lord Simon? He has no quarrel with you. I'll be out of his sight very soon. He's more likely to have his hands full with his father. Especially if he's intriguing for King James, or Bishop Kennedy. I heard some good news today."

This morning she would have forced a thorough discussion on Simon of Kilmirren. Now she let him change the subject, saving her energy. Good news meant more work, likely as not, and she was exhausted. Nobody negotiates with an underling. Everywhere Claes went, she had to go as well, to lead the discussions. Until, Claes said, Felix was ready. And no doubt Claes was right. Felix, master of tavern-keeping, had still to find the incentive to move to less alluring parts of the business. It might take a long time. And meanwhile, she knew, Felix was still secretly practising his wonderful jousting. So she finally answered Claes with some flatness. "Oh? What good news?"

He had no trouble now on a horse. Riding easily, he turned his blue-capped head and grinned. "Four more meetings. No. Seriously. Captain Lionetto, presently with the condottiere Piccinino, is now officially banking with Depositors Thibault and Jaak de Fleury, our own very good friends of Geneva. Don't they deserve one another?"

"I feel less charitable," said his employer. "You say Lionetto was hired by Piccinino? So he's fighting for King Ferrante, as we are. So he, too, is collecting gold hand over fist from the Duke of Milan and the Pope. When the war is over, whoever wins, Jaak de Fleury will be a rich man and Lionetto will make a fortune. That's the principle, isn't it? No matter who wins, the mercenaries make their money. That's why you've persuaded me to send all those extra men to Astorre."

"Yes, you'll make a fortune too," said Claes happily. "But it is good news, all the same. What do you want to do tomorrow?"

"Nothing," said Marian de Charetty with feeling.

"Well, that's all right," said Claes. "I thought I'd take that trip to Louvain we were speaking about. Felix could come with me, with authority to dismiss your new manager. And then we'd go on to Genappe."

She reined in her horse without meaning to, and then kicked it on before her grooms overtook her. She rode better than he did. Her cloak was perfectly pressed and her hood securely pinned over her rolled cap and coif, so that no hair escaped. Her saddlecloth was in the Charetty blue, edged with scarlet, and her bit and bridle were trimmed with silver. She said, "Felix won't go to Genappe if

you're with him. And who said anything about dismissing Olivier?
You've never even met him."

"Me?" said Claes. "I've no feelings one way or the other. But
Felix can hear the case and judge for himself. A taste of pit and
gallows. Seigneurial power."

"And Genappe?" said Felix's mother.

Claes smiled. "I'm going," he said. "And Felix daren't let me go
without him."

Four days later Olivier, the manager of the Charetty business at
Louvain, found himself dismissed. The enquiry which preceded it
took up most of a day, and the dismissal was effected, with aplomb,
by the jonkheere Felix de Charetty. Master Olivier, who had heard
certain rumours from Bruges, had already completed some of his
packing and was allowed to finish the rest, after signing a number
of documents. By evening he had gone.

The young broker's partner whom Claes happened to have
brought along to check the accounting, agreed readily to stay temporarily in the manager's place, which made everything simple.
Felix left Claes to show him the ropes and went off to enlighten his
university friends about life in the business world. When he came
home under a paling sky, the candles were still lit in the managerial office, which was a waste of wax if you like. But he was too
sleepy to open the door and complain about it.

When he got up next day, he found an empty house with some
cold food on the table. Looking out, however, he saw the courtyard, looking remarkably clean, with a group of people in the middle standing listening to Claes, who seemed to be sitting on a
wheelbarrow, talking to them. The broker, a man with ginger hair
he had sometimes played skittles against, was standing beside him,
looking attentive. As he watched, the talking came to an end. Men
began to disperse, and Claes and the broker walked together across
to the pawn booth and stockrooms. Felix went down.

"Ah, there you are," said Claes. "If you've eaten, we ought to
get on our way. People who stay in castles don't like to be kept
waiting. Old Persian proverb. Do we need anyone with us? We
could ride to Genappe on our own. You prop me on my horse and
I'll find dinner for you."

The battle over Genappe had reopened. The initial salvo, in
Bruges, had been delivered by Felix's mother. Felix was to go with
a party to Louvain and examine, with Claes, the way the new

manager was running the business. He was to remain with Claes, who wished to call at Genappe. He was then to come home. Felix had refused point blank and had been sent from the room by his mother.

Second salvo from Henninc. Which men was Felix taking to Louvain and Genappe? He wasn't going.

Surprise of Henninc. Then he supposed he'd have to ask that young busybody Claes which men he wanted. He'd thought the Widow would have more sense, begging jonkheere Felix's pardon, than to send a servant on those sort of errands. Claes at Genappe! My lord the Dauphin'd wonder what Bruges folk were coming to.

Back to his mother. Of course, if Felix didn't care to represent the family, Claes would have to go to Louvain on his own. She couldn't leave Bruges. The matter of Olivier was urgent. As for Genappe, Claes knew more about that than she did.

Out to find Claes. He found Claes. Felix observed to Claes that he understood, of course, that a visit had to be paid to Louvain, to see what this new man was up to. But what was all this about going to visit the Dauphin?

The Dauphin? Genappe. It was a word you could snap, and Felix snapped it.

Ah, Genappe. Yes, quite right. Claes wanted to visit a friend at Genappe, but of course it wasn't the Dauphin, just a man at arms in the Dauphin's household. Raymond du Lyon, his name was. It wouldn't take long. An afternoon's ride from Louvain, and he mightn't get another chance to see Raymond. If Felix wasn't eager, he needn't come with him.

Felix (said Felix) was far from being eager to go to Louvain, never mind underwrite some servant's trip to Genappe. But Louvain, he saw, was important. He could hardly let a base-born apprentice represent the Charetty family. He would go.

Felix dropped plans, broke appointments and left Bruges with Claes and his compact retinue in a foul temper which lasted through two of the three days of the journey. Then Claes found him a good brothel in Brussels and an inn where the cooking was wonderful and the owner's wife wanted to know what it was like to run the best tavern in Bruges. By the time they got to Louvain, Felix was quite in the mood for business.

But now, Genappe had appeared in the programme again. Felix said, "You never think of your employer, do you? Using her time and her horses on some private visit, when her whole business in

Louvain has collapsed and she doesn't know it. I'm going straight
back to Bruges to report, and you're coming with me. And that's
an order."

"All right," said Claes peacefully. April sunshine was browning
his skin and reflecting into his dimples the inexorable blue of his
livery. He added, "I'll have to send to the Dauphin though, and
explain. He's expecting us this evening."

"What?" said Felix.

"You were sleeping," said Claes. "My friend Raymond sent a
message this morning. My lord the Dauphin would like to see us
both. That's a great honour for someone like me."

"It would be if you were going," said Felix shortly. "I'll go. I'll
tell them you're sick."

Claes didn't argue. Felix didn't like that. Claes said, "Well, of
course, you could explain that to them now," in the same propitia-
tory tone. "That's the escort over there, waiting to take us to
Genappe. I'm afraid I've spoken to them already, but they might
believe I've taken ill. I could fall down." He gave the yard a calculating look and moved backwards, his hands smoothing his hip-
bones in readiness.

The whole thing, Felix suddenly saw, was pretty stupid. And
funny. He began to emerge from his sulks. He groaned, and Claes
looked up at once, grinning. Claes said, "Did you think you would
get away with claiming that stupid helmet had been loaned by
Guildolf de Gruuthuse? If it had been his, you'd have broken out
in boils by now anyway. Come on. There's no escape. You always
were a hopeless liar."

Felix said, "Does Mother . . . ?"

"Of course your mother knows you've been up to something,"
said Claes. "So does half Bruges. The theory is that the Dauphin
came here hunting and you met him, and talked hounds, and he
took to you. You've been to Genappe, and he asked one of his
masters at arms to teach you a little jousting. Then someone lent
you some arms that didn't fit them. Why should you have to keep
quiet about that?"

"They gave me the armour," said Felix. "As a little present. I
knew she wouldn't let me keep it. Bad for business. The clients
would think the Charetty were plotting with the Dauphin. That's
what they say, you know. Every country that hates France has
agents at Genappe plotting with the Dauphin. So that he can get

all his lands back from his father. So that he'll give them favours when he's king of France after his father dies."

"You mean you're not plotting with the Dauphin?" said Claes. "That's disappointing. I thought I could join you and get a jousting set too."

Felix burst into laughter. "I don't think you've quite the style," he said. "But you know, I've thought of something."

"What?" said Claes.

"The next deal you do, give me the profit instead of Mother, and I'll buy the armour. Then I won't owe anyone anything."

"That's perfectly true," said Claes. "And then your mother can sell your armour and she'll get her profit."

"Well, hardly," said Felix.

"Then we'll think of something else," said Claes cheerfully. "Later. Come on. Let's go to Genappe, if we're going."

Better than the windswept flats of Bruges, the sweet rolling country round Louvain was known to both Felix and his servant. Now, in early spring, every turn in the path was a delight and, for Felix, a promise. The awkwardness of Claes' presence was forgotten. Felix was a man of stature, invited by princes.

Claes, well accustomed to Felix's ways, watched him engage in conversation one by one the members of the Dauphin's escort who replied politely. None of them quite matched the heir to the Charetty dyeshop in the costliness or high fashion of his apparel. Claes, who had been trying not to look at it in detail, had an impression of furred hems and violet flouncing. Felix certainly had on a very tall hat.

Claes hoped Felix would enjoy the journey, for he was not at all sure what awaited them both at Genappe. Until now, the Dauphin had used Arnolfini as his intermediary. A meeting like this—if it took place—would forge a direct link between Genappe and Milan. If it took place, what would it be like? Princes were not within Claes' experience. The Count of Urbino, last winter, was the greatest noble he had ever met, and their encounters had been brief, and on the exercise field: not a meeting of minds. The minds he was used to, apart from his fellow workers and Felix and his friends, were people like Julius and the Widow. Speaking with Anselm Adorne demanded a little more caution. And also the Greeks: Acciajuoli and the woman, Laudomia. The professor had been something new, but only briefly: his mind fell into patterns. That of Tobie, less so.

Noblemen . . . That was only troublesome because of the difference in custom, which could disguise, at the beginning, how they were going to tackle you. It was certainly true of Jordan de Ribérac who was, one supposed, with proper irony, the highest ranking of the men he had had to do with, apart from Urbino.

Now a king's son. A king's son who made a point, Marian de Charetty had said, of appearing shabby, comradely, even vulgar, and who was ostentatiously religious. But who had led armies at twenty-one; reigned in Dauphiné; plotted to capture lordships in Italy; and had defied his father the King to marry a plain twelve-year-old from the house of Savoy, for the battle-base her father's lands would give him. Defied his father in so many ways that the King of France had terrorised the Duke of Savoy into renouncing Louis his son-in-law, and conceding the King of France as his overlord. Then the flight of Louis the Dauphin to Burgundy. To Genappe, where he was plotting with Milan and the Earl of Warwick against the King his father, and did not, naturally, wish the matter broadcast by dim-witted couriers.

Claes had picked up a lot about the Dauphin from his many sources, but it was the Widow, in the end, who had helped him most. That was when, finally, she had pinned him down and asked him why he was going, and he had told her.

"Messengers are always a danger. We all know too much. And suddenly, not only the Dauphin's own man Gaston du Lyon but the Medici and Sforza are using me. It's only common sense to try to make out why. And whom I see. And what I know."

It had been a shock to her. He had realised why, after a moment, and added quickly, "But Felix, of course, doesn't know he's giving away more than he should. I'm sure of it. But if we warn him, and make him stop going to Genappe, they'll think there's something to hide.'

"So why are you going then?" she had said.

"Not because he's in danger. Only to display that I know what is happening. I haven't asked to see the Dauphin. Just to take Felix to visit Raymond, the chamberlain's brother. It will make the point. If the Dauphin wants to see us, he'll say so."

"And if he wants to see you, Nicholas?" had said the Widow. "Once before, I asked you about him. You said, I think, that he was far too astute, and you'd never expect to deceive him."

When she called him Nicholas, it was because she was either angry or frightened. He remembered the occasion of his previous answer. She had been both, and so had he. He forgot to answer, remembering.

"So," she had said. "You will have to decide, won't you? Claes or Nicholas? Which will you show to the Dauphin?"

Being only one person and not a carnival freak, he had started to laugh. In any case, there was no doubt that, whatever happened, he was going to be thoroughly tested, and at a new level. He had felt gratified, until he realised that this was primary proof of his inexperience. Now the visit to Genappe was upon him. Now he listened to Felix saying to him, yet again, as they rode: "And you kneel *three times*. Going in, going out. For God's sake remember, and don't make a fool of me." And he began to laugh again, because he probably wouldn't remember. Poor Felix. Poor Claes. Good luck, Nicholas.

Chapter 23

It was shortly after this that Claes realised that the impeccable escort sent to fetch himself and Felix had led them well away from the road to Genappe. That they were making their way over fields and through a copse to where, just over a rise of new grass, there came the sound of many voices, and hoofbeats, and the barking of excited dogs. A horn brayed.

Below Felix's towering hat his face, turned to Claes, was ruddy with pleasure. "My lord Dauphin's huntsman!" he said. "It must be. No one else can hunt here. Now you'll see. Jet black horses. He'll have nothing else. And the hounds. He has a new pair . . ."

"Monsieur is correct," said the captain of their escort. He had not spoken for an hour, and Claes looked at him with amazement. The captain continued to communicate with Felix. "It is for this very reason that my lord Dauphin requested you should be brought by this route. It will not displease you to hunt?"

Claes looked at the violet flounces, the quilted skirt with its marten-edge, the tasselled cone on Felix's head that would shear the lower branch off a pine tree. Felix cried, "My dear captain, I'm honoured!"

The captain smiled. The captain kicked his horse from a trot to a canter. So did Felix. So did all the rest of the troop except Claes, who fell off. The captain and Felix, by then well to the forefront, continued over the rise without noticing. The other horsemen, who certainly noticed, went on as if they hadn't. The last man, who had actually to ride round him, leaned over and, collecting Claes' horse by the reins, took it away with him.

Claes sat up in the grass and shouted after him. The last rider, leading Claes' horse, receded impassively, breasting the hillock in a different direction at a good, regular pace. Claes, sitting with his hands dangling over his knees, took a contemplative breath and sent a musical halloo in that direction. The rider began to descend the hill on the other side. The last thing Claes saw of the company were the two ears of his horse on the skyline.

The saddle, which had fallen off with him, lay upside down in the turf some distance away. Dug in beside it was a hoe, with a man leaning on it at an extravagant angle. His feet, nearest to Claes, were in patched and squashed boots, and he wore the felt cap and rolled sleeves and brief dress of a countryman. He turned a tuberous face with no teeth in it. "Now," he said. "Look at that. That new falcon brung down a saddle." He lifted his chin from his clasped hands and eased himself slowly back, raising his watering eyes to the sky. Claes went on sitting.

"Might bring down the horse next," said Claes. "I should watch out."

The hoe quivered. Collected over the gums, the owner's lips writhed apart, and a haze of saliva shot into the air. "Might bring down a man next, I shouldn't wonder," said the old man. "Catch your death, sitting on grass. Other people's grass. Hanged a man last week on that tree."

Claes said, "I wondered what you were planting."

Sunbeams danced on another frothy emission. The old man said, "You hungry then?"

Claes threw back his head and laughed. If it sounded like relief, he didn't mind. It was relief. He said, "I'm always hungry."

"Big fellows like you," said the old man. "I've seen you lot at harvest time. Eat the worth of the harvest at supper-time. They're over there. I've to take your sword off you, and your dagger."

Claes smiled at him. "Where will I find them again?"

The bristled cheeks glittered. "If you come back, they'll be under the hoe."

"And my saddle?"

The old man let his hoe drop. Now he turned, you could see he had a hunter's knife slung at his hip. The two-edged blade looked quite new. He rubbed the dirt off his hands and, wiping them on his tunic, stood waiting for Claes to get up. He said, "You need a horse before the saddle's any good to you. The girth's broken."

The girth, as he was already well aware, had been cut. Claes disputed nothing, but got up and, unbuckling his own unspectacular sword and knife, went across and laid them beside the hoe. The watering eyes met his as he straightened, within a miasma of sweat and unwashed linen, like the smell of pawned clothes. The old man said, "Follow the stream to the trees. Eat well. Eat well, my boy. My boy, you must be hungry."

* * *

Louis, Dauphin of France, was supping al fresco. Within the trees to which the stream led, a light hunting cabin had been erected from last year's timber with two small rooms, at present untenanted. The company, which was very small, was disposed on the patch of turf before it, almost crowded out by the number of wicker baskets and flasks packed between them. Farther off, the jingle of bits told where their horses were tied and grazing.

All of them were plainly dressed, although the cloth of their hunting clothes and the quality of their belts, their boots and their spurs showed that they were not servants, although they were not being served.

No. One man, closest to the cabin, was being served by the rest, and on bended knee. A man who didn't look round when Claes approached. Only one of the company did, and then rose and came towards him. Claes recognised no one, but he knew that the man by the hut was the Dauphin, and that these must be his intimates. The Bastard of Armagnac, then; and the lord of Montauban. Jean d'Estuer perhaps, lord of la Barde. Jean Bourré, the secretary. And someone of good birth for professional bodyguard . . . probably the man now approaching, who, on closer inspection, looked remarkably like someone he had first met in the Savoyard snows.

"Monsieur Raymond du Lyon?" said Claes. "I am happy to meet you."

"And I you, Monsieur Nicholas," said the other. The hair under the brim of his hat was dark, like Gaston's, and he had a jousting man's shoulders. His pleasant, free smile displayed three broken teeth. He added, "You took no harm, I trust, from our method of disengaging you? We tried hard to think of a gentler one."

"It's the one I feel most at home in," said Claes. "As your brother would tell you."

Raymond du Lyon smiled again, but made no rejoinder. Instead he said, "My lord Dauphin wishes to speak to you. Come."

The prince who sat on a cushion, knock-kneed legs splayed before him, fitted well enough the description gossip gave of him. Below the narrow-brimmed sugarloaf hat was the thin, drooping nose, the thick lips, the small chin. *The most suspicious man alive,* someone had called him. Pretty Margaret of Scotland, marrying him at eleven, spoiled by his father, had died defiant at twenty, intransigently childless on a diet of green apples and vinegar. Plain Charlotte of Savoy, married at twelve, was already at twenty twice pregnant and had had no chance to be spoiled by Louis' father. The last time the Dauphin had seen his father was thirteen years ago. Since then he had fled to Burgundy and his father had made his famous quip: *The Duke of Burgundy has taken in a fox that will eat his chickens.*

He was eating them now, wrapped in a napkin. Claes approached and, remembering not to make a fool of Felix, knelt the prescribed three times while the Dauphin laid down his meat and wiped his mouth and hands. Claes kissed his fingers, smelling of both fox and chicken. Placed on the grass, he was given a manchet with a chop and a chicken leg, smothered in sauce. A wooden tankard appeared, with Bordeaux wine in it.

The Dauphin spoke, using French. Some malfunction of palate or teeth or even of tongue made his words thick and not always clear, but never prevented him from speaking often, and quickly. Now he said, "I have this problem that requires a young mind, my good Nicholas. Monsieur le Bâtarde, where is it?"

One of the noblemen, rising silently, opened his purse and handed a paper to the Dauphin. No, a parchment. Covered with diagrams.

The Dauphin held it out. "Of course you were at Louvain with your young master Felix. I saw you, when the good rector was teaching. Monsieur Spierinct. He made this chart for me, but sometimes, when my poor mind is full of business, I cannot remember the key. Translate it for me." It was an astrologer's projection, in both Latin and Greek. Everyone knew that the Dauphin employed his own astrologers. One of them was probably present.

Claes or Nicholas? Nicholas bent his serious gaze on the Dauphin and said, "Yes, my lord. I have broken the Medici cipher."

He could feel the movement behind him. The sharp eyes in front were like the old man's hunting knife. The Dauphin said, "Well now: you make the Knight's move, but you drag me behind you. One step at a time. Can you interpret this document?"

Claes said, "My lord. Forgive me," and took the vellum, running his eye over it. After a moment he said, "To this point, I can read it. After that, I should have to correct it. The transcriber has made a mistake."

One of the company was standing at his elbow. The Dauphin said, "You hear, my lord? My transcriber has made a mistake. Show my lord, Nicholas."

And that had been predictable, too. As he spoke, Claes was

achieving, methodically, the last of his mental calculations. He reviewed them. Then he lifted the parchment, using his meat bone as pointer. "There are the false figures. Instead, it ought to go something like this."

Halfway through the recital, the other man said, "Stop!" He looked flushed. He said, "My lord Dauphin, this is correct."

There was a little silence. The Dauphin looked surprised. "Then give the boy more wine, another dish!" he said. "Has he to hold up a meat bone to remind us of our poor hospitality? My friend Nicholas, we are well met. We are on the same chessboard. The only question is, are we on the same side?"

Claes said, "Sir, Monsieur Gaston would tell you. I am employed by a burgess of Bruges. Her company has been hired by the Duke of Milan to help King Ferrante of Naples. As her courier my services have been retained by the Duke, by the company of the Medici and by yourself to carry dispatches and news. I brought you messages from Monsieur Gaston and from my lord the Duke of Milan, and through Messer Arnolfini have been well paid."

"But that," said the Dauphin, smiling, "is only the first indication of the warmth of our feelings for you. For such a relationship must depend on trust, must it not? For example, it is not convenient that the messages to me from Monsieur Gaston or my lord the Duke should fall into other hands. And yet my illustrious father, we discover, is fully aware that Monsieur Gaston has stayed in Milan, and even that he has paid a visit on my behalf to Savoy." The Dauphin lifted his arm and signed half a cross with the heel of his hand, renouncing anxiety. "Not, of course, that my father the King should find such news amiss. My family is twice linked with Savoy; exchanges of gossip are natural." The hand, darting, caught Claes' arm like a bird claw descending. "As you, my boy, will appreciate. Thibault and Jacques de Fleury of Geneva are your kinsmen, I'm told."

Claes said, "Monsieur Gaston knows my position. I am a baseborn great-nephew. I owe them nothing, and they prefer to have nothing to do with me. There is a legitimate heiress. I have nothing to gain or lose should you decide to win their allegiance."

"Of course I believe you," said the Dauphin. "Although an unkind person might say that a bribe to Monsieur Jacques de Fleury from me might well find its way, some of it, into your purse. And that even accepting a bribe, the family might be so dishonest as to serve my father secretly. As it is—"

He paused, and Claes dropped his eyes.

"—As it is, Monsieur Gaston tells me that Messieurs Thibault and Jacques have refused to move from their allegiance to the Duke of Savoy and my father. He offered them a considerable sum. As I said, my father knows of my chamberlain's visit. He presumably knows because your great-uncle and his family told him. But you say you have nothing to do with them."

"My lord," said Claes. "You are related to Anjou."

Again, the slight movement at his back. Again, the black glance above the long, pointed nose. Then the Dauphin, lifting his hand, tapped it once, sharply on Claes' arm and removed it.

"We are playing chess again," he said. "How very forward we are. But is this the best you can do to convince me of your good faith? Will you not extract what secrets, what coin you may from us all, and then abscond from the good lady your employer? Abscond to Venice, perhaps. I am told on the best of authority that you already have a modicum salted away and we know, of course, of the high regard of the Acciajuoli. How can I be sure that the secrets of my dispatches will remain secure in the hands of such a code-breaker?"

The Dauphin had put his fingers together, his gaze tranquil. Claes considered. The other men had ceased eating. Speaking in murmurs, they paid no apparent attention to the discussion. The astrologer, whose name he still didn't know, had rejoined them. A man emerged from the trees where the horses were, looked round and went back quickly, but not before Claes had seen him.

Claes said, "Well, my lord, that's the trouble about messengers. You can never tell. You can reward them so highly that they'll favour you more than the other fellow; but you can't know if the other fellow isn't doing the same. You can threaten, and if he makes a mistake, of course you have him. But the only sure way is not to engage him. My lord, my mistress is well paid by the Duke and by the Medici. There is no need for you to employ me."

The Dauphin picked a piece of grass and held it at arm's length, studying it. He folded his arm and held it, twirling before him. "You are perfectly right. What advantage could I possibly expect that would offset such a danger?"

Claes gazed at the prince's dark face. "You could retain me for formal messages only, and trust the others to better-accredited couriers, if you have them."

The grass twirled. "Now, here's a sorry lack of ambition! A boy who can outwit astrologers, but cannot see how to turn his talents to money!" The Dauphin looked up. "Jean, mon compère. What do you know about ciphers?"

Bourré the secretary. One of the seated men rose, came over and knelt. "All too little, monseigneur."

"And here we have an expert." The blade of grass indicated Claes.

"My friend," said the Dauphin to Claes, "Your skill is worth money. Do you not realise it? A great deal of money. Provided that it is devoted exclusively to ourselves. Messer Cosimo, Messer Cicco are my very good friends, but their ciphers are already the best in the world. It is we, struggling behind, who need your talents."

Claes looked from prince to secretary. He said humbly, "Of course, monseigneur. I should be honoured. That is, a servant may only achieve as much as his ability lets him, and there may be some matters where my meddling might cause only damage. Monseigneur understands."

"Naturally," said the Dauphin. He smiled at de la Barde.

"And again—" said Claes with diffidence.

"Yes?" This time, the Dauphin was less patient.

Claes said, "I beg the Dauphin's pardon. But the more time I spend on such affairs, the less I have to give to the Charetty business. Monsieur Felix, as you know, is an able youth, and will one day be a worthy head of the company, but at present is much distracted by other pleasures."

The Dauphin flung out his arms. "You hear, my friends! I am being taken to task for my hospitality! Will you deprive me of the company of this charming youth? I flatter myself that he, too, will be grieved. How he has enjoyed viewing our kennels, riding our horses, learning the martial skills!"

Claes said nothing.

The Dauphin dropped his arms. "But you are right. Duty calls. His family need him. I shall no longer seduce him from his dye-vats. But what shall I say to him?"

Claes said, "He will be heartbroken, I know. I wonder if I dare suggest to my lord a final summons for some special feast-day, where Monsieur Felix's presence at Genappe would not discommode him? Say the second Sunday after Easter?"

The eyes held his, then turned to the secretary. "Of course! So it shall be," said the Dauphin. "My friend Monseiur Bourré will note

it. Young Monsieur Felix will receive the invitation. And we shall
see that he does not refuse it. That is what you wish?"

"That is so exactly," said Claes. "My lord, these things should
profit us all. I am grateful."

"Well!" said the Dauphin. He threw the grass away. He put a
hand on his secretary's shoulder and rose. Above the boots his
knees turned markedly towards each other. Above them, thin and
muscular thighs disappeared into his short hunting skirts. His eyes
under the sugarloaf hat rested on the rest of the company, who had
already scrambled to their feet and were beginning to close and
order the baskets. From the trees came the sound of horses stamping. The Dauphin glanced at Claes who had risen also but now,
rapidly, knelt.

The Dauphin said, "We understand one another. You are a good
boy, and will serve me well. Monsieur Bourré here will send for
you, and Monsieur Arnoulphin, whom you already know. You
have, I hope, already been recompensed for the suit of armour?"

"To the last penny of the pawn ticket," said Claes with gratitude.

The Dauphin frowned. "We should have done better than that.
Monsieur de la Barde!"

The best-dressed of the others came forward. "I shall see to it,
monseigneur."

The Dauphin's smile flashed again towards Claes. "You understand, my child. You do not leave this hut dressed in cloth of gold
with rings on your fingers or even gold in your purse. But you will
not be a poor man as a result of this day. Provided only you are
loyal, as you will be. The alternative does not bear thinking of.
Now God speed you."

Claes kissed the hard fingers and rose, and backed, and bumped
into Raymond du Lyon who turned him round by the elbow and
walked a dozen paces from the clearing. His horse was waiting
there with his saddle, mended, upon it. The man at arms said,
"You were stunned by the fall, and a field-worker cared for you.
The hunt is not far away. You know where to recover your arms?"

"Under the hoe," said Claes. "Unless someone has stolen the
hoe. It's late to start back."

Raymond du Lyon showed his three broken teeth. "Your young
Monsieur Felix has had a message already from the Dauphin's
steward, regretting that his lord has changed his plans and a meet-

ing cannot now be expected. But a room has been arranged for you both on your way back at Wavre. There will be nothing to pay."

"That will please Monsieur Felix," said Claes. His arms were soon found. He took leave of Gaston's brother and rode off. He felt slightly breathless, as he had in February, climbing out of the frozen water. Somewhere under the shock, a feeling of pleasure was struggling with a very sensible apprehension.

Chapter 24

Wearing court dress, including a hennin, Katelina van Borselen rode through the streets of Ghent with her parents and a handsome retinue, below the Veere banner. With her, she carried her liege lord Duke Philip's permission to visit Brittany, there to take up her post as maid of honour to the widowed Scots Duchess. Tomorrow she and her party were passing to Zeeland. Tonight they had rooms in one of the great inns of Ghent. They were turning into the courtyard when her father stopped yet again to greet someone he knew, and his wife and daughter and servants halted once more obediently.

Then Katelina saw that the person he was greeting was the son of Marian de Charetty, and that behind him were two grooms and Claes. Claes, whom she had not seen since the morning after the Carnival. Claes, who had taken, very courteously, what she had enjoined upon him, and then had taken it again, she was rather pleased to remember, purely for his own enjoyment. Unless he was rather cleverer even than she had thought.

At no time, either next morning nor later, had she felt ashamed of what had happened. She had chosen well. She had not been roughly treated. Her initiation, she was ready to believe, had, from its circumstances, been more careful than she could have expected at the wedded hands of the seigneur's son from Courtrai, or even Guildolf de Gruuthuse, never mind Jordan de Ribérac and his nasty son. She was grateful to Claes, although he had made one miscalculation. He had, as he had said, wakened her too far.

You would think, then, that she would have been eager, for the first time, to study the renewed lists of suitors, young and old, which her mother was pressing upon her. That she would, with this curious ache which now visited her, have sought the company of the young men who came to her house, and escorted her family and tried to please her. It was ridiculous that she did not. They said that a duckling, born out of sight of its mother, would follow the first form it set eyes on. Heaven forfend that she was to spend the rest of her life looking for someone who, put in a bathtub, spoke like . . . looked like . . . handled her like the boy Claes.

She thought particularly about their next meeting. Despite their difference in rank, Claes and she were bound to encounter one another in the weeks to come. She could trust him, she believed, not to be familiar. But the circumstances demanded some acknowledgment—some change of attitude, a special friendliness, even in public. She had to deal with that, and so had he.

She found, in any case, that she was curious to know what became of him. She discovered that, as courier, his status had risen a little; that his employer was giving him experience about the various forms of her business. Claes was permitted to escort Marian de Charetty nowadays to business meetings and was not treated entirely as a servant, but was allowed to sit quietly behind and sometimes make notes, as if he were Meester Julius. Of course, it suited a respectable woman to have servant and bodyguard both. Speaking of Claes, people still laughed.

But although Katelina heard of him, no encounter with Claes had taken place. Since the night of the Carnival, she had glimpsed him only once, and that on the following morning, when the household had been drawn to its windows by an unaccustomed shaking of bells. Called by their merriment she had gone too, and so had seen Claes skipping by, his creased blue clothes weirdly decked out with goat bells, and a flock of goats trotting behind him. He had looked round in elastic response to the catcalls, returning happily insult for insult, his eyes searching the casements. From her window she had tried to convey in her smile the freedom and gentleness she felt that morning, and made for him a movement of her hands which said, All is well.

And now they were meeting again. He looked older. In six or seven weeks, that was impossible. Different work made people's faces settle in different lines. A life indoors in cellars and dyesheds amid heat and harsh vapours had formed in him an appearance she remembered as rounder and softer. His unusually open eyes, looking at her now, conveyed an expression that was friendly; muted; apologetic; a little daunted. Apologetic because, she assumed, he had not anticipated the encounter. But, clearly, there was no harm done. She was on her way forthwith to Brittany, and he must leave soon, she supposed, for Milan.

The raw, jagged scar no longer leaped to the eye, but was just a heavy pink mark, as if a stick of dye had been drawn down his cheek. He was wearing the same doublet and jacket she had dried for him in front of the fire. The rip had been mended and the cloth well pressed and looked after.

The boy Felix, on the other hand, looked as if some accident had befallen him. Half the flounces on his violet overjacket were torn, and he wore a hat quite at odds with the rest of him. Her father, she saw, was putting questions to him. Behind, Claes was responding, with a small bow, to the smile of her mother. Then his gaze switched to Katelina herself, his smile deepening as he studied her steeple headdress.

Her mother approved of Claes, who had been such an exemplary escort for Gelis on the night of the Carnival. The manservant, heavily bribed, had taken Gelis home that night as if nothing had happened. The porters at her father's house were even simpler to deal with. No one seemed to have suborned them. They had seen a masked escort leave with her, and arrive back. They hadn't seen him emerge because, as Katelina explained to her mother, he had left almost at once by the postern. Her mother, listening, had been inclined to be severe over her rejection of Guildolf de Gruuthuse. Katelina had not made it perfectly clear that the rejection had taken place at the beginning, not the end of the evening. She didn't suppose that Guildolf would boast of it. She hadn't spoken to either parent, after all, about Jordan de Ribérac.

The vicomte de Ribérac had left Bruges the following day. She had found that out herself with some trouble. Claes, she learned, had been enquiring as well. She had felt relief, and a sense of being protected. This was nonsense. If anything in this world was certain, it was the death of Claes, if de Ribérac ever found out what had happened. Claes knew how necessary it was to take precautions.

Anyway, she had her parents to shield her. Except that her parents, again, were discussing suitors. This time there was no escape from it. She was not likely, now, to choose a nunnery. She chose Brittany. If life wouldn't open its gates for her, she would force them.

No. She had already done that.

Her partner in that experience was, at the moment, busy shutting them again. Yes, jonkheere Felix was passing the night also in Ghent. No, Claes regretted that he had not bespoken beds for jonkheere Felix and himself at this inn, but another. Had he not told jonkheere Felix? He must have forgotten.

Her father, goodnatured man, didn't press the young fellows to change their arrangements. The inn was an expensive one. On the contrary, he invited the good son of his old friend Cornelis to join him and his family for supper. And of course, to bring Claes, who had been so protective of their young Gelis. A tribute indeed, thought Katelina, to Bruges' view of Claes' improved prospects. Felix, delighted, accepted, and his harbinger, overruled, said nothing more.

Claes, her father had called him. It was the name all Bruges knew him by: perhaps they would never allow him another. It was the name which, with great determination, she had continued to give him in her mind ever since that night. She had not forgotten the things he had said, which were true.

They parted briefly: Felix de Charetty and his party to settle their horses and baggage in some other inn whose name Claes had some trouble, it seemed, in remembering. Then they returned, as guests, to share Florence van Borselen's supper.

Her father had taken a private chamber for his family, and had invited other guests, all burgesses of Ghent with one or two wives and one daughter. His own clerk was there, considerably placed next to Claes. The room itself was small, with a clean tiled floor and a long table with a good linen cloth on it, striped with drawn threadwork. Seated on trestles along its three sides, the company ate and drank and made seemly conversation, served by her father's excellent servants. Katelina watched the one girl glance at Claes, and away, and back again. He didn't appear to notice, but she knew, positively, that he had. He and the clerk were finding an enormous amount to say to one another.

Her mother, as might be expected, talked of Brussels. Young Felix contributed something, but soon changed the subject and launched into a detailed and rather endearing account of coursing with the hounds of the Dauphin. When that came to an end, her father spoke of the attractions of Louvain and its professors and, politely, of the Charetty business there, and those parts of it about which clearly he thought Claes as well as Felix might feel able and happy to speak.

Katelina said, "You forget, Father. Claes has left that part of the business to carry dispatches."

Her mother tapped her father's hand. "There now, Meester Florence: you did forget that. And the beautiful warming-apple young Gelis received from Milan. A fine city, I'm told. But the princess's chaplain was shocked at the way the ladies whitened their faces. He is a broad-minded man. But the paint was too much for him. He told us about it."

Katelina's father rarely listened to what his wife said, a practice which, Katelina often thought, must have contributed to his sweet temper. Now he said, "Dispatches? That should take you to some interesting places. Do you carry for the Dauphin?"

The two deceiving dimples appeared in Claes' cheeks. The girl—who was she? She had missed her father's introduction—glanced at them and remained looking at Claes. Claes said, "I know jonkheere Felix hunts with the Dauphin's hounds, but there are the limits to the exalted company we keep. I carry for Angelo Tani, though, and the Strozzi bank and the Doria."

"Well, I've met the Dauphin even if you haven't," said Felix. His hair, solidly curled for once, bounced as he turned to his host and hostess. "A delightful castle, Genappe. I expect you know it?"

Since they didn't, he told them about it. Katelina doubted, from the recital, if he had seen much of it, or had been there often. She thought that it was perhaps just as well. Every plot was supposed to start at Genappe. It would do the Charetty business no good to appear too close to it.

Her mother said, "I suppose there is something to be said for a good family life, even if one doesn't trouble with great households of servants and lodgings in every hunting-forest. There is the King of France, unloved and ailing, in spite of his dozens of new silk gowns and red and green doublets; and his own son his bitterest enemy."

Katelina's father smiled. "Hardly unloved, by all accounts, my dear," he said. "Indeed, if you will forgive me, it is the love which they say has caused the ailing. But yes, it is sad. For a son to dislike his father—that passes. That is natural in a growing man. For a man to vent hatred on his son—that is unnatural."

"Then look at the Duke of Burgundy!" said her mother. "What has he but an only son; charming; religious; of the purest habits. The finest landowner in Holland: brave as you wish: sailing his boat in the roughest seas; longing only to show his worth in the field. And see how he hates his father and his father hates him! That dreadful quarrel! But for the Dauphin, they might have killed one another. As it is, the poor Duchess left court. And now, when the Dauphin takes young Charles hunting, the Duke is furious. They said the King of France offered in jest to take the Duke's son for his, since his own liked the Duke better. See what land and power will do!"

The guests, who had met Florence van Borselen's wife before, smiled warily and preserved a circumspect silence. As they always did, Katelina and her father sat through it also. At the end, her father said merely, "I advise you to watch your words, my dear, or you will have Katelina marry a pauper in case her heirs are impelled one day to turn and rend her." He had not mentioned Simon of Kilmirren, whose relationship with his own father he had once called "unnatural." And whom, once, Katelina had toyed with the idea of marrying.

Felix had flushed. Claes glanced at him, hesitated, and then said nothing. Felix said, "I don't say the Dauphin is right, or the Count of Charolais. But men don't always want to obey orders. Whether it has to do with land or power or not."

"You are quite right," said Katelina's father. "Indeed, even womenfolk object to orders at times. But the effects in some families are more far-reaching than others. Discord between princes can ruin a country. A dispute between father and son can of course ruin a business. A quarrel between a fisherman and his son might mean that the boat cannot be launched and a livelihood is lost. Hence a king will have many bastards so that, failing sons, he will have men of his blood he can trust. Hence a man of small family will cleave to his uncles and cousins, for he may need them. Many a man had a truer son in a nephew than the one born to him."

She had not heard her father say that before. She realised that the presence of bastard Claes had slipped his mind, and glanced over to find the same bastard looking at her, mildly amused and mildly reassuring. Then her attention was recalled as her mother exploded.

Her mother often exploded, and they all simply waited until it passed over. It appeared that she was deeply affronted to think that any husband of hers could dream of putting some woman's child before his own two dear pure-bred daughters, and was sure that the other ladies round the table would feel as she did. She thought the number of the Duke's bastards a disgrace. Was her husband trying to tell her that the Dauphin's two illegitimate daughters were also got as a matter of state policy? And what about . . . ?

The principal guest, with great aplomb and a certain amount of experience of the Borselen family, discovered that it was sadly late, and he deserved a chastisement for keeping Meester Florence and his lady from their beds. So kind had been their hospitality, so ravishing their company, they had however only themselves to blame for it.

People rose, Claes among them and Felix, with reluctance. The unknown girl required help, supplied by Claes, to extricate herself from the table. He had stupid eyes like an imported monkey. It was perfectly true. And the muscles inside his sleeves came from pounding cloth in a dyevat. The dimples trembled, and the girl looked up at him, speaking, her eyes sparkling. He replied. The girl was smiling.

Her father said, "Katelina! You're dreaming. Pray escort the ladies." She attended their departure punctiliously and with a certain tart enjoyment. She saw them leave the inn gates and turned back to follow her father and his clerk, and bumped into someone. Claes said, steadying her with a nearly invisible palm to her elbow, "She has the reversion of three bakers' shops in Alost. What do you think?"

As if he had flattened it with a hot-iron, the pain disappeared. Katelina lifted her hand and, when he dropped his, caught it in her own and held it, despite him. The inn-yard lights shone on them both, and showed her his eyes flicker: to her father waiting on the steps, and back to her again. She kept his clasped hand in shadow. He was smiling. He said, "Oh Madonna, you must go in." And within her, another ache had begun.

Her father was returning down the steps, his face impatient. Katelina said aloud, "Tomorrow morning, then. My maid will give you the packet. Father, you don't mind? Claes has been kind enough to undertake a transaction for me."

Her father also was smiling. "You're a good lad," he said. "Young Felix couldn't be in better hands. I'm only sorry you can't stay in Bruges all the time. But youth calls, eh? And ambition. You'll do well. I'm sure of it."

And then Felix, whom Nature rather than youth had called with inconvenient suddenness, reappeared to repeat his formal thanks, and take his leave, and begin, before he left the yard, to berate Claes for not having the forethought to reserve rooms in the same place. Claes, who usually answered back and got him into a good humour again, was less communicative than he should have been.

It was van Borselen's fault. Servants should never be invited to table, or they thought they could do anything.

* * *

Katelina retired to her room. It was a lady's privilege, to test young men, and tease them. If Claes didn't come, the matter was closed. He was a servant, and a coward.

If he came tomorrow to the family room, and made her transaction in public, it told her something else about him. He was a prude.

If he came another way, trusting her maid, trusting her powers of bribery, trusting her discretion, he was too sure of her, and too sure of himself, and ungallant. And false, after all he had said.

He came before dawn. She was asleep. It was her maid who wakened her. By the time he opened the door and closed it behind him with the utmost quietness, she was sitting up, the sheet high and firm round her body. A candle, shielded from the door, had been lit. She had also loosened her hair from its night-pleat. She saw it reflected in his eyes, as if she had only summoned him as a mirror. Her hair, and the sheet, and her naked shoulders.

He stood by the door and said softly, "There is some trouble?" His voice was reassuring, but there was concern in his face of a kind she couldn't mistake. Of course. That was why he had come.

Pride demanded that she should undeceive him and send him away. Beseeching flesh overwhelmed it. Her throat was dry. She said, "Yes, there is trouble."

He left the door at once and came to the bed and knelt, so that their eyes were level. She could see the glint of stubble above the swell and curl of his lips and over the frame of his jaw. His eyes, even unsmiling, still had a crescent pad of laughter tailored to each lower lid and beyond, ready for when he felt happy again.

Her hand lay on the coverlet. She saw him begin to move his own, in simple concern, to cover it, and knew that she couldn't prevent herself from shaking. He touched her, and she shuddered from head to foot.

Taught by one night, she could read his response in his softening face. She watched him try to master it. But when he began to draw away, she snatched at his hand. The sheet dropped to her hips. If he moved to the door he would have to pull her naked with him. And out into the street. Her inner body was springing apart, was beginning of its own accord to scale the peak she had wanted him to drive her towards. She cried, "Oh, *comfort* me!", but thought, even as he let himself respond, that it was too late.

He was experienced. She was brought from the bed to the floor, and in seconds he was with her, and this time with insistent violence. It hammered her, already come to her pinnacle, and kept her there, agonised, dying with pleasure. In the last moments, with a sort of crazy wildness that plunged beyond practised timing, he sealed it by joining her.

She lay, stunned into a sort of oblivion that might have been sleep. When she woke, she was again in bed, the sheet folded over her. Her limbs had melted. Where the ache of longing had been, there was a host of dim, unwonted pangs, quite unlike the small, sharp rending of her initiation. It came to her, an odd thought, that last time she had become merely a ravished virgin. This time, somehow, she had been made a woman.

By Claes, again. Had he gone? No, that would be too discourteous. Then, fully dressed still, waiting for her to awake?

She moved, and found his bare shoulder by hers, and his head deep in the pillow beside her. To comfort and receive her confidences, he had done what was considerate. And for other reasons, surely, too. Even Claes could never have reached that point so quickly, unless he had wanted her.

He moved, feeling her move, and lifting himself on one elbow, stretched not towards her but to the bedside. When, half-sitting, he turned, he held a pewter cup of water, already drawn from her drinking-stand. Instead of offering it to her, he rested the cup on the sheet, and said, "Lie still for a little. Sometimes, when it's like that, the first movements can make your head ache."

She lay, and felt her body settle, and the weight lift from her brow. He made no bones about his experience, even now. After a bit she moved too, and pulling herself up a little, took and emptied the cup. He leaned free of the sheet to place it on the floor, and she watched the muscles play on his body, from shoulder to rib, rib to hip and hip to thigh, and when he turned back, let him see her examining him.

She said, "I saw a young bull once, working a field. I couldn't believe what I saw. How many others have you mounted today?"

He paused, but didn't draw up the sheet, although his expression quietened. "None, demoiselle," he said.

Katelina stared at him. "I see. Hence, no doubt, the—brilliance —of your performance. If I hadn't been here, what would you have done? Gone to a brothel?"

He didn't avoid her gaze. "Single men do," he said. "It's something society allows us. I've just left Felix in one."

"You mean," she said, "I've saved you some money?"

He let another interval pass, one elbow pushed into his pillow, his eyes on his hands clasped before him. Then he said, "You said you were in trouble."

"Yes, I did," said Katelina. She was breathless with anger, and panic. She said, "You enjoy my body."

He smiled a little, at his hands. He said, "I failed to hide it, then."

She said, "If I were your wife, you could do that all night, and all day. Would you marry me for it? Or can you do better with other women?"

He looked up. Then, unclasping his hands, he reached for one of hers and held it to him, folded lightly. He said, "You are without peer. But, demoiselle, there are things to discuss. You didn't tell your parents of Jordan de Ribérac?"

"No," she said. "I told them my escort was the Gruuthuse boy."

"Then they'll expect you to marry him," said Claes.

She gazed at him.

He said, "Didn't that strike you? And if he wants to marry you badly enough, he might happily claim to be your lover. You see, you needn't be tied to me."

He made a pause, not quite smiling. When she said nothing, he resumed painstakingly.

"If you don't want him, of course, then you must tell your parents what really happened. They'll help you if you choose a different husband, or if you decide not to marry till afterwards. Wellborn girls are often sent abroad for their accouchement, and the child put out to foster."

It had suddenly got quite out of hand. She picked on one thing. *"Tell my parents!* They would flay you alive!"

He shrugged a little. "If I were to stay in Flanders, of course. But there are other countries. And unless you want to marry the Gruuthuse boy, they must know the child's parentage to safeguard you. Jordan de Ribérac was alone in your house before I was. The slightest hint of all this, and he might try to claim fatherhood and force marriage on you."

"He couldn't!" said Katelina sharply.

"He probably could, unless I can show him he'd lose by it. Do you know Andro Wodman?"

A banquet for last year's commander of the Flanders galleys at which she had met Jordan de Ribérac. And her father, quoting a

Scot called Andro Wodman in de Ribérac's retinue. She remembered, but said nothing. Claes said, "No? Well, he's an archer of
the French king's bodyguard. I've seen him both with the vicomte
de Ribérac and in the . . . associated with the Dauphin. He tried
to hide from me. Also," said Claes, retrieving his hands and link-
ing them together again, "M. de Ribérac knows more than he
should do about Gaston du Lyon, the Dauphin's secret envoy."

Claes, in the vicinity of the Dauphin? She said, "What are you
saying? That the great Jordan de Ribérac has been bought by the
Dauphin, and the King of France doesn't know?"

"I think so. The vicomte knows far, far more than he should."

How did Claes know? Rumour, picked up in offices, taverns,
brothels? Hints and fantasies, built into some vindictive falsehood?
He had said nothing of this before. He might not have known. And
before, of course, she had had a reputation to protect. The scar of
de Ribérac's blow stood, a glimmering stripe on his cheek. Katelina looked at it, and then at his eyes, which had no venom in
them. She believed him. She said, "You have evidence, then."

"Only a few facts," he said. "I haven't looked for anything more.
But I'll find all the proof that you need if M. le vicomte frightens
you, or tries to make you do anything you don't want. You've only
to tell me. You've only to tell me if there is anything else I can do."
He paused. He said briefly, "I thought you would loathe me."

She didn't loathe him. You don't hate a servant. She had only
been angry with him because she was ashamed and angry with
herself. She said, "After all you've said, it's your turn, surely, to
abhor me. I invited you to do what you did. I told you there was no
danger. A child born of that bedding could ruin your life more
than mine. Unless, of course, you were to marry me."

It was said for the second time, and for the second time she
awaited his answer. She didn't know what gave her away. Her
insistence. The shrewish form of her anger, instead of an outburst
of accusation and anguish. He dropped his hands and looked at
her. His eyes saw to the back of her skull. She looked away.

"You aren't pregnant, and there is no trouble," he said flatly.

She was Katelina van Borselen, who had not hung her head,
ashamed, since she was a child. She looked down, and was silent,
through the swift movement by which he left her. He said, "Why?"

From his voice, he was standing still on the floor by the bed. He
had not fumbled to dress, or to cover himself. When she looked at
him he was standing straight-backed and selflessly natural, like the

men she claimed to be familiar with: a whole man, waiting for an explanation which was due to him. He knew the reason, but this time, he meant her to tell him. She said, "You would not have come otherwise."

He said, "And has it become any easier, now that I've come?"

She shook her head.

He said, "And what, then, is to happen? I am your servant, of course, in every way. But not in this."

She sought for some defence. She said, "It was marriage I was speaking of."

"Seriously?" he said. "No, demoiselle. Only to discover how you ranked in a new field of conquest. You have no peer. I've told you that. I have no wish to marry. I've told you that, too. And marriage with me is the last thing you want." He brought the volley of words to a halt. His expression, which had been less than patient, switched to one of exasperated amusement. He let out a sigh like a puncture. "Katelina, what you want is what you have just had, and any husband will give it to you."

She lay becomingly disposed along the length of the bed, and the ache overwhelmed her. "You don't want it from me ever again, even though I've no peer?"

"Of course I want it. Of course I want you," he said. "But not again. Never again. We're using each other like whores. Can you see that?"

"Yes, I can see it," she said. "And I agree. And anyway, we will never be private together again. But we are here now, for the last time, and we can bring relief to each other. Please come. Please come here. Please come back."

He couldn't deny her, she thought, any more than he could deny his present want of her.

Instead, bending abruptly, he extinguished the light which betrayed it. Then, as if hunger didn't exist, he dressed in the dark and went to the door. From there, he said only, "Goodbye. Goodbye, demoiselle."

Chapter 25

The following day, for the first time in his life, Claes lost his temper in public. Riding from Ghent to Bruges, it was necessary to prime Felix with the report he, Felix, had to make to his mother. Claes reminded him why he had dismissed his Louvain manager and all the changes the new man was going to make, aided by Felix. Felix, languid after the night's excesses, was irritated; a thing Claes normally found easy to deal with.

This time he failed to beguile, perhaps because he himself was not entirely in the mood for inventive raillery. Felix rounded on him, pointing out that he knew perfectly well what his mother wanted to know; that he was tired of the subject, and that it had nothing to do with Claes anyway. From long experience, Claes dropped the whole thing and proceeded to work both Felix and himself into a better mood. They were nearly at Bruges when Felix, now entirely cheerful, mentioned Mabelie.

Everyone, everywhere, teased Claes about his conquests. He accepted it philosophically. What his real feelings were in regard to one girl or another, there was no requirement for him to tell anybody. During the three months of his absence, anyway, his private affairs, if any, had been his own; and since he came back, he had been too busy to pursue personal matters. Apart from those he could not avoid. But on his first day back in Bruges, of course, Felix had told him that John Bonkle had won the affections of Mabelie. Which, since John was a nice lad, Claes had resigned himself to, and had taken trouble, indeed, to make things easy between himself and John, and to make it clear to the girl, who was a sweet thing, that he had no possible claims on her.

He didn't expect, at any time, to discuss Mabelie with Felix, far less on the road home from Ghent. Indeed, it began with what appeared to be a much more dangerous subject. Felix said, as they rode, "I don't see why I shouldn't bring my armour out now. You know all about it anyway. You can say the Dauphin's men lent it to me. You can clean it for me, and I'll put it into the show for the White Bear joust."

"You've put your name down then?" Claes said.

"They accepted it. Before we left. It's only two weeks away. I mean to practise every day. It's the greatest joust in Flanders. In France. In Europe, really now. And they'll all be there. The lord of Ghistelle. The seigneur de Gruuthuse. The Count of Charolais, maybe. As many of the Knights of the Golden Fleece as can get away. You know. The man who wins the lance is made Forestier for the year, and goes from house to house with his party . . ."

"It costs a lot of money," said Claes. He blinked. "Did you get money too?" He kept it low, so that the grooms riding behind shouldn't hear.

Felix grinned. "You didn't guess? Well, it went into things you wouldn't know about. Like Mabelie."

"Mabelie?"

Felix's grin, under the borrowed straw hat, became wider. "I bought Mabelie from John Bonkle."

"You *what*!" said Claes. He stopped his horse dead. The grooms swerved behind him. Felix rode on grinning for a pace or two, and then finding himself alone, turned broadside and came back, grinning even more widely. The grooms faltered, looking at Claes who glanced round, saw some trees and said shortly, "We'll eat there. Go there and wait."

The grooms rode on, not looking at each other until they were out of reach. Felix stayed where he was, his eyes sparkling. "Aha!" he said. "Don't you wish you had thought of it?"

Claes put his fists on the saddle and leaned on them. He said, "Money changed hands for Mabelie's favours? John Bonkle sold her to you?"

"He didn't want to," said Felix. "But he'd bought a fur hat without telling his father, and couldn't pay for it."

"Poor John Bonkle," said Claes. "How did he break it to Mabelie?"

Felix's face was losing its grin. He said, "How should I know? Told her it was the last time, and she was to report to me in future, I suppose. She's to be ready when I come back from Louvain. Tonight." His face began to brighten again as he thought of it. He grinned again, appealingly. "Cheaper than last night, yes?"

Claes didn't move. "What about Grielkine?" he said.

The smile vanished again. "Well, what about her?" said Felix. "Where's the law that says you can't have a different girl every night if you want one? Wherever it is, *you've* never paid any attention to it."

"Tell me," said Claes. "What will you do if Mabelie doesn't come?"

Felix stared at him angrily. "Of course she'll come."

"From John Bonkle to you. Just like that. Knowing that money has been paid for her. If she does come, what does that make her?"

"I'm going," said Felix, and dug in his spurs.

Claes shot out his arm and seized his bridle. Then he transferred all the reins to one hand. Felix's horse jerked and stamped. Felix lifted his whip and Claes chopped his free hand on his whip-wrist. Felix gave a cry and dropped the whip, his fingers hanging limp. "You *bastard*!" he cried. "You've ruined my hand. I won't be able to . . ."

"It will be as good as it was in ten minutes. When we've finished this conversation," Claes said. "If Mabelie doesn't come to you tonight, what do you do?"

Felix was blanched with fury. His breath seething between his shut lips, he glared at Claes. Then he said, "I have bought her. If she doesn't come, I go and fetch her."

"From Adorne's house," said Claes.

Felix gave a nasty grin. "Not necessarily. She has to go out sometimes."

"Then you abduct her bodily, take her somewhere quiet, and force her. And repeat the performance every time you want her? Or do you think she'll give in after the first time?"

"Very likely," said Felix. The nasty grin, which was not natural, was being kept in place by his fury.

"Until someone else wants to buy her, and you sell her to him?"

"You make it sound . . . what's it got to do with you anyway?" said Felix, shouting.

"I make it sound like slave-buying, because that's what it is," said Claes. "You're treating Mabelie as if she were Loppe. Worse. I don't think anyone violated Loppe against his will. You are head of one of the best merchanting companies in Bruges, or you soon will be. And you are buying and selling a young girl like merchandise. Even the noble Simon didn't do that. He took her virginity, maybe, but she went with him for love. Do you think she came to me for money? Or John Bonkle? Of course she ought to be married. Of course she shouldn't move from one lover to the next, any more than—yes—I've had different girls on different nights. But at least there's no deception about it. We're not promising marriage or lifelong devotion to anyone. We're doing it, girls and men, for love only. But this! After what you have done, whether Mabelie comes to you tonight or not, she ranks as a bought whore."

There was a silence. Claes sat, breathing quickly, listening to the echoes of his own voice and thinking what a fool he had been. He had given Felix no exit, no compromise, no way to save his face. He knew very well, even if Felix didn't, what had launched him into it.

Felix said, "Very well. Buy her from me. And not with a note on the Medici bank either. In cash. By tonight."

There was another silence. Then, "As you say," said Claes quietly. "In which case you'll forgive me if I hurry. There's a lot to be done."

He dropped Felix's reins and took his own and moved his horse away. He set it at the road and urged it into a trot and then a canter. He saw, as he went by the trees, the grooms standing staring, and then turning to gaze back at Felix. But Felix, as he expected, did not follow.

It was still daylight when Claes rode through the Ghent portals of Bruges, several hours ahead of the rest of his party. He had planned, and still planned, that Felix should present the first report on Louvain to his mother. He was glad, therefore, to find the demoiselle de Charetty and her young daughters absent, even though Henninc began barking at him as soon as he began to lead his steaming horse towards the stables.

The litany lasted all the way over the yard. The pump had broken down again. There was a leak in one of the vats. There had been a fight between three of the men in the shed and the rest had turned sullen. The man who had sold some of that property to the Widow the other day wanted it back and said he could prove the sale was illegal. A whole sack of woad balls had mould in it. The Widow had appointed a new lawyer. The Florentines and the Lucchese and even the Papal Legate's secretary had been to see the Widow and arrange for the head Charetty courier—that was him —to leave soon for Italy, because their dispatch boxes were filling. There was a packet waiting for him from Milan, with that bald-headed doctor's seal on it. At whatever hour Claes arrived, Anselm Adorne wanted to see him immediately.

"What a welcome!" said Claes. He could see that Henninc

thought he was complaining, but he wasn't. He was filled with uncomplicated delight at the prospect of regulating everything. He hastened to hand over his horse and tore through the building, calling greetings and insults right and left, and scooping up as he went the packet from Tobie.

He read it as he stripped to his doublet, and stopped in the middle to read it again. His expression, as he stood holding it for a moment, would have made Henninc furious. Then he tied a piece of cloth round his waist and bounded downstairs and out to mend the pump again. While he was doing that, four separate men came and told him their grievances until called back to their work by a trig young man with a nose like a scythe and a calf-length black gown, who thought he must be Claes.

Claes admitted it, straightening and wiping his hands on his apron. He had tried to get the Widow to appoint someone to help Julius, and replace him when he was abroad with the army. There had been three candidates, all of good reputation. The Widow had therefore chosen one. He hoped it was the right one.

The sharp-featured man, who looked to be in his late twenties, said, "I am Messer Gregorio. I have sent for someone to deal with the pump. I should prefer you to come straight to my office to make your report about Louvain. The demoiselle de Charetty will be back directly. She wished to hear it as soon as possible."

It *was* the right one. Son of a Lombard, friend of the demoiselle's late father. Law at Padua. A few years as junior clerk with the Senate at Venice. Home to Asti, and then back to Flanders, where his father had been a pawnbroker in Furnes. Used, you would say, to dealing only with his superiors.

Claes said. "Immediately, Messer Gregorio. Jonkheere Felix asked to be present, too, when the accounting is made to the demoiselle. He'll be here in an hour."

The lawyer, who didn't know Felix, paused. He said, "In that case, you may as well finish the pump. Be in the bureau when jonkheere Felix arrives."

Claes nodded his head. He waited until the lawyer was out of sight and then finished testing the pump, which was now working. He called someone to clear away for him, and vanished into the house, by another route, to get himself, clean, into his blue livery once again. Then he thrust Tobie's packet in his purse, borrowed a mule from the stables, and trotted off to the Hôtel Jerusalem. He made two calls on the way.

* * *

The moment she returned, Marian de Charetty was met by her new legal clerk Meester Gregorio with the news that her employee Claes had made a brief appearance, but had failed to report to his office as requested. And that the young master, her son Felix, was said to be on his way but had not yet arrived.

Claes had returned without Felix. Something had happened. Felix had tried to dismiss Claes? Claes had accepted employment with someone else, and had only returned to collect his effects? No. At least he would wait and confront her.

She had given her newest legal adviser the room with a table that Julius used. She thanked him and asked him to wait for her to call him. Then she went to her own office and learned, from Henninc, that the pump was mended but the disquiet in the yard was still going on. He made no reference to Gregorio, which meant he was still angry about that. The fact that the pump had been mended by Claes, and that everyone he had spoken to was, apparently, cheerful, meant, surely, that he wasn't leaving. Which should please young Catherine, even if it didn't please young Tilde. Marian de Charetty thumped down her ledgers and applied her mind to her business.

Then Felix arrived. He appeared to be in rags because, he said, he had been swept off hunting by the Dauphin's men. He began to tell her all about that. She suspected, since he didn't mention Claes, that he had already discovered from Henninc that Claes was back and had not spoken to her. Before she could ask, the new lawyer Gregorio tapped on the door. She had asked him to be present, she remembered. He ought to know what the Louvain branch was doing.

Meester Gregorio had hardly sat down before the door burst open on Felix's young friend, John Bonkle. The demoiselle de Charetty stared at him. John Bonkle stopped on the threshold and blushed. He said, "Demoiselle. I'm sorry. They said Felix was here."

"As he is," said Felix's mother. "But rather busy, I'm afraid. Is it urgent?"

"No. Yes," said John Bonkle, who was not notable for keeping his head. "Felix, he's asking for eight shillings parisis before this evening. I can't pay that, you bastard."

Felix's large, shallow eyes, turning to his mother, showed white.

John Bonkle went pale. "That is—I beg your pardon. Just a manner of speaking, demoiselle. But I can't pay it, Felix."

"Pay what? Why?" said Felix.

"Pay you. For him. For her," said Bonkle. "You know."

"Pay me for what?" said Felix. He then went slowly scarlet.

John Bonkle said, "I'm sorry, demoiselle . . . But Claes says I've to pay him eight shillings parisis before this evening or else."

"Or else what?" said Marian de Charetty gently.

There was a silence.

Marian de Charetty rose. She took a key from the bunch at her girdle and, bending, unlocked one of the chests by the wall. From it, she took a bag and set of scales, both of which she brought to the desk. She tipped the bag, and a pile of silver groats poured onto the green baize. She weighed them, discarded some, and found a fresh bag into which she put the coins she had weighed. The scales she placed temporarily on top of a pile of letters obligatory beside which stood a copy of the dyehouse rate card, the prices copied in carefully beside the row of coloured wool samples. It was all very business-like.

"The scales were tested recently," she said to John Bonkle. "I think you may trust them." She spoke quite mildly, weighing the bag in her hand. "Do I give this to you, or to Felix, or to Claes?"

"To me," said Felix quickly.

She looked at her first-born, now grown. She said, "Willingly. But you must, of course, tell me what it is for."

Silence. Then Felix said, with reluctance. "That is, it really belongs to John. I owe it to him. It's John's."

She looked at John. "Is it?"

Clearly speechless, he nodded.

"Then," said Felix's mother, "I am happy to give it you on Felix's behalf. He can repay me gradually, and I shall ask very little interest. You are satisfied, John?"

John nodded.

"Then goodbye," said Marian de Charetty. "Now, Felix. Tell me what is happening to the Louvain business. In detail. With all the figures you have brought back with you. Begin from the beginning, and tell us everything." She thought, knowing Claes, that Claes would at least have tried to prime him. But Claes clearly hadn't.

By the time Claes trotted into the yard the meeting was over, the office empty, Felix in his favourite tavern, Meester Gregorio returned to his austere pursuits in his office, and the demoiselle de

Charetty was installed before her parlour fire, where Katelina van Borselen had once found her, poring over papers now, as she had been then. The first she knew of his return was her maid, asking if she would receive him. Which was clever, as it avoided antagonising her other, superior staff. She supposed she should not, strictly speaking, receive male employees alone in her parlour. Meester Gregorio, for example, didn't know that Claes had been in her household since childhood. Or that, last year, she had sat by his sickbed. Or stood by while a powerful man scarred him for life.

He was shown in. The large, unencumbered smile. The hair turned to seaweed because he was sweating-damp from the intensity of his day. She wrinkled her nose. The smile widened a little. "I ought to beg your pardon. But it's the smell of money," he said.

She sat up in her tall-backed chair and looked at him. She said, "I would rather have the eight shillings parisis."

He had quick wits. "Ah," he said. "John Bonkle? Who paid him? Not you?"

"It appeared," she said, "to be a debt on the Charetty household. Incurred by whom and for what was not quite clear. Except that you were trying to collect it. I have told Felix he can repay me when he can."

He threw back his head and laughed and laughed. He said, "Felix will never forgive me. We quarrelled on the way. I'll put it right."

"I suppose you will," she said. "I should tell you that I have no idea whatever of what happened at Louvain, except that Olivier has gone, and Felix has installed someone else. Was he ever there?"

"Yes," said Claes. "But it isn't easy for him to pick up the threads. It'll come. Would the demoiselle like me to tell her how I saw it?"

"I should like someone to tell me something," said Marian de Charetty. "I think you should sit over there, not too near. And then tell me also what you mean about the smell of money."

And so he came to tell her not only about Louvain, but about Tobie Beventini and his uncle and Quilico, and the Pope's godson and Prosper Camulio de' Medici, and the relatives in Milan and in Constantinople of Nicholai Giorgio de' Acciajuoli, the Greek with the wooden leg. From whose affairs the first germ of a vast idea had sprung.

At the end, she sat absolutely still. She said, "And Tobias has located this mine?"

"Yes," said Claes. He was flushed and a little breathless, and his eyes shone. He said, "I didn't think he'd do it. Or want to share with us. He got help from Messer Prosper. He's an ambassador in Milanese service, but privately a friend of the Adorno."

"And a friend of Anselm Adorne's?" she said. "Hence your success at the lottery. I thought you said this was a wholly Venetian monopoly?"

"So far," he said. A little of the elation had gone. She was not exhibiting rapture. He said, as if presenting a normal report, "None of the Genoese know where the mine is, except that it's in the Papal States. All the evidence about location and volume and quality is being prepared and tested and notarised this spring for the Venetians alone. Then they'll pay us."

"How?" she said.

"In several ways. It has to be worked out. That's why I have to go to Milan. Or one of the reasons."

"I see," she said. She shifted her position in her chair, and swung her sleeves into two new, uncreased folds at her sides, and placed her hands one over the other on her lap. She said, "What you are talking about is appropriating a share of the profit from the world's only supply of good alum?"

He said formally, "For two years at the most. Perhaps less. But the profit is there to be made. And it would let you develop this business into something worth having."

"Yes. The business," she said. "Perhaps we should descend to the mundane. Perhaps we should see how all this is going to leave the business. For example, you've heard about the mishaps in the yard?"

The white flame of excitement had vanished, but his manner was still wholly natural. "Yes. They couldn't find the man who usually keeps the pump in repair. The leaking vat ought to have been replaced. Small troubles. Your Meester Gregorio should be able to deal with them."

"And you heard," she said, "about the quarrels in the shed, and Henninc's bad temper. That was because of Meester Gregorio. He was one of your suggestions. I am sure he's the best man for the job. He is not yet any use whatsoever with people. You heard about the property claim?"

"I've settled that," said Claes. "I called there on my way to Meester Adorne. They were wrong in their assumption. Meester Gregorio would have recognised that as well. He'll settle down."

"That's what I told myself," said Marian de Charetty. "Indeed, when I saw trouble was likely, I had a talk with him, and with Henninc. I apparently used the wrong words. And what about Louvain?"

He said, "Olivier was cheating, as I told you. Indeed, he was, I think, paid to cheat. That's why I took Cristoffels. Of course, he hasn't been given the appointment. You must see him and make up your mind. But he's good, and he's honest, and I've warned him against possible predators."

She said, "You're talking, I take it, of Jordan de Ribérac? Last time we spoke, you were most reassuring about him."

His lips thickened, and thinned. "I don't know who I'm talking about. But successful businesses do have rivals. It's as well to be careful."

Marian de Charetty sat back and looked at him. She said, "And when do you go back to Italy? Next week?"

This time, he did nothing expressive with his face at all. He said, "Not until after the White Bear joust."

"In two weeks, then," she said. "At that point I am left with a business in Louvain which is under some sort of threat and which is at the moment headed by a stranger whom I have not even met. I have a business in Bruges still suffering from past mismanagement and the lack of its usual notary, and now under another stranger who, brilliant though he may be, is causing my servants to attack one another. I have taken on property whose acquisition is causing legal problems, and have ventured into the courier business where secrets not only mean money, they mean physical danger. I am involved in large loans. My husband's bodyguard, from a modest group hired to protect other merchants and earn their keep serving neighbouring princes, has now acquired men, arms and weapons and has become a unit in an international war, making me responsible for killings and open to claims against losses, including those caused by vendettas between rival commanders."

She looked at Claes, and tried to keep the weariness out of her voice. "You suggested all these things. I agreed to them. I arranged them all with you. I am flattered and grateful. You thought, rightly, that I should like to be rich, that I should like to see the business expand and prosper; that I should like to hand something great to Cornelis' son and mine. You thought that I could direct it, and that Felix in time would run it for me."

She paused, and tried, again, to keep her voice calm. "But, my dear, I cannot direct it. However willing they are, Cristoffels and Gregorio and Henninc, and even Astorre and Thomas and Julius there in Italy, are not clever enough to help me do it properly. And Felix I know, and you must now know, cannot do it, does not want to do it and never, I think, will do more than use this business for money, when he wishes eight shillings for—whatever he wanted eight shillings for."

She looked him straight in the eyes. "I cannot run this company as it is. Your wonderful *coup,* your master-stroke which would make me a fortune, is quite beyond me. There is no possible way I can agree to it."

Claes said, "I thought Felix would develop more quickly." And as she stirred, exasperated, he added briefly, "All right. Yes, I know. He won't come to it soon enough. But the stuff is in him. I've seen it. Don't expect too little of him. That's been part of the trouble."

He had paused. She said, "That is what I want of you. Honest comment. About myself, too."

Another pause. He was looking, frowning, into the fire. He said, "Yes. You're good with a team that's already running, but have no experience of breaking in a new one. Not your fault. Anyway, the business is too scattered. I was going to suggest that, as soon as Cristoffels had put things to rights at Louvain, you should sell the dyeing and purely pawnbroking part of the Louvain business, and bring the money-changing and lending side here to Bruges where you can manage it centrally. In six months your staff will be used to one another, and you to them."

She said, "But we have just agreed, I can't hold things together alone for six months. And even after that, perfect teams break up and require new appointments. I can't face that, either. And even if the most perfect team in the world were present immediately, it couldn't handle a scheme like the one you're launching over alum."

He was still considering. "No. I'd do that," he said. "Travelling would be no disadvantage. But it would need a well-run company here in Bruges behind it: you're right."

She wondered if she was meant to make the suggestion. She said, "When you were being irresponsible, the City Fathers wanted rid of you. Having seen your work of the past seven weeks they would have no objection now, I think, if you wanted to stay."

"No," said Claes. "I seem to have managed to keep out of the Steen. But that's not really the obstacle."

She interrupted. "Your contracts? We could find another master courier, surely?"

He smiled, still without looking at her. "Not one who can deal with ciphers. I know too much already. The Medici won't accept a change. Or the Dauphin. In any case, what I learn is an advantage to the company, not an obstacle. It's even possible that I could arrange a long enough time between journeys to keep things straight here in Bruges until your perfect team can manage most things." He made a movement of economical demonstration. "The *real* obstacle is that not even the lowest workers you employ would take orders from me, never mind Henninc and Meester Gregorio. Or even worse, Felix and Astorre and Tobie and Julius. You need someone like Gregorio, or the way Gregorio will be. Someone clever, with authority. I can't aspire to manage a company. I can't force myself on burghers and noblemen. I'm nineteen; I'm a base-born, chance-lettered workman. And people would talk."

He looked up then, and smiled. She said next what she thought she would never say to him. It came quite simply, because it was quiet, and there was no strain in sitting speaking like this, before the fire. She said, "You can become a burgess by marriage."

She knew him as well as anyone did. She knew that a natural comedian is a natural actor. She would never know, because he wouldn't allow her to see, whether he had thought of that possibility, or had expected her to suggest it, or feared that she would suggest it. She didn't flatter herself that he had ever wanted her to suggest it. So his eyes on her face told her only one thing: that he was searching to understand, in his turn, what she really wanted. She said, "Don't be afraid. Real marriage would be something like incest, wouldn't it? I'm speaking only of formalities."

He drew a quick breath then, as if she had accused him of being incivil, and said, "I'm sorry. A matter like that . . . one doesn't take lightly."

She wondered what his eyes saw in hers. She kept her face, as far as she could, impersonal and friendly. She said, "I've only invited you to think about something. Perhaps you should come slightly nearer. It isn't a subject for eavesdroppers."

He smiled, understanding, she knew. She wanted to see him more clearly. She wanted to show her confidence in his interpretation of her. He knew she meant him to bring his stool and seat himself just so near, and no nearer. He did so, and settled himself, crossing his arms on his knees. In the firelight, the scar on his face wavered like the lash of a whip. He said, "I can give you an impersonal view of it, so far as I'm able. It would appal everyone who works for you. The best of your free employees would be inclined to leave. The worst would stay on, hoping to take advantage of the situation. Those who are in no position to leave would work with the utmost unwillingness for you as well as for me. Your daughters would be upset and frightened, at the least. And Felix would walk out of the house and either look for the sympathy of his friends or take himself abroad."

"You draw a harsh picture," she said. "Go on. What else would happen?"

He said, "You know, of course. The business people of the city would accept me, because they would have to, but their families would be a different matter. You would find your friends rather less hospitable than once they had been, and amazingly unable to visit you here. It would be obvious that your business would profit from the information I collect on my travels: I should be less in demand as a courier by the general merchants at least. As the business improved, rivalry would become much more cutting than normal. Competitors and suppliers who so far have treated you leniently would vie with one another to try and best us both. And as you would lose your friends, so I should lose mine."

"Yes, of course," she said; and rose, rather stiffly, from where she had been sitting for so long. "You have answered me completely. No one would gain. I shall sell, then." He stood up so quickly that she suddenly realised what he must think. She said, "I mean, of course, once everything has been provided for and your future, too, has been secured."

"Great God," he said. "Did you think I suspected you of forcing me into something? You have provided for me since I was a child. I can make my own way now, if I have to. But what would please me most would be to serve you and the company at the same time."

She looked at him. She said, "I'm sorry. But I can't go on. I would rather sell while I still have some pride in it, and in myself."

He said, "Will you sit again?" Then, when she stood, a little uncertain, he moved forward and led her back to her chair, and placed her in it, and this time sank to the floor not far away, his head on the same level as her knee, like Felix when he was younger, playing games on the tiles. He said, "If you sell, what will you do with the money? Buy a grander house? Entertain dyers' wives? Collect books? Give Felix all the horses and armour he asks for? Take up embroidery? All those people out there would be workless, unless their new master employed them. You would have no work, no interest, no place in the community but that of a wealthy widow. Is that what you want? You would die of it in a year."

"What, then?" she said.

Claes said, "In six months I'll have made you a team you can trust. I can always help you replace them. I shall spend all the time I can here. Name me your clerk, your assistant factor, your foot-servant, anything. You can do it."

"Yes, of course I can," she said. "I can tell Cristoffels what to do. Sell Louvain. Bring the broking business—did you say?—back to Bruges and expand it. Train Gregorio. Open the cellars in the new property. Watch out for Felix—if he survives the joust—and see that he doesn't ruin the tavern. And play a part in the world trade in alum. All by myself. Of course I can do it." She could hear her own voice grow hoarse with the pain in her throat. She stopped speaking.

Claes turned his back on her. She didn't need to use her kerchief. Her cheeks were not wet, although her eyes dazzled a little, because of the light. Claes' hair, rimmed by the fire, was dry now. When it was brushed, it would lie straight and flat, with strange bumps and kinks at the edges, as if it had been singed. When he was young, in the apprentice-loft, he had had to make himself neat for Mass like all the boys, and she had always liked to see him, marked out from the rest by his size, and the clown's face with its dimples and the observant, good-humoured glance. She had brushed his hair for him when he lay, fevered after the wound. Tobias had treated him. It was one of the reasons she had asked the surgeon to work for her.

Claes had always been free with girls. She knew that. Of the many unspoken factors in his great disclaimer, she assumed that had been one. She couldn't pretend that it had not been an issue. As her youthful husband, he couldn't have shamed her by intriguing in Bruges. Circumspectly elsewhere, she supposed. She couldn't impose celibacy on him. She might live another twenty years yet. She would be forty this year.

She hadn't said so, but all the repercussions he had described had, of course, occurred to her. To be despised by dyers' wives didn't worry her. She had no close friends. Of course, Tilde would have been distressed and Felix would have been a handful. Of course they might lose people like Julius and the new managers, who would feel their status impaired. But Claes himself, with his gifts, could reduce the impact, could talk people round, could deal with Tilde and probably even with Felix. And if people left, he would be here to find others. He had said that the merchant world would set itself to compete against him. She had no doubt, if that happened, who would win. She wondered, as she had wondered over and over, how clever men had not seen what she had seen.

And remembered that some of them had. And that it was Claes himself who had, in the end, given them the opening. Which meant that he, too, was tiring of simple tasks and simple company and perhaps even of simple friends. If he had taken thought, he might have discovered that he would not really miss them. But then, of course, he had taken thought. Behind the impersonal objections were all the personal ones.

He was giving her time to recover, and she had recovered. She said, "I should have told you that I'm proud of you. You realise that the only failure in this has been mine. You brought me a service I didn't deserve, and don't have the ability to take advantage of. But you thought I did, and I'm flattered."

He had been sitting watching the fire, his hands tight around his updrawn knees. The rip in his jacket, neatly mended, had begun to open again across his flat back. When he heard her voice, he eased round a little without changing his attitude. She thought that his face, queerly, looked older. He spoke as if he hadn't heard her. He said, "You've had suitors."

It was baldly put, she knew; for the answer to it had to be an admission. She wouldn't think of his reasons. She said, "I want none of them."

He said, rather slowly, "Of the two, marriage would be less troublesome in the end than selling the company."

She found she was experiencing a shaky amusement. He saw it and said, with a glimmering smile. "For you, I mean. To begin with, it would be like asking the burgomaster and échevins to lie down with Felix's porcupine. It would need care and forethought and attention and teamwork for a long time, through a lot of rebuffs and some unpleasantness. And I'd have to leave almost immediately, leaving you to deal with whatever developed. But if

Gregorio is what I think he is, I could confide in him a bit of the alum scheme. That would commit him. And he would help you."

Her expression must have been very disturbed, because he stopped there and said, "That is, if I may reopen the subject? I wasn't sure if you had finally closed it. For instance, you didn't give me a chance to produce my impersonal list of the advantages of managerial partnerships. I've always admired and respected and honoured you. That's the main one on my side. Indeed, I don't know if I need any others. What's more, I have an excuse to see Bishop Coppini who, I am sure, could manage the essential dispensation, since there's a relationship. That is, I am the illegitimate grandson of the first wife of your late sister's husband. If I have it right?"

He was prepared to reverse his decision. Placing the relationship before her was his way, however, of reminding her that this, too, was a factor to be considered, on top of the difference in age, and in status. Yet such uneven marriages did take place in great houses, where property must pass and heirs be got, regardless.

With a marriage contract, she would be buying not that, but his skills for her company. She had her heir, Felix, and her daughters. He had, perhaps, as many bastards, carelessly sown. That again, she did not expect ever to know. She realised that she was thinking of the situation as if it were real, as if he had firmly accepted what she had proposed to him, whereas he had not.

She rose from her chair. The moment she moved, he rolled and stood also, not so near, and not smiling. She said, "Can we have it plainly? This company needs a man at its head, and I have asked you to take that place by marrying me. This you think you can do?" She wondered if she looked as exhausted as she felt. He didn't look tired; only quieter than usual. He didn't come any nearer. He smelt of horse, and leather and sweat, but she didn't wrinkle her nose.

He said, "I did think it through. It is the best solution. Best for me, too. Or I think so just now. There are things which may be escaping us both because it's late, and we've been talking so long. Do you think we should say no more tonight? And then tomorrow, as early as you wish, perhaps you would send for me?" His eyes, again, were scanning her face. He added, "This is not ingratitude. I realise what you are offering. I want you to think about it again."

She said, "I understand. I agree. Take as much time as you want. Leave it, if you like, until you are ready to go."

He answered at once. "No. Tomorrow, early."

She said, "I'll send for you tomorrow."

His face, which had been tense, relaxed suddenly. He smiled straight at her, reassuringly. He hesitated just a little, and then said, "Then I wish you a good night, my mistress. Not a sad or a difficult one. Whatever comes of it, nothing shall harm you if I can prevent it."

My mistress, he had elected to call her, avoiding both the informal and formal. He always knew the right thing to do. Or nearly always.

"Good night," she said. And he smiled and, turning, left the room. She wondered, looking at the shut door, what else he could have said, what other gesture he could possibly have made; and realised that there was none.

A night on both sides, to consider it. And tomorrow, an insistently early decision, to save them both prolonged embarrassment. Or—who could blame him?—for entirely practical reasons. If he were now to proceed with this frightening bargain with Venice, he had sensitive information to gather and many calculations to make before he left for Italy. Together with everything else that needed handling. Including Felix.

Marian de Charetty sank back in her chair. She rested her swathed and wired head on its cushion and her sleeves on its arms and found, forlornly, that her heart was beating like a bass drum. She had forced it on him. But he would never regret it. Never. Never.

Chapter 26

The first of the shock waves was sustained by Meester Gregorio of Asti, who had known his new employer the widow de Charetty for only a week. He didn't know the workman Nicholas at all, except for a passing encounter at the yard pump which had shown the youth to be unreliable. He had also understood that the young man was called Claes.

Summoned very early the following morning, almost as soon as he had tied the strings of his black cap and slipped on his robe, Meester Gregorio opened the office door to find his employer seated, a little flushed, behind her desk. The scales were still on the table, and the ledgers, and the inkstand and pens. Also the rate card, displaying its columns of bright tufted wool. At the end of the desk sat the youth of the pump, wearing the ordinary blue Charetty livery. His head was bent, and, surprisingly, he was running a pen down columns of figures, or names, on the topmost of a large sheaf of papers resting on one of his knees.

He looked up and smiled, conveying the smile also to the demoiselle de Charetty, who was wearing, for a small, round, not unattractive woman, an expression quite formidable. The demoiselle de Charetty, clearing her throat, said, "Meester Gregorio. Thank you for coming. This is not in fact a matter of business, although I should like to say, for the company, that I'm glad you have joined us, and hope you will enjoy working with us. Nicholas and I need your help in a personal matter."

Us. We. During his interview, she had spoken of the business as wholly her own. Her son was not present. The boy was. Formerly Claes, and now Nicholas. His help in a personal matter? Meester Gregorio of Asti, who had notarised in his time a great many contracts, a great many bequests, a great many affirmations of one sort or another, waited calmly; his gaze moving from the youth to a spot just below his employer's girdle. Age made it unlikely, but one never knew. Unless the boy was a bastard son, newly recognised?

"I shall be glad to do all I can," he said formally. He noticed that the youth smiled at the woman again, and her nervousness unexpectedly changed into something like unwilling humour.

She said, "It is not, I must tell you, a question of pregnancy or of adoption. Claes, who will now use his full name of Nicholas, is the illegitimate son of a distant relative. This is perfectly authenticated. He has been trained on these premises since he was young in, of course, a menial capacity. He knows the business through and through. He is also, and you must accept this, a young man of quite unusual ability."

Meester Gregorio smiled agreeably. He was certainly a young man of unusual appearance. One saw eyes like that, and inflated, aimless lips like that, among the mentally afflicted. Even the broad, low, seamless brow. He had scored his cheek. Still smiling, the youth had referred back to his papers. Meester Gregorio said approvingly, "I see he can certainly read and write."

The widow of Charetty said, "Yes. You have been over the ledgers, of course. You have seen the transactions undertaken by this company since mid-February, and the notes of meetings attended by me, with Nicholas as my escort. You should know that all these meetings were planned and arranged by Nicholas, that he suggested all these acquisitions, costed them and carried them through in all but the official preparation of the documents and the formal agreements, which were concluded by myself. He is more able, Meester Gregorio, than I am. Than indeed anyone I have employed until now. He wishes to stay with the company. He hopes, with the advice of us all, to make it large and successful. But he is not, as you see, of the degree to wield any power. I have therefore discussed with him how I may give it to him." She paused.

Gregorio of Asti, who was fond of church litany and had a taste for after-supper dramatic readings, felt that he had become part of a dramatic reading, and should take his share. He said, "You wish to marry? But how excellent! I should be delighted, of course, to help notarise it."

She looked at him as if over the rims of nonexistent spectacles. Her sleeves, this morning, were much more elaborate than the ones she normally wore and her hair, although still invisible, was covered with a sort of brocade pumpkin instead of her usual voile, wired and bent like a siege engine. She said, "You are now planning, of course, to approach me after the wedding and present your resignation from this company. I hope you won't. We need you. And we are about to make a great deal of money."

He was sure they were. He wondered what the boy meant to sell off. If he had indeed been behind these transactions he was certainly able. He could marry the woman, milk the company and desert with the gold in a month.

"Some of this money," said his employer the bride, "will come from the normal expansion of the various interests of this, the existing company. Although Nicholas has been the cause of much of this expansion and will continue to help and advise with it, he will take no profit from it. All the businesses and all the property at the moment possessed by me, including the Louvain business, which was my father's, must be fully protected so that the proceeds can go only to me, and after me, to my son. Everything that Nicholas earns as my agent will also be paid into this company, from which he will draw an agreed salary."

This was interesting—she was protecting herself. The youth, from his face, did not seem to be at all abashed. No. Of course, he wouldn't be. Meester Gregorio said, "Forgive me. But you have a son and two daughters? They depend on you for their eventual inheritance and their dowries?"

The boy scribbled something and then looked up at the woman. "That's it," he said. "I knew we'd forgotten something. I could lie on cloth-of-gold cushions all day and you could sell Henninc and hang me with diamonds, so that Felix has to beg in his tavern and Tilde and Catherine have to marry street-sweepers. Your spending and my wages have to be controlled. That means trustees. That means good accounting and an independent check on the ledgers." He turned to the notary. "We'd already reached the conclusion," he said, "that it isn't so much a wedding as a re-write of contractual law. That's why we need you. We want it to take place this morning."

Laymen always said this sort of thing. Gregorio of Asti said, "It's unlikely, I'm afraid, that that could be done."

The boy said, "Mm. I think it might. I've sent a message to Meester Anselm Adorne. Once we've considered the worst of the problems, I'll leave you and the demoiselle to draft out a contract. Messer Anselm can call out the écoutète, the public attorney and perhaps one of the burgomasters to represent the city. I'll call with him on the dean of the Dyers' Guild and on Meester Bladelin, and on the Bishop of Terni for special permission. I've sent a message to him as well. Before noon, we might have enough people at the Hôtel Jerusalem to let us go through with the civil contract in a proper manner. Then the Bishop or, failing him, Meester Anselm's own chaplain, can hold the wedding Mass in the Jerusalemkerk, and it'll be done."

Gregorio looked at the Widow. She looked as if, despite herself, she felt a little dazed. Dazed did not describe how he, Gregorio, felt. She had been right about one thing. The fellow had brains. He was dangerous. A stirring of compassion for Marian de Charetty came to her notary. He said, "I see. You have planned very well. But why the speed, might I ask?"

The young man looked at him with apparent frankness. "Because everyone will think exactly the way you've been thinking, and there'll be a commotion. Once the wives get hold of the story, there won't be a wedding: they'll intimidate their husbands. We want the conditions of a normal business meeting in which to transact a good contract which will protect every party."

"Except, I see, yourself?" said Gregorio sympathetically. "If, as you say, you wish to be excluded from any financial gain directly or indirectly through your future wife, apart from your allotted wages? How will you live, for example, if, God forbid, she were to die? The inheritance would then devolve on her son, and he would be free to dismiss you. I gather, since you don't mention him, that he has had no say in this arrangement?"

"That," said Marian de Charetty, "is the other difficulty. My son is seventeen and headstrong. I want this marriage complete, if possible, before he knows of it." She paused and said, "I may say we disagree about this. We do it this way on my insistence. I will not have my personal decisions interfered with beforehand by Felix. Afterwards, it will be bad enough. And if the law normally requires his consent or his presence, you must get round the law."

Gregorio said, "There are ways, if the Church is sympathetic. But if he is minded to be vindictive, in later years if not now, this contract gives him power."

The young man said, "He needs all the power the law can give him, only reserving the rights of his mother. Let there be no doubt of that. Felix will be no trouble to me or to you, when you get to know him. He's only young. And as for money, I can find that without the Charetty business, Meester Gregorio. I think the demoiselle hinted at a new venture. That will be mine, made with my partners and drawing nothing from this company, although I hope it will benefit from it. You too, if you are so minded. It is why, since I am sure you are wondering, Meester Anselm will be willing

to help us. You may think he is a guarantor of some stature, and
that I am a little less unreliable than I seem. But only time can
prove it to you. Meantime, all we ask of you is your help in making
a contract. Are you appalled?"

Gregorio was amazed. He was filled with horrified admiration.
He felt a strong desire, before this meeting was over, to set his hand
to a marriage contract for this manipulating pair that would do
what they said they wanted it to do—precisely, fully and properly.
One so binding that, no matter what trickery the youth had in
mind, what delusion the woman was under, it could never be broken.

Then, he thought, he would much enjoy staying on for a bit, to
see what happened.

The second to receive the news was Anselm Adorne, to whom a
packet was delivered as he rose from his knees and led his wife and
family and servants from their morning devotions in the
Jerusalemkerk, the private church built by his father and uncle.
The packet proved to contain a densely-written letter of several
pages, whose contents caused him to lay his hand on his wife's arm
and say, "Before you begin your household duties, we must talk
together. Then the hall is to be put in order. We shall have guests
this morning." He had to wait, as he might have expected, while
she hurried to the kitchens with instructions. Then she joined him
in their bedchamber.

She was a little excited. Not worried, for all their children were
about them, even Jan, home from Paris for Easter. And after sixteen years, she knew her careful, courtly husband and his good
feelings. Anything wrong with Father Pieter in his quiet retreat
with the Carthusians, with the uncles and aunts, the sisters and
brothers, the numberless cousins and nieces and nephews of the
Adorne and van der Banck family, would have led him to tell her
immediately.

She didn't think of business. She knew of course of some of his
many concerns. Margriet van der Banck had been fourteen when
she married him, and an orphan, but she had been well trained.
She was a good organiser, a good mother, an expert in household
matters. That was her business and there was no need for her to
meddle in his. Except, of course, when it was a matter which af-
fected their joint future, like this alum affair. He had told her all
about that. She still wished he wouldn't touch it.

So she was alarmed when, settling down to hear of some exciting new prospect, a presentation, an appointment, an acquisition, she heard him speak of the very thing that troubled her. About the alum negotiation, and this dyers' workman, this very decent young man Claes who had been so good with Marie and Katelijne, and who, one was asked to believe, had invented this whole dangerous proposition, with some doctor in Italy backing him. Using him, more likely, to presume on his acquaintance with Anselm. Although Anselm appeared to believe in the youth's capabilities.

But not every man was brilliant as Anselm. Anselm had married her at nineteen, and had become a Bruges counsellor at 20, and won his first prize in the White Bear joust the same year. Anselm was a burgess, but in lineage he was an aristocrat, kinsman to Doges. This was a workman. And now Anselm was saying, "You remember young Claes, of course, of the Charetty household. This is a letter from him. He's coming here in a moment to ask for our help for Marian de Charetty. The business has expanded so much that she now needs a partner. She thinks Claes himself is the best person to run it but, of course, he hasn't the standing. That she's decided to deal with, it seems, by proposing to make the young man her husband."

Margriet couldn't stop herself gasping aloud. Anselm looked up, in the way he had. He said, "My dear, this is their affair. The demoiselle has made up her mind. She wants the marriage contracts written and signed this very morning, and begs my help in arranging it. He says he hesitates to ask, but he knows that she would like the Church's blessing. He asks if we would permit the signing to take place today in our hall, and Mass to be celebrated for them afterwards in the Jerusalemkerk."

Margriet was silent for a moment, because he had reproved her. But she had to burst out with her thoughts in the end. She said, "He thinks he has put you in his debt, or he would never have asked you. This is the first ill consequence of your partnership."

He put the letter by her side and sat down. "Of course that's why he asked. But there is another reason. I know Marian de Charetty is right. He could run her business as no one else could, except that he has no status at present."

Margriet van der Banck said, "But you know that isn't all. To marry her own apprentice instead of looking about for a trained manager, instead of taking a second husband of her own age and rank, will make her a figure of fun in this city. Perhaps he is the finest manager she could ever hope to acquire. But in doing this, she is placing her business before her own dignity. Claes! A charming boy, but so unruly that he spends half his time being beaten. Every time he came back from Louvain, all my friends would lock up their housemaids. What is she thinking of?"

"He has settled," said Anselm. "You let him take our daughters to the Carnival. Perhaps he's ready for marriage. Perhaps, my love, they are fond of each other." He hesitated. "Although the letter, I admit, says nothing of that. A business arrangement is how he presents it."

"Perhaps *she* is fond of *him,*" said Margriet. "That is what rumour will say. There is a young, strong man with an attraction for women. It would be easy for him to trap her. A business arrangement! I'm sure it is. Felix disinherited, and those two poor young girls . . ."

"No," said Anselm. "He is quite specific about that. The business stays with the demoiselle and her family. His own lawyer and the écoutète will draw up a contract which excludes him from all benefits. He wants nothing but the labour of controlling the company, which for him, he says, is reward and satisfaction enough. I believe him. It is that which has decided me."

"You're going to help him?" she said. "Yes, I suppose you are, because of the other business. You admire him. I, of course, shall do what I can because you are my husband and I'm sorry for that poor woman, who will need a good friend. As will her family. What will the son say?"

"According to the letter, he is not to be told until after the ceremony. That is by the wish of his mother, not Claes. Or Nicholas, as I suppose we should call him." He rose, and crossing to her, put his hand on her shoulder. "You will stand by her, then, at the wedding Mass?"

"The church!" said Margriet, starting up. "We shall have to prepare the church! Yes, I shall stand by her. A matron would be better than an unmarried woman, although we could have done with someone of standing. Katelina van Borselen, for example. But she is on her way to Brittany. This is going to put Gelis out, and a few other little girls who have been dreaming."

"And bigger ones," said her husband dryly.

When the noonday work bell rang out over Bruges that day, the Charetty fullers and dyers, the tenters and cutters, the carters and yardsmen and storekeepers and grooms took off their stained aprons under the monitoring eye of Henninc and went off to their homes or to the Charetty kitchens for their midday collation. Because Meester Gregorio and the Widow had gone off on unexplained business, their employees were a little noisier than usual, although they missed Claes, who was usually there to entertain them. One of them tried, when Henninc wasn't listening, to imitate the Widow the way Claes used to do, but wasn't nearly as brilliant.

Inside the single tall chamber of the Jerusalemkerk the bell made itself heard also to those grouped before the curious coloured altar, with its skulls and its ladders, the instruments of the Passion, where stood the short figure of Francesco Coppini, Bishop of Terni, concluding a marriage service. On the table, covered with a cloth embroidered by Margriet van der Banck herself, stood the silvergilt cross containing the fragment of Christ's cross, brought back from the Holy Land by Anselm's father and uncle. On either side of the altar, a double flight of narrow steps led to the upper gallery with its white balustrade, lit by unseen windows far above in the tower; made by the Adornes to imitate and do honour to the church of the Holy Sepulchre, the place of their pilgrimage.

The company did some honour in its attire to the exquisite building. Margriet herself wore her good brocade dress with its high belt that met the point of her wide ermine collar, and her two-horned headdress. Anselm and their friends from the city council and from the guilds had come in proper robes, falling to ankle-height, with lapels or tippets of satin or fur, and sturdy felt hats of all sizes. Of intent, there were no women among them.

The bride wore what she had worn that morning, for lack of time to do anything else: a padded headdress which concealed all her hair, and a stiff little gown with neatly-tied oversleeves and a square neck to which she'd added a very fine pendant. The skin displayed for the first time under her chin was, Margriet saw, fair and smooth and perfectly acceptable. She had good blue eyes and sound teeth and usually, one could say, a fine colour.

The boy, too, was dressed as he had been when he had arrived to make the arrangements. Not, at least, the blue working clothes of the Charetty, which would have made the occasion not just comedy but outright farce. The dark serge doublet fitted well enough to be his own, presumably bought with his wages in Italy. Over it he wore a sideless tunic of the middle length that a clerk might have, but in dark green cloth instead of black, which would be too expensive, one supposed, for his pocket. His hair, well flattened, was struggling against the confines of his tilted cap, which was without ornament. His hose, also dark green, were the only unpatched pair Margriet had ever seen him in. She had never seen him, either, without a smile.

Afterwards, there was a difficult wedding-breakfast at a table laid for them all in her hall. Then someone mentioned the Flanders galleys and the conversation flowed as if it would never stop, because it was the subject nearest the heart and purse of every merchant in Bruges. So Alvise Duodo, the fool, had taken the Flanders galleys to London on his way home to Venice. And of course, the English king had impounded them, needing ships for his war against his kinsmen of York. Angelo Tani and Tommaso were fainting with horror. Not only over the loss of the cloth. Would the London branch get its tennis balls? Doria had sent trumpets and clavichord wire. Jacopo Strozzi had put in toothpicks and playing cards. Would they be unloaded at all, or spend their days in the hold while the ships were turned round and sent out to the Narrow Seas to fight other Englishmen sailing from Calais?

Bishop Coppini said very little. It was his task to proceed to Calais and reconcile the Englishmen there with the Englishmen in England who had impounded the Flanders galleys. A good idea, granted. But the moment that was done and peace declared, the Pope would be able to launch his crusade to recover Constantinople, and the King of France and the Duke of Burgundy and the King of England (whichever lord won the disputed succession) would have no excuse but to launch a fleet or an army and aid him. Then the Flanders galleys might well find themselves impounded next time at Sluys by Duke Philip, along with all the Scots barges, the Portuguese hulks, the Normandy balingers, the Breton caravels and the heavy ships from Hamburg. How was a merchant to survive these days? One needed an astrologer.

"You could corner fish," said the bridegroom, who had up to that point been deferential in his few comments, and not grossly stupid. "Fishing boats are about the only ships you can't send on a crusade. But it's too near the end of Lent, perhaps, to expect much of a backing." It was not too bad a joke, and they had drunk enough of Meester Anselm's Candian wine to laugh quite heartily. Indeed, one or two of them began to think, privately, that the boy might have touched, unwittingly, on something worth looking into.

When they left, they were all in good humour. When they

reached home they would be inclined, from the share they had
been pushed into taking, to be defensive about the marriage rather
than to attack it. And they all knew the terms of the contract, why
it had been drawn up, and whom it favoured. In this way, the only
way it could have been done, the most powerful homes in Bruges
would at least know the facts.

When the Bishop had gone, and the Burgomaster, and the lawyers, Margriet van der Banck put her arm round the bride's plump,
pretty shoulders and drew her into her chamber to prepare for the
journey home. Their new notary, the alert Meester Gregorio, had
already left to go back to the Charetty house. There, as soon as
they returned, the news about the marriage would be broken to her
employees by the demoiselle herself, her partner by her side. After,
that is, she had told her son and her daughters.

A daunting prospect, after a difficult morning. The demoiselle
was white with weariness. There was nothing one could put into
words. Margriet hugged her, and tried to tell her, silently, that she
was a friend. She was a proud woman, Cornelis' small widow. She
had not given way, but had clung a little, in Margriet's embrace.
Then, drawing off, she had stood alone and thanked her quietly.

Later, when the bride and bridegroom had gone, Margriet said
as much to Anselm but, although she waited, he didn't say what
happened when he, in his turn, took the young man Nicholas off.
Indeed, there was nothing to tell. After his guest, Adorne used the
offices of his house and, returning to his room, had been in time to
see the bridegroom, hitherto entirely composed, shiver and sit, as if
a bolt had come through the window. Then, hearing Adorne cross
the tiled floor, he had turned round.

Stopping, Anselm had looked down on him. "How much sleep
did you have last night, friend Nicholas? None, I should think."

Suspended in battle, men inflated their lungs in this way, and
expelled the ache, suddenly, with the air. Nicholas smiled as he did
so, and shook his head, smiling still. Anselm wondered where or
how the lad had passed his last night of freedom. Of youth, in a
way. He said lightly, "Every bridegroom is allowed a night with
his friends."

He had hoped the boy would take up the vein. Instead, his eyes
strayed elsewhere, as if he were already distracted by other things.
He said, "Oh. No. I spent it in my room."

Anselm Adorne looked at him. Then, drawing up a stool, he had
sat on it, looking at the withdrawn profile. He said, "Nicholas? But

you wouldn't wish to go back, if you could? To getting up to the work bell, and stirring cloth in the dyevats, and keeping company with simple people and children? It would be a sin, with what you can give the world with your talents."

"Money?" said Nicholas, to the window ledge. "I was fairly happy with nothing. And I could make other people quite happy as well."

"Of course," said Adorne. "But that was the work of your youth. You needed more. You left of your own accord."

"Yes," said Nicholas.

Anselm Adorne watched him. There was no point in saying: You chose this. Didn't you anticipate what it would be like? Didn't you realise that you weren't yet ready to manage it? He thought: he's going to have to manage it, for the sake of that poor woman in there. What would help? Not to drown it in drink, that's for certain.

Adorne said, "I expect my wife and the demoiselle will have something to say to each other. While you wait, will you let me see if Marie and Katelijne are free of their schooling? They would never forgive me for letting you leave without seeing them." He paused, and added, "Of course, they know nothing, and would care less."

Anselm Adorne was a man who tried to understand the feelings of others. Sometimes Margriet had warned him, *You can come too close. Anyway, Anselm, sometimes you are wrong.* He wasn't wrong this time, although the young man did nothing more than say, after a moment, "I should like nothing better." Anselm Adorne rose, and left, and without overmuch haste found and brought back his children to where their friend Claes, smiling, was waiting for them, a puzzle of wool already half threaded onto his hands.

By the time his bride was ready to leave there was no flaw, Adorne saw, in the bearing of her new partner. Nicholas offered well-considered and, he thought, genuine thanks to himself and to Margriet. With practical ease he lifted the demoiselle's cloak and laid it round the demoiselle's shoulders. She looked up at him, her colour returned, you could see, with her courage.

Dear God, what a marriage. What a marriage.

Adorne stood with Margriet and bade the demoiselle and her husband Godspeed as their barge left for home. Thus occupied, Anselm Adorne didn't observe that his student son Jan had strolled into the house. Ravenous as all student sons, he quizzed the servants while filling his mouth from the ruined feast on the table, and received an unbelievable answer. An answer which wild horses could not have forced him to keep to himself.

Chapter 27

The clang of the noonday work bell didn't even penetrate the hearing of Felix de Charetty who, smarting from the double loss of a lot of money and a girl, had salved his pride by inviting himself into the Poorterslogie, the club house of the White Bear Society. The Society whose emblem, perched in the outside coign of the building, had once been embraced by that silly fool Claes, so the story ran, just after he had swum the canal and hacked to death Simon of Kilmirren's expensive dog.

That was when Claes, though a fool, had been amusing to be with. Before he started telling him what he could or couldn't do with girls like Mabelie. To be truthful, Felix hadn't been sorry to get rid of the Mabelie embarrassment. As it turned out, she hadn't wanted to leave John Bonkle anyway, and John Bonkle hadn't wanted to get rid of her. He and Jannekin had both been a bit drunk.

Felix was trying today to keep off beer, in order to give a proper impression. The White Bear Society, whose great joust opened the post-Easter tournament, was extremely exclusive, restricting its members to noblemen and the upper bourgeoisie. Drapers and mercers and furriers just managed to get in and, of course, real estate owners. Guild members were not approved of, although the Brotherhood made exceptions for the larger brokers and innkeepers. As a son of a broker, Felix just qualified. He didn't talk about dyeing or fulling. It was a little alarming, therefore, to walk into this handsome building by the canal bridge and greet men he had seen in his mother's company, and accept their invitation to take a cup of wine.

It came to him that, if he were to come often, he would need more money. He needed more money as it was, if he were going to practise every day the way he needed to practise for the jousting. He had the armour all right, and some of the weapons. But he needed more lances, and he should have a spare shield. And what mattered most of all, of course, were the horses.

He should have two, and heavy ones. There was one in the stable which had belonged to his father, although his father had hardly seen any fighting and used it more to ride up and down and impress people when it was his turn to be captain of one of the companies on the walls. He had meant to get a loan of another. One of the de Walles had half offered. But a lot of the families he knew were going in for the thing themselves. The Breydels and the Metteneyes and the Bradericx and the Halewyns and the Themsekes. It went down from father to son, attempting the joust and trying to carry off the horn or the lance or the Bear. In the great days, the best of the Burgundian Court would come to Bruges to take part. People like Jacques de Lalain and the Bastard of Burgundy.

A tremor ran through Felix but he refused, valiantly, the offer of another cup. He had to get a better horse. And another shield. He couldn't fight great knights, could he, with rubbish? He plunged, avidly, into discussions about the tournaments, and absorbed all the information he could about how and where to practise beforehand. He should have come with an experienced member of the confrérie like Anselm Adorne, even though Adorne had treated him like a child in his house, that time Claes had tipped the gun into the water, and brought the girl's hat ashore, and broken the man's wooden leg.

He saw Jan Adorne signalling in the doorway and thought that he would do just as well. At fifteen he was very likely too young to joust, but he must have been to the Poorterslogie often with his father. Felix waved his cup, summoning him. His sleeve, waving too, just missed tipping a flask over. He had dressed really well for today, with ribbons all down his arms, and his doublet fully padded under his cloak, which the tailor said, rightly, did justice to his chest. Thinking of the crowd, he had put on a very tall hat, rather than one of his wide ones. He wished only that his collar was not buttoned quite so firmly under his chin. It made it hard to look down, and keep his sleeves from interfering with people sitting on the banquettes.

Jan, signalling again, had still not yet entered. Annoyed, Felix pushed his way nearer and saw the reason. There was a crowd of them. Bonkle was with him, and Sersanders and Lorenzo Strozzi, among others. It was wonderful how Lorenzo Strozzi always managed to get away from his father's cousin's business. Or maybe the bell had gone for the midday meal. No. He had had his midday meal. It must be later. He got to the door and said, "Well, I'm not coming out, I'm busy. What do you want?"

"Felix," said Jan.

That was all he said. The others, round about him, said nothing either. Their faces were peculiar. Well, none of his friends were noted for their good looks. But their expressions were funny. As if they had something to tell, and weren't sure whether it was a great joke or a great disaster. For a moment he was worried, and then one of the younger hangers-on at the back gave a great fizzing snort like a boiling fish-kettle, and doubled up with his hands on his crotch. Some mucus landed on Felix's buttons, and he picked it off distastefully.

Nothing wrong anywhere, obviously, if it was as funny as all that. It looked to Felix like the start of a practical joke. Against him. He said, "If you've nothing to say, I'm going indoors. More fool you, Jan, bringing a rabble like this to your father's club. Goodbye."

He had meant to stride in, but one of the town échevins, patiently rounding the group, arrived at the door just before him and he had to hang back. As the door opened, he realised, to his fury, that Jan Adorne was shouting again. It was intolerable. Stiff with anger, Felix turned for the last time and spat at his friends. "Go away! Away! Go away! I don't want to see you!"

"Felix!" shrieked Jan Adorne. "Claes the apprentice has married your mother!"

The door closed without Felix noticing. "What?" he said.

Another boy immediately said it again, articulating helpfully, like a teacher. "Your mother's got married to Claes."

"Claes the apprentice," said a voice from the back.

The helpful boy said, "In Jan's house. This morning."

This, then, was the practical joke. Felix felt his face swell. Beyond his group of so-called friends a carter had slowed his horse, grinning; and two cloth-merchants striding arguing out of the Tonlieu turned and looked. Behind, the club door had opened yet again and this time stayed open, while inside, heads turned.

Transported with fury, Felix began to walk forward, pushing the shuffling group of his tormentors before him. He said, his face scarlet, his voice low, "*I'll* give you Claes and my mother. *I'll* teach you to come to my club and make a disturbance in front of my friends. When *I've* finished with you all, you'll wish you'd never been born. My mother will see your father, Jan Adorne!"

Before his advance, they had fallen back as far as they could. They stood in a huddle on the other side of the narrow street, looking at him. Behind him one of the really rich seigneurs climbed the club steps with a companion and, laughing a little, walked inside, but left the door open. The companion remained, holding the door, and was joined by two others. Lorenzo Strozzi said, "Well, you ought to go and speak to Jan's father. He'd tell you. It's true."

They'd played jokes on each other before. Getting into scrapes and out of them was normal, and so were storms of annoyance and even pangs of fear. But between boys and among boys, not in front of the Poorterslogie. The monstrosity of the social problem was already, as he struggled to deal with it, paralysing Felix, not the most inventive of youths. At Lorenzo's words, his stomach, glimpsing something quite unmanageable, began to flicker with random pain, like summer lightning. His conscious mind was merely goaded to fury. He pushed, spitting words at them.

This time, they stood their ground, although uncertainly. They let him flail them. Occasionally one would try to speak, and find Felix's fist in his mouth. It was ridiculous. Lorenzo, first to collect himself, leaned forward and tried, with the best intentions, to grasp Felix's arm. Felix hit Lorenzo's hand, painfully. Lorenzo said angrily, "All right. If he doesn't want to believe it, that's his affair," and walked off.

The smaller boys moved closer. John Bonkle, his face flushed said, "Oh, come on. This is just making it worse. You shouldn't have told him here, Jan."

Jan Adorne turned and said, "Well, I had to. He wouldn't come out. He has to know, hasn't he? Otherwise he'll go off home and find—"

"—in bed . . ." said one of the younger boys, the one who had snorted.

"—Felix's new father!" said another. "Claes!" They staggered, holding one another and laughing. Behind, at the entrance to the White Bear Society, a number of men standing quietly looked at one another, and the noise from inside the club was noticeably less. It was Anselm Sersanders who saw it and leaned forward and, this time successfully, took Felix by the elbow. He said, "The rest of you, get out. John, help me. Jan, you'd better come."

Felix's head, which had been very hot, suddenly felt very cold. He said, "What . . . It isn't true?"

He was walking, with Jan Adorne on one side and Jan's cousin Anselm and John Bonkle on the other. His doublet was gaping open, showing a stain on his shirt, and his hose, it turned out, felt clammy. There was a group of men talking on the threshold of the Poorterslogie behind him. His stomach rose. He said desperately, "I need a . . . It *isn't* true?"

It was the very heart of the business section in Bruges, but they found him, ingeniously, a corner to be sick in, and worse, with a group of drunk lightermen to encourage him. Then they took him down one of the canal slopes and sat him at the edge of the water, dipping his kerchief for him. He was trembling. He said, "That was the foulest thing you've ever done. That was wicked. That was a dirty, unfair, rotten . . ." Tears were moving down his cheeks. He said, "You could have thought up some other story." He saw them looking at one another. The boulder that had been in his stomach had moved into his throat. He said, "I'm going to the tavern. I don't want to see you again." Still they didn't move, and neither did he. His body started to heave. Then he put his face in his hands and sobbed.

John Bonkle put a hand on his shoulder and pulled a face at Jan Adorne and said, "Go on. He'd better hear what you know."

It was Henninc, his eyes on his mistress's unusual clothes, who told her that jonkheere Felix had gone to the Poorterslogie. As yet, Henninc and the household knew nothing. Back from the Hôtel Jerusalem, Nicholas had taken the demoiselle directly indoors, and had remained there. The staff could not be told before the son of the house. And the son of the house, Nicholas suggested wryly, might better learn it indoors rather than out.

Felix's mother was silent, thinking of the news spreading from this morning's witnesses. But they would go home, surely, first. And although it was not right that Felix should learn of this publicly, he would be prevented from pride from making a scene in a place like the White Bear Society. And would come directly home. Nicholas had wanted her to tell Felix beforehand, and it would have been wiser. He had not reproached her. She supposed he would never reproach her, any more than Henninc did. It was not his place to do so; although in business matters, when he forgot, he spoke to her as to an equal.

She had thought to put one matter behind her, and had asked Messer Gregorio to find and send Tilde and Catherine to her bedroom. She had rehearsed well beforehand how she was going to tell them, and gave them, simplified, the account Adorne knew, and the others. Because Claes was clever and they all liked him so much, she had asked him to help her run the company, so that he would stay with them always. But men and women who stayed together had to marry. Now Claes, whom they must learn to call Nicholas, was her new husband. But of course he would never replace their father. They must think of him as she did. As a friend.

Catherine had been put out. Now Claes would bring presents for her mother from Italy, and not for Catherine. She was reassured. Everything would be as it was before. If there were presents, of course everyone would have one. Simply, Claes would work in the house and not in the yard. And was to be called Nicholas. Catherine was satisfied.

Tilde, her face white, was different. She said, "None of our friends have mothers who married servants."

Before Marian could speak, her younger daughter had interrupted with indignation. "Claes isn't a servant! Nicholas."

"What is he then?" said Tilde. "Have you told Felix?"

"As soon as he comes in," said Marian. "Tilde, both you and Catherine are right. Nicholas is a servant, because he was born into that class. But has anyone you know married someone as clever as he is? You know he is very different from anyone else in the yard. Even Henninc."

"Did you think of marrying Henninc?" said Tilde shrilly. "Why not marry Oudenin de Ville? He's nearer your age. Are you going to have a baby?"

Horrified, Marian looked at her daughter. She didn't know what she had expected. She hadn't expected this. She heard Catherine say indignantly, "She's our mother. She's had all her babies."

"Has she?" said Tilde. "Well, maybe our new father will supply all the babies, although I suppose we'll never know whether they belong to him or to Felix."

She stared her mother down. A sweet, quiet girl of thirteen. Marian said steadily, "What do you mean?"

Tilde said, "You *are* cut off from what's happening. Don't you know that they sell their mistresses to one another? Claes took Mabelie from Simon of Kilmirren. John Bonkle got her from Claes. And Felix bought her from John. That's why he wanted the eight shillings parisis."

That was when Nicholas opened the door. Marian stood up slowly. Tilde, already standing, turned her back on her mother and walked straight up to where he stood. Then she spat on his clothes and walked out.

Catherine's face began to crumple. "Oh dear, temper," said Nicholas, rubbing carefully with his kerchief. "Do you think that will stain?" He sat down, still rubbing. He said, "I don't know. What do you think, Catherine? Will she get used to it? It's very hard, skating with someone one minute and finding out the next that they're going to skate with you every winter."

Catherine hung on to her mother, but her face brightened. She said reprovingly, "She said you sold Mabelie to Felix."

"I'm sure she didn't," said Nicholas, grinning. "I was disappointed in Mabelie. Do you know she preferred John Bonkle to me? And then one night Felix drank too much, and thought he could buy her from John. But you don't buy nice girls like Mabelie. She's still John's particular friend. Do you have a particular friend?"

"I like you," said Catherine.

"Well, that's good," said Nicholas. "But you've got to share me with Tilde and your mother. And you know Tilde's upset. So we just have to keep very quiet, and be gentle with her until she gets used to it all. Now you stay with your mother. My lady?"

She took Catherine on her knee, their smiling cheeks together. I mustn't forget. I mustn't forget that he's with me. I am not alone. She said, "Yes, Nicholas?"

He said, "I've asked that Felix, when he comes, should be asked to see me, not his mother. Would you allow me this?" Yesterday she would have refused. Today, she knew already that she couldn't deal with Felix. Heavens above, she couldn't deal with Tilde. She nodded.

Nicholas said, "I think Tilde is better left alone today. Catherine, would you mind sleeping tonight with your mother? You see, Tilde is angry, and might say things she doesn't mean. But it won't last."

Catherine looked at him. She said, "I don't know. I hoped you would marry me, but I think Tilde really thought she would marry you herself one of these days and have babies. That's why she was so cross about Mabelie. She was always looking to see if Mabelie was getting fat and having a baby."

Nicholas grinned again. "Well, if she is, it's John Bonkle's," he said. "I don't plan to have any babies, I can tell you. You and Tilde will be enough."

"And Felix," said Catherine.

"And Felix," said Nicholas, looking at her mother over her head.

Because very soon after that the news, as a small and delectable scandal, began spreading throughout Bruges, and because, too, as someone said of him, there was the making of a man in Felix, he came back to his house alone that afternoon, and walked through the yard and into his house. There, Meester Gregorio, who had been watching for him, stepped in his way.

"Young master."

The title surprised him. Then he realised that what had taken place with such secrecy was probably unknown even here. He waited neutrally to hear what the man had to say, his hat dragged off in his hand. Sersanders had lent him his cloak, to cover the ruined doublet and the rest. Anselm had been good, even though his uncle had been one of the traitors. All his friends, when it came to it, had been good, in the end. Any one of them would have put him up for the night. But there was still the morning to face. And their parents' faces.

Gregorio, who had looked like a man with a message, had apparently changed his mind. He hesitated. Then he said, "Forgive me, jonkheere. I think you have heard some news."

Felix's back stiffened. He said, "I see you know of it."

The man's angular face didn't soften. He said, "Merely because I was required to draw up the contract safeguarding your interests. It was your mother's hope that she would find you here when she came back. As it is, she asks me if you will see her after you've seen Nicholas." He paused. "She's had a hard and difficult day."

"Claes," said Felix.

Gregorio said, "I'm sure he doesn't mind which name you use. I was to say that he would come to your room if you send for him."

Send for him. Claes, with his back exposed, waiting patiently for his punishment. Claes, the submissive, who never minded when his schemes failed, or his devices were broken by other people. Until this time, when he would be made to mind in such a way that he would never forget it till the end of his life. Felix began to speak, and then remembered that, to this man, Claes was his mother's husband. He said, "Kindly ask Nicholas to come to my room in

will benefit: not if our workpeople won't take your orders and the merchants turn their backs and make fun of us. Maybe you're clever, but what experience do you have compared with theirs? You'll ruin it, won't you? And then no matter how many shares you're not taking, there won't be anything for me or my mother or my sisters."

Claes said, "If this hadn't happened, your mother would have sold, or would have married Oudenin."

"Either would have been better than this," Felix said. "As it is, we'll make the best of it. You'll leave tonight. You can take one of the horses. I'll give you enough money to get you as far as Geneva. Jaak de Fleury will take you in, I'm sure. You're his niece's bastard. If he doesn't, you'll have to find work on your own. I'm sure that'll be easy. You can find someone's business and run it. Or, now you've been taught how to fight, you might find some work with a condottiere. But keep clear of Astorre and our company. You're not a member of this company any longer. We don't hire you and we've nothing to do with you. Is that clear?"

"Yes, it's clear," said Claes. "You would have to discuss it with your mother. But what if she disagreed? She holds the purse-strings."

Felix stared at him. "Are you threatening me?" he said.

"No," said Claes. "At least, I expect you'd get a job somewhere. You see, for her, you come before me in everything, and always will. But if you ask her to choose between us at this moment, sheer pride will force her to choose me. It would make better sense to try later."

"My father's friends . . . the city will run you out of town," said Felix.

"Maybe," said Claes.

"Henninc will walk out."

"You could get him back, after I've been run out of town," said Claes. "Look. The first mistake, and I'm out, you know that—long before I've had a chance to ruin the business. You don't need to be seen to help or approve. Gregorio can go to meetings with me. I only suggested it because you could keep an eye on me that way. Although I could do with your advice as well. The dismissing of Olivier was the best thing that's happened in Louvain."

He always had the answers. Whatever passage of thought you turned into, he was there, already waiting. He would have worked out everything. An unshakable marriage contract. His mother so manoeuvred that she was convinced that this was best, and he would have the rotten job of distressing her. Unless he could show her . . .

Claes said, "We have to tell the yard and the household before they stop for the night. Your mother will do it. You needn't be there. But why don't you go to her now, and make sure that this is really what she wants? If it isn't, I won't hold out against you both. You can't break the marriage, but I'll leave. Then Gregorio can go and collect people together, and we'll tell them the final decision. Is that fair?"

"Not very," said Felix. "You've had a night and a day to get her to make up her mind. And weeks beforehand, I'm sure, preparing her for it. I've got a few minutes."

"But you're her son," said Claes.

He would go to his mother. He couldn't think how to get Claes out of his room. He finally just walked and opened the door and said to Claes, "Go and wait in your quarters." And Claes went, without fuss, as if he weren't his mother's husband at all. Felix felt his throat harden again. He waited until he had collected himself. Then he went and tapped on his mother's door.

To be alone for the first time at seventeen is a frightening thing.

A handful of times, Felix had stood like this outside his father's cabinet, gathering courage to knock, and go in, and face Cornelis' anger at some piece of misconduct unbecoming to Cornelis' only son and adored heir.

Cornelis had never really known what Felix was like. His mother knew, and had cuffed him often harder than Cornelis, but had always been there, in the background, grimly understanding. Even while he rebelled against her, he felt safe. Not any longer. He was so empty that his hand didn't even shake as he lifted it, at length, to knock on his mother's door. He just felt cold.

When she didn't answer he knocked again, not very loud. Then he realised that the sound he had heard before was her voice responding, and that she was telling him, for the second time, to come in. He cautiously opened the door.

His mother was alone in her office, seated behind her big table. Interviewing Henninc, or Julius, she sat stiffly like that, with all the light from the window falling on Henninc or Julius and very little on herself. The only difference now was that she had planted her elbows on the baize and had folded her hands to her lips as if she were blowing to warm them. Above them her eyes, he supposed, were inspecting his changed clothes, his uneven complexion. He didn't really care if she saw what she had done to him. She deserved to. Then he got a little nearer, and saw that her eyes were shut.

His next steps brought him quite close to the table. Instead of looking, she squeezed her eyes tighter closed. Then she opened them on him, and brought her hands down. Her voice, when she spoke, sounded as if her tongue and the roof-arch above it were stuck together. She said, "Your friend understood you better than I did. Nicholas begged me to find you this morning and tell you everything."

He stood in front of her. He said, "You would say that anyway."

Her eyes had never moved from his face since they opened. She said, "Look at me as an adult looks at an adult. Think of Nicholas as an adult would. Think of all you know of him, and me, and yourself. We three do not lie to one another."

He found he had started to breathe again properly. He straightened a little. He said, "But you didn't tell me. I suppose in case I stopped it."

"Yes," she said. He wished she would go on, and protest, and try to explain, so that he could get angry again.

He said, "So you didn't care what I felt, did you? You just wanted to get the marriage over before I heard about it. You knew it would be . . . I would be . . ."

"I knew that you would find it unthinkable. Yes. That's why I hoped to arrange things so that you would find you wanted to think about it. Felix, you know Nicholas very well. Do you think he would try to trap me into marriage for his own purposes? Really?"

Claes. Claes, year in, year out at his side. But—

"You see, he's clever," said Felix.

Her face relaxed, as if she knew what that cost him to say. She said, "He's wise as well. If you feel you can hardly hold your head up in public, you must know that he feels the same. He knows what people will say. So do I. So our reasons for doing this must be very strong, don't you think?"

"The business," said Felix. He said it flatly, and not with the disbelieving contempt he had felt, when he had feelings. He said, "*He* said just now it was to keep the business straight until I could run it. As if I would want it this way. As if my father would have ever, ever asked you, expected you . . . to . . ."

"Marry one of his apprentices," his mother ended for him. He heard her draw a deep breath. She said, "No. Your father would never have wanted that. But your father is dead. I am here. My life, too, has to be lived. It is not even the company that your father made; it is quite a different one, and will grow more different still. I want to stay with it; spend my days thinking about it. But I couldn't do it without help. Until you are ready, there has to be a man close to the business. Felix, I don't want a man who will take your father's place. I only want a friend." She paused. She said, "And it will be known, I promise you, that Nicholas is only a friend."

He felt his face burning again, because such denials should be remotely necessary. It sounded so reasonable. Except that he was the heir, and Nicholas was hardly older than he was. And Nicholas, everyone knew, was his servant.

His mother said, "Men have different gifts at different ages. Sometimes we must stand by and see others take the prize, but our turn will come. It would be a small spirit which would hold another one back. In Nicholas, you and I have a friend. In you I have a son. What can ever change that?"

Something moved on his cheek, but he couldn't imagine that he was crying unknowingly. He said, "Just now, he said that he would leave if you wanted it. He said that I shouldn't expect you to choose me instead of him at this moment, but I could ask you, and you might, later on."

His mother didn't answer. Then she said, "How could I choose him instead of you? You are my son. Wherever you are, you are chosen. And Felix, how are you better off if Nicholas leaves, with all his opportunities lost, and the company fails, and my way of life has to end? Is that the way a man takes his place in the world?"

He knew then from the cold at his chin that he *was* crying. He said, "It was at the Poorterslogie," and pursed his lips against the pain in his throat. He glanced, through flickering eyes, at the table and saw that she had lifted her hands again to her mouth, and then to her brow. Under their shadow she said, "I would go through this whole day again, to spare you that. You should have been told. I was wrong. To be fair, I should be the one really to leave. Perhaps one day you and Nicholas will decide to leave me. I deserve it."

Below her hands, her lips had twisted as if in a wry smile. But then she took her hands down, and he saw that her face was striped with tears, and that the tears ran over skin already shiny with weeping. Then he was beside her, and they had their arms round each other, and their wet cheeks were pressed together. It was the first time ever that she had admitted to being wrong. Adult to adult. She had said so.

Somewhere during the disconnected exchanges that followed, he heard himself telling her that he wanted her to be happy. Somewhere in the same passage, he learned, without anything being said, that some of his mother's happiness was bound up with Nicholas. It was not entirely news. It was what, after all, had been behind much of his misery. But he had shared Nicholas before, especially with women. His head on her knee, he let her stroke his hair until her composure came back. Then he said, "It's done, I suppose. If you really want it, I'll help you."

An adult could afford to be magnanimous. He was her son, and chosen. She was a woman, and weak enough to need the help of Claes, his servant. He could spare her that. Of what, in detail, it would entail: of how, in detail, he was to face the events that lay ahead, he would rather not think. Today, his poor mother could rely on him.

He waited for her to drop a kiss on his brow. She hesitated, and then just massaged and patted his shoulder, as he got to his feet. Her eyes were wet and anxious, watching him. He sniffed, and bent over and kissed her firmly instead.

Chapter 28

Messer Gregorio, working quietly with one eye on his open door, heard his mistress's step and had already risen when she came into the room. It was to request him, as arranged, to summon all her workers and her household to the biggest of the dyesheds and to put a box there, beside the pay-trestle, for her to stand on. She spoke calmly and without a tremor, although her lids were a little red. She added, "Henninc will help you. I have asked him to come to my room so that he may receive the news first." Impeccable. Impeccable from beginning to end as a piece of sheer human management. Only the deferred breaking of the news to the son had been a mistake. One could hardly see how the son's own servant could remedy that.

Gregorio of Asti did as he was asked, and soon Henninc, his face flushed, his lips pursed, came to join him. Like himself, Henninc, he noticed, answered no questions from his underlings. Soon, noisy as starlings, there streamed from house and yard into the dyeshop the whole sum of the Charetty employees, from the journeymen dyers to the boys who cared for the tack; from the regal authority of the cook to the maids who swabbed floors and cut vegetables.

Then the demoiselle, in her good clothes, came out. Not escorted by her new husband. The youth who followed her into the yard and, catching up, gave her his arm was, Gregorio saw with fascination, her own son, Felix de Charetty, with a rather pale face and a jacket that didn't assort with his doublet. They had reached the dyeshop when a door banged and the architect of the whole affair came purposefully over the yard. Heads turned. The smiles, Gregorio saw, were without rancour. Claes hurtling, late, into the yard. Now a courier and very grand, but still Claes. From a distance, tall and well-built, he had a presence. Close at hand, of course, it was different.

Now he came into the dyeshed, looking about him. On his face Gregorio could detect no shadow of triumph, or shame or embarrassment. He had been looking, evidently, to see where he, Gregorio, was standing with Henninc. They were near to the lady and her son, but not beside them. Pushing through, Nicholas got to the same place and stood, turning his face to the Widow. She mounted her box, and everything got very quiet.

She was not unused to this. She had run the business, after all, since her husband died. She began by thanking them for the help they had been to her, and for their loyalty. She went on to talk about the difficult times after her husband died, and about the changes in the sort of work people wanted, and the sort of business that made and didn't make money. She said that it had been shown, over the last year, that the Charetty business was a very good one, and provided it changed with the times, could be even better. Perhaps one that could be very rich indeed. She was glad to tell them this, because she hoped they were all going to be able to stay with her and share in what was to come.

In all this she had had great help. From her manager Henninc, most of all. From Meester Julius, who was away but who would return and help her still more. But also, from one of themselves. From Claes who, now that he was a courier, they had learned to call Nicholas. For the past six months many of the good ideas about running the business had come from Claes. He had a gift for this. He could take the gift to any company and help to make it a great success. But to persuade him to stay with the Charetty company, she, the owner, had decided on an important step.

Nicholas was a young man, with a fine future. She was therefore making him managing partner of the business. As before, Henninc would manage the yard, and would give Nicholas his very good advice, as he had given it to her. Messer Gregorio would act, meantime, for Meester Julius and help him when he returned. And her son, Felix, would be at Nicholas' side to keep him right and, in due course, take her place as supreme owner.

She paused there, for the murmurs, the head-turning, the ejaculations. With discretion, Gregorio scanned his companions. Henninc, still flushed, stared directly ahead, looking at nobody. The boy Felix, standing very straight below his mother, glared at the crowd as if he hated them. Beside him Nicholas stood quite still, wholly concentrated on watching. Watching everyone, Gregorio saw, from his wife to those people who must have been his friends round the dyevats.

The Widow said, "You will have to be understanding with Nicholas, and help him as much as you can, because he has taken on a very large task for all of us. But I think you may thank me for not bringing in some stranger. You know each other. He has been here for a long time. Of course, his appointment has brought another problem. As you know, I am a widow, and vulnerable as a woman is. I have not wished to take a husband who would be pleasing to me but perhaps not to you, who are, in a way, also my family. Now I am faced with sharing my house and most of the affairs of my day with my new manager."

Felix dropped his gaze. Nicholas, instead, lifted his to the platform. Marian de Charetty looked at him, and smiled. She said, her voice steady, "There seemed to be only one sensible solution. I asked him if, without prejudice to the business, in which he will have no share, he would combine this appointment with marriage. He agreed. A marriage contract between us was sealed this morning."

Silence. Then a sound like a whine, with a murmuring undercurrent. Then a rumble of words. The high notes were from women. The smiling faces, Gregorio saw, were all women's. And the thought, plain as if gleefully shouted. A lusty boy in her bed! Good for the Widow!

The Widow herself stood smiling. A stiff smile, but a real one. If she was trembling, it didn't show. She had courage. But of course she had courage, to agree to the whole thing in the first place.

It was a woman who shrieked, "Three cheers for the demoiselle!" and it was women who began cheering, although the men had mostly joined in by the third. Their faces were diverse as the faces of men about to fight a battle. They didn't know what they felt yet. They wouldn't know until this was over, and they were huddled in some corner together.

Marian de Charetty was saying, "Thank you. It seemed right to mark the occasion. I see the sun is still shining. If you will move into the yard, Henninc will take some of you to help him bring out a wine cask, so that you can drink our health. And your own. And that of the company."

It was over. The demoiselle, helped by her son, was stepping down from her box. Hesitantly, some of her people were already moving forward to speak to her. She began to take their hands, one by one, smiling and speaking briefly. Henninc had gone, busy with his commission, and silent. You could see Nicholas follow him with his eyes, and then one or two of the brasher men stepped up to him, and soon a small group surrounded him, and more and more.

He made no attempt, Gregorio saw, to join the demoiselle and create of the occasion a bridal reception. The experimental jokes he appeared not to hear. The questions about his work and theirs he answered readily, with excitement even, so that some of it infected the professional men among them, who began to press closer and ask more. He finally moved out, in a wide knot of people, and found an old barrel to sit on while they crowded round him. In a while, laughter rose. Others crossed the yard to join him.

There were still sufficient paying court to the demoiselle to make it a fair division. Messer Gregorio walked to where she stood with her son and said, "Demoiselle, my congratulations. The Duke's controller could not have spoken better, or more wisely."

"I had Felix to advise me," she said. "Is the wine coming?"

It had come. Without haste, the crowd around Nicholas dissolved, or rather reshaped so that it came with its nucleus to the trestle where the cups were being laid. The wine was poured. The Widow, raising her cup, gave a toast to the company, and they to her. Then, with her son, she left for the house. Gregorio, interested, waited.

Nicholas said, "Well, of course I should like to stay and get drunk with all my friends, but I suppose you and I ought to go in. I've told Henninc they can drink themselves silly for half an hour, and then he's to come in and join us."

Gregorio kept his face solemn. He subdued, with a great effort, a desire to ask directly how Felix de Charetty had been won over. Or if not, by his looks, exactly converted, at least persuaded to co-operate. Instead, he said, "What made you late?" They began walking indoors side by side.

"A letter from . . . a letter," said his new master. "I'll tell the demoiselle later. I have to leave for Italy as soon as I can. The day after the joust."

"Trouble?" said Meester Gregorio.

"Well, trouble in the sense that I'd hoped to have longer than that to arrange things. It isn't fair to you, or to the demoiselle. I'll get everything done that I can before I go. In one way, it's not bad to leave early. The sensation will have time to die. People will pick a public quarrel with me, but not with the demoiselle."

"Who would pick a public quarrel with you?" asked Gregorio.

"The person you're thinking of," said Nicholas without animosity. "We're to go to the parlour. It's the special wine."

"And Italy?" said Gregorio, hurrying. "What's the trouble in Italy?"

"The trouble in Italy," said his new master, "is that Jacopo Piccinino has changed sides."

It was so remote from dyevats and weddings and wine in the parlour that Gregorio frowned. He said, "The condottiere? He was, surely, in the pay of King Ferrante of Naples. Yes, I see. The Charetty company and captain Astorre are now supporting a weakened army. Piccinino has crossed to the Angevins?"

"Piccinino is now supporting the Duke of Calabria. Yes."

They were in the doorway. "But what can you do?" said Messer Gregorio, staring at Nicholas.

"Turn back the tide of war, single-handed," said Nicholas. "No. There's a fellow with Piccinino called Lionetto. I'd hate to have him on the wrong side."

"I don't understand," said Gregorio.

"No. It's just as well you don't," said the extraordinary youth, cheerfully. "Or you'd turn and walk straight out. I warn you. Don't stay with this company if you like things to be peaceful."

With darkness came exhaustion for Marian de Charetty. The talk, the arrangements had gone on all evening. Tilde, who had not come to the parlour for wine, had appeared there at suppertime, joining Felix and Catherine and Nicholas and her mother at the table. Her face set and swollen, Tilde had at least answered when spoken to and, sitting next to her mother, had held her hand tightly. Nicholas left her alone, and talked about jousting.

You could see the idea enter Felix's head, and take shape there. You could see him, instead of speaking in monosyllables, begin to guide the conversation. It was no surprise when he said, rather loudly, "You did say, didn't you, that Mother and I would find the business doing remarkably well? I presume in that case it would support an extra horse or two, and a shield, say?"

Nicholas's reply, agreeing placidly, clashed with her own sharp refusal. She looked at Nicholas. He said, "I don't see why not. He's the head of the business. He ought to make a show at the White Bear."

She stared at him. She said, "I thought—" and stopped abruptly.

"You thought the business couldn't afford it. So did I. But they didn't drink half as much wine as I thought they would this afternoon, and the wedding came cheap." He grinned at her. Tilde was looking from one side to the other, puzzled. Marian realised that, of course, they would expect him to economise, to reduce their spending. He had tricked her into allowing him an act of generosity.

It was later, when the meal was over, and Tilde and Felix had gone and Catherine was already asleep in her big bed, that Marian found herself alone before the parlour fire for the first time with her husband. He had been with her all day and yet, in a sense, it might have been Henninc. Except that never in a thousand years would Henninc have contrived to achieve all Nicholas had achieved from last night. Or Cornelis.

Although, of course, Cornelis had given her a bridal night. And she herself had made it plain to Nicholas that there was to be none. He had acquiesced: had even arranged for Catherine to stay with her. And had engineered, too, all those joint announcements which made it clear to the world the basis on which his marriage stood. For her sake, she knew.

For the same reason, he would have to leave her room soon, to find the chamber he had arranged for himself in another wing. Returning from seeing to Catherine, she had given him a last cup of wine and saw, by the firelight, that his eyes were heavy. She wondered if his night, too, had been sleepless, or if he had passed it in dreamless, confident rest. He said suddenly, "I'm sorry. You must be tired as well."

He spoke as if they had never been in company except when vigorously and formally entertaining one another. As if she had never tended him, lying in feverish dreams on the pillows upstairs during his sickness. She said, "I don't think there is anything in the world I want to talk about. Yes, there is. The joust?"

"He won't take part," said Nicholas. "Take my word for it."

"After all that expense?" she said, her smile wider. "Two horses? A shield?"

He said, "Notice how generous I was being with your money. It gives him . . . it will help him with his friends."

"You mean," she said, "he can boast about how he is taking advantage of you?"

"Something like that. He deserves it, anyway." His eyes closed. He said, "Dear Christ, I must go," and opened them and got up.

He hesitated. Sitting, aching with weariness, she tried to will him to say nothing more. Not to offer some skilled, manufactured coda to the whole business, to which she would be expected to respond equally skilfully.

He said, "I think you will probably sleep. I'll stay in the yard or the office all morning. Send for me if you want me."

He gave her one of his lavish, sudden smiles. His eyes were still drowsy. She returned the smile and said, "Good-night, Nicholas," and watched him make his way to the door. He turned, his hand on the latch, and drew breath to say something, and then smiled instead.

She should have left it alone. Instead, she said, "What remark was that going to be?"

He stood, still smiling a little. "A favour I decided not to ask for."

She was pleasantly curious. The tone of his voice declared quite clearly that there was no need for her to be disturbed. She said, "Well, now you have changed your mind. What is it?"

He said, "I don't know what colour your hair is."

She felt her chin coming up. Her skin burned with the heat of the fire. The large gaze, dwelling sleepily on her, held every disarming quality: of affection, of mischief, of appeal. The scrubbed face at Mass, with the hair flattened down, and the glance full of merriment over some innocent conspiracy.

Marian de Charetty rose from her place by the fireside and, smiling, held the eyes of the child Claes with her own as she unpinned the round padded hat she had worn all that day.

There had been no time that morning to pin it underneath as she usually did. She lifted off the solid frame and shook the folded hair under it so that it unrolled and fell over her breast and her back and her shoulders. It was the colour of her sleeves: the deep brown of lampblack mixed with yellow earths, with the vermilion echoes of cinnabar. It was the first thing she had learned: how to dye cloth to flatter her hair. When she let it down at night, Cornelis had compared it to Cathay silk.

Now her second husband looked at it with his large, restful gaze, and said, "Yes. I thought I was right" with simplicity.

Remotely she realised that, of course, he had known the shade of her hair. It might be covered, but one day or another a hairline would show under the wiring. And hence he had been sure that there was no grey there, to shame her. It had been, wordlessly, the coda she had dreaded. But even though she might discern his reasoning, she couldn't fault him for the thought that had prompted it. She smiled and said, "Next time, it will be black. I change it every five days. Why else own a dye business?"

He grinned. "I think," he said, "that would be cause for annulment. Until tomorrow."

He closed the door and she sat down, her hair glowing about her.

Chapter 29

Had it not been for Easter falling midway between her astonishing alteration in status and the joust of the White Bear Society, matters might have been harder for Marian de Charetty. As it was, from the morning after her marriage, the owner of the Charetty company doggedly went about her usual affairs in warehouses and markets and offices where the streets rattled with the furious clacking of looms, the wheeze of pumps, the rumble of barrows and carts as the city pressed its business to a close in readiness for the demands of the Church, and the pleasures of the festival to follow.

From sheer curiosity, of course, people welcomed her; and those who were genuine friends did their best to make her feel she had chosen rightly, whatever they privately thought. Businessmen were apt, beginning a transaction, to make a cheerful if cursory remark about having to watch their step now she had that young man to advise her. Those who were friends of the Adorne family, or who respected them, were both polite and careful.

Only the children were neither. There were not many, but she knew, when she heard the giggling from behind a bridge wall, or under a flight of steps, or from a doorway, that it echoed an adult response: the conversation of a shocked mother or an astounded housemaid. Only once was she truly hurt; when three childish trebles set up a chant of *Mankebele! Mankebele!* . . . Limping Isabelle, the legendary usurer and procuress. She didn't look to see what family they came from, and she told no one about them.

As he had promised, Nicholas had spent the first morning after the marriage on the premises, and part of every day since. It was of the greatest importance, of course, that he should do so. Feeling in the yard had to settle: upset dignity be nursed back into health; a new régime created that would be acceptable, and that would continue when he was not there.

For that they both needed Gregorio, and it was on Gregorio that he lavished most of his time and tact. Of the lawyer's ability there was no doubt. But he had to show, too, that he could come to terms with her workpeople and understand them. Nicholas had aroused his curiosity, but it was a cynical interest, she could tell. Before taking him deeper into the operation of the business, his loyalty would have to be engaged. In two weeks, not counting Easter. With Gregorio, Nicholas proceeded with the restructuring of the business that he had already begun. Tenants were found for some of the new property. Workmen were set to repairing and altering some of the rest. He wanted still larger storerooms, more centrally accessible. Hence the dyeshop, under Henninc and Bellobras and Lippin, and with Marian de Charetty in control, stayed in its present sprawling premises on the canal bank, where the discharge and the odours offended less.

The living premises remained there, and her office. But the expensive house in Spangnaerts Street became the administrative centre of the business. There she had a cabinet too, large enough for her to use for clients or friends if she wished. The most commodious room was given over to the secretariat. In it, Nicholas and Gregorio each possessed tables, and two additional clerks were taken on, and a boy to run messages, as well as a housekeeper and a man for the heavy work, and to tend the small stable.

In all that, she knew he was right. Even when the business was smaller, it had been a constant struggle to maintain even the barest of records, and she had hardly helped matters by insisting that Julius spend half his time assisting Felix. Astorre's muster, the first for a year, had made matters worse. Contracts meant registers, and in duplicate at the very least. A man who fought for you must have his name recorded and the place where his home and kinsmen were, as well as his arms and armour and details of his horse down to its markings. The books for that were currently piled on shelves along with the ledgers for the dye business and the pawn business, and the duplicate books for Louvain, which would have to be checked and corrected. Nicholas had asked her, in one of the many brief, concentrated meetings which occurred in those days, if she would object to his sending for the broker Cristoffels, so that the future of Louvain could be discussed.

In all that, Gregorio too had some say. The longer-term plans Nicholas didn't confide in him, but took on his own shoulders entirely. Most of what he was doing Marian de Charetty thought she knew. He reported to her faithfully. But sometimes, as she saw the superscriptions on the letters he was sending to Geneva, to Milan, to Venice, to Florence, she found it hard to control her

Dorothy Dunnett

uneasiness. That particular venture was too big. He had reassured her. It was being done in his name, and if it failed only he and his other partners would suffer. But she was still concerned.

She could imagine, too, that all was not plain sailing. Where he went to do business without her, men often asked his authority, either because they didn't yet know his new standing, or to discomfit him. Once, a runner was sent to ask for her confirmation. She had been angry, but Nicholas had treated the whole business equably. He preferred that, he said, to the dealers who offered him smiles and false figures.

From the English Governor she heard that Nicholas had been seeing Colard Mansion, and had wondered if he was employing his friend for the letters he couldn't entrust to his scribes. It was only later, reading some sheets that he left her, that she realised that his own writing, once too swift for clarity, was changing to a hand equally fast but distinctly more legible.

He had found time, extraordinarily, to do other things as well. The archery society of St Sebastian, which was not an exclusive one, had admitted him as a member, and he spent an hour there every day, shooting at the mark and becoming known to his fellow members. He was also visiting the small founder who had made up some of Astorre's requirements of armour, and who had been a master at arms in his day. It was Felix who told her that Nicholas was apparently reviving his recent brief acquaintance with the military arts. To protect all the money he intended to make, Felix had suggested.

The truce of the marriage-day had not lasted. Now, Felix threw her, from time to time, all the scraps of gossip he could glean about Nicholas. Short of walking out of the room, which she sometimes did, she couldn't prevent him. So far, there was little she hadn't known. Blessedly, in any case, Felix was out most of the time, practising. He had acquired the rest of his jousting equipment, far more splendid and far more costly than was sensible, but she had not objected, since Nicholas hadn't. As the days passed and the time for the tournament neared, she tried not to think of it, even when at every meal Felix related, with glittering eyes, the names of the great ones who were to take part in it.

With glittering eyes and frightened defiance. If he had been vulnerable before her marriage, he was twice as vulnerable now, in his bravado. She ached for him, wondering how he was managing, torn between despising her and defending her. Once, he had come

back to the house with a bruised cheek, but had not explained it.
And the wife of one of her clients had offered her an admiring
account of how her dear son Felix had stood up for his mother the
other day, when one of those ill-bred girls from Damme had forgotten her manners. The pawnbroker's daughter, it had been. The
daughter of Oudenin the pawnbroker.

When at home, Felix spent his time with his sisters, or with
Henninc and his deputies. He ignored Gregorio, assuming (rightly,
she supposed) that he was in process of being won over to Nicholas. Nicholas himself he did not speak to, but he often watched him
for lengthy periods. When he did, there was a look in his eye that
reminded Marian oddly of Cornelis. A calculating look.

At Easter she didn't entertain: she had rarely done so, in any
case, since Cornelis died. Invitations did, however, come. One was
from the Adorne family to spend the day at the Hôtel Jerusalem.
Tilde and Catherine went with their mother and Nicholas. Felix
was otherwise engaged. They were treated quietly and kindly, and
she was grateful.

The house of Wolfaert van Borselen was another matter. For one
thing, he was married to a Scottish princess—one of those six royal
sisters who were meant to ally the king of Scots with half of Europe—with France and Savoy, Brittany and the Tyrol and Zeeland.

Marian de Charetty had met the princess and her husband, and
knew they kept state in Veere, where their residence was, and were
never less than formal in their tall gabled town house in Bruges,
where she and Nicholas had been bidden to supper.

When the day arrived, the demoiselle stood in her bedchamber,
her robes spread about her, and considered what lay before them.
She would expect to see their son Charles, who was eight. She
would probably meet Louis, seigneur de Gruuthuse, whose wife
was a van Borselen, and perhaps Guildolf, the Gruuthuse kinsman
who was so far unmarried. Florence van Borselen and his wife
would certainly be there, but not their daughter Katelina, now in
Brittany. She remembered the incident at Damme involving the
girl, which had ended in a beating for Nicholas.

Felix, Julius and Claes. The trouble they caused.

Her eyes were wet. She turned her mind resolutely to the problem of selection, which was not great. Her finest robe, her most
elaborate headgear. Concealing her own hair, as always. She had
no illusions about that. Nothing bridal; nothing juvenile; nothing
different, to cheat the avid observers. That, alone in the evening,

she unpinned and let her hair fall loose for her own pleasure, was none of their business.

She had, at his own request, inspected Nicholas' wardrobe. It was Felix, again, who had let fall, mockingly, that friend Nicholas was now patronising a tailor. Since what he wore had not changed, she could only assume that he had needed replenishments. Then she noticed that the doublets, the jackets, the hose, although still in the same subdued colours, were of better cut and respectable cloth, such as a manager of her household would wear. He had had made, in addition, one heavy robe, inexpensively trimmed. Seeing, as she had not, that an occasion like this might occur.

She was curious enough to look at the ledgers, but the accounts for none of these things had been entered. It meant very little. He could make a profit and spend it in a morning, and she would never know. But she felt, without knowing why, that he had paid for it in some other way. She had not commented, lifting the robe and approving it. It was correct for the occasion, as he would be.

The evening, as it turned out, was a grand pleasure, at the cost of some strain and a great deal of hard work. The house was full of wax lights and people, and above the noise of the people was the sound of trumpets. All the folk she expected were there, and many more. She spoke to the wife of Louis de Gruuthuse, who was quick-witted and friendly, and told her how intrigued her husband had been by young Nicholas and his interest in gunpowder.

She met Guildolf de Gruuthuse, whom she liked, and who, at fifteen, was in many ways older than Felix.

She met Katelina van Borselen's father, who complimented her on her appearance and said he was looking forward to hearing more of this energetic courier service young Nicholas had got under way. As she could see, Bruges was filling already with Scots come over for the Holy Blood Procession and the Fair, and he would be surprised if she didn't find some new clients there, who would like to send letters to Italy.

There were, she saw, quite a few Scots here as well, as was natural. Wylie. George Martin. The man they called Sandy Napier, to whom Nicholas was talking. Some of these, presumably, had been among Bishop Kennedy's passengers last year at Damme. She wondered if any of them remembered the matter of the apprentice Claes and the gun, and what they would make of it all. Napier's face, she saw, expressed nothing but animated interest.

At supper, she found herself next to Jean de Ghistelles, Grand-

Veneur of Flanders and married to Gruuthuse's sister. Nicholas, whom one did not trace nowadays by explosions of marvellous laughter, was sitting quite far away, beyond Count Franck and next to a very young, very plump girl whom she recognised, after thought, as Florence van Borselen's younger daughter. Gelis, who had so upset Tilde at the Carnival. Marian de Charetty smiled down the table. If Nicholas had been any less of an artist with children, she would have been sorry for him.

Her sympathy, or that of anyone else, would not have been wasted. From the moment he saw the stony face of the fat child surveying him from the next place at table, Nicholas knew that there was very little between himself and disaster. But of course he had known, from the moment the demoiselle accepted the invitation, that this was likely. He had protected himself by meeting Florence van Borselen and his wife on business beforehand, to try their reaction to his precipitous union. The wife, he thought, would have been scathing about it in private, but in his presence she followed her husband's lead, which was to treat it with disinterested courtesy.

Felix, of course, had long since proclaimed the tale of his supper in Ghent. It was even possible to tell, if following closely, that Nicholas was one of the company. But there was nothing in that to upset anyone. There was, however, plenty to upset everyone on other scores. Such as the fact that, on the night of the Carnival, he had been saved from near-death by the Borselen sisters. A fact which had not come to light for a number of reasons.

One of these, which Gelis might know, was that her sister Katelina had chosen to spend the early evening alone with de Ribérac. And that he had attempted, thus invited, to ravish her. The other, which Gelis certainly knew, was that he, Nicholas, and her sister had spent the later hours at her home alone together. Where he had not tried of intent do anything, but undoubtedly had realised all of Jordan de Ribérac's aspirations.

Cajolery wasn't going to work. Neither was charm. Marian de Charetty's new husband arranged his furred robe and addressed the fat child at his side in a voice which could have been overheard by nobody. He said, "Now be quiet and listen to me, or I'll tell everyone about your sister and the seigneur de Ribérac."

She said, "He didn't!" Her face was scarlet.

"I'll say he did," said Nicholas. "And let's get this over with.

One, the demoiselle de Charetty is not going to have a baby. Right?"

"But she will," said Gelis van Borselen.

"Two, it's none of your affair, but this happens to be a business arrangement, so she won't."

"She could," said Gelis.

"She won't," he said calmly.

"So you've got to get rid of Felix," she said. "At the joust next Sunday."

He had wondered if some cynical tongue might propagate that idea. He hadn't looked for it here, at the supper table. He said, "He'll be all right."

"You know he isn't good enough. You tested him specially. Then you bought him all that armour."

Nicholas said, "So I have to stop him being hurt. Or people will blame me."

"So you've disinherited him?" said the fat girl.

She was demoniac. He said, "Why not ask to see the marriage contract? He isn't disinherited. He and his mother still have all the profits of the business. If they both die tomorrow, I get nothing."

Her eyes were on the furred robe. "That's nice," she said.

"I have the receipt in my purse," Nicholas said. "Now stop poking into my affairs and remember that I can hurt your sister a lot more than you can hurt me."

"You have," said Gelis.

More food plates arrived and were settled before them. Skilled hands holding wine flasks reached over their shoulders. Nicholas said, "You've sent messages to her by pigeon, no doubt."

"I've written," said Gelis. "She won't have got it yet. She's sent you a letter. I've read it."

"Presumably she knew you would," he said. "Am I to read it or not?"

She had been sitting on it. A much-folded bunch of pages, now shell-shaped with the seal thoroughly burst, was retrieved with a jerk and handed over. He put it in his purse. He said, "Tell me something."

"What?" said the child.

"Do you consider ʲ   ᵐoiselle de Charetty has hurt your sister as well?"

The face, restored   ʲ norm, stared at him. "What's she

got to do with it? You're the one who did what you did," said Gelis van Borselen.

The situation became clear. "Ah," said Nicholas. "I thought you were expecting me to marry her."

"Marry her!" said Katelina's sister. She gave an unlovely laugh. "Ladies don't marry apprentices."

Nicholas said, "So you'll agree that if anyone is the sufferer in this situation, it's the demoiselle who did marry me."

Gelis glanced down the table. "She's a fool," she said.

"In that respect, perhaps, yes. In every other way, no. Do you plan to hurt her?"

She was shrewd. "You're safe," she said. "I can't do anything, can I, without harming Katelina's good name, or your silly mistress? But you didn't enjoy meeting me. You won't enjoy the next letter from Brittany either, if you get one. And you'll enjoy it still less when Felix gets killed at the joust, and you get the blame for it." He drew breath, but she interrupted him. Her eyes were gleaming. "Oh, I know you say he'll be all right," she said. "But I can tell you he won't. And I can tell you why, if you don't know already. The Scots names have just come in. The names of the Scottish contenders. Including the best jouster they've got. Simon of Kilmirren."

"Now let me think," Nicholas said. "I remember. Something about a dog."

"And a girl called Mabelie," said Gelis spitefully.

That night, in his room, Nicholas read the letter from Brittany.

Katelina, he noted, trusted her sister no more than he did. Even to an over-informed pair of eyes, it contained no message at all that was personal. The journey had been reasonable. She thought the appointment would not be unamusing. She filled in some snippets of court gossip, including the information, which he already knew, that the Duchess's son had acquired the King of France's mistress who, the court thought, would have passed on the pox by September.

September? He paused over the intrusion of the date, and then recalled that the Carnival had been on Shrove Tuesday so that, even to calculating small sisters, the reference had no hidden significance.

The main item of news, and patent purpose of the letter, made him laugh quite a lot, which he had not expected to do. He put it away and promised himself a visit, somehow, tomorrow to Lorenzo Strozzi. The news about Simon he didn't pass on to Felix's mother. She would hear soon enough. Oddly, it was Gregorio who brought it up when Nicholas joined him in the new building after a morning which had started at dawn.

With less than a week to his departure Nicholas had begun calling at last for his dispatches. On Jacques Doria, colleague of Adorne and coolly authoritative, who had given him a satchel for Genoa. On Angelo Tani and Tommaso, the one business-like and the other pointedly reserved, and both offended by his refusal to leave before Monday. On Arnolfini for letters for Lucca and Sforza, delivered with pallid amusement, but no comment. It was Arnolfini who had passed him the Dauphin's promised gold, for services about to be rendered. He had bought his clothes with it, and a man. Or he hoped so.

Now, in Spangnaerts Street, he walked through the new building to his large office, touching each busy clerk on the shoulder and greeting Gregorio at the other desk, as he dropped to a seat and pulled forward his papers. They worked until noon, when the bell sounded and the youths were given leave to go below and eat. Gregorio said, "I have to ask something."

Nicholas said, "Yes?" without lifting pen from paper.

Gregorio said, "About the joust on Sunday. Gossip says that our Felix is going to have a hard time. Some Scotsman who regards himself as a personal enemy."

"Simon of Kilmirren. Yes." Nicholas powdered what he had written, and looked up to meet a singularly hard black gaze. He said, "He's one of the people I have to warn you to watch while I'm away. He's more anxious to harm me than Felix, but he won't manage either if I can help it. I've promised Felix's mother that he won't enter the joust, and he won't."

Gregorio said dryly, "Then you'll have to kidnap him. He won't back out now."

"Oh, you never know," said Nicholas. "And now I've something to ask you. You weren't in your room all last night, or the night before?"

The black gaze became even harder. Gregorio sat back in his chair. "You pay me by the night hours as well?"

"Bruges," said Nicholas, "is the living heart of good Flemish gossip. If you install a lady in such a way, it usually means a permanent arrangement. If you have a permanent arrangement in one direction, it occurs to me that you might intend a permanent arrangement in another. With the company that employs you, for example."

He waited, letting the other man study him. Gregorio said, "You spy on me?"

Nicholas grinned. "I wouldn't need to. Tommaso's mistress lives in the next house to your friend's. Tommaso Portinari. You can tell when he leaves in the morning by the clash of his rings. I don't suppose I could meet her?"

It was early to broach such a thing, but he hadn't much time. He knew the lawyer was quick. He would dismiss, he hoped, the notion that in some way his mistress was being inspected. He would grasp, he hoped, the fact that his mistress was being invited to inspect Nicholas. About whom, no doubt, she had heard so much. And about whom, for certainty, she had profound reservations. Gregorio had raised his eyebrows. Gregorio was not smiling: he seldom did. But he was not frowning either. Gregorio said, "Now?"

"Why not?" said Nicholas.

After the first shock (she was washing her hair) the encounter went off amazingly well, and she cooked and served them both an excellent meal. Her name was Margot. She was distinguished. She was not unintelligent. She followed all the bantering conversation except for the three occasions when Nicholas mentioned a place, or a person, or an object concerning the Charetty business. On those three occasions, he was satisfied she was at a loss, but expected to be.

Leaving afterwards, he said, "I like her very much. As the business grows, you'll be able to house her better."

Gregorio was walking slowly. He said, "I'm not sure if I like what you did."

There was nothing much one could say. Nicholas continued to walk beside him.

Gregorio said, "I suppose there was no other way to prove it in time. Does it mean she would be under surveillance?"

"My God, who by?" said Nicholas. He grinned. "By Tommaso, perhaps: she's a prize. But no. I told you I might make you an offer, and I'm making it. It's concerned with a business of mine, not the Charetty one. That is, I take the risk but the Charetty company will share in the profits. The problem is, it has to operate in absolute secrecy. I have one associate, now in Italy, and I need a lawyer whose silence I can depend upon. If my enterprise fails, you'd still have your work with the demoiselle—unless, of course, it fails because of you. I don't think it would. But people have been known to break trust."

Gregorio didn't answer at once. Then he said, "No one can say they won't fall out with one master and take up with another. It happens. You may not like my ways when you get to know me better. I may not like your plans when I hear about them. But I will tell you this. I happen to find law more interesting than money. And a lawyer can't stay long in practise if he passes on secrets. I might leave you, but I won't betray what you are doing."

"Well, that's good," said Nicholas. "Come to my room when you get back tonight, and I'll tell you what you don't know, and you'll pack your boxes, most likely, and leave. Meanwhile I have to call in here and see Lorenzo Strozzi. It was a *very* good meal."

"You must come again," said the lawyer. He seemed to mean it.

Lorenzo Strozzi, who hadn't spoken to any member of the Charetty household since the painful episode outside the Poorter-slogie, tried to get the Ridder Straete gateman to say he was out, and then, angrily resigned, glared at Nicholas when he entered the office and took a seat without being asked. Equally without being asked, Nicholas told him why he had come.

By the third word, Lorenzo had ceased to interrupt. By the tenth, only horror remained in his expression. At the end he simply gazed at Nicholas and repeated, *"Shipwrecked!"*

"Off the coast of Brittany. So I am told by an informant. But rescued, and in good health. The only ostrich to be brought safely ashore. But the trouble is that it has been impounded until the claim for insurance has been settled, because of the counter-claims, you know, for wreckage and flotsam. A real difficulty. Very few people in Brittany know how to feed an ostrich."

"Its keeper?" said Lorenzo. "It must have a keeper. In any case, surely someone has appealed? It's for the Duke of Milan. An envoy. We should send an envoy."

Nicholas said, "But do we want the Duke to know of our difficulty? Remember, it was the House of Medici who undertook to get the Duke an ostrich, and it was you who said . . ." He broke off. "They paid you for the ostrich and you've spent it?"

Lorenzo Strozzi stared at him. "What could I spend it on here?" he said bitterly. "I sent it to Florence for my mother to put aside for the business. The business Filippo and I are waiting to start up in Italy. With our own money. Not by marrying an old woman."

"I don't know anyone who has," said Nicholas. "And if the lady were sensible, she certainly wouldn't hand over any money belonging to herself or her family to a new husband. Don't be an idiot. Do you want me to find out what's happening in Brittany, or will you do it? If you can't get another ship it may have to walk. Unless it's granted to someone local. He might sell it to you."

Lorenzo gazed at him. He said, "Do ostriches walk?"

"I don't think they fly," said Nicholas. "Although I suppose it might learn, given a week or two. It'll stop the English war if it flies over Calais. Ship will collide with ship."

Lorenzo said, "It may not be serious to you—"

"All right," said Nicholas. "Message to Brittany. Where is it, who has it, is it being fed and can it walk. They'll think we're discussing the Duke's latest bastard . . . Lorenzo, it's all right, don't take it so seriously. I'll find out for you, and I'll arrange it so the Medici don't worry you. What about Caterina and your mother? I'm leaving on Monday, if you want me to take letters. No charge. Pay me in ostrich eggs."

He wasn't sure if, in the end, he left Lorenzo looking less worried than when he found him, but he thought that he did.

Chapter 30

There were then four days left to Sunday. Nicholas told Gregorio about the alum mine, and the lawyer went very sallow and stayed that way for half an hour. At the end of that time the blood began coming back into his face and he started writing things down. After that, Nicholas noticed, Gregorio frowned every time he looked at him. Marian de Charetty, informed that he was now a fully-fledged member of both companies, asked him to spend some time in her office talking about it, and he emerged from that looking slightly calmer. He still frowned, however, whenever he came across Nicholas.

On the Thursday, Felix's mother searched out the final list of White Bear contestants and found Kilmirren's name on it. The further discovery that her household already knew this made her angry. Pointedly, she made no renewed or anguished appeal to Nicholas, on the few occasions he was there to appeal to. And after Sunday (whatever happened on Sunday), she was going to lose Nicholas anyway. When she wasn't thinking about Felix, she thought about that.

Nicholas had to go, she knew that. The remarkable fees he had received, the even greater fees he was promised, depended on the information, of all kinds, he was taking with him to Milan. He had to see the Medici about the money they had advanced for Tobias to buy handguns and for Thomas to recruit his fifty extra gunners. He had to collect the revised condotta, and arrange how the money for it was to be re-invested.

He had to discover, from messages Tobias and Thomas and Julius and Astorre should have left, where the company was positioned and what its needs were, and its prospects.

He had to glean, officially and unofficially, from all his new acquaintances, the information he would bring back with him along with new dispatches. Some of it in difficult codes, and of greatest importance. Some of it merely market prices, of use to their own business as well as others. And some of it, from the

Acciajuoli and the others, to do with the scheme she was frightened of.

He would take a good, strong bodyguard, although not the compact fighting-force which had gone with Astorre. And this time it was summer. He would travel quickly. But however quickly he travelled, he would be away for two months at least: perhaps longer. Leaving her alone to face the unfriendly Simon. And perhaps even Jordan de Ribérac. The prospect disturbed her. It struck her after a little thought that there was an alternative.

Had she not been so troubled, she might have gone about her plan differently. As it was, she waylaid Nicholas at dawn on Friday morning as he was running, fresh and cheerful, down the stairs, and said, "Sit down there."

They were alone. The rooms all about them were empty. He sat with promptitude on the step that she pointed to and looked attentive. She seated herself well below him and folded her hands in her lap. She said, "You trust Gregorio?"

He said, "Yes, I do."

"To run the business alone for two weeks? Could Gregorio do that?"

"No," he said.

"I thought—"

"No, you're not coming with me," said Nicholas. "Demoiselle."

She released a hiss of exasperation. *Always* the short cut. She said, in the tone she used to Henninc, "Not to Milan. I propose to come with you as far as my sister's husband at Dijon, and then to my brother-in-law Jaak and his dear wife in Geneva. Don't you think I ought to tell them whom I have married?"

"No, I don't," he said.

"My only relatives?" said Marian de Charetty. She watched him making up his mind how to handle this.

He said, "Your sister's dead, and Thibault must be nearly seventy and hasn't been in his senses for years. It would only distress you, and probably him. He's shown no interest in me since my unfortunate mother died."

She said, "He had a daughter by his second marriage. By my sister."

His face was quite composed. "Adelina. She was five when they sent me to Jaak's. She'll be married now."

Marian de Charetty said, "And you don't want to see her? Or

your mother's father, before he dies? Do you blame him so much for sending you to Jaak? He did something for you later, at least, when he found how they were treating you. He had you sent to Cornelis and me."

His face changed then, and he said, "Yes. I have to thank him for that. But not to see him. Would you forgive me, would you allow me that? If you feel very strongly that you must visit him, I could leave you there, with an escort to bring you safely home again."

"And Jaak in Geneva?" she said.

He suddenly smiled. "I don't know what you have in mind there. Not a sickbed visitation at least. Are you by any chance trying to dazzle them on my behalf?"

She smiled too. "Partly," she said. "Why not let me have my amusement? What could Jaak do to me or to you now?"

He said, "Insult you. And I couldn't stand by and let it happen."

"Then you're still afraid of him?" she said.

There was a pause. Then he said, "I can understand him now."

"But physically?"

"Oh, physically I'm afraid of him. Yes. Still."

"You would like to be able to fight him? To beat him? To over-power him?"

The large gaze was empty of everything but surprise. He said, "Jaak de Fleury is thirty years older than I am. At least. If I'm afraid of him, I'm afraid for all time. What can I do about it, physically, that would make any sense?"

She swallowed. She began to speak, and swallowed again. She said, "I asked you how you felt about him, but that doesn't mean I expected the pair of you to lock jaws over my marriage. I have a strong wish to visit him. I don't think it would harm you either. And if he insults me, you can protect me verbally. You know you can."

He was silent.

She said, "And Thibault is older, and sick. To see him is just an act of clemency, surely. He kept you and your mother. You were only turned out when he couldn't look after you."

She paused. She said, "I know you can probably argue me out of it. But I do want to go. To both places. I wouldn't suggest it if I thought it was wrong for you."

His elbows on his knees, he had sealed his lips with both hands and was staring past her, into the shadowy hall. She relied on him to perceive all the arguments she hadn't used, and to form his own impression of her motives. If it was a wrong one, so much the better. She saw him decide, eventually, as if he had spoken. *Yes. I can carry it.* But he didn't agree immediately. He said, "What will Felix think?"

"Nothing that will flatter you or me," said Marian de Charetty. "You have demanded a circuit of triumph and I have weakly agreed. Petty revenge on Jaak de Fleury. And, of course, a warning. Now Jaak can't touch little Claes, who has the widow de Charetty behind him."

He had long since identified that as her real reason. He said, "I wish Felix knew us as well as we seem to know him. Yes. Of course. If you want it so much, let us do it." After that, he spent an hour in the yard and then left unexpectedly to follow Gregorio to Spangnaerts Street. Midmorning, she knew, he had an appointment to confer with Jehan Metteneye.

Gossip had indicated to her the means Nicholas had probably used to draw Gregorio into their interests. How he had overcome Jehan Metteneye's natural prejudice she had no idea. His wife had not spoken to Nicholas or herself since the marriage. Nicholas and a pretty girl, caught in a cellar. She tried not to think of it. Men were men. Sometimes she had wished that Cornelis had been less staid. She supposed Jehan Metteneye had his secrets as well and, properly seasoned at the baths or the butts, had exchanged them for Nicholas' confidences. To get Jehan Metteneye's vital interest, a young man would have to use what means he could. What she didn't know wouldn't hurt her.

And meantime, there was Felix and the White Bear meeting to think of. Her son was asleep. She wouldn't help him by worrying. She must plan as if he were about to emerge unhurt, happy, successful, from Sunday's joust. As if she were really likely to be free to set out on Monday, to travel through Burgundy and Savoy for two weeks.

In which case, there were fearsome lists to be made, arrangements to be thought of. The business she usually handled would have to be supervised by Gregorio. Which was why, of course, Nicholas had gone to Spangnaerts Street so early. She must remember that he was human, and there must be limits to the burdens she laid on him. But so far, she could see none to his capacity.

When, later that morning, three riders rode into her courtyard, she was busy in her office with Henninc and paid no attention to the small commotion outside. It was five minutes later that Felix burst into the room, his cheekbones flushed. "Mother!"

Behind was someone very grandly dressed indeed, in velvet riding dress with a draped hat and scarf pinned with jewels. She knew him. Roland Pipe, of the household of Charles, Count of Charolais, the Duke of Burgundy's difficult son.

She rose, curtseying. Henninc melted back to the panelling. The Receiver-General bowed. Felix said, "Mother! The Count has asked . . . Der Roland brings an invitation to me from Monseigneur de Charolais. A personal invitation. To a grand hunt. A special hunt at Genappe on Sunday. I have to leave now. Right away."

"Such an honour!" said Marian de Charetty. She seated her guest, signed to Henninc for wine, and sat herself, flushed and smiling and breathless. The picture of a bourgeois mother overwhelmed by the favour shown to her bourgeois son.

The picture of a mother thanking God that her son need find no excuse, now, to face enemy lances at the White Bear jousting on Sunday. For when the heir to your liege lord commanded, no excuse was acceptable. Thanking God, she thought, and someone else.

When Nicholas came back much later, Felix had already gone. The yard was full of the news. Nicholas sat and let the dyeworkers tell him. They were disappointed, mostly. It was fine, of course, that the great lords should see, at last, the worth of the good Charetty family. But where now was the special pleasure and pride of standing there in the crowd at the jousting and saying, There! There's the young master!

Someone who used to share his cabbage with him said, "Why not take his place, Claes? There's the armour."

"Now, there's an idea," Nicholas said. "I'd win every bout. I'd be Forestier. I'll show you. Come on, why don't we all go in for it?"

When his mistress looked out of her window to find the reason for all the shrieking and laughter, they had rigged up a rope line for the barrier and were charging one another in pickaback pairs, with kettles for helms and stirring-sticks for their lances. They broke a rod, and Henninc's voice roared over the yard, berating them. Then one of the charging figures took off his helmet, and Henninc, faced with his mistress's husband, fell silent.

Nicholas jumped to the ground. "I'll pay for the stick. No. I was wrong to take them off their work. We were just glad about the honour to jonkheere Felix."

Grinning, they were clearing up quickly and scattering. They would work late, if need be, to make up for it. She saw their spirits were high and that Henninc, who knew his people, had the sense to recognise it. He smiled too, if stiffly, and said, "It's a pity about the jousting but an honour too, as you say, friend Nicholas."

Then Nicholas came quickly up the stairs and tapped on her door and opened it. "Reward?" he said. She wrinkled her nose. "I know," he said. "It's the smell of relief, this time. I thought my deep-laid plot had gone wrong."

"But you had contingency plans," she said.

"Oh, yes. Three dog handlers and Gregorio's mistress. That is, I hadn't asked Gregorio yet." He smiled lavishly at her. "Do I deserve some special, strong wine? Felix has gone, then?"

Her chin trembled while she was smiling at him. She stiffened it. She said, "Will they treat him well?"

He said, "Of course they will. It's the Dauphin he'll see, really. Probably for the last time. But they're well bred. They won't stint." He paused. "The drawback is that you'll be gone when he gets back. Did you tell him?"

"About the tour of triumph? Yes." Her back to him, she poured wine in generous measure.

"When he thinks about it, he'll be pleased. He'll be master until you come back. And he won't have to see me leave, either."

She gave him his wine and stood for a moment, holding her own. "I don't know. He's not very complicated. I think he feels a little like Tilde. They both like to see you here slaving for them."

He *was* relieved. The ridiculous dimples, missing for a day or two, had returned. He said, "If I don't know when to keep my place, then I might as well pay for it here, rather than tread primrose paths in the distance? He ought to see the primrose paths. Especially this time. He should have lent me his armour for Geneva. I've had an idea."

She went and sat down. "Now I can bear it. Yes?"

He said, "Why don't we leave on Sunday, during the joust? The roads would be clear. Unless you still want to be present?"

She shuddered. "No."

"Well?"

She said, "There would be no one to help. Everyone will be

watching. You won't even get a bodyguard to come away, I shouldn't wonder."

Even as he began persuasively to answer her, she knew that he had it planned already. Another contingency. He had cancelled the bodyguard. He had found another, and an escort for herself from the former master at arms who ran the metal foundry. Her personal servants were willing to come, and the cook from Spangnaerts Street: Gregorio would find a replacement. The packing could all be done tomorrow.

She watched him, and at the end said, "And when does Simon arrive?"

He grinned. He said, "Tomorrow. But I can't get us away quite so early. And the roads would be packed."

She said, "He'll still be here when I come back. And perhaps de Ribérac."

The benign smile was still there. "They may have threatened you, but I'm the object of their real esteem, remember. Anyway, they won't come together. They dislike each other. And even if they do, I've told Gregorio what to do about it. While I'm away, he'll move back to Julius' office. In the evenings, you let no one in."

"Really?" she said.

"Except by invitation, of course. There are primrose paths everywhere, or should be."

His large smile defied her to take him seriously. She wondered, with humour, who was supposed to travel the aforesaid paths with her. Gregorio had his mistress. Metteneye was suited. All her clients had wives already. That left Oudenin, she supposed. Or possibly even Henninc. She reproved herself. He had taken thought for her safety, returning. Concern for what she did, once returned, was too much to expect.

Side by side with an extremely handsome young woman and followed by a double line of attendants, Simon of Kilmirren rode through the clamorous highways of Bruges on Saturday. Behind him, page, squire, grooms carried his shield and his weapons and led his fine horses. Liveried riders conducted the sumpter mules and bore the gold-tasselled pennants which had surged and flapped all the way from Calais.

Simon himself wore his jousting-armour and carried his helm, the green plumes trailing over his arm. His face, with its fair skin and pure, finicking bones, expressed well-bred boredom. People turned to look. The gold of his uncovered hair and the silver dazzle of engraved plate beneath it were not what you saw every day, even among the great cavaliers. Especially among the great cavaliers, who often had gifted an eye or a set of good teeth to the god of mock battle.

When he had gone, the tumble of business resumed. Competitors, servants and horses, ladies and escorts, spectators from miles around Bruges—all that, every year, meant hard work, flourishing trade and, of course, money. Acclaim, too, for the influential city of Bruges, host to the flower of chivalry. Pride as well as self-interest inspired the carpenters hammering day and night to erect the lists and the tribunals in the market place, the painters completing the blazons and banners, the city officials hurrying everywhere with the officers of the White Bear itself, seeing to the dressing and clearing of the streets, the preparations for the feasts, the protocol for processions and ceremonies and presentations, the entertaining and ruling of the scattered company of élite challengers.

Tomorrow the jousters, each with his train, would wind in procession from the Abbey of Eckhout there, behind the house of Louis de Gruuthuse, to the lists in the market place. Tonight, Simon of Kilmirren was lodging, as usual, at the house of Jehan Metteneye, with his banner and hatchment and crest dressing the windowsill of his chamber, as was the custom.

He had got rid of Muriella and her ladies first, at the house of her hostess. He was quite pleased with her. She was rich: her brother was a Scotsman turned Englishman trading in the Staple at Calais. She was dark, in contrast to his fairness, and striking, in crimson and that extraordinary headdress like some sort of butterfly. Although none of that could compete, he was aware, with golden hair and green plumes and silver armour.

The brother, John Reid, had not been unattracted by the idea of a marriage contract, although it was clear that he would prefer to hand over the girl to a title. But, as Simon had happened to mention, his titled uncle in Scotland was old, and his titled father in France, although unfortunately set apart by affairs from his only son and heir, had a well-cultivated seigneurie. That, of course, was a double-edged weapon. His father's fortune had probably been signed away already to some parcel of monks or a mistress, to deny it to his unpopular son. And although his father could not, probably, alienate his heir from his land, the French king certainly could, if he heard what Simon had been up to in Calais. Nevertheless, John Reid had been interested. Simon had been allowed to bring Muriella, properly chaperoned, as his lady of honour on the strength of it.

The presence of the chaperone didn't disturb him at the moment. Tonight was the great formal feast at the Sign of the Moon in the market place. Already the Forestier, last year's champion, would be parading the town with his heralds, his pipes and his drummers, and calling on the grand ladies and well-born maidens whom the Brotherhood wished to come to the banquet.

Muriella would be his partner at the feast, which would finish prudently early, so that he could escort her prudently home. After that, he had a well-tried welcome already awaiting him somewhere else, as he always did before a contest. Something easy, expert and quick. That way, you didn't waste time before you began, or in trying to get away when you'd finished. He wished to do well tomorrow, after all, for his lady's sake.

Then when the lady had watched him win in the lists, and had danced with him, and had shared his cup at the banquets before returning each night to her cold bed, she might begin to think of that short journey home in his company. She would admire his chivalry. She would dream, as ladies do, of perhaps testing it. And in some inn on the way she would find the means, he felt sure, to relieve him in some sweet, thoughtful way, of the minor impediment of the chaperone.

And then, if he still felt like it, he would ask the brother for her hand, and the dowry he had been three-quarters promised.

Meanwhile in Metteneye's house, arranging for his servants, his horses, his gear, Simon was chastely polite to Jehan Metteneye's wife, as arch and as pendulous as he remembered. The girl Mabelie had, of course, gone. The woman didn't mention that, or the affair with the knave Claes. After he had left Bruges on the last occasion, travellers to Scotland had sought him out for quite a while, regaling him with the heartening news of his youthful friend's promising recovery. And later, of how he had been encouraged to depart from Bruges, and had gone off to soldier in Italy. The end, he supposed, of a trouble-maker.

It was John of Kinloch, the Scots chaplain, who disillusioned him. Master John, in stained black, met him on the stairs and, instead of stepping aside, took occasion to compliment him on the splendid armour he had heard so much about, and the exquisite doublet he had now assumed with, he saw, a left sleeve fit for a king. He then remarked, without stirring, how interested Simon must be in the latest news of young Nicholas.

If the fellow was trying to find common ground, he was failing. Simon said, "Forgive me. I can't think whom you mean." He glanced down the stairs. Metteneye was approaching. Rescue.

"Oh," said John of Kinloch. "You'd remember him as young Claes. Who would have thought, when his life was despaired of, that all this would happen?"

The quality of Kinloch's smile was explained. Simon smiled in return, at the chaplain and at Jehan Metteneye, now starting up the stairs. He said, his tone one of civil amusement, "I heard he was in Italy. Then he's made his fortune, has he? A commander?"

Both men laughed. Kinloch moved to one side and Metteneye took his place on the same step. Metteneye flicked Simon's chest with a finger. "Now we've got you," he said. "You'd never guess. No. Here in Bruges, the young rascal. He's married the widow Charetty, and he's managing the whole of her business!"

"Married!" said Simon. "Surely not."

"Oh, quite legally," said the chaplain. He was smiling more widely, God damn him. He'd got what he wanted. Simon stopped even attempting to disguise what he felt. The chaplain said, "Of course, they're related, but there's to be a dispensation. I wonder Bishop Coppini didn't mention it when you were both in Calais. He took the wedding Mass. With Anselm Adorne's chaplain."

Coppini, the bastard. No, of course: he would know nothing about Mabelie, or the gun, or the dog. Or the shears. But Anselm Adorne did, and had supported the marriage. Marriage! And who else now found Claes entertaining, of the men he would meet during the tournament? Metteneye had spoken with tolerant amusement. Metteneye, who had tried to thrash Claes with the best of them.

They were both still gazing at him. Simon said, "In view of all the trouble he's caused, you do surprise me. There must be twenty years between Claes and the poor woman. He's running all the business, you say?"

"Aye," said Metteneye. "And you wouldn't believe what he's done for it. Bought arms and artillery and formed a big company and sent it off to the Naples wars. Started a private courier service between Flanders and the Italian states. Expanded the dyeing and pawnbroking business. Bought property and added new management . . ."

"All with the widow's money? I didn't know she was worth as much," said Simon.

"Oh, she had a fair bit," said Metteneye. "But most of it's being done on loans and promises. That's the beauty of getting old Astorre's company and the courier service started early. The Medici are backing him, and the others he's contracted to. It's in their interests to make him loans, you see."

The chaplain stood, grinning. Other people were coming into the passage below. Simon said, "It seems he must have entranced the poor lady. I hope she doesn't wake up one morning and find her husband and her business and her money all gone together."

Jehan Metteneye nodded. "That's what my Griete says," he said. "And maybe there's truth in it. But they've done wonders to that place of theirs. You should walk past it before they go off tomorrow."

Simon said, "Go *off*? You mean the bridegroom is abandoning Bruges before the jousting! I thought to find him in cloth of gold at the best window. Or even breaking a lance for his elderly wife. They seem to have admitted her son to the lists, so there should be no trouble about a landless by-blow."

It had not been a very wise pronouncement. The Metteneye, like the Charetty, were of bourgeois stock, and landless, however long their line. Metteneye said, "I've nothing against the jousting. The Metteneyes have always taken part, and young Pieter will be there tomorrow. But sometimes affairs have got to come first. The young man is taking his wife, I understand, to call on the Fleury hôtels in Dijon and Geneva. Kinsfolk, and no doubt important clients. And as for young Felix—"

The chaplain, smiling, nodded and pushed past. Metteneye, his face slightly flushed, continued to impart information.

"Young Felix did better, some might say, than take part in a joust. He had a personal invitation to hunt with the Comte de Charolais. Delivered by the Count's Receiver. Unfortunately for the same Sunday, so what could he do? But I dare say," said Jehan Metteneye, "that you'll find someone worthy to break a lance against come tomorrow. Now we're blocking your way, and you'll be in a hurry."

He was in a moderate hurry, but he still took time to walk, as recommended, past the large, well-maintained and orderly premises of the Charetty behind its long wall. He made a few calls. And then he went, thoughtfully, to call on the dark and stately Muriella.

His evening passed agreeably. The banquet was lavish, and his immediate company suited him. He entertained it with ease, and continued his bantering courtship of the young lady his partner, whose jewels certainly did nothing to reduce his standing with the nobles of Bruges. He had brought Muriella a rose, from someone who stored such things for him, and she had allowed him to caress her fingers when he kissed them. Then he avoided any growing complacency by paying particular attention to the lady who partnered his neighbour. She responded warmly.

As he had hoped, the banquet was not a long one. He escorted his lady home, well-attended, and took leave of her with gentle courtesy. She turned as she entered her lodging, the rose crushed in her fingers. He was, of course, still in the roadway. He bowed. That done, he dismissed his attendants and walked through the less busy streets in the anonymity of his hooded cloak. Idle, his thoughts turned to the white skin and dark hair of the Reid girl, and the explicit comforts that the rest of her might have to offer. He reached Betkine's house hot with an awkward energy which, put to use, gave a few moments of extreme pleasure, but refused repeatedly to disperse.

He couldn't stay all night. He stayed twice as long as he meant to, and left well after dark. By then, the lamplit hammering and the voices of straining workers had come to an end. The market place was brightly lit, and you could trace, by the occasional murmurs, the places where the town had posted its guards to watch over the confections of wood and lath and canvas until the jousting day dawned. There were other noises. The snuffling of the ubiquitous pigs. The squeal of cats. The muted wailing, behind a lit window, of a demanding infant. A batch of snores, from between open shutters. The lap of canal water. The shifting, in wind, of some litter. The hollow sound of lonely footsteps, crossing a bridge. From several places, the subdued barking of dogs.

He had lost a fine dog here, once. And a pretty, plump girl.

The wind had risen. It brought an odd noise which, standing still in the market place, Simon considered. You would think that tomorrow's joust was being rehearsed at the edge of the city. A replica, in miniature, of the screams, the roar of the crowd, faint as the sea in the breath of a mollusc.

The wind brought it again. He listened intently, every sense fine-tuned to magnify the one sense of hearing. The blow of the bell overhead, when it came, struck him deaf for the moment, and nearly out of his senses.

Then it came again, a violent boom, shaking the bell-tower. And again. And again.

Someone shouted. A light bloomed in a window, and another. A door banged. The bell tolled and tolled. And over it now, a magnified voice proclaiming what appeared to be an injunction of the Almighty from the top of the bell-tower. A man, gabbling through the great trumpet. The great bell for fire. And the speaking trumpet telling the place: the dyeworks and house of the Charetty family.

Of course, at one time every building was timber and thatch, and a fire could reduce a town in an hour. Now brick and stone and tiles and slate might resist, but stairs and penthouses were of timber, and inside beams and panelling.

The city had proper regard for its responsibilities. In every quarter you would find a deposit of buckets and brooms. On the call of the speaking trumpet, men knew what to do. For Bruges was a city which made its living from cloth; which sat day and night upon the canvas bales wedged in its cellars, with all the other stuffs a merchant needed to store.

A pawnbroker's stockrooms would be full of cloth, in the way of pawned clothes. And a dyeshop of course would have more than bolts of cloth and bundles of yarn. It would have the dyes themselves. The kegs of yellow crocus. The sacks of dried gall-nuts for fine, costly blacks, and the sacks of brazil wood blocks for crimson. The parcels of herbs: bunches of weld hanging from rafters. The trays of powdered woad and caking granules. The bladders of buckthorn and sap green and mulberry. The barrels of lakes and gums and resins. The sheds full of ashes, and empty wine-casks for scraping and burning. And scattered through the yards, the wooden vats and tools and stretching-frames; the teasel bats piled high for napping. And the lines of strung skeins and stretched coloured cloths joining house to dyeshop to warehouse in one endless pattern, like some magical puzzle in wool.

Simon of Kilmirren turned and made his way to where, now, the distant noise was more distinct, despite the sharp sounds increasing all about him. And where, now, you could see by a colouring in the sky that there was indeed a fire, and a growing one.

People began to run past him, half-dressed, with racketing buckets. He stood for a moment and then moved in their wake, without hurrying. Whatever was going to happen would have happened before he could get there.

Which was true, of course. When he got there the fire had just gained control of the house and was advancing through the yard. The street, as he turned into it, was a mass of moving, shouting, half-naked people.

The gateway to the yard and the yard beyond were thronged with jostling men. Horses were being led out. Buckets flashed. Silver arches and cascades of water crossed the air and dissolved in white, fizzing steam. As the line of fire advanced, the bucket-line and the beaters began to fall back. Blazing stuff from the house began to spring through the air, alighting on sacks and boxes dragged into the yard. Pushing farther in, Simon passed a middle-aged man in a nightcap, struggling out with a sack of insect-dye, his great naked belly blotched scarlet. Simon said to someone, "What about the folk in the house?"

The man he spoke to was collecting ledgers, tumbled over the ground as they must have fallen from an upstairs window. He said, "The dogs wakened us. I think we got everyone out." He wore a black doublet, open over his small-clothes. His scoop-nosed face was black, too, and hollow with effort.

Simon said, "Look. I'll see to that. Go and see what else you can save."

He waited until the man had turned away, and then tossed the ledgers one by one, carefully, into the heart of the fire. After that, the heat drove everyone back and he was content to stand in the road with the rest and watch the Charetty business burn, while the shouting and thumping moved to either side, where the nearest houses were being soaked and emptied.

Around him, the crowd had separated into small groups, silent except for muffled crying, where women clung, being comforted. In one such group he saw the man he had just spoken to, standing close to a small, comely woman with beautiful hair. Two attractive young girls, their faces swollen, were clasped to her sides. He noticed them first because of the empty space left, as if by deference, all around them. Then he realised who, of course, they must be.

The beauty of the fire was now at its height. The fusion of strange and precious substances created a red and yellow pyre of extraordinary brilliance, shot through with salt greens and acid yellows and an unsettling violet. Now and then, above the crackling roar, a report or a hiss would herald a ribbon of silver or a plume of gamboge or an arrowhead of crimson, spitting sparks. The yard, pooled with water, reflected it.

Then the wind turned, and the black pall of the cloth smoke found its way, with the stench, to the roadway. As if awakened, the crowd started to move. The house, half ash, half fire, offered no threat now, with the altered wind. The nearby houses were safe, and the swarming figures began to leave them one by one. The woman who must be Marian de Charetty stood still, looking towards them. Simon saw the man in the black doublet speak to her gently and then, moving away, begin to look about him. Soon he was surrounded. He would have shelter to find, of course, for all the Widow's people.

But of course, she was a widow no longer; and it was perfectly plain what she was waiting for. Something more important than the mere distress of her employees and their losses. And, sure enough, a figure separated from the last group of soot-blackened men coming back from their labours, and trod with strong, bare feet towards the woman and her two daughters. This immortal young bastard; this Nicholas.

Whatever expression he wore, a gum of soot and sweat concealed it. There was burned skin as well as dirt on his body where the untied shirt didn't cover it. Then Simon saw the flash of his teeth and the taller of the two young girls left her mother's shoulder and ran towards him suddenly. Nicholas put his arm round her tightly and kissed her forehead. Then holding her at his side, he walked forward and, one-handed, drew the woman and the younger child into the same wordless embrace. The mother's long, ruffled hair blew about them.

What he said after that could not be heard, but the woman's eyes as she listened spoke for her. Indeed, no one watching could doubt precisely how she had been induced to marry. Then her juvenile husband, breaking carefully away, called to the man in black, who turned and replied, and then looked about him, and then saw Simon, and pointed.

In his black cloak and satin feasting-clothes, slightly ruffled by Betkine, Simon waited while Nicholas walked over and stood before him. Below the dirt, the youth's face was colourless.

Simon said, "With the world full of fat little businesses, why marry one so ill-smelling when heated? I hear you planned to scurry to safety tomorrow. But see, we've met none the less."

They might call him Nicholas now, but the boy who took all the beatings still stood before him. He said, "Gregorio tells me that he left all our ledgers in your care."

"Gregorio?" said Simon. He looked about.

"The lawyer in black. He did not, of course, know who you were," said the youth.

Simon located the man in black and smiled at him. The man began to come over.

"Oh, another gallant employee drenched in urine. Tell him not to come," Simon said. "If, of course, that's the man whom you mean. I've never seen him before, or your poor ledgers. Are you sure, my dear Nicholas, that your lawyer didn't find it convenient to throw them back into the fire? It's been known."

The man Gregorio had arrived. He turned to the youth who, God save him, he must be forced to regard as his employer. He said, "What did he do with them?"

"Flung them back in the fire, I imagine," said Nicholas. "This is a gentleman called Simon of Kilmirren. It allows me to repeat what I said the other day. If he attempts to enter any building of ours, or interfere with any employee of ours, or speak to the demoiselle against her wishes, you are to call Meester Metteneye and Meester Adorne immediately."

Simon looked at the fellow's clown's eyes, large and white as blisters in the blackened face. He said, "There must, surely, be some insult that would force you into a manly attitude. But, by God, I am at a loss to think what it could be. In a somewhat varied life, I have never met, Meester Gregorio, a servant quite so craven as the one who calls himself your master."

He smiled and moved off, and no riposte followed him. He did not look round to see if the youth was gazing after him.

After a moment Gregorio said, "I take it you have your reasons."

Nicholas turned. He said, "I don't know whether I have or not. There is more to think of than a squabble."

"The ledgers . . ." said Gregorio.

"They're not irreplaceable. And if you're going to ask whether he started the fire, I don't know."

"But you *are* going to try and find out?"

"No. You are," said Nicholas. "You'll have a lot of help. The city takes these things seriously. But I don't expect anything will be found."

"And the loans," said Gregorio. "The security for all those loans, and the income you needed to repay them . . ."

"Oh, yes," said Nicholas. "It couldn't have come at a worse time. Whoever started it counted on that. They probably counted as well on half of us burning to death. But no one did. And that, really, is all that matters."

The demoiselle had come up, with the girls. She said, "That wasn't . . ."

"Come to say how sorry he was. Not exactly. We'll talk about all that later. Now, let's see what has to be done."

Nicholas left for Geneva on Tuesday, only two days later than he had originally intended. With him went the hired escort he had already arranged, with the mules and his own horses rescued from the stables, with their harness. Also salvaged from the stables were his saddlebags ready packed for the journey, and (against strong advice) a single cart stacked with bales of cloth for Jaak de Fleury.

He left behind the bags and boxes which Marian de Charetty had prepared for the same journey, and which now represented all the clothes and trinkets she had. There was no question now of her expedition. With Gregorio, she had assumed at first that his also was cancelled. Through that, the longest night of her life, there was no chance to think of it. With ready hospitality, folk took in her homeless people. One of the burgomasters came, in his nightcap, bringing the town doctors to see to their burns. A guard was set round the flaring, smouldering building to protect anything that might be worth rescuing once the ashes cooled. Winrik the money-changer took his friends and stood by that part of the house where, somewhere in the ruins, was a heap of melted silver from her coffer of groats. Tomorrow the Mint would send its officials, and she would perhaps get the return of some of its worth. The rest, promissory notes and pledges, had all gone. And all the stock of the dyeshop, save for a sack or two of the most valuable dyes, which Henninc had dragged out himself.

Then, at dawn, she and Nicholas and Gregorio had gathered blackened and exhausted in the unpaid-for, miraculous refuge of Spangnaerts Street, sitting about a scrubbed table with soup in their hands, and talked. It was not very sensible but, too tired to sleep, Marian de Charetty had earned the right to exorcise her worst fears by attempting to plan, while she had men willing to listen and help her.

Gregorio, kept awake by the persistent oddity of the relationship, watched Nicholas making up the demoiselle's mind for her. The May Fair was less than two weeks away, but something could be contrived. The Louvain business would supply them with some stock to sell. The Guild would help them with credit for purchases, and very likely with some sort of shared premises. Spangnaerts Street and the other property Nicholas had bought were no use for dyeing. But the first would now become their home and office, and the other buildings, where not already let, could house some of their workers. The wine tavern perhaps could take some. The rest could go to Louvain.

Louvain, instead of being reduced, would be kept meantime, under Cristoffels. In Bruges, the large sprawling yard with its numerous lines of business was not worth replacing. They should look for quality work now, in dyeing, dealing and broking. Dyeing better than Florence's. Valuable pledges requiring secure but not extensive storage. Opportunities for loans at high, well-concealed interest.

It was, Gregorio knew, the view Nicholas favoured. He had gathered as much long before the fire. Gregorio said, "You're talking of money-dealing linked with luxury trade. I've nothing against it. But where is all the money to come from to set it up now? You've numbers of people to support. You're in debt for these buildings and the others. Customers' cloth has been burned: people will expect refunds for that, and for your own cloth delivered on credit. Your confiscated pledges have gone, leaving every loan as a loss; and those who want their goods back will have claims on you. You've bought weapons on credit. The costs still to come from the mercenary company may be more than its earnings. If your commander is captured, or your soldiers badly defeated, you may have heavy bills for ransom or compensation to pay. You may find yourself without the means to replace men and armour and horses and fulfil the rest of your contract, or certainly to win another. You're now exposed to that risk, too, without a business to cushion it."

Gregorio paused, and dropped his eyes from the drawn, set face of the Widow. At some time in the night she had twisted up the rather attractive brown hair, and had pinned a riding-cloak over her bedgown. He had wondered whether to allow her to retire, comforted by a young man's fantasies, but he had seen that, in the long run, it would be kinder to face the reality. He said, "Demoiselle, I'm sorry to say it. But all you can really afford is to dismiss your workpeople, including me, and retire to Louvain, having resold all the new property and repaid some of your creditors. And, of course, Nicholas cannot now contemplate his alum project."

He looked up, genuinely regretful, as he finished. The demoiselle's blue eyes were fixed on him. Then she turned them to Nicholas.

Nicholas said, "Nicholas is not only contemplating his alum project: he is leaving on Tuesday to complete it. That one scheme alone will restore us. You would think a ship had never gone down, or there had never been a flood or a famine. This is a disaster to us, but not to the rest of the community. They'll uphold us. They'll extend our credit. And if they don't do it from brotherhood, they'll do it from self-interest. I'll see to that. You forget the famous courier contracts. We may not be able to deal in very much cloth, but we can deal in information."

He had forgotten those. Gregorio said, "The dispatches?"

"Here, in Spangnaerts Street," said Nicholas. "I would be wearing rather a different face if they weren't."

"Tuesday?" said the demoiselle.

Nicholas turned to her. "The dye business was always under your management. You know the Guild, you know the problems better than anyone. We have tomorrow and Monday to plan it all, you and Gregorio and Henninc and myself. Cristoffels is on his way. And in a few days you'll have Felix back." He paused. He said, "It really is best for everyone if I go now. Not to Dijon of course. But I'll take the cloth to Geneva, and go straight to Milan. I shall be back as soon as I can, depend on it."

The demoiselle said sharply, "Geneva!"

Nicholas said, "The cloth was ordered. The money will be useful."

Gregorio, his eyes drooping, sat up firmly. He said, "If it's Thibault and Jaak de Fleury, they haven't paid for the last delivery. We'd be better, surely, keeping the cloth for the Fair."

"Perhaps you're right," Nicholas said. He was looking at the demoiselle and reading, it seemed, something Gregorio had missed in her face. Nicholas spoke to her. "You'd forgotten Felix? We were lucky that he wasn't here, committing acts of foolhardy bravery. He'll tell you, when he comes back, just how badly we've handled everything."

The demoiselle smiled, and soon, rising, made her way slowly to where a pallet had been made up in her small parlour.

When the door had closed, Gregorio turned on his companion. He said, "She owes you a lot. So does the business. But listen to my advice. Intelligence is not enough to steer a way through this mess. It needs experience, and it needs caution. These schemes were always risky of their nature. You still want to pursue them. You've learned fast. You've gained confidence even faster. But you still haven't the experience."

Nicholas looked at him. He produced, surprising Gregorio, one of his larger, more encompassing smiles. It ended in a jaw-cracking yawn. "Goro friend," Nicholas said. "Do you think I don't know all that? But if all you've said is right, and it is, we need a great deal of money from somewhere, quickly. And whether I've the experience or not, I'm going to get it."

Chapter 31

Stolidly unaware that the Charetty business lay smoking behind him and that, even worse, the Charetty widow was no longer a widow, Thomas her under-captain proceeded south to do battle, accompanied by four squadrons of lances and fifty men willing if not yet fully able to use the handguns wished on him by that young terror Claes.

With him also went the two fellows, Godscalc and Abrami, also chosen by Claes. Thomas found he was glad of them. Abrami, a Hungarian crossbowman trained in Germany, knew more than he did about handguns. And Godscalc was not only a clerk but quite a bit of an apothecary. When Thomas's horsefly lumps went rotten, as they often did, Godscalc was a wonder with pastes and powders. Thomas quite enjoyed the journey south, in spite of the rabble of horse-boys and camp servants and the rest that always had to come along for a long campaign.

That was the bad side of it. The good side was the women. The Widow always left that bit of it to Astorre and him, and didn't often query the bills either. After all, you'd never expect a fighting man to forage for food, or grind his own corn, or wash his own linen. That was women's work. And when a man had stopped fighting, he wanted more out of leisure than a game of dice and a drink.

There would, of course, be no shortage of women in Naples. An army waiting to fight attracted them like those God-damned horse-flies, and they bit you as bad—or if they didn't, the fights over them did. So it made sense to bring along a few good girls of your own. There were even one or two wives in the carts, one of them giving suck. Hers was the only infant he'd seen, but sometimes others turned up. That was up to the father. A man only got one lot of pay. It was up to him if he wanted to feed more than one mouth with it.

Thomas, and his cavalcade, crossed the Alps without incident.

In Milan, he picked up the handguns. He also received a surprise, but one that didn't distress him unduly.

He reached Naples at the end of April, after a fair amount of tactical dodging, and found the city nearly invisible behind sheets of clammy rain. He had sent a runner ahead to warn Astorre he was coming, and hoped there were still some reasonable billets left with dry floors and no more rats in the thatch than a man might expect to deal with.

The castle was big enough to hold all the commanders and captains as well as this bastard Aragonese king called Ferrante. But lodging the men was another matter. Some towns put you outside, between the walls and the outer defences and built wooden huts for you. Sometimes you had to use your own tents. Sometimes you were shoved in with any family they could force to take you.

He was glad to see Julius, the Widow's notary, waiting at the gates when he rode up, with a well-dressed man who turned out to be the Neapolitan commissary. Thomas watched with some satisfaction as the man rode briefly along the neat file of troops and carts and baggage and, returning, nodded. Then Thomas was given a clerk and a man at arms and, with Julius, started the work of getting everyone settled.

During all that, you couldn't chat. Astorre, his captain, was off on a raid. That he learned. Then the notary asked him how the journey had gone, and if things were all right in Bruges, and Thomas had said they were, and was captain Astorre still the same old bastard. To which Julius, smiling briefly, had said yes, he would recognise him all right.

Glancing at him on and off, Thomas saw quite a change in Julius. A well-set-up man for a clerk, he'd always been, with the sort of thick bony face you'd expect in a professional fighter. Astorre had said more than once that he wouldn't be surprised if the Widow didn't take him to her bed one of these days, and then they'd all be under Meester Julius. But if that was so, she'd made no fuss about sending him off to Italy, and he'd made no fuss about going. And if there was a woman in Bruges who'd got any nearer to Meester Julius than the inkpot on his desk, he'd yet to hear of her.

So what had changed now? He'd lost that glint of devilment, that's what. The spark that got him into all those scrapes with Claes and young Felix. Perhaps he was missing them. Or perhaps he was jealous of Claes, in his decent blue courier's clothes, and bankers giving him the nod instead of old Henninc clipping him over the ear. Or he could have got himself on the wrong side of

Astorre, which wasn't hard, especially if you weren't a soldier. Or
perhaps he was just tired of Naples and rain. You would get tired
of Naples and rain, if you weren't a man who liked women.
Thomas, who had run through all the girls in the carts twice over
on the trip from Bruges to Naples, was sorry for Julius.

So was Julius. He was tired of Naples, tired of rain, and especially wearied of the ferocious company, for three months, of Syrus
de Astariis, showing him how to keep his senior men on their toes
while waiting for the rest of the company to arrive.

Like the rest of the King's motley army, the nuclear group of
Astorre's bowmen and cavalry had spent most of the winter inside
Naples, apart from the occasional sortie to dog the very few movements of the enemy, who were led by Duke John of Calabria and
the Orsini fellow, the Prince of Taranto.

When they were inside the walls, they took their share in the
various violent inter-company engagements, not to mention outright brawling, that kept them in training. From time to time they
were counted by the powerful gentlemen who controlled the various armies fighting for King Ferrante. None of the byplay bothered
Astorre, who simply got on with controlling his own little group, a
matter in which he was extremely competent. But through the
weeks Julius found himself longing for the arrival of Tobias, who
was supposed to come south when Brother Gilles was cured, and
who had not so far come south at all. In three months.

Julius realised he missed Tobias. He missed Tobias because he
was the only civilised person with whom he could discuss the
Charetty family. The Widow and Felix. And the terrible, much-
beaten Claes who ought to be here, keeping him company, and
ready to listen to him. And, somehow, to improve himself. Late at
night therefore, in the small captains' room at the castle, Julius
thumped down at last with Thomas and the two new men, Godscalc and Abrami, and said, "Well. Now tell me all the news."

And Thomas had said, "Well, I thought you'd be wondering.
Three hundred florins a month over what's been agreed. Now what
do you say to that?" Julius stared at Thomas. "For the handgun
men," Thomas said. He frowned. "What did you think it was going to be? Nine hundred florins, the captain was promised in the
condotta. Now we've added fifty trained men. I got the promise of
the Duke's secretary. Three hundred florins extra. Wait till the
captain hears."

Carefully, Julius trained his mind in the direction of Thomas. He said, "Astorre will be delighted. And so will the Widow. Thomas, that's good news. You negotiated it all with Meester Tobias?"

Thomas was in an expansive mood, and in any case scorned to pass as someone who bothered with reading. He said, "With the help of Meester Godscalc. Meester Tobias wasn't there."

Julius gazed at him. "He isn't still in Piacenza? Or Florence? Is Brother Gilles still in Milan, Thomas?"

Thomas grinned. "You should hear the tales of Brother Gilles. But no, he's cured and sent on to Florence, so they say. And Meester Tobias did go to Piacenza, because he got us the hand-guns. But he took his time. He didn't come back to Milan till the end of February, we were told." He paused.

"Well?" said Julius sharply.

Thomas grinned again. "Well, he left again. For the Abruzzi."

Julius stared at him. In his mind's eye he saw the west coast of Italy, from Rome all the way south to where he was now, in the castle of Naples, preparing to fight for King Ferrante. And in his mind's eye he saw the opposite, eastern coast of Italy, and the corresponding stretch of coastal land called the Abruzzi. A stretch of land of great interest, since towards it, rumour said, was marching the army of Jacopo Piccinino, now paid by Duke John of Calabria, and intent on joining his force to Duke John's in preparation for an all-out assault against Naples.

Julius said, "Why would Tobias go to the Abruzzi?"

Thomas's grin appeared to be fixed. He said, "Oh, there's no secret about that. He's gone to join captain Lionetto. He's gone back to Lionetto, the fellow he was with before he switched to captain Astorre. Wait till captain Astorre hears. There'll be no holding him. They'll have to tie him with chains, or he'll be off to fight Count Piccinino and captain Lionetto and Meester Tobias single-handed."

All that night Julius, sleepless, thought about it. It should have come as no surprise. Ever since Bologna, he'd got used to being let down. He knew every man looked after himself, and you should expect nothing more. He hadn't known Tobias well. He'd found him short tempered and impatient and often intolerant, but reasonably fair in his dealings and accurate in his judgments. He had come to rely on his company more than he realised. He should have known that money would talk, in the end.

When Astorre came back with his small fighting group, it turned out that he already knew about Tobias. After a few casual obscenities, he dismissed the matter. The loss of the horse-master would have worried him more. Anyway, now they had this fellow Godscalc and he was an apothecary, wasn't he? Used to salves and wounds? One medical man was the same as another.

It was, if you thought about it, the way a man like Astorre would react. But to Julius' eye, accustomed to interpret the tilt of the beard and the glint of the sewn eye, there seemed to be something else. He waited until he got him alone and said, "What's troubling you then? A real attack on the horizon? A proper battle?"

"Oh, I shouldn't think so," said Astorre. "Duke John's got a big force out there, and a lot of strongholds with barons in them who don't like Ferrante. We're not strong enough to break out and wipe them up yet."

"Can we afford to wait?" Julius said. "There's Piccinino marching down the east coast. And they say the King of France has troops massed in Lyons, waiting to cross and help his cousin Duke John."

"Maybe he has," said Astorre. "And maybe he hasn't. A man would say he has his hands full with England and Burgundy just now, without being free to throw armed men in the direction of Italy. And as for Count Piccinino—he's got to get to the south of Abruzzi, and then cross Italy to get to his friends here. He'll find that harder than he thinks, especially if the Milanese army comes chasing south after him. No. If it's battle you're waiting for, you'll have to wait a while yet."

Julius said, "You've had some other news then?"

"Oh yes," said Astorre. "News I've had. Thomas, come and sit down. Meester Julius here wants my news, and he ought to have it. You too. Then you can decide whether or not you're going to join Lionetto as well as that fellow Tobias. Now I know why he did it. By God, now I know."

Thomas was gazing at Astorre. Julius, every chamber of his brain empty, gazed at him also. Astorre said, "Claes."

Thomas said, "Claes?"

Julius said, very slowly, "Claes has turned spy?"

"Spy!" said Astorre. Heads swivelled. He replaced the roar with a volley. "Maybe he has. I'll believe anything of the little brute now. Anything. Thomas, how do you fancy working for Claes? Toadying for drink-money? Thanking him for a new pair of boots?"

Thomas began to turn a puzzled red. Julius also flushed, think-ing furiously. Claes, the obedient courier; the most beaten, most cheerful servant in Bruges. Claes, who was clever with numbers, and who had perhaps taken his good advice at last. Julius said, "Has he begun to help with the business? Has the demoiselle brought him into the office?"

"Into the *office*?" yelled Astorre. "Holy Mother Mary, the mad-woman's *married him*!"

Julius began to laugh. He laughed all through Thomas's worried questions and Astorre's consequent fiery exposition which cata-logued every disaster awaiting them, from the insult to their dig-nity to the coming bankruptcy of the business which would turn them all into beggars unless they could face taking orders from a cocky young stud who had one skill, by God, which everyone knew about, by God, and which he had used, by God, to get where decent men couldn't.

Afterwards, Julius remembered recovering enough to point out that Tobias, at least, must have left Milan for reasons other than the demoiselle's ill-chosen nuptials, which had not then taken place. But Astorre, shaking with rage, would have none of it. "If there's been a marriage, it's because there've been couplings enough for a scandal. That bastard Claes! Maybe Tobias put him up to it! Maybe *Lionetto* put him up to it! Maybe Lionetto's the new Charetty captain, on his way south to wipe us all out and save the newlyweds paying our wages! I'll kill him!"

"Who?" had said Julius.

"Them all!" had roared Astorre with perfect logic, retiring thereafter to drink himself to the pitch of picking a fight with the biggest man he could find, and winning it.

Julius spent two days calming him down and succeeded after a fashion, without eliminating, for the benefit of King Ferrante of Naples, the core of a simmering animosity that bid fair, as Thomas had once conjectured, to destroy the entire opposition single-handed.

For himself, Julius felt neither anger nor envy but a growing pleasure, and a growing curiosity. For whatever reason, it had be-gun. And now, what would come of it?

A week before the news of his marriage reached Julius, Nicholas set out for Milan. Behind him in Bruges he left a courageous woman and two weeping children. He also left Gregorio, with

Cristoffels hourly expected. He had confidence in them both. Between them, they could begin, without him, the work of restoration. And within three or four days, Felix should have ended his stay at Genappe and be shortly restored to his mother.

In fact, three days after the departure of Nicholas, the young broker Cristoffels arrived in Bruges from Louvain. He knew nothing of the fire, and expected to find the Widow and her new consort already gone to Dijon and Geneva. Stunned by the news of the dyeshop, Cristoffels did not at once respond to the Widow's pointed enquiries about her son Felix. Then, collecting himself, he reassured her at once. The jonkheere was well. His entertainment at Genappe had evidently been most agreeable. On leaving Genappe, he had called at Louvain to change horses before riding south with his servants. That is, ignorant of the fire and consequently of his mother's changed plans, jonkheere Felix had taken the notion of riding after herself and Meester Nicholas. Of riding, that is, to Dijon. And straight to Geneva, if he failed to encounter them there.

At that point, Cristoffels had paused, mistrusting the look on the demoiselle's face, and had glanced at Gregorio, who gave him no guidance. Then the demoiselle said, "I am glad to know where Felix is. I thought for a moment that it might be worth riding after him. But he will meet Nicholas soon enough, and learn how things are. I expect we shall see him next week."

Cristoffels had remained discreetly silent. He had described with accuracy what Felix had said, when planning to join his mother and his mother's new husband. He hadn't described the look on Felix's face when he said it.

Felix himself, riding towards Dijon, showed the same face to his servants who, as a result, refrained from their usual chatter and resigned themselves to the sort of grim journey you always got when the jonkheere was sulking.

At Dijon, he didn't stay long and came away without his mother and Claes. No. Nicholas, you now had to call him, or you'd get young Felix's whip. In a state, the jonkheere was, and no wonder: all pride so that the old woman mustn't be criticised, and crazy with anger, of course, over Claes. Nicholas. Holy God, how were you to remember to call him Nicholas when you'd won a girl's garter off him at dice only two months ago?

So he'd missed his mother at Dijon and they had to go all the way to Geneva. And it wouldn't tax you to know why. The old woman was showing off her new bridegroom, and the jonkheere wanted to spoil it for her. Or that was the way it looked, if you knew young Felix. Not a bad little bastard. To tell the truth, you felt sorry for him now and then. When he wasn't lashing out with his tongue and his whip, at any rate.

It was mid-May, season of lambs and new-dyed greenery, of orchard blossom and fine, rushing rivers and deep forests full of bustling wild life. Riding south, Felix saw none of them. He slept at the inns his servants found for him, and put his hand in his purse for food and drink and bed and tolls and charity, and thought about his mother and Claes. Nicholas.

He arrived at Geneva and started to look for the house, yard, warehouse and stables of Jaak de Fleury, whose niece had borne Claes to a servant.

Felix had never met Jaak de Fleury or his wife Esota, for whom Claes had worked as a child. And whom Claes was coming to visit now, no doubt in all the finery the Charetty money could buy. Not Claes but Nicholas, married to the owner of the Charetty business and rich.

For everything, of course, was quite different from what Felix had expected that day in his mother's cabinet when, adult to adult, he had accepted the presence of Nicholas in the family circle. Nicholas wasn't in the family circle. He was head of it. He wasn't his mother's friend; he was her master. Nicholas, Felix's servant, who had so bewitched his mother that she had begged him, Felix, to stand aside and give Nicholas his chance in life! His chance to parade his cheap triumph in front of their kinsmen. *This is the old woman my wife. That's her boy Felix, but pay no attention to him. I'm running the business now.*

He'd heard through Cristoffels of this expedition of his mother's. At first, the shock had been so great that Felix hadn't known what to do. But now, if he wept at all, it was from anger. He tried to stop his thoughts before they got as far as that. A merchant never showed his feelings. That was how bargains were made. That was how you got the better of the man you were bargaining against.

When the house was found, the porter didn't want to let them in, and Felix had to go forward himself and use all his authority. Jaak de Fleury might think himself a great merchant and broker, but he took Charetty cloth and bought and sold just like the Charetty company. And Felix's mother, for what it was worth, was his sister-in-law. Although Jaak de Fleury set no store by the kinship, it seemed, and there was certainly no desire on the part of Felix de Charetty to claim any sort of concessions.

But still, you let in the heir to the Charetty business without any arguing. Unless his mother and Nicholas were already inside. Unless Nicholas was behind the delay, or even the refusal . . . ?

No. Someone was coming. A tall man in a fine brocade gown with trailing sleeves over a high-necked doublet of figured silk, and a draped hat larger than his own and twice as expensive. There was a golden chain round his shoulders and a lot of discreet jewellery. His cheekbones shone, whorled like the masks on a misericorde. Only his eyes, large and dark and densely lashed, didn't shine at all, despite the short smile which showed his fine teeth.

"They tell me," said Jaak de Fleury, "that a young kinsman has arrived at my door. I came immediately. I am most harassed with business. My desk is laden. I have visitors due in an hour and many letters to write, but for these words I stop. A young kinsman, wishing to speak to me. And you, I take it, are he?"

Felix gazed, fascinated, at the good teeth. "Yes," he said.

The good teeth showed themselves in a second smile, behind which was a hint of weariness. "Yes," echoed Jaak de Fleury. His voice was encouraging. He said, "You will, I hope, allow me to compliment you on your excellent hat. Indeed, it is uncommon to see such a rare confection in Geneva. And the distinguished cut of the jacket."

Behind Felix, one of his servants shifted. He felt hot. He wondered why the man was keeping him on his threshold discussing clothing. He said, "Thank you, monsieur. I've been hunting at Genappe."

The dark eyes sharpened. There was the breath of a pause. Then a smile of true spontaneity enlarged the small mouth. Jaak de Fleury said, "At Genappe! My young kinsman has been hunting with the Dauphin! Now here is reflected glory indeed for your poor relative in Geneva! And now tell me, what is your name, my boy?"

Felix said, "I have already told your steward. I am Felix de Charetty from Bruges. I called expecting to find my mother here."

"Your mother!" said his overwhelmed kinsman. "Now here is a knot! You are Felix de Charetty—of course, there is a relationship somewhere by marriage. You are right. And you expected to find your mother in this house?"

"She isn't here?" Felix said. As well as hot, he was growing angry. The man might be rich and might be, on the face of it, friendly, but he was still standing inside the courtyard, one ringed hand laid on the open gate, and Felix de Charetty was still standing at the entrance, with his men and his mounts.

"Never!" said M. de Fleury. "Nor sent word she was coming, poor lady. No doubt she needs help of some sort."

"Then," said Felix, "you have made a mistake. She is in no need of help. She was merely travelling south with her . . . She was merely proposing to call on you."

"My dear young man," said Jaak de Fleury. The tone he used was so changed that Felix, forgetting his pique, simply stared at him.

"My dear young man, if you have spent some days at Genappe —is it possible that you have not heard from Bruges? That you did not call at Bruges before setting off south? That, in fact, you have not heard the terrible, terrible news?"

"What?" said Felix. At either elbow his servants moved forward. All three stared like imbeciles at the prosperous figure before them.

"My poor, poor boy," said Jaak de Fleury. "The Charetty business no longer exists. It burned to ashes last month, on the eve of the White Bear tournament."

They got invited inside then. The servants and the horses and baggage disappeared. His heart thudding, Felix followed Jaak de Fleury up stairs and through passages, ramming into him when the merchant stopped to answer questions, and getting left behind when he lost himself thinking up more to ask.

The dear lady his mother was alive, and his sisters. No one had been killed. The house, the yard, the stock had all gone. A tragedy. A tragedy when the lady was, by all accounts, already deeply in debt because of some incautious commitments. And M. de Fleury had heard rumours of another kind, although he did not propose to offend the lady's son by relating them. About a marriage to a certain scullion. Although nonsense, these tales injured the reputation of a company, along with that of its officers. "But of course," said Jaak de Fleury, entering a parlour at last and signing his bemused visitor to a settle, "there is no Charetty company now, alas. So rumours have no importance. Some wine?"

Felix said, "I'll have to get back."

"Yes, of course. But after some wine, and a rest. My wife will bring it. Esota! Esota! Here is Felix de Charetty, whose business burned down in Bruges the other day. My wife," said the merchant, turning tenderly back to Felix, "loved your mother with devotion. Here she is."

His spirit in Bruges, Felix stood and remained mindlessly standing. There entered the room a cake of a woman, pale as a pudding packed into a gut of stretched silk, with a head of dyed hair rolled in ribbons. She trod towards him, lifted two draped and powdery arms, and encased him. His nose sank into flesh, found a vacuum, and plugged it. He freed himself with a gasp.

"Felix!" said Esota Fleury, her hands on his shoulders. "Motherless child!"

Renewed fright in his eyes, Felix turned his head. Jaak de Fleury's smile was soothing. "Esota! The boy will think his mother dead, and she is unharmed. Ruined, but unharmed."

For such a large face, Esota's eyes were bright but meagre. They remained fixed on the boy. Sliding one hand down to his, she led him to the settle and seated herself at his side, his fingers clasped in both her palms. She said, "But motherless still! That wretched marriage, forced on an innocent widow. How can you forgive us? Your mother raped by a knave from our kitchens!"

Jaak de Fleury turned from where, instead of his wife, he was preparing wine for his guest. He said, "But that is merely rumour, Esota. We will not speak of it."

"It's true," said Felix.

They stared at him. After a moment he realised it, and pulled himself together. He drew a deep breath. He said, "Not rape. If that's the rumour, I'd be obliged if you would deny it. Nicholas and my mother recently drew up an instrument of marriage purely as a business arrangement. Despite his base beginnings he has, my mother thinks, great business acumen and can help her manage the company. This contract gives him proper authority."

The woman released his hands. "Nicholas!" she said, amused.

"I suppose it is his given name," said the merchant thoughtfully. "We, of course, think of him as he was known in the kitchens. Such a change of fortune can happen to few boys. A turn for business, you say? And so he owns it jointly now with your mother?"

"No. He gets nothing but a salary. Got. There won't be much in it for him now," Felix said. "There's nothing to own."

"Except debts," said Jaak de Fleury. He sat down, glass in hand, and gazed at it thoughtfully. "Unless there is money we know nothing of? Business acumen, you were saying."

"There's property," Felix said. "There's Louvain. There are

other investments. Something could be done. We'll put our heads together."

"You don't think there is money somewhere? No cash? No investments? I only asked," said Jaak de Fleury, "because in cases of arson, it is usual for someone to benefit, and here apparently no one does."

"Arson?" said Felix. His stomach, which had begun to settle, started to disturb him again. His hair, which had been rolled up tightly that morning, had begun to come down in the heat. He said, "Someone *started* the fire?"

"So they say," said the merchant. "Not your mother or yourself, it goes without saying. Someone with a grievance against their new young master, perhaps. What else could it be? Although I must say I have been wondering . . . Ah. I hear voices below. That will be your stepfather now."

Felix didn't even repeat the word. He merely gazed at his tormentor.

Jaak de Fleury smiled. "Nicholas. He *is* your stepfather, you say? You didn't know then that he was in Geneva, calling on Francesco Neri of the Medici? I wondered if my poor house was to receive his next call. And after you arrived, dear boy, I sent to Francesco's to make quite sure Nicholas made his way here. You wouldn't want to miss him. And I must admit. I must admit," the merchant repeated, rising and setting his glass on a table, "I am full of curiosity. Why, after such a disaster, is he not in Bruges, helping his wife in her hour of need with this great business acumen we have heard of? What can bring him to Geneva? And where, I wonder, does he plan to go when he leaves? However generous his managerial wages, there is a limit, I imagine, to what they will fund. How interesting it all is."

He remained standing as the door opened and Felix, too, got to his feet. Jaak de Fleury smiled down at his wife. "Esota, my dear," he said. "You remember Claes, who is now Felix's stepfather? For the sake of Felix, I want you to receive him in your parlour. He will not presume. I'm sure of it."

The tall man in the doorway moved inside and it was, Felix saw, Nicholas and not Claes. Nicholas with the brown of the open air on his skin and not the pale sweat of the dyeshops. Nicholas dressed not in Charetty blue but stout brown and green, with a sleeveless jacket over his doublet and serviceable riding boots and a leather cross-belt with a sword in a plain scabbard. Nicholas, with a brimmed beretta pulled over the damply crimped edges of his dust-coloured hair, and whose open eyes scanned the room, observed the woman and stopped at Felix. In them, Felix read a number of expressions. The last one, plain to see, was concern.

Felix said, "You're not surprised?"

Nicholas said, "Not if you came straight here from Genappe. Your mother is still in Bruges."

"So I hear," Felix said. "The house burned down. So what are you doing here?"

"Collecting debts. And selling cloth," Nicholas said. He didn't imitate anyone, or pull a face, or make a joke or even grin. He spoke, now, the way he'd spoken ever since his mother had started taking him into the business. He spoke like all the dreary merchants he and Felix and Julius (sometimes) used to poke fun at.

"Collecting debts? Who from?" Felix said. He had forgotten Jaak de Fleury and his wife, one standing, one seated behind him.

"From Thibault and Jaak de Fleury, I hope," Nicholas said.

Behind, Jaak de Fleury spoke. "My dear Claes! I can see the necessity. But I fear we owe your mistress nothing."

Nicholas looked past Felix. He said, "I had a word with your steward, M. de Fleury, on my way in. He is asking your clerk to prepare a list of what is owing. For what you cannot settle immediately, I shall require a notarised document establishing the debt. I have also brought, monsieur, the cloth you ordered. Payment for this, too, would be appreciated by the demoiselle. You will, I am sure, be anxious to help her in every way."

Jaak de Fleury smiled. The bosses of his cheekbones shone: towards his wife, his wine-pouring servant, and to the two young men before him. "Come," he said. "Let us be seated. These are not matters to be dealt with hastily. For one thing, money is tight in Geneva just now. Indeed, I am surprised that you brought your cloth so far south. I should have thought the Bruges Fair would have brought you a better price. It depends, of course, what use you have for the money. Or indeed, the promissory notes."

Nicholas said, "I should have thought that was obvious. The business has to be rebuilt."

Jaak de Fleury said, "Of course. So you are returning to Bruges with whatever money you have collected—from me and, no doubt, the Medici. And the debts still outstanding? Do you return for these too?"

Nicholas said, "Monsieur, you will be told where and how to fulfil your obligations."

"I hear," said Jaak de Fleury, "that you favour Venice. Is that where the cloth money will go?"

Felix said, "It will go to Bruges. If there is money owing us now, I will take it."

"Without a guard?" said Jaak de Fleury. "Your skilful Nicholas and his men at arms won't be with you. You talked of returning to Bruges, but he has said nothing of it. I am told by the Medici that, on the contrary, he is on his way south to Milan. After that, who is to say where he, and the money, will find themselves?"

Nicholas stirred, but made no effort to sit. He suddenly did pull a face, of the kind Felix remembered when he was making up his mind, against his will, about something. Nicholas said, "Did he tell you I started that fire?"

"Did you?" said Felix. It seemed likely that the merchant was right. Nicholas had married his mother, cashed what he could of their assets and lodged it somewhere, and then destroyed both the business and the evidence. He would hardly admit as much if he meant to come back to Bruges. But, confident of escape, he might just confess it. In which case Felix would kill him.

Nicholas said, "No. There are other candidates. Your mother knows of them. Since I can't prove it, you'd better go straight back to Bruges with the money. Take my escort: they're Bruges men. I'll hire others."

"You won't," said Felix. "You're coming back to Bruges as well. Now. Tied into your saddle if need be. M. de Fleury will help me, I'm sure."

Jaak de Fleury got up, and with deliberation strolled to the door, where he turned, blocking the exit. "Why, gladly," he said.

Nicholas looked sadly at him. "That's awkward," he said.

"That's stopped your tricks, you mean," said Felix angrily.

"No," said Nicholas. "Of course, it would be quite easy to leave, but you can't really collect the debts and the documents without me. That is, I am sure M. de Fleury's officers are beyond suspicion, but I do know what is due, and how to check it. Perhaps I could be taken, under heavy chains, to where the ledgers are kept? Or could the clerk bring them?"

He sounded solemn, as he had before, but there was something about his face Felix distrusted. Felix hesitated. If Nicholas was here to collect money, then no one, it was true, could extract it

better than he could. After that, all he had to do was take it into
his, Felix's, care and march Nicholas back, under guard, to his
mother. Then they'd see about these mysterious caches in Venice.
Venice!

In the end, clerks and ledgers were brought to the parlour, and a
table carried in at which Nicholas seated himself, opposite an
amused Jaak de Fleury, with his officers standing about him. During the half hour that followed the merchant continued to show
amusement, although at times clearly bored as polite question followed polite question, and page after page was consulted so that
the finger of Nicholas could trace, with gentle clarity, the proofs of
his argument. Or rather, his discourse. Nicholas entered into no
arguments. The objections, such as they were, came from de
Fleury's officials, looking from time to time at their master when a
point appeared to be lost.

When that happened, the merchant allowed the concession without interfering. The final list of money, as a result, owed by
Thibault and Jaak de Fleury to the Charetty family was double the
steward's first estimate, and there was even some silver in earnest
of settlement. It was put in a box with the documents, which had
been signed and witnessed by public notary. Felix, biting his nails,
watched the box being locked. Then Nicholas turned to him. "Felix. You wanted to take the box back to Bruges. I'll come with you.
There is the box, and there are the keys. The sooner we get back,
the better."

The clown's eyes were holding his. Felix hesitated. He longed to
get away from the fat, scented hands of the woman and the dark,
amused gaze of her husband. They said Nicholas had meant to
cross into Italy. Perhaps he still did. Once on the road, there was
nothing to prevent him from wresting the money from Felix and
turning back south. He had men at arms.

Apparently Nicholas thought all that was behind him. That,
somehow, he had induced Felix to trust him. Smiling, Nicholas
said, "You wanted to tie me into my saddle, I seem to remember.
M. de Fleury would certainly help. He might even send some men
with you, if you don't want to trust mine. But perhaps you feel that
isn't quite necessary."

Like all servants, he'd got over-confident. Felix, as it happened,
thought that all these precautions might quite suitably be put into
effect, and he turned to M. de Fleury and said so. Nicholas looked
very surprised. He still looked surprised when M. de Fleury not

only agreed, but took immediate action. A jerk of M. Jaak's head, and his steward was standing in friendly fashion close beside Nicholas. M. Jaak left the room with his clerks to summon men and arrange for provisions and weapons and horses. The box was still on the table, so Felix remained. He endured, with abnormal patience, the patting hand of Esota de Fleury.

Nicholas stood still, with his guardian beside him. After an interval the clerk came back for the steward and the lady of Fleury. He carried with him a key for the parlour. The steward scowled at Nicholas and went out, but the lady was in no hurry. She waved the clerk off, and again, more angrily, when he hesitated. Felix was sorry for him. He was even slightly alarmed when, with his mistress's leave, the clerk went out without her and, shutting the door, turned the key in it from the outside. He left the box, so Felix stayed, in the uncomfortable company of Esota de Fleury and the servant his stepfather.

Felix waited for Jaak de Fleury to come back. He seemed to be away a long time. Nicholas walked backwards and forwards and Felix watched him. He even saw Nicholas stroll to the window and nod to someone he knew in the courtyard as if there was nothing to worry about. Indeed, it was not until Nicholas walked back, kerchief in hand, to bend courteously over the demoiselle that something struck Felix as odd, and he turned.

But by then the kerchief was, he saw, bound tightly over the demoiselle's full, tinted lips and Nicholas' arm was already swinging towards his, Felix's, head with a thick wicker flask at the end of it. Felix tried to shout, too, but his mouth was blocked by a large and familiar hand, smelling of new ink like Collinet Mansion.

The blow presented him with one ridiculous thought, before every thought left him. If Collinet Mansion was there, Claes must be somewhere about.

Claes would help him.

Chapter 32

Felix de Charetty, who had left his home in the middle of April to go hunting at Genappe with the Comte de Charolais and the Dauphin of Vienne, did not return. In Bruges, it was generally known that the boy had ridden south, thinking to overtake his mother and the young fellow he used to go about with. Nicholas, who married the demoiselle.

There were those who thought it a bit funny that Nicholas went off like that after the fire. Although, of course, the Widow had very good help, what with that busy new notary Gregorio, and Cristoffels, who had a reputation with the brokers who used to deal with him. Indeed, it was amazing what they had all done to pull the business together in a few weeks.

But all the same, you saw the difference in Marian de Charetty. Whatever you thought about the marriage, that young man had a head on him, and was useful to her. And now he was gone, and her son as well. And there was a mystery. For one way or another, surely the boy Felix had caught up with Nicholas. And learned of the fire. And had been desperate, as any boy would, to get back and comfort his mother, and help set things to rights. But May ended, and the first week of June arrived, and Felix didn't come.

In Spangnaerts Street Felix's two nubile sisters saw no reason for worrying. As their mother pointed out, he and Nicholas might have missed one another. Felix might have ridden a very long way before he learned of the fire. Catherine rather enjoyed the May Fair and the Holy Blood Procession without Felix, now she was getting over all the nice things she had lost—her gowns and her oldest toys, and the coverlet she had made, and the box a man from Danzig had given her.

Now people gave her more things because they were sorry for her, and in return she told them all about the fire, and especially the frightening bits. As she remembered more, the story got better and better, and there were always new people to tell it to.

Tilde, too, was recovering, although rather more slowly, for there were things of her father's that she would never see again.

And sometimes, at night, she thought of Felix, and remembered the little knife Felix carried and how short-tempered he was. She hoped, when they met, that Nicholas would remember to say the right things to Felix, the way he used to. At first, she had thought Nicholas had done such a terrible thing that none of them should speak to him again. Then she began to think that it was all her mother's fault. Now, since the fire, she felt so sad for her mother that she had forgiven them both. At least, when he came back, Nicholas would be living in the same house, and her mother would be happy.

Only neither Felix nor Nicholas had come back by the beginning of June, and Tilde hoped they wouldn't stay away long. She had a new robe, since the old ones were burnt, and they had to put buckram into it. But of course her mother wasn't talking of husbands at the moment, for husbands meant dowries, and the company had to be set on its feet first. And although at times she looked pale, and spoke sharply because she was working so hard, her mother had said, just the other day, how well everything was going: just as Nicholas planned. Tilde had thought then she would talk about suitors, but instead she just got up and left the room.

The Adornes also spoke about Nicholas, but not so freely, since Anselm and his wife were not in perfect agreement over the scheme which drew them and the young man together. But when outside his home, Anselm Adorne spent a good deal of time on the subject, especially when among the Doria and Spinola in the Genoese consulate.

In the Medici establishment, Angelo Tani and Tommaso his under-manager received the Widow's representatives and proved to be actively helpful in the matter of loans, and forbearing in the face of indebtedness, as Nicholas had said they would be. They also, from time to time, requested news from Jacques and Lorenzo Strozzi on the progress of the Milanese ostrich. For news of the ostrich, Lorenzo Strozzi had taken to relying on Katelina van Borselen's little sister. According to the last letter from Brittany, the ostrich was still alive but impounded, and could not be set on board ship until a legal case had been settled.

Gelis van Borselen, who found it necessary to visit Bruges a great deal at this time, and who was a frequent caller at the Hôtel Jerusalem and at Spangnaerts Street, had summoned Lorenzo Strozzi to her father's house to hear that bit of Katelina's letter. She thought Lorenzo Strozzi moody but romantic. He had sworn never to marry, they said, until he had a business of his own. She looked forward to several more talks about ostriches.

About the rest of the letter from Katelina she said nothing, either to her parents or to Lorenzo. It was the first to come from Brittany since Nicholas married the old woman. But when Gelis burst the wax and flattened it, there was nothing about Nicholas and the wedding at all, because her letters hadn't reached Katelina. Nor had anyone else's. Some ship must have sunk.

She would have to write it all down again. And this time add the news about the mysterious fire at the Charetty, and how Nicholas had run off south three days later, and how the Charetty boy had disappeared. Not been killed in a joust (which, as Nicholas himself pointed out, he would be blamed for), but simply sent out of Bruges and never seen again. For which, of course, no one could blame Nicholas at all.

That was the person she and Katelina had taken all that trouble to fish out of the canal on Carnival night. Katelina should never have taken him home. It wasn't as if Katelina was married yet. And if she wasn't careful, her reputation would get spoilt, and even Guildolf de Gruuthuse would start looking elsewhere. From what she wrote, the court in Brittany was as bad as courts anywhere, with Duke Francis and the King of France sharing the same mistress. Antoinette somebody. Katelina spoke as if she saw her all the time. Mind you, she was probably a relief from the old Duchess, the Scottish king's sister, who sounded bad-tempered as well as dim-witted, and wouldn't go home to be married to anyone else now her husband was dead.

Katelina said the court was full of Scotsmen calling to try and get the rest of the old Duchess's dowry, which had never been paid. Katelina said that Jordan de Ribérac had come to court one day on business of the French king, who owed him money and who relied on him for everything. Katelina said that Jordan de Ribérac often rode through to the coast to check over his shipping. Katelina said that she acted as if she didn't know him, but he had had the conceit to kiss her hand and chat in front of the Duchess as if he had never insulted her, or tried to kill Nicholas. Katelina asked her to ask Nicholas to write to her.

Katelina was a fool.

At the end of the first week in June a messenger arrived in Bruges from the Medici manager in Geneva with papers for Angelo Tani. He also bore a letter which he delivered to Marian de

Charetty. It was from her husband Nicholas. It hastened to assure her that all was well, and Felix safe in his company. It added that, because of the money they carried, it seemed best for Felix to travel with him to Italy and come home at the same time. The experience, it further added, might do Felix some good. There followed some detailed information and other cogent suggestions on trading matters. The greetings with which it closed were all that they should be. It was a pleasant letter. Marian de Charetty, reading it, deduced that Felix was misbehaving and that this was the way Nicholas had chosen to deal with it. She had no fears for Felix. The concern she felt sprang from the same source as Tilde's. Felix, when thwarted, could harm people.

Being unconscious on the banks of Lake Geneva, Felix de Charetty was incapable of harming anyone at the time the pleasant letter to his lady mother was being composed and written. Nor, in the days that followed could he be said to be a danger to anyone but himself, as he tried to release himself from the horse to which he was tied, or drive it out of the convoy on one side or the other, his head still thunderously sore from the blow which had felled him in Jaak de Fleury's house.

How Nicholas had got him out of the house and out of Geneva he still didn't know. The precious money-box, of course, was in Nicholas' hands. The men at arms around him were all hired by Nicholas. His own two servants were there as well, more lightly bound than he was since they had less incentive, he supposed, to escape and attempt a moneyless journey back home. From the moment he returned to consciousness, gripped on the back of someone else's horse, they had been travelling as if the devil were after them.

Of course, Jaak de Fleury would have sent those armed men of his to follow and rescue him. Or at the very least, would have enlisted the help of the Duke of Savoy's handiest officer. At any moment, they would be overtaken and stopped.

They were not. Whatever trick Nicholas had used, no troop of avenging horsemen swept past them. When, on stumbling horses, they left the lake and began to tackle the rising ground which led up to the pass, Felix saw that no one was going to help him. If he was going to take home that box, and find the rest of the Charetty money he had been cheated out of, he would have to do it himself.

That night his new enemy felt safe enough, it appeared, to risk taking a room at an inn. Sitting on a led horse, with his hands tied together and his feet roped beneath him, Felix saw the man at arms dispatched ahead to arrange it.

He had refused to give his word not to escape. He had refused to speak to anyone. At the first halt he remembered, he had spat back the wine Nicholas offered him, and when they loosed his hands he had used them to do his best to throttle him. So they didn't dare take him indoors. They rested and took their food in the open air, well concealed from the road. Until now.

He had wondered how Nicholas expected to prevent him from making a disturbance in a public place, but it was simple: he was gagged as well as bound and helped in, cloaked and hooded, as if he were drunk. He smelt food and charcoal and ale fumes and heard a confusion of languages and the clatter of booted feet, and the banging of trestles and platters and tankards. His feet found stairs and he hit on the idea of kicking them, but before he could do it, powerful hands took him under the armpits and carried him bodily upwards. He remembered Claes being lifted like that. On board the Flanders galleys, it was. Just before they flung him into the sea.

Had he resented it all as much as that? All the time? Hating and resenting him, and Julius, and Jaak, and his mother?

A door opened, and he was set down beyond it, held by the grip of a single hand. The door shut, cutting off the noise from below, and a key turned in the lock. Felix dragged on the restraining arm and tossed his head like a warhorse, to dislodge the muffling hood. His head began to ache wildly. The second hand returned to his other arm. Resisting, he found himself stumbling backwards and then pushed down, with a jolt, on a low bed. His hood was grasped and folded back, but the cloth round his mouth remained there.

Nicholas stood looking down at him. Nicholas said, "You hear how quiet it's got? That's how thick the door is. And anyway, my fellows are just outside. So don't waste time shouting. I need some food, and some sleep, and so do you. And I want to talk first."

It had puzzled Felix for some time: why Nicholas hadn't killed him and his servants immediately. But that, of course, was merely because he was afraid of pursuit. Now he'd shaken it off, he could arrange for Felix to die more conveniently, and perhaps attach the blame somewhere else.

Felix had no wish to talk to his murderer. He made an elaborate show of closing his eyes while the other man was still speaking, and lying back on the bed, stuck his chin up. The mark of a merchant was his dignity. He hoped he also looked bored. His heart and his lungs, which were not bored, refused to cooperate.

Nicholas said, "Well, if I'm going to apologise to you, you might at least keep your eyes open. Is your head still as bad?"

Silence. The scrape of a stool. The voice of Nicholas, again, from a lower level. It sounded submissive. He said, "I don't suppose I'd have the nerve to lie there, in your place. You must think I'm going to carve you up and send the pieces to your mother. I hit you on the head because I had to get you away. I had to get you away because I couldn't let you go back alone with the money, and I couldn't go with you. I couldn't go with you because I've got to get to Milan. I've got to get to Milan because your mother and Anselm Adorne and a lot of other people are involved in a highly secret piece of trading which is going to make you so rich that the fire doesn't even matter. But only if I get to Milan. And only if other people don't get to hear of it. Other people like Jaak de Fleury."

Felix lay still. His head ached.

Nicholas said, "Now you've heard that much, I'm coming to untie the gag. I've got a dagger, Felix. I know you're not convinced, but you can't overpower me. I only want you to listen. After that, I'll answer any questions you like. And after that, I'll give you my dagger. If you want to walk out, you can."

Fingers pushed his head up. Felix opened his eyes. The gag came away from his dry mouth. He retched, and swallowed, and retched. Nicholas was pouring something from a flask to a cup. Nicholas said, "Spit it out if you want, but it's good Candy wine and you need it. Look, I've drunk some. Now you drink the poisoned half."

There was a smile in his voice. Felix didn't smile. He drank when the cup was put to his mouth. His hands were still tied. He said, "Now I wait until you give me the knife, and I open the door, and your men kill me on my way out."

"But you'll have killed me first," Nicholas said. "Come on, pay attention. Have you had a blow on the head or something?"

"I'll begin to believe you," said Felix, "when you untie my wrists, send your men away, and let me call the landlord of this place to help me get you back under guard to Geneva. You can talk all you want in Geneva."

"Not about an alum monopoly," Nicholas said. His gaze had concentrated and his forehead got lined in the way it did when he wanted you to remember something. He said, "You've got a reputation, you know, for being headstrong. Not like John and Sersanders and the rest of us. There was a feeling that you might forget the scheme was so secret and talk about it. But you're a merchant, and it is your business, and since you're here, you might as well be in Milan when it's settled. Do you remember the Greek with the wooden leg?"

The Candian wine was very good. Nicholas had refilled the cup, and Felix drank that off, too. His headache lessened and his stomach felt warm. *"Do you remember . . . ?"* Nicholas had begun in the way he had so often begun to recall some exploit and embroider it. With a twitch of his shoulder, he had conjured up the austere, bearded Greek and his limp, and the whole hilarious business. Of the gun in the water, and the rabbits. Of the night in the Steen. Of the time the waterpipes burst.

Felix sat, cup in hand, against pillows and echoed, "An *alum* monopoly?"

"Yes." Nicholas had seated himself again on the stool, the flask in his two hands. He seemed to be studying it. Without warning, the silly dimples appeared in his cheeks and disappeared again.

"What?" said Felix.

Nicholas looked up. "Nothing," he said.

Felix waited angrily.

"That is," said Nicholas, "I was just thinking. Wishing that you were sitting here and I was Felix de Charetty."

"With a mother," said Felix, his anger increasing. Why tell him now that he wanted to be Felix de Charetty? Most people did.

He had succeeded, anyway, in reminding the bastard who was who. The open eyes clouded over, and lowered. Nicholas said, "That was stupid of me. I'm sorry. About the alum. You've seen it. Casks of white powder in the dyeshop. Everyone needs it, to fix colours in cloth. It makes hides supple, and parchment last longer. It makes better glass, and better paper."

"I know all that," Felix said.

"I didn't know if you did," Nicholas said. "Then you probably know where it comes from. The poorer stuff from Africa. Spain. Up and down the west Italian coast in volcanic places like Lipari and Ischia. The best stuff from the Byzantine and Turkish end of the Mediterranean. And for hundreds of years, that's been in the hands of the Genoese. You know that, too, of course. It's been coming into Bruges for years in Genoese ships, and being handled by Adornes and Dorias, second cousins of the Adornos and Dorias in Genoa. That's the connection between Anselm Adorne and Scotland. Antoniotto Adorno, Doge of Genoa, was visiting Scotland last century, collecting debts due him for alum."

"That's why you try to murder Scotsmen?" said Felix. "Over an alum monopoly?" A merchant would never show himself to be attracted by this kind of preamble. A kidnapped merchant might be forgiven if his heart was thumping with excitement.

Nicholas said, "When I've finished, you must make up your own mind about that. But listen a bit. You have to understand more about alum first. For instance, the purer it is, the better and costlier. And the best stuff, as I've said, comes from the eastern end of the Mediterranean. Deposits round the Black Sea used to be handled by Genoese trading colonies there, who had set up in Caffa and Trebizond under the Byzantine emperors.

"The best alum of all is south of Constantinople, in the Gulf of Smyrna, in a place called Phocoea. It was worked nearly two hundred years ago by Genoese brothers called Zaccaria, who had been agents in Constantinople. But the family lost its grip, and the Byzantine Greeks jumped into Phocoea and Chios, the island beside it, which didn't suit the Genoese merchants at all.

"So just over a hundred years ago, an armed Genoese fleet arrived and took back Chios and Phocoea and established a sort of merchants' cooperative, based on Chios, and run by the families and later the heirs of the original merchants who had paid for the fleet. Including the Adornos of Genoa."

Felix said, "Thanks for the lesson. That was all ages ago, and anyway the Turks have it now. Have you done a deal with the Turks?"

"The Adornos did," Nicholas said. "And the rest of the Genoese working the mines from the island of Chios. The Turks mastered most of the area, and the Phocoea Alum Company, to survive, had to pay 20,000 gold ducats a year to the Sultan. Then five years ago, Phocoea itself fell to the Turks, and the Genoese company kept Chios, but lost all the alum mines."

"So you've done a deal with the Turks," Felix said. He remembered, as a boy, being driven out of doors by the monotony of his father's voice talking of subjects like this. Listening now, he forgot even his hunger. Trade, and money. A monopoly, he had said.

Nicholas said, "A Venetian merchant in Constantinople did a deal with the Turks. He had a dyeworks there, and he knew about alum. He told the Turks he could work the Phocoea alum mines if they gave him a concession, and they said they would think about it, provided he could raise enough money for his ransom. His name was Bartolomeo Giorgio or, as the Venetians pronounce it, Bartolomeo Zorzi."

He stopped. He often did that, meaning that he had said something important. Felix thought. He said, bursting out with it, "The Greek with the wooden leg!"

Nicholas smiled. He said, "Nicholai Giorgio de' Acciajuoli. Collecting a ransom in Europe to free Bartolomeo Giorgio, his brother. And especially collecting from places like Bruges, and like Scotland, which need alum."

Felix said, "He liked you because you broke up his leg. He's offering us special cheap rates of alum through his brother?"

Nicholas said, "He's offering us special cheap rates of alum. And regular supplies of alum. And, indeed, a stockpile of alum if we want it. Which we do."

"Why?" said Felix. And then, as Nicholas failed to answer at once: "Oh," said Felix. "I suppose that's the secret?"

"Secret?" said Nicholas. "It's the business expedient which will make your fortune, and your mother's. If you tell it to one other person—just *one*—your mother will lose everything but a pittance. I am going to tell you, but you must understand what it means."

"In exchange for my silence. Oh, I know what it means," Felix said. He wished Nicholas would look somewhere else.

Not looking somewhere else, Nicholas said, "When you get to Bruges, Gregorio and your mother and Anselm Adorne will all confirm the truth of what I'm going to tell you. In Milan, I've had Meester Tobie to help me."

"Tobie?" said Felix.

"The doctor. Because he knew about herbs. And because the Acciajuoli and the Adorno know people who have worked in the Phocoea alum mines, and Tobie had an excuse to be in Italy, where he could look about and talk to them . . .

"Felix, listen. No one knows it yet, but in the hills north of Rome is a huge deposit of perfect alum. The best ever known. Better than the alum of Phocoea."

Felix felt his heart swell. His voice was hoarse. He said, "Tobias is buying it for us? That's what the money's for?"

Nicholas looked down. He said, "Felix, no one could buy it, because it's in the Papal States. The family who own the land are tenants of the Pope. As soon as the discovery is made known, the Pope will buy the rights and lease the mine, keeping the profits. The profits will be huge. Enough to launch a crusade."

Felix said, "But if you've discovered it, Pope Pius would pay you. Us. Tobias."

"I am sure he would," Nicholas said. "But that would be all. Someone else would develop the mines. The Charetty business hasn't the capital. Even before the fire, that was true. And once the mines are producing, the Pope has an alum monopoly."

"He hasn't," said Felix. "You said it yourself. Bartolomeo Zorzi is producing in Phocoea. For Venice, paying tribute to Turkey."

"That's true," said Nicholas. "And I suppose some misguided Christians, such as all the merchants in Bruges and Genoa and Florence, are buying from him. But once Papal alum is on the market, what faithful follower of the Cross will buy from the Crescent? Especially if the papal alum comes with a remission for sins, and the Turkish alum comes with excommunication. He'll hoist the price, too."

"So?" said Felix joyously. *What game? What prank?* his mind was asking itself. Life was for having adventures. Life was for taking chances, accepting offers, making profits. Life was not for staying at home with your mother.

"So we sit on the discovery of the new papal alum mines," said Nicholas blandly. "And the Venetians pay us for doing it. And give us all the alum we want, at knockdown prices, for as long as we want. Or until someone else makes the discovery. We might get two years out of it, and an alum reserve that will serve us when the price starts to rise."

Felix thought. He became aware that he had been thinking for a long time. His heart was thudding. Nicholas, he saw, was watching him and smiling a little. Felix said, "And that's why you're going to Milan?"

Nicholas said, "I do have courier business to do. Dispatches to deliver and collect, and fees for both. But yes. Tobie sent me the proofs. Adorne has seen them, and your mother. Now I have to talk to the Venetians. Not the Florentines, who would instantly expose the papal mines and exploit them themselves. But the Venetians, who control the Phocoean alum."

"And that's why you invested money in Venice?" said Felix dreamily.

Nicholas said, "Partly. When I started, I didn't know all this would happen. Or that I should be staying in Bruges."

"You were going to leave?" Felix said.

"I was sent away," Nicholas said. "For improper behaviour. You must remember."

"But you came back and married my mother instead," Felix said.

They had been talking, man to man. He thought for a moment that, man to man, Nicholas was going to answer him. But although he hesitated, in the end he only said, "Yes."

After that, there were other questions and answers. At some time Nicholas, still talking, untied Felix's hands. Food was brought, and eaten. The bed, which was broad enough for five, was prepared for the night. At that point Nicholas said, "I've told them to free your two men, and tell them that you've decided to travel on to Milan of your own free will, but that if they doubt it, they can come and speak to you. Apparently they fell asleep without troubling. Was I right?"

"I suppose so," said Felix. Between food and warmth and wine and sleepiness, the words had some trouble forming themselves. He said, "You were supposed to give me your dagger."

"I forgot," said Nicholas. "There it is. Which side of the bed do you want?"

But Felix was already in bed, and although he thought he answered, he didn't.

Chapter 33

This time, the cavalcade of the Charetty entering Milan caused no shutters to open. For one thing, it was too hot. For another, the rival captains had mostly departed long since for their respective battlefields: some south to Naples, and some spurring east after the renegade Count Piccinino.

Those who were not captains were not impressed by the appearance of a merchant's young son and his factor, however strongly escorted. What gained Felix immediate entrance through the Porta Vercellina and a ready welcome at the Inn of the Hat was the safe-conduct carried by Nicholas, with its manifold Medici and Burgundian signatures.

But of that, Felix was unaware. For seven days he had ridden at Nicholas' side discussing business, the way a man should with his manager. To his questions, Nicholas had given long, careful explanations which he had found not at all boring. They had talked about Henninc and Bellobras, and about Gregorio, and Cristoffels at Louvain. Nicholas had asked his opinion about many things. Nicholas, anxious that he should follow all the negotiations they were going to have, annoyed him from time to time by trying to teach him Italian.

Arguing with Nicholas, echoes of his mother's diatribes and inquisitions had come back to Felix, together with some of his father's impatience. Nicholas was not deferential, but had dropped into the same reasonable, commonsense voice that Julius had habitually used with his employer. Felix approved of that. Some of the shame and the anger and the fright of the last eight weeks began to ebb away.

In the city of Milan where, instead of air, they had marble powder and brickdust, Nicholas had four calls to make for the Charetty company, and Felix, if he so wished, could attend him on each. Felix so wished, once he had got his boots off and his doublet unfastened and a good night's sleep and a lot of wine behind him. He flopped on the inn bed, leaving Nicholas to order food and see to their escort.

Nicholas, who still had his boots on, looked quite pleased and said he would arrange it all for tomorrow. And meanwhile, did Felix want to come and watch him deliver dispatches? Weariness fought with the dregs of suspicion, and weariness won.

"You do it," said Felix; and fell asleep almost at once. When he woke, it was dawn and Nicholas was slumbering peacefully on the truckle bed and refused to waken. He had arranged a cold meal, half of it eaten, on a chest with a guttering candle. Felix demolished it, dropping things now and then, but as Nicholas still didn't wake up and the wine was excellent, he decided to get back into bed with a bottle. After all, he had to be fresh for business tomorrow. This morning.

Later that morning Cicco Simonetta, head of the Milanese chancery, might have been alarmed to find himself discussing Charetty business with a sharp-featured eighteen-year-old with a more than uncertain grasp of his language, had he not received ample warning beforehand. As it was, the required payments for the revised condotta were smoothly computed, and the necessary papers changed hands. What other papers had changed hands the previous night, when the reports oral and written had been delivered, did not fail to be mentioned.

Messer Cicco, busy man that he was, was disposed to be friendly. He was interested in all Felix had to tell him of his recent visit to Genappe. He asked Felix if he had met the Dauphin's chamberlain, M. Gaston du Lyon, in Geneva. Felix's negative clashed, to his surprise, with an affirmative from Nicholas, who had not only met the man, but owed him a favour.

They were joined by another member of the ducal household: Messer Prosper Schiaffino de Camulio de' Medici, the Duke's right hand (said Messer Cicco, smiling) in diplomatic missions abroad to the French. They talked of the defence of the kingdom of Naples (which the captain Astorre was so ably assisting) and the growing hopes that the enemy would find himself starved of money and troops as France and Savoy found themselves unable to keep their fine promises.

Felix mentioned the lavish armour and weapons of the Charetty squadron, and the excellence of Astorre and his secretary Julius and his physician Tobias Beventini of Grado.

Cicco Simonetta di Calabria, who couldn't be expected to remember everything, said that it had been much admired, Messer Tobias' help with captain Lionetto.

Felix, who was already encased in buckram and bombast as in Egyptian bandages, couldn't sit up more stiffly. But he did say, "Lionetto!" in a voice of alarmed astonishment.

Nicholas said, "Messer Tobias, knowing captain Lionetto of old, was entrusted by His Holiness the Pope with a message entreating him to leave the wicked forces of Count Jacopo Piccinino and cross to our side. He was successful. Captain Lionetto changed his mind. He deserted Count Piccinino and is with the Count of Urbino at this moment."

"But you forgot to mention it. And Tobias?" demanded Felix.

Lifting languid fingers, Messer Cicco replied instead of Nicholas. "The brave doctor has lost his chance, I fear, of fighting in Naples. If I know anything of my lord of Urbino, he will have kept your Messer Tobias in his service. If he has, you will be paid his worth, to enable you to hire another physician. Meanwhile, the service you and he have performed will not be forgotten. Do you join the fighting, Messer Felix?"

Messer Felix flushed. He said, "There's nothing I'd like better."

"Why, I commend your courage," said Cicco Simonetta. "And we should honour it. You have had a long journey, and perhaps feel your skills require refreshing? I should be happy to make you free of the tilting-yard, and of any practice our masters might offer you. Our gossip Niccolò here knows what exercise we can provide."

Felix didn't need Nicholas (Niccolò?) to tell him what the Milanese masters could do for him. Deep in making appointments, he heard Nicholas humbly accepting for them both an evening in the company of Messer Prosper de Camulio de' Medici. He was angry with Nicholas. Nicholas should have told him about the doctor. At the same time, the ducal chancellor seemed very pleased. And an evening with a ducal ambassador might turn out to be dull, but business was business. He hoped the women's booths stayed open late. Sometimes, in a new town, you could buy lists. But when he had mentioned it to Nicholas, Nicholas had only begun to laugh, but wouldn't say why.

With Nicholas, he left the Arengo and issued into the frying-hot Milanese sunshine. He forgot, for the moment, his complaints. Everything in Milan was huge. In front was the biggest church Felix had ever seen. It was half-built and covered in scaffolding, with brown-backed workmen in breech-clouts moving from plank to plank like seagulls on the Crane. You had to watch, in case a pulley stuck and a bucket emptied before it should. The hammering behind came, Nicholas said, from the workshops, where they brought the marble in from the pool.

Felix wanted to see the wonders of the Medici Palazzo, which was supposed to be their next port of call. He had put on parti-coloured hose and his best tunic, which was yellow, and had bought a straw hat that morning, to protect his complexion from the sun. He looked forward to meeting Tommaso's brothers, whom Tommaso envied, and to whom Felix, nonchalantly, was confiding a box of silver and draft bills to be transferred to Tommaso in Bruges.

On the way to the Medici, Nicholas called at the bench of a notary and retrieved three packets of papers, which he paid for in silver. Then, finding a tavern near the Piazza Mercanti, he took Felix inside and ordered wine, while he opened the packets and examined them. They proved to be two complete sets of the credit notes supplied by Jaak de Fleury, copied to the last word and fully notarised. One copy for themselves. One copy to be lodged with Maffino, the Fleury agent in Milan, as a convenience for any future exchanges. And the originals, which they were taking now to be sold to Pigello Portinari of the Medici.

"To be *sold*?" Felix said.

Nicholas, refolding the packets, seemed unaware that he'd said anything worth remark. "Well, it's the best way of getting our money," he said. "Or at least the bit I got Monsieur Jaak to acknowledge. Maybe you want to come trailing down to Geneva every six months to try and collect, but I don't think it's worth it. Instead, let the Medici squeeze the silver out of Jaak de Fleury through their Geneva branch."

Felix stared at him. He said, "Why should the Medici do it?"

Nicholas put the packets away and signed to the landlord. "They're always doing it. It's their business, debt-collecting. They handle papal bulls in the same way exactly. And anyway, they owe me a favour. I've composed them a cipher that no one living can decode. Including me."

Felix continued to stare at him. He said, "You mean the Medici are going to pay you all the money Jaak de Fleury owes us?"

Nicholas said, "Well, all he's admitted to owing us. That's why we're here, isn't it? To raise money to rebuild your business. That's why I couldn't go straight back to Bruges."

"I thought it was because—"

"It is. As well. But don't think in public," said Nicholas. "Come on. Pigello and Accerito await you."

The Palazzo Medici turned out to be a long, low edifice with a row of very fancy windows above a sort of bastion wall of squared blocks. Felix thought that they would be given wine Italian-style from a big copper cooler in the loggia, but the loggia was only just being built and wine would have turned into mud anyway, he could see.

They were met by Pigello Portinari, who had the same nose as Tommaso, but had been stuffed and packaged at a different shop, which probably happened when you became purveyor and financier to a ducal court. He had a sloping brow, and bags under his eyes. He looked as bald as doctor Tobias, but the top of his head was concealed by a sort of roofed pillbox, below which he had on a short tunic with his shirt and hose because of the heat. It had a low belt, to disguise the thickness of a good trencherman's waist. Felix felt very cordial towards him.

Messer Pigello, too, was charmed that Messer Felix had honoured him with a personal visit, and led the way to his office. He had on his table, ready for inspection, the box of silver from M. de Fleury, which Niccolò had brought him last night for safekeeping, but which Messer Felix himself was to check. To add to these, he now saw, he had several more bills from the ducal chancery. And were these the credit notes of which Niccolò had spoken?

He used Arabic numbers, Felix saw, adding quickly on scraps of paper; and so did Nicholas, counter-checking. The bills themselves registered sums in stately Roman numerals, less easy to tamper with. Accerito, the other brother, came in at some point and Felix was glad to cease looking as if he, too, were counting, and to join him in small-talk. He had seen enough anyway. Whatever else was happening, Nicholas wasn't cheating him. He was making him rich.

They didn't stay long, just enough to finish the transaction and take (indoors) some sugared nuts and some extremely good wine, served in heavy goblets decorated on the outside like orange segments. Messer Pigello, bowing to both Felix and Nicholas, made a graceful compliment about the marriage of the demoiselle de Charetty, and suggested that, despite the sad news of the fire, the company under such shrewd management would go from strength to strength.

News travelled fast. The subject, so painful at home, was re-

duced by its business setting to nothing. Felix had hardly bowed or
Nicholas murmured his thanks before the talk had veered again.

Afterwards, Felix remembered trying to follow an amiable exchange about eastern silk markets. Since Chinese silk was hard to
come by, Constantinople was crying out for silk to sell. Chios
could get rid of it anywhere. A Florentine consul at Trebizond
could pick up a fortune. It was Greek to Felix, in that he understood half of it. But even if it were no business of his, he always felt
warmly towards anyone who was by way of making a fortune. Of
course, the Medici in Florence had a silk *botteghe*. Marco Parenti,
married to the Strozzi sister, was a silk merchant. So were the
Bianchi of Florence.

The names, which Nicholas had not mentioned to him, meant as
yet nothing to Felix. He listened, but was equally eager to accompany Messer Accerito on a tour of the half-finished palace. He
returned, deeply impressed by the paintings on the walls and the
ceilings and the marble floors and the way none of the clerks
seemed to be impressed by them. He found Nicholas on the verge
of departure, and smiling, the two dimples deep as buttons, at
Messer Pigello.

Nicholas said, "How surprising! The Duke mentioned it even to
me. You didn't know he wished a trained ostrich?"

"Not," said Pigello, "until I received word from Tommaso. Apparently it has been necessary to send to Spain for the animal."

"Bird," Felix said. He looked from Nicholas to Pigello.

"And there has been some delay in conveying it."

"A shipwreck," said Nicholas. "Unhappily involving some liti-
gation. But the bird, I am told, is alive and well."

Pigello Portinari was not, it seemed, deeply disturbed. He said,
"And I am sure Messer Strozzi and my brother will contrive that it
reaches Milan in the end. Of course, anything you can do to the
purpose will be warmly acknowledged."

"Well, thank you for the confidence," Nicholas said. "But I seem
to have my hands full. And the last thing I should wish is to
deprive Messer Tommaso of his triumph. The ostrich, alive and
well in Bruges, and able to leave as Duke Philip's gift to Duke
Francesco. There is an achievement."

Out in the via dei Bossi, Felix said, "The ostrich."

"Yes?" said Nicholas. He skipped as he walked, winding his way
between sweating people and under awnings, and when he passed a
pretty girl, he grinned at her.

Felix said, "The Medici had never heard of the ostrich. Messer Cicco never mentioned it either."

"No," said Nicholas, from behind. He emerged from a booth with three oranges and started to juggle them as he walked, disrupting sundry groups of housewives, and well-dressed nobles and merchants, and hot men in cassocks, and servants and labourers, and stallkeepers and children. Two men playing chess on a balcony looked down as an orange rose by their ears and descended.

Felix said, "But the dispatch you brought to Tommaso said the Duke wanted one."

"Yes," said Nicholas. Three dogs were following him, and several children.

Felix said, "So you made it up? You made up the whole thing? No one wants an ostrich at all?"

"Nonsense," said Nicholas. "I do. Tommaso does. Lorenzo does. And once I've told the Chancery that it's coming, the Duke will as well. If no one wants it, we'll put it into the lottery like your porcupine. We'll harness it to the waterwheel and watch it eat all the buckets. We'll make it run in the Crane. We'll use it to dredge the canals. Winrik can keep his money in it. Everyone should have an ostrich. Or an orange. Catch."

He didn't catch it, and it fell in the wall-fountain they were passing, so that the splash went up his nose.

Felix didn't mind. For a moment—for how long?—Claes was back amongst them.

But it was Nicholas, not Claes, who accompanied Felix that night, to the house of Prosper de Camulio de' Medici.

A warm, strong breeze had risen which made it pleasant, in spite of the dust, to walk through the narrow streets under the shade of the crimped red eaves and the balconies and between the crooked steps with their pots of bright flowers. Swifts swirled overhead, random as gnats, their distant fluting turning into a thin, snarling whistle as they swooped. The house of Messer Camulio was in the southern quarter of the town, and close to the inner, encircling canal. Between that and the outer ring of water were some important churches and hospices, lodged on the specially-cut channels that brought freight-barges close to the heart of the city. The brothers Portinari supported two of such churches and, in return, were given favours.

Trade. Wealth. Renown. With high spirits and a new confidence,

Felix de Charetty trod the paved streets beside Nicholas, who listened receptively to Felix's detailed account of the afternoon he had spent at the Duke's tilting-yard at the (half-rebuilt) Castello, with the Duke's jousting-master.

Then they arrived at the Casa Camulio, which had a coat of arms over the entrance and pillared arches, underlit by the sun, in the small, warm courtyard within. Here, since the sun had lost its heat, they were invited by Prosper de Camulio to sit by the fountain and take their ease. He had one companion only. Four men, eating and talking, with no ladies present. A group of men talking, in low voices, about money.

Prosper de Camulio de' Medici, a man in his mid-thirties, possessed what Felix was beginning to recognise as the style of a diplomat and a politician. He was lightly dressed in a linen shirt and fine overtunic, and he wore a silk scarf embroidered with violets which had certainly come from France. With him was a Genoese called Tomà Adorno. Camulio and Adorno. Felix knew what they had in common, for Nicholas had told him.

Tomà Adorno was short and meaty and middle-aged, and his pale hair was bleached to wrack by the Levantine sun. Nothing of the slender, quizzical beauty of Anselm Adorne was visible in him, yet (said Nicholas) Anselm and he must be related.

So long entrenched in Bruges, so well-thought-of, so splendidly Flemish, the tribe of Adorne might have known no other roots. But six generations ago (according to Nicholas) the loss of Acre had driven the Adornes' merchant ancestors from the Holy Land: one branch to Flanders, and one branch to their native Genoa. And even sooner than that, the shrewd seamen and traders of the Genoese fishing village of Camoglio had begun to settle in the Genoese colonies, and one Vivaldo de Camulio had a trade in cloth in Byzantium.

Four generations ago, in the time of Anselm of Bruges' great-grandfather, Gabriel Adorno had become the first Adorno Doge of Genoa, and his kinsmen and fellow merchants had mastered the island of Chios and the alum trade of Phocoea. Within a couple of years, a Niccolò de Camulio was also living on Chios. In later years the family were to intermarry (said Nicholas) with the heirs of one Antonio de' Medici, to produce Niccolò de Camulio de' Medici, notary to the Commissarii of Genoa with the duty of reporting on rights and taxation in Phocoea and Chios. That was the line of their host, Prosper de Camulio.

Today the Turks owned the Phocoea alum mines, but the trade of Chios was still controlled from Genoa, and the Genoese merchants on Chios still included Baldassare and Paulo and Raffaele and Niccolò and Giuliano and Tomà Adorno.

Today the French occupied Genoa. But among the exiled Genoese still with an interest in Chios was Prosper Adorno, Count of Renda, seigneur of Ovada and of the two Ronciglioni, and the man with the strongest claim to be the next Doge of Genoa. He was Tomà's cousin. He was kinsman, many times removed, to Anselm Adorne. He was a longtime friend and supporter of Prosper de Camulio their host, and bore the same Christian name. He was the first of the Genoese rebels whom the Duke of Milan was supporting in secret since the Duke, too, wanted the French driven from Genoa.

He was also the man whose estate the doctor Tobias had recently visited to discuss, according to Nicholas, the interesting matter of alum.

Alum linked Tomà Adorno and Camulio. Alum and republican politics on a scale which cast Felix, when he thought of it, into a state of frightened excitement. The excitement came from the prospect of riches. The fear came when he looked at Nicholas and, now and then, allowed himself to realise that there was something here that he could not recognise.

Fear as well as his vestigial Italian kept him quiet, too, while the others were talking. The talk was not social. An undercurrent of resentment disturbed him. Nicholas appeared not to notice it. He went methodically about his business, which was to describe and produce for his Genoese hearers a written survey of the alum deposit recently found by the Charetty company in the Papal States, together with an estimate of its quality. The survey and the estimate were both signed and countersigned by Venetians. Felix had never seen them before.

It was Prosper de Camulio who raised his head from the paper and said, "This tells us, of course, that Venice has already seen the deposit and is aware that it constitutes a threat to its monopoly of Turkish alum. If, that is, the signature is genuine."

Nicholas said, "The man who signed it, Caterino Zeno, is in Milan. He is waiting not far away to be summoned once I have your agreement to his terms and mine. If, that is, you consider him a reliable spokesman for Venice."

Adorno answered. He said, "His forebears ruled Constantinople.

If Venice has sent him, then they are taking you seriously. You don't say where this deposit has been found. But Venice, it seems, has been shown it."

Nicholas said, "It is Venice who is being asked to pay in return for concealing this mine. It would have suited Venice to make these arrangements direct with my company; to pay me for my silence, as they will do, and to guarantee me concessionary alum, as they will do. Unless I insist, there is no need for them to include Genoese merchants in their special terms."

"But you include us, in return for a handsome payment. Why Genoa?" said Tomà Adorno. "Why not include the merchants of Lucca? Of Mantua?"

Nicholas sat, his big hands between his knees in their serviceable cloth, and rested on the Genoese his large and innocent gaze. He said, "The demoiselle de Charetty has always found the Adorne and the Doria and the other Genoese merchants in Bruges to be fair in their dealings with the dye trade. I confined the concession to Genoa, otherwise it would have been worthless. You wouldn't pay me for including your rivals."

"And profit, of course, is what you want," said Messer de Camulio. "You didn't think of approaching the Pope? With the money from a mine as rich as this, he could finance a Crusade and free the Phocoea mines. Then there would be a world of cheap alum and no monopoly."

Felix looked at Nicholas. Nicholas smiled. "I thought of it," he said. "But would a Crusade free the Phocoea mines? Would there even be a Crusade, while Naples and England and France and Burgundy have found such urgent need for their armies? A lot of Christian wars have to finish before the Turks need fear the Pope."

"What of Christian conscience?" Messer de Camulio said. "In protecting Venetian trade, you are protecting Turkish trade."

"And who isn't?" said Nicholas. "The West needs what Turkey can sell. Turkey needs the trade even more, and unless she's pushed, won't go too far in her wars in case she forfeits it. Kings make war, but traders, you can rely on it, are suitors of perpetual peace."

"I see," said Messer de Camulio. "Then why not demand your concessions direct from the Turk?"

Felix's mouth had fallen open. He shut it. Nicholas said, "I could, of course, if I were a larger company. I could demand almost any sum for my silence, and force any concessions I wanted, for anyone I wanted, including a change in the franchise. I don't have such power, but Venice has. I can't approach the Turk. But I'm rather expecting Venice to do it for me."

"I wondered if that would be your answer," said Prosper de Camulio. "So your plan will in the end favour Venice?"

Nicholas said, "Venice has the Turkish franchise. I can't alter that. Our concession will mean she takes less profit from us. It's only fair that she recoups from the Turk. You are still better off, and so is my company."

Tomà Adorno rubbed his chin. "True," he said. "You've been lucky, Messer Niccolò. You've been enabled to make a discovery which holds to ransom a great many rich institutions, for a short time at least. And I think you are right. The price the Christian church will set on its goods will far exceed the tribute exacted by Turkey. But in the meantime the price of alum to you and to Genoa must fall, and in some way all clothmakers benefit. I've no quarrel to find with your terms. I should like to know, however, how you mean to exclude the Florentines. Once the Medici observe our concessions, they'll begin to ponder the reason. Remember, they're papal bankers. If the existence of this mine comes to their ears, they'll proclaim it from every tower."

"I thought of that," Nicholas said. "But concessions are made for many reasons. Venice and Florence themselves, for example, are constantly in some such negotiation over the price of Italian silk. Florence could well be persuaded that our cheap alum was a matter of trade adjustment. You can make ledgers say pretty well anything."

"I daresay you can," said Tomà Adorno. "I think you should produce your terms in detail and let us have done with it, before you decide to add Lucca and Mantua to your list of the favoured. Then we can send for your patron Caterino Zeno. A friend, I take it, of Alvise Duodo of the Venetian galleys? A kinsman of Marco Zeno who commanded the Flanders galleys himself?"

"Gentlemen," Nicholas said, gently respectful. "You know him better than I do."

No one mentioned, because they didn't know, or they thought it irrelevant, the most important element in the history of Messer Caterino Zeno of Venice; which was simply the identity of his beautiful wife Violante. It played no part in the conversation the following morning, when the arranged meeting took place, and the agreement was ratified which made the Charetty company immedi-

ately wealthy, with the promise of healthy future assets in the way
of concessions and fees.

Prosper de Camulio supplied the Milanese agent who was to
transfer the payments to Bruges. Felix, hollow-eyed from a night in
which he had hardly slept and barely stopped talking, counter-
signed what had to be signed, and escaped, when he could, to shed
some of his pent-up excitement at the Castello.

Much later, Nicholas joined him at the tilting-ground. Of
course, he had spent some weeks there in the winter. That explained the shouts with which he was greeted, and the laughter as
he clowned his way through the first practise bouts. Then the jousting-master came out, and flung a sword at him, and then an axe
and a lance, and later got him on a horse and ran a course with
him.

Nicholas, amazingly, didn't fall off. Screaming at him with the
rest, Felix became gradually thoughtful. When he was told, at the
end, to mount and break a lance against his one-time servant himself, he lifted his weapon with none of the angry elation he remembered from that silly mock jousting in Bruges. The fight was different, too. He tried his hardest, but this time he didn't dislodge
Nicholas, although Nicholas rocked him twice in the saddle. Then
someone came from the Chancery asking for him, and Nicholas
took his leave of the master and left.

He didn't come back. Felix supposed there were arrangements to
make for the homeward trip. It would be a fast journey this time,
with the great news to take to his mother. The Medici credit notes
were already on their way to Bruges by Medici messenger. The
Venetian and Genoese money orders they would take to Bruges
themselves. Stripped to the waist, Felix ate under the trees with his
new friends, and chatted, from duty, to someone he recognised,
and dressed rather thoughtfully and called in his turn, when summoned, at the office at the Arengo of Cicco Simonetta. Then he
went back to the inn.

Nicholas was there, under the vine canopy in the garden, with
some of their men at arms. Felix located him at once because of the
laughter. When Nicholas didn't rise to his call, he went out and
joined them, and took some ale, and found he wanted to laugh
quite a lot as well. Much later, in the room that they shared, Felix
peeled off his sodden shirt once again and set out to obtain some
answers.

Nicholas always gave answers. Nicholas said, "I've told the escort to be ready to set out for Bruges tomorrow. I've hired some extra men for security, but all the bank drafts have been copied in case of accidents. I wondered if you'd object to going back on your own."

Felix stood, shirt in hand, and glared at him.

"You've got all the money," said Nicholas.

He'd forgotten about Geneva. He'd forgotten all his suspicions. Felix said, "Where are you going?"

Nicholas said, "I thought someone should find Tobie and thank him. He arranged all of this. I expected to find him here. We owe him a lot, and I want to make sure he's all right."

"Tobias?" said Felix. "He's on the other side of the country. With the Count of Urbino and Lionetto."

"So they think," Nicholas said.

"And what about my mother?" Felix said.

"You'll be there," Nicholas said. "She has good help as well. Now the money will solve everything."

Felix said, "She doesn't need me, does she? Only the money."

Nicholas said, "Which do you think she would choose?"

And Felix said, "Are you coming back to Bruges at all?"

Nicholas grinned. "I've got to come back, haven't I? Or you'll spend the whole fortune on jousting-armour. Of course I'll be back. I haven't got any money, for one thing."

Silence. Felix stood, pleating a handful of shirt. He said, "Why did you marry my mother?"

The large eyes didn't avoid his. He could see no guile in them. After a while, Nicholas said, "Because it was the right thing to do."

Felix looked down. He said, "I see." After a moment he said, "I suppose she wants us both back. But she's got help. We could get someone else to take her the money."

Nicholas said, "We could, of course. Why? Do you want to stay in Milan?" The floor was littered with papers. He sat down, crossed his legs, and began to collect them together on his knee, shuffling them into order. He didn't say, "Do you want to come with me?" In Felix's mind, a vagrant desire recently provoked became, unexpectedly, an intention. Felix said, "I want to go down to Naples. I want to join Astorre and Julius and fight."

Nicholas tapped his papers together and looked up. He said, "Well, I don't see why not. You ought to have the experience."

Felix stopped pleating the shirt. "You think I should go?" he said.

Nicholas balanced the paper pile on his scissored ankles. "If you want to. It's unfair to your mother, but she's used to it. So long as you don't salve your conscience with me. I'm no substitute if you're killed."

Felix stood and frowned. Nicholas returned to scanning his papers. Felix said, "I'm not going to be killed. Not with all that money there. Do you think I'm going to leave you to spend it? But—"

He didn't explain any more. Nicholas apparently understood. He said, "Well, you know how Julius needs keeping in order. I dare say it might be quite a good thing in the end. I'll probably get back to Bruges before you. You don't mind if I buy myself some nice jousting-armour?"

He leaned his head back, his gaze owlish. Felix laid down the shirt, and grinned, and walking round the bed sat on it, looking down at Nicholas and his papers. He said, "You just want to get rid of me. You don't know what happened today at the Chancery."

"No, I don't," said Nicholas obediently.

Felix said, "I was called in by Cicco Simonetta, and asked if I would accept a gift from the Duke to take back to the demoiselle of Charetty. He offered money."

He had, from the floor, Nicholas' entire attention. "And you told him we were tired of money?" Nicholas said.

"I told him," Felix said, "that in place of money I should like to ask a great favour. Such as the return of the singing Guinea slave whose services my mother had come to miss sorely."

The scarred face below him changed a little. "Loppe?" said Nicholas. "I didn't know he'd seen you."

"For some reason," said Felix, "he enjoyed being with us. He doesn't like Milan now Brother Gilles has gone away. He's afraid he'll be sent to Cosimo in Florence. I think," said Felix dreamily, "an African, properly dressed, makes a good impression in any company."

"So?" said Nicholas.

"So Messer Cicco offered to return Loppe with pleasure. And I said that I hoped to send in his place something that would give the Duke even more satisfaction."

"You did?" Nicholas said. "A sack of duty-free alum? A fancy helmet? A jacket with ermine tails on it? Or . . . Felix? What did you think he might like?"

"What you said he'd ordered, and he hadn't. I suggested," said Felix, "that what the Duke ought to have was an ostrich."

Below, they wondered if the two young men from Flanders were killing each other, such was the outburst of thumping and shouting that came from above. But when they descended a little while later, red-faced and rather dishevelled, the older had the younger by the shoulders and they both appeared to be laughing.

Chapter 34

The Dowager Duchess of Brittany, whose childless marriage had occurred when she was very young, was neither very old nor very wise. Her late sister Marie, who had married the neighbouring monarch in France, had been basically silly as well, although brought up with a liking for letters and poets. Indeed, her young court had acquired a certain notoriety because of its liking for poets, but this was less a matter of orgies, it was thought, than mere childish levity.

The Dowager Isabelle, although much given to rages and passions, was a lady of shallow mind who could be easily diverted from most things, always excluding her strong desire not to be sent back to Scotland. Her little court, unlike that of the young Duke her nephew, was a backwater, and public affairs seldom intruded. She was allowed, therefore, to include among her cats and her ladies a member of the family van Borselen, whose affiliations were Burgundian. This was a concession. France was Brittany's overlord, and no friend to Burgundy. And Burgundy, it was rumoured, was no friend to France's protégé, the English king who was a Lancastrian.

Nevertheless the Duke of Brittany, having cast a practised eye over Katelina van Borselen, was heartily in favour of allowing her to stay to wait on his aunt. She would learn nothing dangerous. They might even convert her to a Breton way of thinking. He would like to see that glossy hair out of its pleats, and the rest of her, but Antoinette would deny him her bedroom again. And he liked his women, as a rule, with more colour.

In April, it was true to say, the Dowager's new maiden of honour had possessed a brighter complexion. The change, along with several others, had begun during May. And by now, the middle of June, Katelina could be left in no doubt at all what had happened. She had begun to carry the child of a bastard servant called Claes. It shouldn't have come as such a shock, for in a blaze of wilful defiance she had flung the possibility at the feet of the gods. She had lied to Claes. She had said whatever would make him do what he had done.

And now, what? The Dowager's poor silly sister had consumed green apples and vinegar to preserve her from motherhood. She could try these, or harsher remedies. She was in Brittany, far from home, and no one would know. Every court had a servant who knew someone—a barber, a midwife who could interfere with nature. But it would have to succeed. Sometimes the child persevered, and was born mangled. Sometimes you died yourself.

Suppose she allowed the child to finish its term? Then she would have to leave court, find friends to hide her, and foster it. It had been done, by women with money. She had no resources. She could see no way of keeping such a thing secret. And the shame for her family would be terrible. For their sake, she must provide the child with a father. So she needed, quickly, a rich and powerful lover. Or, of course, a husband.

There was a rich and powerful lover at hand. She guessed her father's dreams that one day she might be the mother, married or unmarried, of a Burgundian prince. He would think no harm in a liaison with a profligate duke with a permanent mistress. But the more high-born the lover, the less flattered he would be at the arrival, after seven months or less, of a son or a daughter. And the less inclined, from experience, to acknowledge and rear it. Whereas a husband, contractually bound, might well ignore the calendar, and be happy with whatever heir he had so quickly begotten, rather than be labelled a fool.

She had wanted a husband. She had hoped to make up her mind here in Brittany, free of family pressures. And she had certainly been free of those. No letters had reached her since she left in April. In the early weeks, indeed, before she was sure where she stood, she had enjoyed the sort of life she had envisaged: of undemanding companionship to the Dowager; of becoming acquainted with the dramas, the actors in yet another court; of choosing her own rôle to play in it. She learned to evade the Duke, and to make friends with his mistress. The first visit of Jordan de Ribérac had been therefore doubly unpleasant.

Later, she was to be glad that she had then been ignorant of her condition. She had had no warning. He had arrived on an April morning in the Dowager's audience chamber. The room, which was small, became simply a shell for his bulk and his height. His robe was of Lucca velvet. The scarves of his hat were embroidered with gold. His face with its many chins was fresh and smiling, but the eyes scoured her naked.

The last time the seigneur de Ribérac had visited Bruges, Claes had nearly died in the fire at the Carnival. The last time she had met the seigneur de Ribérac, he had proposed, placidly, to requisition her virtue on her kitchen floor, preparatory to marrying her. What she had denied him, she had presented, the same night, to Claes. But that Jordan de Ribérac couldn't know. Or he wouldn't just scar his face, or order his death by two inept assassins. He would personally kill him.

Now, it appeared, he was merely in course of a courtesy call on the Dowager. He spent half an hour and spoke to all the ladies of honour. She couldn't leave. She hardly believed he would address her but he did, his eyes cold, his smile delightful. "What, mademoiselle! No suitor yet for your charms? Or none we know of in Bruges, where they keep their fools in barrels like fish, so I'm told. You are wise to come to Brittany. Make your choice here. Wait until the air is clearer and fresher before you venture to Flanders again."

She said, "Even in Brittany, monseigneur, the air is not as fresh as I would wish."

It was childish. It made no impression. He merely spread his smile blandly among all his audience. He said, "Bruges! A place for small artisan businesses and coupling servants. A wise man would clear the city of both. Forget Bruges. Wait until you savour Carnival evening in Nantes, my dear lady. Whatever your past experience, I promise you this will exceed it."

He had turned away before she could reply. He knew. He knew something.

Afterwards, when he had gone and the Duchess and her kittens were sleeping, Katelina left the Dowager's suite and went to the reception rooms where she might find the Duke's mistress. The King of France, it was clear, was satisfied that no French secrets could leak through to Flanders from the Dowager's court. That a Flemish secret might leak through to France ought to give him great pleasure.

Antoinette de Maignèlais, when she found her, naturally knew all about Jordan. France was full, my dear, of these Scots who came and fought in her wars and then stayed on to become rich. Grateful kings gave them seigneuries, like this Ribérac. A clever man with a good eye for trade didn't take long to make connections, acquire fleets, amass property. And the reward? The King of France's ear, my dear, on all matters financial, and some of the darker little secrets of his treasury. His present Majesty often sent him to Brittany, to disentangle the affairs of his first wife's sister. Personally, said Antoinette, she preferred men who were not quite so obese.

Katelina agreed, as most people did with this lady. When Agnès Sorel, the French King's great mistress, died ten years ago, her place was filled by her cousin Antoinette, Madame de Villequier: some said before she was widowed, some said after. When the King's taste became jaded, she found him younger bedfellows. She still did so, and was as often at the King's side as at the Duke's. She had carried to the Duke, rumour said, the King's ulcerous leg. She was sharp-witted, forthright and practical.

Katelina said, "It's not so much the fat. Is he trusted?"

The lids fell, in mock pain, over the bright, painted eyes. "My dear, you know better than that!" said Antoinette. "If there is one person to be trusted at court, we do not rest until we have changed him. But, having the strings of the Mint in his shirt, I suppose our dear Jordan has all the money he wants. But, let us think, now you mention it. What else would attract him?"

"The same position under the next king?" said Katelina.

The painted eyes wandered. "Ah," said Antoinette. "Tell me. Is this hearsay?"

"No," said Katelina. "He has been seen at Genappe. He has information about the Dauphin's chamberlain which could only have been learned at Genappe. He takes with him one at least of the Scots Guard of archers."

"How do you know?" said Antoinette.

Katelina said, "He has no hold over me or my family. But he is trying to persuade me to marry him."

"Why?" said Antoinette. "Of course, you are very beautiful. But he is a rich man, with many to choose from in his own country."

"To oust his Scottish son from the inheritance," Katelina said. "He wants heirs. Once he has them, his present son may not long survive."

"And he chooses a Flemish, a Burgundian lady," said Antoinette. "How fortunate that he is fat, and did not attract you. Doubly fortunate. Fat men are noticed, when gossip starts."

"Gossip is none of my business," said Katelina.

"I am aware," said Antoinette. "But, my dear, you know very

well that in Bourges, where the king is, gossip is what makes the walls and the ditches and mans the embrasures. Gossip, my dear, not bricks and mortar."

That was when Katelina wrote her letter to Gelis, to be passed on to Claes. To a casual reader, the missive appeared mostly concerned with the astonishing shipwreck of an ostrich. In the weeks that followed, Antoinette didn't return to the subject of Jordan. Later, when Katelina knew she was pregnant, she did nothing to correct or cancel the rumour she had started.

From what Claes had said, there was truth in it. Antoinette would report to King Charles. And King Charles would have his own way of testing the loyalty of the vicomte Jordan de Ribérac. If the rumour was correct, if he was the Dauphin's man and a traitor, she would be amply revenged for his treatment of her. And for what he had done and tried to do to Claes.

Claes. She had wished to call him Nicholas, and he had shown her that the wish did her no credit. Now, when she had even more cause to slaughter her pride, she found herself resisting. She remembered what Claes the man and the lover were like, and he bore no badges of servitude, and many of joy. In his own right, he was Nicholas.

From there, she was moved for the first time to wonder what he would make of the child. He had no reason to expect this would happen. She had convinced him otherwise. He had said, and she believed him, that he had no wish for marriage. He had dismissed, with finality, the alternative. But if there was a child coming?

If its coming were interrupted, what would he feel? But to dispose of it was her right, as it had been her decision to risk conceiving it. If she bore it in secret for fostering, would he want to know? He might not. Or he might, if told, take the child. Even proclaim, for the child's sake, who its mother was.

What was his own rearing? She knew so little about him. He had had his mother, she thought, for a few years. Then he had gone to some distant relative, who had been harsh. No. A man brought up like that wouldn't see his child given away. He would have, then, to be made to believe that it was not his. Unless . . .

Unless. The second month passed, and her eyes became large and profound, and her cheekbones sharpened a little. Sometimes she was late for her morning duties, but she never missed one. She met many men, but none she liked. She took no lovers, but kept thinking of the one she had had.

In the second week of June, when she knew she must do something, Jordan de Ribérac returned. This time, the Dowager was closeted with her astrologer and her companion on duty was absent. But for the page at the door, Katelina sat alone in the outer chamber. The fat man, with sketchy formality, sat down beside her.

The eyes again stripped her naked, from fichu to high waist and below. And this time, there was something to see. Jordan de Ribérac said, "Well, demoiselle. Where is your husband now?"

Katelina said, "You think I should have one? Are you proposing yourself again, M. de Ribérac?"

He smiled. He said, "The number of suitors is not so great, is it? The Duke, I am sure, would make an accommodation, but he cannot marry you, and the state of his leg, I am told, is truly distressing. As for the others, you know the situation, I'm sure, as well as I do. You hear the news from home?"

The tone of his voice urged her to say that she had. Instinct kept her to the truth. She said, "No. Letters seem to have been lost."

He raised his eyebrows. "I see. Then perhaps I can give you first news of these promising friends of yours. My son. Let us begin with my son. Simon, it appears, is on the verge of a most advantageous alliance with a lady called Muriella, the daughter of John Reid, the Staple merchant. Will she be fecund? I wonder. Simon is not fond of children. But you must, I am afraid, dismiss the charming illusion that once we shared. My sweet Simon will not run to your call.

"Who else? The Gruuthuse family, I am told, have begun actively pressing young Guildolf to make his final choice. He is young. But he would I think have swallowed his rebuff and come to you, except that he and his parents are in Bruges and you have abandoned him to come here. Poor Guildolf."

Jordan de Ribérac sighed. "And there is really no one else, is there? You disliked your parents' other two candidates, so that you won't be sorry to hear that they have each made a contract with the girl of their choice. I know of no one else who has been able to pierce the magic circle of your maiden reserve. Unless, of course, you count the young workman Claes."

Katelina said, "Hardly."

"Hardly?" said the fat man. "After you and your sister took such trouble to lift him—*twice?*—out of our canals? An act of mercy I commend, of course. If he had actually killed my son with his shears I might have felt differently."

"I thought the fate of your son was the least of your worries," said Katelina.

"No. No!" said the fat man. "I concern myself with him very much. I may not wish him in health, but I should like to be consulted as to the time and manner of his departure from it. I do not like to have my paternal rights in this matter pre-empted. Not that Claes, I believe, would have given me much concern. Claes is the underdog. He has beneath him the treadmill of perpetual ambition and perpetual failure. Look at his latest contrivance."

She wouldn't answer. She raised her eyebrows. The fat man sighed.

"Would you believe that he has induced his employer to marry him? Witnesses bribed, the son kept safely in ignorance, notarial documents prepared for all her property. With her loving acquiescence. I am told she is besotted. And that the only heir has now been tempted south, where he might discover a warrior's grave. A scheme worthy of modest congratulation save that he made the error, in his excitement, of burning down his bride's business, her house, her money and every one of her ledgers. It seems unlikely that she can rise to her debts. All is lost, save the marriage."

Her stomach rose to her throat, and with anger, and hatred and fear and pride, she controlled it. She knew, from his face, that he could identify all these emotions, and was not abashed. She said, when she could speak, "I congratulate you. It's a skill, carrying small items of news from one place to another. I trust your accuracy. I'm only surprised that the Charetty fire was an accident."

He considered that, his face earnest. "You think it may not have been? Certainly, the young man had rivals. The pawnbroker Oudenin. Perhaps others. She's a pretty woman, if no longer young. They made a touching picture, I'm told: the young husband, half-clothed, embracing his wife in her bedgown outside their shrivelling love-nest. So you understand why I say to you, Where is your husband?"

"I have no difficulty in understanding you, M. de Ribérac," Katelina said. "And I repeat. Are you proposing marriage again? Perhaps I should be interested."

The pupils of his eyes, sharply black, pinned themselves to her face. "Would you now?" said Jordan de Ribérac softly.

"But on the other hand," said Katelina, "I might prove to be barren, or you might prove to be incapable, and all your plans would come to nothing. No. On mature reflection, I really cannot imagine the circumstance which would bring me to stomach it. Now, what shall we talk about? Or perhaps there is nothing more we have to say to each other. Let me find out if the Dowager will see you now."

He rose when she did and stood, without moving, looking down at her. For a moment she wondered what she would do if his hand rose, as it had done to Claes, and the ring cut its way down her cheek. But he simply turned on his heel and crossed the small room to the door, where he took up his courtier's stance, prepared to be led to his audience. Afterwards she didn't see him leave the rooms, or the building.

Antoinette de Maignélais found her later in the room she shared with the others, and taking her to a window seat, embarked on a harmless discourse. Halfway through she observed, "M. de Ribérac contrived to see you alone. Does he suspect you?"

"He wondered if I still wished to marry him. No. He showed no suspicions," said Katelina. "But I trust him less and less."

"You have an instinct," said the Duke of Brittany's mistress. "And you are correct. Discreet enquiries have been made. Messengers have been followed. Banks have had tales to tell. The story is not yet complete. Records have to come from Burgundian sources, and time and money are needed. But in two months, I fancy, it will not be a new wife that my lord of Ribérac has to think of."

It helped, a little, to know that he might suffer some of the devastation that he visited with such ready artistry on his fellows. He had been angry, she thought, that Claes had aspired, even briefly, and to a small widow's hand. But the anger had been soothed by the pleasure of telling her of it. He couldn't know, surely, the use she had made of Claes. Of course she had used him, and should expect nothing more from a servant than this, that he should jump from her bed into that of the first person who could help him into the bourgeoisie, even if she were an old woman with a grown family.

Half-naked, he had embraced the widow. Perhaps she, too, had drawn him his bath, and kept his clothes from him. However old she was, however ugly, he would perform for her. Every girl in Bruges knew that. Mabelie. Herself.

And his name was Claes. It had never been Nicholas. Her first-born had Claes for a father, the bastard workman with the beguiling tongue and the vast and innocent gaze which concealed a cunning, a ruthless ambition. The treadmill of ambition but not, surely, of failure. There the fat man was wrong. Building carefully, woman by woman, man by man, Claes was raising the staircase that would take him from apprentice to merchant and from merchant to whatever pinnacle his self-esteem demanded.

He hadn't needed Katelina. Her name and rank without money were useless to him. He needed what he had got: the owner of a small business whose standing, however minor, now became his. Arson might check him. There might be other attempts to hinder his rise. But unlike the fat man, she could judge Claes from many aspects. News of his marriage had completed the picture. Now she knew him. Short of death, nothing now would hold him. He didn't need her, and still less would he want the baby she carried. The problem was solved.

Katelina van Borselen went quietly about her business. Those who knew and liked her noted that she was a little withdrawn, and spent more time in her room than had been usual. They had to call her from it to act, as she often did, as interpreter for one of the interminable talks about the Dowager's dowry.

There was to be a meeting in France. The Scots commissioners, assembling their claims, were calling to discuss the King's case with his sister. Sir William Monypenny, of course. Bishop Kennedy later. Flockhart, perhaps. And the handsome, yellow-haired man the Dowager claimed to favour, who had not called since Katelina had come, but who would put the roses back in Katelina's pale cheeks.

"Come, Katelina!" said her friends. "Come and meet Simon of Kilmirren!"

June was then in its second week. All over Europe, forces already set in motion, like a game in a wooden box, began to hop and roll to their destiny.

Before June ended, Felix, heir to the Charetty company, arrived in Naples and joined his mother's troops under captain Astorre and the notary Julius. With him as personal servant he took a magnificent negro called Loppe. With him also came a gift to the King from the Duke of Milan: eighteen hundred horsemen destined to reinforce the Pope's army and help King Ferrante clear his foes out of the land about Naples. Emboldened, King Ferrante moved out of Naples and challenged the enemy.

It wasn't wise, but the King of Naples was fortunate. Duke John of Calabria, with unusual caution, refused battle. When threatened, he fled with his army to the small town of Sarno, built on a river-girt hillside just thirty miles south of Naples, and allowed himself to be besieged. The army of King Ferrante, aided by the troops from the Pope and the Duke of Milan and their many hired companies, including that of captain Astorre, settled down to starve them out, as was usual.

They would have succeeded. It was unfortunate that King Ferrante's mercenaries, in particular, had not been paid for quite some time, and that King Ferrante, at that moment, had no prospect of paying them. Attractive offers began to arrive from the enemy camp. Men began to desert.

King Ferrante decided, with a certain amount of regret and a greater amount of reckless optimism, that instead of prosecuting the siege, he ought to attempt an attack. He meant it to be a limited one, or so he said afterwards. But, bored and unpaid, his soldiers thought otherwise. That was in the first week of July. That a decisive battle had been fought at Sarno was unknown for some time.

Decisive battles were being fought elsewhere at the same moment. A bloodless one occurred in England when, led by Bishop Coppini and the Earl of Warwick, the white-rose Yorkists crossed from Calais and entered London in triumph. It remained only to locate the person of the Lancastrian king (to whom, if roses were given, a red would be appropriate) and his queen, the sister of Duke John of Calabria.

The Duke of Milan was delighted. The Yorkists gave full credit to the advice and leadership of Bishop Coppini, Papal Legate to England and Flanders and secret agent of the Duke of Milan. Bishop Coppini, working hard for his Cardinal's hat, ran out of sympathetic ink in his happiness.

James, King of Scotland, had long ago reached the conclusion that he ought to be dealing with both sides in the English war, in order to have a friend with a rose when it finished. A long-standing grievance was the English occupation of two good Scottish towns: Berwick on the eastern Borders, and Roxburgh to the south. It seemed to King James and his advisers that, while the English were currently so very busy, there might be something gained from a short, sharp attack on the English garrison in, say, Roxburgh.

King James and his artillery master had a serious talk, as a result of which the two great cannon from Mons were run out and prepared for a journey. King James went to see them himself: old Meg and new Martha. He fondled them. No one had guns like these. No one outside the Sultan of Turkey. If he had not been a King of Scotland with six stupid sisters, he would have been crowned master gunner.

Chapter 35

Pursuing also his solitary course, Nicholas, once Claes and never solitary, made the long hard journey east and south across Italy from Milan to Urbino, and from there tracked, by the scars on the land, the route of two armies. To a man riding south through the Papal States in the choking heat of mid-summer, there were everywhere to be seen the ravages of Count Jacopo Piccinino and his troops, hastening to help in the destruction of Naples.

In early July, Nicholas reached the river Tronto, and crossed from the Papal States to the Abruzzi, the eastern territory between the Appenine mountains and the sea which belonged to the Kingdom of Naples. Here the burned farms and smoking castles were the work of the pursuing papal and Milanese army under the Count of Urbino. It was this army that Nicholas overtook and indeed almost overran, for it had stopped.

South of and parallel to the river Tronto ran the river Tordino. And by the banks of the Tordino the forces of Milan and the Pope were encamped on level ground, confronting the army of Count Piccinino which had halted also, arrayed on the opposite hillside.

It was dusk when Nicholas reached the end of his journey. On his right the sky was still tinged with the dying sunset above the black spine of the mountains. Before him, lamplit in snapdragon silks, was a city of tents, the hosts of its banners stiffened like hogthorns. He could see the viper and eagle of Alessandro and Bosio Sforza; the cross and crescents in azure and gold of the papal banner, and above all, the eagle of Federigo, Count of Urbino, the flag of the commander. On the hill, the tents of the enemy lay like embers, and the banner of Count Jacopo Piccinino could only be guessed at.

Nicholas had planned to defer his entry until morning, but he approached too near, and was challenged. His safe conduct was not the kind to be lightly ignored. He and his grooms and his horses were allowed into the camp under escort, and a little later, he was conducted to the pavilion he sought.

Tobie Beventini of Grado, the candlelight on his bald head, was seated in his doublet and drawers, with one foot in a bucket. The other was saddled between his two bony hands and he was studying it. Beneath the neat double curl of his nose, his lips appeared shorter than usual. Behind him was a camp bed, and to one side a field table with his medical box lying on it, as well as a litter of jars, a bowl and a sheaf of assorted papers. There was no one else in the tent with him.

Nicholas said, "Five is the usual number."

The doctor looked up. His pale eyes, already round, didn't alter. He said, "And about time. Unless you've got haemorrhoids."

"My grooms have," said Nicholas helpfully. "Are you specialising?"

"I'm buttock man to the Holy Roman Empire," said Tobie. "They don't want a doctor. They want a man to design a new sort of horse. You took my advice and married the woman."

"I always take your advice," Nicholas said. "Anyway, you took mine and persuaded the Count to bribe Lionetto. For a nice sum too—I checked at his Milan agent, Maffino's. Astorre must be very annoyed. He probably thinks you've got half Lionetto's glass rubies. May I come in, or will your leg run away?"

Tobie the doctor released his foot and placed it carefully beside the other in the bucket. He said, "You're alone?"

"Apart from two grooms with haemorrhoids," said Nicholas. He came in and dropped a saddlebag on the straw by the truckle bed. He said, "I've sent Felix on to Astorre in Naples."

The tent was stifling. The staves of the bucket had misted. "More fool you," said Tobie.

"He can't stay a child," Nicholas said. "A big Milanese contingent was leaving. They don't expect fighting."

A sequence of small, contemplative splashes emerged from the bucket. "You had a fire," Tobie said. "Deliberate?"

"I know who did it," Nicholas said. "I'm the target. While I'm here, they'll be all right in Bruges. Now we have all this money, they can put the business together again."

Tobie's short mouth widened. His round, pale eyes stubbed themselves on his cheeks. He placed two hands on his stool, and lifting both dripping feet deposited them tenderly on a towel. He said, "Pray sit down. Take my bed. But don't go to sleep before you've told me. How rich am I?"

Nicholas sat, with the care of a man who has ridden sixty difficult miles in extreme heat, and who is not feeling his best. He said,

"Not as rich as I am, but you can hope to leave buttocks behind you. Why the sore feet? A new cure for piles? Are you vatting your patients and treading them?"

Tobie lifted one foot and started to dry it. "I'm glad you're so happy," he said. "And I only hope I'm worth as much as I deserve to be, after riding all over Lazio with those two drunken miners of Zorzi's. Messer Caterino Zeno was impressed, then."

"Everyone was impressed," Nicholas said. "We share the concession with the Genoese."

Tobie caught his little toe in the towel and screamed, *"What?"*

"Why d'you think I put you onto Camulio? We've got to work with the other merchants in Bruges. We need Adorne. We need the Adorno. Venice and Turkey may always fall out. And we could do with friends on Chios to keep an eye on what the Venetians are doing."

The doctor's bald head had flushed. The wispy hair by his ears swelled and released drops of sweat. He said, "I should have arranged it myself. You should have crawled all over those hills with two alum miners and an enlarging glass. The concession's worth nothing once Tolfa's discovered. That adventurer da Castro's begun prospecting already with his astrologer friend. Did you know that?"

"No," said Nicholas.

"And the name of the astrologer friend, my numerate colleague, is Zaccaria. Did you know that?"

"No," said Nicholas.

"No," repeated the doctor. "Then think about this. The French are already governing Genoa. The French would like to attack Burgundy. The French would like to get Sforza out and put their own man into the duchy of Milan. And the rumour is that they're asking Venice to help them. So no Adorno, no Sforza, and no way of frightening Venice with the new alum mines. If Venice helps France to conquer half Italy, the next Pope will be French and Venice will work the new alum herself."

Nicholas had opened his purse. He sat holding with both hands the paper he had drawn from it until Tobie paused, and then he leaned forward and offered it to him. It was covered with figures. Tobie took it and read them.

"Your share," said Nicholas. "It's banked as you wanted it."

Tobie rubbed his nose, which was running, with the back of his hand. He read it again, his fingers making wet marks on the paper.

Nicholas said, "I don't think, do you, that Venice will agree to help France? I don't think France can afford to attack anyone unless perhaps the Lancastrian side wins in England. But they would have to win quickly, because they say the King of France is unwell. If he dies, the Dauphin would be king. Gaston du Lyon is travelling backwards and forwards because Milan and the Dauphin are planning an alliance already. And then—of course, someone will find the Tolfa mine. Maybe Zaccaria. But not quite yet. That's the payment we've already got for our silence. And if we get only one consignment, a really big one, it will help. And there's the silk deal."

"What silk deal?" said Tobie. He was still staring down at the paper.

"To reassure Florence. I've arranged it with the Venetians. Florence gets a certain amount of cheap alum too, but in return for equal exports of cheap silk to Zorzi in Constantinople. Florence also wants to trade in the Black Sea, but they haven't a consul. Venice doesn't want them to have a consul. If the Emperor of Trebizond and the Medici insist, Venice will see to it that the agent proposed is the Charetty company."

Tobie slowly laid down the paper. "Breaking ciphers," he said.

Nicholas grinned. "Honest trading," he said. "We could invest in a ship. Felix would like it. Julius could run the whole agency. He would probably have to learn Turkish."

The doctor's pale eyes examined him, as if for an infection. The doctor said, "You're half serious, I think. You're thinking of outlets in case I'm right and you're wrong and France expands into Italy? But soon the Dauphin may be king."

"One day Felix will be head of the Charetty business," Nicholas said. "And a sterner master, I suspect, than old Cornelis ever was."

The doctor got up. He walked in his bare feet to the tent door and rattled on the post, and when his servant came, sent him off with the bucket and a list of instructions. He turned back and, sitting down, picked up his hose. He said, "They skirmish on the plain sometimes at night. Daytime too. Nothing serious. They shout at one another and issue challenges but that's all they can do. Until someone sends us more troops, we can't get past that bastard to Naples. Do you like hens?"

"In their proper place," Nicholas said. "Why? Do you have some?"

"Twenty thousand," Tobie said. "We took a lot of mules too.

Oxen. Sheep. You probably noticed the fields after you got over the Tronto. The corn all cut clean and threshed. Good farmer lads, these Urbinati."

The door opened. He went on dressing as a table was unfolded and set, and platters laid on it. A wine-jug and cups made an appearance. Someone carried in and propped up a second bed. Nicholas got up and sat down at the table. He said, "What did they do with the corn?"

"Took it to market," said Tobie. "And sold it to the needy peasants and their needy lords for a lot of money. And that's just for their living expenses. You should see what the commanders have picked up in the way of treasure. You haven't asked if I'm with Lionetto."

Now he had started eating, Nicholas was so hungry his jaws ached. He said, "I don't need to: you're sober. Why did you stay in the Abruzzi?"

Tobie said, "Count Federigo asked me. The commander."

Nicholas said, "And?"

The doctor said, "For a condottiere, he's fairly uncommon. You've heard. He rules Urbino, and Urbino's no paradise. His only riches are soldiers. They're good, too."

Nicholas looked at what he could see of the other's face over a chicken. He said, "You don't owe anyone anything."

"That's what I thought," said Tobie sharply. He tore the fowl to pieces.

The meal was long over and they were asleep in the darkness when there came the only alarm of the night, and that was not from the enemy. It was Lionetto who ripped the tent lacings apart and kicked the beds, one after the other, the lantern swinging in his hand. The first thing Nicholas saw, turning over and looking up through narrowed eyes, was the bush of shoulder-length carroty hair, the bulbous nose, the skin uneven as tweed in the lamplight.

Lionetto's smile rarely displayed, as now, his obelisk teeth. He said, "There's Greek for you, and names for all the unnatural vices. That's the brat I flung in the sea. It didn't cleanse him."

Nicholas returned the gaze, lying quite still as he was. His skin sparkled with sweat.

Tobie jerked into sitting position. One lamplit nostril had curled like a snail. He said, "The lord Federigo has sent for him perhaps?"

"Now I'm sorry to hear that," said Lionetto. "So Urbino is

tainted as well. Is this wine? You don't mind. The news has made
me thirsty. Oh. There now. I spilt it."

The trail of wine crossed the floor, and the wrinkled sheet on
Nicholas' bed, and ended in a pool at his throat. Lionetto laughed
down at him, the goblet tilted still in his hand, and Nicholas continued to gaze back, saying nothing. "You look better now," Lionetto said. "Wet."

Behind, Tobie was on his feet, scalp glittering, eyes round and
threatening. He said, "And he's got more patience than I have.
You're drunk. I'll report it."

"Drunk?" said Lionetto. He strolled back to the table, hauled
out a stool and sat on it to refill his cup. He said, "Half the camp'll
be drunk by tomorrow, illustrious medical man. Drowning our
sorrows. Hiding our poor little fears. What'll the high-handed
widow do now? The pawnbroker's daughter that thought she was a
man. But you showed her she wasn't, didn't you, wet boy? Married
her. Didn't bed her. Couldn't bed her. But got the business. What
business? Burnt business and all her little soldiers gone and dead.
Poor old bitch."

Nicholas sat up. "News from Naples."

The doctor, arrested staring down at Lionetto, suddenly leaned
forward and knocked the wine out of his hands. "Is it? News from
Naples?"

Lionetto roared. Nicholas acted, scooping up the fallen cup, filling it, and thumping it in front of the captain. Then he stood, his
hand on the doctor's elbow, holding him. "Tell us," he said. Veins
of wine crawled and trickled over his skin. He shivered.

Lionetto said, "If you go outside, you'll hear Piccinino's men
starting to cheer in a minute. The survivors are just coming
through. Naples is lost. Ferrante's dead. The army's smashed. And
you know why? Because the handgunners hadn't been paid, and
crossed to the enemy. Ferrante had Duke John and all his army
penned up in Sarno. Instead of starving them out, he attacked
them. And the handgunners stood on the walls and shot red holes
through their helms and their cuirasses until there was no one left
to fight."

He drank off the wine and looked up grinning. "Astorre's men.
Using handguns you bought for him. Now he's dead, and you're
both safely here with the condotta money."

"Be quiet," said the doctor. He was looking at Nicholas, who
had shivered again.

Nicholas said, "No. They were fully paid. Julius would see to that. And Astorre had control of them."

Tobie said, "It hardly matters."

It didn't, of course. Astorre. Julius. And Felix.

Lionetto said, "Well, it matters to the statesmen, I dare say. Now France can put their candidate into Naples. But I'm all right. A contract till September and I can go back home. Or cross back to Piccinino."

Tobie said, "What'll happen now?"

"Here? Piccinino has nothing to do but stay there on his hill, blocking our way. Maybe in a week or two, the Duke of Milan and the Pope will raise more troops and try again. Another thousand and we could offer the little Count battle. We could march south and take back some of the towns that used to be under Ferrante. But we couldn't take Naples. That needs a whole new force on the east." He cocked an ear. "I told you. Listen."

Through the stuff of the tent there had appeared, bright and dim, the blooming of many lamps, and the red of revived fires. You could hear the confused sound of talk, getting louder, and a braying and barking as livestock were roused.

"I thought you'd like to be among the first to know," said Lionetto. "That's not a bad wine. I'll take the jug with me."

He left. No one spoke. Nicholas released the doctor's arm and moved alone to stand where the doorway canvas hung open. As Lionetto had said, the news had now reached the enemy camp. The cheering from the hillside was faint, but getting louder. "And now?" said Tobie's voice with deliberation. "Another set of figures?"

Nicholas stood in the doorway and listened. The cheering that was getting louder was different from the cheering on the opposite hillside. You could never mistake it for a victory shout. It was a straggling, sympathetic acclaim, accorded to men who had fought well, and lost. It came from their own encampment. Under Nicholas' grasp, the tent flap gave way. He stared at the ripped cloth in his hand, and then let it go. He said, "I was wrong. I should have hit him."

"My God," said Tobie. "Is that all you can think of?"

Nicholas didn't answer. Sweat and wine seemed to be running all over his body, and his heart beat like a cannonball bounding on hide. Then he said, without turning his head, "Come and look."

As soon as he came, Tobie stood still as he had done, listening and looking as all about them the tentless spaces filled with shouting men, half-dressed or naked. And then, as he had done, began to catch sight of riders, filing through the gates of the encampment and pushing through the crowd and one by one dismounting, among the cries and the torchlight. Weary men; wounded men. Men who had survived the rout at Sarno and who had ridden, not safely back to their homes, but here, to join the flag of their other army.

Brands clustered about them, offering glimpses of unknown faces and unknown features. Then, suddenly, something familiar: the moustache of a man called Manfred, a horse-master. The black, helmetless head of a Hungarian crossbowman with his neck wrapped in white cloth. Two men in tattered black: one sunburnt and thin, and the other straightbacked and muscular with slanting eyes and a classical nose, who slid from his horse one-handed, the other wrapped in a sling.

"Julius," said Tobie aloud. His voice sounded odd. "And there. Behind him. Astorre. Holy Mother of God, you should have hit him. I should have killed him. I will kill him. Lionetto knew they were safe."

The words followed Nicholas but he paid no attention to them, being already deep into the crowd with his head down, making his way to the battered file of men still stumbling in. He touched them all as he reached them and passed—Manfred, Godscalc, Abrami— the shoulder, suddenly come on, of Thomas, whose grey face turned, full of surprise. Astorre, who dismounted heavily, chin in air, eyes half-closed on each side of his nose-piece. Lukin. And black Loppe, his face empty. And then Julius, standing still and looking at him.

Beyond was Felix.

Felix said, "Oh, there you are. I said he'd be here. We've had quite a battle. You really should have been there. How many men did I kill? I forget."

"Eight, you said," said Julius. He hadn't moved.

Nicholas stayed where he was.

Tobie's voice said, "That's my tent over there. They're putting up another one beside it. I'll help Nicholas see to the men and your horses. There's plenty of food. Ask for what you want. Have you seen the Count?"

Astorre said, "We've just come from his tent." His voice creaked.

Tobie said "Go on, then." Nicholas saw a glance passed between him and Julius. The knot of men began to dissolve. Tobie's voice said, "Pull yourself together. Wait for me. I'll see to all this."

It was dark by the carts. Nicholas sat on the baked dirt and failed to pull himself together. The voice of Julius said, from above him, "Well, idiot, what's wrong? Were you hoping we wouldn't come back?"

It was no use trying to answer. He could feel Julius bending over him. With broken bones, that was probably painful. Footsteps, and another voice. Tobie said, "We're all sorry you're back. We were going to get rich on your dead-pay. Don't you know marsh fever when you see it? Tell Godscalc to come out."

Nicholas opened his eyes. Tobie was kneeling beside him alone. Tobie said, "Amazing. You're human. It *is* marsh fever, as a matter of fact; saw it coming. You'll throw it off."

Nicholas tilted his head back against the cart and, as well as his chattering teeth would allow, returned a shaky, unfocused smile.

"Although," said Tobie, "we'll never know, will we, what brought it on? Relief or disappointment?"

Chapter 36

When you had good enough health, but had spent your whole life inviting beatings of one sort or another, it was nothing new to feel alternately hot and cold, to run a small fever, to feel sick until the pain passed. It didn't matter, because it always passed. It was the same now, in Tobie's tent, after a blurred interval where Nicholas saw very little, but sometimes heard voices. Sometimes when he woke it was dark, and sometimes it was light. He was not greatly troubled about whether he woke or not.

The voice that finally reached him and kept him awake was that of Felix, arguing. The voice answering him appeared to be that of Julius, but he couldn't make out what the dispute was about. He was still dreamily listening when a shadow fell over his bed and he saw it was Tobie, with a cloth in his hand.

Tobie said, "Ah. Don't speak, or you'll have them both over."

His lips didn't want to smile and his tongue didn't want to move, but central authority at length prevailed. "Why not?" Nicholas said.

The pale eyes, ringed and pin-pupilled, studied him. "Why not, indeed?" said Tobie. "Piccinino is getting bored. Urbino is getting bored. The brilliant young noblemen leading the skirmishes on both sides have taken to throwing out personal challenges. There's to be a joust in two days, and Felix wants to take part."

"A joust?" said Nicholas hazily.

"On the battlefield. On the plain between the two armies. All properly supervised, with the appropriate truce declared on both sides. Chivalry. Lunacy," Tobie said.

Felix's voice said, "He's talking. He's better. Nicholas? Tell them to let me go."

Felix came up to the bed. He had under his arm the amazing helmet the Dauphin had given him, with the red plumes and the face of a sour-looking eagle with carbuncles for eyes. He must have brought it in his luggage from Genappe.

Felix's face was different: the neck thicker, the nose and cheekbones firmed and broadened. The wavering curl had gone, too, from the ends of his hair. His hair, cropped below the ears, had reverted to its natural straightness, except where bent by the weight of a helmet.

Nicholas said, "Someone said you killed eight men. A lie. You talked them to death."

Julius had come over too. The sling was still there, and the strong face was paler than usual. He spoke straight to Nicholas, notary to apprentice, as if they'd been at home in Bruges. "He's right. He fought very well for a brat who never listens to what he's told. Did he train in Milan?"

"Yes. Who are the challengers?" Nicholas said. He didn't look at Tobie, but felt the heat of his glare.

Felix said, "I was going to fight in the White Bear. You know I was. If I could fight in the White Bear, I can manage a few jumped-up mercenaries."

"Who?" repeated Nicholas. He kept his eyes, with difficulty, open.

"Well, no one great," Felix said. "Nardo da Marsciano. He's fighting Francesco della Carda. And Serafino da Montefalcone issued a challenge to someone called Fantaguzzo da San Arcangelo. So I issued a challenge too. The Count said I could."

"The Count," said Tobie through his teeth, "said that any of the survivors of Sarno was welcome to break a lance, and he would double the prize. Felix could draw anybody. Piccinino himself."

"The Count? The Count'd be scared," Nicholas said, his eyes on Julius. Julius obliged with the faintest shrug and a nod. Nicholas said, "The Count'd probably get one of those Braccian cross-bowmen and they'll pick Felix off on the way to the lists, and good riddance. What's the problem? If Felix has killed eight men already, I don't see how mortal man can prevent him."

"I said you'd say that," said Felix. "And you've to come and help me arm and write down the names of all the jousters. I haven't finished."

"For posterity. You haven't, but I have," said Nicholas, his eyes finally shut. He thought he was in control of the matter and would open them after Felix had gone, but his central authority proved to be of a different opinion.

It was, however, his last involuntary withdrawal. The next time he wakened, it was for several hours: long enough to manage some solid food and to hear at last the tale of Sarno. Sarno, which should have been a long, bloodless siege but because of desertions turned into an ill-advised attack on one tower. And the ill-advised attack having succeeded, further spread into a major assault, unplanned, disconnected and leaderless. The attacking troops, as Lionetto had said, had been shot down from the walls by their own handguns.

Astorre had got out with almost all his force, alone of all the army. The handgunners who deserted were not his. King Ferrante had escaped with twenty horsemen to Naples. The Milanese ambassador had lost all his papers but got away safely to Nocera. So had the Strozzi (said Julius), who had already exported everything of value from Naples, including his savings. And now Duke John of Calabria was left victorious in the field. He had only to regroup his army, obtain some reinforcements, and march on Naples and take it. This army, stuck in the Abruzzi playing at jousting, was not going to stop him. Julius was scornful, but Astorre the veteran made them listen to common sense. The puckered eye had regained its gleam and the bow legs their spring.

"What can we do? Can't dodge Piccinino. Can't beat him. But if he's blocking us, we're stopping him rushing off to Duke John. The longer we keep him here, the more chance of reinforcements from Milan. Keep him jousting, I say. Sing to him. Do anything except fight, till we're ready."

Watching Astorre from the depths of his pillows, Nicholas was aware that none of this was being addressed to him directly. Since he came back, Astorre had been avoiding him. He was the demoiselle's new husband, liable to jump up and give Astorre orders, whereas yesterday he'd been Astorre's much-beaten pupil. Astorre hadn't yet decided how to handle it. Nicholas could see the difficulty. He hoped Astorre would have the sense to take the problem to Julius, who had been remarkably incurious about his marriage so far, perhaps because of the régime imposed by his snarling doctor. A talk with Julius was indicated, as soon as might be.

The chance came on the day of the tournament, which was no barnyard contest. It was the Count's contenders against the cavaliers of the Duke, and the honour of both sides demanded nothing less than magnificence.

The Brotherhood of the White Bear at Bruges couldn't have bettered it. Spurred by rivalry, the carpenters of both armies had set up the stands and the banners, the workmen erected the painted pavilions hung with shields. Sun gleamed on trumpets and tabards and blazed and glittered on the rippling shells of plate armour. Horses paced, their embroidered cloths sweeping the grass in brilliant primary colours, and their manes plumed and tasselled. Birds and animals, grotesquely decked, sprang from the helms of the competitors and, taking the pace of their wearers, trotted the length of the lists like some bestiary distressingly animated. Behind the tents on both sides of the lists the opposing armies sprawled at ease. Nicholas was there, helped by the one good arm of Julius.

The captain himself was arming Felix. They could see the Charetty blue in the distance, from the seats Julius had found them. Julius said, "He'll be all right. He's quick. Even Astorre was surprised."

Nicholas said, "I spoiled the White Bear joust for him. He doesn't know."

Julius looked at him down the bone of his nose. "You sent Felix to Naples. Don't tell me you couldn't have stopped him. If he swallowed your marriage, he'd swallow anything."

"Has Astorre swallowed my marriage?" said Nicholas.

Julius grinned. "Shall I tell you what he said when he heard about it?"

"No," said Nicholas.

"He thought Meester Tobias had gone back to Lionetto as well. The other ear nearly flew off. So in a way, when Felix told him you were just manager, and Tobias hadn't gone back on his word, he felt better."

"I could see him feeling better," said Nicholas. "The back of his head nearly scorched me. Tell him the Widow is happy to leave everything to him and Thomas. How should I know what to tell him to do?"

"I'll tell him," said Julius doubtfully. "But what happens when you want him to do something?"

Nicholas said, "Felix will tell him."

The tilted, narrow eyes looked at him.

Nicholas said, "Felix is heir to the Charetty company. Never forget it. He and his mother are the owners. I'm only someone who owes them a debt."

"Like you owe Jaak de Fleury a debt?" Julius said. "He brought you up as well. And there's Simon of Kilmirren. He taught you to swim. You've been nice to him, too. And I expect you're planning to thank the person (who was it? A strong-minded lute-player with a daughter?) who gave you the elegant mark on your cheek. I gather you owe Lionetto, even, a debt. According to the way you let him do what he likes to you."

It was six months since Nicholas had parted company with Julius in Milan, and Astorre had taken the army to Naples. He had grown out of the habit of understanding Julius. And Julius had never understood him at all. Nicholas said, "I was saving him for Astorre. Have they met?"

Diverted, Julius gave his irresistible, reminiscent smile. He said, "On the first morning. Honours were even. No, in Astorre's favour. He had more to defend than Lionetto. But so far, the battle is verbal."

Nicholas said vaguely, "After all, they're on the same side. Will Astorre want to stay with the Charetty, then?"

"Handle him tactfully," Julius said. "And yes, he'll stay."

"And you?" said Nicholas. He waited.

Julius was not watching him. His eyes were on the lists, where a pattern had formed; the familiar pattern of the formal joust. Between the barriers the grass was smooth and empty and green. At either end the competitors, armed and helmed, waited in readiness. The sun flashed on lifted trumpets and the air carried, ominously, the tuck of the drums.

Julius turned. "I'll stay," he said. "Until I've worked out how you do it."

"Do what?" said Nicholas.

"Make money. What else did you think? There's Felix," said Julius.

And they both fell silent, and watched.

The honours of the day fell to Count Federigo's contestants, and no harm befell Felix. His face, luminous under the dirt, crowned with laurel, turned dazed and beaming from side to side as he marched with the victors, led by the drums and whistles and trumpets of the joint armies. Loppe, in Charetty blue silk, carried a prize purse of gold coins behind him.

The procession wound twice round the field and divided. Slowly, like the parting of the Red Sea, the spectators withdrew, one half to the hill and the other half to the tents on the plain. The workmen, hurrying, began to bring down the lists. The suites of the commanders, briefly acknowledging each other, set off, banners flying, drums beating in opposing directions. Felix, breaking away as the ceremonial procession entered camp, gasped and bellowed beneath the thumping fists of his friends, while keeping a firm eye on Loppe and the purse.

Tobie was missing. "Well, of course," Felix said. "Didn't you *see*?"

Not being privileged as Felix was, his friends had not seen.

"Well, didn't you *hear*?" said Felix, astonished. "One of the Milanese sergeants lost control of his horse and was pounding straight across the course just as da Marsciano was galloping up to the lists. They nearly collided. They could have been killed, but Count Federigo saw it. He threw his battle-horse straight into a gallop and got between them and veered the sergeant's horse away. But his own horse gave such a bound when he spurred it that it just about shattered his spine. He got off, but he can't move. He's in agony."

"Count Federigo?" said Thomas.

Astorre, bustling past, stopped at his shoulder. "What are you standing about for? Jonkheere Felix, get yourself unstrapped and rubbed down. Count Federigo? He's not dead. He's only hurt his back, so it's painful to move. Meester Tobias and Meester Godscalc will see to it. We got our prize anyway. Messer Alessandro handed it out. A good purse won by the Charetty family. Three cheers for . . ."

"Waste of time," Julius said. "If I know Felix, he won't hand over a penny. What do we do now without our good commander, the lord Federigo of Montefeltro, Count of Urbino?"

"Sforza of Pesaro will take over," Nicholas said. "Messer Alessandro, the Duke of Milan's brother. The lord Federigo's good father-in-law."

"They say," said Julius, "that Alessandro's spoiling for a fight. You don't suppose he'll create one?"

"I don't know," said Nicholas. "Although I'm trying to care, for Astorre's sake. I'm planning, before anything happens, to get ready to set off for home. I hope that Tobie, once he's cured the Count, might come with me. And I think that Felix, at long last, might be content to come back to Bruges with his laurels."

He waited. Julius said, "Tobie?"

Nicholas said, "We've been doing business together. He's almost as good as you. Better at purges."

"Thank you," said Julius. He paused. "What business?"

"Making money," said Nicholas. "If you hadn't joined Astorre, I should have asked you to join us. It's Charetty business, but in my hands more than the demoiselle's. I found a notary for her. Gregorio of Asti."

"Felix told me. I've heard of him. Does Felix know what you're talking about?" Julius said. He looked surprised.

Nicholas grinned. "It's the first secret I've ever known him to keep. I warned him if he told a soul about it, he'd lose all the money."

Julius said, "It doesn't sound as if you need me. Whatever the deal is, you've already carried it through?"

"Well, you were winning wars in Naples," said Nicholas. "Now it needs running, and I *am* asking you to join us. If you're not interested, never mind, I won't burden you with the details. If you are, tell me. But take your time. Tobie has to put Count Federigo together before we can go. At least he doesn't sing."

He was glad to reach the tent, for the fever had weakened him more than he liked. Julius left him. He had been rather silent and had made no commitment, but Nicholas thought on balance that he would come back to Bruges. Lying still on his bed, he began to consider Astorre and his officers, but fell asleep almost at once.

When he woke it was dark, and Tobie was in the other bed, reading by candlelight. He stirred, and Tobie said, without looking up, "Did you convert Julius? I suppose you thought it worth it."

"I laid a trail," Nicholas said. "Time enough to ask him how his Turkish is. What about the Count?"

"He'll live," said Tobie. He tossed down his papers. "One-eyed, broken-nosed, weak-backed and thirty-eight years old. He's laddered the inside of his back like a piece of old quilting and he can't move an inch, but he'll live all right. He'll be up in two weeks."

Nicholas said, "According to Julius, Alessandro wants to fight."

"Alessandro," said Tobie, "wants to march out while Urbino is sick and command a successful battle. They've just had a council of war at the Count's bedside. There's nothing wrong with my lord Federigo's brain or his mouth. He spent half an hour pointing out that we haven't the men for an attack, and that we're already stirring them up with constant skirmishing. We have to hang on and wait."

"But?" said Nicholas.

"But he's married to Alessandro's daughter. He had to make a concession. In two days' time, Sforza can make a limited attack on one wing of the enemy, using three squadrons only. He might reduce their supplies and their numbers. If he loses, the whole army hasn't gone."

"Astorre?" said Nicholas.

Tobie said, "No, thank God. The Sarno men have done enough. It's the fresh squadrons he'll use; the restless ones that haven't been blooded."

Nicholas said, "I want to get back to Bruges."

Tobie said, "You could, in a few days. If you wait a bit longer, I'll come with you. Otherwise you'll walk off with all the money. Does Julius know I'm involved?"

Nicholas said, "He didn't cry out when I told him. As far as the money goes, the predatory eyes of Felix will be on it. You needn't worry."

Tobie said, "Of course. He's proved himself, hasn't he? I don't suppose he really wants a life roving round battlefields. You have a certain genius, you know. To persuade Felix that home is Bruges, that he's really running the company, and that you're merely his mother's manager is quite a feat. He can't even dismiss you."

"No. But I can dismiss other people," said Nicholas.

"You don't like being dissected?" said Tobie. "But that's my business. And you'll have to get used to it, won't you? I know too much."

Nicholas said, "You know what I trusted you with. If it's money you want, you haven't lost by it. If it's amusement you want, don't cut too finely too often, or there'll be nothing left to amuse you with."

The next two days were unpleasant because of the turmoil in the camp, as one squadron after another squabbled over the right to take part in the coming attack, and win glory and booty. In his tent, locked in pain to his bed, the Count of Urbino tried in vain to resolve the muddle, but couldn't overrule the command he had himself given to Alessandro Sforza. By the date of the attack, the whole camp was partially under arms, and not only the three favoured squadrons Sforza proposed to lead over the plain.

Nor had it been kept secret from the enemy. Not only the fact of the attack but its scale seemed to be known. When Sforza burst from his encampment it could be seen that Piccinino in turn had begun to move from his hill. As Sforza's three squadrons raced forward from one side, a matching force spurred out on the other to meet it.

Waiting outside the Count's tent Paltroni, his secretary, carried news to the Count as runners brought it. Before the Count's instructions could come back, a group of his less intelligent officers decided on further action. The gates were opened. A fourth squadron, hurriedly mounted, streamed out and set itself, galloping, towards the heart of the battle. On the hill opposite, the gates opened in answer and horsemen began to pour out.

On the plain, the two initial forces crashed together without plan, without strategy. To the shaking thunder of hooves was added the rattling thud of shield and lance and pike and the anvil clash of steel meeting steel. The continuous shouting of men and the squeal and whinny of horses hung over the encounter, hardly travelling. Veils of red dust rose, and lingered, and falling, began to cloak the dark sparkling mass on the plain.

Through the haze it heaved, like bees swarming. Knit together, it moved from place to place, its edges shaped and reshaped by the stamping hocks and round, swinging hindquarters of the battle-chargers. The fresh squadrons, first from one side and then from the other, galloped straight up and, dividing, pressed their way into the struggle.

The mass spread, and loosened. Where the fighting had been worst, dark gaps appeared, their cause invisible. The flock of living men, swirling, formed new skeins and masses, the battle line stretching. From the hill, the stream of horsemen was now almost continuous.

Astorre, standing watching from the highest ground in the camp with the other captains, suddenly turned on his heel and spoke to Thomas. And soon after that, in common with the rest of the camp, the survivors of Sarno were armed and mounted and drawn up, watching and waiting.

Tobie was not among them. Julius was, in a cuirass and helmet with his left arm out of its strap. He saw Astorre's eyes rest on him, but the captain said nothing. He could hold a lance or a sword, and guide his horse with his knees. If he had to.

No orders had been given for a general engagement. If any more squadrons were allowed to ride out, it would become a general engagement. But if they didn't ride out, it might become a carnage, out there on the plain, with Piccinino's whole army sweeping over to take them. The word up till now had been "Wait." But Tobie wasn't here, which meant something else.

Felix had put his fancy helmet on. His face was white and his eyes, grey and shallow-set, shone in its shadow. Heat from his armour shimmered. They all wore gloves, and Astorre's force carried the blue ribbons of the Charetty. Astorre himself wore his best helmet also, with the nosepiece. The plumes, so brave in Milan, hung over his bearded face, which was working with passion. He kept flinging words at Thomas on his other side, who stood without answering, his hand smoothing the hilt of his sword.

Julius kept looking round. Abrami. Manfred. A big man in good half-armour behind him said, "I don't see Lionetto. Has he gone yet?"

Under the helmet was the familiar face of Nicholas, with the unfamiliar scar and both dimples. Julius said, "What do you think you're doing?"

"The women threw me out of the cart," Nicholas said. "Before I could do anything, too. Tobie isn't here."

"I know. That means . . . By God, there he is," Julius said.

No one thought he meant Tobie, although the doctor had appeared outside Urbino's tent. What he was looking at was the figure of Count Federigo himself being manhandled, stiff as a funerary figure, to sit his war horse.

The Count wore no armour. He had borrowed a leather jerkin and someone had laced it over Tobie's bandaging, which encased him from neck to waist. Instead of a helmet he wore a light cap over the receding waves of his hair, still pressed flat from his pillow. Below it his great broken face jutted out, the sunken eye and gapped nose unmistakable among men.

It was not his only injury in a lifetime of wars, but it had come nearest to killing him, and that from a friendly jousting bout. Now his back was his weakness. He was grey with pain, catching his breath as he rode forward. But he made for a piece of high ground, and reined, and got their attention so that he could address them all. And then, despite the pain, he inflated his lungs, to make sure his strong voice would carry.

He laid no blame with Alessandro Sforza. Merely, the enemy had cast or was casting all his troops, bit by bit, into the field and they must therefore do the same or lose the day. Already their own troops had been forced to spread themselves too thinly for comfort. Soon, unless they were supported, the enemy would break their way through. Then the whole encampment would be taken, and their hopes of reaching Naples and assisting King Ferrante to defend his capital would be ended. He had hoped that some of those who had already fought hardest might be spared a battle, but it was not to be. God would reward them.

There was not time for much more. They mounted. To his former apprentice Julius said, "For Christ's sake. This is your first battle?"

"It's easy," said Nicholas. "Stay on the horse and keep ducking. What are you doing here? You're a notary."

"The same reason as you. I feel safer with Astorre than I do left behind with the baggage. Keep beside him, and do what he tells you."

Nicholas started to laugh. Before Julius could ask him why, they were out of the barriers and picking up pace as they began to trot and then canter over the plain into battle, with their banners snapping above and the trumpets braying before them.

The battle of San Fabiano, so fecklessly brought into being, went on for seven hours. By the time dusk put an end to the bloodshed, it had earned its name as one of the costliest encounters of its time. Four hundred horses were killed. How many soldiers lost their lives was less easy to count, as both sides removed their own dead. With the charge of the reserve under the Count of Urbino, the immediate threat to his camp was removed. But by that time, or very soon after, the whole of Piccinino's army had come to give battle against everything that Sforza and Urbino had, and no quarter was given.

No longer confined to one massive struggle, the fighting split and surged in one direction or another, sometimes threatening Urbino's encampment, and sometimes pushing Piccinino's men towards the slope of their hill. Fallen horses lay like boulders. Others, felled and struggling, trapped and brought riders down. Men lay everywhere. Fighting, you could hardly look down to see what to avoid. Later, as the sun began to sink, you might trample on the dying or overrun dismounted men fighting or running or standing dazed, half unconscious with exertion or wounds, or the effects of the heat.

Julius lived through it, and so did Astorre. He had not spoken lightly of Astorre's gifts in the field. It was what he did best, leading men into battle, marshalling them and keeping them in high heart, and intact.

He couldn't keep his company intact today. No one could. The handgun men had suffered most, being less used to close fighting. They had not even brought their guns, which would have been useless. The crossbowmen on both sides, on the other hand, had inflicted slaughter. Too much slaughter. Julius had seen Abrami go down, and Lukin, the best cook and forager Astorre had ever had.

The smith Manfred had lost his horse early, and had jumped clear and caught another. Later, Julius saw he had Nicholas beside him and was glad.

At one point he saw Felix with them as well, and then the boy dashed off, his helmet bobbing until Astorre called him back. All through, everyone watched out for Felix, and kept beside him when they could. He was their employer's son, and precious and brave enough, damn him, to take quite considerable risks. Julius spent quite a large part of his time, when he wasn't fighting, looking out for young Felix. Nicholas, he saw, did the same. Even Tobie. His greatest moment of astonishment was the sight of Tobie, with no helmet on at all, standing holding his horse with one hand and helping to heave the bandaged figure of a dismounted Count Federigo into the saddle again with the other. Then the fighting swept Julius away, and he lost the bald head to view.

In time, his arm had suffered so many blows that he couldn't feel it, and his hand inside his glove felt like meat. Then Julius lifted his head and stretched open his dry, burning eyes and saw that the sun had started to sink, and the plain was dark with the fallen.

The riders who were left moved slowly, on stumbling horses, and blocked their enemy's path by their bodily presence rather than by driving lances or whirling swords. The skirmishes languished, and broken companies began to gather together, merging into obstinate blocks but no longer challenging. The air, tinted with rose, was decorated with the swooping of small chiselled birds, but their twitter was lost in the groundswell of men's voices crying.

Astorre said, "Form up. Make a line. The Count is having the retreat blown."

Tobie was still with the Count. Manfred. Nicholas, his head turned, and beyond him, by God, Lionetto. Thomas was there. Felix? Julius craned round. A glitter caught his eye. Across the field, Piccinino also was withdrawing his men, and his trumpeters also were waiting.

The field was still full of men returning on foot, or indolently fighting, unaware as yet of the disengagement.

Among them was Felix, bare-headed and horseless. He wasn't fighting, but appeared to be searching for something. Julius yelled. Astorre's voice, even louder, made Felix look up just as the trumpets began, and he realised the fighting was over. He straightened, grinning, and waved. He had his helmet under his arm, the scarlet plume trailing, the eagle's head glaring up at the sky. Julius said, "Run, you fool!"

He meant it for Felix. It was Nicholas who jabbed his spurs in his horse and launched it out into the field and across to where Felix was walking. He rode in an arc, to come between the gathering enemy line and Felix's back. Felix, suddenly aware, gestured quickly and started to run. Nicholas turned his horse, to overtake and gallop beside him.

The retreat was not quite complete. The trumpets of Piccinino had not yet answered, although his troops were almost all back in line. It was probably the stray rider dashing out from Urbino's section that drew the eye of some skilful crossbowman. Even in the dying light, a horseman was an easy target.

Julius, watching the little rescue taking place, caught the gleam of the weapon and screamed. Nicholas heard him. It made no difference. The bolt was already on its way.

Nicholas, stopping his horse, had already leaned down to swing Felix into the saddle when Felix gave a small gasp. His mouth opened. Instead of jumping he sank slowly down to his knees. A moment later Nicholas had flung the reins from him and dropped beside him. They saw him kneel, and take Felix by the shoulders, and then hold him, looking down at his back. The bolt between Felix's shoulderblades was quite distinct.

Julius began to urge his horse forward and then instead dismounted and ran, and saw that Tobie was doing the same. After the single shot, the living had drawn back from the field. No one on either side moved, except to sway, or shuffle, or shift to hold up the wounded. The trumpets went into the last cadenza of their call. Julius reached the injured boy.

Tobie was already there, behind Felix. He didn't even touch him; only looked up at Nicholas, and then Julius, and moved his head a little, from one side to the other.

Nicholas had been speaking to Felix. The murmuring voice went on after Julius came to his side, but he couldn't hear what it said. Now and then, Felix asked a question and Nicholas answered. He had one hand under the boy's arm, supporting his weight. The other was spread behind, above the murdering bolt, holding Felix's head forward, his cheek resting on Nicholas' shoulder. The cut brown hair blew a little, in the sunset breeze.

Tobie said, "You can lay him down when I've drawn it. Then he'll go, Nicholas."

"He knows," said Nicholas.

He looked down. Some message must have passed. He looked up from Felix's face and found Tobie, and said, "Yes. Before the pain gets any worse."

Other men were whimpering in other parts of the field, but Felix made no sound when the bolt was drawn, although Julius heard the rush and spatter of blood. Tobie unlaced the cuirass and Nicholas, changing his grip, lowered the slight, wiry body until it lay on the ground.

Felix looked gaunt, the way he did when he had drunk too much the night before, or become too excited, or spent too much time with Grielkine. His eyes, large and shallow and dull, were only on Nicholas. He said, "Why did you marry my mother?"

"Because I love you both," Nicholas said.

A little later, Tobie said in his quiet voice, "Close his eyes."

Nicholas carried Felix de Charetty from the field to his tent, although Loppe came to his help at the last part. Then the doctor closed the flap and didn't come out for a while.

Nicholas didn't come out at all, and so must have slept there. The next day, when he did appear in Astorre's pavilion, he had his saddlebags already packed but passed Julius and the others without saying anything. It was Tobie who said, "Nicholas feels, and I think he's right, that the lad's mother should be told as soon as possible. After the burial he's going off, fever or no. He'll take Loppe, but I'd feel better if you were with him as well. If, that is, you want to go back to Bruges at all."

Julius knew the date. It was Wednesday, the twenty-third day of July. However promptly anyone left, Marian de Charetty wouldn't know of her son's death for many weeks; perhaps not until September. He said, "What about you? No, of course. All the wounded."

The doctor's eyes were swollen with sleeplessness. "I've got my hands full. A useless tragedy, if ever there was one. We came off worst, it seems. But Piccinino isn't likely to attack again soon, if ever: he's lost too much. Astorre will stay to the end of his contract and I'll leave Godscalc with him, of course. I'll get to Bruges when I can."

Julius said, "I'll go. Felix, Claes and I. Nicholas. We went about a lot together, and Felix was a good lad. But I wouldn't have said . . ." He stopped.

The doctor fixed him with his odd kestrel gaze. "That Nicholas

would respond in the way he did to what happened? You and I
have seen death in battle. It was his first time."

"Yes. And, of course, he has the boy's mother to face. The
Widow. His wife," said Julius rather blankly.

Chapter 37

In Milan, M. Gaston du Lyon, deeply bored and deeply frustrated in the Hospitio Puthei, discovered to his surprise that two members of that extraordinary little Charetty company had come without warning into the city.

Enquiry showed that they were passing one night in a tavern, although not their usual Inn of the Hat. They had made one call, to report to the Duke of Milan's secretary on this unbelievable news of the rout at San Fabiano (which on top of the losses at Sarno was enough to make the Duke weep). The young men had then returned to their inn, so his informant said, without attempting to visit the Castello, or the Acciajuoli, or the Piazza Mercanti, or even have a pleasant evening walk about the piazzas.

They were leaving for the north in the morning. One of them was the likely youth interviewed by Gaston's master the Dauphin while hunting outside Genappe. If he was carrying dispatches, Gaston wanted to know what they were. And there were some of his own he could add to them.

Gaston du Lyon, chamberlain, chief equerry and carver to the most serene and excellent lord Dauphin of Vienne, first son of the Most Christian King of France, sent a gift of marzipan and five household servants to collect M. Nicholas and his companion and deliver them both to the Hospitio before it grew any later.

They came without having changed, which was disrespectful but not unknown when men rode hard bringing news. They had even taken part in the actual battle. The merry one, Nicholas, had altered quite a lot since the memorable episode of the avalanche. It was not surprising, considering what he now was meddling with. The other, a well-built fellow whom he remembered seeing on the same occasion, was the Charetty notary, M. Julius. They had a black servant with them, a huge fellow, who waited for them outside.

M. du Lyon was given, briefly, an account of the fighting in the Abruzzi. The notary did most of the talking. Disappointingly, the boy Nicholas was not carrying papers, and wouldn't accept any.

He didn't rise, either, to the news that Prosper de Camulio was in the city and about to leave for Genappe. Gaston du Lyon, who had a fine ear for rumours, rather wanted to know why this fellow Nicholas had spent some time, it was said, with Prosper de Camulio and the Venetians before going south to the Abruzzi. Laudomia Acciajuoli, delicately sounded, had professed not to know or to care. The Duke's doctor, Giammatteo Ferrari, on the other hand, had shown a mild interest.

Gaston du Lyon was disappointed in Nicholas. He himself had, after all, performed several services for him. But for him, M. Nicholas would never have got that youngster Felix away from Geneva in May. The boy was dead. He had asked. In any case, the Dauphin had finished with young Master Felix. He had not been discreet.

Piqued, the chamberlain didn't at once take the trouble to pass on his own news. He ignored Nicholas and spoke of the Naples war: after Sarno it seemed that Duke John, unexpectedly, had failed to take advantage of his victory and march straight in Naples. They might save the city yet, with the fighting season soon ending. The merchants would be glad. So would the Duke of Milan. He had expended 100,000 gold ducats, it was said, on keeping Duke John out of Genoa and Naples. Or trying to. And the Pope, they said, was already planning to avenge what happened in Sarno by sending a new army under San Severino.

In England, the Yorkists were in London. So that King Henry looked like losing the war, and his Most Serene Majesty the Dauphin's father was unlikely, one supposed, to attempt anything against Burgundy now.

The notary, who was bright enough, responded suitably, and asked intelligent questions. The youth Nicholas continued to say very little. Since Geneva, the scar on his cheek had faded considerably. And one must not forget. He had broken the Medici cipher.

Gaston du Lyon said, with courtesy only slightly exaggerated, "I shouldn't keep you both, tired as you are. Is your mission to Burgundy urgent, friend Nicholas? Or do you have time to spend at the Geneva fair?"

The response this time was quick. It reminded Gaston of the evening at cards with Monna Laudomia. The youth Nicholas said, "Should we call there?"

Gaston du Lyon gave him a glance which might have come from the Dauphin's amused face. "If you do business with the de

Fleury," he said, "claim your dues before the rest of the creditors empty their boxes."

The youth said, "I see."

M. du Lyon hadn't expected to be embraced on both cheeks, but he was disappointed. It was the other one, the lawyer, who straightened and said, "Monsieur? What did you say?"

Gaston du Lyon turned his head. "Only a little item of news. The depositors Thibault et Jacques de Fleury have been declared bankrupt."

The notary said, "Are you sure?"

Taken aback, M. du Lyon paused, but forgave the man on reflection. He was certainly in a high state of excitement. "Yes," said M. du Lyon. "There is no doubt. They have lost everything. It has caused a great disturbance, I'm told. They had many creditors."

"Nicholas?" the notary said. "Nicholas. Jaak de Fleury."

"Yes, I heard," the courier said. "I'm obliged for the news. M. du Lyon, forgive us. We have to set out early."

"You go to Bruges," said Gaston du Lyon. "But you will have time to call at Genappe? My lord Dauphin, I'm sure, would be happy to receive you. News of affairs. The death of that poor boy, whom he loved as a son."

"I shall do what I can," Nicholas said. "But I think the debts on both sides have been honourably discharged. Monsieur, I am grateful."

In diplomacy, one recognised the end of a contract. Another, more lucrative, had clearly offered elsewhere. He would warn the Dauphin. He wondered if the youth knew just how feeble the Dauphin's father had become. Smiling, Gaston du Lyon saw his visitors to the door.

Had he gone with them he would have been amused to see the notary, exercising none of the restraint of his calling, literally capering in the street beside the large, silent figure of the former apprentice, with the black servant following disapprovingly behind.

"Jaak de Fleury!" Julius was saying. "Lord of the money-boxes. The pompous bastard who used to wring his servants dry. Including me. And used that poor woman for all he could get. And worked you like a dog. Don't tell me he didn't. Bankrupt! Can you believe it?"

"Yes," said Nicholas.

"Well?" said Julius.

Creeping over him was the irritation which had been with him, illogically, ever since they left Urbino's camp at San Fabiano. He didn't expect Nicholas, God knew, to be the crazy clown of the lighter at Damme, or the Waterhuus joke, or the escapades with girls and with goats and the rest. But he hadn't expected him, either, to have grown in eight months into a married version of Lorenzo Strozzi.

He said, "I suppose you're worrying about all that cloth you delivered, and the money they owe us. All right, you can't rebuild the Bruges shop, but there's still Louvain, and the condotta. You can't do everything right. My God," said Julius. "Isn't it worth the loss just to imagine Jaak de Fleury's face?" He paused, stretching his imagination. He said, "And it'll help the demoiselle, surely. At least she'll know she's free of the de Fleury family and all their intriguing. D'you want to go inside already?"

Nicholas had turned into the gates of the inn without saying anything. In the afterlight of the sunset, a pair of sedate, well-groomed horses stood in the courtyard, held by liveried servants. Their harness was embroidered in silk, and the emblems worn by servants and horses were familiar from the falcons and diamonds and feathers all over the inside of their owners' palazzo. And the motto woven into the horsecloths. *Semper* meant always. And *always* meant the Medici.

Nicholas said, "We have visitors. We could go away and wait until they've gone. But I don't know. I'm tired."

Once, you never had to bother with how Claes felt. Indeed, you never knew. But of course, the frantic energy had been sapped by the stress and the fever, and he had to take thought if he wanted to keep up the pace of this journey. Nicholas had always been good with plans. Julius said without much conviction, "They may be waiting for somebody else." Then Loppe, who seemed to have transferred his mind-reading from Felix to Nicholas, slipped indoors and came out with a grimace and a report in his elegant, ducal Italian. The visitors were not only theirs, but had been installed in their private room to await them. The landlord had known what was due to the seigneurs Pigello and Accerito Portinari, of the local filiale of the Medici.

Loppe said, "They won't wait all evening. I could get you a chamber elsewhere."

He was speaking to Nicholas. He often spoke to Nicholas, Julius noticed, as one man to another, and not as a slave to his mistress's husband at all. And Nicholas, he saw, did not even notice it but stood in thought, and then said, "No. We'd better see them. But you needn't wait up."

Loppe did not move. He said, "If it is late for one person, it is late for three. The seigneurs Portinari could come back tomorrow."

This time, Nicholas looked at him, but failed to show either surprise or annoyance. He simply said, "No. I want to leave early." And Loppe gave way at once, only watching his masters, as Julius saw, until they had entered the inn and begun to climb the stairs to their chamber. There, awaiting them with no sign of impatience, were Pigello Portinari and his brother and factor Accerito.

Messer Pigello, in a short gown of light material and a low belt which flattered his paunch, carried a high colour tonight in his bare, sunken face with its long nose. His puffed hat bore a large goldsmith's piece with a table-cut emerald in the middle of it. He had even more rings on his fingers than the time Julius had seen him last, when he and Astorre had called at the palazzo to lodge the ducal bill for the condotta. The air of amiable condescension had risen to something like outright amiability. Accerito, with a smaller brooch, looked complacent as well.

Julius wondered if Messer Pigello recalled Claes, the lad who had delivered Pierfrancesco's horses; and then remembered that, according to Felix, he and Nicholas had called on Pigello since then. On business, unspecified. On, then, the mysterious business Nicholas wanted him for, about which he'd heard nothing more? Certainly both brothers Portinari acknowledged Nicholas' presence equally with his own. They were affable.

They were affable but reproving, like the Dauphin's chamberlain. Since the Charetty company favoured the Casa Medici with its business, Messer Niccolò and his lawyer might be kind enough to call when in Milan. Messer Niccolò had, of course, heard of the closure of Thibault and Jaak de Fleury?

At once, Julius felt better, despite the mistake they seemed to making about Nicholas' status. *Messer!* Or no, he ought to remember. The ridiculous marriage. Well, despite that, he was glad he hadn't dodged the encounter. He thought of dispatching Nicholas to see to refreshments, and then realised, with a moment's annoyance, that he should do it himself. When he excused himself, Nicholas hardly looked round, never mind stopping him.

Julius hurried. He was longing to know just how awful the

Fleury disaster had been. When he and the servant came back, there was no room to put the goblets down, there were so many papers on the table. All the writing on them appeared to be in columns. The puffed hats of Pigello and Accerito moved up and down, almost chiming like wedding bells, as their owners discussed them. Nicholas, his hair frizzed with heat, sat in his travel-stained, decent jacket, apparently watching them. When their voices stopped, he sometimes commented.

Julius, who seldom found a reason for examining faces, noticed that Nicholas did look tired, and not very responsive. Julius, pouring the wine, made a point of brightening the atmosphere. After all, the downfall of Jaak de Fleury was something to celebrate.

The brothers Portinari, with Ambrosian courtesy, accepted the wine and went on turning pages and referring to Nicholas. Julius said, "Have I missed something?"

Everyone looked up. Messer Pigello glanced from his face to that of Nicholas and back again. He said, "A great deal of money is involved. I am happy, of course, to take the responsibility, but I should prefer you and your colleague to check it. And of course, there is the consignment of arms at Piacenza. The order placed with Messer Agostino by Messer Tobias."

"That was for Thibault and Jaak de Fleury," said Julius quickly. They looked at him. Suddenly his face began to burn. Julius said, "These lists are . . ."

"Bills for moneys owed your company by M. de Fleury," said Messer Pigello. His voice, always polite, almost concealed his impatience. "And corresponding credits for the gold and the property of Thibault and Jaak de Fleury in possession of their agent Maffino in Italy, impounded on your behalf and on our own as soon as the bankruptcy became known. All these are in addition, of course, to the debts which, as you know, were purchased by us in June from the Charetty company. We were fortunate in having early warning of the failure in Geneva and have been able amply to recoup them.

"It is usual, of course," said Messer Pigello, "for a far-seeing company to insure against disaster at sea. It is seldom that a merchant thinks of the consequences of disaster on land, and makes corresponding provisions. The demoiselle de Charetty is rare among persons of business."

Indeed. "How did the Fleury fail?" said Julius abruptly. Nicholas, chinning the rim of his empty cup, didn't return his gaze.

"A large, a very large withdrawal of capital. That is all we know.

Coupled with an immediate demand by creditors, as the deficit became known. The August fair, as you know, is due at this time. Small tradesmen already committed to purchases can risk failure themselves, if they cannot call on funds they have lodged, in good faith, with such a company. Companies like your own, who have sold cloth on credit, may well never see cloth or money." Messer Pigello, pausing, looked at his brother. "It is a lesson every dealer must learn, including our branch in Bruges. Not to extend credit, no matter how great the firm or the personage."

"So we have all Jaak de Fleury's undelivered guns in compensation," Julius said. "And how much else?"

Nicholas put his cup down, and lifting his elbow, pushed a paper before him. "That. Enough to buy the business if there's anything left."

"Not the business in Geneva," Pigello Portinari said. "They've wrecked it. I told you, word got about. There were a lot of small creditors. Some hothead started a rush, and the crowd broke in and took everything they could find and then set fire to the building. The owner got out. Jaak de Fleury. There's an elderly brother, a sleeping partner called Thibault near Dijon. Our filiale in Geneva think he went there. I have to tell you to call, of course, on our manager, on Francesco Nori in Geneva. He has cloth of yours, and other things."

Julius said, "That's extraordinary." He felt dazed. His natural elation receded. What had seemed an act of celestial retribution had turned into catastrophe. Nicholas, his unmoving hands on the table, was gazing at the manager in a way that transformed his whole solid face into an instrument of inspection. Julius realised there was a question no one had put. He said, "And what about Jaak de Fleury's wife? The demoiselle Esota?"

Messer Pigello wished to gather his papers. He shot a look of enquiry round the table, and then began, unimpeded, to collect them and form a neat pile. He said, "Alas, it was sad, according to what reports say. The crowd meant no harm. But the lady was, it seems, heavily built, and excitable. Instead of leaving quietly, she tried to bar the way to some, and urged others to help her. They paid no attention and pushed past. She fell, she was trampled. But it was her own weight which killed her. You knew her?"

"Yes," said Nicholas. "She wouldn't be able to deal with that."

Messer Pigello looked at him. He said, "Some might say her husband should not have left her. But one should not condemn.

People do strange things from fear, and from greed. As bankers, we know that. Now. The assets?"

Nicholas said, "It is for the demoiselle to agree, and for Meester Julius to advise. But I suggest the guns stay in Piacenza, the silver is lodged with Messer Tani in Bruges and the cloth is sold by your filiale here and Geneva, and the profit, less your commission, added to our account here with you for any use captain Astorre may have for it. Messer Julius?"

Messer Julius agreed. He could hardly do less. He said very little as the manager of the Milanese Medici and his brother, with formality, began to take both their lists and their leave. Then, seeing that Nicholas didn't propose to cross the threshold, he himself accompanied the noble bankers downstairs and over the yard to their horses. Outside it was dark, and the swifts had gone to rest.

Returning, he heard the crash of glass breaking as he made the last turn of the staircase, and his foot crackled on splinters as soon as he entered the room. The wine flask, fortunately empty, lay under a window where it had arrived with such violence that the entire floor was glittering.

"I'm sorry. It slipped," Nicholas said. He looked dyeshop pale, but otherwise perfectly stolid.

Julius said, "Well, you've made a sty of the floor, haven't you? If you hadn't also made a fortune at the same time, and if you weren't married to my employer, I'd think about beating you. That's either Loppe or the landlord coming up to find if we've wrecked his windows. You explain. And once he's got the place cleaned, I want to hear what's been going on. Everything."

But he didn't. While Loppe, completely silent, swept glass, Nicholas went off belatedly to make all the arrangements for their morning departure. Before he came back, Julius had commanded another flask of wine, this time of pewter, and was holding a personal celebration which led him at last to his bed.

He lay for a while, thinking. Being amused by a youngster who has the audacity to marry his employer was one thing. But working with or under him was quite another. The way the doctor handled Nicholas might have warned him. If he was going to join them all in some new venture, he would have to learn to think of Nicholas as what Portinari had called him—a colleague.

He had left the Abruzzi ready to accept whatever appointment was going, while the army was laid up at least. Nicholas, easily tired to begin with, had put off describing the venture, but before their arrival at Bruges he would certainly know all about it. From what he'd seen tonight, he had no doubts that it was something profitable. This was a very young man with gifts which, of course, he had noticed. But now there were signs of something much more. The curious thing was that Felix, too, had begun to partner the servant he'd once used so carelessly. Had taken part in these negotiations. And more amazing still, had kept his own counsel.

Felix had gone. Now the heirs of the company were the little daughters, and the men they would marry. But that was only the Charetty company. Already, Nicholas was venturing out on his own. Soon, with the right people behind him, he might accomplish more than anyone dreamed. Which would mean sinking one's pride. Becoming his colleague. And helping to guide him, perhaps, a little further than he might have gone on his own.

Had Nicholas been older, there would have been no question. Sheer curiosity would hold him. As it was, it remained to be seen if he could tolerate Claes, the demoiselle's husband. But it was worth trying. By God it was.

He rolled over, and by the time Nicholas returned, was asleep. It would have pleased him to know that Gregorio in Bruges, much before him, had reached the same conclusions precisely.

That year, the Flanders galleys came early to Bruges. In the first week of September they floated under blue skies outside the harbour at Sluys, and the crowds on the headlands watched the light sails come billowing down. Then, straight and precise as if painted, in gold and red and blue and sparkling white, they rowed in to their berths, the light starring their trumpets.

In their holds they carried Barbary wax and elephant tusks and brown sugar. They had gingers this year from Damascus, and violet camlets from Cyprus. There were forty caskfuls of currants. There were jewels, as always: rubies, turquoises, diamonds, and seed pearls to powder for medicine. There were wimple silks and lake gum and white comfits and thirty bags of good cotton. There were tabby silks packaged in Syria. Messina had sent astrakhan lambskins. There was also sulphur from Sicily and porcelain from Majorca and rosewater from gardens in Persia. There were Mass bells and missals and music books and glass drinking-cups of several colours, including pink. There was indigo from Baghdad, and oak galls and madder and kermes. There were one hundred and fifty butts of Malmsey wine; and a ballast of alum.

The commander this year, it was well known, was a Venetian nobleman named Piero Zorzi.

Marian de Charetty, with her household, was as usual in Bruges for their coming. Nowadays most of her interests were in Bruges, and now she had a good man at Louvain, she spent less time there. Everyone said how drawn she had looked after the boy Felix went off in April, and of course the terrible fire. She hadn't looked herself for a month or more, until word came in June that the boy was safe in Geneva with that young rascal Nicholas. And then four weeks after that had come this letter, brought to Bruges through the Medici.

Young Nicholas, the boy she married, had gone off somewhere in Italy and was not coming back as expected (or at all, like as not). And her precious Felix, who wasn't even allowed to joust when he wanted, had ridden off to war, if you please: gone south to Naples to fight for King Ferrante.

Now who encouraged him to do that, you might wonder? And whether he was encouraged or not, what else could you expect, if you set aside proper womanly matters and thought you could run a soldier company? Sooner or later any boy worth his salt would want to put on armour and show what he was made of. She had only herself to blame. Herself and that terrible boy.

All the same, you missed Claes. She was probably missing him too, and the jokes. If nothing else.

She knew, of course, what was being said. She was helped a great deal by the need for hard work, and by the men Nicholas had chosen for her. Gregorio was her right hand. But she had the devotion also of Bellobras and Cristoffels as well as Henninc and Lippin. Everyone worked to restore and reshape the business in the way they had planned, in those early days after the fire.

To begin with, it was bitterly hard. But then, in the first days of July, Tommaso Portinari had come to her, bringing both good news and bad. With the letter which said that Felix and Nicholas had gone beyond her reach, to the Italian wars. And the package that contained bills drawn on the Medici bank for sums she had never expected. Money for the condotta: for the extra soldiers so skilfully raised and armed at minimal cost. And sums, unbelievably, which appeared to originate with the Fleury company. Somehow, Nicholas had obtained a reckoning of Fleury debts, and persuaded the Medici to pay them. At the time, it had seemed miracle enough. She hadn't recognised the later visitor for what he was, because she didn't deal with the Venetian merchants called Bembo. It was only when he was alone in her office that her visitor of that name had drawn from his pouch the paper that was more amazing than all the rest.

After he had gone, she had called in Gregorio, and shown him what Felix and Nicholas had sent. It held their signatures, as well as those of names Genoese and Venetian she did not wholly recognise. The sum of money it represented was enough, of itself, to clear every debt. The sums it promised would make them wealthy.

She realised that she had been looking for a long time at the signatures. That of Nicholas, black and firm and exact, because he had been taught very young, and then tutored in late months by Colard. Felix's sprawl, because he had never wanted to learn, and wouldn't be tutored by anybody. But the presence of his name showed that he had begun to learn now.

She said, "They seem to have concluded the alum deal. Even if some authority finds the Pope's mine tomorrow, we have this."

Gregorio hadn't come near her since the word came about Felix's destination. He was a considerate man. He said now, "It's a good thing for the jonkheere, getting involved in the business. I'm not surprised either that he went off to Naples, or that Nicholas let him. Every boy should set foot on a battlefield once, and the risks are very small. They can't afford to fight. And the season will soon be over."

It was what she told herself. She could understand, too, why Nicholas felt it necessary to go after the doctor Tobias. Without Tobie, his letter had said, they would have had no alum money. He hoped to bring Tobie back, and perhaps Julius.

Tobie. They must be on good terms. Now the yard, and her household, had got used to referring to Claes as Nicholas. They gave him no prefix, because he had no claim to the "Master" of the academic, or the "ser" of the better-born. She didn't mind. It would be hard enough for him to conduct himself at all these levels without the artifice of a title.

She noticed that those close to Gregorio had taken to calling him Goro. Three months of working with people had taught him a lot. There had been no more disturbances in the yard. The nicknames people produced for Bellobras she pretended not to hear. She became, as the presence of money lightened her load, able to meet people and laugh again and sometimes take Tilde and Cather-

ine on trips to other towns, visiting friends and finding small adventures which would give them pleasure.

The girls were beginning to be invited in their own right, and
someone took Tilde to join a family sailing party out of the harbour. Every now and then, the thought of her son and of Nicholas
weighed down her thoughts. In August, news came. There had
been a battle south of Naples with heavy losses. For a day she
thought about nothing else. Then, indirectly, she heard the details.
The Charetty company, with Astorre, was quite safe. They had
gone north, to join the Count of Urbino. She hoped they would be
safer there. She hoped that Felix, now blooded, would be persuaded to come home, and Nicholas with him. She tried not to
hope anything, but just to go on with her business.

Keep busy. The ultimate anodyne. Nicholas had been right. If
she had given up, if she had sold off and gone to sit in some
cottage, making lace and gazing out from the shutters, she would
be dead.

By mid-August, the new property was rebuilt and furnished to
their design, and she was stocked again with cloth, but of finer
weave than before; and with dyes, but only those of high quality.
She had increased the quality, too, of her staff, but not by releasing
anyone. People who had bought from her out of sympathy continued to buy because they appreciated what she sold. Then they
found that she was also accommodating in financial ways.

That, Nicholas had said, was the line the company ought to
take, and Gregorio was best fitted to deal with it. Usury was forbidden. But loans on security was what pawnbroking was about,
and it was very simple to adapt the same principle to the exchange
of finished goods and raw materials. And from there, to other
things. The ledgers never showed loans: only late payments. She
found Tilde interested and let her sit beside her once or twice and
listen.

The rest of August went by. She remembered it afterwards as a
strange time; three-quarters happy. The hammering on the door,
the hammering that ushered in all the change, fell in the last days.

She was in the new warehouse built behind the great house in
Spangnaerts Street when it came. The porter who answered the
summons went for Gregorio and Gregorio came through the house
and into the yard himself, and saw where she was standing, tablet
in hand, watching two of her storekeepers check over stocks. When
the Flanders galleys were due, work was always heavy. The voice

in which he said "Demoiselle!" was not a casual one, and made her turn quickly. He said, "May I speak with you? You have a visitor."

He didn't mean to frighten her, and she mustn't be frightened. She spoke to the workmen and came out, the tablet still in her hands. Gregorio said, "The firm we used to do business with. Thibault and Jaak de Fleury?"

She nodded, mystified. "The Medici settled their bills."

Gregorio said. "Yes, I remember. And Monsieur Jaak de Fleury is a kinsman of yours?"

"My sister married his brother," she said. "I thought you knew that. There's never been any love lost between us. Quite apart from his unpaid bills. So what is it? A message from him?"

"He's here, demoiselle," said Gregorio. "I left him in the house because I'm not sure if you should see him. He is not in command of himself."

"Now that is something new," said Marian de Charetty. "If ever there was a man in command of the whole world, including himself, it is Jaak de Fleury. What is wrong?"

Gregorio gave a hint of a smile. "I am not, apparently, fit to hear. I'm sorry, demoiselle. I couldn't get him to tell me. But he has a dozen horses in front of the house, and two carts and a string of servants. Whatever it is, it must be serious." He paused. "I thought perhaps—if you would allow me to say you were out, he could find a tavern and return alone when he's calmer."

She said, "You think he wants to stay here?"

Gregorio said, "I don't know. But I think he would be better elsewhere. If it can be arranged easily."

She stared at him, and then made up her mind. "No. I'll see him. If I don't want him to stay, I shall tell him so myself. He can hardly force his way in."

Gregorio said, "Would you like me to stay within call?"

Marian de Charetty ran through her mind all she remembered of her sister's unpleasant brother-in-law. Physical assault upon grown adults did not feature. Not unless they were servants, which she wasn't. Mental cruelty was another thing. She had in mind that Nicholas had been brought up in his kitchens. And that, to Jaak's mind, she had married his scullion. It was not going to be a pretty interview. She didn't want even Gregorio to hear it.

"No," she said. "If I can't manage my own sister's kinsman, I shan't know what to do with Astorre and Felix when they come back from the wars. Tell me where you've put him and I shall go in. Have no fear. I am known for my speed with a fire iron." She smiled at him and went in, rather slowly. The door of her small business cabinet was open. Jaak de Fleury was inside, seated in her chair at her table, with all her ledgers open in front of him.

"This is where I will sit," he said. "And I'll take the large bed-chamber. That one. I told your man in the yard to find a place for my grooms and the others. They won't complain. They've learned not to. So. You're doing well, I see, my lady. We must see that continues. You know, of course, why I'm here?"

She had never seen him before other than well-dressed and lav-ishly jewelled. Now, although he bore himself like a prince of the Church, the gown he wore was marked and flattened and dusty with riding, and the plumes of his cap frayed and dirty. His face, too, had sunk about his large eyes and under his rounded cheek-bones, and the narrow lips were blistered and dry. He wore rings. But the habitual gemmed chain was missing, and there were no pieces pinned to his gown or his hat. He looked like a man flying from battle.

Marian de Charetty said, "What has happened?"

"You have no idea?" he said. "Ah, me. Women. A different species. When it happens to you, there will be a crying and scream-ing such as no one has heard, as if no one had ever suffered treach-ery before in their lives, or envy or spite. What has happened? I have lost my business, dear sister-in-law. The Duke of Savoy has lifted from me—has stolen—a sum of money under some pretext which has left me unable to meet all the demands on me. And my creditors, strangely prescient, have taken the rest, so far as they were able." Jaak de Fleury, smiling, looked down. He snapped shut, one by one, the ledgers he had been scanning and made two even piles of them and placed one shapely hand upon each.

"I have no business. I have no house. I have only the money you owe me and the chance to avenge myself on those who thought I was finished. To bestow on the Charetty business my wisdom and my experience. To regain my capital and return and show those beggars what a successful businessman is."

His smiling gaze remained on her face, blandly confident. She felt her heart beating. She said, "I am sorry, of course. But you're mistaken. This business owes you nothing. The debts were on your side. I received payment for them from the Medici."

The lustrous eyes flickered once. "Ah," he said. "From young Claikine your husband, perhaps? He collected them in Geneva, after he had successfully half-killed and kidnapped your son. He did not, perhaps, tell you that the amount you were in credit was less than half the sum owed by the Charetty to me?"

Marian de Charetty walked forward. She rested her hand on the tall chair she kept for her visitors, and then moved round and sat on it. She folded her hands. She said, "You had better speak plainly. I have already heard from my husband that he and Felix were in Geneva. And I have since had papers signed by Felix himself in Milan. I am not therefore inclined to believe you."

"Oh, you may believe I am bankrupt," said Jaak de Fleury. "The news will be all round Bruges in a day or two. And you may believe that your son called at my house, and that your husband drew a weapon and felled him, rather than allow him to come home to you. Any of my men will confirm it. Even those who fled home and deserted me. Even the friends of this rascal you married."

"And the signature in Milan?"

"Under duress, I dare say, poor fool. Now, of course, your husband has sent your son Felix to Italy, but so far his efforts to remove his rival have failed. The boy, I am told, survived Sarno. He may not, however, survive life in the Abruzzi alongside Monsieur Nicholas. You will permit me to ask your kitchen for food and hot water? I have ridden, as you might think, a considerable distance."

Marian de Charetty got up. "I know a tavern that will suit you very well," she said. "And will give you both food and hot water. I am sorry your business has failed but you are not persuading me, I'm afraid, to rush to help you. You have a brother in Burgundy. I suggest you shelter with him."

He remained, smiling, where he was. "But Thibault, dear lady, has no money either," he said. "And a wild daughter to provide for. No. If I have to earn my living, it must be in Bruges. If you won't help me, I must go elsewhere. To the dyers' guild certainly. I hear they supported you after the fire. They may find loans for me. Or they may hesitate, when they hear how their gold found its way out of the country in the purse of the servant you married. Until he saw the proofs, your poor son could hardly believe it. He protested most bravely. He was protesting when he fell. The dyers of Bruges will be proud of him, although it may worry your clients somewhat." Jaak de Fleury shook his head sadly. "After such a fire and such thievery, public confidence in the Charetty company will not encourage investors. You would do better to make me your partner. You will make money. And no disagreeable rumours need ever upset your friends or your business."

She stared at him.

He said, "You still find it hard to believe me? Take an hour. Ask my men what you like. I shall be here when you come back. Perhaps, on your way, you could bring yourself to send to the kitchens, as I suggested, for some hot water and food? With reasonable speed. Like your little company, your staff does not inspire confidence."

She said, "I am not only going to question your men, I am going to speak to my man of law. When I come back, I shall have several men with me. You may therefore take one hour, sitting here. I shall have someone bring you a refreshment. I shall remove, if you have no objection, the private ledgers of my company. And I have to remind you of this: that whatever threats you think you are holding over my head, they will vanish the moment that my son and my husband walk through that door."

"My dear woman," he said. "They are not coming back. One is at war and the other has money to spend. Your Nicholas dare not return and face what he owes me. My ledgers may be burnt, but who will take his word against mine? Make up your mind. You have no heir and no husband, and will have to look out. If nature cannot now provide you with the first, at least the second is here to hand."

She saw then the full extent of the plan, and her touch on her chair became a broad clasp. She said, "Your wife? Esota?"

"Oh, they killed her," he said. "I think your husband had left when it happened, so the hands which did the deed were not his. In any case, she would never have survived the journey. She needed to pack so much, poor Esota."

He was smiling when she left. She went downstairs, and found Gregorio, and together they questioned the men who had come from Geneva. They confirmed, as she had expected, what Jaak de Fleury said. They confirmed it, as she had not expected, with anger and sullenness, and every appearance of truth. When she finished, and went with Gregorio into her parlour, she was shaking.

Gregorio said, "Put him out."

"I've told you what he will say. And these men saw Felix and swear that Nicholas felled him. Do you think they're lying?"

"No," said Gregorio. "But I can think of good reasons as well as bad for silencing Felix."

That was when, for the first time, her fear was checked. She stared at Gregorio. Then she said, "Let me leave you in no doubt. There is no one on this earth, far less Jaak de Fleury, who can shake my faith in Nicholas and his loyalty. What we are talking about are ways of protecting Nicholas as well as this business. Not everyone knows him as I do."

Gregorio said, "You would allow this man to install himself in your house until they come back, rather than spread rumours?"

"Yes," she said. She thought he would protest again, and when he didn't, she said, "You agree, then."

Gregorio gave an impatient sigh. "No man in his senses would agree," he said. "Except that I think you're not mistaken in your trust. I think Nicholas will come back if he can, and the jonkheere with him. But there's another thing. You say M. de Fleury saw all the ledgers?"

"They were all there," Marian said. "He isn't a layman. Better than anyone else, he could make them out instantly."

Gregorio said, "If he's seen the entries, he knows that you're thriving, whatever opposite story he means to tell. He wants the company. He's sketched how he hopes to acquire it. He had another means he may not yet fully realise. If, that is, he's seen the size of the payments from the Bembi."

Marian de Charetty was silent. There in that entry was the only hint of the long, precarious negotiation which had brought them the alum money. To protect that, she would have to agree to anything, or lose all she had.

Gregorio had known that. "Put him out," he had said; but only to test, as was reasonable, her belief in the youth she had married.

She said, "Then he stays until Nicholas comes. But what can be done about the Bembo entry?"

Gregorio said, "Leave it to me. A temporary disguise of some sort, I'm sure, can be come by."

She said, "He's a very unpleasant man."

"But it will be for a short time," said Gregorio. "Don't do anything. There's a lot of goodwill in the yard, and they understand hints. Henninc and I will see that everyone is encouraged to be patient. Perhaps you'll want to send your daughters away for a little. The burden will fall mainly on you."

"Yes," she said. Now it was decided, she felt a small return of courage, and of resolve.

She had to wait, in any case. She might as well fight as she waited.

Chapter 38

By the time they and their servants had reached the Ghent portals of Bruges, Julius had stopped trying to converse with Nicholas.

On the way from Milan, Julius had heard about the alum mine. If the news about the de Fleury credits had amazed him, this revelation of cunning and opportunism had virtually stunned him. He assimilated the fact that Tobie had been concerned with the idea from its beginning, and that the new lawyer Gregorio was aware of it, and the demoiselle, who had apparently given the venture her blessing. And again, that Felix had known, and had kept it to himself. It confirmed what he had told himself before they left Milan. If he could put up with Nicholas there was, clearly, no end to the possibilities.

Putting up with Nicholas was already proving a mild irritation. There was no excuse now that the boy was ailing. A week ago, he had thrown off the last effects of the fever and, although taxed as they all were (except Loppe) by the journey, he was otherwise in normal health. Physically, at any rate. But, having thrashed out the alum business and run briefly through the other matters now occupying the house of Charetty, Nicholas had fallen silent.

Felix, of course. Julius, who was himself tired from some extremely hard riding, recognised that he and Nicholas were bound to see the death of Felix from different viewpoints. He mourned Felix, of course, as a schoolmaster mourned any lively youngster he had taught, and helped out of scrapes. Nicholas mourned him as a fellow-schoolboy. On top of that, Nicholas had to break the news to the mother in the ludicrous rôle of the boy's stepfather. But he had put on that cap when he married the Widow, and Julius saw no reason to squander sympathy on him.

Then they got to the gates of Bruges and the porter, an old enemy, said, "Ho! You'll see a difference in the Charetty, you two."

Nicholas was sorting out permits. Julius said, "Well, I should hope so. They tell me the doormen held a party and burned it to the ground in the spring. They wouldn't have had the chance, I can tell you, if I'd been about."

"There's worse than fire," the porter said. He grinned evilly.

"Such as?" Nicholas said. The permits were sitting on top of a canister of good German beer. The porter grinned to the point where all his teeth stopped and removed the canister, leaving the papers in Nicholas' hands.

"Such as the Widow giving you all up for dead and about to marry again," he said. "Or that's the story. Otherwise it's not right, is it? That fellow staying there day and night, and going to all her meetings, and doing the deals? Where's the youngster?"

"When we've seen the demoiselle, she'll tell you," Nicholas said. "What fellow?"

He sounded calmer than Julius felt. Julius was running names through his head. That pawnbroker Oudenin. One of the dyers. The other lawyer, Gregorio.

The porter said, "They say he's related. So you was related, wasn't you, Claes? Likes her own kinsmen around her. Jaak, he's called. From Geneva. Jaak de Fleury."

Nicholas said nothing. Then he said, *"Staying* with her?"

"And running the business," said the porter. "Got the experience, you would say. A real merchant. The kind a woman could lean on."

Julius said, "Look. Steady. Not straight to the house."

"Yes, straight to the house," Nicholas said. His face, already different, had drained from sepia to buff under a patchwork of dirt. He said, "If she's taken him in, it's because he's compelled her." He'd already left the porter behind, moving forward over the bridge.

"Told her you were dead? Felix? Or what?"

"Told her I knocked Felix unconscious in Geneva and forced him to come to Milan with me. Did Felix tell you?"

"No," said Julius. He was immensely weary, and annoyed at having to bring his mind to bear on what was surely a simple legal problem. Jaak de Fleury was bankrupt. He had no claims on the Charetty, and could be got rid of. If he'd felt fresher, he would have looked forward to the prospect of getting rid of him personally. It was a pity the woman had taken him in, but that might be from misguided philanthropy. Perhaps she had no real idea what Monsieur Jaak was really like. He remembered him, very distinctly, threatening to cut Claes' hands off.

Julius said, "Did you knock Felix unconscious? I'm sure, if you did, it was for the best of reasons; and even if it wasn't, you would persuade her it was. Or do you mean that he's threatened to blacken your character?"

"He could shake public faith in the company," Nicholas said. "Or . . ." He broke off.

Julius said with annoyance, "All right, what? At this rate, we'll be there in a minute."

"There's only one secret you and I and the demoiselle would prefer Jaak de Fleury not to know," Nicholas said. "Or no, there are actually two; but the second one is no business of yours."

The alum mine. Julius, realising what he meant, felt his face, too, losing colour. He said, "How can we stop him if he's found out about that?"

"There are several ways," Nicholas said. "Just as there are several ways of telling someone her only son has been killed. What about thinking for a bit, instead of talking?"

Never in his life had Claes spoken to him like that. A little discipline was required here, and Julius turned to apply it. But then he saw the look on Nicholas' face, and had the good sense to say nothing.

The streets in Bruges, like the roads outside, were crowded because the Flanders galleys were in. However hard they and their small retinue pushed, it was difficult to make headway with horses. Also, they kept glimpsing people they knew. Nicholas kept his head down, responding to no one and urging his horse yard by yard through the press. Julius, who had been away longer, found himself smiling blearily back at the friendly, familiar faces, and mouthing greetings and promises.

That was how, he supposed, Nicholas became separated from himself and Loppe and the few men they had hired for the journey.

It hardly mattered. They were going, according to Nicholas, to a newly-bought house in Spangnaerts Street which the demoiselle now used as headquarters. Julius arrived at Spangnaerts Street and discovered the house, and was impressed by it.

In the yard there was no sign of Nicholas or his horse. With some misgivings, Julius wondered if the first encounter with Jaak de Fleury and, worse, with Felix's mother, was about to fall to himself. He had begun to question the gate-keeper when a slight man emerged and crossed the courtyard. He seemed to be about the same age as himself, with hollow temples and a lean face and a lath-like nose of great length, its austerity somewhat relieved by a prodigious scoop at the end. He asked, with sonority, if he could be of assistance.

The black clothes proclaimed him. This was no doubt Gregorio of Asti, the lawyer, who had been occupying his desk for five months. Introducing himself, Julius plunged through the formalities and discovered that Nicholas had not appeared, and that both the demoiselle and M. de Fleury were out: the demoiselle to the Flanders galleys and Monsieur to make a call in the city.

The lawyer, supplying these details, was civilly guarded. Julius said, "We know about Jaak de Fleury. We think we can guess what's behind it. It's time it was dealt with. Meester Gregorio, how is the demoiselle?"

The astute black eyes assessed him, and the question. Meester Gregorio said, "She has thought of little else, of course, but the boy's return. Bad news would be better than nothing."

Julius said, "She should hear it from Nicholas. He'll be here soon. It isn't something to tell in the streets."

"Her son is dead then," said Gregorio. "Poor lad. Poor lady. But she may hear it in the streets. In fact, I was just setting off to try and find her. Tell me. Was he killed at San Fabiano?"

Astrologers might have divined the name of that battle. There was no other way for the news to have reached Bruges already. Julius opened his mouth.

Gregorio said, "The report of the battle arrived just an hour ago. Another captain from Count Federigo's army apparently called at the house here with news of it. The door-keeper told me. The man said nothing of Felix. He asked for M. de Fleury and left to find him."

"Another captain? Who? Not Astorre?" said Julius. He felt cold.

"No. Not the demoiselle's captain. Indeed, his rival I believe," said Meester Gregorio. "A mercenary called Lionetto."

His own safety was not, that day, in Nicholas' mind. If it had been, he would have dismissed it. No one knew he was coming to Bruges. He didn't give thought to the Ghent gate, and the fleet-footed friends of its porter.

From the moment Nicholas passed over the drawbridge, the problem of Jaak de Fleury occupied all his thoughts. When he let it go, it was to prepare for the other, more important thing he had to deal with. He rode with his head down because he didn't want to be accosted, and to answer questions about the war, and about Felix. He didn't even notice at first that his horse was not being pushed entirely by chance, but by two others, one at each flank.

The riders wore city livery, and were offering, smiling, their escort to the demoiselle's house. He refused, but tried to be polite when they insisted. It was the degree of insistence which made him glance behind for the first time for Julius, and find that there was no one behind him.

The nightmare of the canal and the barrel oddly returned to his preoccupied mind and he dismissed it. It arose, he thought, from the two cleanshaven faces at his side which bore some likeness to the two bearded, drunken faces he remembered from the mists of that night.

They were the same faces.

He realised it only as he hurtled past them, for his horse had slipped and fallen, inexplicably, throwing him heavily to the ground. He rolled over and found himself in a dark archway, beyond which lay a piece of waste ground and the canal bank. Behind, a strange voice in good Flemish was speaking. Not to him: it was assuring passers-by that the rider had come to no harm, and was being cared for. He rolled over again and two solicitous figures appeared above him, one of them with a knife.

He had not been the dullest pupil of the Duke's master at arms at Milan. By that time his own sword was in his hand, and when the dagger came down he parried it, and twisting, got to his feet. He couldn't burst past the two men to the street, but he could and did run on through the passage to the unpaved ground beyond it.

By that time he knew perfectly where he was. The tunnel through which he had come belonged to the half-ruined house which had been neighbour to the Charetty dyeshop. He stood in what had been its orchard. Before him was the canal. To one side was a wall with no footholds. He would be dead before he had scaled it. To the other was the broken wall which had once divided this garden from the dyeyard. The wreckage beyond was the range of sheds in which all his fellow-workers had once gathered to hear the news of the demoiselle's wedding.

The two men in city livery had rather more experience than he had in fighting, but not quite his reach of arm. They didn't like the sweep of his sword. On the other hand, there were two of them.

His cap had already come off in the fall. He shed his jacket as he ran, which stripped him to shirt and hose and left nothing to ham-

per his movements. He did it spinning, with his sword cutting the
air, so that they had to fall back. He had time to think that what he
felt was not fear, but relief. Instead of the burden of responsibility,
he was being invited to show his prowess in physical play.

So he did. As he got to the broken wall he feinted. The man
nearest him ran into his sword. The other rushed with his knife.
Nicholas ducked, found the lowest part of the wall and tumbled
over, pursued by one angry assailant. He swiped at him as he went,
and sliced his shoulder. He would have made a perfect landing as
well, had he not been tripped by the toe of Jaak de Fleury. He
sprawled, twisted, and found the sword of the merchant at his
throat, and his own weapon gone. The remaining assailant, bleeding, jerked him to his feet.

In front of him was the uneven field that had once held the
trestles and tenting-frames. It was patched with seeded plants, red
and blue and yellow and violet. Beyond stood the blackened bricks,
bushy with grass, of the house where he had worked and slept
intermittently since he was ten. Facing him was the man who had
been his master in the years before that.

A calm, smiling, cruel master. A merchant who had tried to ruin
the Charetty business and who, in his own extremity, was now
intent on acquiring it. An unpleasant merchant with a sword in his
hand, who wasted no words on him at all, but simply walked
forward, with purpose, to kill him.

There was a hand gripping his arm, and a knife at his back. Both
belonged to the man whose shoulder he'd stabbed. The grip on his
arm was numbing in its strength. But the knife was in the grasp of
the weakened hand.

Nicholas flung all his weight backwards, not forwards. His elbow ground into the man's wounded shoulder. He felt the blade
slide into his body, but there was no force behind it. The man
holding him yelled, and let go. And as he yelled, Nicholas dragged
the knife from his enemy's hand and used it on him.

The man fell. Jaak de Fleury had a sword. His own weapon lay
on the ground just beyond. Nicholas dived and got it, and swerved
as Jaak de Fleury's blade hissed over his head. He stood, sword in
hand, as he had learned to hold it, and parried, and heard the
orderly clash, as you heard it on the practise ground, over and
over.

In this, as in everything else, he had no experience to set against the long lives of his betters. He had only his brain, which absorbed instruction and held it, forever.

On the broken field where once he had struggled, his nails blue, to push virgin cloth in a vat, to nurture blithely the glories of the maligned urine tub, to share meat and ale and obscene and shattering jokes with his gossips, he was stepping, shifting, sliding, sword in hand, protecting himself as best he could from the great-uncle who was trying to kill him.

Who was thirty years older than he was.

"You would like to be able to fight him? To beat him? To overpower him?" Marian de Charetty had said.

And he had answered, *"If I'm afraid of him, I'm afraid for all time."*

It was true. The fear beaten into him at seven would never go.

Despite the fever, despite the strain of that miserable journey, despite Jaak de Fleury's powerful frame and trained, tutored grasp of his weapon, he, Nicholas, was thirty years younger, and had been recently placed in possession of some very select tricks of swordsmanship. But what had that to do with it? If he killed Jaak de Fleury, he killed his own blood, his kinsman. And left untouched his fear.

He parried and parried again. He didn't know what to do.

Jaak de Fleury, his face a shining confection of sweat, pink as sugar, saw it and, panting, smiled. He shifted position, agile, muscular. He fought without his robe, broad-shouldered in his splendid doublet. The puffed silken sleeves of his shirt swung against the great muscles of his upper arms, and the jewels on his high collar sparkled. The point of his sword arrived again and again. And again, Nicholas parried.

From the ruined house, far behind him, a man's voice screamed at full pitch, and went on screaming, louder and nearer. Jaak de Fleury glanced round. In a moment Nicholas, too, looked over his shoulder.

The figure springing from the tumbled stones, red hair beating, was Lionetto. *Lionetto!* And the two figures running behind, drawing their swords, were Julius, blessed Julius, and Gregorio.

How had they found him?

The horse.

What in God's name was Lionetto doing here? That was easy. Looking for Nicholas. Lionetto had good reason, too, to want to kill Nicholas. Only Nicholas hadn't known that he knew it . . .

He couldn't fight two men. He hadn't the skill to defeat Lionetto by himself, never mind with Jaak at his side. And however fast they ran, Julius and Gregorio couldn't get to him in time. So he was going to die. Not from a beating. From the adult equivalent of a beating, which you got when you meddled with adults' affairs.

"Traitor!" Lionetto was shouting. *"Whoreson! Rascally scum!* Steal a soldier's money, then! Break your trust! Empty his purse and betray him! Oh, yes. Do all of that. But not to Lionetto. Not to Lionetto, my friend."

Captain Lionetto had arrived. He stood, sword in hand, the third point of a triangle formed by himself and by Nicholas and by the glittering form of Jaak de Fleury. The merchant, one eye on Nicholas, stepped back a little, his sword disengaged. Nicholas watched Lionetto.

But Lionetto's eyes were on Jaak de Fleury. He said, "I didn't believe it. Rumours, I said. But I thought I'd make sure, with all that new money I'd sent. The Pope's money. The cash from all the booty. And there was your Milan agency closed. Your man Maffino absconded. No money. No money for Lionetto." He smiled. His nose spread, glittering among the wholemeal crumbs of his skin. "So I asked about my money in Geneva. All my money. All the savings I'd lodged there. And what am I told? Gone as well. All gone. And why?"

He said the word gently. As he said it, his right arm flashed out. A splash of blood appeared on Jaak de Fleury's shoulder and the merchant made a sound and jumped back, his sword lifted.

Lionetto lowered his, artfully. "Why? The Duke of Savoy, they say, has told Jaak de Fleury to hand over all Lionetto's savings. That's what they say. That's what they want me to believe. But was Lionetto born yesterday? No."

Again, he moved. The sword flashed. It pirouetted past the merchant's sword, wildly lifted, and touched and entered the merchant's arm. Lionetto said, "I think you have all my money."

The pink in Jaak de Fleury's face had altered, by measure of a small beaker, say, of diluted woad. He was gasping. He said, "Of course I haven't. It's your own fault. You changed sides. You moved from Piccinino to the Aragon side. The French heard. They gave orders. Everything you had was to be confiscated. Savoy ordered me."

"Really?" said Lionetto. He danced forward. The merchant

moved back. "Perhaps they did. But of course, you got compensation."

"No!" said Jaak de Fleury. "They promised. They didn't pay. I'd invested it all. The withdrawal bankrupted me. I'm a bankrupt."

"So I see," said Lionetto. His sword flicked. A jewel flew from the merchant's collar. "Penniless," said Lionetto. "So where is my money?"

Nicholas said, "It's true. The King of France told Savoy to confiscate it. He *is* bankrupt. It's Charetty money he's living off."

Lionetto turned. "No money?"

"No. Leave him alone," Nicholas said.

Julius said, *"Nicholas!* He was going to kill you."

"Oh?" said Lionetto. "Why was he trying to kill my little Nicholas? Perhaps I will spare him. I wouldn't mind killing Nicholas now and then, myself. I nearly killed your doctor, did I tell you? I met him riding north. Your doctor Tobias. It was the money he brought that made me leave Piccinino. But he pointed out that he'd meant me no harm. He'd made me rich, which was true. Except that I'm not rich, am I? And whose fault is that?"

Jaak de Fleury was not a cowardly man. His self-esteem had never made courage necessary. He stood, breathing quickly, and said, "I see no point in continuing this." And turning his back, he walked away.

Lionetto, on the other hand, was a mercenary. He said, "Nor do I, my dear monsieur." And taking three unhurried steps after him, ran him straight through the back.

Standing over the sprawled, athletic body, he tugged out his blade, examined it, and then wiped it carefully on a patch of grass. "I hope," said Lionetto, "that you all observed. This poor Nicholas was fighting for his life when I saved him. What are all those people doing there?"

"Watching you save Nicholas," Julius said. He was breathing rather quickly as well. "Do you have urgent business in Bruges?"

Lionetto cast his glance round, and scowled at Nicholas. "Not now," he said. "Don't I remember having cause to complain of you once as well?"

"You did," said Nicholas. "But another man fought me on your behalf. I think you could call the matter fully closed."

Lionetto grunted. "Did you win?"

"No. I lost," Nicholas said.

Lionetto's fiery eyes swept the field beyond Jaak de Fleury, to where a dead man lay on one side of the wall and another just over it. He said, "Well, you seem to have got the knack now. If you want to claim the old fellow's death, I won't contradict you. I need a coin to get me a lodging at Ghent."

Gregorio said, "Take my purse," and threw it.

Lionetto caught it and stared at him. So did the other two. Lionetto grinned. "Did you a service, did I?" he said. "Well, remember it. Some day I might want a service in return. Demoiselle?"

He bowed to someone walking forward from the crowd that had gathered on the street side of the site. Then, sheathing his sword, he strolled off, hat in hand.

The person walking forward was Marian de Charetty.

Julius said, "Oh, Jesus Christ."

Gregorio turned from watching Lionetto. He said, "I think she saw who did the killing. I think perhaps Nicholas . . . ?"

Nicholas said, "Could you . . . Perhaps you could clear the crowd and get hold of the people who have to be told? I'll bring the demoiselle back to Spangnaerts Street."

His heart beat heavily after the fighting, and his hands were shaking. He fought to stop the beginning of dizziness. He stood where he was, and collected his wits, so far as he was able. The farther she came from the crowd, the more private they would be. She would still have to accept what he had to tell her in public. The spectators couldn't hear, but they could see her.

The fact that he waited for her, of course, told her what the news was. She was dressed as strictly as he had ever seen her; her gown tight to the wrists and the throat, and voile swathing her ears and her chin below the brim of her hat. The bright blue eyes were set in darkened skin, and her lips and her cheeks were both pallid.

She stood beside him, looking up, and said, "He hurt you?"

There was blood on the grass where he was standing. He remembered the blade in his back. It had been no more than a flesh wound, soon stanched. He said, "No. Julius and I—we bring you bad news."

"I've lost Felix," she said. There were no tears in her eyes.

"He had grown up," said Nicholas. "Quite suddenly. He helped with the business at Milan, and wanted to fight at Naples. He did fight, and well. Astorre will tell you. Then instead of coming home, he chose to cross to Urbino's army. The Count of Urbino and Alessandro Strozzi. They were fighting on the east."

"I know," she said. "In the Abruzzi. You were there?"

"He even had the chance to joust in the field," Nicholas said. "And won. And was very happy. He died just after that, in the field. There was a battle, and he was hit by a crossbolt. It was very quick. We buried him there."

He could see her flinch. She didn't want details yet. She looked at the other dead man lying limp on the grass. She said, "He wanted the business."

Nicholas said, "He hated the Charetty. He hated women, I think. Thibault married twice, and he despised him, and your sister, and my mother. He isn't worth thinking about."

"No. Later," she said, "you'll tell me more. And about where he is buried. And—oh. The girls. They're not in the house."

He said, "We could go for them now."

The house in Spangnaerts Street, redesigned since the fire, was familiar to them and unfamiliar to him. Tilde and Catherine, sought and brought back, showed none of their mother's restraint but gave her work to do, soothing them. To Nicholas they behaved as they'd done when he was the familiar companion walking in and out of their lives. His marriage to their mother might never have happened.

Marian de Charetty behaved, too, as if her rôle of widow had never changed. She had known Claes for ten years. She had borne Felix, and bred him, and seen Cornelis melt, at last, in pride over his child, his son.

Nicholas saw it, and without interfering went on with the business of clearing up the day's wreckage.

The reckoning over Jaak de Fleury he left to the two lawyers, who seemed to think it no trouble in such a case of unprovoked attack. His body was taken elsewhere. Gregorio, with efficiency, began to arrange for the release and disbanding of Jaak's few servants. What the man had left would go to his brother.

With circumspection, and without troubling the demoiselle or her family, Gregorio and Julius between them removed all the small valuables that had begun to accumulate, bought with the demoiselle's money. Turned to silver, they would find their way back to her account. Towards the end, the effects of the journey made Julius stupid, and he was thankful when Gregorio agreed he should go off to bed.

Nicholas, of the unimpaired engine, continued to work. Gregorio visited him, and was told to go home, which he did. The bereaved family had his sympathy. But he was not married to his employer.

The demoiselle was aware of these things. From time to time, a tongue-tied Henninc or one or other of her household would appear and transmit an offer of help or notify a visit from someone. She returned polite thanks, but felt that today her place was with her daughters.

She gave her remaining children supper in her own parlour, but didn't have any herself. After a while, the girls ate with the appetite of the young. They were already recovering. Tomorrow or the next day, they would want to know all about the battle, and the joust.

Later, after she had seen them to bed, she heard Tilde weeping, and went in and sat with her until finally she dropped off to sleep. Then she undressed herself, and put on her nightrobe and went to the chamber and sat at her unshuttered window, wanting Cornelis.

But that was wrong, because Cornelis would have suffered terribly. His son. His heir. She had only lost her baby.

With mild kindness, she remembered Cornelis. He had been as good a husband as any woman might expect. When her father had gone bankrupt, *faute van den wissele,* like Jaak de Fleury, Cornelis had taken the company, and made it thrive. He had never troubled her with it. The child and the household were her business.

And so they would be today, if Cornelis hadn't died. Of course at times she was lonely. She was lonely tonight. Only Tilde and Catherine knew Felix as she did, and they were too young to console her. So were his friends. She thought of Margriet Adorne with sudden thankfulness. She did have friends of her own age, who would understand. Tomorrow. But tonight had to be suffered first.

In Felix's room, she knew, was a chest with all his belongings, and a helmet with a red plume and an eagle's head on it. She had found it for herself. Whoever had put it there hadn't locked it away. She was being treated by the senior members of her household as a grown woman who could face a crisis, and ask for help if she needed it. She realised that someone had been near at hand all day, whatever she happened to be doing. Not speaking and not in the same room very often, but near at hand. Especially Nicholas.

Until now, she had given no real thought to Nicholas. While he was away she had missed him. She had missed his strength to lean on, and his understanding. She had blamed him, secretly, for abandoning her and the company, as she used to blame Cornelis, she thought, when he went off to Antwerp and left her to deal with something.

She had wanted him back for the same reason. No. She had wanted him back for the sort of intermittent companionship which had come to be part of her daily pleasure. If he felt the same pleasure, she didn't know. She did know that he had found a taste for affairs, and was experimenting with it. Until recently, she supposed, he could, if he wished, have slipped back into anonymity. Instead, he had stepped forward and committed himself to the Charetty company and to her.

So what must he be thinking tonight? He'd been with Felix. He hadn't learned of his death in the yard among wool caps and stained skins and stinking aprons. The way Felix had met his end owed something to him. Guilt as well as thoughtfulness had sent him dragging Julius on that breakneck journey to bring her the news with least pain.

Instead, his arrival had caused her to learn of Felix's death in the most brutal way possible. Whatever he thought of Esota, he had learned of her death on his way. He had heard of the ruin of Jaak de Fleury. He had lived with them both, and had survived cruelty without apparent bitterness. It was not his fault that Jaak de Fleury was dead: Lionetto had killed him. But today he had learned that his life as well as his happiness meant nothing to Jaak. And today he had killed. Nicholas, who emerged ruefully from the Steen with the stripes red on his back, his face cloudless, had taken two lives.

But she was forgetting. Men didn't go to war and stay merchants. He had been taught to kill now, and so had Felix. And one of them had paid the price.

She thought for a long time. The house was quiet. Along the passage, the door to the handsome chamber Jaak de Fleury had adopted as his own was shut and locked, his possessions piled in the empty room. Beyond it was the room Nicholas had taken when he and Gregorio made this house their office before the night of the fire. No light came from it, but the door was open.

It had been open when she passed. She knew why. He was the man who had taken Felix from her. He was her husband. He was neither. There was no rôle for him in this tragedy, unless she wanted to make him one.

Did she? Her memories tonight were of her family, of Cornelis and Felix, Tilde and Catherine. However long she had known the boy Nicholas, he was outside that small, tight circle. To admit him was a kind of betrayal. He had been to Felix what Julius had been: a mentor, a tutor if you like. He had been to Cornelis an apprentice. To her, he had shown the face of the ideal steward: loyal and hardworking and thoughtful.

Outside in the street, someone passed with a lantern. The little glow swept her room, printing her hands and her robe with frail lozenges. Her hair, falling coiled to her lap, briefly gleamed. She looked down, smoothing it.

I am a fool, she thought. Gregorio is an ideal steward. Julius is loyal and hardworking and thoughtful. But I made Nicholas marry me. And then I became the child, and he became the parent.

She thought, Now I have no other child. And he has no one else, either, to understand the day it has been.

The door was still open when she walked along the passage, shielding the small flame of her candle. He was resting, as she had done, at his window, but had turned his head from it on hearing her step.

All the daytime energy had gone, pressed down below the surface to give room to the thoughts that had to be dealt with.

She knew what they were. She walked to the window and looked down at him, so that he could see her dry eyes, her command of small things.

He didn't rise: a thing she found touching. But his face eased a little.

She had handled children and husbands. She knew how to give comfort as well as receive it. She saw him recognise what she was about to do just before she blew out the candle, and laid it down, and sat, gathering her robe, at his side by the window.

There was enough light to see where his hand lay. She took it lightly in both her own.

He said, "I didn't know what you wanted."

She said, "I need someone who needs me."

She was wiser than she knew. As it turned out, in this one thing she was the stronger. As doctors do, she forced him out of his composure and then, as she did with Tilde or Catherine, took him in her comforting arms.

But he was not Tilde or Catherine, and she too was astray and bewildered and suffering. His embrace, gentle as hers, held within it something else, which she realised he was silently controlling. That was when she lifted his hands in hers and ran them through the warm, shining weight of her hair. Then she held them to her breast, in the hollow where the robe fastened. "Nicholas?"

His fingers escaped hers but stayed, touching her robe. In his anxiety, he spoke in French. "Think."

"No," said Marian de Charetty. "Don't think."

Chapter 39

How or where Marian de Charetty passed the first night of her second bereavement did not escape notice. Tilde, her daughter, disturbed by some small sound, rose before dawn to find her mother's room empty. Nicholas had closed his door. Tilde had paused there only a moment when she heard her mother begin to say something inside. Whatever it was, she broke off almost at once, as if she were out of breath like Catherine, and crying. But the sob had not been one of grief. Tilde stole past the door. Then, curled tight in her bed, she wept not like her mother, but like Catherine.

In the days that followed all the household grew to realise what had happened, for neither the demoiselle nor her husband tried to pretend that her bedchamber was not being shared. During the day, it was a house of black cloth and tailors and mourning. At night the demoiselle accepted the comfort that was legally hers. Where once her servants would have felt discomfort or resentment and would have resorted to obscene jokes and even hostility, now they excused and forgave. The death of Felix changed everything.

Julius, consumed with curiosity, watched it happening. Not only was the marriage accepted, he saw, by Henninc and the men who used to work with Claes, but even the burghers they dealt with were apparently reconciled to the union, and had been even before this development. He spoke to Gregorio about it and heard a little, from the other lawyer, of how the marriage had been achieved. He was wary still about Gregorio, as any man was entitled to be with another in his own line of business, but he liked what he had seen of him at the time Jaak de Fleury was killed, and he had found him an unassuming, hard-working partner during the unpleasant tasks that had followed. In subsequent hours over the ledgers he had had to admit, as well, that the man was more than competent. At times, he thought that there was something more than competence behind the disconcerting black stare; but after he found that Gregorio had a mistress called Margot, he realised that he was just like everybody else. The woman was a good cook, as well. He wondered, after Gregorio had invited him, unprompted, to meet her, why he had the impression that Gregorio was secretly much amused.

To the rest of Bruges, of course, Nicholas was the new hero. Now everyone knew what a rogue Jaak de Fleury had been. Several had spotted it right away, when the man appeared so suspiciously, taking over the demoiselle's business and claiming to own it. Nicholas and Julius between them had the facts and figures to show that he didn't, and what's more, had been cheating the poor Widow for years. And young Felix's servants, if you questioned them, were very ready to tell just how and why Nicholas had got Felix safely away from M. Jaak in Geneva, and how well Nicholas and jonkheere Felix had got on from then on.

Everyone, of course, was sorry about what happened to the jonkheere, but agreed that his city and his family could be proud of him, fighting for King Ferrante and winning the laurels in a great joust in the Abruzzi. It was only a pity it hadn't been here, so that his own friends could have cheered him. But if a young man had to die, what better way was there?

And as for Nicholas, who used to be Claes, who would have thought it? Held his own against two armed men and killed them, and then fought that bandit de Fleury to the death, no matter if another man had finally finished him. And so careful of his new wife, you wouldn't believe, as well as showering her with all the money he'd made in Italy. You only had to hear the stories of the money credits he'd sent her through the summer, so that all her debts were paid, and the two girls could look forward to fine dowries. A good boy, Nicholas had turned out to be.

The only person who didn't seem to want to rhapsodise about all this was Nicholas, who spent a dazed morning being slapped on his bandaged back and congratulated, and then took desperate refuge in work. Julius and Gregorio shared his long hours and the succession of hard-bargaining meetings without objection. Decisions made by Jaak de Fleury were corrected or reversed and new ones made in their place. The courier service was inspected, renewed and reorganised. Everything Gregorio had done since April was assimilated and discussed, including the purchasing programme for the Flanders galleys. And the vital meetings began with Bembo and the Venetian merchants.

Within a week, sanction should come from Venice for the acquisition by the Charetty and the Genoese merchants of the prescribed amount of the Flanders galleys' cargo of alum. Being only ballast, it was not great. But the principle would be established, and the next round ship carrying bulk supplies from Constantinople would put in here, and the demoiselle's new stockrooms would begin to fill up. Even if the authorities found the new mine tomorrow . . .

The only people in Bruges who didn't seem happy about Nicholas were all the girls he used to go about with, who must have been hoping that he would get tired of the Widow and begin to chase them again. Once, Julius had passed the time of day with a high-ranking party from Veere with whom he thought he had no particular quarrel, until he saw the venom on the face of a fat little party he remembered as the younger Borselen girl. Nicholas, at whom she was staring, looked back at her with no expression at all, which was one of his commonest gambits these days. No longer were you able to track down Nicholas by the sound of other folks' laughter. But, of course, it wouldn't be right anyway, when you remembered poor Felix.

In the middle of all of this, the bald-headed doctor Tobias arrived from the Abruzzi, having presumably patched up Count Federigo and all those of his army susceptible to cure. Like Julius himself, Tobie was red-brown from the Italian sun and impressed, you could see, by the Spangnaerts Street house which, like Julius, he hadn't seen before; and also by Gregorio, who was new to him. Gregorio and Tobie weighing each other up was a study which Julius rather enjoyed. He thought they might be a match for each other.

Nicholas wasn't there, so Tobie had a session alone with the demoiselle about Astorre and his winter quarters, and the winding up of the contract and, presumably, Tobie's recruitment to Nicholas' alum venture and his share in it. Of them all, the doctor had shown least interest in the demoiselle's marriage, but that was presumably because he hardly knew her anyway. After all, their only previous encounter was ten months before when he had applied to join Astorre instead of Lionetto.

He emerged from the meeting apparently unscathed, and from the way he walked into the office, evidently had reason to think he belonged to it. The clerks were away at the time, but the room looked business-like enough, with its tables and cupboards and orderly litter. Tobie glanced round, nodded to Julius and Gregorio, and said, "And where is the young master?"

Julius frowned. Gregorio remarked in a voice of truly organ-like pitch, "You will find that, in this house, the young master is dead. Nicholas will be back soon. He is presiding, with some reluctance, over the burial of a great-uncle."

Tobie lifted a hand and passed it over his bald head, removing his sober black bonnet. He said, "I nearly had to be buried myself. That's why I didn't exactly hurry here. My late captain overtook me on the road and tried to make out I'd deliberately ruined him. I left him looking for Jaak de Fleury instead."

"He found him," said Gregorio dryly. "If your late employer was Lionetto."

Julius noticed that Tobie and Gregorio were staring at each other. Tobie said, "It's Jaak de Fleury who's being buried?"

Gregorio nodded gently. "Killed by Lionetto. Who departed the same day at speed. He must regret he changed sides. If he'd stayed with Piccinino, none of this would have happened."

Julius said, "Never mind Lionetto. Have we got a new condotta?"

Tobie looked back. "Oh, yes," he said. "At least, we've been offered one. Astorre is everyone's favourite captain, since he got himself safely out of Naples and rushed straight to the feet of Urbino. This year's campaign against Piccinino is over. Urbino's accepted a renewed contract as well, and is taking his army to winter just north of Rome, in Magliano, so that he and Alessandro can see the Pope over Christmas. Astorre will go with him until he hears what we . . . what the demoiselle wants him to do."

Julius said, "If you mean Nicholas, why not say so?" He was saying it when Nicholas came in, but he didn't seem to have heard it, and was looking instead at Tobie, and then greeting him.

Tobie's eyes, returning the look, were round and pale with a nasty black dot in the middle: the kind you saw if you were a weasel with a goshawk coming for you. Tobie said, "What's all this about Jaak de Fleury?"

"He's dead," said Nicholas. "What's all this about Astorre and a new contract?"

He got his answer, but didn't really go on to force Tobie to talk about business, when there were much more interesting things to discuss. Nicholas himself sat listening, as usual these days, instead of saying very much. But, immersed in a bath of news and gossip, Julius sat chatting with the other two straight through the noon break, stopping only for visitors. People called at the house all the time to offer sympathy to Felix's mother. And after they'd seen Felix's mother, they walked through all the time to open the office door and speak to Felix's friends.

They'd already had visits from Sersanders and John Bonkle and Colard Mansion (to ask about Godscalc) and even Tommaso Portinari, who had hardly been in Felix's circle but who seemed to be experiencing an unwilling compulsion to cultivate Nicholas. He'd asked Nicholas all about the joust and the battle at San Fabiano, and Nicholas had told him.

The friends of Felix, Julius noticed, didn't seem to blame Nicholas for what had happened, but were privately very keen to hear all about the fighting. Having been told so often, Nicholas' account had acquired a rather truncated form, but Julius was able to add to it. He had also a lot of very good stories about Sarno. He found it all rather stimulating and was a little ashamed. But after all, the dead shouldn't be forgotten. One should talk about them.

He did, to Lorenzo Strozzi, who called just after Tobie had arrived. Lorenzo wanted news of his brother in Naples, and to be reassured that King Ferrante would stay on his throne and the Strozzi business would be safe. Julius, as an equally anxious depositor, gave Lorenzo what tidings he could, but few reassurances. Lorenzo then began to talk about the meanness of the Strozzi in Bruges, and how the expanding Charetty company must be looking for bright young factors. When no one followed up this line of conversation, he reverted to talking about Felix. Nicholas told him about the battle. Lorenzo began, at last, to take his leave. At the door he said, looking at Nicholas, "I owe you something for getting that bird back."

For a moment, Nicholas looked entirely blank. Then he said, "The ostrich? Where is it?"

On Lorenzo's gloomy face there spread a rare grin. "Tommaso has it," he said. "They fed it on shellfish in Brittany. It arrived in a very poor state, and he's trying to get it well enough to cross the Alps before winter. I got paid for it."

"Good," said Nicholas.

"Is that all?" said Julius as the door closed. "According to Loppe, Felix told him some story . . ."

"Yes, I know. Let Tobie finish what he was saying first."

So Tobie resumed his discourse, but was still in the middle when they all had to get up because the door had opened on Giovanni Arnolfini, the Lucca silk merchant, who had brought some black velvet for the demoiselle. A gift from the most serene and excellent Dauphin to console the sorrowing mother for the loss of her gallant young son.

They talked about Felix, and Nicholas explained about the battle. After Arnolfini had gone, Tobie looked at Nicholas and said, "Why don't you lock that God-forsaken door?"

Gregorio said, "Because the work bell's just going to sound, and we rather want all the clerks to get in. I haven't had any food yet. Shall we take Meester Tobias and see what we can find? If the demoiselle can be persuaded to excuse us all?"

Nicholas said, "You three go. I'll tell her. I'll see you all later," and got up and left. And Tobie and Gregorio, who didn't know each other, exchanged glances again.

In the tavern, they had the room to themselves because they were late. It was an inn Julius had known for a long time, and he got them to spread the board with food in the doctor's honour, and add as much good Rhenish wine as he could drink. Though in the end, Tobie didn't drink all that much, but requested instead a complete account of why Jaak de Fleury had come to Bruges, and what had happened to him.

At the finish, he sat for a moment, and then swallowed a lot of wine all at once. He said, "And how has Bruges taken that? Do they blame Nicholas?"

"Blame him!" said Julius. "He's redeemed himself at last. You won't remember. He never stood up to anyone. And now that he and the demoiselle . . ."

Gregorio said, rather quickly, "The merchants have come to accept the marriage as well. Nicholas has a good standing. Enough to do all he wants in the way of business."

Tobie, without paying attention, was still looking at Julius, who could feel himself flushing. Tobie said, "I see. And what does he want to do? Has he told you yet?"

Julius said, "Well, it's hardly a matter, yet, of Nicholas running the business. Once the alum sanction is through, I dare say we shall all be asked to help plan for the future. All I can tell you is that we might be raising two squadrons more for Astorre next season, now we have all the extra weapons and money for equipment. I suppose they'll ask you to go back as his surgeon, if they haven't already. The dyeshop will stay under the demoiselle, but the credit side, and the property, including things like Felix's wine tavern, will be looked after by Gregorio and myself and perhaps expanded."

"And Nicholas himself?" said Tobie.

Julius said, "Well, there's the courier service. That's getting well established, with a good team. He'll run it mainly from Bruges, but do some of the riding himself between Bruges and Milan to keep in touch with the Milan side. I dare say he thinks you can help too, if you're to be in Italy with Astorre."

He stopped and looked at Gregorio, but Gregorio didn't seem to want to add anything. Tobie said, "And that's all he's talked about? Nothing about ships, or setting up branches abroad, or going into trading in silk?"

"Ships!" said Julius.

Gregorio said, "No. Nothing about any of that. But of course, there's been a lot to arrange and overhaul these last days. As Julius was saying, there hasn't been a meeting yet to plan anything. The demoiselle probably wanted to wait until you were here. And the alum sanction had come through. I've certainly had the impression . . ." He hesitated.

"What?" said Tobie.

"That Nicholas is waiting for something," said Gregorio.

"And you're not worried?"

Julius said, "What about?"

"About the future of the business, of course," the doctor said. He tore bits off his pheasant and put them all in his mouth with one hand, tidily. He said, "Felix was the nominal head. He's gone. The demoiselle is the legal head. She's a good, capable woman, but an affair this size is beyond her. Until the two daughters marry, who runs the Charetty company?"

Gregorio said, "I should have thought it was fairly obvious. The same people who together will be running the alum venture. The three of us, together with Nicholas. Except that Nicholas, being the demoiselle's husband, has the strongest position."

"He certainly couldn't do it without us," said Julius.

"Couldn't he?" said Tobie. "I've been thinking of all I've seen of friend Nicholas. I listened to the demoiselle talking about the business today. I don't think that Nicholas needs us to run anything. He needs us to help him, that's all. Whether we like it or not, Nicholas is the master of the Charetty company. So how does that strike you? Is he the sort of person you want to work under?"

It was exactly what had been worrying Julius. He said slowly, "I know what you mean. He's young."

Tobie said, "He's just under twenty years old. That's up to ten years younger than the oldest of us. It means that, gifted as he is, he has no experience."

"We can supply that," said Gregorio. He was watching Tobie closely.

"And he'll accept it," said Tobie. "He's good at taking advice. And he's good at management. He's won the goodwill of everyone who has ever beaten him, by being cheerful, placid, long-suffering, and, above all, by bearing no grudges. It makes him attractive to work with. For me, it would make him attractive to work for. But I've begun to wonder about this submissive role. Is it genuine?"

Julius grinned. He said, "Have you seen Nicholas putting up with a beating? It's genuine."

"Oh, he puts up with it, at the time," Tobie said. "But what if he doesn't immediately forget it, as you seem to think? What if every slight, every punishment is being quietly registered, because he is really a different sort of person altogether?"

"I've wondered," said Gregorio.

"Yes. So have I," said Tobie. "Is he what he seems? And then, from wondering, I started to notice things. The chief being this: whom friend Nicholas dislikes, it seems to me, friend Nicholas kills."

Julius stopped eating. Gregorio said, "Yes. I think we should talk about it."

The warm weather had brought in all the flies. Julius batted them away, and untied and flung off his jacket and unhooked the top of his doublet and turned to Tobie and said, *"Now* what are you talking about?"

The doctor laid down the bone he had finished and, splashing his fingers in the water bowl, scrubbed his hands clean on his napkin. Then he pushed his plate away and collected his wine cup in both hands. He said, "Jaak de Charetty and Lionetto."

Julius gazed at him. He felt angry and breathless at the same time. He said, "That's ridiculous. What are you blaming Nicholas for? He killed two servants who were trying to kill him. He didn't kill Lionetto, and he didn't kill de Fleury although, by God, he had every reason to. What he did do is free Bruges—and the company —of the lot of them."

Tobie said, "I'm not saying for a moment that the people he

hurts don't deserve to be hurt. Or most of them. I'm talking about building puzzles and creating ciphers and laying trails and then sitting back while other people explode them."

Tobie picked up his wine, took a hard swallow, and put it down smartly. He sent his eyes round both Julius and Goro.

Tobie said, "Let's take Lionetto. I don't like Lionetto. Lionetto, incidentally, abused Nicholas too, during the flood in the tavern. And then, later, he forced a fight with Astorre, and Nicholas found himself one of the contestants, and all but died. So we may suppose Nicholas doesn't like Lionetto very much either. So you would think Nicholas would be glad to hear that Lionetto was fighting on the other side in the Naples war, under Piccinino."

"He wasn't," said Gregorio, "I remember when the news came that Piccinino had changed to the other side. Nicholas didn't like it. But he wouldn't tell me why."

"Because he didn't care what Piccinino did," Tobie said. "But he wanted Lionetto on our side. So much that when the Pope sent bribery money to Milan, Nicholas asked me to try to persuade the Duke to use some of it to tempt Lionetto away from Piccinino. I did, and he came back to the Milanese side."

"Why should Nicholas want Lionetto on our side?" said Julius.

"That's what I wondered," said Tobie. "Then I began to wonder where Lionetto was putting all this gold he was getting for bribes. And guess what?"

"He used to bank with the Medici," said Julius. "I remember in Geneva that Nicholas joked with the Medici about Lionetto's glass jewels."

"And encouraged Jaak de Fleury to yearn for Lionetto's future deposits," said Tobie. "Of course, Jaak de Fleury knew how lucrative a soldier's business could be. He'd been handling captain Astorre's money for a long time. Until, that is, Nicholas came along."

Julius said, "Nicholas?" But he was already remembering. He said, "In Milan. Astorre transferred his business to the Medici because they offered him amazingly low rates." He paused. "But how could Nicholas influence the Medici?"

Tobie said, "Nicholas had the Medici in the palm of his hand. He makes and breaks ciphers. He's an informer. There's a limit to what the Medici would do for him, but offering low rates to a mercenary captain to capture his trade is well within them. So Astorre's money was safe, and Lionetto, despising his enemy and courted by de Fleury, transferred his money in turn to Maffino. M.

Jaak's agent in Milan. Nicholas was quite relieved when it happened. He checked specially on his way through Milan. He told me."

Gregorio spoke. He said, "So that Lionetto would be ruined when Jaak de Fleury went bankrupt?"

"So that Jaak de Fleury would become bankrupt," said Tobie. "Jaak de Fleury was the target. Lionetto was only the buffer that set the missile off at the right angle."

Was it possible? Julius sat staring at him. Jaak, who had shamed and abused the child Nicholas and the grown Nicholas. Could he have planned such a revenge?

Gregorio said, "You didn't say why Nicholas wanted Lionetto on our side, and not the enemy's."

Tobie's pale eyes turned to Julius, and then back to Gregorio. His short, pink mouth looked sulky. He said, "So that he could betray him. Lionetto is French. All anyone would have to do to ruin Lionetto is to get word to France that Lionetto is fighting for the opposition, and has a large sum of money salted away with a disloyal firm in Geneva. The King of France doesn't have to set out to ruin Thibault and Jaak de Fleury. All he has to do is confiscate Lionetto's huge deposit, and the house of Fleury fails automatically."

Julius said, "You're implying that Nicholas thought of that. How could—"

"Nicholas not only thought of it, he arranged it," said Tobie. "He needed a third party to tell the King of France about Lionetto, so he thought of Savoy. Remember the avalanche in the Alps? It wasn't planned. I saw the idea come into Nicholas' head. He saw the monk was going to shout, and encouraged him. A piece of childishness he came to regret. But back in the hospice he'd been collecting gossip. And I'd swear that he knew that among that party of English was an officer of the Dauphin, the King of France's son and worst enemy.

"Nicholas and M. Gaston du Lyon met and talked then. They would have contrived to talk, I'm sure, even without the avalanche. They met again in Milan—I was there. M. Gaston was supposed to be interested in the Charetty courier service on behalf of his master. In fact, of course, the Dauphin would be hoping to buy information. And Nicholas would have it to sell, or perhaps barter. If in return, for example, the Dauphin would help betray Lionetto to France through the Dauphin's Savoy connections.

"Don't you see?" Tobie said. "The Dauphin would enjoy doing it for all sorts of reasons. He hates his father. He'd get Lionetto back on the Milanese side. And he wouldn't mind helping to destroy Jaak de Fleury. The firm had always favoured the Dauphin's father although, out of greed, M. Jaak didn't refuse Lionetto's custom. And that's what the Dauphin did. He gave the necessary orders. Gaston du Lyon was in Savoy himself that last time Nicholas passed through with Felix. That, I am sure, is how Jaak de Fleury was ruined."

It was still impossible to connect Nicholas with that sort of cunning. Struggling with his disbelief, Julius began with reluctance to search his memory. He recalled an incident. He said, "In Milan —it was Gaston du Lyon who told Nicholas and myself about the bankruptcy. And then . . ." He stopped.

"And then?" said Tobie.

Julius said, "The Medici were waiting for us. They were able to offer us full payment of all M. Jaak owed us, in money or goods, and return of all the unpaid-for goods Jaak was holding. Nicholas had already sold them all the debts previously outstanding. The Medici were pleased because they'd been able to recoup everything, having . . . having prior warning of the bankruptcy."

"Quite," said Tobie. "Nicholas told me, too, to tell the gunfounder at Piacenza that Jaak de Fleury was in no hurry for the weapons he'd ordered. In fact, I was to ask Agostino not to send them to Geneva, even when ready."

"So that they would be here for us, when the house of Fleury fell," said Gregorio. "Julius . . . you were with Nicholas in Milan, you say, when the news of the bankruptcy came through. How did Nicholas take it?"

Julius said, "He was as horrified as I was about the demoiselle Esota and the wrecked business. He . . ."

"What?" said Tobie.

"Smashed a flask," said Julius lamely.

"But," said Gregorio, "was he surprised at anything else? At the bankruptcy? At the money he was collecting?"

And into Julius' mind came the memory of that hot night in Milan, with the two grotesque heads wagging over the sheets of figures, and Nicholas sitting passively by, saying nothing; drained, he had thought by the fever. Julius said, "No." Then he said, "I'm sure he didn't mean to harm the demoiselle Esota."

Unexpectedly, Gregorio said, "I don't think he meant to harm M. Jaak physically, either. He was only parrying in that fight."

Julius didn't say anything. At the end of a weary journey, after killing two men, what did lack of energy prove? Was it possible? Was it possible that after all his exhortations *this* kind of retaliation, this long, quiet, vindictive trail of destruction, was the way Nicholas had picked to assert himself? After a long time, Julius said, "He protected Astorre. He could have left Astorre's money in Geneva too."

"Perhaps he needs Astorre," said Tobie. "He didn't protect Felix."

"No!" said Julius violently. "I don't believe that!"

"And he needed the demoiselle," said Tobie, as if he hadn't spoken. "To begin with, at least. Just as he needs us, to begin with."

Gregorio said, "Wait. I think this is going too far. I don't know Nicholas well, but I would swear that his regard for the demoiselle and for Felix were real. This past week, his feelings have been beyond disguising. Julius will bear me out."

Julius said, "Of course that's true. My God, Tobie. You saw him at San Fabiano. That wasn't all fever, surely? I saw him when he heard about the extent of the disaster at Geneva. He could hardly speak all the way back to Bruges, and he still hasn't got over it. How could he feel like that, if he were the sort of monster you're talking about?"

"Remorse?" said Tobie. "He's not twenty yet. It's his first experiment. The next one will probably set off its explosions more neatly. The question is, do we want to wait until it happens? It might be one or all of us another time. Deliberately, or—if you want to give him the benefit of the doubt—accidentally. I put him down at first as an innocent cursed with an overwhelming intelligence, and liable to blunder in any direction. I thought you and I could control that. But suppose he's not an innocent at all? Suppose he knows very well where he's going, and proposes to get there in this fashion?"

A silence fell. Julius didn't want to speak. He twisted his hands on the table, slowly, one inside the other, and still couldn't imagine Nicholas doing all those things. And then could, quite easily.

Gregorio said, "There isn't any absolute proof, is there?"

Tobie said, "Only by consulting the Dauphin or the Duke of Milan, who are unlikely to tell you."

Julius said, "What are you going to do?" directly to the doctor.

Tobie's hands were still, his lips pursed, his eyes on the opposite wall. He opened his mouth. Without warning, he sneezed.

"May God bless you," said Julius.

To his surprise, the doctor went patchily red. Then he said brusquely, "I'm staying. If he's already turned the wrong way, I'm fairly confident that I can outwit him. If he hasn't, I might be able to stop him. I don't think you or I would be in any danger at the moment. He needs us. What I *am* going to do, however, is warn Marian de Charetty."

Julius said, "I would stay, too." Then he said, "Perhaps the demoiselle knows."

The light gaze came back to him. "And that's why he's . . . No. She wouldn't have acted the way she did with Jaak de Fleury. Goro?"

"No," said Gregorio. "I'm sure she doesn't know how M. Jaak and Lionetto were tricked. She wouldn't have allowed him to do it. She's a very honest lady. I would stay. I will say this, too. He can't be wholly innocent. But I don't think he's evil."

Tobie said, "Or not yet. As a matter of interest, was it Jaak de Fleury who had the dyeshop burned down?"

Gregorio said, "Not that we know of. The man we caught there was the Scotsman. Simon."

"So she has more than one possible enemy," Tobie said. "I've had an idea. Why don't we set them at each other's throats?"

"They're there already," said Julius.

Chapter 40

Isolated in his wooden box, where the triggers for the moment had ceased to act, Nicholas was not only waiting; he was adrift.

He gave no appearance of it, being endlessly industrious on the concerns of his business by day, and taking on himself, by night, the charge of the demoiselle's happiness.

Marian de Charetty was happy. He had known since their marriage the triple rôle he had played, sometimes as Claikine, the child whom she pitied; sometimes as Nicholas her steward and factor, to be relied on like Julius or Gregorio. And sometimes as a substitute for Cornelis, who would take her burden when she was tired, and whom she could trust, because she was married to him.

He had known, too, what pity could lead to, and loneliness. Because of it, he had kept one private rule since his marriage. It was not a popular one among the girls who thought they knew him.

He no longer suffered a servant's life, and so no longer, you would say, needed compensations. Instead, he found himself with a new, densely organised career, but no means of relief. He endured it, but not easily. What part this had played in his surrender on the night of Jaak de Fleury's death he didn't want to know. But he could hardly fail to see, in the morning, the result of that night spent with Marian: her fresh colour; and the calm with which she spoke lovingly of all that had to do with Felix. To Nicholas she used the same voice exactly. He was to be Felix. He was to receive comfort, and not bestow it.

And so it had continued. The first days for her had been bridal: to wait until nightfall a penance. He had to be wise for them both: to remember that night-long pleasure was something that only the young can withstand for long; to be gentle; to recognise that the relationship must diminish, and settle sooner or later at a level much less intense. He was ready, he thought, to deal with that as well. The real world demanded tolls of all kinds. To drain off his energy, he had the exercise ground and the archery butts to return to. He got Julius to go with him to both, and forced even Tobie and Gregorio into joining.

They didn't thank him, although once they were there he thought they enjoyed it. He had hoped, for the sake of the business, that they would all three get on together; and for the sake of the business, unloaded on them everything he could think of, so that they got used to helping each other.

They did get on well together. They were roughly the same age, and all professionals. He had expected to be regarded as the outsider, and he was. He thought that once he felt better about a number of things, it would be time to start handling them. And then to make plans.

Soon after that, the alum sanction came through. It was the first of the things he had been waiting for. The arrangements were already poised, and only needed to be put into action. Nicholas set Tobie to do some of that, and went on himself to visit the Hôtel Jerusalem.

He had seen something of Adorne since he came back: there was no need to talk about Felix. Nor had much been said about the death of Jaak de Fleury, which officialdom had dealt with so remarkably smoothly. Since the wedding here in this hall, Margriet Adorne had been a good friend to Marian, sustaining her in the first days of her loss, and helping her now with her daughters.

It was to be expected, he supposed, that Tilde and Catherine, jealous and angry, should want to enjoy what their mother was now enjoying, and should bid fair to run wild with the young of their circle. Someone had to restrain them, since attention and restraint, in the end, were what they wanted. He himself was the one person who couldn't help. But Marian and Margriet were managing, between them.

Adorne was as glad as he was about the papers from Venice, and they spent a long time making arrangements. Adorne, the long, fair, quizzical face unaltered, was wearing a dark robe and doublet out of deference to his Scottish clients, whose king had just died. It had struck Nicholas at once that there would be a demand for black cloth. Once a dyer, one thought like a dyer.

Adorne said, "You know Prosper de Camulio is coming to Genappe?"

A hot night in Milan, and Tomà Adorno. And, of course, Felix. Nicholas said, "On Genoese business? Or for Duke Francesco?"

"As envoy of the Duke of Milan," Adorne said. "An alliance

between the Dauphin and Milan is under negotiation. I can't imagine that's news."

"No," said Nicholas. "Is he staying long?"

"Long enough," said Adorne, "to give you the introductions you may be waiting for. As with Milan and the Dauphin, circumstance seems to be making bedfellows of Venice and Genoa. I only hope, if you lie on that particular bed, that you will live to get up from it." He waited. Nicholas, who had learned when to say nothing, made no comment. Anselm Adorne smiled and, taking ribbon, began to tie up his papers. He said, "The requiem Mass tomorrow for the late James, King of Scotland. Are you and your wife brave enough to attend?"

He went on tying the ribbon. Nicholas said, "Why?"

Adorne pushed the packet aside and looked up, folding his hands. He said, "I thought you mightn't have heard. Don't you know how the King died?"

Nicholas sat very still. He said, "I knew he was young. I assumed he was killed in battle. He was fighting the English, surely?"

Adorne nodded. "At a place called Roxburgh. He was besieging the castle with all his artillery, including the two cannon from Mons. One of them burst as he stood beside it, and killed him."

Nicholas said, "Not Meg, I'm sure. But Martha?"

Adorne said, "The one that sank at Damme. Of course, that had nothing to do with it. It left Sluys for Scotland in perfect order—if it burst, it burst for quite different reasons. But you should be prepared for certain remarks if you go to the service. When you go. I think you should attend."

He waited. Nicholas said, "How many others were killed?"

"Only the King and one other man," Adorne said. "Not a massacre. A piece of bad luck, that was all. They were both fascinated by guns. The King and Kilmirren. The other who died was Alan of Kilmirren, the uncle of your old acquaintance Simon. I'm told Simon is delighted. He now gets everything his own way in Scotland."

Nicholas heard the words, but they were a long way behind the place his thoughts had arrived at. He realised that Adorne was speaking again in a different way.

Adorne said, "But, in fact, you did plan to sink that cannon, didn't you? Monsignore de' Acciajuoli saw you position the barge before it entered the lock. And found the pattern of jet-holes in the wall afterwards."

Nicholas said, "I thought of a way to do it. That was all."

"And did it," said Adorne. "Why?"

"To see what would happen," said Nicholas flatly.

He got back so late that he thought Marian would have retired, but there was light still to be seen, rimming the bedchamber door. At night, instead of wearing mourning, she waited for him in a fine robe the colour of her loosened hair. The gown had no fastenings, and there was nothing below it. There were ceremonies he had invented to do with that. There was no ceremony in the world he wanted to take part in tonight. But he couldn't pass her door either. He paused, and then tapped and went in, fully dressed as he was.

Since coming back, he had grown to know this room well. The narrow windows with their studded shutters and the squares of latticed glass. The stone fireplace, with the settle piled with cushions standing with its back to the empty hearth. The painted chests which held her possessions. The sturdy table, with a bowl of figs or pomegranates on its lower shelf, and a spouted wine-jug in silver standing on top, with two goblets ready. A shelf with her silver plate, and a porcelain jug with some late roses. A round mirror, and another table with a basin of water on it, and a towel hanging beside it, on a bracket.

Two stools, and a carpet, and some cushions on the floor, which became pressed flat with their weight, and had to be lifted and shaken before morning. And of course the bed, its frame reaching up to the coloured rafters, with the hangings and coverlet Marian had embroidered for her marriage to Cornelis and which, tactfully, she had not changed. That had been a marriage, and so was this. The bed was wide enough for any sort of ceremony.

She had been sitting on the window seat, and she was fully clothed also. So he introduced the subject himself. "I've just heard. About the cannon."

She had taken off her daytime headdress, and her hair was pinned, loosely coiled, at her neck. Her gowns now were lighter and prettier than those she used to wear for business. This one had brocade sleeves with glints of gold about them, and she was wearing a long string of fine pearls. She rose from the cushion and walked forward a little, saying, "I was waiting to tell you. Where did you find out? At Anselm Adorne's?"

She didn't say, as Adorne had done, "The sinking at Damme had nothing to do with it."

He closed the door, while he thought. Then he said, "Yes. And about Kilmirren."

She nodded. She was standing before the little table with her hands lightly clasped in front of her, looking at him. She had an open face, clear-skinned, with particularly bright blue eyes, which he had learned to read quite well. He said, "What has happened?"

She rarely stood perfectly still, like this. Her face was a little drawn. She said, "I heard another small piece of news. All France, it seems, is talking about the downfall of the vicomte de Ribérac."

Jordan de Ribérac. A pain ran through his cheek, as though the ring had scored it again. He cleared his throat and said again, "What has happened?"

Marian de Charetty said, "It seems he had been caught trafficking with the Dauphin. The King was very angry. M. de Ribérac has lost, of course, all he had. Land, houses, money, all his possessions."

Nicholas said, "What is going to become of him?"

And Marian said, "I imagine he'll be locked in the dungeons at Loches. Perhaps they'll put him in the cage. Perhaps they'll behead him at once. Did you arrange that as well?"

He realised how stupid it was, simply standing staring at her. He said, "I expect so." With a great effort he said, "Marian, *what has happened*?"

And she said, "You chose some very astute new men for the company. The doctor, Tobias, has been to see me. He and Julius and Gregorio have been troubled about the future of the business. So they decided, quite rightly, to place their doubts before me and ask my opinion."

"Tobie," he said.

"Yes. And Goro. And our good Julius. I thought you were fond of them, and they of you," said Marian his wife. "But now, they're afraid of you."

A large sigh stretched his chest, and he got rid of it. It left an ache behind, as bad as a blow. Nicholas said, "You don't need to be afraid of me. Ask me anything you like, and I'll tell you. Will you sit? On the settle, and I'll sit over here. But some wine, first. Will you let me give you some wine?"

She sat, nodding. When he took her the cup, the wine in it trembled, but whether from his hand or hers no one could have known. He saw it, and thought of the pink goblet in the grasp of Astorre and Lionetto. He was cold with fear. He had been, for weeks.

While she drank, he chose the bedside stool to sit on, elbows on knees, laced hands pushed into his lips. Then he dropped his hands and said, "Will you tell me what Tobie said?"

It was about Jaak de Fleury and Lionetto, as he had expected. They had pieced it all together remarkably well. And, of course, Marian herself could match it with her own knowledge. Of his dealings with the Dauphin, for instance. They didn't know that he and Gaston had tried first to bribe de Fleury to the Dauphin's side and failed, but that of course had had no effect on the final issue.

And they didn't know, either, about Jordan de Ribérac. Only Marian and the van Borselen girls knew of the war between himself and de Ribérac. Marian had guessed that the vicomte's downfall might owe something to him, but she couldn't know how it had been done. Katelina was in Brittany, and he had been careful to ask no one about her. Gelis would say nothing, for her sister's sake. And Felix, who could have been curious about that last meeting in Ghent, was, of course, dead.

What had spurred Tobie to come to the demoiselle had, in the end, been the news of the death of the Scots king. Telling of it, Marian paused, as she had often paused during the long recital, but he had made no comment yet. She resumed, speaking quite steadily. "Up till then, you see, they had assumed that, whatever you'd done, it was nothing that need concern anyone else. They thought it was finished. They were only concerned about the future. But there was the gun."

Then, for the first time, Nicholas spoke. He said, "I didn't even mean to be in the lighter when it went through the lock. It was pure chance that someone asked us to help with the Duke's bath and Julius and . . . and Julius agreed." He stopped. He said, "If I hadn't gone, I shouldn't have met any of them."

He was talking to himself, really, not to her. After a moment she said, "I suppose you knew that the soaking couldn't possibly affect the gun's performance. People may still say that you might not have known; that you hoped it would do just what it did. Tobie, I think is not quite sure. But discussing it, Julius and Gregorio came to realise something else much more likely. By sinking the cannon, you delayed its arrival in Scotland. And if that was deliberate, if you were hired to do it, then you are concerned with matters which could not, after all, be kept amongst ourselves."

She paused. "You were a boy when it happened. People thought nothing of it. But even mischief begins to look sinister when, later, other connections are made. Because Scotland was supporting the Lancastrians, the absence of the gun was an advantage to the opposite side. The Dauphin, the Duke of Milan, Bishop Coppini, King Ferrante in Naples, Arnolfini and the English Governor—all these are people who oppose the King of France and the Lancastrians, and you have been involved in some way with all of them. And once people notice such things, it must seem that you are not only spying for merchants, it must seem that you are a political informer as well."

Nicholas said, "The vicomte de Ribérac was on the Dauphin's side."

"But," said Marian, "you had overwhelming reasons, hadn't you, for punishing him? And then, once word gets about that you are not what you seem, that you're not to be trusted, people will begin to imagine things. About the dismissal of old employees and the taking on of new ones, all of your choice. About . . . your marriage, of course. About they might say, the way you kept Felix involved in escapades, and away from anything prestigious or responsible . . . and the way he died."

Her voice broke off, then. He didn't look up. He didn't want to see her crying. He said, "I wish I were Felix. I told him that, once, in Milan." His elbows still on his knees, he found himself slowly rubbing his face, as if pressing in some miraculous, analgesic ointment. Then he remained, his nose deadened between his two hands, his closed eyes spanned by his fingers. Then he said, "And what was Tobie's conclusion?"

This time, the silence lasted so long that he did, in the end, open his eyes and look at her. She had been crying, but only a little. She had been waiting for him, that was all.

She said, "He said they had talked about it all day. They couldn't reach a conclusion until they knew what I thought."

"And what is your conclusion?" he said. This time, he couldn't read her expression.

She said, "I knew about de Ribérac, which the doctor didn't. I knew a number of other things, Nicholas, which he didn't. But I also had a great advantage. I knew how you really felt about us. About Julius. About Felix. And, I think, about me."

"So?" he said. His teeth wanted to chatter.

"So I confirmed what was, in the end, his own view, I think," Marian said. "I told him that you were the truest, most loyal friend he or anyone else was likely to have. That nearly all that you had done had been done for the company, and not for any political reasons. That you had put Felix and the training of Felix above everything else, and that he would never have become more than a child but for you. But I told him, too, that you would have to be watched day and night because you had gifts more dangerous than Meg, or Martha, or any weapon of war yet invented. And you didn't know yet how to control them."

His throat closed. He couldn't answer her.

Then she said, "I told him that. I thought if he knew that, he deserved to know everything. So I also told him who you are."

"They spent the night apart," said Julius.

"Oh?" said Tobie. All anyone could see of Tobie was the rump of his black gown as he knelt on an office stool, peering out the window.

Julius said, "So why not tell us what happened? Come on. You saw the demoiselle. You told her everything. What did she say?"

"I told you," said Tobie. He sounded angry. "She wanted to speak to Nicholas first. Then she'll see me after the service. Then I can tell you."

Julius said, "But if they spent the night apart . . ."

Gregorio said, "There might have been all sorts of reasons for that. We might as well wait till Tobie can tell us. Anyway, if he knew anything he wouldn't be hanging out of the window to see if they go off to Nôtre Dame together."

Tobie's rump remained uncommunicative. Then it jerked. "They're going!" he said.

Julius bounded to the next window and threw open a shutter. Below, indeed, was a group of well-groomed servants in the Charetty livery, Loppe towering head and shoulders over the rest. His face was expressionless, which Julius had learned to recognise as a bad sign. There were also two horses. Marian de Charetty, in a white headdress and a dark cloak, was already mounted, and, as he watched, Nicholas came out and turned to his stirrup.

Julius came away from the window rather abruptly. Tobie, he saw, had done the same. Tobie said, "It isn't all that amusing, is it, when you see the effects?"

Gregorio, walking quietly to the window, looked out as well. He said, "They would have to go anyway, to keep up appearances in front of their friends."

Julius said, "And not only their friends. The noble Simon of Kilmirren will be among the Scots mourners."

Tobie pulled his hat off. "How d'you know that?" he said.

Julius made a wry face. "Because I pick the right clients," he said. "Liddell. Secretary of Bishop Kennedy and tutor to the small Scottish prince. They're all staying at the lord of Veere's house, and I went there for a signature yesterday. Liddell told me Simon had come for the Mass. Brought his wife, too."

Gregorio said, "I remember. At the time of the White Bear tournament. My lord Simon was escorting the sister of Reid, the Staple merchant. Muriella, her name was."

"And no doubt still is," said Julius. "But that's not the lady he married. Simon's been married for nearly four months to Katelina van Borselen. I saw her. Very pregnant."

"*Very* pregnant?" said Tobie.

"As I say. I would reckon," said Julius cheerfully, "that Simon got there about four weeks before the priest did. He's delighted, says Liddell. Been trying to get children, as we all know, for years. What was that girl's name?"

"Muriella," said Gregorio dryly.

"No," said Tobie. "The one he's thinking of was called Mabelie. Oh, Jesus Christ. Nicholas. He doesn't know Simon's married?"

"No," said Julius, sobering suddenly. "I should have warned him, shouldn't I?"

"Yes, you should," said Tobie grimly.

Delight was, indeed, the mood of Simon of Kilmirren these days. Waiting while his wife's servants dressed her to go to Nôtre Dame, he felt hardly any impatience. He was almost sorry that her train was as long as it was. Swept about and held bunched to her breast as the fashion now was, it hid the rounded, rich swell of her belly.

In which kicked his child. The heir to Kilmirren, now that his father was surely done for, and his wretched miser of an uncle had met his end at last. Kilmirren was his, and the title was almost his, and in due course would pass down to the child.

Katelina was sensitive about the size of the child. Simon didn't mind. After all her maidenly protestations in Silver Straete, he had been surprised at first when he had discovered the sort of welcome he was being drawn into in Brittany. On reflection, he quite understood it. The lady Katelina van Borselen was starved for elegant company, and courting, and expert dalliance.

He brought out, that first evening in Brittany, his handsomest doublet, cut short to the waist in the French style, exposing silk-covered haunch and fine codpiece. For the silk, he had chosen his shapeliest hose in two colours, embroidered from knee to thigh with spiralling roses. It was as if contrite angels had remodelled, for him alone, that humiliating episode in the smoke-ridden garden. What Bruges had denied him, Brittany now gave with both hands on that first night. In the drowsy company after the meal, close by Katelina, he had filled her glass over and over, introducing one by one the invisible, critical caresses, the hints of desire in his murmuring, until he saw that the moment was coming already.

The Duchess had no objection to his leading the lady Katelina to take the air in the warm moonlit garden. This time Katelina's trembling fingers were already deliciously wooing him as he moved down the steps from the house, and the last of the lamplight from its windows showed him the anxiety in her face. Then they were alone in the bower, and no man knew the art of forcing anxiety to the point of anguished exultation better than Simon of Kilmirren.

In a fortnight, she had suspected she was pregnant. Half reluctantly, he had heard her frightened appeals, and had married her. Only half reluctantly, because already he could not have enough of her. When the pregnancy was later confirmed, his cup was full.

He didn't mind who saw that he had fathered a child before marriage on Katelina van Borselen. He would give her one a year. Day and night, he would give her reason for one. She was, now, the way he spent his time.

The church of Onze Lieve Vrouwekerk, when they got there, was shrouded in black and already filled, except for the chief mourners. The Duke's representatives waited at the door for the party from the house of Veere. The Duke whose niece, Mary of Guelders, was now Dowager Queen of Scotland.

The Princess Mary walked first, led by her father-in-law Henry van Borselen, comte de Grandpré, seigneur de la Veere, Vlissingue, Westcapelle and Domburg, together with his wife Jeanne de Halewyn. Next came the Princess's husband Wolfaert van Borselen and the Scots Bishop James Kennedy. Between Wolfaert and the Bishop walked the two children: Alexander, Duke of Albany, middle son of the late Scots king, and Charles van Borselen, his nine-year-old cousin.

Alexander, Duke of Albany and Lord High Admiral of Scotland, was only six. Conducted by his father's cousin, Bishop Kennedy, he had arrived this summer at Bruges to be reared at the Burgundian court. Now his father was dead, but no one had taken him home. Bishop Kennedy, detained by an illness, was still at his side: skilful ambassador; agile diplomat, reporting back all the nuances of Burgundian response to the new Scottish régime.

Perhaps the child, thickly dressed in dark jewelled doublet and bonnet, had no desire to go home. He looked harried and sullen, walking there with his cousin. The Scots in the party studied him and the Bishop, and pondered. Including Simon of Kilmirren and his lady, walking behind with the others. The fifteen years between them could hardly be guessed at. Ripened with marriage, his wife now looked older than twenty. And he, all his life, had kept the style and looks of his golden youth.

Politics mattered. But once pacing down the aisle with his wife, Simon had remarkably little thought for the dead king. He could feel people looking at Katelina, beautiful even under her veiling. And at himself, in cut black velvet tied with grey ribbons, and the hat of cocks' feathers which he held in one hand.

The Mass was a long one, and the music tedious, but afterwards they would go to the adjoining palace of Louis de Gruuthuse and his wife, Wolfaert's sister. Simon looked forward to presenting his Katelina to the noblesse of Bruges for the first time since returning from Scotland. It was possible, because of the degree of haste in the marriage, that not all of them knew of it. He had noted some curious glances. And one stare that he thought he recognised, but failed to find and identify.

He was careful not to reprimand Katelina when she shifted on the uncomfortable seat. He would, however, be happy when she had given birth to the child and had a body less cumbersome. He remembered her breasts as they used to be. There was a girl, across by the ambulatory, who had smiled at him as they came in, and who had small, heaped breasts like that, separated under the stuff of her gown in the Florentine style. Simon smiled back at her in a kindly way, and patted Katelina's hand as she shifted again.

As they slowly filed out at the end, he was able to smooth his hair and put on his hat at the proper slant, while Katelina put back her veiling. Then they passed across the yard in the sunshine and, with the other, select guests, entered Gruuthuse's palace.

Louis, seigneur of Gruuthuse, greeted them on the threshold. The style was ducal, but the lined cheeks, the thick eyelids under the fringe, belonged to a long line of wealthy burghers from Bruges and Brabant. Gruuthuse, courtier, statesman, man of business, was about to leave for Scotland himself, carrying Duke Philip's greetings to the new child king, James the Third. He knew every Scotsman who entered and so, Simon saw, did most of his family. The boy Guildolf, it seemed, had got married. The bride, curtseying to Katelina, had what he would call an impudent smile. It reminded him of his young sister-in-law Gelis who, blessedly, had lumbered home.

They crossed the tiled hall and walked up a staircase between men in livery. The windows were very fine, and the woodwork, and the fireplaces. He glimpsed what looked like a library. The Gruuthuse motto and cannon were everywhere. So, of course, were the Scots. All the merchants, fat and lean, and their hôteliers. Jehan Metteneye and his wife. That fool John of Kinloch. Wylie, the archdeacon of Brechin. Mick Losschaert, with some of his relatives from the Scottish branch of the family, and the Bonkles also, from both sides of the water. Anselm Adorne, of course, with his wife and older children, and his married sister and her husband Daniel Sersanders of Ghent with their son Anselm. Napier of Merchiston. Stephen Angus. Forrester of Corstorphine. And various Scots just returned from Bourges and the French conference over Denmark, Spain, the Breton dowry: Monypenny, of course; and Flockhart with one or two Volkarts from the Flemish side for good measure.

Attending the requiem for their late master with proper sobriety. And rushing off afterwards, he had no doubt, to plot and plan for the next struggle for power back in Scotland. A Flemish queen dowager, and a crowned king aged eight, and all the battlefield of Lancastrian and Yorkist England to make capital out of, if you played your cards right. All you needed to look for were good card-players.

Simon found he was little interested in his own countrymen. He spent some time with the Duchess's secretary, his brother-in-law, who complimented the lady Katelina on her appearance but not on her fecundity, which was deftly disguised by a swirl of brocade in her fingers. Señor João introduced the bride to some other ladies, and prepared to fulfil Simon's wish to meet the commander of the Flanders galley, Piero Zorzi.

Simon brightened. He had some business to do with the commander, a short, personable man in a magnificent outfit of ash colour and silver. He could see him through the crowd, his arm held by the seigneur de Gruuthuse, who was steering him to meet a tall man and his wife on the far side of the room.

The wife Simon couldn't at once place, except that she must be Scots, in view of the severity of her mourning. The man was in dark clothes as well, but very plainly cut with no jewels, although you could see that his belt was expensive, and his tunic of good cloth. His face, turning towards the Venetian, was vivid with interest and when he smiled suddenly, a disarming pocket appeared in each cheek.

He smiled and Simon, arriving with Vasquez, halted and looked at him with disbelief, with amazement, with a growing fury that, for a moment, deprived him of speech.

At the same moment, the other man glanced across and his face changed also, radically. João Vasquez, arrested, stopped on the verge of introducing him. Gruuthuse looked round with an air of enquiry. Simon stared straight at his host. He said, "M. de Gruuthuse, I cannot think you know what you are doing. We are here to mourn the death of our king. You insult us by inviting the man who caused him to die."

Like Anselm Adorne, Louis de Gruuthuse was a master of awkward situations. He smiled at the commander and made a little move, so that Zorzi was no longer quite in the circle, and Marian de Charetty, moving with him, was able to distract him. Vasquez stayed.

Gruuthuse said, "Well now, you might as well blame the good men who made that cannon in Mons as pounce upon Nicholas here. And the name of Gruuthuse is guarantee enough, I should have thought, of good faith. I should never shame any guest. Come. There are others who want to meet you."

Simon made no move, nor did he look at anyone but the youth he had last seen in tatters outside the burning wreck of his dye-shop. Simon said, "How dare you appear in this company? How dare you dress as a burgess, as if your stinking clothes and your clogs were forgotten? I'd like to teach you a lesson."

"You already have," said the boy Claes. He had changed colour.

He began to back away, with the encouragement of that meddler Gruuthuse.

Simon followed him, lounging. "You think I would fight you again? Hardly. But when you tempt Providence as you do, you should look out for acts of God. They do happen. Another fire. The sad expiry of a business deal. A lack of confidence, shall we say, in the house of Charetty? It might be awkward, you know. How would you live, after all, if there was no business? You would have to go back to the dyevats, wouldn't you? And take your elderly lady along with you?"

Louis de Gruuthuse said, "Kilmirren. That's enough. Señor João, I'd be obliged if you would see to your friend."

Simon paid no attention. Simon said, "What are you going to do, *Nicholas*, when you're tired of her and she can't support you any more? You got rid of her son quickly enough, they tell me. You may be sorry. A young man can support his elders if he works hard enough, and is well beaten."

He was getting home to the boy. The boy looked stupid. He said, "Ser Louis, forgive me," and tried to turn on his heel, but Simon caught him hard by the elbow, willing the fellow to try and hit him. The youth wrenched, and then stood still. Simon's hands were used to a sword. He could grip to draw blood, when he wanted to. People were looking round. Simon saw Katelina turn as well. He hoped she would come over.

The boy said, "Let me go."

"You didn't hear me," Simon said.

"Yes, I heard you," he said. Bleated, perhaps. Their host, giving up, had moved away, his face rather grim. After a moment, Vasquez left too, leaving them isolated.

Simon said, "And you have nothing to say?"

The boy said, "I have nothing to say here. If you use your imagination, you must know what I think."

"I don't know why I think it worth the trouble," said Simon. He released his grip. He said, "Ah. There you are. Come and look at this turd who has married his employer and can do nothing in front of gentlemen except stand and quake."

"You mean Claes?" said Katelina van Borselen. "But no one expects Claes to be brave, unless someone pays him."

The boy and she stared at one another. Simon, pleased, thought he had never seen her look more handsome than she did now, in her scorn. The emeralds he had given her jumped and flashed round her throat, and gold shone around the edge of her hennin, whose veils framed her face.

After what seemed a long time the boy said, "You're back from Brittany."

She said, "I hope you received the ostrich. I did my best for poor Lorenzo, you know."

It seemed a pointless remark. Simon had expected her to join in the baiting. The boy looked as if he didn't know what to say. Eventually he said, "It came. I have to go and look at it today. Thank you."

"And," said Katelina, "I hear you are married now? That is your wife?"

He didn't turn round. He said, "Yes. You are with . . ."

"I am with my lord and husband, of course," said Katelina. "My lord Simon. Tell me, is your wife bearing yet? But no. I suppose those days are behind her. Indeed, you will be marrying off your stepdaughters soon. Tell me if I may help find them husbands."

Simon stared at Katelina. He said, "What have you to do with scullion marriages? Are you playing some game?"

"I suppose I am," said Katelina. "And I'm tired of it. Shall we go home? You know how you like me to rest." She looked at the fellow Claes. She said, "My husband, you see, cannot care enough for my health."

Simon hadn't finished with the boy. He had planned to say a lot more, in spite of Gruuthuse. But when Katelina leaned her weight like that on his arm, he always grew a little alarmed, just in case. Just in case, after all these years, he might be robbed of his heir.

So he smiled at the imbecile Claes instead, conscious of the picture he and Katelina must make standing close, romantic as lovers in some superb Book of Hours. Then, taking time, Simon let his eyes travel to the dumpy figure of the boy's wife, still standing behind, anxiety plain in her eyes. Simon laughed. Then, bowing with mockery, he led his lady away. As she moved, Katelina threw down the heavy folds of her train. It fell behind her as she walked, dragging against her swollen stomach. The stomach of a woman some five months gone with child.

It destroyed the graceful illusion he had created. At first Simon felt annoyed at her carelessness. Then he realised that it was not carelessness. It was contempt. It was there, on her face as she

walked. And the boy, standing behind with his wife, looked as if
she had stunned him.

Simon turned to his Katelina and, lifting a beautiful hand,
traced her size caressingly with his palm. Then he looked over his
shoulder. He conveyed disdain, he hoped, and certainly triumph.
And the look on the fool's face behind him was better than anything else that had happened that day.

Usually, he didn't much enjoy leaving company because Katelina
felt unwell. But this time, what with the conspicuous frowns of
Gruuthuse and a few other people, he knew he had better depart,
and work out in a day or two how he should apologise. He had a
short temper, and he didn't suffer fools gladly, especially when
he'd had a little to drink. People were always claiming to be upset,
or insulted, but his steward usually made it all right, or he could
arrange an invitation for someone and flatter them, or if it were
someone like Gruuthuse, he would send round a charming gift
with a grovelling note. Keeping one's temper was for women.

Usually the fresh air cured Katelina's upsets, but this time they
got back to the house of Veere and she was still trembling. He was
going to get her maid when she stopped his leaving the bedchamber. She said, "What did you mean about the Charetty business?
Another fire?"

Simon thought back, and smiled. He hadn't known she was listening. He said, "Did you see his face? I thought that would
frighten him."

She was sitting where he had placed her, not yet in bed, but in
the tall wooden chair, with cushions behind her. She said, "You
didn't mean it, then?"

He couldn't understand what she was talking about. He got a
flask of wine out, and gave himself some. He said, "Well, I'm not
likely to put any bargains their way, am I? It depends. It depends
how he behaves. Why? What does it matter?"

Katelina said, "It doesn't, of course. But she's a good little
woman, Marian de Charetty. It isn't her fault."

"Of course it is," said Simon. "She shouldn't have married him.
Do you know what I heard? He's not such a fool as you'd think."
His glass was empty. He filled it.

"Who?" said Katelina.

He got irritated when she was obtuse. "Claes, of course," said
Simon. "The Charetty servants have some great tale of what he'd

been up to in Milan. Did you hear about Jaak de Fleury, the great-uncle that tried to take over the business?"

She had heard. It was surprising sometimes what she heard about the Charetty business while she remained regrettably ignorant about his.

"Well," said Simon, "the story runs that it was Claes who bankrupted M. Jaak. He not only bankrupted him, but he ruined that captain, Lionetto, and got Lionetto to blame Jaak de Fleury. So Jaak de Fleury not only lost all his business, but Lionetto came to Bruges and killed him. I don't believe it," said Simon. "But they do. They think Claes—they call him Nicholas, now—was behind the cannon that killed the King and my uncle. They talk about his being a Yorkist agent and carrying messages for the Dauphin and inventing a magic that means that the Medici can talk to each other without words any more. Infantile rubbish. I tried to shame him today and you saw him."

"I saw he wouldn't fight," said Katelina. "But maybe . . ." She broke off.

Simon frowned. He said, "It did strike me. He got Lionetto to kill his great-uncle. He didn't do it himself. I don't much like the idea of someone saying nothing to my face and then creeping about planning disasters."

Katelina said, in a rather odd voice, "Your father. His whole life came to an end in the same way."

"Fat father Jordan?" He wondered what had put that into her head. He said, "Well, Claes can hardly have ruined Jordan de Ribérac, can he? Unless he's really trading services with the Dauphin."

"Perhaps he is," said Katelina.

"Well, if he is, he's done me a favour," said Simon. "And if he was behind the gun that killed Uncle Alan, then he did me an even bigger one. You know, there's something strange about that. But of course, it can't be."

"What can't be?" she said. She looked green, the way she did when she was overtired.

Simon said, "You've done too much. Never mind this nonsense. I'll get your woman."

She actually caught him by the wrist to stop him. "No," she said. "I want to know. What do you think is strange about Claes?"

He was surprised, but he dropped into the other chair and poured himself some more wine and then, as an afterthought, some for her. She didn't take it. He said, "Well, just that if he really did all those things, you would think he was getting rid, one by one, of all his family."

She said, "All his family?" and he wished he had gone when he said he was going.

He said, "Well, Jaak de Fleury. He was his great-uncle. And the woman he married was related, and he got rid of her son."

She said, "Did he? I didn't hear that." She looked even more distracted. She said, "And who else? I didn't think Nicholas—Claes—had any family."

With no food and a pleasant amount of wine inside him, he thought that was funny. He said, "Well, that's Jaak gone. And his wife Esota. And old Thibault the brother ruined, and his daughter, whatever she's called. And old Jordan, my revered father done for. And Alan my uncle. I'm the only person he hasn't succeeded in harming, if you don't count Lucia, and she's in Portugal. It's amazing. He hasn't been able to touch me. All he's done is get me my title."

You would think she was drunk, the way she persisted. He hoped she wasn't drunk, because it would harm the baby. He realised, hazily, that she hadn't drunk anything. She repeated, "But I didn't know Nicholas had any family. I thought his mother died."

He wondered how she knew that. He said, "Yes, of course the stupid bitch died, and good riddance. The whore produced him and dandled him for a few years and told him a few lies, and died. Don't you see how he looks like her? Don't you see?"

Katelina was whispering. He wondered why. She said, "You knew her then? Nicholas' mother?"

They were all bitches, and all stupid. He stared at Katelina.

"Knew her?" said Simon. "She was my wife. That's why that stupid bastard won't fight me. Claes. Nicholas. He thinks he's my son."

He got to her as she started to slip off the chair. Her face looked terrible. He shouted for her maid and held her weight against him on the floor, patting her back to reassure her. "It's all right," said Simon. "It's all right. Four months to go, and you'll see a fine, fat, beautiful baby. Claes is brainless, you see. He never dreamed I'd marry and get a child on you. A real Kilmirren, to inherit all he thinks he's entitled to. He may have outguessed the rest of the family, but he couldn't best me."

Chapter 41

Gregorio, who never swore, said, "Oh Christ Jesus."

"My feelings entirely," said Tobie. "Simon, who tried to kill Nicholas at Damme, should have been his father. And Jordan de Ribérac his grandfather. De Ribérac who, in case you don't know, apparently scarred him for life with his ring. Now tell me Nicholas wasn't right to lay as many trails and traps as he liked."

Julius said, "But Jaak and his wife were the only ones who were hurt because of Nicholas."

Tobie dragged his hat off and polished his scalp. "No. Evidently Jordan de Ribérac's fall had something to do with him too. The demoiselle didn't know what. But you're right otherwise. Simon hasn't been touched. Neither could you blame Nicholas for the cannon killing Simon's uncle. Not really. And the demoiselle is adamant that the death of Jaak and his wife were unintentional. I'm inclined to believe that," said Tobie.

"For what it's worth, so am I," said Gregorio. He said again, "My God. Poor bastard."

Julius said, "But that's the point, isn't it? He is a bastard. His mother had a child—Christ, to Simon, it must have been—which was stillborn, and went off to her father, old Thibault, to recover. Her husband—Simon—never went near her again. Then Nicholas gets himself born. There was nobody to blame for it but the servants, but which one fathered him they never found out. Meanwhile he grows up . . . I suppose . . . longing to be accepted as a Kilmirren."

"As Nicholas de St Pol," Tobie said. "That's the Kilmirren name."

"Claes vander Poele," said Gregorio. "Of course. So there's a stubborn streak. He wouldn't let the name be discarded. I can see the point."

To Julius, there was only one point that mattered. He said, "So what did the demoiselle say?"

Tobie was silent. When he answered, it was in his clipped, professional voice. "She said that I was to tell you who Nicholas was.

That I was to ask you not to tell anyone else. That I was to say that Simon was likely to pursue this feud of his, and that we should be warned that working for the Charetty company might become dangerous. And finally, to say that she believed in Nicholas, and his character and his loyalty, but that we should have to decide whether or not we could act as his keepers, so that there would be some restraint on the way his intelligence worked. She used the word *keepers,*" said Tobie.

He paused and then said, "She also said that the Venetian Piero Zorzi is holding festival on the Flanders flagship this evening, and has invited herself and her husband. She hasn't seen Nicholas since, but she thinks this is what he's been waiting for."

Julius said, "Hasn't seen . . . Didn't he come back from the church with her?"

Tobie said, "Come back here? Knowing that we were going to be told what we've been told? I should think we'll be lucky if we see him this week. And I can't imagine how, if I were Nicholas, I could find a way to face us."

"That's because you're not Nicholas," said Gregorio. "Tobie. You're the doctor. He's exposed now, to us at least. What difference will that make to the way he works in future? Do you have more faith in him, or less?"

For a long time, Tobie said nothing. Then he said, "I don't know. I don't think it's changed the way I felt before. I think I can out-guess him. I'm curious enough, at any rate, to want to try."

Julius said, "Here? Do you think he'll stay here?"

And Tobie said, "I don't know if it will be here. Not if Venice is involved. Would you go overseas? Goro? Julius?"

Gregorio said, "I don't mind where I go. But the demoiselle would need someone here. And I thought you and Julius were returning to Astorre next year anyhow. You'd be safe from Simon there."

"But Nicholas wouldn't," said Tobie. "Not if he stays here in Bruges. I wonder what he wants. I wonder what he's thinking now."

"I wonder where it is now," said Julius. He wrinkled his brow. "The ostrich."

"What?" said Tobie.

"He said something about going to see the ostrich. It's to go to the Duke of Milan, and Tommaso keeps complaining that it's dying on him."

"That sounds like Nicholas," Gregorio said in his solemn, rumbling voice. "If he can't bear to face us, depend on it that he's gone to look at an ostrich."

Nicholas had indeed gone to look at the ostrich.

The principal problem, to begin with, was that there was nowhere to go.

Confining the problem to Bruges and not allowing it to assume cosmic proportions, there was nowhere, that is, where he could be sure of avoiding Tobie, Gregorio and Julius, now in possession of knowledge about him that they should never have had. He couldn't go home without meeting Marian, now aware of his . . . engineering, and struggling somehow to trust him.

The rest of Bruges was occupied by people who had seen and heard what happened at the Gruuthuse palace this morning. Or who wanted to talk about Jaak de Fleury, or Lionetto, or Felix. And finally, somewhere in Bruges were Simon of Kilmirren and his fertile wife Katelina, whose mood he could guess, but whose plans he did not know.

So Nicholas thought of the ostrich, which was supposedly in the stable compound of the house of the Florentine merchants, and set off to inspect it. It seemed fairly certain that he would find there none of the Charetty employees. And Florentines had been largely absent from the morning's High Mass for a Scottish monarch. The Flanders galleys occupied them far more seriously.

And since the Flanders galleys occupied them, he might not have to consider ciphers, or dispatches, or any of the alluring, dangerous strands that might lead to a new set of devices or echo old ones. Just the simple matter of an ostrich to be dispatched to Milan.

He met Angelo Tani, the Medici manager, before he had crossed the threshold of the handsome, towered building by the Bourse. Tani said, "I'm off to a meeting, but go in. Tommaso's there somewhere. There was a message for you—why here, I don't know. A boy brought it. You're wanted at Silver Straete this afternoon, at Florence van Borselen's house."

Nicholas heard his voice saying, "I thought he was away."

"He is. His daughter Katelina wants to see you. Hangings for the accouchement, perhaps. They've bought some fine christening silver from me already. They pay, too."

"So they do," Nicholas said. He stood looking after Tani, and was bumped once or twice by people coming out or in. A boy of fourteen, a *giovane,* said politely, "If you want Messer Tommaso, he's gone to the stables."

The civility was not unmixed with something else. Looking again, Nicholas saw it was the boy he and Felix had spoken to, the day they had taken the Medici barge with Lionetto to Damme. Nicholas said, "I hear you're keeping the whole company right these days. What's Messer Tommaso doing? Taking a journey?"

The youth became a little less guarded. The power of Milanese manager Pigello, it was easy to see, hung over the Bruges branch of the Medici. The boy said, "Oh, no. He's gone to look at the ostrich again." One of his eyes gleamed.

Nicholas said, "Again?"

"To look at its droppings," the youth said. Both eyes gleamed.

With a gigantic effort, Nicholas detached his mind from everything else and said, his chin on his chest, "Messer Tommaso is doctoring it?"

The Medici *giovane* gave a sudden and seraphic grin. He said, "No. He's just watching its droppings. It's eaten Messer Tommaso's hat jewel and two of his rings."

Nicholas said, "I should have thought it was the *giovane*'s job, to help your under-manager with a problem like that."

The boy looked at his face, and then, relieved, grinned again. "He tried to make me, the first day. But he got the idea I wasn't looking closely enough."

"Poor Messer Tommaso," said Nicholas. "Well, suppose you and I both go and help him? We could hold his jacket. I suppose he takes off his jacket?"

"One of the grooms gives him an apron," said the boy. "But some of them say the rings could stay inside the ostrich forever."

"Or emerge as an extra, late gift for the Duke of Milan," Nicholas said. They were walking through the house to the stableyard. He said, "Is the bird better, then?"

"They say so," said the boy. "You heard about the shellfish?"

"Yes," said Nicholas. "Who on earth fed it shellfish?"

"It ate them itself," the boy said. "Wading ashore from the wreck. Then it worked through a whole field of corn before they could catch it. It runs very fast. It took eight horsemen to get hold of it, because they had to watch not to damage its feathers. It likes little birds."

"That's rather charming," said Nicholas.

"To eat. And insects. And grasses. They've had to keep it in its travelling box, or it steals all the feed from the horses. It has this very long neck. And long legs. It kicks with its legs when Messer Tommaso tries to look in the box."

"How did—how did it get hold of his rings?" Nicholas asked. They had emerged into the yard. From the farthest stables came the sound of thudding, accompanied by a low, booming roar. Nicholas said, "Not the bird?"

"That's the ostrich," said the boy. "It roars when it's unhappy. It usually hisses when it sees Messer Tommaso. Sometimes it cackles. His rings came off when he pulled his hands too quickly back from the bar."

"I expect it cackled then," Nicholas said. "This stable? Well, the horses look all right. And that's the travelling box. It's very tall."

"It's a big bird," said the boy. "Five feet to its back; eight feet to its head. A cock. You tell by the black and white plumes. That's what makes them so valuable. The big black and white plumes."

Tommaso Portinari was not, at the moment, peering into the box where the ostrich stood. He was not, either, inside the box inspecting its droppings. He had not even replaced his jacket with the leather apron which hung from his hands as he stood, his back to a post, contemplating his feet. He looked up, with deliberation. Adversity suited him. He was pale. The dark, ruffled hair, cut round his brow and across the top of his ears, framed the long-nosed antelope face with its fine arched brows and high cheekbones. His expression was one of a man pushed beyond endurance.

Nicholas said, "Your boots. It's eaten your boots?"

For answer, Tommaso Portinari merely turned his head on one shoulder and nodded towards the box. It was an extremely stout box, as befitted a cage for a 300-pound bird. The sides were solid, with windows let into them. The top consisted of open spars. The whole contraption stood filling a horse-stall and emanating a smell of rotting fruit, bruised grass and ostrich. Nicholas jumped for the frame of the horse-stall and straddled its wall, looking down at the far-travelled captive. Then he started to laugh.

It was what Julius saw as he crossed the yard into the stables, having set out with many misgivings to track down someone called Nicholas de St Pol who was still married to his employer. He expected to find him in some sort of extremity. Instead he heard the fearsome sound of Claes in a fit of idiot laughter. A sound which had enticed him into many a scrape in the past, and had maddened him equally often.

The noise came from the top of a horse stall. Claes . . . Nicholas was sitting there, bowing up and down and exploding, while down below, Tommaso Portinari and a boy were gazing up at him. Next to the stall was a strong-smelling box from which came thudding noises, accompanied by spitting and hissing. Julius reached Tommaso and looked up and said, "What? The ostrich?"

"Go and look," Nicholas called. He stooped for a hay-rake and pointed. "There's a window at the side."

Julius went and looked. The boy was already there. The boy's face had gone red. Tommaso stood where he was, apparently studying the rafters. Nicholas, whining with laughter, handed himself to the front edge of the wall from which Julius could see his expectant face, the dimples like nutshells. Julius peered into the box.

The ostrich hissed back at him. It had a small, fuzzy head, a beak like a hinge and pale, hostile eyes that reminded him of Tobie. The head topped a long twitching neck like a bellrope. Both were being carried up and down the box by a pair of thick, stalking legs with powerful elbows. Between neck and legs was something like a large chicken joint crossed with a pincushion. A shell-pink naked flap depended from either flank.

The pincushion was its plucked body. The sore-looking rump, the silly flaps, were where forty snow-white plumes and a mantle of fine glossy black had once proudly been flaunted. Someone, in the night, had pruned the Duke of Milan's present. The ostrich was there, but there wasn't a feather left on it.

It danced on its strong legs. It darted its beak through the spars, its eyes flashing. Every now and then it would kick, and the side of the box would vibrate and echo. Nicholas, weeping with laughter, reached down with the hay-rake to prod it.

And the door of the ostrich-box opened.

Tommaso, lost in bitterness, didn't notice. The boy whooped. Julius leaped but was far, far too late. Neck stretched, the bird took its first step outside, and then its second. Tommaso whirled round. The boy ran forward shouting. The ostrich delivered its low, booming roar. And Nicholas, just as it took its third step and swung a leg for its fourth, launched himself from his perch and landed fair and square on its back as it passed him.

Julius yelled, and started to run. Nicholas yelled too, but in a different way—in a crowing sort of way that was all too familiar. The ostrich burst from the stables, toed its way over the paving and sprang, like a haunch escaped from the oven, through the big double doors and into Vlamynck Straete, with Nicholas crazily bouncing and hugging it.

Julius gave a gasp. He raced for the street where the ostrich, not yet into its stride, was darting from side to side in a haphazard way, impeded by vehicles trundling down from the Waterhalle. The ostrich boomed. The street blossomed, like a garden of sun-flowers, with pale, turning faces. Capped heads and white-coifed heads began to surge up steps on either side, vanish through doors, squeeze between houses. A man with two bales on his back stag-gered out of the way and found himself jammed under the jut of a building. A wheelbarrow, left overturned, disgorged a torrent of round, glossy cheeses. One of them struck the ostrich on the leg and the ostrich lifted its foot and kicked irritably. A cask of quick-silver, left at a trapdoor, began to spout a glittering stream of liquid which almost certainly spelled ruin for somebody. Nicholas, still clinging, looked round as it happened. His face was pink with effort and happiness.

Julius croaked. He turned and raced back into the stables, send-ing grooms staggering. He wrenched open stalls and jumped bare-back on the first horse he found with a harness. Then, already followed by others, he made out into the street and after Nicholas. Claes. After another mad escapade.

By then the ostrich wasn't in sight, but you could tell where it had been from the split bales and dropped parcels. Balconies sported a sequence of cropped vines and munched pot-flowers and, twice, empty bird-cages hung drunkenly open. A corner shrine had toppled, leaving only a vase with some stalks in it.

Julius turned his horse and rode for the canal and was in time to see the ostrich emerging from the Augustinians' gateway with Nicholas still on its back. It was moving extremely fast but was now wearing some sort of rein. It looked, from the distance, like the cord from a cassock.

One of the reasons why it was moving so fast was that there were by now several dogs at its heels. Every now and then the ostrich would pause to kick, and the dogs would skid out of the way. Then the ostrich would set off again, hissing and cackling. Julius, still some way behind, could see Nicholas clinging on with one hand

and wielding the looped cord with the other, trying to prevent the bird from crossing the bridge into Spangnaerts Street.

He failed. The bird set off up the street, kicking bales as it went and stabbing grilles with its beak. Two quilts, hung out for airing, started to fall in a cloudburst of feathers. Nicholas caught one of them and, single-handed, attempted to stuff it between the cut quills and his bottom. Julius, crying with laughter, raced behind him. Towards the Tonlieu. The weigh-houses. The market.

The bird checked now and then: for a stall loaded with berries; when, twice, groups of determined men barred the street or attempted to corner it. The delays were only brief. Two swipes of those powerful legs, and everyone scattered. The Crane went by, and the Hall and the belfry. The bird darted over the bridge to the Steen, with screaming people running before it. Soon it would come to the fields and gardens between the Ghent and Holy Cross bridges where it would be free to run as fast as it liked. An ostrich could cover forty miles in an hour, so they said—fast enough to kill any rider it threw off. Nicholas didn't seem to be worrying. Every now and then he turned upon Julius a wild, ridiculous grin, and once he freed a hand and gestured ahead and to the left. What he meant, Julius couldn't yet fathom.

Behind, now, other horsemen were coming. They'd halt the creature by converging on it from side streets, and using thrown rope to hamper, then bind it. Except that ahead lay open ground. Julius spurred his horse and slewed round a corner and saw, at last, what Nicholas was trying to tell him.

Ahead was the shallow, turgid water of one of the spoke canals that joined Bruges' encircling river. Pushing hard, Nicholas was shoving the bird off the road and down one of the slopes in the canal bank. The ostrich galloped into the water and slowed. Its head swung from side to side. A group of swans, busily feeding, came upright with an agitated splash, stared, and then rose to tread water hissing round the intruder. The intruder hissed back, struck, and a swan hurtled into the air. The others, necks outstretched, advanced uproariously. The ostrich, outnumbered, struck twice more and then set off up the canal, wings labouring. Occasionally it dipped and rolled, with a streaming Nicholas so far still adhering.

By now there were half a dozen horsemen with Julius. Ahead, the canal flowed under a bridge to join the circling river. Ahead, also, the ground rose to a broad embankment on which the windmills were planted. Horses could move quicker, now, than the bird in the water. Julius sent two ahead, to cross the bridge and threaten the bird from the east. Then he drew the others carefully back in a half-circle beside the only place it could leave the water, a sloping ramp leading to one of the windmills.

He forgot that the purpose of windmills is to grind, and that the ostrich was hungry. Up to a point, the ruse worked perfectly. The bird, scared by the horsemen on the left bank, turned for the ramp on the right. It emerged, its naked pink body effulgent; its rider a living cascade of canal water. Julius and the rest moved gently forward. The ostrich saw the sacks of corn in the yard, and the grain heaped and strewn all about it, and ran straight under the wheel of the sails to get at it.

Julius yelled a superfluous warning. He expected Nicholas to kick; to drag the bird away by its rope; to abandon it and roll off its back. The sails, creaking and thudding, moved round; missed the bird; threatened it; missed it once more. The ostrich lowered and raised its neck, feeding, looking about it, diving to feed again. It moved a little, one leg and then the other, but always close to the mill, mesmerised by the feast spread before it. And, as all action and all need for action came to a halt, so Nicholas returned to his senses.

Julius had no means of knowing. Filled with alarm, and even anger, he saw Nicholas sit, his face blank, his hands loose on the cord and do nothing.

The horsemen with Julius, staring, hung back. Julius didn't. Julius, his head down, his body clamped in the saddle, forced his horse forward and under the sails to where the ostrich was feeding. He used his spurs, bloodily, to push himself between the bird and the mill. And then, disregarding the open beak, the stamping feet, he rammed his horse into the flank of the bird, so that the creature came flailing out into the yard, hissing and kicking, to where the other horsemen were waiting.

It took five minutes more to corner it between them and truss it. Before then, Nicholas left its back. He couldn't, at first, stand at all. Julius relinquished him, and went to help with the bird, and saw it set off, safely held, on its journey back to the Florentine stableyard. The riders, drunk with excitement, did an admiring lap of honour round Nicholas first and Julius had to say to him *"Wave!"*

He looked up then, and gave some kind of a wave. He was shaking like a man with a disease; but after exertion, or a fright, men often did that, and they would think none the worse of him. But of course it wasn't that, or marsh fever. And yet . . . Nicholas had, he knew, tripped the latch of the bird's box himself.

To begin with, Julius had been happy to think that he was in the company of lunatic Claes, restored to them again. But of course, that freedom could never come back. If it had come back even for an hour, it was for the wrong reasons. A moment's reflection had told him that. A moment's reflection, added to what had happened under the windmill.

Now Julius said, "Why don't we get the miller to find a spot where you can rest? We'll send a boy for dry clothes."

He expected, and got, no reply. Speech had no part in this sort of crisis. He was ready for anything, but in fact Nicholas neither fainted nor wept nor collapsed in any spectacular way. Simply, once in the mill, he sat on some straw, curled tightly and erratically shivering. Someone brought a blanket for him and a drink, and then sensibly went away at a gesture. Julius sat down beside the demoiselle de Charetty's former apprentice and tried, unusually for him, to fathom what had happened. And then, to conceive what to do about it.

Trained to deal at second hand with critical events in the lives of others, he seldom found himself, like this, a participant. He cleared his throat. He looked at what little he could see of Nicholas, which consisted of segments of arm for the most part. Julius said, "Well, some people get drunk and some ride ostriches. But we all have to get back to real life some time. I don't see that you need be afraid of it. We all agree, you know, that you were quite right to do what you did, under the circumstances. Tobie thinks so. And Goro. There's no reason why we shouldn't all go on just as we did before. The demoiselle would agree."

He paused. From what he could hear of his breathing, Nicholas was still unlikely to speak. On the premise that his ears must be working, Julius studiously went on with his monologue.

"The trouble is, of course, that you get carried away. You know. Like . . . Like Felix did. The demoiselle understands that as well. In fact, she's asked us to help you. Whatever ideas you have, you won't be alone in acting on them. If they go wrong, then we'll all be to blame. Soon, you'll have as much experience anyway as we have. So forget what you've done. In the future, it's going to be different."

While he was speaking, he could see Nicholas compel himself to be still. Elbows on knees, he sat with his palms over his face. His hair, in wet coils and rings, dripped over his brow and neck and shoulders, where the blanket had shifted. He spoke at last. He said, "You don't know what I've done."

Julius paused. Then he said, "Then I don't want to know. Start afresh. You can."

Silence. Nicholas cleared the wet from his face with one hand, then brought up a corner of blanket and rubbed his face and hair slowly with it. He said, "I suppose I can."

It was an agreement for the sake of form only. But at least it meant that he had a grip of himself again. Nicholas with his brain working was easier to deal with than Nicholas defenceless, when you had no idea how to help him.

Julius said, "Don't do anything silly again. It isn't worth it. It's unfair to the demoiselle, too."

"Yes. Of course you're right," said Nicholas slowly. He stopped rubbing his hair and found a smile, quite remarkably. "But I'll pay for the damage, not the demoiselle. I only hope none of the dogs belonged to Simon."

If that was how he wanted to construe the remark, Julius was willing to let him. Very soon, the boy arrived back panting with a set of dry clothes and Nicholas stripped and dried himself and dressed, fumbling only a little over the doublet fastenings. Then Julius gave him the wine the miller had brought, and he drank it all in one swallow and was immediately sick.

Julius said, "Come on. Back to Spangnaerts Street. It's not every day you get your backside pricked by an ostrich."

"You go," said Nicholas. "I'll follow as soon as I can. I've got a call to make."

Julius said, "Why? Where? I'll take you, wherever it is."

"No. I'll manage," said Nicholas. "It's only to Silver Straete. Katelina van Borselen wants to see me."

Chapter 42

To Nicholas it seemed fitting that on this, the worst day of his life, he had to pay for all his sins by meeting Katelina van Borselen.

After some argument Julius left him alone and, all too clearly confused and annoyed, went back to Spangnaerts Street. To report, no doubt, to Tobie and Gregorio. He would also have to say something, one supposed, to Marian, since the career of the plucked ostrich would be the talk of Flanders by now. Nicholas thought that Julius, not necessarily the most discreet of men, might have the sense to keep to himself what had happened after its capture. He knew very well that, but for Julius, he wouldn't be here. Julius had done the same thing for him once before, in the water at Damme. He wished Julius would either keep him out of trouble or stop rescuing him.

Walking to Silver Straete was a trial. He felt stupidly weak, and no matter what back ways he chose, people kept hailing him. He hadn't been able to decide beforehand what he was going to say to Katelina, and now, on the way there, he was given no time to think. He simply arrived at the gates, and the porter let him in.

It occurred to him, at the door, that he knew his way to the kitchen, and to her bedchamber. Even though her father was away, it was unlikely that she would interview him there. She would recognise him, at least, with his hair wet. Straight from the canal again. The whole history of their relationship had to do with water.

There was, this time, a manservant on duty. He was taken to a large parlour and shown in, and the door closed behind him. It was the room from which she had sent him that sober salutation, full of contentment, the morning after the Carnival. The morning he had run past with his goats, and bells on his doublet.

He turned his gaze from the window seat, which was empty, and found the rest of the room equally vacant. Then the tall chair by the hearth creaked a little.

No one rose from it. Of course, she was with child, and heavy.

With his child. Nicholas walked forward instead, and stood before the chair, cap in hand.

The gross body filling the chair he had half imagined, and the tumble of velvet disguising it, and the animosity in the face above both. They were all there. Except that the face, the body, the hatred were those of a man, not a woman. Seated in the chair, sneering at him, was Jordan de Ribérac.

Already cold, Nicholas felt himself become perfectly bloodless. He stood idiotically, as if paralysed. Then sensation came flooding back, and he could feel all the colour return to his face.

Jordan de Ribérac, back from the dead. Alive, alive. But well aware now, one supposed, of the name of the person who had ruined him. Whom he did not like, very evidently, to think of as his grandson. It was necessary, too, to consider very quickly what else the vicomte de Ribérac might know.

Seated there, the trader and financier, companion of kings, didn't look like a man broken from Loches, or a refugee from the executioner's axe. There was a gold chain of some weight round his shoulders, and the vast, pleated doublet under his gown was buttoned with jewels. He was wearing a large, cuffed hat of brocade with a collapsed crown, below which his broad cheeks shone, healthy with colour, and his cold, bright eyes glittered.

He said, "Well, Claes vander Poele, killer of men. Pray be seated. I am sorry, of course, to have brought you here in the name of my daughter-in-law, but I felt it wise, and so did she. Who knows what assassins you mightn't have brought with you otherwise? Or what ingenious way you might have found to capture me? I am, as you might think, an embarrassing and therefore very discreet guest of Burgundy, and have no desire, just yet, to find myself back in France."

Nicholas sat. He said, "You escaped, then."

The small mouth smiled. "From Brittany, with the help of my daughter-in-law. That is, she had not yet married Simon, but she saw, I am sure, the advantages of keeping the French land in the family. I may be exiled now, but I am still alive. And when the Dauphin becomes king, Ribérac will, of course, be restored to me. An argument which outweighed, as it turned out, even the lady Katelina's unreasonable distaste for my company. Simon, of course, doesn't know how she helped me in Brittany. He would be most displeased with her if he did. His greeting this afternoon when I appeared alive before him was not filial."

"He isn't interested in Ribérac?" Nicholas said. He kept his voice as calm as the other's, and sat perfectly still.

"He is more interested in Kilmirren. It has been, naturally, a great blow to him to discover that he has neither the land nor the title, and indeed is about to lose all the freedom he enjoyed under poor Alan in Scotland. I have to thank you, by the way, for disposing so ably of Alan," said the fat man. "As an older brother, he was always a great inconvenience to me, and should have been got rid of years ago."

Nicholas said, "It had nothing to do with me."

"No, of course not," said the fat man his grandfather. "What a large number of deaths you have had nothing to do with. Alan. Poor Esota de Fleury. The unfortunate M. Jaak. That sad young bumpkin Felix de Charetty. All your dear friends or relatives. As I heard it, even the famous Lionetto was happy to save your life with his sword, quite unaware that it was you who had ruined him. No wonder Simon fears for his life."

"He needn't," said Nicholas.

"Oh, not directly, of course," said de Ribérac. "I hear that you almost ran away from him at the Hôtel Gruuthuse this morning. Yet you invite his attention, don't you? A little matter of stealing a whore of his. And a remark you made as you did it. Now she knows what it means, it has added a good deal, I'm afraid, to the violent antipathy in which the lady Katelina holds you."

Now she knows what it means? Nicholas waited.

De Ribérac smiled. "You are really the most passive opponent I have ever met. I thank God there is no blood of mine in you to be ashamed of. Don't you remember the comment you made? *The conduct of an oaf and the talents of a girl and a mortification to your father.* It cut deep at the time, poor Simon. After the dead weakling he got on your mother, he never found a girl he could quicken until Katelina. You know she is bearing? You are ousted, poor bastard.

"I'm glad," continued Jordan de Ribérac. The surfaces of his face, reflecting back into each other, bespoke a vast and undisturbed serenity. "There was a time when I thought I should have to resort to her myself, but really, a man wearies of animal pastimes. I am glad Simon has achieved something at last."

Nicholas said, "So you don't want me to take care of him any more? I was looking forward to it."

It was an arrow at venture, and it pierced the arrogant calm.

Nicholas received a look so quick and so sharp that he felt it. De Ribérac said, "That is why you are here, M. l'assassin. To warn you to attempt nothing against me, or against Simon. Especially against Simon."

"In case I marry Katelina?" said Nicholas.

It brought his answer, at last. "Katelina!" said Jordan de Ribérac. "I thought I had told you. Didn't I tell you she is your bitterest enemy, your most vicious opponent, the person who will not rest until you are punished? I never thought to see Simon confess his cuckoldry, that festering secret from his past. But of course, he was in his cups. Simon told her, this morning, who you are. The son of her husband, you might say, if you had been legitimate. The half-brother of her coming child. Oh, I tell you. If Simon thinks you are a devil, she thinks you are Satan himself. With what they are planning to do to you, and your wife, and your little company, I have nothing to fear."

The clean-shaven chins quivered as the fat man chuckled. "I was to tell you that. She was insistent that I tell you that. Now she understands everything you have ever done."

Nicholas said, "The demoiselle de Charetty has done nothing. Or the others in her company."

The fat man said, "I believe you. Indeed, Katelina herself pities the lady. But for you, the demoiselle de Charetty would be safe."

Nicholas said, "She will be safe."

The fat man smiled. "Dead, she would be safe. But not once I'm in Kilmirren and Simon has to look for another arena. He should have married the Reid girl and gone to England like her brother. With all the double-dealing he's been involved in at Calais, the Yorkists would welcome him. He could set up his business in Southampton, in London, in Burgundy. He might do it yet, with Katelina to spur him on. And all the merchants who don't like losing trade to an elderly widow and her clog-wearing child lover might well feel like joining him. Jealousy wrecked my business, and jealousy will ruin yours."

Nicholas said, "How could jealousy ruin you?"

"Antoinette de Maignélais," the vicomte said. "You'll never have heard of her. She thought, no doubt, that the King was paying me too much attention. She got wind of some connection I had with M. le Dauphin, and suddenly, the word had reached the King. But for the warning I got from the lady Katelina, I should have been taken. You could say that you, too, helped me escape."

"In the same way, I expect, that I helped kill your brother," said Nicholas.

"Oh, indirectly, of course," said de Ribérac. "However else do you always act? Katelina knew she had to smuggle me out. She also knew there was a ship of mine in St Malo. The *St Pol.* I should be grateful, by the way, if you would refrain from using our family name. Claes vander Poele is already too close for comfort."

"I shall remember," said Nicholas. "And she arranged for you to board the ship and escape?"

"Because she happened to be there on business of yours," said de Ribérac. "Something to do with an ostrich. Have I said something more witty than usual?"

"Yes," said Nicholas. "You have completed my day. Is that all you wanted me for?"

His grandfather looked at him. "My dear fool," he said. "What else should I ever want you for, except to tell you whom to kill and whom to leave alive? When you cease to be useful to me, I shall cease having you summoned."

"I understand," said Nicholas. He got up. "But next time, perhaps, you might have the courage to summon me in your own name."

The fat man laughed aloud. "Don't speak of courage as if you knew what it was. Certainly, I can tell you, you won't receive another summons from Simon's lady wife. Or if you do, you would be well advised not to answer it."

Going home, he offended no doubt a great many people, because this time he saw and heard nothing until he was entering the house in Spangnaerts Street. Soon after that, he did notice Julius, who asked him how he was and then went away. He must have reported to the others because neither Tobie nor Gregorio came near him, although he became aware of a number of broadly smiling faces about the house and the yard. With a jolt, he remembered the ostrich.

His own room, which he had kept, was empty. He stood there for a while, thinking, and then, because there were things to be settled, he went to Marian's cabinet. She was there with Bellobras, whom she dismissed. He had braced himself for explanations but she seemed to know everything, presumably because Julius, after all, had not been reticent. Everything, that is, except about his last interview.

She said, "Never mind about the ostrich. Gregorio and Henninc have gone to put it all right, and even Tommaso is reconciled. I've told him to tell Duke Francesco that it's sick, and keep it for eight months till its feathers grow."

"If he can keep it for eight months," Nicholas said. He sat down. "I seem to need keepers."

She said, "Julius told you?" She had less than her usual colour, but her eyes were clear and steadfast and affectionate. It came to him that she was magnificently dressed and he remembered that she, too, had been invited on board the Venetian flagship.

He said, "He told me that they're all ready to stay. In spite of everything."

He had expected her to answer at once, but she didn't. Then she said, "And, Nicholas, do you want to stay?"

At first, he wasn't sure how to answer. Last night, after he knew she had been told all about Jaak de Fleury; after she had broken the news that Julius and the others knew his connection with Simon, they had talked, but carefully. And when, at the end of it, she had used, flushing, a woman's excuse to sleep alone, he couldn't have told whether or not it was genuine, but was glad she had used it. What degree of courtship, what fervour is proper when bestowing only tender affection, and not affirming or courting some new and ambiguous pledge? He hadn't known, and had been afraid to put it to the test.

So now, he listened to the tone of her voice, and tried to read her face, and remembered, of course, what else Julius would have told her. He said, "It wasn't Katelina van Borselen who was waiting for me at Silver Straete. It was a trick. It was Jordan. Jordan de Ribérac."

Her face coloured as she felt, too, what he had felt. She said, "They didn't kill him."

"He escaped. Katelina van Borselen helped him. She hasn't told Simon."

He hadn't been sure whether or not to tell her that. But her mind was on something else. She said, "But he knows you betrayed him?"

"Not even that," Nicholas said. "He only wanted to warn me not to touch Simon. Since I began murdering all my family, he has had to concede me some small ability. He has an idea, too, that Simon and Katelina together may represent a threat to you and the company because of me. I think he's right about that." He stopped. Then he added, "I do want to stay."

Marian de Charetty said, "I think you do. But we are, aren't we, going on board the galley tonight?"

And he said, "Yes. But whatever happens, the choice is going to be yours. Whatever you want, I will do."

"Yes. I know that," she said.

They had, now, a household barge of their own, so that they could set off in style with all the other boats making for the harbour at Sluys, their oarsmen smart in Charetty blue and Loppe, finely dressed, looming behind them. He had wanted to come. Exactly one year before, Loppe had been chained on board a Flanders galley, and forced to dive at the captain's command. He had served the Duke of Milan since then, and Felix. But if he returned to Sluys now it was not out of pride but—had he been asked—from a sense of foreboding.

Before leaving for Sluys, Nicholas went alone to the office where he knew he would find Julius and Tobie and Gregorio. By then he had had to change clothes. For the Flanders galley, it was necessary to wear the robe he had had made for Easter at the Veere house. Since then, it had mysteriously acquired embroidery and a better sort of fur than he had thought right at the time. Marian had done that, and had also had made for him the doublet he was wearing, which was as well-tailored as her own damask gown. It had taken a certain amount of hardihood, since he couldn't claim courage, to walk into the office and confront them all, knowing what they all knew. He said the first thing he thought of. "Pray that I don't fall in the water this time. I'm wearing all next year's profits and your salaries, too."

Tobie trained on him, unsmiling, the basilisk scrutiny of Pavia. He said, "Prosper de Camulio has arrived. You may meet him."

"Yes. I know," said Nicholas. "Look. About the company. You've said you want to remain with it. But it's perhaps going to be more than you bargained for. Simon is going to cause trouble. And de Ribérac . . . his father is free. I saw him this morning."

He could see Julius thinking. Julius said, *"Silver Straete?"*

"Yes. That was Jordan. He just wanted to reaffirm that my . . . that the family is out for my blood. Ruining the Charetty company if necessary."

Gregorio said, "It would take quite a lot to ruin the Charetty company. Although I say it myself."

You wouldn't think, looking at the black cap and the comedian's nose, that Gregorio had the steel in him that he had. Nicholas gazed at him with the first, faint stirring of optimism. He said, "I think I feel the same. That is, I don't mind fighting. The question is, where will it do the most good?"

"I can imagine," said Tobie.

"I'm not asking for any more promises," Nicholas said. He met Tobie's pale eyes and tried to read them.

Tobie said, "I'm not making any. I suppose you know what you're up against? Whatever happens, you'll have to keep Adorne on your side. You'd have the Bishop and some of the Scots preferring Simon. And the Duke of Milan and his allies are friends with the Dauphin just now, but that mightn't last."

Julius was looking in an annoyed fashion at Tobie. He said, "If you're afraid, go back to Lionetto."

Tobie pondered. "I don't think he'd welcome me," he said. "He's probably found out about Nicholas by now. I may have to stick to Astorre."

"We may all have to stick to Astorre," Nicholas said. Three pairs of eyes turned on him. It was the moment he thought it better to get up and leave the room.

Loppe was waiting to board the barge with Marian. Her daughters had wanted to be rowed to the galley as well, but Marian had explained that the visit was a matter of business.

Nicholas had changed in Catherine's eyes yet again. From her mother's lover, he had become the amazing person who had rampaged through Bruges on a featherless ostrich. Even Tilde, reserved and watchful, looked at him a little differently. He wondered, rather wildly, what change of attitude the same event might have wrought among the great men of Venice and their confederates. All offers cancelled and all communications cut. And perhaps as well, at that.

It was dark, by then. Julius saw them off in the barge and stood looking after them, the lamplight on his brown, well-turned face. He looked puzzled.

Sluys, when they got there, was like Carnival time all over again, with the canal banks hung with lanterns, and torches flaring all round the moated town walls and towers, while the fortress, the belfry, the castle blushed and flickered with light in the distance. But the crowds who had come by foot, by boat or on horseback, stood with their backs to the town looking out over the harbour where a hundred ships, small and large, lay rocking at anchor, beaded with lamps. The banners and pavilions and pennants glowed under the great lanterns at masthead and rigging like flowers in a hedgerow: azure and indigo, vermilion and alizarine, cinnabar and earth-green and vermilion. And alone in the centre, with its burden of lights and flowers and music, of unreeling silks and swaying fringes, lay the flagship of the Venetian fleet, like a garland made by a goldsmith.

Receiving his guests with his noblemen, Piero Zorzi welcomed on board the small, wealthy woman Marian de Charetty, about whom he had received his instructions.

Under the rose colour of the awning her face looked less strained than it had done in the Hôtel Gruuthuse, when she had had to witness the insulting of her artisan husband. Reporting the incident to his fellows, Zorzi had mentioned again his own misgivings. In the maintenance of its empire, the Signory of the Republic of Venice used, of course, what tools came to hand. Their quality varied. But they were such, as a rule, that men of breeding could tolerate.

About this youth, one had doubts. Some feckless escapade had been reported that very day by Corner and Bembo and the other Venetian merchants. Senseless children ran races and upset their betters. The young man might be a foot taller than Messer Piero Zorzi, and decked today in furred robe and damask, but he was still a dyer's apprentice.

One had, however, to think of the good of the Republic. Conducting his two incongruous guests through the chattering, jewel-prinked company, the Venetian commander hoped (in Italian) that they would accept the hospitality of his cabin, where Messer Prosper Camulio of Genoa would shortly join them with two of his friends.

They knew Italian. "And yourself, commander?" the Flemish woman enquired.

"Alas, my other guests call. But later, certainly, I hope to give myself the pleasure of joining you. Madonna, through this curtain."

Marian de Charetty walked past his arm. Behind the curtain was a small panelled chamber lit by silver wall sconces. There was carpet on the floor, and a table fixed to it, and cushioned seats round three sides. She walked in, thinking of Prosper de Camulio, who would shortly join them, and who would condole with her on the death of her gallant son Felix, whom he had entertained in his Milanese villa. She heard the door curtain close, and the commander's stiff walk retreating.

Beside her, Nicholas suddenly checked. The cabin was not empty. From where he had been sitting in shadow a bearded man rose, his two hands on a stick, and stood studying them. A black-haired man dressed in Florentine robes, whose olive skin and dark eyes fixed on Nicholas were not Italian, and whose red lips parted now in a slow, amused smile. He said, "Have no fear, my friend Niccolò. There is nothing I can take from you. There is nothing of what I am going to offer you that you need accept."

There was a pause. Then beside her, Nicholas said, "I am glad to hear it."

Disturbed by his voice, she looked up at him; but could not read his face. He said, "Demoiselle, you remember Messer Nicholai Giorgio de' Acciajuoli, who passed through Bruges on his way from Scotland last year? Messer Nicholai: the lady my wife."

"I have to felicitate you," said the Greek. The Greek with the wooden leg, who had witnessed the sinking of the cannon at Damme. Who had given Nicholas that first, teasing hint about Phocoean alum. Who had divined from the beginning—was it possible?—that here perhaps was a man he could use.

Nicholas said, "Messer Prospero . . . ?"

"He will join us later," said the bearded man. "With Messer Caterino Zeno and his wife. Messer Caterino ratified the alum agreement, demoiselle. You have seen his signature. You will enjoy meeting the man. And Violante his wife. The princesses of Trebizond are famed for their beauty."

"We should sit, then," said Nicholas. "I dare say you will want to come to business quite soon." His voice was peaceful again.

The Greek smiled, making way for her. She seated herself between the two men, and facing the curtain. The Greek said, "Our friends will not come until I seek them. In any case you know what we are to discuss. The Duke of Milan has offered your company a renewal of the condotta for next year, but you have not yet accepted?"

She realised Nicholas had left her to answer. She said steadily, "No. But we expect to do so very soon. After San Fabiano, the lord

Federigo was most pressing. Any alternative would have to offer much more."

The Greek said, "How soon would you expect to sign your Milanese contract?"

It was Nicholas, this time, who replied. "Before the end of the year, monsignore. I plan to go to Milan in November."

She hadn't known that. She waited.

The Greek said, "But you wouldn't object, personally, to taking your company farther afield? You have a developing business, which breeds jealousies. No one would wish to harm a lady, but the more successful a merchant, the more he invites retaliation. There is much to be said for moving a share of the business elsewhere. You've already thought of Venice. You have a rapport with the Genoese. Through your courier service you have commended yourself to the Florentines. It remains to select the theatre in which you may capitalise on all these new assets. Naturally, I speak of Trebizond."

When talking affairs, you learn to give nothing away. Marian de Charetty rested her gaze on the saturnine face as if it was of no account, this proposal to send a young man, not yet twenty, to the other side of the world. To Trebizond. The jewel of the Black Sea. The prized trading-post with the Orient which Venice feared to lose to the Turk. Which, now that Constantinople had fallen, was the last fragment on earth of the Empire of Byzantium; the last imperial court; the last treasure house of royal Greece.

Caterino Zeno, who had signed the alum contract for Venice, was married to a Byzantine princess. It was all planned. None of this was an accident. It was war, and not trade, that Nicholas was wanted for. But war and trade both were the foundation of the Charetty business.

Nicholas said, "We have an excellent company, but I doubt if captain Astorre could hold off the Turks single-handed. That is what you are asking?"

"I?" said the Greek. "I expect nothing. I demonstrate what is possible, that is all. Venice has her own hired soldiers in Trebizond, poor though they are, to protect her traders. The Genoese merchants have some sort of bodyguard. It is likely that they will never be needed. The Sultan requires trade, and the mountains do not encourage Ottoman armies. No. I had in mind a business opportunity. If you ask your captain Astorre to accompany you, he will of course be sure of a welcome. The Emperor himself would be generous. But it is a matter of trade. Trade and money."

She was aware, again, that Nicholas preferred to be silent. She said, "And the business, precisely?"

The Greek's eyes, in the lamplight, seemed softened. He said, "This winter, Monna Marian, envoys from the East are due to reach Italy, begging help to drive out the infidel. Among them will be a Venetian merchant, Michael Alighieri. The poet Dante was one of his forebears. His home is in Trebizond, and he is spokesman for the Emperor David. It is his task, when in Italy, to arrange for a Florentine agent in Trebizond."

She said, "A trading-station on the Black Sea for Florence? Then Florence will choose the Medici to run it."

The Greek smiled. "But what Florence proposes may not suit Trebizond and the Emperor. He is threatened from Constantinople. Sultan Mehmet has shown his distrust of the Genoese. The Emperor David may therefore insist that Florence appoints an agent of his own choice: a company which the Medici and Venice both favour. A company already blessed with its own private army. Quartered in Trebizond, such a force would be priceless. To the traders. To the imperial family. And the fees it might command would reflect this."

He stroked his beard, watching them. "I do not doubt your success in the Milanese wars. Perhaps you owe the Duke of Milan more than I know. I would only mention, my friends, that a Trapezuntine contract could be yours for the asking. And a share —perhaps a major share—perhaps one day a monopoly—of the whole silk exchange from the Orient."

The breathing she could hear was her own. Nicholas stood, his eyes like coins, without breathing at all. He had talked to her, a little, about this possibility. It had then seemed a dream, a bookkeeper's fantasy. And even then, it had been Julius he had envisaged as leading this branch of the company. Julius who would go to Rome, and to Venice, and finally far off, beyond Constantinople, to the shores of the Black Sea.

But it was not Julius who was being spoken of now. It was himself.

The silence stretched, and then he dropped his gaze. He said, "I see. Well, you won't expect an answer from us just now. We need to know very much more. But I shall be in Italy in November. I undertake at least to see Messer Alighieri. Unless—"

She felt his eyes, and tilted her head, to meet his enquiry. "I have no objection," the demoiselle said.

"Then," said the Greek, "I shall fetch our friends, and we shall take wine together. Without commitment, it goes without saying. Venice, Florence and Genoa. The Turk makes strange bedfellows, my friends. But of such things are fortunes created."

He was skilled at rising, despite the faint sway of the vessel. Nicholas sprang to his feet also, and held the curtain aside as he left. Then he dropped the heavy cloth, and stood looking down at her. He said, "It means nothing, to see Alighieri. We can decide here and now to accept the Milanese condotta instead."

She said, "He has planned for this."

Nicholas said, "Then he will have planned for our refusal. It is for you to say, when the time comes."

He looked as he always did. As he always used to do. Affectionate and a little anxious, with the glow of excitement behind it. Excitement at the prospect of a great escapade. The greatest ever.

She said, "Nicholas, don't be foolish. It's the finest opportunity the company has ever had. You aren't afraid of it?"

A merchant has to disguise what he feels. So she had said, over and over, to Felix. She withstood the enveloping, generous gaze trying to sift through her mind; trying to discern her real motives. He knew that trouble lay ahead for her if he stayed at Bruges and invited Simon's attentions. He didn't know, or guess, the real trouble that lay before her. He said, "I don't want to leave."

She said, "And are we all to depend on what you do or don't want?"

His brow had puckered. He said, "We have until winter."

And she replied, "No, my dear. We decide now. You go to Trebizond. And, one day, come back to me with your profits."

It was a fair offer, with its own sort of justice. She had said as much to Felix, after he had suffered at the Poorterslogie. She had said that he and Nicholas might want to leave her.

Her eyes were not as clear as she would have wished, and she was shaken to find Nicholas dropped to her feet, and her hand snatched as if he would break it. Then he kissed the palm formally and rose, holding it tightly. She studied the strong, workman's fingertips, remembering when they were blue. The footsteps they had both heard came nearer. She kept her eyes fixed on their interlaced fingers, and heard the distant voice of the Greek, ushering several people to join them. Prosper de Camulio, they had said.

And Caterino Zeno and Violante his wife. Violante, princess of Trebizond.

Their twined hands fell apart, and became memory. Nicholas moved to her side and they waited. Someone lifted the curtain. She didn't know what to expect. Then she smelled the perfume: harsh, expensive, disturbing; and knew what she had given up; and to whom; and why.

And then she walked forward and smiled; for she was a merchant.

Rebels and outcasts, they fled halfway across the earth to settle the harsh Australian wastelands. Decades later—ennobled by love and strengthened by tragedy—they had transformed a wilderness into fertile land. And themselves into ...

The Australians

WILLIAM STUART LONG

___THE EXILES, #1	12374-7	$3.95
___THE SETTLERS, #2	17929-7	$3.95
___THE TRAITORS, #3	18131-3	$3.95
___THE EXPLORERS, #4	12391-7	$3.95
___THE ADVENTURERS, #5	10330-4	$3.95
___THE COLONISTS, #6	11342-3	$3.95
___THE GOLD SEEKERS, #7	13169-3	$3.95
___THE GALLANT, #8	12785-8	$3.95
___THE EMPIRE BUILDERS, #9	12304-6	$3.95